A FAMILY
THAT WAS

By the Same Author

A FAMILY THAT WAS

BY
ERNEST RAYMOND

CASSELL AND COMPANY, LTD
London, Toronto, Melbourne and Sydney

First Published 1929

Reprinted 1967 by Cedric Chivers Ltd., Portway, Bath,
at the request of
The London & Home Counties Branch of The Library Association
ECM - ANTON HAIN K.G.
Printed in Germany

CONTENTS

PART I

PART II

PART III

PART IV

PART V

PART I

A FAMILY THAT WAS

CHAPTER I

SUNDAY SITS FOR ITS PORTRAIT

THE hour between breakfast's close and church-bell was always a silent space in the long road where the family lived. The pavement kerbs ran straight as railway lines, from their wide beginning, as they turned out of Kensington Road, to their narrow end where they pierced into the vagueness of Uxbridge Road, whose happy transversion at that point, it would seem, alone prevented them from meeting. And in all that vista which lacked but one quarter of the complete mile, there was nothing seen except the morning light of Sunday; which, to the English, is a light different from all other lights—a sad, hushing, and faintly disturbing light. And never more so than on this dry, wintry, sunlit morning, in the year 1893, in the winter of the Great Queen.

It was Sunday; and no two-wheeled butcher's chariot rattled behind its cantering pony up to the area gates; no milk float, pushed by the milkman, tinkled its churn and its cans along the gutter and stopped to the cry of "Milko!"; no sedate van from the Army and Navy Stores, with its glossy brown hood and well-behaved boy on the tail-board, brought provisions and delicacies to its long array of clients in this decorous road; no closed brougham, purling behind its silky bays, came to fetch Lady Castlewaite (the street's one title) from No. 203; nowhere to-day reeked the apricot-coloured dustcart, with its dustmen in their sou'westers, and its fine inscription "Royal Borough of Kensington;" no top-hatted men hurried down to the city omnibuses in the Kensington Road; no long-skirted ladies, with household cares behind their veils and purses in their muffs, set out to their barter among the deferential tradesmen; and no errand-boy, as he kicked a stone between pavement and gutter, whistled the new, universal air:

> " After the ball was over,
>   After the break of morn."

It was Sunday.

The long road—its cambered metal of rolled flints, its pavements dotted with coal-holes, its shallow areas, and its tall house-fronts—waited in an anticipatory silence for the church bell. Such house-fronts, with their spotless hearthstoned steps mounting to porticoes of stucco, with their pretentious little pediments over the windows, and their green-painted window-boxes on the sills, *would*, in that year, and under the ægis of the Great Queen, have made proper submission to the church bell. The dust lay quiescent in the sags and the cracks of the pavement-flags where it had blown, or in little mounds against the kerbs where it had been swept at dawn; and because the horses in those days possessed the streets of London, it was nine-parts hay from the country-side. And this very dust seemed to know it was Sunday. Far up the road, back in the break between the blocks of houses, waited the church of St. Austin's, till it chose to ring its bell. Standing at the bottom of the road, one could not see it with the eyes, but one was seeing it with the mind, just because Sunday filled the street. It was towerless, but its high walls of grey stone and its steep roof gave it an imperious presence; and about its silence now there was an air of especial sovereignty. This was its day and its reign: let the pavements and the areas and the house-fronts stare up at it as expectantly as they liked, not one second before the half-hour would it sound the Matins bell.

Behind every window in that street, no doubt, was a story well worth the telling, but nine hundred and ninety-nine of these have been shelved into people's memories, where their characters are dimming and their piled chapters are waiting to be destroyed. This is the odd one. And through all those stories that long wide road must run—remembered in many guises but never more clearly than as it lay on Sunday mornings in winter, looking the longer and the wider for its emptiness and its stillness and its dry sunlight. Very straight and clear it will be, if the people whose memories hold it were children on this November day, thirty-six years ago.

Footsteps tapped into its silence, coming round that corner where the pillar-box was, with its monogram " V.R."; the footsteps of a single person; light steps but hurried, and ringing unusually loud as they drew near. From the quickness of their beats one would have imagined that they belonged to a tripping girl and would have erred just about as widely as possible, for it was a very little old man with a grey, walrus moustache, a black overcoat, black trousers and a bowler hat; but he was so spare and sprightly, and so hurried, that his feet could twinkle like a girl's. As he walked he was encouraging himself with words spoken almost aloud : " Come along, dear man. It's getting on. Time's getting on. . . . Cruets . . . Wine and water . . . Paten . . . Bread . . . Violet stoles . . . Come along, dear man; hurry, hurry"; and his hand, to save time, went into his trouser pocket for a key. He turned up an alley by the side of the church and came to a side door. While fitting the impatient key into the lock he found time to read, not without pleasure, a white lettering : " *To Vestries and Crypt*. Head Clerk and Verger, Mr. Flote, 15 George Street." Mr. Flote was sixty; but one does not easily tire of seeing one's name painted on a door.

Entering a vaulted passage that had the curious quality of striking cold and damp even as it sent towards him the warmth of the church's heating system, he hurried along its darkness to a Gothic door which, yielding to another key, admitted him to an oblong cell lit from a shallow, mullioned window, high up in the wall. This was the Verger's own room, or Office; and so long and compressed and lanky was it that it gave the appearance of having resisted and fought the church's architect till he, defeated by its obtuseness, had pushed it, angrily and anyhow, between the large Clergy Vestry and the important Muniment Room. It held a good oak table, a raffish desk, a decrepit armchair, and a gas stove which Mr. Flote hastened to light. Down the whole of its south wall were fixed with drawing-pins the dusty and curling photographs of choir-boys, choirmen, sidesmen and clergy who had worked with Mr. Flote during the last twenty years, and liked him, and given him their pictures on departing. Everyone who entered this room looked along this picture-gallery, and Mr. Flote would leave his desk or his

armchair and look along it too, and say contemplatively :
" Yes, the dear boys. . . ." and explain who had been who,
and what had become of him.   Did you ask information of
this one or that one, and learn that he had carried his career
to the Episcopal Bench, or to Africa, or to gaol, Mr. Flote
always began his reminiscences with : " Ah, that dear boy . . .
Yes, yes . . . poor, dear boy . . ."

This morning he applied the term to himself : " Come along,
dear boy.   Fifteen minutes past ten."   He removed overcoat
and jacket, and, taking from a hook an old serge cassock of
which all the lower buttons were done up, stepped into its
skirt, drew on its sleeves, and secured it by the button at the
throat.   From a cupboard he took the sacred vessels for the
Mid-day Communion and a big black bottle ; he replenished
the cruets with wine and water ; he laid a napkin on the paten
and cut reverently and carefully some squares of bread into
little cubes and placed them on the napkin.   Then he put a
kettle to boil on a slow trivet of the gas stove, for he was partial
to a cup of tea.   Then he hastened into the Clergy Vestry and
laid out the violet stoles and a clean surplice for the Vicar, and
opened the Preachers' Book at the First Sunday in Advent.
Back in the passage, he unlocked the Muniment Room and
extracted certain marriage and baptism registers.   Back in the
Verger's Office, he put the Banns Book under an arm-pit and
his gown over the same arm, and took the cruets in one hand
and the chalice and paten in the other, and caught up the front
of his cassock-skirt with some spare fingers, and climbed up
the stone stairway to the door of the Chancel.

In the lofty, echoing chancel he stepped more quietly, and
soon the carpet of the Sanctuary stayed all sound of his feet, as
he laid his cruets on the credence table and opened the Office
Books on the deacon's and sub-deacon's prayer-desks.   Now
down the long Chancel he went, putting the Banns Book on
the Vicar's stall as he passed, and down the nave between the
clustered columns of the arcade, pulling on his gown and
buttoning the overdue cassock-buttons.   The last button was
fixed as he reached the west end of the church and stood by the
main doors.   He looked at his watch and waited.   Already
he could hear the people outside the locked doors, and in
exasperation muttered aloud :

" He's always late.   Always late.   I said ten fifteen.   I
wonder what'd happen if *I* was late.   They never think of *that*,

neither assistant vergers nor curates nor vicars nor any of the like of them. 'Don't you worry. Flote'll see to all that.' But they'll rely on the little man once too often, I shouldn't wonder. Have a stroke, I might—half an hour before the service; *then* what'd happen? . . ."

So he muttered on one side of the oaken doors, looking repeatedly at his watch; while on the other side shuffled the feet of the assembling people, and their voices whispered together.

This was a parish of fifteen thousand souls, and, to judge from the congregation that would assemble for Morning Prayer, a fashionable parish; but ten thousand of those souls lived in the poorer streets to the north and knew little of their church. Once, twice, or three times in their lives they established a contact with that big, grey Gothic ark, and then it was necessarily through Mr. Flote as a gateway. Him they knew; they could remember those few times, happy and sad times, when they had been obliged to visit the little white-haired verger with the grey, walrus moustache; and because he had not been unkind to them then, they remembered him with grateful thoughts. Who realized—not the portly and successful vicar, Dr. O'Grogan, and not the curates, churchwardens, sidesmen, district visitors and fashionable congregation—that ten thousand of the parishioners, if they thought of the Parish Church at all, thought of Mr. Flote? And, to be sure, Mr. Flote himself had no such knowledge.

But it was so. In the nature of things it was he who had seen to it that innumerable babies from the surrounding streets had been safely baptized into the faith as he knew it (and in water of an innocuous temperature) on Sunday afternoons when the shadows were long in the aisles; it was he who had shepherded to the altar innumerable panicky swains and brides, there saying their responses for them when they were reduced to speechlessness (so that none could now tell how often Mr. Flote had been married—how many strange women he had accepted as his wedded wives and how many gaping louts he had accepted as his wedded husbands); it was he who had made the antique jest to innumerable giggling bridesmaids, " That it'd be their turn next; " it was he who had first administered to thousands of brides up and down the land the pleasant shock of being called " Mrs." (for he had a trick, in which he fancied that no one had surprised him, of bottling their husbands' names in his memory and then, the minute the ceremony was over, saying : " This way, *Mrs. So-and-So ;* this way, *Madam,* if you please ") ; it was he who had given to thousands of minute-old husbands and their attendant best men a happy liberation from nervousness by his loud laugh in the vestry, when he called to them : " Now, dear boy, you've got to sign the crime sheet ; come along, please ; " it was he who had knelt in the Lady Chapel by the side of bewildered young mothers, just out of child-bed, and said their part for them (so that none could now tell how often Mr. Flote had been churched) ; and it was he who had often, in the last twenty years, made comely his church with purple hangings and white flowers for those who had known him at the gate and were now entering it for the last time.

And every evening at six o'clock, down in that crypt beneath the church, where it smelt so vaulty and damp and his peculiar burrow lay huddled between the Clergy Vestry and the Muniment Room, a queue of people might have been seen awaiting an audience of him, for they had read in the *St. Austin's Parish Magazine* that Mr. Flote was then at his desk, ready to expound the law as it touched such dark subjects as matrimony and banns and licences, or to issue hospital letters in days of sickness, and bread tickets in days of want.

" Five and twenty past ten," he muttered. " This is later than he's ever bin. It's a scandal."

But then a youth leapt irreverently the three steps of the chancel and ran down the nave, buttoning up his cassock.

" Well ! " called Mr. Flote ; and most of the reproach in the world nestled in the monosyllable.

" Good morning, Mr. Flote."

Mr. Flote tried sarcasm.

" Perhaps it's the afternoon service you're coming to, George. If so, you're too early. It's at three o'clock, the Children's Service."

" No, it's Matins," assured the youth, tying his cincture.

" Matins, is it ? And a lot you've done towards preparing for Matins ? Perhaps you're the churchwarden. Perhaps I'm mistaken in thinking you're the Assistant Verger. . . . Why, the congregation's out there, before you've finished your breakfast."

" Yes, 'ark at 'em ! " said the youth. " Aren't they in a hurry for a good seat ? St. Austin's is getting popular, Mr. Flote."

"It's the attractions of the Assistant Verger, I shouldn't wonder," Mr. Flote suggested.

The big doors shook as someone pushed against them.

"Now just you wait," the youth ordered, in an imaginary address to the people outside. "At half-past ten we open them doors, and not a minute sooner. For Queen Victoria we might open them, but not for you. . . . Eh, what's that?"

A clock gave a premonitory clicking before it rang the two quarters. Mr. Flote straightened his gown and smoothed down his moustache, stroking both its drooping wings. The clock struck.

"Open up, George."

George, who loved, like all boys, this prompt and punctual response to the commands of a clock, shot back the bolts and flung the doors apart. Mr. Flote, standing where all must pass him, smoothed down his moustache again: ready to welcome the People of God.

The bell, high up in the church's gable, said "Clink" once, "Clink" again, and then "Clango, clango, clango, clango, clango," without change or intermission. To that long and dignified street, now dotted with worshippers approaching the church, there was always a vague disappointment in the sound of this single bell; it seemed an unworthy sound to come from so superior a pile; it gave to its listeners a tiny shock of personal shame like the shock which comes when a very tall and important gentleman on a platform rises and addresses an audience in a thin little voice, pitched high in his head.

In two houses only did it sound loud and bruisingly, those to right and left of the church. The house to the right was the Vicarage; like all its neighbours, it was as upright and narrow as the spine of a book, dividing itself into a basement, a bay-windowed ground-floor, a bay-windowed first story, a flat-breasted second story with a pedimented window, and a third story with a dormer. Its hearth-stoned steps mounted to a stucco portico with corinthian columns and a balustraded balcony above. And now the bell was clanging into its stairways, landings and bedrooms. It clanged into the head of Mrs. O'Grogan, the Vicar's wife, who was at her dressing-table in the second-floor front room. It sent her with a muttered, " Good gracious ! *There !* " to the bannisters where in a high-pitched voice to defeat the clangour she called down the well of the staircase : " Children ! Children ! " and, receiving no answer, raised her voice to a still higher treble and called again : " Children, Children ! Are you ready ? For goodness' sake get yourselves ready. It's half-past ten."

From a door on the ground-floor a boy of eleven came out and called :

" What ? "

" Oh dear ! I said, are all you children ready. The bell's begun."

" We had remarked it," said the boy of eleven.

" Well, for goodness' sake see if those children are getting themselves ready, Keith. It's——"

" They are not so employed," said the boy.

" Tut, tut . . . dear, dear . . . well, tell them to, for pity's sake . . ." and she worried back into her room.

" I will do what I can," her son called after her. " I have a predilection towards helpfulness."

This boy of eleven had, it will be seen, an idiom of his own —though hardly his own, perhaps, for there is a period of disastrous humour through which many boys, who are in the higher forms of their preparatory schools and beginning to sip the joys of language, find it pleasant to travel. Boys who are tall and good-looking are particularly likely to seek this happy country where the berries of language are so large and luscious, and to browse among them ; and Keith O'Grogan was certainly tall and good-looking. He had dark hair that, because of its slight coarseness, stood off his head in waves ; grey-blue eyes in which a lazy humour peeped ; and good straight features that promised in time to become the commanding, seigniorial features of Dr. O'Grogan himself. His body was already thinning to lankiness, and now he carried it with something like a cynical weariness into the breakfast room. " Now then ! " he shouted to four other children who were busy at play in the room. " Bestir yourselves. The lady upstairs is getting impatient." He took the gun-metal watch from his waistcoat pocket and consulted it. " Yes, the tempus fugit's all right. Look alive, all of you. Equip for Divine Service."

The four children began to lift themselves sulkily from their play.

" Come on ! I never speak twice," said Keith, standing at the door like a sergeant.

The tallest of the four children, a girl of nine years and a half, and as handsome as Keith, though her expression was as spontaneously lively as his was studiously languid, came towards the door.

"He's trying to be clever," she scoffed.

"I take no impudence from you, young Joyce," Keith answered. "Go and wash."

Joyce showed him a brilliant red pennon of a tongue and danced from the room. She was followed by a thick-set boy of eight, whose advance into the hall Keith encouraged quite gratuitously, and on the inspiration of the moment, with a kick.

"Hell to you!" said the child.

"Go and wash, young Derek," commanded Keith.

"I shouldn't do it for you," Derek explained from the hall, that his independence, about which he had heard a great deal, might be vindicated. "I do it because I want to."

"You do. You want it badly," Keith agreed.

Derek was followed by Peggy, a little girl of six and a half, who passed her eldest brother with the promptness of a healthy fear. Lastly came Tony, a very small boy of five, with impudent eyes, to whom Keith said, "*Br-r-r-r!*" and feigned a blow, thus shooting him into the hall.

"That's the lot," Keith sighed. "'S'blood! what a crowd!"

Keith, Joyce, Derek, Peggy and Antony—those were the five O'Grogan children. And their ages were eleven, nine and a half, eight, six and a half, and five—eighteen months, or as near as made no difference, dividing each of them. And they came in a perfect alternation—a boy, a girl, a boy, a girl, and a boy—so there was little wonder that Dr. O'Grogan, whose pulpit vocabulary would sometimes stray in from the church next door and invest his dinner-table observations with the grand manner, had more than once given the following address to his guests: "There's a beautiful rhythm about my family. There's something cosmic about such a rhythm, which passes our understanding. It's the rhythm of the tides and the seasons and the stars. Keith, Joyce, Derek, Peggy and Antony—why, it's a perfect work of art. And they pattern off perfectly in other ways. Keith and Joyce, the two eldest, both have brains and make a good pair, for young Joyce has all the liveliness and vanity to meet Keith's *imperium* with a desirable insolence, and so they get on splendidly; young Joyce takes nothing for nothing from Keith; for every *quo* of elder-brotherly rudeness he gets a *quid* of sisterly vitriol from Joyce ! And then Peggy and Antony, the two youngest, are much alike in many ways and make another good pair; and meanwhile, young Derek stands in the middle, quite apart, which suits him exactly—for young Derek is as different from the others as chalk is from cheese; he's *sui generis*, completely self-sufficient and completely self-satisfied; going his own way, with no brains, and therefore as conceited as they make 'em. Oh, ho, Derek: I've no fear for Derek's future; brains or no brains, he's certain to be successful in life; no one so cocksure and self-centred could possibly fail."

As if in illustration of this talent for success and this apartness Derek emerged first from the cloakroom, and emerged alone. Joyce was still within, paying considerable attention to the mirror, while Peggy and little Antony shared the vacated basin together.

" Is it going to be decent this morning ? " Derek asked of his elder brother.

" I will ascertain," said Keith.

He walked up the stairs to the closed door of the first floor front room, which, being the best room in the house, was the Vicar's study. Here, since the landing was dark, a fortunate hole in the door enabled him to see much that was happening in the sunlit study beyond. He returned with news of what he had seen.

" The sermon will be by Dr. O'G. He's walking up and down with it, and looking out of the window as he spouts it off."

" Oh, bother ! " said Derek. " I hoped it'd be the Crab's Farewell Sermon."

" No, it's the dear vicar this morning. And it's pretty sound stuff, I fancy. He looks as though *he* were going to enjoy it, at any rate."

" Does he always learn them by heart ? "

" Course he does. He learns them by heart and pretends that he never uses a note. It's a sound scheme."

" Is he going to read the lessons ? "

" Does he ever if he's preaching ? Idiot ! "

" Yes, he does sometimes," retorted Derek, unperturbed and self-confident as ever. " If it's a hot lesson he always bags it for himself. So *had on !* "

" *Had on !* " was the current expression at Derek's preparatory school for that emotion of triumph which other boys at other times have expressed by " *Sucks !* " If you had defeated your opponent in argument, you were held to have " had him on," and were entitled to announce the fact.

At this point Joyce burst out from the cloakroom, and having heard something of Keith and Derek's conversation, demanded in her bright and lively manner :

" What's the programme this morning, Keatings ? "

" Your father's preaching," Keith answered.

" I guessed it ! I guessed it ! He's preaching at St. Paul's this afternoon, as he's told everybody a million times, so he was certain to try out his sermon on us. That'll mean the Crab'll take the service for the last time, bless his heart ! "

" The Crab's no good at taking the service," Derek interpolated, for no other reason, probably, than that it would annoy Joyce.

" Course he is ! "

" Course he isn't ! Daddy often says so."

" Daddy's probably jealous of him. He's sweeter than any of them, and takes the service beautifully."

" What piffle——" began Derek ; but Keith, as the eldest, adjudicated between the combatants.

" He doesn't," he said. " He can't sing for nuts, young Joyce. His sermons are worth a hundred of Daddy's, though Daddy doesn't think so, but singing the service isn't his forte. Your love has blinded your eyes, my child."

" And anyway," added Derek, with his quiet superiority, " the Crab won't be there at all. He's gone away on a preaching job that Daddy didn't want to do, because it wasn't big enough. So *had on !*—all."

" Oh, blow ! " bewailed Joyce. " Then there'll only be Hugo. That'll mean that Daddy'll take the first part of the service, so that he can have all the second part to swat at his sermon."

" It'll be precisely thus," Keith promised.

These three elder children were now drawing on their overcoats, Joyce punctiliously, and Keith and Derek indifferently, so that the necks of their overcoats lay at strange inclinations along their Eton collars. The lining of their preparatory school caps, too, when they put them on, peeped down at the Eton collars. And the double breasts of the overcoats swung unbuttoned, as the boys wandered back into the breakfast-room, leaving Joyce to gaze into the mirror of the hall-stand.

Since the dining-room, the drawing-room, and their father's study were normally forbidden territory, the breakfast-room was the room where they had lived most of their lives, if their bedrooms be excepted. And the hall was almost its annexe. The breakfast-room was a fairly large room at the back of the house, overlooking the narrow garden. On its cream wall-paper, striped like a newly-mown lawn, hung some large steel engravings of Doré's pictures and one, more recent, of Queen Victoria's Golden Jubilee, which had been celebrated six years earlier. On the marble mantelpiece stood several photographs of the family in plush and silver frames, two nondescript brass candlesticks and an ash-tray, and a tall overmantel, elaborate with shelves and mirrors. A large mahogany dining-table with piano legs filled the centre of the carpet, and a green saddle-bag suite stood against the walls. Heavy plush curtains hung from the abraded brass rail above the windows, and gave something of the appearance of a shallow stage to the balcony, whose green boxes, in summer, were gay with scarlet geraniums, white marguerites and blue lobelia. That pink geraniums also should hang in wire baskets from the awning was an offence to Derek, who held that it would be more patriotic to limit the balcony flowers to red, white and blue.

The chequer-board linoleum of the hall was very narrow as it passed the door of the basement and the flank of the stair-case; but it spread out into a broader oblong on the space before the front-door. Round the lower half of the hall walls ran a dado painted chocolate, and above it a paper that imitated Dutch tiles, and then the cornice of the ceiling began with a strip of applied leaf ornament. On the left of the front door was the hat-and-umbrella stand, and often several pairs of goloshes, and Keith's cricket bat or hockey stick, and perhaps a toy perambulator belonging to Peggy. On the right were two hard-seated oak chairs for the spiritual or financial invalids who might await an interview with the vicar. Above these hung a text, "GOD IS THE MASTER OF THIS HOUSE," to which Joyce, this morning, was turning her back, as she adjusted her coat in the hat-stand mirror. To the youngest two children, Peggy and Antony, who were by far the most imaginative, the front door itself was the most clearly marked feature of the hall: about its bolts and its chain, its letter-box which could click with such alarm or such promise, its leaded lights stained the greens and the blues of the sea's depths or painted in the centre of one window with a bird on a branch and in the centre of the other with a brace of pears—leaded lights which could darken with the shadows of strange visitants, there was an interest and a fear, and the fascination that is born of these.

Mrs. O'Grogan now called down the stairs to Joyce that she was to see that Peggy and Tony were properly dressed; and Joyce, without giving a glance at the little ones, called back that they were all right; and Keith, from the breakfast-room, shouted a genial " Liar ! " and Dr. O'Grogan made an angry but invisible emergence from his study, to send a petition both up the staircase and down the staircase that there might be less noise in the house.   So Keith, in a subdued voice, summoned the family into the hall, and arranged them according to their heights.

" Little Tony'll go first ; and Peggy, you jolly well keep close behind Tony ; and Derek close behind Peggy ; and Joyce, just you tread on Derek's heels ; and you can rely on me to tread on yours.   And just you keep close behind each other like that, all the way up the nave ; otherwise we shan't get the Organ Pipes effect."   He looked at the gun-metal watch. " Hang ! It's only a quarter to.   It's no good having the Organ Pipes effect unless there's a full congregation to see it. You'd better hoof off for a bit.   Here's Mother all ready to go."

Mrs. O'Grogan was descending the stairs : a tall, slender woman in a well-made black-silk dress, a large hat and veil, and drawing on her gloves as she came.   In her outdoor dress she seemed a handsome woman, for the veil softened the lines she had worried into her forehead and the look of sad resignation that dwelt in her eyes.

" Where are the children ?   I thought I asked you to get them ready, Keith.   Can you *never* do anything to help ? "

" Such is gratitude ! " Keith sighed.   " They're ready for the fray."

" Well, where are they ? and don't call Morning Service a fray."

But Keith was meditating on his hurt, and found it worse than he thought.   " ' Never do anything to help,' " he repeated. " By jove, that's a bit thick, as thickness goes."

" Oh, don't stand there playing the fool !   Where are they ? And your coat and cap are all on one side, both of them.   Can't you even get yourself ready properly? I don't know what people'd take you for, sometimes; upon my word I don't."

"They'd take me for a gentleman, no matter how I was dressed," answered Keith, very readily, submitting as his mother readjusted his cap and pushed his hair from sight. "But damme! 'Never do anything to help'—after I've been slaving with them! Gorblimey! as thickness goes, it's the thickest thing that ever was. I shan't forget it in a hurry. . . . Yes, they'd know me for a gentleman anywhere, which is more than I should care to say about Derek, or about your youngest son, the infant Tony. . . . No, I shouldn't go so far as to say it about *them*."

Mrs. O'Grogan, in no humour for his pleasantries, slightly stamped her foot, while she slid a shilling into the palm of one glove, subcutaneously.

"Oh, *don't* stand there acting the fool like that. I've told you not to. Where are the children?. . . Children, children!" she cried, putting her smelling-salts into her muff. "Oh, where are they? Joyce dear! . . . Derek. . . . Peggy. . . . Tony. . . ."

"You'll have your husband out, if you call like that," warned Keith. "He's not in his happiest vein this morning. That's why I sent the kids away. But there you are! I'll round them up if you want them. It's my happiness to oblige."

He gathered them together, with as much delay as possible; but the brake could not be applied for ever, and in due course the family passed into the dry sunlight of the street. The bell was clanging with a slower and more wearied rhythm now, as if it knew that the end of its long exercise was at hand. And there were only a few people on the pavements approaching the church, because people needed to come early who wanted a good pew in St. Austin's, Kensington, during the ministry of Dr. Ernest O'Grogan. In the far distance the brougham of Lady Castlewaite was returning to its mews; no other vehicle could be seen, for not many of the congregation, though it accounted itself well-to-do, were among the "carriage-folk." The long wide road was taking back the emptiness and the sabbath silence which for another hour must occupy it—a silence only heightened by the dim, imprisoned murmur of a congregation singing.

In the vestibule, after sundry grimaces of Keith's, the children fell into his prescribed order; and here was Mr. Flote in cassock and gown, smiling a welcome to them. Mr. Flote always looked forward to the entrance of the Vicarage family; they came rather late, when every seat in the nave was filled except the roped-in Vicarage pew, and the sidesmen were escorting the last arrivals into the side aisles, and thus the church's central alley was free for him to conduct them in an important little procession, as was proper, down through the hushed respect of the congregation to their royal seat in front. It was the most impressive event before the service. This morning with a step becomingly slow he brought them, as usual, into the centre of the parochial picture; but he did not know, never turning his head, that they were coming in an especial formation; Tony first; then Peggy, a little taller; then Derek, a little taller yet, and self-assured and unsmiling; then Joyce, a little taller and inclined to giggle; then Keith, the tallest of them all; then the tall, thin, tired mother; a perfect similitude of an ascending series of organ pipes. He unhooked the cord that secluded the Vicarage pew; and the family, in exactly the same order, filed in. Keith was satisfied: his row of organ pipes, in their decent regularity, could be observed of the congregation throughout the service.

St. Austin's, Kensington, had " uses " of its own, warranted by no higher authority—but who cared for a higher authority ? —than Dr. Ernest O'Grogan; and one of these " uses " was the trooping of a " processional hymn " round the church on every possible occasion. Let tradition say what it liked, was not the First Sunday in Advent a magnificent opportunity for the choir and clergy to burst out of the vestry doors with :

> " Lo ! he comes with clouds descending,
> Once for favoured sinners slain ;
> Thousand thousand saints attending
> Swell the triumph of His train " ?

There would be no announcement of the hymn; the choir would just break it on the people, who would rise to it in their multitude. So, at the last clang of the bell and the first stroke of the clock—for Dr. Ernest O'Grogan had as boyish a delight as George, the assistant verger, in a promptness like that of a gun to its trigger—the vestry doors flung wide, and the processional cross and the choir boys brought this great roll of song down the side aisle—" Alleluia ! Alleluia ! Christ appears on earth again "—behind the choir boys came twenty choirmen, some young and round-faced, some middle-aged and with long curling moustaches, some grey-whiskered and grey-bearded, and all boyishly pleased with the drama of their entry and with the richness of their voices in " Every eye shall now behold Him, Robed in dreadful majesty ; Those who set at naught and sold Him, Pierced and nailed Him to the Tree, Deeply wailing, Deeply wailing . . ." ; then came the banner of St. Austin of Canterbury ; then came the junior curate ; then Mr. Flote in his gown, and carrying his silver wand (another " use " peculiar to St. Austin's, and designed to give a proper dignity to the office of the vicariate) ; then—and the faces of the people fluttered towards him, so fine a figure was he—Dr. Ernest O'Grogan himself, wearing his scarlet hood. Dr. O'Grogan was a tall, broad man, whose immense vitality, after impressing itself on the greater part of cheaper Kensington, had plenty to spare for running to flesh. His neck had the round ruddy thickness and his mouth the straight thinness of a man who was developing aggressiveness and obstinacy, but in his other features he was most handsomely blessed : the nose, chin and brow had an imperial dignity ; the eyes were dark, bright, and with those persons who would yield to him, always playful ; and his hair, most blessed gift of all, crowned him with that exceptional distinction which silver hair can give to a man only forty years old. As a witty lady of his flock explained : " Dr. Ernest was not a saint, but then how could he be with such features and such hair ? God would surely take into account the insuperable difficulty which they presented." He was not singing, as the procession drew him like a fine conclusion round the church, but looking to left and right that he might drink satisfaction from the massed attendance, and smiling as he remembered that the same witty lady, in whom he delighted, had once called these thousand people " The Ernest Worshippers." The worshippers were rejoicing in the hymn, which had now entered upon its last verse and was rising, according to the directions in the book from *forte* to *fortissimo* :

> " Yes, Amen, let all adore Thee,
>   High on Thine eternal Throne ;
> Saviour, take the power and glory ;
>   Claim the Kingdom for Thine own :
>   Alleluia ! Alleluia !
>   Thou shalt reign, and Thou alone."

It expired before the clergy had reached the chancel steps, and the organist played the Vicar with a thunderous roll into his stall, and, immediately the scarlet hood was there, stopped: as if the main business of all this triumphant inauguration were now achieved. The Vicar faced the congregation; he waited till the silence was perfect; he administered a dramatic snub to two later-comers by prolonging his wait till they had attained their pews and following them into that refuge with his eyes; and then, in his good Irish voice, began:

"I acknowledge my transgressions, and my sin is ever before me."

After the service that long road smelt of roasting potatoes and steaming winter greens; and the smell poured out on the noon air as strongly from the basement of the Vicarage as from any of the other houses. The children met it in their dining-room, where it had solidified into the form of Sunday dinner. The father sat at the head of the table with the joint; the mother at the foot with the vegetables; Keith and Joyce, as the larger children, on their father's right; Derek, Peggy and Antony on his left. A parlour-maid, in a cap with long streamers, carried the plates around; and Keith and Joyce finished their mutton and vegetables and red-currant jelly long before their father, who had to carve for seven persons upstairs and two in the basement, and, moreover, did a deal of talking about the thing uppermost in his mind—his recent sermon. At last their father had finished; and their mother, who had given but a simulated interest to his talk, interrupted it with the suggestion that he rang the bell for the pudding; and he rang it, and continued his talk. Up came the apple tart, and best of all, the cream; and, not many minutes later, repletion was the fact most sensuously felt in the dining-room.

"You're to go to the children's service, understand," said Dr. O'Grogan, wiping his mouth with his napkin, and pushing back his chair. "Your mother and I will be away. I am preaching the first of the Advent sermons at the Cathedral. I don't know but what Keith and Joyce might come too."

A sudden alarm showed itself on Joyce's face, and a grimace turned down Keith's lips.

"Would you like to, Keith?"

" Well . . ." Keith was beaten.

" It'll be the same sermon as you preached this morning, won't it ? " asked Joyce, with her ready wit.

" Yes. Something the same, I suppose," answered the vicar, who knew it would be word for word the same, but sought a reputation, even among his children, as an extempore preacher.

" I rather wanted to hear the Crab's last sermon this afternoon."

" I wish you wouldn't speak of Mr. Crabb like that," her mother protested ; but her father, paying no attention to his wife, broke in :

" All right, my dear, and so you shall. He is great with children, is Crabb." His tone left a clear impression : that, when it came to a question of preaching to a vast and intelligent adult congregation, there was no one on the staff in quite the same class as the vicar, and so the vicar could afford to praise generously the lesser gifts of his juniors. " Yes. Go, by all means, and hear his good-bye."

The father and mother retired upstairs, and the children to the breakfast-room, where Keith recovered his ascendancy.

" That's all nonsense about *us* going to Children's Service— you and me, Joyce, I mean. The Kids can go. We shan't. He didn't put us on our honour to ; I carefully noticed that."

Joyce seemed frustrated again, and began hesitatingly :

" Still, I think we ought to. . . ."

" I don't. . . . It's absurd to make us go with all those smelly Sunday School children. . . . Here, Peggy and Tony, *you'll* jolly well go, and Derek'll look after you."

" Shan't," said Derek, occupied, after his fashion, on some solitary business.

" What if I make you ? "

" Shan't go with Peggy and Tony."

" Oh, won't you ? "

" No."

Keith stared at him threateningly, like a lion-tamer hypnotizing a rising beast ; and the child was overawed.

" I may look in," he conceded. " On my own."

" You may," agreed Keith.

Now Peggy intruded herself excitedly : " Keatings, *I'll* take Tony. I'd love to. I'll look after him, I promise I will. Do let me."

Keith studied her with a humorous scrutiny. "Strange child," he commented.

"Keatings, may—may I? Oh, may I?"

"Certainly. Certainly."

"Oh, good! Come on, Tony." She rushed to the child, took his hand and led him, unprotesting, towards the door. "Come; I'll get you ready."

Peggy, at six and a half, had a fringe of brown hair nearly reaching her eyebrows. The rest of her hair reached her shoulders where it turned round in a curl. Her mouth was large and moist, and her eyes large and moist. One feature of her attire seemed ever the same; though weekday frocks might give place to Sunday frocks, and playroom frocks to party frocks, the left leg of her white drawers was always hanging low down, and always visible. This insecure funnel of drawers was as inseparable a detail of anyone's portrait of Peggy as the lustrous remoteness in her eyes; and both details, maybe, were fathered by the same pensiveness. All people remarked her pensiveness and would say that if she had not the vivacity and beauty of her elder sister, Joyce, she had, at any rate, an exceedingly interesting face. They said that both these two younger children had exceedingly interesting faces— faces that made you wonder what they would do in life; and Dr. O'Grogan, when his pulpit brilliance was invading his dinner-table talk, would say so too. "All the three elder children have just ordinary good looks and, as far as I can read them, utterly objective minds; and therefore they'll probably be fairly successful in the world. But little Peggy and little Tony, anyone can see, are subjective creatures; their minds are inward—especially Peggy. They can be impudent enough —at least the small boy can—but their eyes, when the sparkle of impudence has left them, turn inward at once. Yes, the shadows will fall deeper and the lights shine brighter in the lives of my Peggy and Tony. Especially Peggy, I fancy."

So, lest he were right, watch her as she carried off Tony to an afternoon's worship. She quickly arrayed herself and turned and ordered his toilet; she buttoned his reefer coat and dusted his knickers; she straightened his hair and, wetting the corner of her handkerchief with her tongue, removed all traces of the apple-tart from his mouth; she put a prayer-book in one of his hands and took the other in her own and led him out of the vicarage to the church. The November afternoon was sharply cold and had turned misty, so that when they passed into the church, its sudden warmth struck like the warmth of an oven door. But some of the mistiness had entered the church before them, and the windows shone opaquely, and the unlit chancel, behind its screen, seemed very dark, and Peggy could feel that she was leading her little brother into an atmosphere of God. Mr. Flote smiled at them as they walked up the nave, and the few adults, scattered here and there in the hinder pews, smiled too ; for they were amused to see a small girl, with one of her drawers insecurely depending, dragging a smaller boy up the whole length of the nave and pushing him into one of the pews reserved for " The Children of the Congregation." She pushed him on to his knees, that he might perform a private devotion, and then sought her own hassock and knelt too. But Peggy alone knew that this was a mere concession to appearances and that she wasn't really praying. Peggy alone knew that, for a long time now, appalled at her secret sins, she had withdrawn from the insincerity of prayer.

From every door the Sunday School children were pouring in, their teachers pushing them and their Superintendents shepherding them into allotted pens. The church was full of the sound of shuffling feet and noisy whispering. Much interest in the dirty little Sunday School children was being shown by the " Children of the Congregation," where they sat very clean and well-behaved, their nurses and governesses among them. Before the last of the children were in their places, Mr. Crabb, middle-aged, fat, and jolly, came to the Chancel steps and beamed over all. There was rustling and craning and neck-stretching among his audience. He announced the first hymn, and smiled as if he were announcing a great game :

> " I love to hear the story
> Which Angel voices tell. . . ."

Out boomed the organ, and many hundred children slithered from their seats to their feet. They were singing now. Perhaps it might be said that the older boys were roaring, but Mr. Crabb only directed on them a beam of gratification and they, who had been under the impression that they were doing something bad, began to wonder if they were doing something good. The hymn had hardly started before Derek " looked in," as he had promised. He came through the West Door and seated himself alone in a back pew, after the manner of the

solitary adults.   Having a high sense of the proprieties he
knelt for ten seconds, and then rose to assist in the current
hymn.   Almost immediately Joyce, having escaped (who knew
how ?) from Keith, rushed in, anxious not to miss a minute's
vision of her beloved Mr. Crabb.   She saw Derek and pushed
beside him, with the idea of spending the service, like a friendly
sister, at his side.   But he, annoyed at being thus converted
from a single adult to one of two children, moved out of the pew,
singing, " I am glad my blessed Saviour was once a child like
me," and chose a lonelier seat behind.   Joyce turned and smiled
broadly at him for such pomposity, and then, rather out of
breath, added her shrill and happy voice to the uproarious song :

> " He never will forget me,
>   Because he loves me so.
> I love to hear the story
>   Which Angel voices tell
> How once the King of Glory
>   Came down on earth to dwell."

When Mr. Crabb ascended the pulpit stairs and six hundred
children with shuffle and slither sat themselves down in the
pews, Peggy placed Tony in a sitting position and herself beside
him, and took one of his hands in hers, as she had seen other
governesses do.   And she stared up at the preacher.   Mr. Crabb
was leaning over the pulpit to make his first point—leaning
over so far that it seemed he was thinking more about the
effectiveness of his opening words than about his safety.   Fat
and jovial, he looked—in this thrilling moment before speech—
rather like a benevolent snail extending itself out of its shell.

" There's a lot in a door," he said.

Having said this, he drew himself in, and stood upright, and
smiled.

" There's an awful lot in a door," he repeated.   " The door
of this church, for instance—" six hundred children turned
round to have a look at the big West Door—" Yes, there it is,
children ; the door of this church opens on to very great
things.   It admits to the greatest things in the world.
Ahem !——" he coughed humorously, and leaned out again :
" I daresay you think it leads to greater things when you
approach it from within, at the end of a children's service, say.
Eh ?   Well, well, well.   Time'll be when you'll know that it
leads to greater things if you approach it from without, and
you'll remember that I told you so, one misty Sunday in

November. . . . Our subject this afternoon is Doors, and one door in particular. And we'll begin by saying this : *Open the doors more often than you shut them.* On the whole you're more likely to do right if you open a door than if you shut it. . . .

"Now should we say that three times ? "

They said it three times, with immense willingness and immense indifference.

"And that reminds me that my old father often says——"

Surprise quieted the children to a sudden interest. They conceived of Mr. Crabb as old himself—corpulent and jolly, but old. And here was talk of Mr. Crabb's father. Peggy, listening with taut interest, pictured a palsied Methuselah, nut-crackery and mummified.

"My old father often says, when I have most inconsiderately left him sitting in a draught, that doors are made to be shut. Well, in such a circumstance as that they *are ;* once or twice in life they *are ;* but on the *whole*, children—speaking *generally*, children, you do a glorious thing nearly every time you open a door, and a harsh thing nearly every time you shut it. And that reminds me of the story of Rhoda——"

The congregation sat up. It always did when Mr. Crabb smiled his most expansive smile and said that something reminded him of the story of someone. One little girl, sitting among the children of the Moon Street Sunday School, sat up more abruptly than the others. Her name was Rhoda Bell, and she was suffering a horrid fear that the Reverend Crabb was going to talk about her.

"You all know who Rhoda was, don't you ? " cajoled the preacher over the pulpit.

Quite fifty little girls turned round in their pews and looked at Rhoda Bell and giggled.

"Well, Rhoda was a serving maid in a very nice household. Quite the nicest household in Jerusalem—turn round, you little girls. It was Mrs. Mark's household, you know, about which you can read in the twelfth chapter of the *Acts*. Mrs. Mark was the mother of John Mark, who was our dear Lord's disciple. And she was an extraordinarily nice person, Mrs. Mark." (At this point a lady who disapproved of making children laugh in church got up and walked out ; while the huge majority of the congregation turned round to study her exit.) "She was an extraordinarily nice woman, Mrs. Mark," continued the impenitent Mr. Crabb. "She used to keep open house for the apostles. And once, you know, when Peter was in prison and in serious danger of being put to death, she and her friends, and Rhoda, her serving maid, were all together—and what do you think they were doing? You boy, what do you think they were doing?"

The small boy, thus addressed, promptly stated the only business which, in his thinking, could assemble a lady and her friends together. "Eatin'," he suggested.

"No. Oh, no," Mr. Crabb reproached him. "Hardly eating. It was past the time for eating. Besides, I can't think such loving people had much appetite for eating so long as poor Peter was in prison. Not eating, I think."

"Washid' up," ventured another child, taking the next event in the natural order of life.

Mr. Crabb shook his head.

"Sewin'," tried a little girl.

Again Mr. Crabb shook his head, smiling his forgiveness.

"Readin' the Boible," called a large boy. Not that he was a pious child, but because he believed in giving the clergy the answers they wanted, and so avoiding unnecessary delay.

Mr. Crabb smiled patiently.

"Remember," he said, "Peter was in prison—in trouble. Surely there is only one thing to do when your friend is in trouble."

Then happened the thing that shamed Joyce so intolerably and made Peggy blush brilliantly and sink lower in her seat by Tony's side, who was now asleep: Derek called out, "*Pray for him*"—and called it out quickly, lest anyone else should get in with the true answer and away with the honour before he did. Who but Derek would have been such a brainless idiot, and so secure from shyness, as to do a thing like this, when everyone knew that only the Sunday School children were expected to answer the questions from the pulpit—not the ladies' children?

"Precisely!" acknowledged the preacher, radiant with approval. "They were all together praying for Peter. And—even as they prayed—the doors of Peter's prison far away, huge, studded doors, were swung open by an angel. So often —so often, my children, they are angels that open doors. . . . Should we say that three times? . . . Thank you. So the doors were swung open, and Peter found himself in the street. And, standing there, he saw in his mind's eye Mrs. Mark's household, and the warm welcome he would get from Mrs. Mark and from young John Mark, and from charming Rhoda, the bright-eyed serving maid. So he turned naturally towards their door. There was something beautiful about Mrs. Mark's door. (I told you this sermon was going to be all about doors.) You see: all doors are beautiful to which people turn first in trouble or in joy. . . . Yes, I think we'll say that three times. . . . Thank you so much; you said it very nicely. . . . Well, Peter came to that door and knocked. . . ."

Mr. Crabb knocked three slow and awful knocks on the pulpit. The silence in the church was sepulchral.

"Knock . . . knock . . . knock," declaimed Mr. Crabb, only half reminiscent of Macbeth.

He leaned over the pulpit and whispered with great dramatic power : " Rhoda heard that knock. . . . She rose. It was her duty to go to the door. . . . She was a little startled, I think, or she would have opened it at once. It can be a startling thing, a knock at the door—and the sound of a man's footsteps on the threshold. ' Who's there ? ' she asked. Wonderful words ! *Who's there ?* "

The words were so wonderful that they stilled the whole congregation to silence. The children were staring with wide eyes at the preacher. Peggy's jaw was drooping, and her hand, holding the sleeping Tony's, pressed it excitedly.

" Who was there——"

" Peter," answered Derek, anxious to pursue his recent success, and lacking the imagination to distinguish between a rhetorical question and a friendly test of memory.

" Yes, yes." Mr. Crabb rebutted the unwanted answer and continued the rhetoric. " ' Who's there ? ' she asked. ' It's me,' said a voice. Was it—could it possibly be Peter's voice ? Yes. It sounded like it. She thought it was. But how could it be ? Peter was in prison, and they had just been praying for him. If anything was outside the door, it must be Peter's ghost. Oh, what was she to do ? What would she see if she opened the door ? O Rhoda, what are you going to do ? Won't you have faith, and overcome your fears, and open that door. What happiness may come in, if you open it ! What are you waiting in that passage for ? . . ."

Like insubstantial things the grey walls of the church had faded out, taking with them the lofty windows, opaque with the November dusk ; and the walls of Rhoda's passage had closed in and bounded each of six hundred waiting minds. Each child was standing in Rhoda's passage, looking at her hall door. Each child was Rhoda, standing alone. There were six hundred passages, all different, and yet all the same. Peggy stood in a hall that was indistinguishable from the hall of the Vicarage : the lower half of its walls had a dado painted brown, and the upper half a paper that imitated Dutch tiles, and the cornice a strip of applied leaf ornament ; on the left of the front-door was the hat-stand, with her father's black Inverness cape and soup-plate hat hanging on a peg ; opposite was a framed text, " GOD IS THE MASTER OF THIS HOUSE," with a brass gong beside it ; a lantern of coloured glass, suspended on chains, surrounded the incandescent gas mantle under the centre of the ceiling ; and the front door at which she was staring had leaded windows above the letter-box and the chain, and the street light was illuminating every coloured diamond and lozenge of those windows, except where a shadow moved —a patient shadow—the shadow of a man. The door was bolted, and the chain was up, and she stood there alone. But somehow Mr. Crabb had passed very quietly through that bolted wood and was somewhere near, talking. Himself was invisible—a voice in the passage where she stood alone, staring at the closed door, and the shadow beyond it. He was saying that, just as Peter, when the angel opened his prison, came to Rhoda's door, so Jesus, now that an angel had rolled away the stone from his tomb, came to your door. He was saying that it was natural to have doubts and fears of the miracle, and if you knew in your secret heart that you were always sinning, to be afraid lest He were angry ; but if only you would open the door straightaway, instead of doubting and worrying and arguing as little Rhoda did, you would just know—just *know* that He was no ghost but your best friend, and that He didn't come in any terrible form, but like a friend who had been in trouble for your sake and was now seeking shelter and love ; he was suggesting that they all went on their knees and said just what they liked to Jesus, and then they would all stand up and sing a very joyous hymn, because they would be very happy about what they had said to Him.

There was a far-spread rumbling noise, as of six hundred children exchanging their seats for the hassocks. Six hundred church interiors had come back and become one church interior ; and Peggy slipped to her knees in it—her father's grey church, filled with children, and strangely dark now, its windows all put out by a November twilight. The day that had been bright with pale sunlight was burning down into darkness and mystery ; and little plump Mr. Crabb had vanished in his pulpit —no, the crown of his head was still visible, for he had simply sunk down in it, and buried his face in his hands.

And in that minute of silence while the children knelt in the falling darkness, and Mr. Crabb knelt, and Mr. Flote put a match to the long taper with which he would light the gas brackets all up the aisles, the O'Grogan children held their own thoughts : Keith, enjoying the privileges of his seniority, was reading *Peter Simple* at home ; Joyce, in one pew, was thinking how much she loved Mr. Crabb and wondering if she were as attractive as Rhoda ; Derek, in another pew, was enjoying his solitariness and thinking that the service had not been so bad and that he had acquitted himself rather well ; and Peggy, her face buried in her hands like Mr. Crabb's, was welcoming Jesus back again ; and Tony was asleep with dreams that have been lost.

CHAPTER II

SUNDAY, in the memories of the O'Grogan children when they grew up, and just such a wintry Sunday as this, stood out as a vessel that held much of the essence of their childhood. Other days, having no such isolation, merged into one another and made hazy patches; for example, did Tuesday, as a word, mean anything at all? Not even Saturday, the holiday, had a character so essential, because on Saturday, as on other weekdays, the family fell apart; it was only Sunday that forced all the family to jostle together within its strict enclosure. On weekdays Keatings, as all called him now, went to his day-school at Colet Court, where he was in the Lower First and preparing for his entry into St. Paul's School; Derek went likewise to Colet Court but went there alone, Keatings having refused to convoy a " kiddy brother," and Derek being completely satisfied with his own company; Joyce went to Cottenham, a High School for girls; and Peggy and little Tony sat in the breakfast room with a daily governess. Common, uncharactered days, they died in memory.

Joyce, like her brothers, walked alone to school, having loudly protested against being taken there by a mother or a maid. She had protested with blandishments, with kisses, with tears and with sulks; and beneath such artillery her parents had capitulated. " Oh, let her have her way," Dr. O'Grogan had said, sealing it with a hug, " and Lord! how I pity her husband!" When bicycles became familiar spectacles in the streets, and the " New Women " impudently bestrode them in bloomers, and even the decorous ladies of St. Austin's Road had quiet lessons up and down its long stretch, reclining at alarming angles against their gentlemen teachers and often embracing them round their necks; and when Ken Williams, of No. 185, flourished his "Child's Model" to Colet Court and back, and Maisie Thomson, a Cottenham girl, pedalled hers past the Vicarage windows and, removing her hand from the controls to wave it to Joyce, crashed on to the crown of the road, Joyce opened a second campaign to be allowed to go to school on a bicycle. But this campaign dragged on for years before it issued in success.

If Sundays isolated themselves as single days, rather dark in colour, the Summer Holidays, the other quintessential patches of memory, isolated themselves as long stretches of time; and they sparkled beneath the sun, and were green with country foliage and blue with the sea.

It was the First of August, or the Second, or the Third—one or other in that string of lovely dates. The trunks were in the Vicarage hall; the labels were on the trunks—wonderful labels, "O'Grogan, Passenger to Freshwater, Isle of Wight, via Lymington;" the travelling rugs, strapped round, were lying floppily on the trunks; a luncheon hamper was in the charge of Derek (by his request); the noses of little Peggy and Tony were flat against the dining-room window, searching the length of St. Austin's Road for the first appearance of the bus—a private, one-horse, black affair, like the buses still attached to old hotels; Joyce, who was in the midst of a "pash" for her father, was following him wherever he went, lest she should lose her chance of sitting next to him throughout the journey; the bus was descried by Peggy and its horse-hoofs heard—and the hoofs of a cow-hocked horse clattering up a metalled road have sounded an overtone of beauty from that day to this.

They piled up the luggage on the bus-roof; Keatings, the senior, bagged the box-seat next the driver, before Derek could get there; Derek requested that he might be allowed to sit on the luggage-pile on the roof, but his father forbade him, saying "Certainly not! I am not going to take an Albert Memorial through the streets of my parish;" the children clambered inside; Mrs. O'Grogan said worryingly, "For mercy's sake try and be quieter. We shall have the neighbours complaining;" and the neighbours did indeed come to their windows; but returned to their work, announcing, "Oh, it's nothing; it's nothing. It's only the Vicarage children going away."

The vehicle lumbered off, and Peggy turned green and was put near the window, and Joyce, Derek and little Tony had an immense, staring interest in the sickly changes of her complexion. "*I* don't feel sick," Derek bragged, and his father suppressed him with a "No, it's only children with imaginations who turn sick." Here was Waterloo Station; the luggage was unloaded from the bus-roof, great efficiency being displayed by Keatings; the porter wheeled it off, all the children crowding after him, to see it labelled; the bus clattered away; and nothing was left on the pavement, except the breakfast of Peggy, who was now feeling perfectly well and happy. Tony, running by his mother's side, kept looking back at that breakfast, till it was out of sight. He was wondering what people would do about it; and wonders to this day.

Four hours in the train, staring out at the country, or reading the highly-coloured comic papers. Extraordinary how delightful could be the first approach to these comic pictures, and how depressing the second! The journey palled, and Father wondered when they would invent a corridor coach and a Dining Saloon. He drank something from a flask. The younger children fell asleep—to be awakened by "Look! Look! It's Southampton Water." And they crowded to the window and saw the first ships and the first gulls, and smelt the seaweed and the sea.

They stayed at the window now, for the train was smoking through the New Forest, and they hoped to see the places where the children of Marryatt's story played; or the tree from which the arrow glanced that slew the Red King; or a wild pony; or some of the deer that the King loved as if he had been their father. Then came Lymington Town, and that marvellous slow run of the train on to Lymington Pier. "There's the boat! There's the boat!" "Where? Where?" "There, you idiot!" They were beside it; they were on the platform, standing by its gangway. And there, over the Solent, was the long heave of the Isle of Wight, with the new Tennyson's Monument standing like a tiny stick on one of its summits. We must climb up and see it to-morrow.

On to the ship, and watch *our* luggage being carried aboard. The engines have started; the paddle-wheels are moving; the boat forges out into a smell of sea-weed and a strong wind; down a winding channel between the green-haired flats and the squatting sea-gulls; past the white yachts riding at anchor, and the tubs on poles growing out of the water; out into the open sea, where the wind is stronger still and the buoys, in the running waves, float slantwise. Spray hits our cheeks and the smuts dirty us as they fall from the funnel. Look at the Needles, marching in Indian file out to sea! The Isle of Wight draws nearer, and the long white Yarmouth pier enlarges from a toy pier to a towering pile, with people on it, waving. Now watch the boat coming alongside without hitting anything, and the sailors running the gangway aboard. Keep close now, everybody. Joyce, keep an eye on Peggy and Tony. What a crush! "People are not seen at their best at such times as these," Keatings is heard to remark, as he is pushed and sandwiched to the gangway. We are ashore; we may run down the pier to see if the Freshwater coach is at its foot, and if it has the same two horses as last year, Prince and Nippy; we race, except Keatings, who is too old for that sort of thing; Derek is at the pier-gates first—he would be!—and shouts that the coach is there—the pig! we wanted to discover it without being told about it first. We scramble on to the front seats; and the coachman, with the lump over his eye, who knows us well, says, "Back once more?"

All the family's aboard, and all the strangers too, and the horses start for Freshwater. Joyce trumpets shrilly: "Tara-tara-tara!" Past the Lonely Tree and over the Toll Bridge that spans the Yar and down the lovely familiar lanes, past old villagers quickly recognized and hailed—see, the friendly coachman is allowing Derek to hold the reins and Tony to hold the whip! There is secret alarm in the soul of Peggy, lest Derek should overturn the coach; but there is little danger, for Derek (to be truthful is) holding them very gently.

Here are the outskirts of Freshwater. Here are some of the shops we know so well; and we begin to see everywhere the holiday-making children, hatless, sunburned, bare-legged, —the very spirits of Freshwater Holidays. This is School Green; in a few minutes we shall have reached our cottage— our other home. The coach spanks past the Station and round the Vicarage and round Victoria House, where the draper's is —and at once all fingers are pointing to the thatch on our cottage roof. The coachman gathers his reins and draws them in. We are there.

Yes, but Derek says he is going on with the coach as far as

the Bay. Oh, may we *all* go on with the coach as far as the Bay—may we? We want to see the Arch and the Stag Rocks, and the tamarisk, and the broken esplanade. May we? Yes, Mother and the maid and the luggage will get out here, and we and Father will travel on to the Bay, and return afoot. So on we roll, past Tennyson's Lane and Gubbins', the stationers; past the Apartment houses—there's where the Baldwins stayed last year, and there's where Dick Galway used to hang out his bathing togs—past the drinking trough that is so like a standing lion; and so into the Bay of chalk cliffs, with the breakers foaming at their base; of purple beach littered with the chunks and fragments of the esplanade; of bare-limbed, pink-brown children who run shrieking to meet the coach, waving prawn-nets and towels and spades. The sun glistens on the sea, and there are people bathing. Oh, couldn't we bathe *this afternoon?*

During this holiday Peggy passed through a spiritual crisis to a conversion. Not the first conversion in her life, nor the last, but one of the most striking. A miracle played its part in it; or she thought it a miracle at the time; and if in later years she was to invoke coincidence to explain it, the hour was past then for altering the bias it had given to her childhood.

It happened that Joyce had gone away to spend a fortnight with a school friend she had discovered at Totland, and Peggy, not liking to sleep alone, was sharing the bedroom protected by Derek. This was a little slope-roofed chamber, whose chimney stack abutted like a bluff headland on to the floor-space, and whose low window peeped under the thatch at a meadow dotted with cows. There were two narrow bedsteads on either side of the chimney stack, and a *Tit Bits* presentation plate on one wall, and an engraving of the Good Shepherd on the other. Here she was converted.

Her Christianity, for many months before this event, had been a Christianity of the mind entirely, her will having receded from it. Her mind accepted without question all that her father and mother told her about Heaven, and all that the maids told her about Hell, and all that Derek, who spoke with much confidence and authority, told her about Satan. Her mind endorsed the omnipotence of God, even to maintaining angrily that of course he could make a door open and shut at the same time. But this faith was producing no good works now. The period of good works which she had enjoyed after Mr. Crabb's sermon about Rhoda had not lasted long; which failure her secret heart had awaited from the beginning.

Her faith, truth to tell, was precisely the faith of the devils: she believed and trembled. And this meant, as always, that if she had no moral works, she had plenty of superstitious ones. In the bedtime concerts, for example, she insisted on a careful divorce between the sacred items and the secular. These concerts were held in the long summer evenings after they had been dismissed to bed; it was impossible to go to sleep while daylight was on the other side of the blinds and the voices of their father and mother, and of Keatings, came up from the room below, so they passed an hour with music. The items would be either instrumental or vocal, provided always that Derek conducted them. If they were instrumental, they were produced by the issue of a buzzing hum through Peggy's teeth and of the word " twang-twang " through Derek's nose. But whether they were instrumental or vocal, a sharp distinction, so Peggy insisted, had to be maintained between the rendering of comic songs and the rendering of hymns; they should always count twenty before passing from " I bet my money on a bob-tailed nag, Doodah, doodah, day " to " I love to hear the story which Angel voices tell; " and if the comic song were excessively comic, they must increase the twenty to fifty. Sometimes they continued their singing till after Keatings was in bed, and then he, either of his abounding high spirits or as a protest against being kept awake, would suddenly bellow his part of the chorus from his room; which would bring their mother to the foot of the stairs with that sentence inseparable from her: " Quiet, *quiet!* children. *We shall have the neigh-bours in!* " And again: Peggy insisted that if she and Derek told tales about fairies, or about people who didn't really exist, it was necessary to preserve them from being lies by prefixing the title " Pretend " to these fictitious characters when first you mentioned them. That done, one could invent the wildest tales about them; she had told Derek some incredible stuff about her " Pretend Uncle " who was staying at the Freshwater Bay Hotel.

But Peggy was inclined to wish she had never given birth to her pretend uncle, when Derek produced his formidable

pretend cousins who lived in the Western Caves. The western
arm of Freshwater Bay is the Redoubt Cliff, which has caves
like a cathedral underneath it, and in the furthest of these caves
is the Frenchman's Hole, a natural but terrible little corridor
leading up into the dark interior of the living rock. Derek
had taken Peggy and shown her the place, affirming that it
was here that his cousins retired at night. To reach it was
not easy. When the tide was out you footed it along the rocks,
walking delicately, because they were both sharp with jagged
ends and slippery with sea-weed. It was best to have your
legs bared for immersion, which might be intentional or un-
intentional ; but to keep your rubber sand-shoes on, so as
to save your feet from the knives of rock or the upturned
mussel-shells, from the pinch of a crab or the tickling of the
prawns. You entered first the Great Cave (St. Austin's
Church), with its apsidal end, its natural piscina and sedilia,
and its Gothic roof, so high where the great entry spanned
the sea and so low where its drooping vault met the shelving
beach. Keatings had once confirmed Joyce, Derek, Peggy and
Tony here, and had more than once tried to church Joyce.
After the Great Cave you passed into a smaller cave, The Vestry,
and then bent your head to the Emergency Exit, a sea-worn
tunnel, little wider than a crack ; you went through it hurriedly
lest this were the moment (which must one day come) when its
walls fell in and either crushed you to powder or enclosed you
alive for ever. From it you emerged into the light of the
third cave—and your breath quieted. The thing to look at here
was the dark and sinister opening of the Frenchman's Hole.
It fascinated you. Derek had one morning decided to climb
into it and report its nature ; but he had only, while Peggy
watched, taken two steps into the hole's dark heart, and then
come down again. The time was getting late, he explained,
and they mustn't risk being cut off by the tide.

Derek's cousins lived only by night in the Frenchman's Hole.
During the daylight they left it for their operations all over
the island. Wherever the O'Grogan children went, Derek
always justified the fact that he accompanied them by explaining
to Peggy that he was really going to meet his cousins, who were
invisible to all but him. Sometimes the family passed through
the gate of the Military Road to go and picnic on Afton Down,
which was all a-dance with cat's ear and scabious and thistle and
harebells ; and Derek generally walked on one side alone,

keeping, it was to be presumed, his ghostly company. Sometimes they descended the southern flank of the down, where all the grey grass blew one way and shimmered delightedly under the tickling breeze, that they might have tea at Compton Farm ; and Derek always got to the bottom first, partly because he liked to beat other people and partly because his relatives were awaiting him in the farm. On calm and dazzling days they got into single canoes and paddled them at high water into the Eastern caves ; and Derek drove a lonely vessel to his assignation in the green, submarine light of the cavern behind the Arch Rock. Quite often he disappeared for a whole morning, leaving the others to play among the tumbled chunks of the old sea-wall, which the ruthless tides had shattered ; or to bathe under the supervision of Andrews, the blonde and genial fisherman ; or to go out in a boat and hook up the rock-whiting, under the charge of Munster, the dark and surly fisherman, reputed to be the poisoner of his wife. And great adventures he enjoyed with his cousins in those solitary hours, and rehearsed to Peggy at bedtime. So far as she could make out there were three of them : two boys and a girl. But their numbers varied strangely, and their ages and heights too. It was this atmosphere of the unknown and of variableness, together with certain occult powers they possessed, that made them grow rather uncanny to Peggy, rather terrifying. She at once longed and dreaded to hear stories of them.

The weather was hot that August. Weeks had passed without rain ; the grass was burned yellow ; the country roads seemed to bake one's bare legs, and the water in the rocks to dazzle one's eyes. The nights were too sultry for sleep ; and Peggy would toss restively, hating to be still awake after Derek began to breathe long and rhythmically. Sometimes Derek had a way of not being asleep when he appeared to be, so that, if he suddenly spoke to her, after she had rolled round in her bed, it gave her a nasty turn.

" Are you awake, Peggy ? " he asked one night.

" Yes," she answered, as her heart accelerated and decelerated.

" I say," continued Derek, rather mysteriously ; and Peggy, alarmed into looking at him, could see his eyes staring into hers. " Would you like to meet my cousins—to *see* them, I mean, as *I* can ? "

" Yes," Peggy answered, feeling socially obliged to do so.

" Well, I was talking to them this afternoon. And they

told me how it could be done.   They know you well, of course.
They've often been watching you, when you didn't know they
were there.   They were invisible, of course.   Perhaps they're
in the room now, watching us, being able to see in the dark."

Peggy set her teeth.

" They told me there's only one way of your being able to
see them.   And that is to visit the cave at midnight.   I'd do
it.   I'm not afraid, are you ? "

She guessed at once from what dark pool Derek, the unoriginal, had lifted this horrid idea.   Of late he had been reading
" Eric, or Little by Little," where the boys broke from school
in the middle of the night and went through the darkness to
strange places.   And the book had captured him so completely
that many of his solitary journeys had been in search of secluded
coppices where he could read it undisturbed ; and the last
sad chapter, as Peggy well knew, had sent him like a sick animal
out of the sight of men, to cry in a green corner ; from which
he had returned to her, red-eyed, but with brave tales of a
meeting with his cousins.

" I shouldn't be afraid of staying in the cave—with you,"
she said.

This expressed accurately a fine shade of the truth.   Peggy
was not afraid of the cave, or of the tide, or of the moonlit
darkness, or of any tangible things ; she shrank only from some
awful materialization of Derek's cousins.   Out of the black
Frenchman's Hole they would come.   And she knew that
when these fears got hold of her, the correcting principle in
her brain, which ought to keep reminding her that it was only
a game, would fail to work.   That was the terror : Derek's
worked ; hers did not.   To her it was real.

" Well, when shall we do it, Peggy ? "

" I don't know."

" Guess."

She failed to guess, having an idea that if she named a day,
she would increase the chances of its all happening.

" Why, there's only one day possible," said Derek.   " Thursday, when Father and Mother are going to London for the
night, and it just happens it's low tide at eleven-forty—so
Andrews says.   The Fates are with us.   I think my cousins
must have arranged for the tide to be out that night."

" Derek . . ."

" Yes ? "

"Derek, we could only go if it's fine," Peggy pointed out, in a burst of hope that it would be wet.

"Oh, it'll be fine all right. My cousins'll arrange for that. Good-night."

"Good-night."

There was moisture on Peggy's brow as she lay in bed. This was an awful game of Derek's, and she would have to go into it quite alone; Derek would not really accompany her, because he would be able to remember that it was all a game, but to her it would be real. If only the weather would break, and the rains set in. She lifted her lids that she might see through the open window what the night promised, but her eyes met a sky blue-black and sheening like velvet, and brilliant with stars.

By the evening of the next day, Peggy, who had begun by being afraid of something in the cave, was so obsessed by her fear that she had almost forgotten what it was about. But nothing existed save in its relation to that dark, incomprehensible fear. The hours that marked off time were only important in so far as they meant that she was getting nearer and nearer to the awful moment. London, for which Dr. O'Grogan would leave to-morrow to fulfil a preaching engagement too flattering to be missed, she thought of only as a city which might conveniently be burned down between now and to-morrow, or be visited by another Great Plague, which would slay its tens of thousands and postpone Dr. O'Grogan's visit. In which circumstances, Derek, she knew, would spend Thursday night in his bed. And all these thoughts showed her how frightfully selfish she was, and how worse than useless it would be to do the thing she was now longing to do; which was to call in God to her assistance, to apologize for eight months of deliberate rebellion, and to strike a bargain with Him for the future. He was omnipotent, and could invent something remarkable to stop Derek going. Perhaps He would undo the past, and make it as if this idea had never been born in their minds. But Peggy's spiritual eyes were too bright for her to do this: God, she saw, would know that it was only in fear that she was approaching Him, and that she would not abide by her bargain longer than a month, at most; He might even treat her negotiations as insolence and punish her by sending the exact opposite of what she asked; and if, anticipating this, she purposely asked the opposite of what she wanted, He was too clever not to see through it.

Wednesday came, and Dr. and Mrs. O'Grogan left for London; and Thursday succeeded Wednesday, swift as a weaver's shuttle. It was like the last day on earth of a condemned criminal. All day, as she kept up an appearance of playing on the beach, she was really envying Keatings and Derek and little Tony, who had no reason to dread the coming of the night. She wondered what they would think if they knew of her sufferings. Once or twice she got relief by hoping that something big would happen to prevent the visit to the cave. She employed a favourite test: Derek's conversation having lapsed, she said to herself: "If he doesn't speak before I count twenty something'll happen." And by counting twenty very fast she succeeded in getting through before Derek was again moved to speech. But once, when she was at "'leven-twelve" he caused her a sharp sickening by shouting suddenly: "Ahoy! A ship! A ship in the bay!"

With the fall of evening and the gathering of the darkness, Peggy's terror became intolerable. No matter if it were futile; no matter if it would bring on her the punishment of the frivolous and the profane, she *would*—she *must* ask God to do something to stay the carrying out of Derek's plan. "O God, make it rain—make it rain!" she prayed at her bedside; and lest God were not prepared to send rain and spoil other people's enjoyment just for her sake, she explained that she was quite ready to be taken ill in the night. She knelt long on the floor to make her knees hurt and thus add a value to her prayers.

Rising from crushed knees she felt better. But it was only the despairing calm that comes from having taken a final step. She had not much hope; especially when Derek, showing no new control by God, said cheerfully: "You'd better try to get some sleep now. I'll call you about eleven. *I* shall be awake. And the night's absolutely perfect—hot as hot." Ten thousand to one that God would do nothing, unless he punished her. The night was indeed as fine and hot as ever. Phew! It was overpowering! She sighed a deep sigh, and lay down with the bedclothes no higher than her waist.

She woke with a horrible start, to hear a voice summoning her in the darkness.

"Peggy! Peggy!"

Her heart leapt, and at the same time a frightful noise like an explosion rent the air outside, and ran echoing away. A brilliant light lit up all the room; she saw the washstand, and the coloured " photograph " of the fishmonger's boy reading *Tit Bits,* and the uncoloured " photograph " of the Good Shepherd. The curtains blew with a shudder into the room. Dogs barked over the countryside, some near and some far away; voices spoke the other side of the room wall; and a very late, or very early, market cart clattered down the distance as if it were escaping from a terror.

" Peggy, are you awake ? " It was Derek's voice. " Look at the lightning ! Isn't it splendid ? "

He jumped to the floor and ran to the open window, which was at the foot of her bed. She too sat up, with a heart like a caught bird, and looked out. A flash shaped for her, with the clearness of a woodcut, the white road, the black elms and the hedgerow beyond, and the meadow with its standing cows.

" My ! " exclaimed Derek. " The cows are all huddled together. And they and the old horse are all looking the same way. Do you know why that is ? " And, in case she knew and got her answer in first, he hastened to tell. " They're turning their backs to the way the weather's coming from. They're expecting it, you see."

Crash came another thunderclap. And lightning again. Peggy did not mind. She loved it. She had no fear of concrete thunderstorms but only of fantastic chimeras. Crash again. Then a curious sound of rushing, of something tearing through the elms, and beating on the road; a sound of many waters in the gulleys. It was the rain. Sheets of it.

" My ! " Derek greeted it. " It's raining cats and dogs."

There was another crash of thunder; and the noise of its reverberation was sharply diminished as Derek slammed the window.

" Pho-o-o-o-o ! " he whistled.

The rain-spines stormed against the glass; and the lightning lit them up into long knitting needles.

" I expected it," said Derek, sitting up in bed and staring at the frame of the window. " I was afraid all the evening that the weather was going to break and spoil all our plans. It *would*. I felt all along my forehead that thunder was coming. Of course it *had* to, sooner or later, when it's as hot as this."

But it was useless to talk to Peggy about the inevitability of the weather-break. She knew that the secret of that noisy downpour was in the possession of two people only—herself as she lay in bed and Him who wielded the storm. She lay exhilarated. It was, in germ, the experience that older people call conversion. There was a sudden new revelation of God's intense personal interest in her ; a sudden conception of a love for her so great that it was always ready to treat past offences and wicked blasphemies as though they had never been. She lay vowing within herself : " Oh, I will try. I will try." And suddenly she remembered with widening and wondering eyes, and with fear at the thought that, perhaps, she was a chosen vessel, the story of St. Paul and the dazzling light from Heaven.

Until that train journey to Freshwater, Tony, the youngest of these children, had been an electric tram ; that is to say, he had run at an even pace along the walks of Kensington Gardens, drawing electricity for his motive power through a toy walking-stick which he extended so that it sizzed along the low railings at the grass's edge. While his right hand held firmly this transductor, his left turned imaginary brakes and controlling handles. The result of such expert driving was a steady, smooth run from stopping-place to stopping-place, accompanied by a droning *siss* from his teeth that did little more than emphasize the exquisite silence of his engines. The halts were about a hundred yards apart, and sometimes the brakes had to be jammed down very sharply, so that he could pull up in record time on the crunched and dissipated gravel. He would wait for thirty seconds while the passengers got aboard, and then, after a *ting-ting*, a slight jerk that no doubt shook the passengers, and a suggestion of grinding, the vehicle moved again.

But now the attributes of an electric tram were fading out, and he was developing the parts of a steam engine. On his return from Freshwater to Kensington, he found that the narrow and precisely straight pavement, stretching from Kensington Road, past his front door, to Uxbridge Road was really the permanent way from Waterloo to Lymington Pier. The gas lamps were stations which, when he was an express, he ignored with a shriek and a whistle. Sometimes he swung round the curve into Uxbridge Road (with a menacing list more in the character of a heavy-sailed frigate than a locomotive) and whistled very loudly here, rather than drive to the public danger.

Tony, in these days, was a round-faced, round-bodied boy, all of whose features were quite indeterminate, except his eyes and his hands. His eyes were remarkable, so his father would maintain, because at one moment they could be as unseeing and remote as Peggy's, and at the next as impudent as Joyce's. And to his hands, with their long fingers, his father would often point as earnests that height must one day come to that tub of a body, and artistry claim its life. But the indeterminateness of all else about him was made clear by the fact that Dr. O'Grogan would shake a sad head to his men friends and say: " I'm very much afraid he's going to take after the wife's people; " and Mrs. O'Grogan, in her drawing-room *At Homes* would bewail that he was getting so like her husband's mother. " Again and again I see the grandmother in him—she was a wild, feckless Irish creature, you know. All impulse . . . no order in her life. . . ." Tony was the only one of the children who had not yet weaned himself from a fawning, clamorous dependence on his mother. All the others had vaguely apprehended that, for some reason which they might one day know, there was a strange ossification of emotion in their tall, thin, tired mother which left her little to express sincerely except a resigned querulousness. But Tony could still hang about her, clamouring that he didn't want her to go out. Once he had begged her, if she must leave the house, to slip away while he wasn't looking; and when she asked how that could be any good, he replied: " Well, it's all right, once you've really gone."

Life was heightened for Tony when his godmother promised that she would give him an engine for his birthday. This godmother was Aunt Adelaide, his father's sister, and the wife of the great Archdeacon Gabriel. She was a big, plump, well-dressed woman, tight-laced in body and still more tight-laced in mind; and she appeared always with a deal of gold chain resting on the slope of her bosom and depending down the bluff. Even at this age Tony had perceived that her figure, in spite of the whalebone corsets which he had so often experienced, was more cubiform than it ought to have been. And he could remember sitting in his more babyish days on her knees, holding on to her chain and likening it to a cable hung over a cliff by the coastguards at Freshwater to draw a lee-shore mariner to safety.

"It's Tony's birthday next week, isn't it?" Aunt Adelaide asked him one day, with her silly habit of speaking to him as if he were a third person. "What would he like for a present?"

Now it was an accepted convention among the adults that between Tony and Aunt Adelaide, since she was his godmother, a link of peculiar affection existed; and Tony, so far, had been quite prepared to believe all that they told him about his love. But he had a poor opinion, none the less, of her discernment in the matter of presents. Last year she had given him a cannon that was fired by nothing more exciting than a very feminine spring.

"Please, I want an engine," replied Tony, with such readiness that for a second he feared she might guess that his answer had long been prepared. But then he remembered that Aunt Adelaide had scarcely understanding enough to detect the subtler shades of expression.

"An engine?" echoed Aunt Adelaide patronizingly. "What sort of engine?"

"An engine like the one we went to Freshwater in. . . . Only a toy one," he added, to help her out.

"Hasn't he got an engine?" asked the stupid woman of his mother.

"No," said his mother. "I don't think he has."

"No, I haven't," Tony hastily corroborated.

"Then that's settled. An engine it shall be." And she drew Tony against the whalebone and kissed him. "And now you must forget all about it. . . . He doesn't know what I'm going to give him," she explained to his mother, pushing him away and rearranging her chain. "Don't tell him what it is. It's a secret. Sh!" She put her finger to her lips. "Sh! Sh! Not a word!"

This impressed Tony as rather a good joke; he was aware of a certain surprise that Aunt Adelaide should come out so strong.

During the long, slow-rolling days before his birthday—days that had their interest, though, because glamorous with anticipation—the furniture of Tony's world, such as chairs and tables and beds, seemed to pale a little and become subservient to one sharply defined article that, though small, had more individuality than anything else; which was strange, because the chairs and tables really existed, whereas the sharply-defined article could scarcely be said to exist as yet. It was the engine; Aunt Adelaide's birthday gift. Tony saw it always; a wonderful model of the Waterloo locomotive. The steam would be produced by an oil-lamp, of course, not coal—he wasn't going to be such a fool as to expect more than a small oil lamp. And it would *siff* in the little boiler and *chuff chuff* through the pistons; and when you turned a tiny handle at the whistle, it would give a faint, sibilant sound—not like the shriek of a real engine, doubtless, but good in its degree. The funnel would be squat and stumpy, like all true funnels. The little hand-rails, hardly thicker than his mother's knitting needles, would run along the sides of the cylindrical boiler. And the boiler—Tony had determined to err on the side of expecting too little—would probably be about as big as the smallest of the sugar castors. But it would be long: all true boilers were long.

Every afternoon before his birthday Tony suggested to his governess that he and Peggy took their afternoon air along Kensington Road and Kensington High Street. The children conceived of Kensington Road as the chief street of London. Its terraces of flat-fronted houses, so different from the bays and porticoes of St. Austin's Road, stared between their tarnished trees at an endless head-race of green omnibuses, red omnibuses, hansoms, four-wheelers, victorias, broughams, tandems, drays, Army and Navy vans—among whose horses shot the red-coated scavengers, always busy. It had Olympia at one end, to which came Barnum and Bailey's Freaks, and Buffalo Bill's Wild West Show; it had the Roman Catholic Pro-Cathedral in the middle, where Father Bernard Vaughan denounced contemporary society; and then the great shops and the huddled corner of St. Mary Abbott's, where the Black Maria could often be seen, with the policeman standing on its step.

From there it was but a step to Kensington Gardens, by the side of whose railings the road ran on and on, ennobling its condition and improving its society with every yard, till it attained to nothing less than gorgeousness in the fine place where it gave one hand to the Albert Hall and the other to the Albert Memorial. Once or twice the little old bonneted Queen drove down this way in her open carriage, with four horses and postilions in front, and truly royal C-springs beneath, and two Indians or two Highlanders perched on the flunkeys' seat behind. Ahead of the carriage and astern of it rode a Sovereign's Escort of the Life Guards, their helmets, swords, and breastplates glittering.

Tony gave no reason why he vociferated so loudly for Kensington Road, but it was because of a famous toy-shop which chanced to have the exact engines in its window : beautiful little models, running on eight wheels and bogeys ; with pistons and cranks and shining brass piping each side of the long boilers, and whistles whose handles invited turning, and the true stumpy funnels. Every afternoon he stared at them and wondered which of these it would be like. He chose the smallest. Even if it were no larger than that, it would be very satisfying.

The vigil night of his birthday he slept little. But then he did not want to sleep ; it was so pleasant to think that every tick of the clock was bringing him nearer to the engine. He felt sorry for Keatings and Joyce and Derek and Peggy who were lying in bed without the prospect of a birthday in the morning. On the same score he felt sorry for his parents, his governess and the servants. And when he suddenly opened his eyes and saw sunlight pouring through the holland blinds, he could not understand. Had he been asleep then ? He was sure he had not. Yes, he had, though, for he could hazily recollect a dream in which he had tried putting coal-dust beneath the boiler, just for an experiment, and it had been a great success, smoke coming from the funnel and steam escaping from the exhaust-pipes. And now it must be to-morrow morning, already.

In honour of his birthday Tony's egg at breakfast was distinguished from those of Keatings, Joyce, Derek and Peggy, by its cochineal tint. And all his presents, except the engine, which Aunt Adelaide was to bring with her own hands, were spread about his plate, packed up in brown paper. There were soldiers and chocolates and a fireman's complete uniform. The soldiers were the best, for they could be put into the tender of the engine and steamed away to war. Yes, these things were very nice, but mere curtain-raisers before the great event of the day.

With a fidgeting impatience, and much pressing of his nose against the dining-room window, Tony watched for Aunt Adelaide. And when he saw her coming his legs kicked in

an excited autonomy, and his breath came short and quick.
The ringing of the door-bell caused his fist to rush to his open
mouth and remain there, as if he were petrified by his own
anticipation. He listened to Aunt Adelaide being shown into
the breakfast-room. Why the breakfast-room? He listened
to steps approaching his door. He watched the door open and
heard the maid telling him to go and see his Auntie in the
breakfast-room.

Along the passage he went, slowing with nervousness as he
drew near the room. He was almost loath to give up the
poignant joy of anticipation. Turning the handle, he opened
the door six inches. But Aunt Adelaide gave a humorous
shriek and called out: "No, no. Not yet. Not just yet.
Stay outside a moment longer. Mother and I are getting it
ready. Only one minute, dear."

Instantly he shut the door, eager to join in the game. Fancy
Aunt Adelaide having the imagination to start it going on the
dining-room table! He had seen, just as he shut the door,
that the cloth was off and the table bare. Aunt Adelaide
was entering into it with as much excitement as himself. It
was absolutely—he used a word he had just learned from
Keatings—it was absolutely top-hole of Aunt Adelaide. He
would give her, though he did not care for the experience much,
the huge hug and kiss she would expect. In his excitement
out there on the landing, his legs began to fidget of their own
accord, and he caught himself *chuff-chuffing*, and moving his arms
like pistons.

"You can come in now, dear," called Aunt Adelaide's voice.

His skin hot with expectancy, Tony entered. Aunt Adelaide
and his mother were standing with folded hands to enjoy his
first sight of the engine. And there on the bare table—there
was the . . . A twist at his heart; a catch where his breath
came from; and a gathering warmth at his eyes. His mouth
dropped and his lower lip twitched. The engine was humming
along the mahogany, for Aunt Adelaide in her playful delight
had started it going. And it was only set in motion by winding
string round a fly-wheel and pulling the string sharply away.
Aunt Adelaide was holding in her hand the string she had
used.

He stared at it with raised eyebrows. Whoever saw a real
engine like that, with a fly-wheel where the boiler ought to be,
and a body much too short, and a funnel as tall as a factory

chimney? And that funnel a fraud, because it could never smoke.

He glanced up and saw them beaming at what they conceived to be his open-mouthed wonder and delight.

That moment he learned something of the beauty of social duplicity: he saw that, because Aunt Adelaide was obviously so excited about her gift, he must pretend to love the engine and must say it was perfect; he saw, however dimly, that life could run in a channel quite indifferent to one's dreams, and that since the mistake lay with one's dreams rather than with life, there was little sense in feeling angry or displaying pain. He gave his Aunt the big hug and the kiss, which she accepted with a bending graciousness.

" There, there. I'm glad you like it." And she turned to his mother. " It was safer to get him one like that. They don't notice the difference." For Aunt Adelaide, as Tony had noticed, was one of those who always thought that children weren't listening unless they were personally addressed. " Now, dear," she concluded, " you'll like to play with it on the table. And your Aunt Adelaide has a lot of shopping to do. Good-bye, dear. So glad you like it. And a very, very happy birthday."

Escorted by his mother, she left the room, quite flushed with her triumph.

Tony wound the string, pulled it, and set the engine going; and as it purred along the table-top, he supplied from his mouth the absent *chuff chuff* and the *sissing*. But he could not do it with any zest. Only when his mother returned did he begin a loud and lively humming, lest anyone should be disappointed.

CHAPTER III

IN the Autumn term of '97, when he would be just nine years old, Tony was to go to Colet Court. So Colet Court, as the summer of that year drew to its close, loomed very near, very massive, and rather dark; and its largeness and darkness, somehow, were increased by the news that Derek, who was now in one of its higher forms, had actually won a prize. This gave the school an unusual solidity: Tony's mental eye could always see its great red-brick buildings on one side of the Hammersmith Road, with the still greater red-brick buildings of St. Paul's School on the other side, and the river of traffic rolling between; he could see the small knicker-bockered boys going into the gate of Colet Court, and the tall trousered boys swinging into the gardens of St. Paul's (Keatings one of them now); and he had his own impression of the large Main Hall of Colet Court, with its galleries of class rooms all round, which would frame that fine scene wherein Derek, in his Eton suit, would walk up to the platform and take his prize, while a multitude applauded.

No one seemed quite to understand why Derek had been given a prize. Such a thing had never happened before. Keatings was of opinion that the mental level of the Upper Second must be lower than in his day; and Joyce suggested that they had really given a dull child a prize for perseverance. Derek himself employed the news as a release for his congenital pomposity and at breakfast one morning, when the prize was being wrangled about, proclaimed, " Well, anyhow, I'm glad it has happened. I feel I've made it easier for Tony when he comes next term; " at which Dr. O'Grogan roared with laughter, inquiring what possible advantage could accrue to Tony, and

Keatings commented, " Don't be more of an idiot than you can help, Derek. You've done nothing very wonderful." Derek was unabashed, and retorted, " Of *course* the kiddy brother of a fellow in one of the Firsts has a better chance than an *absolutely* new boy. So *had on !*—all."

Was the summer holiday at Freshwater a little spoilt that year, by the day-by-day approach of the huge school ? Certainly there was nothing in Tony's face, with its sparkling, irreverent eyes, to hint it ; he was liveliness itself—never before so noisy or so enthusiastic. Almost there was something ostentatious about his gaiety.

One sharp day—a day of misbeatings and fluctuations of the heart—and the boundary was crossed : Tony was a Coletine, wearing a dark blue cap with a Maltese cross worked above its peak in silver tinsel. Now a knickerbockered Norfolk suit, with an Eton collar and a made-up bow tie, had dismissed for ever the white sailor suits and brown stockings of a governess's child. One rather nervous week, most of whose fears were started by smells, such as the smell of hot pipes and radiators as you entered the school, or the smell of varnished lockers and desks and brand-new text books, as you entered a classroom, or the smell of cedarwood pencils and indiarubber and dusty plaster models in the Art School—one such week, and all the fears were overpast : he could wonder what they had been about. He found that his form master, Mr. Spaull, considered him " quick ; " and on a day towards the end of the first month he scored his first goal at football, which drew from an enormous boy who was captaining his side the word, " You'll come on, O'Grogan Minor ; you've got speed." A potent semen, that word of the enormous boy ! Tony who had been within an ace of disliking this football now discovered that he loved the game and wished to talk of nothing else, so there can be little doubt that this first goal and the captain's encomium were the primal cause of Tony's getting his First XI colours, four years later. And the honest truth is that the goal was accidental.

Tony's cap with the Maltese cross was no longer new ; that was the symbol. Purposely he had kicked it about the asphalt of the playground to destroy its damning newness, and now when he put it on its head, the silver tinsel was tarnished and bristly, and the lining hung down behind.

Most of the days that followed, becoming " samey " like the

old days with his governess at home, sank out of memory's sight. A few stood vividly embellished : the days when he took prizes, the sunny afternoons when he distinguished himself in the School Sports, the two famous half-holidays when his father took the family to the theatre, once to see *The Sign of the Cross*, with Mr. Wilson Barrett as the Roman officer and Miss Maud Jeffries as the Christian girl ; and again to see *Julius Cæsar*, with Mr. Beerbohm Tree as Mark Antony, little Mrs. Tree as the boy Lucius, and Mr. Lewis Waller as Brutus. Of these two plays the children much preferred *The Sign of the Cross ;* and for weeks after seeing it, Tony, who had quite misunderstood the nature of the Roman officer's assault on the Christian girl, would seize a pen or a poker, whensoever Peggy threatened violence, and hold it above his head like a cross, and declare, " Thou canst not harm me now ! " But one day there was which stayed in memory, lit with a troubled brilliance : it was the day when he first saw the new boy, Wavers.

Something that was to be an ascendant factor in Tony's youth came alive that day. It had been waiting to come alive for years. It had peeped in strange imaginings which he had revealed to nobody, because he was rather ashamed of them. Was it to be believed, for instance, that at one time when he had persuaded himself, thanks to a story just read, that he loved his father better than anyone else in the world, he would devote the long hour of Morning Service to creating a fine drama in which his father charged him with a crime he had never committed—say one of Derek's—and took him into his study and caned him—this scene would thrill Tony as much as the scene in *The Sign of the Cross* of the whipping of the Christian boy, Stephanus—and he accepted the punishment with a wonderful dignity, refusing to betray Derek and forgiving his father the mistake ? But this love for his father and a later love, deliberately induced, for Peggy, had been secret gifts to his imagination, in which he had never really believed. Something different, something much more real, entered him this day, when at four o'clock he came out of the school buildings and saw little Wavers standing on the gravel.

Tony was now eleven years old and flowering well as a schoolboy. His fellow Coletines seemed to like him, and adults found attractive the way in which he would utter the slang and enthusiasm of a boy in a girl's soft voice, more beautiful than it would have been good for him to know. Social success was coming as easily to him, it appeared, as to his father. And to-day he was feeling extraordinarily successful, for he had spent the last hour of the afternoon under Monsieur Manise, the French master, and by some excellent clowning had reaped the laughter of his class-fellows. The music of that laughter was still in his head ; he was feeling somewhat as Dr. O'Grogan would feel when leaving St. Austin's church, with the phrases of a successful sermon dancing in his memory.

The clowning had played around the matter of an imposition due from Tony to Monsieur Manise.

" O'Groh-gahn," called M. Manise at the opening of the class, " please shoah me your ten French vairbs."

With a man who pronounced like that how could one do other than clown ? Tony, his mien expressing alternately protest and resignation, walked up to the master's platform and dramatically laid upon his desk a couple of sheets of white foolscap. Then he opened his coat, put the fingers of each hand in a waistcoat pocket, and stared at the ceiling.

Now M. Manise had a rule that impositions must be written on a special brand of blue paper that could be purchased from the Office at ten sheets a penny ; which rule the boys most strongly resented because it added to the writing of the imposition, which was punishment enough, the gross injustice of a penny fine. Alone among the eccentricities of a French master this one passed beyond amusement. Tony, in full accord with this indignation had therefore deliberately written all his verbs on white paper. It was the first act in a little comedy that he was staging.

M. Manise picked up the imposition and glanced at it.

" But this is on hoo-ite paper," he complained ; and turned the foolscap round, rather as if he expected it to be blue on the other side.

Tony continued to gaze in abstraction at the ceiling.

" But this is on hoo-ite paper," repeated M. Manise.

" Is it, Moss-soo ? " asked Tony in surprise ; and, bringing his eyes down from the ceiling, he took the foolscap and examined it inside and out, now holding it up to the light and now extending it at arm's length. There was no rebutting the master's allegation, so he allowed it. " It is hoo-ite, certainly, Moss-soo."

The boys giggled.

" Hoo-igh have you not done it on blue paper ? "

Tony shrugged. "No money, Moss-soo. Dreadful poor."
And he dropped his head sadly, his toe describing a coy, girlish
circle on the floor.

"I will not accept it," M. Manise declared. "Noah, noah."

"No?" inquired Tony, aggrieved.

"Noah, certainly not." The laughter of the boys had angered
the master, who pushed the foolscap back into Tony's hands.
"You will do it all again."

"Oh, Moss-*soo!*" protested Tony. "Moss-soo!" In his
note rang a mingling of shock, disappointment and forgiveness.

"It is so. I have said it. Go to your seat."

"But Moss-*soo*——" began Tony, appealingly.

"Go to your seat. I do not argue."

"But, Moss-*soo*, had I had the pennee, I would have bought
the blue paper." Tony, like all the boys, had decided that, to
penetrate the intelligence of a French master, he must speak
very distinctly, rather loud, and in a pidgin-English. "Look
here, Moss-soo. *Regardez.*" Into the pocket of his knickers
went Tony's hand, drawing out a palm full of coppers. "Look.
I did receive my pocket money yesterday. Here is one penny.
Please take it yourself, and say no more about it."

M. Manise glared at him, his brow flaming.

"That is vary impudent."

"Oh, no, Moss-soo!"

"You are the most impudent boy in the class."

"*Noah, noah!*" protested Tony.

"You are. You will now do the imposition too-ice."

"But, Moss-soo, that is not fair. That is mouldy. You
see——" and Tony began an analysis, in which he hoped to
make clear the difference between English customs and those
of France.

"Go to your seat," roared M. Manise, tearing up the imposition and dashing it into the waste-paper basket. "Vun more
word, and I say tree times.

"Three times! Golly!" Tony considered the situation,
and finally shook his head over it. "No." No, three times
was more than the fun was worth, so he shrugged his shoulders,
framed with his lips a disgusted "Well, well!" and walked to
his desk, where he sulked, but not without dignity, for the
remainder of the afternoon.

School over, the boys filed out to the playgrounds or the
street. Tony had delayed behind to buy M. Manise's blue

paper, and when he passed through the big doors on to the gravel between the main buildings and the boarders' house, he was arrested by the sight of a very small new-boy who was waiting there shyly and unhappily. Little Wavers was one of those boys who have the perfection of an immortal's child; his hair was very fair, his features small and straight, his eyes large and wistful, his mouth rich and quick to tremble. Above a face on which " eight years old " was written the school cap sat ill, and its silver Maltese cross shone dazzlingly new. Tony stopped. Though he did not know what had happened to him, he had, in truth, been stayed and stabbed by beauty of form and feature. Compassion surged in him. He felt compelled to speak to this little boy, to be very kind to him, and to put his arm, should opportunity offer, with paternal encouragement about his shoulder.

" Hallo, what's your name ? " he demanded, something roughly, his brain unconsciously seeking to correct this dubious softness.

" Wavers." The large, timid eyes stared up at him.

" Oh. Are you waiting for someone ? "

" Yes. I think I must have missed him. Kanes Major said I was to wait for him, as he would take me home. He promised my "—the child flushed with shame—" my mother to do so."

" I see. I understand," Tony answered, generously. " Yes, that's all right. You needn't be afraid to tell me. Somebody's supposed to see you home. Well, look here, *I* will, if you like." A thrill went through him at the idea. " My name's O'Grogan. I've been here three years now, but I remember how beastly it was in one's first few days. Come on. Where do you live ? "

" In Comeragh Road, West Kensington."

" Well, that's right out of my way, but I'll go with you just the same."

" Oh, thanks."

It was an early day of the Lent term, and the sun at four o'clock was already setting. A rosy glamour lay along the Hammersmith Road, and washed the red walls of St. Paul's School. Colet Gardens, the road that ran beside the brick wall of St. Paul's playing field and was the road for Tony and Wavers now, had assumed the only beauty it could ever know, a beauty of light. The stillness that ever seems to partner the sunset filled it from end to end, the tree branches staying motionless above the long brick wall, and the houses on the opposite side gazing at them in a trance.

Neither Tony nor Wavers spoke. Tony was striving for courage to say some words which he was afraid might sound ridiculous; they seemed to have, most strangely, something of the quality of the heightened light in the street; they didn't belong to normal day. After some hundred yards there was a bend in Colet Gardens, and all people walking round it were then hidden from the windows of Colet Court. For some reason it was not till he was round it that he was able to clear his throat and say the words. "If ever there's anything I can do for you, you must tell me. I feel I should like to help you. I felt it somehow directly I saw you. Funny, wasn't it? Will you let me?"

"Yes, thank you," agreed the little boy, who did not seem at all surprised.

"Good. If ever you want anyone to see you home, I will."

"Oh, thanks awfully."

"Yes, I should like to. Kanes Major doesn't seem very keen on the job, does he? Expect you'd rather I did than he did. Wouldn't you?"

The boy did not answer.

"*Wouldn't you?*" Tony demanded, almost angrily.

"Yes, I think so," agreed Wavers.

"All right, I will."

"But it was only for the first day or two that Mother thought I ought to——"

Tony interrupted at once, his tone nervously huffy. "All right. I won't if you don't want me to."

And as Wavers did not answer this, they walked on in none too happy a silence till they reached the foot of the railway bridge beneath which, in later days, Baron's Court Station was to appear. Here Tony, who had been wondering how to win a response to his interest from this little Wavers, suddenly suggested, "Let's go straight on down Talgarth Road."

"Why?"

"Oh, it won't make the way much longer. And I want to buy something in the North End Road. . . . But hang it, don't do it if you don't want to."

"I don't mind."

" You don't seem very keen on it——"

" Oh yes, I am."

" Sure ?   Honour bright ? "

" Yes."

" Come on, then."

And on they went, Tony glad that he had pushed further from him the moment when he must give up Wavers.   Their silence was uncomfortable down Talgarth Road, because Wavers had nothing to say and Tony had to worry his courage before it would strengthen him to say things which some part of his mind was whispering to be ridiculous.   In North End Road was a confectioner's shop, and he walked in and bought four ounces of " Satin Cushions " at two ounces a penny.   With these in his hand to give to Wavers, he felt that at last they had a subject of conversation.   Wavers was to keep them for himself and give him one as he needed it.   Sucking the sweet-meats, they turned at length up Comeragh Road.   It was a quiet road of uniform private houses, and empty in this hour of tea-time, when the heightened light of sunset was deepening into a gas-lit dusk.   They were very near the end of their journey now, and Tony summed up courage to do what he had been hungering to do from the beginning : he put an arm around Wavers' shoulder and pulled him against him lovingly.

From that evening Tony had an outer life and an inner life, strangely contrasted.

His outer life was that of a high-spirited preparatory school-boy just entering upon the spacious places of his seniority and sipping the new wine of athletic success.   His success at football was a thing which Derek, who had achieved far less at eleven years old, found difficult to explain.   " It's just his speed, that's all," said Derek, implying that his young brother was really no better than most but just chanced to possess this quite extraneous, and perhaps not wholly creditable, gift of speed.   Speed Tony certainly possessed.   At the School Sports he won the Under 12 Hundred Yards, the Two Hundred and Fifty Yards, and the Quarter Mile ; and Derek hinted that it was because he was so light.   Joyce would have none of this.   She insisted that there was no getting away from the fact that Tony was a brilliant kid and growing more attractive every day; and with this as her standpoint she proved a sore embarrassment to him throughout the sports meeting. She was fifteen now, a gushing age; and on this sunny day her small brother's appearance in his shorts and vest bound with pink ribbon troubled her heart so pleasantly that she kept saying, " Doesn't he look perfectly sweet ? " or " Tony, you look perfectly adorable ! " and once she tried to put her arm round his neck. Dr. O'Grogan also, in these days, was awakened to the positive qualities of his youngest son, and inclined to accord him that affectionate banter one reserves for one's favourites; and Tony responded to this treatment with his own make of affectionate, clowning impudence.

His inner life was a corridor that ran behind all this gaiety; a corridor lit with a curious and unreal brilliance, of which he was rather ashamed. Why ashamed he could hardly tell: perhaps it was because he supposed no other boy in the world's history had indulged such thoughts as he. What would Keatings or Derek or any of his noisy schoolfellows say if they knew that he would dawdle about the school gates before the morning prayers to watch for Wavers's arrival; that he fixed his eyes on him during the whole of Prayers; that, during the Break, he would wander about the playground alone, in and out of three hundred boys, till he had found Wavers, and when he had found him, could do nothing but toss him a greeting and walk away; that, when he took Wavers home in the evenings, he would wait till they were in the quiet streets and then put his arm round the little boy's shoulder and hold him close, covering the action with jests; that he drew an odd delight from calling him by pet names; that he spent absurd hours at home worrying out the question, did Wavers like him better than any other boy, or did he not? Was it to be known that he devoted day-dreams to the creation of dramas in which he dived to the rescue of a sinking Wavers and brought him safe to land, perishing himself; or took Wavers's crimes upon him and their punishment, keeping his silence till the end of life; or lay on his death-bed in a hospital and summoned Wavers to his side to hear his last farewell ?

No, these things could never be published. If one detail of them leaked out, he would die of shame; he would kill himself, so terrible would be his humiliation before the world.

What did Wavers really feel for him ? His own thoughts about Peggy, for example : were Wavers's thoughts like those ?

For Peggy, since the fashion had begun of trumpeting Tony's achievements, had become almost oppressive with her affection ; he guessed that in her passionate schoolgirl way she had worked herself up into a feeling for him no less secretly blushful than his for Wavers ; and yet—and yet he could feel little more than pity for her. He liked her ; liked her best of all ; but certainly didn't love her with the love she was offering to him. How odd, thought he, that one could be hungering for the adoration of one person, and feel only pity for another who was offering exactly what one desired. Was it possible that Wavers felt no more for him than he for Peggy—just a liking, and a gratitude for favours received, and a self-preening at being a favourite, and—and a suspicion of contempt ? Oh, no ! Wavers was fonder of him than that, surely. But was he ? Did he know any of the unrests and aches that Tony knew ? " Of course not," answered the saner part of Tony's mind, " of course not ; " and at the answer his heart fluttered, sank, and died a while.

How could he win the adoration of Wavers ? By a display of his accomplishments ? By a period of neglect, coupled with the flaunting of another friendship ? Then would Wavers be jealous and suffer ? Strange how pleasant it could be, this thought of inflicting pain on the beloved person ! Perhaps Wavers, in a torment of jealousy, would be savagely rude to him, and then he would punish him—shaking him, perhaps, and giving him a stern blow, and reducing him to tears. His body stirred at the picture. Strange ! Why was it sweet as a forbidden drink to imagine himself hurting Wavers.

It was early night as Tony played with these disturbing thoughts ; and, worried by them, he went to his bedroom window and looked out upon the narrow garden of the Vicarage. The moon was just rising, and the shadow of the church's apse lay diagonally across the lawn and up the garden wall. As if to counter the advancing moonlight, the lamp from the open window of the breakfast-room flung a splash of golden brushwork over the shadowed grass and lit the individual leaves of a laurel near by. A plane tree beyond spread a few branches towards this illumination and caught it in saucers of light. And in the darkness of the inner branches which missed the sprinkled light he could see a congregation of starlings plumply asleep. Happy birds, free from the bewilderments of men !

It was a Friday night and, as on every Friday night that he

could remember, the sound of the organ and of the choirboys came from the dimly lit windows of the chancel. From his earliest days this music had worked a melancholy in him, though he could not tell why. To-night he half perceived that its melancholy was bound up with its unreality: he could picture the dark, empty church with only its chancel lamps alight and the boys and the men singing dully and flippantly, because the music had not even a congregation to justify it, still less an emotion. But this was not his chief thought to-night: he thought how normal a thing in his life was the murmur of Choir Practice, and he seemed to see, as in a picture, the stream of normal and natural life flowing on steadily and indifferently, while he alone stood to one side with doubts about the sanity of a secret thought. He envied the choir boys and the choir-men, as he had envied the starlings; they would soon leave the church to go talkatively home, no rooted bewilderment in their minds.

Why did it stir his body to think of hurting Wavers? What would people say if they knew? Resting his elbow on the sill, and his cheek in the support of his palm, he stared down upon the garden, and told himself, while his brow furrowed, "No, I couldn't do that; I couldn't deliberately hurt him;" and yet he knew he *would* do it, so pleasant was it in contempla-tion. And the knowledge made him afraid. "It's not un-kindness. . . . It's just because I want him. . . . Oh, what would people say if they knew? . . ." Defeated, in this darkening land of thought, he turned back into the room, leaving the future to bring what it would.

Not Wavers alone, and others of the day-boys, but Mr. James also, the Master of the Upper Fifth, walked to his home after school along Colet Gardens. Tony knew of this, and generally allowed all homeward boys, and Mr. James, time to be well out of sight, before he assured Wavers that he was ready to start. Then they dawdled along together, he unruffled by the fear of censorious or ridiculing eyes.

But one afternoon Mr. James had himself been detained at the school and started up Colet Gardens five minutes after Tony and Wavers. He swung round the bend that concealed the further sweep of the road from the windows of the school, and saw two boys sauntering along, a taller, neat-figured boy of about eleven, and a smaller one of between eight and nine. That the elder had his arm along the younger's shoulder did not entirely surprise Mr. James; he had remarked that many Coletines walked in such a fashion with their "chums;" though the difference in these boys' ages made their chumminess strange. On overtaking the two boys he was prepared to give them a nod and a good-night. But recognizing the elder as Dr. O'Grogan's son, he was moved to ask laughingly, "Hallo! You don't live this way, do you, O'Grogan?" and the boy blushed so quickly and hotly and became so tongue-tied that Mr. James was surprised. A kindly man who disliked the sight of discomfort, he only smiled encouragingly and passed on. But a sidelong glance as he rounded a further corner showed him that the two boys were no longer walking linked; and he wondered as he went on.

CHAPTER IV

FINANCIAL OPERATIONS AND A TRADING FAILURE

THE Easter holidays broke across the daily lives of the O'Grogans, playing a merry shaft of light on three weeks; and then were gone; and the opening of the Summer term brought them back from the Freshwater cottage to Kensington and its day-schools. It was now that Earl's Court Exhibition began to call to them. That famous enclosure of white palaces, illuminated band-stands, and sixpenny side-shows, once it was opened in May, loomed large to the south of their world. Down certain streets its Great Wheel could be seen revolving above the house-roofs, its shape, after dark, picked out with two concentric circles of light. Sometimes a captive balloon soared up into the sky above the happy gardens. Paulines and Coletines, whose homes were in West Kensington, and therefore nearer the enchanted gates, spoke much of the Water Chute, the goblin grottos, and the Venetian Lake with its gondolas; of the long bazaars with their Oriental stalls and their smell of joss-stick everywhere; of the pleasure to be derived, in the summer darkness, from extinguishing the rows of gas-lit fairy lamps by poking them out with a walking stick; and (if they were older boys, with a bent that way) of girls who would meet them in the Western Gardens and flirt in the illuminated dusk. This made Keatings to deplore and deplore that he had no season-ticket like them, and no pocket-money worth the name. And one morning at breakfast he broke a remarkable conversation on his mother. It was at a time when Dr. O'Grogan was away on a preaching tour in America, and Keatings, now seventeen, was running his peculiar humour into the assumption of a

delegated authority, a power of attorney, or—to put it in a word
—a regency.

"Mother," he opened.

"Yes, yes?" Mrs. O'Grogan, that wearied lady, was
paying more attention to the bread-board than to her eldest
son.

"Mother. You may remember that it was always your desire
that I should go as a boarder to Winchester after Colet Court,
but that I put my foot down and decided to go as a day-boy
to St. Paul's."

"I remember that you quite failed to get the scholarship
we hoped for, and so we had to send you to St. Paul's."

"I had no intention of going anywhere else. I—I may say
I engineered it."

"Oh, did you?"

"Yes. And it occurs to me now that, since I have saved you
such a terrific lot of expense, the least you can do is to increase
my pocket money."

"Half-a-crown a week," he added as a suggestion, when his
mother seemed in doubt. "And that's letting you make
heavily on the whole transaction."

Mrs. O'Grogan looked at him, and probably began to think
that it was rather ridiculous to offer anyone so long in the leg
the sum of a shillling a week. So she said she thought he might
have two shillings every Monday.

Keatings accepted this compromise as a basis of argument,
and proceeded to the question of back-payments.

"I've been at St. Paul's four years, and therefore you owe
me two hundred and eight shillings, which is more than ten
pounds. Still, we'll call it a tenner, if you'd rather."

"You can call it what you like," said his mother. "There'll
be no back payments."

"Oh, won't there?" Keatings threatened. "It's a debt,
nothing less. I have not pressed for it before, but I need
the money now, because I'm going to take Joyce to Earl's
Court Exhibition, on the day you go off to meet Daddy. We
shall spend a hell of a lot—if you will excuse my manner of
speaking."

"*Coo!*" exclaimed Joyce. "O Mummy, *may* he?"

Up to this point she had been hurrying over breakfast to
escape to some imperious occupation that called her; but
now she had eyes only for Keatings and her mother.

"It's not a question of 'may,'" Keatings objected. "The whole thing is decided. And as I shall need at least five shillings of my rights, I proceed to call 'em in."

Joyce adopted the feminine method: she jumped up from her chair, ran to her mother, and flung her arms about her neck. "O Mum, *do* let him. Do give him five shillings."

"A truce to these 'lets' and 'gives,'" protested Keatings. "It's not a matter of giving, it's a matter of taking. Mother, what's to prevent me selling some of the furniture to get my rights? I mean, I reckon I've got a claim on some of your furniture now."

"H'm," scoffed his mother, disentangling the arms of Joyce, "and what's to prevent me refusing thereafter to give you any pocket-money at all?"

"Only your sporting sense," Keatings admitted.

"Very good, then. And I don't think my sporting sense would survive the robbery of the furniture."

"Robbery!" Keatings was indignant at the word. "Quite apart from your manifest debts to me, there's the question whether the furniture isn't more mine than yours, and whether in Father's absence I couldn't dispose of some of it according to my discretion. If you won't pay a family debt, I may chose to exercise my discretionary powers and pay it for you. Though it'd be a poor business, paying a debt to myself with furniture that is really, in the long run, mine. It *is*, Mum. Father paid for it, and I'm a nearer blood-relation of his than you are. In fact, you're not related to him by blood at all. You should consider that very carefully when you feel inclined to do the heavy with me—*and* the stingy."

"I'm his blood relation, too," put in Derek.

"So'm I," reminded Tony.

"You don't count," Keatings snapped, "so shut up. You're simply washed out by my existence. It's a case of what's called primogeniture."

"You may die," Derek suggested.

"I think not." Keatings dismissed the point. "And now, Mum, what about it?"

Mrs. O'Grogan's humour was passing into irritation.

"Don't be absurd, Keatings, and don't worry me. I'm not going to give you any back payments; and if you argue any more, I shall take back my offer to give you two shillings a week."

"Oh, you couldn't do that," Keatings reproached her. "You've given your promise. It's on your honour now. And please, I particularly want two and a half weeks' payment in advance, if convenient. I'll forgo all my other rights, if you'll give me this. Five bob, and I shan't expect anything more for two and a half weeks. There; if that isn't magnanimity, I don't know what is."

"Yes, *do*, Mummy," pleaded Joyce, standing at her side. "Mummy, be intolerably exquisite."

To avoid further pestering—for she well knew that Keatings would walk all round the house after her, into bedrooms and kitchens and pantries, pistolling her with his little slugs of humour—she gave him the five shillings. Joyce skipped with delight.

"I say, thanks awfully," said Keatings. "I'm very pleased with you, as I shall tell Dr. O'Grogan when he returns. Joyce, you can kiss your parent for me."

Joyce did so extravagantly; and a few minutes after was lost in the occupation for which she had been anxious to escape from breakfast.

This was her letter to Mr. Anthony Hope. Joyce, for some time past, had been allotting much of her leisure to a correspondence with the novelists of the day, in which she besought their autographs for her album. At first she had begun this practice as a very diffident experiment, but such success had rewarded her efforts, that it was now become a thrilling and engrossing hobby. Hardly one novelist in twenty had ignored her letter; most had sent along their signatures on postcards, but one or two had replied with friendly and humorous letters. Probably there was something in her naïve superlatives, penned in a round schoolgirl hand, which they found irresistible; and probably, as she advanced in the art of throwing the fly that was to bring the autograph to land, she grew more conscious of this. "I think your books are absolutely some of the best I have ever read, and lots of my friends agree with me," she would write. "I have read 'A Child of the Jago' three times and am just going to begin it again. My especial friend and I used at one time to call ourselves Dicky Perrott and Kiddo Cook after your characters, and we most frightfully want to know how much of them is founded on fact. We simply can't believe that Dicky Perrott never really existed, and we sometimes wonder if you weren't Father Sturt yourself. If you could just tell us when you send your autograph how far we are right in this guess, we should be most awfully grateful. But I daresay you won't take any notice of this letter, in which case I can only apologize for having taken up your valuable time, and, though I shall be very disappointed, I shall at least have the pleasure of thinking that I have said ' Thank you ' for all the lovely hours you have given me. Please write a lot more books. Yours truly, Joyce O'Grogan, aged 15."

Arthur Morrison, Sir Walter Besant, Seton Merriman, S. Baring Gould, Marie Corelli, L. T. Meade, Edna Lyall, R. L. Stevenson, Annie Swan, George Meredith, E. Nesbit—she valued all their signatures equally; it was enough that they had written stories, whether between the linen covers of a book or the paper covers of a magazine, for her to deem them immortal names and offer them their niches in her album. Already she estimated that this collection would soon be worth many thousand pounds and that thus her old age would be provided for.

One of the authors had evidently been so pleased with her letter that he wrote in reply : " No, my heroine had no prototype in life. When I began to create her, I rather intended her to be a portrait of a little friend of mine, but quite early in the story she most impudently burst into an independent life of her own and had the sauce to reduce me to the position of a mere reporter. But I found her, let it be confessed, much more attractive in this new development than in the one I had planned for her. Her impulsive enthusiasms and her ready impudence gave me much pleasure, and I was quite happy to write at her command. Might I whisper that in these qualities she seems to resemble my present correspondent ? "

Here was an exciting compliment which could only be acknowledged in a long letter. Joyce settled down to it, and it quickly became an obliging analysis of her own character. " I only wish I *were* as attractive as your perfectly adorable heroine, but I cannot think I am—no not in my most sanguine moments. I tried to think so all the time I was reading the book, but I was not deceived. I have really only just ordinary intelligence and a little more than ordinary good looks, but not very much more : nothing like as much as I should like. (How badly that is written and how dreadful it must seem to *you !*) No, I've resigned myself to the fact that I am not a Helen of Troy for beauty nor a Sappho for brains. . . ." The name

Sappho had involved her in a long hour of research, chiefly in the accumulated knowledge of Keatings; and after she had written it and sent it off, she was less than content with it.

Her correspondence with Mr. Anthony Hope was only just about to be opened, because it was only in the last weeks that she had discovered his books, but " The Prisoner of Zenda " and " Rupert of Hentzau " once read, had enlisted some of the noisiest suffrages she had ever accorded to the works of man, and now she was looking forward, perhaps more than ever in her life before, to the composition of her introductory letter. She hurried from the dining-room to the breakfast-room to give it her quiet consideration.

Meanwhile the mind of Tony, after hearing Keatings' talk of Earl's Court Exhibition, had been filling with its own private picture of those illuminated gardens. He saw the dense ring of people parading slowly round the brightly lit band-stand, where the scarlet grenadiers were playing; he saw the gay Oriental stalls and smelt their cedar-wood and burning joss-sticks; he saw the long lake with the white palaces around it and the white bridges spanning it, and the golden fairy-lamps throwing their reflections upon the water—a water troubled, now and then, by the passing of a gondola. And with this picture came, quickly and exhilaratingly, an idea. How splendid it would be to play the generous and wealthy patron with Wavers; to give him a memorable day there; to thrill with him down the Water Chute and up and down the Switchback; to visit the side-shows; and, at the end of it all, to parade in lordly ease round the band-stand! Surely—surely such a treat would wake in the boy the adoration he desired. Three or four shillings would go a great way with himself and Wavers, because they would pass every turnstile at half-price. How to raise three shillings? How on earth could one raise such a sum?

The incidence of the Colet Court Sports, which brought him three prizes and made the subject of flat-racing for a while the enthralling interest of his life, gave him the dawning of an answer. And the answer grew into an elaborate plan. As a plan, it seemed flawless at all points. That Saturday, when his mother would be gone to meet his father, and Keatings and Joyce would be away at the Exhibition, why should he not have a Sports Meeting of his own, with an entrance fee of sixpence? Competitors could be tempted to enter if he promised valuable prizes; and these prizes could be books from off his private shelves. At a second-hand bookshop they would fetch nothing (he had tried that market before) but half a dozen of them, employed to lure eight boys, or perhaps four boys and four girls, at sixpence a head, would be spent to very good purpose. At first he thought of organizing this meeting in Kensington Gardens, but when he looked at his selected prizes and saw how obviously second-hand they were, and when he remembered how few boys of his acquaintance would produce a sixpenny entrance fee without much stronger attractions than these, he decided that he must throw in " Refreshments " as well, which would involve the services of Cook and the use of the Vicarage dining-room. So the races had best be run along the pavement opposite the Vicarage, and round the block of houses. And—oh, yes—Peggy would help in the business and bring, say, four Cottenham girls to balance his four Colet Court boys ; each of them could surely raise four competitors, and it could well be a Mixed Meeting. And since everyone else would be away, the whole affair could be a secret of his and Peggy's ; all that Mother and Cook need know would be that he and Peggy were having a few friends to tea. Yes, the plan was perfect at all points.

Peggy, when approached, looked dubious, though palpably eager to please her favourite brother ; the idea of securing four girls and four of their sixpences seemed far less rational to her than to Tony ; but of a sudden a happy thought came to her. Thanks to a doting godfather she was at that very moment in possession of several shillings, and she would pay her guests' fees herself ; it would only be like spending two shillings to give four of her friends a treat ; and Tony need never know.

At once she became enthusiastic. " Oh, it's a topping idea," she said. " But, Tony : you'd better let me collect the subscriptions of my lot myself."

" Yes," Tony agreed. " I'm keen that you should be Treasurer for the whole show. I shouldn't have liked, somehow, taking the money from the girls myself, though they'll get jolly good value for their money. And I've a sort of feeling that the boys'll hand over their subs. to you quicker than to me. I'll tell them they've got to bring the chink with them."

" Oh yes, yes." Peggy accepted everything. " And, Tony : let's map out the course—*now*."

" Why not ? " Tony endorsed ; and together they hurried

out of the hall-door on to the pavement, and looked up and down their long, straight road.

" It's nearly a mile long, I'm sure," reflected Tony.

Peggy contemplated it. " Tony : the Mile course could be from one end of the road to the other, couldn't it ? "

" No." Tony gave thought to this, chewing a thumb. " No, *that* wouldn't work, because when they found themselves at the bottom and saw they had all that way to walk back to the house, they might go home, especially the losers. And then there'd be nobody for the winners to compete against, and they might want their sixpences back. Of course we could make the Mile the last event," he added dreamily, " but even so, we can't have anything going wrong, or they may feel we got their sixpences on false pretences, which would be absurd, considering what we're giving them. Refreshments and all. No, we'll run the longer races round this block of houses, so that they finish where they start. Let's step out the distance."

Starting immediately in front of the Vicarage steps, they began their measurement of the pavement, taking strides that were meant to be a yard. They followed it round the first corner into Upper Ottley Gardens, and round the far corner of that road into Bolingbroke Terrace, and round the point where Bolingbroke Terrace meets Lower Ottley Gardens, and so to St. Austin's Road again and the hearth-stoned steps of the Vicarage. Tony decided that the racing track was five hundred and twenty yards long, but Peggy made it nearer six hundred.

" Never mind," said Tony. " The simplest way will be to say it's just about four hundred and forty yards, and call once round a quarter mile, and four times round a mile. Four times round. Phew ! By gosh ! "

By two o'clock on the Saturday he was standing on his steps awaiting the arrival of the competitors. The road of tall, uniform houses, with its clean pavement and metalled road, lay hot and glaring under the midsummer sun. Neither windows nor pavements showed signs of inhabitants, and he was glad of this ; he hoped that the oppressive afternoon would hold them indoors, and even commit them to sleep. Pedestrians would be a nuisance. But he was not completely at ease. He had found it even more difficult than he had at first imagined to obtain competitors at sixpence a head ; and as he stood clog-dancing on the Vicarage steps, his conscience was accusing him of having exaggerated beyond all reasonable limits the prizes and the refreshments.   And now the nearer the moment came for the boys to arrive the less confident he felt about everything.   At last he ran back into the hall, and established a communication down the basement stairs with the cook.

" I say, couldn't you put some sugar on those cakes ?   Icing, I mean."

" But they're rock cakes, Master Tony," she protested, the perspiration moistening her forehead, as she stood at the foot of the stairs.

" Never mind.   Put some sugar on them.   And make some other showy things, if you can.   It's really rather important."

He hurried back to the doorstep just in time to see three of the boys coming briskly up the road.   Two of these, the Hewett brothers—good heavens ! they had turned out in their dark-blue running shorts !   Beneath their jackets he could see their white vests, and in their fists their cork handgrips.   The sight of these seriously minded sportsmen so increased his worry that he was almost running back to the cook to inspire her still further.   But there was no time.   And now there was a row : the fourth gentleman competitor, arriving, had seen the Hewett brothers' kit, and was arguing indignantly that they had taken a mean advantage over the rest.   Tony took little part in the quarrel, because he was anxiously scanning the road for sight of the lady competitors, whom, since they were so late, Peggy had gone to find.   Quite likely they wouldn't turn up at all : Peggy's conscience was a restive thing and might have forbidden her to emphasize the prizes and the refreshments. No—gosh !—here they were !   Here was Peggy breathlessly running with four other girls, all of whom were in their dark blue gym. costumes.   As he saw this fine team with its black-stockinged legs flying, he was so pleased that he yelled : " Don't run.   Don't run yet.   Keep your wind.   Keep your wind, you fools."   Then, lest they had not yet paid their subscriptions, or Peggy's conscience had been obtrusive, he called out : " There are some jolly fine prizes."

" Tony : it's all right," assured Peggy quickly.   " *I've* got their subs."   And she showed him four sixpences.

" Good ! " said he.   " My hat ! "

The competitors, boys and girls, were now assembled about his steps ; and a fox terrier, belonging to Winnie Riley, sat on its tail amongst them and, like the rest of the visible world, stared up at him for further instructions.

" Now then," said he to the boys, flushing in spite of himself. " My sister is the Treasurer.   Will you give her your entrance fees ?   As soon as they're all paid, we'll start."

And he turned away from his guests, to conceal his disquietude.   The gentleman competitors produced their sixpences, giving them shyly to the Treasurer, who looked twice as shy about receiving them.

" Well," continued Tony, after he had seen from the corner of an apparently uninterested eye the last of the sixpences go into Peggy's hand, " well, now we'd better start.   The first race is the Gentlemen's Hundred Yards Flat.   I'll take you to where you begin ; you finish exactly opposite the church."

One of the two brothers in running shorts hereupon took off his jacket and displayed a white vest whose edges were bound with cerise ribbon.   Tony gave it a look.   " Help ! " he exclaimed.   " You do look a fool."   And the boy, since his fellow competitors were likewise inclined to ridicule him, replaced his jacket rather sheepishly, while his brother, observing the public temper, never so much as unbuttoned his jacket.

Peggy and one of the girls were told off to hold the tape at the winning-post, and all the rest marched to the starting-place. Here Tony drew from a bulging pocket a service revolver that he had borrowed for the occasion.   He cocked it ; and two of the girls, on first viewing the weapon, decided, with giggles, that they would rather witness the finish than the start, and ran up to the tape, with black-stockinged legs flying.

" Keep your *wind*," roared Tony, impatiently.   " Keep your *wind*, you idiots ! "   And to the lined-up boys he said, while still staring at the girls :   " Isn't it funny that all girls run like cow-hocked horses ? . . . Now then, are you ready ?   I shall say ' One—two—three ' and fire.   One.   Two.   *Three*."

He pulled the trigger.   The report in that road of house-fronts, stone pavements, concrete areas and metalled roadways, reverberated like a thunderclap.   It sufficiently demoralized most of the boys to make them forget what it had been for, and enable one of them, who otherwise could not possibly have won the race, to gain a start of some yards and win easily.   A few people came to their windows and disappeared into their rooms again, having doubtless informed their households, " It's only the Vicarage children."   The hall-door of the house opposite the starting-point opened, and a man came on to the doorstep and called: "Don't you fire that thing again, you young scape-grace!"

"Righto!" Tony smiled back to him; and he replaced the revolver in his pocket, without much disappointment, because he had hardly supposed it would survive its first report.

The next race, the Ladies' Hundred Yards Flat, was spoiled by the fox terrier, who, attracted by the flying skirts, persisted in running on the inside lap and barking at the legs of the girl in that favourable position, who would otherwise have won. As it was, he won himself, or so the boys, shouting with laughter, maintained; and the incommoded girl looked rather sulky.

The Gentlemen's Two Hundred Yards and Four Hundred Yards were both won by the elder Hewett (together with the unofficial terrier). And after the Ladies' Four Hundred Yards, which no one finished, came the great event of the day, the Gentlemen's Mile. "Four times round!" shouted Tony, and the girls clapped stupidly.

The four boys were soon jogging at an easy trot round the blocks of houses; and the girls stood to watch each competitor and tick off his laps. Tony had insisted on this precaution, because he had clear memories of a similar event, at a Family Race Meeting in Freshwater, when the Mile Handicap had been won by Derek, whom most people believed to have run a lap less than Keatings, who came just behind him.

"What ho, Peggy; let's see about tea now," said he. "I'm not very happy about the prizes—they're so obviously books that I've no further use for—so we'd better give 'em tea first to put 'em in a good temper. But really they'll have had more than their beastly sixpence-worth—there's no getting away from that."

The cook and the parlour-maid had done their part well; tea for ten lay down the long dining-table. Temples of bread and jam alternated with tumuli of rock cakes; and Cook, in the goodness of her heart, had iced a big Madeira. Tony contemplated the spread. "I reckon they're jolly lucky," he gave as his opinion.

Returning to the doorsteps he inquired of the watching girls, "Anyone doing the fourth lap yet?"

"No, only the third."

"Gosh! How slow they are!"

Two of the boys, whose score of points left them no chance of winning a prize, had dropped out after the second round,

and there were but two remaining, who intended to stay the
course, lest they endangered their prizes. Tony looked at
them with some compassion, when they appeared round the
corner of Upper Ottley Gardens, and laboured past his steps
and the Church to the corner of Lower Ottley Gardens ; they
looked as if their hearts must burst, but went jogging on, their
mouths parted for panting, their faces greying, and their legs
breaking at the knees. He thought with less and less satisfaction about the prizes and with more and more relief about the tea.

They finished the mile, these two, and as they broke the tape
received an ovation which, so exaggerated was the cheering
and cat-calling of the non-competitors, brought some critical
and fretful faces to the neighbouring windows ; observing
which, Tony hastened to call : " Refreshments now. We
mustn't have the neighbours in. Come inside. Plenty of tea
and several cakes each ; and all—all for nothing."

The company trooped indoors—indeed, there was something
rather disturbing about the way they trooped into the dining-
room and sat themselves at the table, without so much as a
murmur of approval for the generous fare provided. They
must not miss this sense of the food's value, if trouble was to be
mitigated later, so he repeated, as he started the bread and jam
on its rounds : " All free, gratis, and for nothing."

He delayed over the tea, wishing to postpone the revelation
of the prizes. But it could not be postponed for ever, and, after
a period of abstraction, he suddenly assumed a jaunty confidence
and announced : " The Prize Giving now. If all you people'll
go out on to the pavement again, we'll bring the prizes and
present them properly on the steps."

They rushed through the passage with " whoops ! " and cries
of " The prizes ! the prizes ! Fall in ! ; " they scuttled down
the steps and clicked and heel-tapped on the pavement, waiting ;
and Tony, who had closed the front door between them and him,
heard their voices and footsteps as the beating of a sea of trouble.
The books were in the breakfast-room, tied up in brown paper
parcels, and with a despairing lift of his shoulders, he picked
up two and gave them to Peggy and carried the other two himself
towards the noisy menace without. He opened the door, and
as a silence fell on the assembly, said : " Well, here are the
prizes. We'll do this part in style. They will be presented
to the successful competitors by Miss Peggy O'Grogan."

" No, no," Peggy interrupted. " Tony : you give them."

" All right," he accepted. . . . " Well, the ladies first."

The girls came up, giggling, and took their prizes. Tony was astonished that they only made wry faces and said nothing ; he was unaware that they had paid nothing. Then the boys came and took their parcels and began to undo them ; and he prepared for the worst.

" Gee ! what a swizz ! " cried one boy ; and another muttered : " They're only his dirty old second-hand books ! " and a third (he had won no prize at all) shouted : " I vote we all get our tanners back. It's a bally fraud ! " which remark, firing their imaginations with a vivid picture of an attack on O'Grogan's house, drew yells of happy agreement ; so that Tony's last desperate appeal, " You've had huge refreshments as well," was lost in the chorus of : " Riot ! Vengeance ! Rescue ! Come on ! Massacre the garrison ! " and they rushed up the steps, just as he slammed the front door behind his back and stood ready to receive them. With instant presence of mind he whipped out his revolver and addressed its nose to theirs.

" Now then, you ! " he threatened. " Steady ! This revolver is only loaded with blank, but if I fire it at close quarters it'll make a nasty mess of your faces. Not that they could be made much worse, as faces go. . . . We'll have an attack by all means. It'll be rather fun—a jolly good finish to a jolly good day. But we'll organize it properly. You can attack the house, and Peggy and I'll defend it against the whole measly lot of you."

Peggy, at the first onrush of the trouble, had hurried down the steps and joined the other girls who, having no great quarrel with the afternoon's entertainment, were standing on one side and assisting the attackers with no more than a benevolent neutrality. But now, flattered by Tony's words and deciding that a defence of her home, if it were really only a game, would be indubitable fun, she ran through the boys and stood by her brother.

" *That's* the idea ! " shouted Tony, replacing the revolver in his pocket. " Now then, you chaps ! Come on ! Don't be afraid ! And he began to dance on the footstep and sing :

> " I'm the king of the castle,
> And you're a dirty rascal. . . ."

The attackers rushed for the door, and Tony laid about him, feeling his fist or his palm crash into faces and studs and coat-buttons. As he fought he yelled gaily : " Here we go ! Come on, my lucky lads ! . . ." Peggy had as much to do to escape her brother's flying arms as to administer punishment on the enemy ; but whenever she could, she pushed someone off the invaded territory. One boy tried to seize her and pull her down the steps, but Tony collared him round the middle, as he had seen the Rugby players do at St. Paul's, and hurled him against his fellows. " Don't be so beastly rough, O'Grogan," grumbled the victim. But Tony puffed : " Can't be helped. Can't be helped, man. Plenty more where that came from." The boy charged angrily, and the two were locking themselves in a serious tussle, when Tony became aware that a third figure had joined the defenders and was charging the enemy down the steps. His own assailant was pulled from him and dispersed confusedly, and another was disentangled from Peggy and sent with a truly fundamental kick to the pavement. Derek had arrived ; Derek in cricket flannels.

Derek was only fourteen, and less tall than square, but he loomed big, heavy and formidable to these prep-school urchins. All paused to recover their breath and stare at him.

"I won't have a row like this outside my home," he panted. "It's a scandal. You'll have the neighbours in. What's it all about ? My father is away, and so's my elder brother, so I reckon it's my business to stop this sort of thing. Tell us what it's about."

They all explained together, and Derek listened to them and cross-examined them properly, being rather pleased with his office of arbitrator ; from one faction to another he turned ; from the attackers who were declaring that they had been cheated of their sixpences ; from Peggy who was loyally shouting : Oh, they *hadn't* (though she was doubtful) ; and from Tony, who was describing the refreshments. The word " cheated " Derek disallowed at once.

" ' Cheated ! ' I'll thank you not to use words like that about anyone in *my* family. There may have been mistakes, but we don't cheat in this house." Having solemnly heard the full case, he solemnly found for the defendants. "I reckon you've done jolly well for sixpence. Anyhow, it was your agreement, and you've jolly well got to stand by your engagements. Haven't you any honour ? If you have, you'd better shoo off."

They drifted away ; and Derek, Peggy and Tony returned into the house. Peggy was disposed to smother Derek with her admiring gratitude, and Tony to enfilade him with further wordy explanations, to neither of which he listened : he just said loftily : " I wasn't going to have words like that used about the Family. And strictly they had no case. But I must say I think it pretty mean, selling tea to one's schoolfellows in one's house. It's a pretty awful let-down for us all. I should have thought you'd have had more sense of decency ; " and disappeared to his private occupations.

It was ten minutes after two on a Wednesday afternoon, and Tony was back again in the inner and secret corridor of his life. He was standing on the pavement of North End Road, outside the gates of Earl's Court Exhibition, waiting for Wavers, not doubting that it was a shameful, unpublishable matter that his heart should be beating so excitedly. Wavers was coming at half-past two, having agreed that it would be much jollier if they kept the adventure secret. Over a shop across the busy road there was a clock whose hands Tony studied whenever he was not directing a searchlight glance to the corner round which Wavers would first appear. But he was telling himself that he must accept a long wait cheerfully, because it was due to his own stupid impatience in coming twenty minutes too soon. He rattled the money in the pocket of his knickers. One minute of savage, almost tearful rebellion passed over him, when a leaden cloud obscured the sun and speckled the pavement with thunder-drops ; but it passed with the cloud, and he clod-hopped his relief and thanksgiving, to feel the sun pouring warmth on his cheeks again. The clock now pointed to twenty past two, and he could legitimately play the beam of his gaze on Waver's corner and dodge it round the carts and buses which tried to cut across it, because Wavers would surely be before his time, rather than after it. Any moment now, and he would be in sight. . . .

The minutes, from passing slowly, suddenly began to pass quickly, alarmingly quickly ; already it wanted but two minutes to the half-hour and Wavers had not appeared. " Always a rather unenthusiastic little beast, Wavers," thought Tony ; why couldn't he come early and be as keen as his treater. Ah, perhaps his lunch had been late. Resolved to be cheerful, Tony accepted this as the certain explanation. Any moment now !

He might even be a quarter of an hour late. The minute hand left the half-hour and climbed towards three o'clock; and Tony, refusing to admit a sinking of the heart, walked merrily to Waver's corner and looked up the road. It was empty.

Still holding grimly to happiness, he wandered back to the Exhibition gates. Evidently Wavers was coming by some other way. A quarter to three. Well, a quarter of an hour was nothing. Just once more he would walk to the corner of Charleston Road, and, this time, the little figure of Wavers would certainly be seen in the distance, hurrying towards him, probably running. Tony's breath halted as he neared the corner—halted with anxiety—then—oh, contemptible idiot that he was! the tears of anger welled up and his heart seemed extinguished. The road was still empty, except for a woman toiling home with a string bag of parcels.

Back to the Exhibition gates, anger now mounting higher; and, mounting with it, the old pleasurable idea of punishing Wavers. . . . No, he pushed that thought from him; he was afraid of it; it heightened his imagination so. And he was *not* a bully. In every school story he had read the bully had been the villain whom he had hated and despised; and how utterly absurd it would be to call him the bully of Wavers, when his one desire was to make a fuss of him!

Five to three. If Wavers came before three o'clock, even though only one minute before, he would forgive him, not so much as standing on his dignity, but treating the unpunctuality as a pleasant jest. " Ding-dong-*dang'd*-dong." A church with a cracked bell was beginning to strike the four quarters; and each of its blows, especially that on the cracked bell, struck on Tony's nerves and *clang'd* among his heart-beats. Till the last stroke of three he would keep the door of his forgiveness open. Racking seconds, as the bell went mechanically on! The last beat of three o'clock dissolved into the air above the traffic, and the street was just the same as before: shoppers loitering on the pavement, a coster crunching his barrow of fruit in the gutter, and carts and omnibuses lumbering along the roadway.

Angrily, miserably, he swung into the Exhibition entrance, paid his half-price at the turnstiles, and passed through. He found himself in pleasure gardens that seemed deserted of everything except the bathing sunlight. The empty green chairs round the empty white band-stand, and along the rustic front of the Western Club enclosure ; the unlit fairy-lamps outlining the white façades of the side-shows and the circle of the bandstand and running in a serpentine arcade before the Club grounds ; the stillness of the Great Wheel where it towered above the canvas scenery at the vista's end—all these things oppressed him with a heavy melancholy. Set against his own unhappiness, they revealed to him, probably for the first time in his life, how artificial was much of men's pleasure, and therefore how pitiful and how courageous. He walked on dully, between the empty bandstand and the empty chairs. Dull ! Well, he wasn't going to be made miserable by a little idiot of a nine-year-old. Just imagine : if anyone sitting at home could read his thoughts across the distance and was watching his mind now and knew all that he was thinking ! A shudder passed up him. They would put him in a lunatic asylum, surely. No, he was not going to be made miserable ; he was going to enjoy himself. He could spend all his money on himself now.

So he visited the side-shows that attracted him, and was surprised that performances which, undoubtedly comic, must have lifted him on other days to loud laughter, this afternoon only saddened him. He had a run on the Switchback, and, though he would not allow it, the reaction into sadness after the breath-arresting, thought-inhibiting rush, was as miserable a collapse as he had known. He visited the Lake and the turn-stiles at the foot of its dizzy Water Chute ; and in loyalty to his fiction of happiness, decided to spend his last sixpence here. Following a score of other thrill-hunters, he entered the lift and was drawn up the steep incline of the Chute to its platform high in the air. From this eyrie he could overlook the whole of London, and he leant an elbow on its rail and did so. How depressing, how pitiable seemed that vast, huddling congregation of little houses, whose meagre smoke wormed up into the sunlight and died ! There were the red towers of St. Paul's School ; there was the round roof of Olympia and, a little march away, the steeple of St. Mary Abbots, Kensington, and somewhere among the roofs between them was his home. What flies the people looked where they moved in Lillie Road ! Gosh ! what an infinitely tiny thing was the disappointment of a prep-schoolboy down there ! And here at the foot of the Water Chute—Tony's head went a little swimmy as he looked down—the white palaces of the Exhibition and its blue lake, set in the midst of that huddled, boundless, smoking multitude of houses, spoke to him once again, and with cutting potency now, of a tawdriness, and a pitifulness in much of the pleasure men shaped for themselves. That moment, while his elbow rested on the rail, he was apprehending something of the world's grief. What though the June sky was reflected in that lake and the sun was gilding the cupolas of the palaces and burnishing the sea-wide swarm of slate-roofs all around and lighting dots of fire in a thousand attic windows? It seemed only to stress a sorrow that it could not heal.

" Ain't you comin', Kiddy ? "

The sailor who would pilot the boat down the Chute and over the lake was addressing him.

" Oh . . . rather ! "

Quickly Tony stepped into a seat behind six giggling girls and beside two young men who removed their straw hats, guards and all, and put them between their knees for safety. " Hold tight, all." The boat tilted forward ; the girls shrieked at the movement ; they shrieked louder as it slid down the steep de-clivity ; they held their shrieks as it gathered speed and plunged through an air that battened down one's breath in one's lungs ; the young men's hair was flying backward and their lips com-pressed ; for an unbearable second no one did aught but hold tight to the rails ; and then the girls screamed again, half in terror and half in delight, as the boat hit the water with a mighty slap and shot its head into the air, plumes of spray breaking to its left and right, and bumped and bumped along the water, and bumped more quietly, and bumped a last time, and slowed into a smooth motion under the low arch of a white bridge.

All, the girls and the young men, breathed " Ah ! " in relief, and straightened hair or hats, and laughed out a description of their experience.

" I'm glad I done it, mind you, but never agyne ! "

"Lor-lummy, I thought I was dead ! My heart didn't arf cop it, on the bump—sorta jerked it into my throat, kind of speaking. It hasn't gone back right yet."

" It wasn't my heart that was chucked up into my throat so much as my dinner. I thought I was going to cat over your back, Nell, straight I did ! "

" Oh, you horrid ! "

" I'm not sure I shan't do it yet."

" You better ! . . . I didn't like it. It was like what you feel going down in a lift, only ten times worse. When

I go down in a lift, my stomach always goes down with me, but not my dinner—at least not at once."

" Oh, ain't he *awful*, Nell."

But Tony, sitting alone behind and beside them, had never for one moment been caught up into jollity by their screaming and laughter : only stabbed into dejection. This day there seemed to be little but an unreality and a despair in the world's laughter. If any emotion other than his settled sadness had accompanied the boat's abandoned career, it was a feeling of desperate abandonment in himself : " What does anything matter ? What does it matter if we're overturned at the bottom and drowned ? Go fast as you like, *I* don't care."

His last coin spent, he left the Exhibition, and, declining to accept the fact of his depression, walked the roads between Earl's Court and Kensington, to a tune of his humming.

CHAPTER V

THE PUNISHER

NEXT morning he went to Colet Court with a little programme of private theatricals spread out in his mind. He had prepared a rôle for performance in front of Wavers and conned it well; and though he despised the rôle, he knew he would play it. He would not speak to Wavers nor notice him, and when the child came up with his explanations he would walk away; he would keep the child dawdling around him in search of reconciliation; and at last he would grant it. And then perhaps a richer intimacy—something a few degrees nearer the perfect thing he desired, would be the fruit of this forgiveness and this reconciliation.

He acted the part in the playground during Eleven o'clock Break. Espying where Wavers was, he contrived to pass him with an arm linked through the arm of a distinguished boy of his own age; when the older boys began their game of "Hot Rice" and some of the younger boys, including Wavers, sat on the wooden rails and watched them, he made it his task to appear the noisiest, happiest, and most successful player; and finally, the game over, he strolled with unseeing eyes near Wavers, that the offender might approach him with apologies, and he act his majestic "walk away."

But Wavers did not move. He simply sat on his rail, a smile of greeting ready to break over his so troublingly beautiful little face, should Tony look his way. Good heavens! Wasn't he even going to apologize? Did he think it a little matter to have failed in his appointment? Had the offer of a whole afternoon at Earl's Court Exhibition seemed so small a thing to him? Extending his stroll, Tony looked quickly back, only to learn that Wavers had not moved from his rail, nor was watching him as he went ; and his next few minutes were pain —an ache of pain—in which angry pride struggled against his longing for Wavers, but struggled at losing odds. Time was short, and in two minutes the longing had won. He strolled back and passed Wavers.

" Hallo ! " he exclaimed, as if noticing him for the first time. " You didn't turn up yesterday afternoon."

" No. My people wouldn't let me."

" Oh—why ? "

" I don't know. Some silly idea of theirs."

" But why did you tell them ? We agreed it was going to be a secret. What was the sense in telling them. . . . Oh, but it doesn't matter——"

He wasn't going to continue ; he walked slowly away. It was something very different from the haughty " cut " he had imagined. There had fallen on him the final certainty that Wavers was quite untroubled by any real affection for him, and he felt he must walk back in search of his pride, with whose aid he would worry out the misery of it alone.

After Prayers that afternoon the Headmaster was waiting at the door of his study as the boys poured past it through the vestibule, on their way to freedom. His appearance was that of a person waiting for a particular boy. And to Tony, of all that streaming crowd, he beckoned. " O'Grogan, I want you to speak to me a minute. I want you to do something for me, if you will." This explanation was offered in a manner of marked kindliness, perhaps to save the boy from any suspicion of disgrace. Tony caught its note and followed the headmaster into his study unsuspectingly. The room seemed friendly, too, with its thick red carpet offering to the feet a softness that was strange within the walls of a school. The afternoon sun slanted through open windows on to a chair pleasantly littered with books. There was a vase of flowers brightening the large desk, and two more on either side of the clock on the mantelpiece. For no clear reason, however, Tony turned a little afraid, as the headmaster closed the door ; possibly it was because he and other curiously excited boys had sometimes, as they loitered in the vestibule, watched this door close on a delinquent about to be caned.

This chill of fear the headmaster quickly dispersed by tossing off his gown on to the revolving chair behind the writing table, as if all official duties were done, and sitting down and crossing his legs, and beginning a most interesting conversation about Tony and Tony's family. He talked about Tony's success in his class; he asked how he liked his football and cricket; he inquired after his parents and whether his father was back from America and how he liked Americans as an audience; and he expressed a hope that Keatings was doing well at St. Paul's and that Derek had quite settled down there. Then, just as Tony was telling him of Keatings' prospects of getting into the Second XV at St. Paul's next term—in the scrum, of course, because he wasn't fast enough for the three-quarter line—the Head, who seemed to have wool-gathered and missed what he was saying, broke in on the subject of Tony himself, and declared that he was sure he was going to do well at Colet Court—very well indeed. He spoke of making the most of good abilities, and divulged that Mr. Giveen had described him as " one of the clearest minds that had ever passed through his hands." He said, why not aim at a scholarship *and* the First XI? There seemed good reason for hoping that he might do both; then would he indeed be an honour to his school. He asked who were his chief friends, and Tony mentioned the two Hewetts and Candler and Soule Major. " Yes, yes," nodded the Head inattentively, " Candler and Soule. . . . Candler and Soule. . . ."

Suddenly he smiled. " But you seem very fond of young Wavers, don't you?"

Tony had no answer, and oh, hateful! he felt the warmth rising over his face and steaming under his hair. Happily the Head did not see it; one could suspect he made it his business not to see it.

" Well, that's excellent," continued the Head encouragingly. " Only . . . only . . ." and after a cough and a clearance of his throat, he began again, " I don't think, O'Grogan, if I were you, I would make a favourite of a young new boy—and walk home with him—and give him sweets, you know—and invite him to the Exhibition. It's very nice of you—exceedingly nice of you—but we think—his parents and I—that it's better for him to be left alone to—er—fight his own battle in his own ranks in the school. You mean well, I know, but the favouritism of an elder boy is not always the best thing for a young one; it might hold him up to ridicule, you see . . . and takes him away from those who ought to be his companions . . . and all sorts of things.   You with your clear brain can see all that, I am sure."

Tony still stared, unanswering, while the heat distilled to drops on his brow.

"So this is what I want you to do for me.   I want you to give me a definite promise now that, for this term at any rate, you will leave young Wavers entirely alone.   By that I mean that you are to have no dealings with him at all.   We want to see how he will shape, if he is left quite undisturbed among the boys of his own age.   Do you see: you've said your last word to Wavers for the remaining six weeks of this term—that's the experiment.   It's for his own good, so I am sure you will help us, if you're fond of him, won't you?"

Still no answer came from Tony, in whom language had congealed.   His brain was clear enough to see that however the Headmaster, of his good nature, might pretend otherwise, he really disapproved of his affection for Wavers; which meant that some of the lunacy in his secret thoughts was suspected and talked about and probably ridiculed; and that was awful —unthinkable—shiveringly unthinkable!

"That's right," accepted the Head, just as if Tony had given the promise.   "I think that's all I wanted to say.   Except that I thank you for all the help you've tried to give a new boy.   It was good of you, O'Grogan, but more would be a mistake."

Since Tony did not reply, the Head got up and, putting his hand on his shoulder, said: "Well, you can go now," and patted his back encouragingly.

When the school assembled for Prayers next morning, with the usual back-chat and horse-play passing between boy and boy and class and class, there was nothing in the manner of Tony, where he stood far back among the enlarging boys of the upper forms, to show that the searchlight of his gaze was playing among his incrowding schoolfellows for a sight of one figure only.   And since he laughed often there was nothing to show that he sought a view of this person in order to rest his gaze on him and heighten the aching of a bruised place in his heart.   A fixed look in one direction throughout Prayers there was, and nothing more.   And in class that morning there was nothing in O'Grogan Minor, who dealt very creditably with Ovid's *Tristia* and had many bright moments in his Divinity hour, to show that he was indulging a sick despair.   Nothing, because he lapsed into inattention no more often than he always did, and as a day-dreamer he had quite a reputation.

During the Break he kicked a tennis ball about the asphalt playground with, apparently, as good a will as the rest; but, in truth, he was enduring a miserable quarter of an hour, because he had seen Wavers playing in happy indifference with some of his class-mates. His pain blew up for anger.

At four o'clock that afternoon when the school was dismissed he drifted to the entrance and waited to see the passing of Wavers. Last night he had pictured for this hour a following of the boy along Colet Gardens, a hailing of him in the quiet round the corner, and then a parting, not unsentimental in its language and hand-clasps. But he did not expect that now. What he expected he did not know. Just for this evening he had suspended his will from control; he was an ungoverned city, listless, and awaiting the chances of the night.

It was an ill chance that Wavers should come out, merrily laughing, with a chum to whom he had lately been showing all the concentrated devotion that Tony had tried to buy. Like a pair of puppies these two romped on the gravel, before separating with such shouted abuse and thrown stones as only the best of schoolboy friends accord each other. Wavers, satchel on hip, was now walking up Colet Gardens alone; and Tony, unseen of him, followed. For what purpose he could not have said; he was too unhappy to know. When Wavers rounded the bend, Tony broke into a velvet-padded sprint, and in ten seconds was within a few yards of his quarry. Quieting to an easy walk, he called naturally:

" Hallo ! "

Wavers swung round. " Hallo, O'Grogan."

Tony opened genially.

" You're a fine chap, aren't you ? You've barely so much as thanked me for my invitation to the Ex. Even if your people wouldn't let you go, you might have behaved like a gentleman."

" Oh, I'm sorry," said Wavers. " I wanted to come."

" No, you didn't."

" Of course I did."

" Well, what did you want to tell your people all about it for ? We arranged that it was to be a secret. You're a little sneak."

" I'm not."

" How did they know about it, then ? "

" I told my kiddy sister and she sneaked, and Mother asked me straight out if it was true. I've often talked to them about you, you see."

" Oh, have you? And what did they say? "

" Shan't tell you."

Tony seized his arm above the elbow, and crushed it in his grip. The pleasure this brutality gave him bewildered and distressed his mind.

" Oh yes, you will."

" Don't ! You're hurting."

" Tell me what they said."

" You wouldn't like it."

" Never mind that ! Tell me ! " He gave the boy a sharp shake that nearly threw him off his feet.

" I—I'll tell you. . . . They said you were rather absurd. Daddy said you were soft, and the whole business was sammy."

" Oh, did he? . . . did they? . . ." Under these contemptuous words Tony concealed the knife-thrust that Wavers' revelation had given him, and the throbbing of the wound that resulted. " Well, look here, young Wavers : I'm not so soft that I don't punish people who betray my confidence. I'm going to give you a lamming. Now. See? "

Wavers tried to wrench himself free.

Excited, exulting, Tony seized Wavers' other arm above the elbow and pushed him backwards against the red-brick wall that surrounded the playing fields of St. Paul's. He pinioned him there by resting his weight on his arms.

Wavers stared at him, terrified ; and shame and pity began to move in Tony at the sight of that stricken face.

" All right. I shan't hurt you much, kid," he began.

At the word " hurt " Wavers, in his fright, made another quick effort to escape ; and Tony, taken by surprise and enraged at the trick, gripped him more savagely and thrust him so sharply against the wall that the back of his head struck the bricks with a stunning blow. The child turned suddenly pale and looked as if about to faint.

" Oh ! . . ." cried Tony, in alarm. " Wavers, I didn't mean to do that. I swear I didn't ! "

He had instantly released the boy, who now turned on one side and put his hand against the wall to save himself from falling. His head hung down.

" Wavers ! . . ." begged Tony, almost shouting, as if to reach a retreating consciousness. " I'm frightfully sorry. Are you all right ?   Shall I help you along ? "

Wavers turned on him.   He was only stunned and dizzy, but looked terribly sick and ill.   Proud of his wounded state and conscious of his perfect security now, he hissed :

" Beast !   I think you've killed me."

" Wavers ! " pleaded the beaten Tony.   " It isn't really bad, is it ?   I didn't mean to, I swear I didn't."

Wavers put his hand to the back of his head, and drawing it away, saw a red stain in the hollow of his fingers, which terrified him more and turned him paler.

" Let me bind it up for you.   You'll be all right soon," Tony assured him, for his own comfort.

" My skull's cracked, I think."

" O Lord ! " cried Tony, tears of desperation now welling up.   " No, it isn't.   It can't be.   You didn't go hard enough for that.   You'd have to go an awful crash to crack your skull. It only feels like it.   But I say, I'm awfully sorry."

" What's the matter, O'Grogan ?   What's happened ? "

Tony looked up into the face of Mr. James.   Not an unkind face, but a Gorgon's face to Tony now, petrifying him.   His brain stood still.

" What's happened, O'Grogan ?   Speak, boy.   Tell the truth ; don't stare ! "

As in front of the Headmaster, Tony was dumb.

" Wavers, what is it ?   Are you ill, Wavers ? "

" My head hit against the wall."

" How ?   Turn round and let me see. . . . Yes, it's bleeding a little.   How did it happen ? "

Two months earlier Wavers would not have hesitated to explain passionately how it happened, but he had just been introduced to the schoolboy ban on sneaking and he hesitated to disclose the truth, at least while Tony was still present.   He looked at the ground instead, and soon it was plain from a lifting and falling of his shoulders that sobs had forced their way up, at the call of this new sympathy.

" What's happened, O'Grogan ? " persisted Mr. James.

But Tony was still dumb.   Dumb with horror : would Wavers tell ?

" O'Grogan, tell the truth ; you are the elder.   This child's hurt.   I shall have to walk back with him to his parents.   Did he just fall or something? . . . Speak, boy. Don't you see, O'Grogan, if you keep silence, I shall suspect you've been hurting him. Are you going to speak?"

How could he speak? He had nothing to say. How could he tell of love, and love's desire to hurt?

"Very well, then. Go home. I shall take Wavers home. We shall have to get to the bottom of this. Go along."

Tony went. There was little thought in his mind, only fragments and starting fears and sudden sick horrors, as he walked along Hammersmith Road and into Kensington Road and up his own familiar pavements, like a dazed bird, homing instinctively. Wavers would tell; of course he would; they would say that they would have to know—or that it would make no difference if he told or not, because silence meant the same thing. They would explain that it wasn't sneaking, and he would tell. He was telling now. In his sitting-room in Comeragh Road he was telling his parents and Mr. James.

Life was collapsing around the youngest O'Grogan.

As soon as Home Work was finished that night there were games in the Vicarage breakfast-room, and its hall, and up and down its stairs; and Tony played in them with an artificial gaiety that he had raised like a lath-and-plaster screen between the eyes of men and his inner fears. If Derek or Peggy glanced his way during his periods of inattention, he quickly provided them with a wide smile. At nine o'clock the younger children went to bed, and Tony escaped to his with relief. He was impatient for the warmth and the darkness and the silence. This desire for warmth, though really a mental need, became a suggestion of physical cold, and he shivered as he removed his shirt and vest. He hastened into bed and hunched up his body and gathered the clothes tight about him. Ten o'clock came, and the steps and laughter of Keatings and Joyce, as they too mounted to their rooms. Eleven o'clock, and the house was quiet, except for the intermittent opening and shutting of his father's study door. His father was writing his letters, as he nearly always did at this hour, and soon he would take them to the pillar-box, fifty yards down the road, in time to catch the midnight post. Then he would return, bolt and chain the door, and creak upstairs to bed.

Tony waited for this last episode. For some absurd reason such as only a child's mind can hold, he felt that he could not think out his fearful pass till all these noises were over and the house abed. So he arrested his thinking, till he heard his father open the hall-door; heard his steps diminishing down the pavement; heard him returning—but after how long a time!—heard him slide the bolts and the chain and climb the stairs to his room. Now Tony could release the machinery of his thought. He rearranged his position in the bed, the movement making him shiver again.

The naked Fact: let him look at it. He had been caught bullying. And Wavers would reveal the exact truth—let him admit no spurious consolation—Wavers would reveal that O'Grogan had been bullying him. Tony's despair at the knowledge, for he believed from his school-stories that bullying was a crime which met with no social forgiveness, was not a shade less black than that of a man who had embezzled his thousands of trust funds and knew that his theft must be discovered in the morning. By nine o'clock to-morrow the Headmaster would know; possibly he would announce it to the whole school at Prayers. By lunch-time his parents would know, and Keatings and Joyce and Derek—Derek! Derek, with his heavy conscientiousness, was the most alarming of all. The servants would know, and their presence in the dining-room would be awful. The congregation of St. Austin's would know and flutter its sea of heads when he entered church on Sunday. The long, quiet road, whose pavements he must daily tread, would stare at him from a hundred curious, hostile windows. And there was nothing he could do—nothing. Nothing could put back the clock. Time would not retreat behind four o'clock in the past afternoon, so that what had happened then might be as if it had never been. It was securely set in the imperishable metal of time.

Only eleven years old, and he had ruined his life. Probably he would be expelled, and expulsion, so every school-story warned you, was the hall-mark of ruin. From now onward it was his sentence to wear a disgrace that would be pointed at and whispered about, among whomsoever he walked. The Fact was ice-cold.

The despair was so complete that it led him to the sleep of exhaustion, only to draw him back from it, after flushing his dreams with unhealthy, brain-heating visions. Again and again it dipped him in this hot sleep, from which he was glad to wake with a start and turn round in his bed. Often he opened his eyes and stared into the darkness, and once he saw that the darkness was greyer than it had been. Was it the dawn—yes—and as the grey light directed his perceptions to the bird-song in the plane trees, his breathing became short and quick like asthmatic breathing : he realized that the day of his exposure was creeping over the world.

At the breakfast-table Keatings was humorous and Joyce was lively, and Peggy lost her temper once and was so rude that everyone, from her father downwards, roared with laughter at her. Tony smiled dutifully at the fun, and once provided an audible laugh ; but this laugh sickened him, and his throat nearly closed to his porridge and his toast. Only hot tea seemed a welcome thing.

In the hall he put on his Colet Court cap, immediately wondering if it would be the last time he would wear it. The furniture of the hall, and its front door, took on a new individuality, as he wondered with what experience behind him and with what news in his pocket he would return to that door of crude stained-glass windows and hang his cap on that crowded hat-stand and see those eternally recurrent people in the Dutch tiles of the wall-paper and read that framed text : " GOD IS THE MASTER OF THIS HOUSE." A dull, painless ache settled at his cheek-bones and his temple-bosses, as if both were made of wood, and he picked up his satchel, flung it over his shoulder, and stepped into the street. His body went cold in the changed air. As he walked down Kensington Road, his thinking had slowed to the thinking of a dull-wit, and his eyes stared widely and unintelligently at the stream of buses, cabs, carts and cycles, rolling citywards. All these people were going happily to work, none to disgrace. The red-brick façade of Colet Court, and the red-walled railings of St. Paul's opposite, with the small, knickerbockered, Eton-collared boys going into the one, and the tall, trousered, high-collared boys going into the other, hardly added to his fear, for he was chilled to immunity. He began to understand how mere women, condemned to death, could walk to the scaffold without the appearance of fear ; some petrifaction of thought, some dull, staring acceptance of the inevitable, chilled them from terror, and they walked on dully ; there was nothing else to do. In such a condition he walked into the Large Hall of Colet Court and took his place for Prayers; where he stood, picking his fingers, whistling quietly to himself, and sometimes swallowing with difficulty.

In his state of nervous anticipation he had arrived too early, and the next quarter of an hour seemed twice its length, as the boys poured into the Hall and diverged to their places, and the masters wandered in, drawing on their gowns. The later minutes he gave, with mounting anxiety, to watching for the arrival of Wavers. Not yet was there sign of him. They must be nearly all here now, and still no Wavers. He kept craning his neck and steering his gaze down avenues in the crowd to distinguish that small, fair head. Once he saw Mr. James instead, and straight withdrew his body behind the screening body of another boy. Now all three hundred boys stood in their places, waiting for Prayers—all of them, except himself, free from the sickness of doubt and the threat of disaster. All of them here, but no Wavers. Was he not coming? Could he have been hurt as much as that? . . . Hallo, was that him? . . . No, that was only young Rose. . . . Could Wavers, then, be seriously hurt?

Prayers began. The Headmaster announced his favourite hymn, "Brief Life is here our portion," and its words were not empty of comfort for Tony. Life with its pains would be short. . . . It would be all the same a hundred years hence. Then he read the story of the Feeding of the Five Thousand, but Tony, try how he would, could not squeeze from the familiar words anything like a special message from God to him. Then Mr. Spaull said the Collects, and they certainly rang out with a strange appropriateness—not those for the Queen and for Albert Edward, Prince of Wales—but such a one as said: *We humbly beseech Thee, O Father, mercifully to look upon our infirmities; and for the glory of Thy Name turn from us all those evils that we most righteously have deserved.* . . . Now Prayers were over, and he was being drawn by the file of boys to his class-room. He cast a last look everywhere for Wavers, but the boy was not there.

The sharpest moment in Tony's early years was at about half-past ten that morning, when the door-handle of Mr. Giveen's class-room turned, bringing in the Headmaster who walked up to Mr. Giveen's desk. Indeed, it is doubtful if in all his life came another moment which shot at his heart and cancelled its normal action as this one did. Always such an entry, because it teemed with possibilities, lifted the boys' faces from their writing and stilled the atmosphere. They stared to-day and wondered. Tony looked too—and yet didn't look. He kept his pen-point above his paper and moved it up and down, but it was writing on a plaque of air, for, though his head, resting on the palm of his hand, was bent over it, his eyes were swinging between the black groove on the desk-top, where the pens and pencils lay, and the gowned Head-master, where he stood conversing in an undertone with Mr. Giveen. How strange that this solid, hard, round, untrembling body of his could encase a heart that was inflating and de-flating, like a frog in a hole as it stares at a threatening dog! The Headmaster had spoken quite a while with Mr. Giveen before both of them went out of the room on to the gallery beyond. The door did not quite close after them, because Mr. Giveen was holding it, as they stood talking together; and Tony, whose desk was near the door, could catch the high-lights of their conversation: "Monsieur Manise . . . impu-dent but affectionate. . . . Irish, I suppose, all of them. . . . No, no; can't be overlooked; besides, it's flat disobedience. . . . After the Break is over; then the others won't see." Mr. Giveen answered distinctly: "Yes, I understand," and came back into the room, while the Headmaster's steps receded along the gallery. Now Tony's heart changed to a new speed, waiting to take the words of Mr. Giveen. But Mr. Giveen never once looked Tony's way; he went straight to his desk and continued his work. And the rest of the hour passed.

Not till the bell for Break was drawing the boys in a stream through the door did Tony hear from his master: "O'Grogan, just a minute. I'd like to speak to you." He stopped; and at his side stood Panic as a companion, which returned with him to Mr. Giveen's desk. When all the boys were gone and Mr. Giveen had made sure that they were out of hearing, he began:

"The Headmaster, O'Grogan, wants you to go and see him, but not till the Break is over."

"Y-yes, sir."

"Right. Er—that will do."

Almost the first thing that caught Tony's eyes as he wandered out to the playground was a white bandage round a small boy's head. Wavers, then, had come, and was now a centre of interest to an enlarging crowd of boys. One showman called out: "Come and see the 'Gentleman in Khaki,'" and all understood his allusion, for this was the first year of the Boer War, when patriotic schoolboys wore in the lapels of their coats and the peaks of their caps button-portraits of General Buller and " Bobs " and " Fighting Mac," and sang arm-in-arm " The Absent-Minded Beggar," and dressed up with bandages round their brows as " The Gentleman in Khaki ordered South." They hurried up to gaze on this wounded Wavers and to hear his tale. The sight of a crowd with what looked like a bleeding accident in the middle drew yet more enraptured boys from all parts of the playground—from the giant-stride and the bridge-ladder, from the asphalt football pitches and the fives-courts, and from the green expanse of cricket field. They came shouting " What's up ? " and " Anyone dead ? "—and Tony slunk back into the Hall.

The bell sounded for Second Hour, assembling the boys in groups outside their class-room doors. Tony, when the doors had shut on the boys, walked to the Headmaster's study. What was the use of waiting till his heart, his breathing, and his nerves steadied ? He had best go now. Perhaps, such is the fascination of pain, he was almost anxious to go.

" Come in." The Headmaster's voice answered his knock. " Ah, O'Grogan," he greeted, " come in, come in."

His voice was as friendly as before, but not, somehow, his gown, which instead of being tossed aside, as in dismissal from duty, was in its official place, on his back. And not the room : this morning the flowers on desk and mantelpiece had ceased to express its essence, and had handed over that task to the upturned mortar-board on a side table, and to the leather-bound book in which the Headmaster was writing an entry, and to the wall-cupboard, which was known to hold the cane.

The Headmaster laid down his pen and sat back in his chair.

" You know what I want to see you about, I expect."

As before, Tony only stared dumbly.

" *Do* you know ? "

Tony looked at the carpet.

" Well, well," soothed the Headmaster. " I understand."

Neither spoke now for a little. The Headmaster, lifting his pen up and down on his desk, seemed to be building up his sentences.

" I see you know all, or you would tell me you didn't. . . . Well, O'Grogan, I am going to cane you for this——" Tony's heart now raced—" because I must punish you for two things :

first, for deliberately disobeying my order that you were to leave Wavers alone, and secondly for something that looks like bullying, though I'm sure the severity of what happened was mainly an accident. . . . But I want you to understand, O'Grogan, that I don't believe you are, or ever will be, a bully. This has been a momentary lapse into cruelty, to which we are all liable, especially—er—in youth. I want you to believe that it will be very easy for you, once we have got this business over, to rehabilitate your good name with me. Will you remember that?"

He seemed to realize that his answer, and his only answer, was coming from Tony's eyes; so continued:

"After this sharp lesson you will be properly afraid of the more selfish and brutal parts that are in your nature as in everyone's. They are the only things of which you are ever to be afraid. Do you see?"

Standing up he took the leather-seated chair, which last night had looked so pleasantly relaxed under its litter of books, and placed it against a bare wall.

"Kneel there, and bend over."

Tony knelt against the chair, his disordered brain causing him to stumble as he knelt; and he bowed his head over the leather seat, and its grained pattern dimly interested him. A cupboard door swung to, and the floor creaked. Came the first stinging cut, and five more after it; to which he gave no tears, but only an involuntary quiver.

"All right," said the Headmaster's voice. "Stand up." Tony stumbled to his feet, and stared at the Headmaster, who touched his shoulder gently.

"Well, that's all, O'Grogan. It's all over now; do you understand? We're just where we were before. . . . And now I think you'd better go home. You don't look as if you could do any good work this morning. Come back this afternoon and begin again. . . . Good-bye, good-bye."

Gently he guided Tony to the door.

CHAPTER VI

THE WANDERER

WHERE seven sit down for lunch, a father and mother and five assorted children, there is no great anxiety about an absentee, and no waiting. The first course was nearly completed when Mrs. O'Grogan said, "Tony's late;" but the subject, thus introduced, was treated by the other children as an uninteresting guest and neglected. The maid cleared away the ruins of the large cottage pie, while Dr. O'Grogan discussed parish gossip with his wife, and Keatings discussed Pauline politics with Derek, and Joyce broke brightly, if ludicrously, into both conversations. Now the maid was bringing in a hillock of suet pudding in a pond of treacle, and Dr. O'Grogan continued his talk over the arriving dish and the following plates.

"Tony's very late," repeated the mother, an extra and embarrassing plate recalling the absentee.

"Kept in," suggested Keatings.

"Even if he'd been kept in, he ought to be back before this. It's a quarter to two."

"He may have gone off to lunch with the Hewett's," Derek offered. "He did once before."

"Yes, and I made him promise he would never do it again without letting us know."

"All right, Mum, he isn't dead," Keatings grumbled, with all an elder child's impatient criticism of his mother.

And again the subject lapsed, not to be revived during the meal. But in the moment of general dispersal one tidy and unoccupied place on a disorganized table stared up at Mrs. O'Grogan and prompted her to call after her receding husband :

93

" What can have happened to that boy ?   Ought we to inquire at the school, do you think ? "

" What ?   Tony ? " said her husband, as if he now, for the first time, realized that a child was absent, and which one it was.   " Oh, well, he'll turn up, I expect.   He's probably disobeyed you and gone out to lunch."

" There can't have been an accident, I suppose ? "

" Gracious no !   Gracious no !   Tony can look after himself.   If there were anything wrong we'd have been informed before this."

" He's only eleven."

And in those words from the tall, thin, tired mother was heard the woman that had once been, and the woman that might have been.

Tea, being the direct descendant of Nursery Tea, was always spread on a large white cloth in the breakfast-room.   And Dr. O'Grogan, business permitting, liked to come into it and chaff his children, as once he had chaffed and diverted his babies. This afternoon he was turning his verbal pea-shooter on Peggy, while Keatings and Joyce, the only others who had so far arrived, gave occasional flank support, and the mother listened —or didn't listen.

" What a pity.   What a pity ! " he deplored as he scrutinized her.   " To miss beauty by so little, but to miss it so surely ! But there you are, Peggy dear ; a miss is as good as a mile.   It's your mouth that does it——"

" It *is* awful, isn't it ? " agreed Keatings.

" Good eyes, good nose, not at all a bad little chin, but dear, dear ! a mouth like a—like a—well, honestly, I don't know what it's like——"

" It's like nothing on earth," suggested Joyce.

" It's out of all proportion : too wide, too full——"

" And it's always so beastly moist," added Keatings.

" Yes, I've noticed *that*, when she's kind enough to kiss her father.   And the trouble is, I see no signs of it's getting better, Peggy.   I always hoped that as you got older, you'd grow up to it, as it were, and it'd be less conspicuous.   But here you are, seven already, aren't you ? "

" Thirteen," corrected Peggy, with her mouth full.

" Thirteen ? Holy Moses, that makes the situation more desperate than ever !   Every morning when I come down to breakfast I give it a glance, in the hope that there may have been some improvement overnight, but——" Dr. O'Grogan lifted a despairing hand from the table-cloth and let it collapse again—" it's always there, just the same, *just* the same. . . ."

" Oh, well, never mind," Peggy retorted. " It eats."

" Crikey, yes ! " emphasized Keatings.

" And it talks nine hundred to the dozen, when it gets going," said Joyce. " My hat, you should see it going at full speed."

" And I've heard—I've *heard*," continued Dr. O'Grogan, a thought mysteriously, " that when it loses its temper and vilifies its enemies, it—I hardly like to say the word—it is inclined to *spit* a little."

" Quite right ! " Keatings endorsed, cheerfully.

" Well, one must resign oneself to it, I suppose. I should have liked a pretty younger daughter (the elder having been such a failure) and should have grown fond of her ; but as it is, I shall do my duty by her—feed her and educate her, and all that. I shan't throw her out. But, Peggy, you'd better resign yourself to a life of good works, or art, or something——"

" Why ? " demanded Peggy.

" Why, because—— Well, I *mean* to *say*—I *mean* to *say*——"

" Exactly ! " nodded Keatings, taking the point at once.

" Mean to say what, Daddy ? " Peggy persisted.

" I mean, you can't expect that any handsome young blade is ever going to invite you to—No, no ; no, no. Not with a mouth like—— "

At that moment Derek entered, preceded by a noticeable scent of peppermint, for he was dissolving a bull's-eye. His lateness was deliberate—so deliberate that he had delayed in the road till sure that all the others were seated. He was in the triumphant and glowing condition of possessing exclusively a sensational news item, and had been rehearsing all the way home the nonchalant words and the unruffled manner that must grace its publication. It would be a striking performance, and like other stars he desired a full house. Finding a full house now, he walked to his place, sat down, helped himself to some bread and butter, and asked :

" I suppose you've heard about Tony ? "

" No ! " exclaimed his mother. " What about him ? Has anything happened ? "

Derek drew the jam dish towards him.

" He's been caught bullying, and been whacked by the Head-master ; and now all the boys are only waiting to catch him to give him a ragging. But he didn't turn up at Colet Court this afternoon. Seem's he's a coward as well as a bully."

The effect was all that Derek had pictured : his mother stared, his brother and sisters stared, and his father burst out :

" Good Lord ! I—I don't believe it."

" Nor do I," said Keatings. " Tony's a piffling little idiot, of course, but he's not a bully. At least, I never supposed so."

" Of course he isn't ! " echoed Joyce, who looked frightened.

" All right," conceded Derek, pursuing his business with the bread and jam. " I'm a liar then."

" Certainly," said Keatings.

." Good ! " shrugged Derek. " Now we all know where we are."

" Yes, we know that you're not only a liar but a sneak. You enjoy sneaking on your brother."

" Oh, then you believe he did it, since you say I'm sneaking ! " triumphed Derek. " But I'm not sneaking. I wouldn't breathe a word of it to anyone else, but this was something the Family should know—surely. Our name stood pretty high at Colet Court till this happened. Now I imagine it's mud."

" Don't be a pompous idiot ! *You* did a lot to make it illus-trious, didn't you ? "

" Be quiet, Keatings," commanded his father. " Derek, tell us what you've heard."

" I've met at least a dozen Paulines this afternoon whose kiddy brothers are at Colet Court, and they've been telling me all about it. It's a nice thing to have thrown at you at every turn. One sidey ass came up and said, ' So you've a bully in your family, O'Grogan.' I asked what the dickens he was gassing about, and he told me that Tony had been bullying a new boy called Wavers and cracked his nut against a wall. I went over to Colet Court and had a look at the kid, and his head's all bound up like a wounded soldier and stinks like a hospital ward. He's absolutely the star exhibit over there just now ; you can't get near him for the crowds. But they made way for me as I was Tony's brother. I said what I could in the way of apology. I said that if there was anything any of us could do to make amends, we'd certainly do it ; and I hope

I've undone some of the harm. The kid doesn't look more than seven years old, and he's as pale as death."

" And did he sneak on Tony ? " demanded Keatings.

" No, old James caught him red-handed, and Tony went to the Headmaster's this morning and had no end of a whacking. Since when he's not been seen or heard of."

" *What !* " cried his mother.

" I don't believe a word of it ! " said Joyce. " Tony isn't a bully."

" Well, why has he run away ? "

" *Run away !* " cried his mother.

" Yes, I suppose that's what's happened."

Dr. O'Grogan pushed back his chair.

" This is all true, is it, Derek ? "

" Honour bright."

" Then I go and see the Headmaster at once."

" And should Keatings and I and Joyce make up a search party ? "

Derek had been looking forward to this suggestion.

" Oh, yes ! " Joyce endorsed, forgetting dismay in excitement. " Oh, do let's."

" You can do what you can to help, certainly."

" Come on, Keatings ! Come on, Peggy."

And Keatings rose too, concealing a very real enthusiasm under the words, " Yes, we'd better do something pretty quick. Come on ; we'll work out a plan of campaign."

" Oh, my Tony ! " cried Mrs. O'Grogan suddenly. " Ernest, you don't believe any of it, do you ? And you don't believe that he has run away ? "

" No, no, no, no," he impatiently soothed. " He's probably shy of coming home. . . . Or if he has, we can recover him in no time, these days."

When Tony left the Headmaster's study he rambled out into Hammersmith Road, with a mind stunned from consecutive thought. No plan spread itself before him, except a dull certainty that he would not go home, and would not return to school that afternoon. How could he go home and face his family, some of whom would infallibly hear the tale from the newsmongers before the day darkened ; how could he enter his father's church next Sunday morning; how could he ever enter the playground of Colet Court again and meet the gaping of three hundred boys. He did not see how he could do any of these things—or how he could not. So he just walked on.

That the whole school had heard about Wavers he knew from the throngs who had been catechizing the wounded hero in the playground; and that the whole school must soon hear of his flogging he knew from fate's last merciless blow: as he had come through the Headmaster's door, he had seen a boy standing in the passage with an ear most obviously given to the stimulating sounds within and an eye waiting for a glimpse of the victim. This eye had followed him as he escaped it hurriedly, running to find his cap.

In his present witless and uncaptained drift, he kept naturally to the main road, walking on and on, but rather slowly, up Hammersmith Road and Kensington Road, with the current of the pedestrians and the traffic, and catching a depression from the long terraces of smoke-greyed houses, whose few London trees were already dark and autumnal in June. On and on, past Kensington High Street and over the huddled corner of St. Mary Abbot's, till the blocks of shops on his left hand abruptly stopped, presenting a side like a cliff-face to the sea of foliage which was Kensington Gardens. The tall, immobile tree-trunks and the serene grass drew him as a forest might draw a hermit to his healing. He wandered up the Broad Walk, glancing over the railings at the ragged sleepers beneath the trees or at the dogs gambolling over the turf, and remembering how, in his childish days, every hummock crowned with elms had been a mountain screening mystery and every close plantation of shrubs had hidden a fairy wood. He reached the Round Pond where, for a while, he stood in listless contemplation of the children sailing their toy yachts. And his dreaming smudged the scene with a glimmering haze.

Waking from this half-coma, he strolled round and round the pond, sometimes picking up a pebble from the gravel and examining it before losing interest and tossing it away. The population round the pond was diminishing: the nursemaids were calling to their children, the big boys were drawing out their ships, and the old gentlemen on the green chairs were struggling to their feet; it must be one o'clock, when Lunch called all London indoors. Now he was almost alone; the half-heard voices and laughter that had come through the air were withdrawn to their happinesses at home; in their stead came the fluting of birds, the breath of the breeze among the leaves, the fluster of a duck on the water, and the deep diapason of the traffic on the High Street.

He turned away and walked along a wide path between carpets of flowers; and the flowers troubled him, because he remembered that only the undishonoured could enjoy their loveliness. He crossed into Hyde Park, and feeling a weariness in his limbs, sat on a seat and gazed at the red and green buses as, behind the railings, they dazzled along to Knightsbridge. The only people on the seats were the sleeping tramps, and he suddenly felt a kinship with them and saw a rest and security in the vagabond life, when you plodded on and on, down the hedged roads, with no possessions to give you anxious care, and no name to be disgraced. He shivered; not with the cold, for it was a perfect summer day, but with a quick, sharp, diaphoretic memory of his disaster; and the shiver made him rise and move towards the footwalk beside Rotten Row. A few riders were in the Row now: well-tailored, top-hatted men astride, and neat-habited, bowler-crowned women side-saddle, on their shining horses. Derek was always talking about blood-horses, and Tony, without understanding what the term meant, wondered if these were blood-horses. They and their riders, like the flowers in the carpet gardens, hurt him: surely this was life at its happiest, and such happiness was possible only to the undisgraced. He sat and watched them; and something of the beauty of women and of spirited horses and of all graceful movement; something of the beauty of happiness and of social fellowship showed itself to him this day earlier than it would have done had he never set it against the dark background of an exile's thoughts.

Unaware that he had sighed he wandered on, till he came to the park's end and the Achilles statue, round which he walked in dull examination. He turned out at the gates and seeing the equestrian statue of the Duke of Wellington, in the midst of the diverging traffic, crossed the road to make a study of that too. Never a boy of eleven but has dreamed of statues in his honour, and certainly not Tony, who had heard his gifts so loudly trumpeted of late; he shrank again as he bethought himself that he had thrown this fine hope for ever away. Oh, everything had the same stab for him. He would like to die, but death had it too. The story would remain behind; he could take it with him into death.   It was written in history for all eternity.

On up Piccadilly, where the traffic from Hammersmith blent with lordlier strains, the red and green omnibuses mixing with victorias and landaus and broughams.   One of these broughams turned many heads, because it was electrically driven and whispered along without horses, its cockaded coachman on the box steering it with a tiller.   One or two of the new motor cars attracted attention too, but they were nothing like so fine as the electric brougham—high ungainly traps with a chunking coal-scuttle thing in front, or a box of works behind.   There were clocks in the shops and Tony wondered that minutes could pass so slowly.   A quarter-past two at the last shop, and now only twenty-past !   In Piccadilly Circus it was half-past.   School had begun at Colet Court, and what was happening there now ?   They must have learned that he was absent ;   did they suspect that he was staying away without permission ?   " Playing truant ; "   would that mean another caning for him, if ever he went back ?   But how could he go back ?   He did not see how he could, or how he could not— but just walked on.   He came to a German band, six musicians with wind instruments playing patriotic war tunes at the corner of a private street, and the words of " The Absent-Minded Beggar " fitted themselves in his head to the music, and he walked on listlessly humming :

> " Cook's son, Duke's son, son of a hundred kings ;
>   Fifty thousand horse and foot going to Table Bay ;
>   Each of them doing his country's work, and who's to
>   look after the things ?
>   So pass the hat for your credit's sake and pay, pay, pay."

Appetite did not visit him, but only thirst ; and he drank more than once from the public fountains, though he had always been forbidden to do so.   But what did it matter if they were full of disease germs ?   Disease meant death, and that was the least of all the evils.   Weariness registered in his limbs, but not seriously ;   it is easy to walk when you are miserable.

Much of London did Tony see that day, and a thousand of its phases ;   he saw a fire-engine being galloped along by its magnificent horses—blood-horses   these, if any !—and   heard   its firemen clearing a channel through the middle of the traffic with their " Hi ! Hi ! Hi ! Hi ! Hi ! " he saw what always stirred him curiously—a Black Maria hastening to the prison with the policeman on its step, but to-day he knew the souls of the captives within; he watched the scavenger-boys, in their scarlet coats and peaked caps, scraping up the horse-droppings under the very shafts of the carts and the very noses of the horses, and he envied them as happier than he; he waited while a turncock turned up a gush of water into the street; he watched the bare-foot children dancing round a barrel-organ as it played the eternal war-tunes, " Good-bye, Dolly, I must leave you, For I can no longer stay," " O Tommy, Tommy Atkins, you're a good and hearty lad ! "; in the Mile End Road he watched a contortionist performing on a mat in the gutter, and wondered what his home-life was like; at the corner of Old Ford Road and Stratford High Street he heard the beating of a drum and the whistle of pan-pipes, and, walking towards the noise, joined an audience of ragged children who were gaping up at a Punch and Judy show; he stared unsmiling while Mr. Punch sat on the shelf of his high-pitched theatre, with legs dangling and a club in his arms, and cracked the beadle on the head every time he popped up from below, and then cracked his joy and his triumph on the shelf itself, shrieking at every blow in his raucous falsetto, " Oh, dear ! " . . . " Oh, dear ! . . . Oh, dear ! . . . Oh, dear ! . . . Oh, dear ! " And when the showman put his theatre on a barrow and wheeled it away, followed by a herd of children, Tony lifted his eyebrows and walked on.   He was in the Essex outskirts, among trees and fields again, when the dusk of the coming night drew about him.   With it came bewilderment; and he stood still in the empty road—a child without a will—a brain beaten.   Should he go forward or backward ?   What was going to happen now ?   Something would happen sooner or later; it was known to God who could see the future, but it was not in Tony to do anything to shape it.   Going backward was more painful than going forward, so towards what destiny had written, he walked on.

Keatings' search parties returned in time for a late supper with nothing achieved except large appetites and talkative tongues, and minds lustrous with alarm and excitement.   They had made judicious inquiries at the homes of Tony's friends; they had stood at the gates of Colet Court and " reconstructed the crime ; " and they had even, on a bright inspiration of Joyce's,

" combed out " Kensington Gardens. And now they returned, eager to publish their complete, despairing defeat.

" It's a bad business," said Derek, as he sat down to supper.

" And the worst part is," Keatings told his mother, " that it's all true. Tony *has* been bullying the kid."

" Yes, and when he turns up," added Derek, " we shall have to do something about it. We can't have this sort of thing in the Family."

" I can't believe it yet," Joyce declared. " But if it's true, I shan't be able to speak to him. I simply *couldn't*."

" Unfortunately it *is* true," Keatings bemoaned.

" Of course it is," Derek corroborated, who now felt justified of men. " But I'll lay it won't happen again. Is Father back, Mother ? "

" No, he came back in a cab from Colet Court and when he heard that Tony was still missing, he went off again. We've not seen or heard anything of him since that."

" Good Lord ! " exclaimed Keatings. " Don't say *he's* lost now."

Peggy was out of the conversation. Her imagination had long been giving her a vivid sense of Tony's pangs, and she was listening with astonishment to these unimaginative hints of further punishment for the runaway. Did her brothers lack some vision that was easy to her ? Did Joyce ? Surely— surely it was daylight clear that if Tony had already had one flogging and was now in such misery that he had run away, there was nothing but cruelty in adding to his punishment. Why couldn't they see it as plainly as she could ? Derek— you wouldn't expect *him* to see it ; but Keatings and Joyce— why were they so blind ?

In the absence of their father, Keatings, as usual, assumed command.

" Joyce and I will sit up all night, if necessary. But Derek and Peggy'll jolly well go to bed. The servants can go to bed too. Too many cooks spoil the broth," said he, and wondered whether this concluding citation were wholly felicitous.

Derek protested vigorously, as well he might, for he felt that the whole mystery was his peculiar property. But he went to bed a few inches in front of Keatings' following boot.

Peggy, who slept in the same room as Joyce, thus lay alone. Often she looked at the blue night behind the lace-work of the holland blind, and thought of Tony out there in the darkness alone; and as her mind created his pangs with increasing sharpness, her heart did sickly jumps and slips under her small, maturing breast. And her vision, playing freely now, gave her a sight of the difference between herself and Keatings and Joyce; it was not that they had less imagination than she, but that they were so lost in imagining themselves the ministers and instruments of justice that they had no time to project themselves into the victim's mind, whereas she had leapt there instantly.

Tony was in disgrace for having bullied a little boy; he had been whipped, and his schoolfellows were waiting to vent their contempt in persecution, and from this humiliation—not from the mere threat of pain, as that idiot Derek supposed—Tony had run! Two problems puzzled her head now. One, that this idea of Tony being whipped should be so stimulating; wasn't that a rather awful wickedness in her? And the other, that if *she* had been in disgrace and persecuted, she would not have run from it but would almost have enjoyed it. If, for example, she had been in disgrace with Miss Gibbon—a mistress at Cottenham whom she was disposed to worship—and if Miss Gibbon had severely punished her, she would have—yes, there was no doubt of it—she would have found it rather thrilling. Her body, as she conceived of such punishment now, endorsed the idea with a pleasant tremor. (Peggy had glimpsed, from the episode of Tony's cruelty, the difference between herself and Keatings and Joyce, but she could not see the difference between herself and Tony. It was beyond her sight that Tony, in his blindness, had wanted to wield a whip, whereas she, in the same blindness, would have liked to put herself under one.)

Oh, poor Tony! what was he doing? Bed is ever a rich soil, and darkness the right light, for the rearing of black fantasies, and she saw her brother leaping into the Serpentine . . . jumping over London Bridge. . . laying his head on the rails as the express thundered up. So perfect was her identification with him that she gasped as the water closed over her head, or the train approached. "O God, make him not do that. . . ."

"O God. . . ." Of course, she must pray hard for Tony, and keep on praying, like the Importunate Widow, or like—like—what was this old memory struggling to the surface? A Sunday afternoon in church, and the winter dusk creeping over the heads of six hundred children, and Mr. Crabb beaming from his pulpit. . . . Like Mrs. Mark and Rhoda, who prayed for Peter when he was in prison awaiting death, and, even as they prayed, heard his footsteps approaching and his knock at their door.   If she prayed now for Tony, hour after hour, with tireless perseverance and unshakeable faith, she would sooner or later hear his footsteps echoing up St. Austin's Road.   She saw the long road, abandoned by everybody to the occupying starlight ; its paraded houses staring at each other from their blinded windows, its gas lamps dotting a zig-zag line from pavement to pavement.   And then she saw a figure turn out of Kensington Road, and walk up the pavement, till its steps became audible : *pat, pat, pat, pat, pat, pat*. . . . By persistent prayer she would bring Tony round the corner like that.   Mrs. Mark and Rhoda had done it with Peter.   But——

Oh, how often she had turned to God, offering him promises of amendment in exchange for some signal favour, and after no more than a few days of holiness, abandoned its pressures and strains with extraordinary relief !   So what was the use of praying now ?   Prayers, as she had heard in her father's church a hundred times, were of no avail unless associated with these promises of amendment ; and in common fairness what could she do but refuse to sign such a blank cheque on her credit when she knew it would never be honoured !

From her earliest days Peggy had seen the beauty of holiness, and loved it.   The characters who appealed to her in her books and lessons were those who went about on works of mercy, binding up the wounds of the broken, visiting those condemned to death, and receiving illegitimate mothers into their houses. Peggy—though she found it difficult to put a penny of her weekly pocket money in the alms-plate, and loathed having to say her prayers at night, and could not stop stealing fruit or biscuits off the sideboard, and had fibbed at school and at home with heart-breaking aplomb, and always enjoyed saying punishing things to her brothers, even finding that the delightfulness of these taunts bore an exact ratio to their beastliness— Peggy, despite all this, in her dreams of the future, saw herself as a nun with a serene face framed in a wimple and a crucifix dangling on her breast—or a sister with a basket of comforts under her arm—or a nurse with a lamp in her hand.   A sister ! It was a lovely word ; she would like to be a sister to the whole world, but one who accounted as her favourite brothers the bedraggled, the old, the wicked, the smelly, the spurned. Always she would be walking among them with her basket, or her lamp.   Always she would be knocking at their doors with new gifts ; and in their profoundest griefs she would even kiss their grimy and revolting brows.   One of her greatest ambitions in life was to have kissed a leper.

And now with all her heart she wanted to pray for Tony, but what was the use ?   God could see right into the back of her head, and was probably at this moment resting His eyes on her secret certainty that she would backslide into rebellion.   But perhaps he would listen to a prayer for Tony, if offered simply for his sake.   " O God, make it all right for Tony, and bring him safely home, not for my sake who am but dust and ashes, but for his, Amen."   Ten, twenty, fifty times, she repeated it, but her doubts of it grew with repetition.   Was she so poor a sister that she could not make the effort to be good, even though her brother's safety depended on it ?   Pausing, she listened for footsteps in the street.   Not a sound came through the open window and past the unstirring blind.   *Could* she make the promise to try again ?   No, not with intent to keep it, and God was not mocked.   She could promise to *try* to try again ; that was all.   " O God, I promise to *try*, but I will not deceive Thee by pretending to think it will come off; nevertheless, with Thee all things are possible.   I pray Thee, accept my prayer that all may come right with Tony ;   forgive him his iniquities and bring him safe home, Amen."   This twenty times, counted on her fingers.

Any footsteps in the street yet ?   No, only the night silence. Perhaps Importunacy was not reached till you had said it a hundred times.   She said it eighty times more, and the effect was almost to send her to sleep.

In common with the ascetics of all ages Peggy held the curious idea that prayers uttered in a comfortable position must be less effective than those uttered in acute discomfort.   And it was warm and comfortable in bed.   Let her get out and kneel in the cold.   Let her say her prayer fifty times by the bed's side, till she felt the cold chilling her body.   She leapt out for the exercise, quite as pleased and delighted with the game (though this was unrecognized by her) as were Keatings and Joyce and Derek when they started off as a search-party.   Fifty times at the bed's side she said her prayer, never once sitting back for the support of her heels, or collapsing forward into the soft invitation of the counterpane.   And she was most abominably cold when she finished, and not a little stiff in the knees; which satisfied her so much that she added ten more repetitions, and, rising, felt really hopeful. She went to the window to look out, not expecting immediate results, but just in case a miracle might be happening. The road stretched emptily away.

Still, she felt strangely confident now, and climbed back into bed. Since Tony would be back soon, she dropped into the pleasanter occupation of considering how she would greet him. That all the others were against him was a cruel fact, but she was not insensible to the fine ebon background this hostility would provide for her gentle pity; nor, though she would have repudiated this thought, was she over eager that it should be at once removed: she wanted to be able to contrast against it her love and forgiveness—to be able to visit his prison bedroom and say with full effect something like: "*I* do not condemn thee; go and sin no more." And as he lay on his guilty couch she would put an arm around his shoulders and draw him close. It would be the nearest she could get, for the present, to kissing a leper.

The picture proved so attractive that she fell to her prayers again for the return of Tony. The prayer became a set form; and as her familiarity with the words and with the necessary lip-movements increased, her repetitions, leaving her conscious control behind, acquired a velocity that passed belief and a rhythm that was one with the rhythm of the universe.

Stay!—oh, too wonderful!—was there not the sound of a horse in the road? Yes! *clapper-clut, clapper-clut, clapper-clut* —a cab was coming. Oh, silly that she had been! of *course* Tony would return in a four-wheeler with his father; and here he was! It was a little disappointing perhaps that the footsteps which were to resemble Peter's should be the footsteps of a cab-horse, but it was the same in essence; God had granted her prayer as he had granted Rhoda's; in his unconquerable forgiveness he had once again turned his face from her sins. But wait! if it wasn't to stop at their door? Her fingers flew to her lips in a spasm of doubt—but it *was* stopping. Yes, it was they. Gratitude to God and conditional promises poured from her till they acquired the velocity and rhythm of her previous petitions. There was a bustling in the hall, as Mother and Keatings and Joyce hurried to the door. And Tony's voice. Oh, pray God that they didn't forgive him before *she* could!

After the voices had dwindled behind the door of the break-fast-room, she had to wait a long time, seemingly an endless time, before they emerged again and the family climbed to their several rooms. Tony's room was on the landing below, and she heard him go in. She would count a hundred, so as to give him plenty of time for undressing, and then set forth on her sisterly visit. Reaching the hundred sooner than she expected, she decided to give him another fifty. Thereupon she got up, lit her candle, and holding it in her hand, looked out into the passage; nor at that moment did she think of her likeness to the Lady with the Lamp. The passage was dark and deserted, and she tip-toed quickly and guiltily down the stairs and knocked at her brother's door.

" Come in."

Entering, she saw that he was already in bed, huddled up in the clothes.

" Tony: I'm so glad you're back. I thought you would like to know there's somebody siding with you. I'm siding with you through thick and thin."

" *I'm* all right," Tony muttered, mixing a sad fatalism with a proud independence.

He was blinking his eyes at the candle, so she laid it on the washstand, before sitting on his bed and putting her arm around his shoulder. That done, she sank—and sank with a sinker's alarm and gathering despair—into a horrid and embarrassing speechlessness. Tony said nothing, and even betrayed his discomfort; and she could not think of a single possible sentence, or, if she did think of one, could not force it past her lips. She had fondled the idea of strengthening him with a verse of poetry that had often garnished her father's sermons:

> " Beware of desperate deeds;
> The darkest day
> (Live till to-morrow)
> Will have passed away;"

but all courage for uttering it had finally evaporated. So they both stayed awkwardly there, Peggy holding an embarrass-ment in her arms, and Tony in the grip of one.

" Tony: you're not awfully unhappy, are you? " she essayed at last.

" No," said he. " Not particularly."

And then a happier idea seized her, of something much easier to do than to speak consolation and strength.

" Tony : would you like me to come into your bed and sleep with you ?   I will if it'd be any comfort to you."

" No, thanks," said Tony.

" Well. . . ."   These sinners were always a little sullen, and she refused to sigh about it.   " Well, Tony : I'll leave you now.   Good night."

" Good night."

She had not even the courage to kiss him now.   Holding her disappointment at bay, she took up her candle, gave him a doctor's bedside smile, and on her bare feet drifted from the room, soundlessly as a child's ghost.

Though Peggy's will had failed to produce a recitation of

" The darkest day
(Live till to-morrow)
Will have passed away,"

it remains the aptest comment on Tony's twelve black hours. The entanglement and the knots in his life which had filled those hours with bewilderment simplified themselves in a manner too easy, one might say, to be consistent with the dignity of the preceding pain.   It had been easy for Dr. O'Grogan, once he had accepted the conviction that he must use the police, to find Tony.   About ten o'clock that night, a Romford police-man had dropped his eyes on the silver Maltese cross of a Colet Court cap, and, under cover of an amicable smile, charged its wearer with being Antony O'Grogan.   And Tony, too brain-sick and indifferent to meet this with anything but the truth, answered simply, " Yes."

" You're lost, ain't yer ? " inquired the policeman.

" I suppose so," said Tony.

" Sort of run away, eh ?   Well, I should come back 'ome, if I was you.   You have a better time at 'ome, all said and done, than you do at sea.   At sea, you know, they string you up to the mast and wollop your bare back with a rope's end, till they have the skin off yer.   You don't want none of that. It's no life for a gen'l'man, relly—not when you can have bacon and eggs every morning for your breakfast at 'ome. Yes, you come along, sonny, and let's phone to your pa.   I'll lay he don't give you a hiding, now he's found you again.

They never do, bless yer heart. We see a lot of runaway nippers in our time, and their pa's and ma's, after threatening to strap 'em no end, are all over 'em, once they get 'em back. Kissin' 'em and cuddlin' 'em as if they were two-year-olds. So don't you worry about that. You come along o' me, and we'll give you your tea."

Tony, for want of any other solution, was now walking along by the policeman's side, who applied himself to sustaining their first cordial association by a prop of friendly chatter.

"My missus lives along of the station, and she'll look after you properly, till I come off my beat myself, which'll be in half no-time now, when I'll come and have a crack with you too. Yes, there was one nipper we had: his pa had come 'ome rather the worse for his drink, and was all for taking a strap to him, just—as far as I could make out—to keep his eye in and pass away the time; and the nipper—'e done a guy like a good 'un through the scullery window, while his pa was undoing his belt in the kitchen; and when the kid didn't come 'ome for hours and hours, the father come rolling round to us and says we've got to find 'im, or what was taxes for? 'But don't you do the punishin' of him,' he says; 'you leave that to me,' he says. 'I'll learn 'im to run away from a good 'ome.' And when we pointed out that runnin' away wasn't an indictable offence, he says, 'Oh, *isn't* it? It *is* at No. 7 Barford Buildings'—which was where he lived—'*I'll* indict the seat of 'is pants for 'im, so that 'e won't run away again in a 'urry and make a police matter of it. Gratitude!' he says, 'Gratitude —they don't know what it means.' Well, he sat there on the bench, bletherin' away to himself like that, and the missionary come in to speak to him about his habits and he just stares at the missionary, and says 'Oo are you?' and when he heard that he was the missionary, he says, 'What do we want with missionaries in England? It's savages you ought to be preachin' to. England's a Christian country, and always has been. And it's a free country, too, I'd 'ave you remember. Not all the coppers and all the missionaries in England can come between a man and his own flesh and blood,' he says. 'If I intend to give my kid a tannin' what's richly deserved, I give it 'im, and ask no one's permission. And if runnin' away ain't a case for a tannin' that 'e won't forget for a twelvemonth, I don't know what is.' And just then, while he was goin' on like that, there was a call for the ambulance, and he saw the

stretcher being wheeled out of the door. 'Christ!' he says—
I beg yer pardon, sonny, but that was what he actually said—
'Christ!' he says. 'Is that for our Paul?' We knew it
wasn't, but we didn't let on. 'Our Paul ain't run over, is 'e?'
he says. 'That ain't for our little Paul, is it?' I seldom see a
man as pale as 'e was then. Well, the long and the short of it is
'e was there for hours bletherin' about ' his bairn ' and reckonin'
'e'd always bin a bit on the rough side with him, and cursin'
the pubs as the cause of it all and wantin' to have them all shut
up by the law of the land, and then, all of a sudden, we produced
the nipper, and you should 'a just seen 'im then. God's
truth! he was all over 'im like a woman, and carried 'im off
'ome on his shoulder. The missionary kep' his eye on his house
after that, and the N.S.P.C.C.—they did a bit of watchin', and I
won't say as how he never touched a drop of the drink again,
because we 'ad 'im once as a ' drunk and disorderly,' but I
know 'e was mighty shy of touchin' any of his kids again.
However, I expect your pa's a different sort to that."

They were now at the station, which was quite a homely red-
brick building, behind a hedge of euonymus. Its front had
big official doors opening on to an asphalted drive, but its
western wing showed curtained windows looking on to runner-
beans and cabbages and sweet-peas and evidently held the
quarters of the married policemen. Into a sitting-room, as
small as the living-room of the Freshwater cottage, but housing
twice as much furniture and bric-à-brac, most of which seemed
to be either draped in lace or enclosed under glass, Tony was
shown, and into the smiling welcome of a ruddy, full-bosomed
woman. They gave him tea in a white cup ringed with gold;
and as he drank it, though bruised from thinking and soft with
sleep, he found himself wondering that the stately policemen
of London should have a cottage life at home so little different
from that of Andrews, the Freshwater fisherman, and that the
head and face of his present rescuer, now he had come in and
doffed his helmet, should seem so small. It was not half an
hour before the wheels of a cab halted outside and his father,
his black Inverness cape flying open, came into the little room
and spread out his hands towards Tony, in a pantomime of
surprise and delight at this strange meeting.

"Well, Tony, God bless my soul! fancy seeing you again!
Now isn't this jolly?" He put an arm round his shoulder
and drew him rather lovingly against his side, looking the

while at the policeman. "And this good friend of yours, you owe him very considerable gratitude, don't you? You'd like to make him a present, I expect. . . . Trouble at school," he explained to the policeman, while he fumbled at the little sovereign-case in his waistcoat pocket; and Tony guessed that he had mentioned this, that no shadow might fall on his own reputation. He put something into the palm of the policeman. "That's but a poor expression of our gratitude, but it carries a full heart with it—a very full heart——"

"That's all right; that's nothing; don't you worry about that, sir," demurred the policeman, but putting the gift in his trouser pocket none the less. "Pleased to 'a bin a bit of service to you."

"A very big bit of service indeed. However——" he quickly changed the subject; patting Tony's arm as he held him, he laughed out, "Got five of these young animals at home, and they seem like fifty. You wouldn't think you'd notice one more or less, but there you are! you do. The disappearance of one leaves quite a draught; and this knave here was rather my Benjamin, you see—he and his sister." Altogether Dr. O'Grogan stood in that little room, a lofty monument of gratitude and jocosity; and what with the huge policeman standing opposite him, and his large wife standing on one side with her arms in her apron, and Tony standing squeezed into his father's Inverness cape, it was difficult to recall afterwards on what part of the floor they could have been assembled. "Yes, five of them, and none of them earning their keep. I suppose you've got some, too, constable, to make your life a burden and a reproach."

"Three," answered the policeman. "Leastways, three alive; but they're all off me hands now. My girl's out at service; my younger boy's in the Army and already got his first stripe; and my elder boy's with the florist here, and married. The eldest of all we've just lost, in South Africa there." He cocked his big thumb over his shoulder, as if South Africa were in the next room.

"Really? Really?" Dr. O'Grogan queried, in his most sympathetic voice. "That's dreadfully sad."

"Can't be helped, sir. But, as you say, it's a sad business to bring 'em up and educate 'em and all, just for them to be knocked out at the very moment when they ought to begin to put it all to some use. I'm glad your nippers ain't old enough to go; and I don't expect, after this business, we shall have another war in a hurry.   Not in their time, let us hope."

"I hope not.   I sincerely hope not. . . . Well, constable, if ever I can be of help to you at any time, remember you have a special claim on me.   I—er—I am not without influence.   I daresay you have heard of my church : St. Austin's, Kensington."

"Can't say as I have, sir.   Kensington : that'd be in the Metropolitan B Division.   I'm never that way, sir."

"No ?" Dr. O'Grogan smiled.   "Well, we flatter ourselves we're rather well known that way.   I wonder if I were to write to my brother Vicar here, if he could be of any service to you."

"I don't think so, sir, thanking you very much all the same. What with night duty, and Sunday duty, and a bit of sleep, we don't get too much time for going to church."

"Of course not.   Of course not.   Well, Tony, it's abominably late.   We must be making tracks for home.   Say goodbye to these exceedingly kind people."

At home, and at Colet Court, everything was simplified by the slight fever which Tony's temperature revealed in the morning.   The mountains went down before this sickness. At the Vicarage the children, after sitting by his bed, expressed themselves as surprised and delighted that he could make such a good case for himself.   And at Colet Court, though his absence gave currency to a rumour that he had been expelled, or, alternatively, that his pater had given him such a flogging that he was likely to be confined to bed for weeks, Wavers's white bandage came down ; with the odd result that the lynchlaw which had been smouldering in wait for Tony's return, simply expired, for want of this important fuel.   Moreover, Derek threw some excellent sand on it.   Having heard these disgraceful rumours, he felt that the honour of the Family demanded a personal visit from himself to some of his friends who were still at Colet Court ; and to these powerful people he averred that, now he had heard his kiddy brother's tale, he didn't feel at all sure that Wavers wasn't a filthy little sneak and deserved all he got.   And he'd thank them, he said, to publish this fact broadcast, so as to make it all right for Tony when he would be back at school.   With the utmost readiness they engaged to do so.   And Derek returned in dignified triumph to his brother's bedside, and quietly explained, " It'll be all right at Colet Court, kid. I've seen to it that you shan't be molested when you go back."

Tony was nervous the morning he went back, but a few hours at school showed him that the boys, so were their heads by now flooded with new interests, had consigned their thoughts on the Wavers episode into the dustbin that had received the white bandage. His appearance did not draw a single sidelong glance.

And then, almost as soon as he was comfortably resettled at school, they were all at Freshwater, under holiday skies, canoeing into the caves at high water; climbing Afton Down to take tea at Compton Farm; chaffing and being chaffed by Andrews, the boatman, as they rocked in his boat a mile from shore, fishing up the rock-whiting; bathing from Rogers's sandy machines; accompanying the dour Munster as he pulled towards his lobster-pots—a dangerous adventure, this, since he was reputed to be the poisoner of his wife; sitting on the broken esplanade to watch the soldiers in their fatigue dress firing from the Redoubt at the targets towed in the channel—when the bay thundered; and walking out of an afternoon, Peggy and Tony, to Alum Bay to continue work on their painting of the blue bay at the hour when its Needle Rocks went marching in Indian file towards the westering sun.

These laboured pictures—begun for a competition inaugurated by the *Western Wight Chronicle*—lifted Alum Bay this summer into a place of almost greater appeal than Freshwater Bay itself.

Day after day, in August's close, Peggy and Tony, with folding three-legged stools under their arms and satchels on their backs, trudged to Alum Bay along the turf road that rolls at the inland feet of the Downs, between the chalk-pits and the hedge. They came to know every yard of that hedge, and to think of it as of no other hedge in England; they greeted each part of its tangled make-up as a shepherd his individual sheep—its elder and privet and hawthorn and ash, its hemp-agrimony and woody nightshade, and its signal points of cuckoo pint, made of berries red as a fire-engine. This hedge and the turf road it flanked were a tramway guiding them straight to the chine, whose steps and steepways dipped down to the beach of Alum Bay. And a figure haunted the road, either treading its tussocky turf itself or walking above it on the sky-line of the Downs—the figure of Captain Alum.

Captain Alum was the famous character of Western **Wight in** those days : a little stumpy old man, with a waving black beard resting on his red jersey and waving black hair touching the shoulders of his blue jacket or blowing in the hill-side wind. He tramped the turf, disturbing the butterflies and the bees and the thistledown, with a stick over his shoulder and a bundle on its end, exactly like the traditional luggage of Dick Whittington ; but sometimes the likeness was marred by a pair of disreputable old boots slung abaft the bundle ; this was when Captain Alum, so fine a soul was he, liked to feel with his bare feet the soft, moist springy turf and praise the God who gave it. His jersey was red because he had once, in his enthusiasm for the Dear Lord (said by the local scoffers to be religious mania, but more probably assumed for brilliant effect, for Captain Alum was little if not a great creative artist), enlisted in the ranks of the Salvation Army ; but they, it seemed, had quickly cashiered him from the service, and Captain Alum had forgiven them their blindness and blessed them in parting, and unpicked the words " Salvation Army " from his jersey, and removed the ribbon from his peaked cap, and worn both in his office as a private merryman of God. " He must have been pretty bad, if the Salvation Army wouldn't have him," the coachman with the cyst over his eye used to say to the children when, on their arrival at Yarmouth, they asked first after Captain Alum. " Yes, he's still going strong. The other day, just before my coach started from Freshwater Gate, and the people were crowding on it more than it'll rightly hold, he stood a little distance off and sang something about ' Yes, there's room, yes, there's room, room in that far-off beautiful land,' or some gammon like that. Sing ! there's no mistaking he can sing. And when the horses got going, he broke into ' Home, Sweet Home,' and the passengers were so moved, what with their holiday being over and all, that they threw out pennies and sixpences, and the kiddies waved to him till we was out of sight. The last I saw of him he seemed to be blessing us. Well he might ! there was three-and-a-tanner on the road if there was a penny. 'Sno good having him moved on, because he goes so quietly, putting on his hat and turning away with a sigh, that the people run after him with tears in their eyes and give him money. Some say that he promises ten per cent. of his takings to someone if they'll push him roughly away, but I don't rightly know that there's anything in that."

All over the island tramped Captain Alum, with his bundle
and his boots and his apostolic hair waving in the wind, singing
in the loveliest tenor voice ever heard on those hills :

> " When upon Life's billows you are tempest-tossed,
> When you are discouraged, thinking all is lost,
> Count your many blessings, count them one by one,
> And it will surprise you what the Lord has done ; "

or, if the wind beat about him and the sea roared beneath the
cliffs :

> " Peace, perfect peace, with sorrows surging round ;
> On Jesu's bosom nought but calm is found."

Newbarn and Brading Down and Culver Down and the hills
above Ventnor and Blackgang had heard his song, and the
people at their feet had contributed their coppers and their
crusts to his maintenance, but it was ever to Alum Bay, where
the Needles carried the Island to its furthermost western reach,
that he harked back at last.   There the wind blew north and
south of him, and the sun set in his face, and he sang it to its
rest, while the soldiers from the battery stood at their doors to
listen :

> " The day Thou gavest, Lord, is ended,
> The darkness falls at Thy behest ;
> To Thee our morning hymns ascended,
> Thy praise shall sanctify our rest."

Sometimes there were no soldiers in the hill-top battery, or
children down on the distant beach, or visitors on the terrace
of the Alum Bay Hotel, to study his figure dark against the sky
and catch the falling of his voice, and then he sang it alone ;
for he was like all great artists, and, while much preferring an
audience and a fee, was ever ready, did love and remuneration
fail him, to create his beauty for himself alone.   It is possible,
of course, that he always sang to the Dear Lord only, so that
all æsthetic appreciation, whether from the people down below
or from his private heart within, was alike irrelevant ; but who
shall say ?

One day the whole O'Grogan family was lunching in the big
saloon of the Alum Bay Hotel, and he stood without the pre-
cincts and sang to the many munching visitors " of Jesus and
His love ; " and at the conclusion of his testimony, visited three

of the open windows with his peaked cap extended for alms, before the manager could hurry out on to the terrace and bid him begone.   Nothing bitterly, he turned and left the gate, and sitting in a free and public place beyond, changed his hymn to " No, never alone ; no, never alone ; He has promised never to leave me, And He never will leave me alone ; " which so affected the hotel visitors that they went out, one by one, and gave him of their substance.   Dr. O'Grogan most deliberately went out, with his table-napkin in one hand and a shilling in the other, and gave the shilling to his brother evangelist ; expounding on his return that, even if the old fellow was a scoundrel, he merited recognition as an artist who was creating for their amusement, and in the free and open air, as delightful a comic character as any Dan Leno or Herbert Campbell were creating on the boards.   " All artists put their genius for effect out to market, and if he chooses to market his creations in this way, well and good ; it behoves us who have enjoyed them to pay for our entertainment.   Most great humbugging scoundrels have been well worth the price they have cost the world, because they've contributed so much to the gaiety of nations ; there was Dizzy . . . and Charles Bradlaugh . . . and now there's the German Emperor."   And well pleased with his aphorisms, Dr. O'Grogan attacked the pudding.

Never did Peggy and Tony set off with their folding stools and their drawing blocks but they hoped to see Captain Alum sitting under the hedge by his bundle, ready to smile on them as they passed, and to give them a " God go with you, my dears.   God bless your going out and your coming in ; " or, on their homeward journey at nightfall, to hear his voice falling from the summits of Tennyson Down with the words, " Sun of my soul, Thou Saviour dear, It is not night if Thou be near," and at length to discern his figure silhouetted against the sky.

He visited them once when they were sketching.   Unheard on his naked feet, he came down the chine to the shore and stood behind their rounded backs, to study the pictures shaping beneath their brushes.   Peggy became aware of him first, and was straightway possessed by a violent interior giggling, which bent her face over her block, charged her cheeks with blood, shook her shoulders and her hand, sang in her nose, and finally burst through her lips, sprinkling her sea-scape and her sky-scape with a rash of spots.   Tony caught the giggle and suffered no less.   But Captain Alum only fingered his silky black beard, and nodded, and blessed them in their work, saying, " May the Master guide your hand."

The southern wall of Alum Bay is a sharded cliff down which the sands and clays of a dozen formations, the strata being vertical, lie in cataracts of colour—deep purple, rich red, light yellow, and pink and white and brown; so that, in the old days, when the pier was still unbroken by the sea, and before the hotel was burned down and left for the skeleton it now is, and before Captain Alum disappeared over the hills to be heard of no more, the ships from the mainland towns used to come into the bay, bringing their crowds of visitors to gaze on a precipice with a rainbow face.   The northern wall is a rounded hill, patched with gorse, overhung with purple saddle-cloths of heather, and sloping in easy steps and spurs to the beach.   On an evening when the ship against the pier had taken its last passenger aboard, and Peggy and Tony, having folded their stools, were standing to watch it cast off and put to sea, and the sun was low behind the Needles, and there was assuredly no money to be made out of the gospel anywhere, Captain Alum appeared on a spur of the northern hill as suddenly as if he were the figure of an Arabian *djinn* incarnated from the air around him and the dust at his feet; and he waited there, his black locks taking the wind, till the siren boomed, and the ship swung its stern, when he lifted his peaked cap high above his head, holding it there for a few seconds, and then letting his arm fall to his side, as he lifted his big chest and sent his voice after the ship, singing it into the open sea :

> " God be with you till we meet again ;
>   By His counsels guide, uphold you,
>   With His sheep securely fold you :
> God be with you till we meet again.

> " God be with you till we meet again ;
>   Keep love's banner floating o'er you,
>   Smite death's threatening wave before you :
> God be with you till we meet again."

Great was the fascination possessed by Captain Alum for Peggy and Tony; for Peggy, perhaps, because deep down in her heart lurked the idea that it must be the loveliest thing in the world to wander about despised and rejected and destitute, with the sky for roof and the down for pillow, and singing to such as would hear of the goodness of God; and for Tony, because he had already glimpsed a beauty in the vagabond life, when a man takes to his own road, shaking his shoulders free of property and praise alike, and claiming the liberty of the artist to be whatever his genius calls for, whether a saint or a scoundrel.

PART II

CHAPTER I

THE SUCCESS OF THE GABRIELS

IN the O'Grogans' world there stood a most oppressive phenomenon, a perdurable fact whose shadow none might avoid or gainsay; and it was the success of their kinsmen, the Gabriels.

Success seemed to be the Gabriels' by prescriptive right. The Venerable John Gabriel, Archdeacon of Putney, and brother-in-law to Dr. O'Grogan, was a good captain for the Gabriel phalanx, for in the intervals between his capturing of most of the ecclesiastical prizes within his reach, he had trained and equipped his four children, with much personal labour, for the capturing of as many as possible of the scholastic benefactions of the ages. The two elder were boys and the two younger girls; and it appeared as if these four children had only to approach their school prizes and scholarships and exhibitions, for the valuable things to drop from their branches and roll to meet them. John and Warner Gabriel both took Winchester scholarships, and New College scholarships, and Elsa and Theresa Gabriel did equally large things in their quieter feminine places. And if the Archdeacon went in front of this advancing phalanx, setting a high example of unresting work and complacent achievement, Mrs. Gabriel may be said to have come up behind somewhat hotly and breathlessly, not making any conquests of her own, but advancing under the cover of her children, flattering them with talk about their gifts and their steadiness and their father, and publishing their successes, like a good liaison officer, to less successful companies in the rear. This Mrs. Gabriel—the Aunt ·Adelaide who, on a faraway birthday, had presented Tony with his toy engine—was, in fact, as Tony had perceived then, a very ordinary woman, if not something of a fool; and it was natural that she should be secretly astonished at the cohort of young conquerors whom she had produced with the Archdeacon's aid, and should fall to descanting, rather too often and rather too liberally, on their attainments at home, their good discipline at school, and the methods that should be employed by others who desired a like result. To Mrs. O'Grogan, as the mother of an undisciplined rabble, she was especially generous with these hints and homilies; and to the O'Grogan children also, as members of that rabble. They always thought of her as coming into their drawing-room, looking very fat and fashionable in contrast with their thin and tired mother, and sitting fatly in a creaking chair to report a new success. Always they saw her in the same hat, a toque with a high, wide front, anchored on the uplifted waves of her silvery hair. The gold chains that lay on her expanse of bosom she fingered idly as she spoke of the Archdeacon's invitation to the Royal Garden Party, or of Warner's election to the Union.

John and Warner Gabriel were of much the same age as Keatings and Joyce, but there any resemblance ceased; for Keatings and Joyce were as unsuccessful in their intercourse with school examinations as their cousins were successful. The only examination which Keatings ever met and conversed with on friendly, if undemonstrative, terms was that slim janitor which permitted him to pass from Colet Court to St. Paul's. It is not recorded that Joyce ever passed any important examination; though, had she been examined at Cottenham on the things that delighted her—dress, bicycles, an adored girl friend, one or two curates, and such divine novels as " King Solomon's Mines " and " The Silence of Dean Maitland "—she would have sent up some very lively papers indeed.

Keatings' attitude to the Gabriels' success was to accept it as unquestionable and to use it as an opportunity for some indecorous satire, and thus to turn an evil thing into a good. To him this towering success, this huge overweening Fact, was as a mighty tree-trunk into which he could shoot his arrows of humour, after he had cut them carefully and dipped them in poison. If over the dinner-table there was a request for information which no one could supply, he would offer but one remark: " Ask the Gabriels." If the conversation threatened to move towards some difficult and controversial subject, he would strive to hold it back by submitting : " Why worry ? Ask the Gabriels." In fine, a debate might develop on any topic, political, religious, literary, scientific, or sporting, and the atmosphere might heat with friction, but he never broke his silence except to murmur : " Why quarrel, children ? Ask the Gabriels." From his talk, with which he was frugal as he grew older, it appeared that he had no ambition in life for himself or for his family, except that they should one day " flatten out the Gabriels." This exception made him more appreciative of any little success of his brothers and sisters than he might otherwise have been. When Joyce did so small a thing as to earn by her appearance an honourable mention in the newspaper's report of a ball, he remarked : " Well, that's something towards flattening out the Gabriels, at any rate. Mother, take it round and show the fat lady." When Derek played scrum half for the Second XV of St. Paul's, he waited till Derek was out of hearing and then said to his mother : " It's not much, but it's something. You'd better let the Gabriels have it in the chest. John and Warner Gabriel may be able to get scholarships, but they could no more kick a ball straight than they could fly. Only don't let Derek know we're puffing about it ; he's conceited enough already." When Peggy was chosen to impersonate " Little Em'ly " in some Dickensian tableaux at Cottenham, he commanded : " Take it round, Mummy. No one'd ever put Elsa and Theresa Gabriel into a tableau, unless it were as Mrs. Gummidge or Jane Murdstone." And when at last the Family did quite a big thing, Tony entering St. Paul's, not by shaking hands with that slim janitor, the Entrance Examination, but with that proud pass, a Junior Scholarship, Keatings was moved to exclaim : " Praise God, ye peoples ! It's a priceless jar for the Gabriels. Perhaps Tony, at any rate, will do something in life that will properly flatten them out."

His satire, more than once, trespassed along the pleasant hedges of profanity. He would maintain that there could be no other explanation of the Gabriel perfections than that the Archangel himself had, on a day of long ago, accepted the favours of a mortal maid, and so founded the astonishing family. He would pronounce of the Archdeacon, when Aunt Adelaide had visited the drawing-room and left the air rumourous with his great achievements, " Children, at last a

Man has appeared upon the earth. Now is Creation and all its travail justified. The Archdeacon is certainly the one far-off divine event to which the whole of creation has moved." He called his uncle Empedocles; and when his brothers and sisters invited him to unfold the riddle, explained that Empedocles was a Sicilian philosopher who, after being the "big noise" in his parts, had suddenly decided that he was too great for this world and forthwith plunged into Etna's fire. "And that seems to me a thoroughly sound and not un-humorous thing to do," said he; "I can't think why the Archdeacon stays amongst us. It must be terribly lonely, living in the world without one's equal anywhere."

Joyce's vindictiveness was less vocal, but harder, because less modified by humour. The blaring of the Gabriel girls' intellectual triumphs raised in her a hard, unreasoning contempt, which could only spit at their dowdiness and plainness; nor justly then, for though Elsa and Theresa lacked charm, they sat well this side of ugliness, and had much of the quiet dignity that goodness and learning give. But Joyce, in her hidden places, thought herself a far finer creature than either Elsa or Theresa. Academic success? What mattered all the academic success in the world when she knew that, if Joyce O'Grogan and Elsa and Theresa Gabriel were to go together to a dance, then Joyce would have more partners than her card could hold, while Elsa and Theresa would sit by the wall?

Derek, as usual, differed from the rest of the family in his attitude to the Gabriel noise. In the mind of Derek, notwithstanding he had announced, soon after his fifteenth birthday, that he and Tallboys Major were Agnostics, the possession of a much-paragraphed Archdeacon for an uncle seemed capable of use as an appendage to his own dignity; and he accordingly made large play with the Archdeacon's name among his fellow Paulines. So also with his cousins' tale of successes at Winchester and Oxford: they seemed excellent matter for rehearsal at school—even for enlargement.

It was in Peggy's nature to savour keenly her own loyalty to the Family, so she endorsed Keatings' idea that they must erect something soon which would equal the beetling superiority of the Gabriels; but she doubted much the righteousness of wanting to annihilate it. That was to covet other men's goods; that was to speak unkindly of those who despitefully used you. Unlike Keatings, who was ready, apparently, to steamroll the Gabriels' flat, with or without pain, so long as for ever; and unlike Joyce, who found a consolation for their scholastic brilliance in the dullness of their features and the incoherence of their dress, Peggy resolved that she must bear them no malice and must only allow herself a few private pictures of what she would do, if their overthrow *should* come to pass. Oh, if it did—if only it did—why, then she would hasten to the Gabriels with her sympathy, thus heaping the coals of fire on their heads; she would defiantly associate with Elsa and Theresa if ever they were ostracized by society for having " stooped to folly and learned too late that men betray "—which seemed unlikely, somehow; she would take her basket of comforts to John and Warner Gabriel in prison, should they ever be sent there for fraud; and she would provide for the whole family when they were thrown into poverty by the sudden death of the Archdeacon.

This vindictiveness against the Gabriels was often rebuked by Dr. O'Grogan, but only with a laughing tolerance, an amused appreciation, which suggested that it really woke an answering chord in him. After all, his brother-in-law was two years younger than he, and his congregation at Putney could not be compared, either in numbers or in fashion, with his own at Kensington; and yet the man had been made a gaitered Archdeacon in his thirties, while Dr. O'Grogan himself, though nearing fifty, had not so much as a prebendal stall in the Cathedral. And always he was hearing: " Your brother-in-law, the Archdeacon, is sure to be a bishop some day; " while of himself, as he knew very well, the people were saying: " Dr. Ernest would certainly have gone much further, if only . . . if only . . ." For the wide-spread of that " if only . . ." he was inclined to blame his wife. She should have more dignity than to let people see her embitterment and her distrust; not easily had he forgiven her when it came to his knowledge that she had answered one of the " Ernest worshippers," who had gushed: " Oh, what a beautiful, *beautiful* sermon your husband preached this morning, Mrs. O'Grogan," with a sad: " It is easy to preach, Mrs. Paget. . . ." Still, that " if only . . ." had probably heightened his fame and lit his figure to a picturesqueness; just as the breath of scandal, if it solidified into nothing tangible, only increased the commercial value of an actor, so the " if only . . ."

that flitted from Hammersmith to Hyde Park had helped to cram the pews of St. Austin's Church.

Dr. O'Grogan saw to it that his figure found the limelight quite as often as the gaitered legs of his brother-in-law. How he contrived to do it was a source of perpetual speculation to Keatings, his son. Sometimes the doctor would startle and faintly shock the air of Kensington by preaching a series of Sunday Evening Sermons on current stage plays or on the best-selling novels of the hour ; and Monday's newspaper would show an inch or two allotted to the meatier morsels of his discourse, under some such heading as " Vicar and Modern Morals ; " and Keatings, pondering this insertion, would inquire of Joyce : " Now how did *that* get in ? There were no reporters in church last night ; I was careful to see that. Do you think the old gentleman has a publicity agent ? I fear it. I fear the worst." Once the *Daily Graphic,* under the heading " Striking Attitudes of a Popular Preacher," published six studies, side by side, of Dr. O'Grogan's gestures in his pulpit ; and Keatings brought the pictures into the breakfast-room, summoning Joyce : " Joyce, come here. That's our pulpit, without a doubt ; which means that these portraits were only taken by flashlight. Dr. O. has a bounce, hasn't he ? I rather admire it." St. Austin's, Kensington, was one of the first churches to use the " moving pictures " as a handmaid to religion ; an innovation which pleased every sub-editor in London and earned an honourable half-column, entitled " Biograph in London Church." Keatings was pleasantly titillated. " The old gentleman's brought it off again," he crowed. " 'Struth, it's wonderful ! I tell you, Joyce dear, our Dr. O. is worth his money, if only for the amusement he gives us—as he used to say himself of Captain Alum." And Joyce read the half-column, and exclaimed : " The darling ! Bless his heart ! " Indeed, Keatings sucked unfailing joy from his father's existence ; filial irreverence, he had found, was the surest stage-laugh in the breakfast-room or the dining-room ; so he would stand at the window and look down the street for his father's return from a preaching engagement, and when he saw him coming, would announce : " By Christopher ! it was a dam-good sermon. I always know ! When he's a bit springy at the knees like that, and swings his umbrella, and lets his cape fly open, it means that he's highly satisfied with his performance. By gad ! there was *one* person who enjoyed the sermon this morning!" And the rest of the family rushed to the window, and gathered round Keatings, to study the spectacle of a victor returning.

The success of the Gabriels infected Tony, the youngest O'Grogan, with a secret, tingling ambition to be the one who should carry the Family's standard miles beyond the furthermost advance of the Gabriels'. Tony, by the age of fourteen and a half, had a secure confidence in his own abilities. This was no heady inflation due to his rapid advance at St. Paul's, but just that consciousness of power which is sometimes alight where power is. He could *feel* that he saw at once and brilliantly things that fogged the brains of others and furrowed their brows. And with this confidence went swelling, tingling ambitions. At fourteen and a half he carried on his shoulders, in the place of a head, a sealed box packed with dreams and schemes and ambitions. On the whole he most favoured the idea of being England's national poet and having a large estate like Tennyson's Farringford at Freshwater, and a barony. Certain strange emotions, hidden away, because of their strangeness, in his sealed box, encouraged him to hope that he had that quality of difference which makes a poet. Neither to his schoolfellows or to his brothers, who would think it ludicrous, could he publish the instant and almost painful response which trembled in his throat and eyes and lips, not only at the sound of lovely words, but at the description of anything that attained sublimity—were it the immense and patterned achievement of Newton, or the prodigious disturbance of Napoleon, or the pioneering vision of Kepler among the stars, or the unending reverberations of the French Revolution. When one of his masters, a Mr. Jamieson, who had much influence over him, waxed enthusiastic on these things, surely it was in Tony alone that tears struggled to break their prison behind his set lips and his shut teeth.

About another " difference " in him he felt less happy. How was it that that self-torturing love which he had given to Wavers, just because the boy's face had agitated him, now struck him as absurd, and he could look upon Wavers, who had recently arrived at St. Paul's as a leggy twelve-year-old, with complete indifference; and yet, in spite of this, he should be always seeking, and sometimes finding, the same experience again? Was it a shameful thing, or was it not, that he should always long for these secret loves which, though he knew them to be only transient and self-suggested, could yet make his life resplendent for a month or two, while he thought eternally of the one person, and hung about waiting for him, and tortured himself with doubts of him?

It was when he was nearly fifteen, and had lately read in "The Mill on the Floss" of Maggie Tulliver's love for her brother Tom, and in "The Revolt of Islam" of the love of Laon and Cythna—who, so Mr. Jamieson told him, had been brother and sister in Shelley's first draft of the poem—that he began to consider the possibility of making Peggy the object of his adoration. He had always liked her the best of his family, and could see now, for the first time, that beauty was coming to birth in her; for Peggy, at sixteen, had the grace of a timid gazelle, and the colour of a peony when she was shamed (which was often), and a large full-lipped mouth (to the nauseation of Keatings) and big eyes in which pensiveness was finally set, because behind them was her quaint conscience, as sensitive and shivering as the hinder half of a wasp. He could like her immensely; he could admire her and be proud of her; but could a sister ever give him the sweet aches that he desired, and the long inward hours. It was very difficult to believe; but he resolved that the experiment should be tried.

Of late he had discovered the River. Most Paulines held that Rowing, of all the sports offered to them, was the one that appealed to gentlemen, and that thus the Boat House at Hammersmith skimmed for itself the cream of the school; and Tony, soon baptized into this creed, set himself to row like a Blue, and, finding that the art was shaping in him, became a frenzied lover of the river. To build his intimacy with Peggy, he would sometimes put her in the stern of a double-sculling skiff, and display his own accomplishment, and teach her to row; or, having moored the boat to a tree, would loll there with her, discussing whether Victor Trumper or Tom Hayward or Ranji was the best batsman in the world, swearing that each of them was "absolutely too wonderful for words," and explaining to her how their batting averages were come at. She was always delighted to go, because she was flattered by her younger brother's advances and very ready to adore him. But Peggy's adoration, since she was a girl, was a serener thing than any Tony could have indulged, and untroubled by secret shames. The only shadow that fell across it was the shadow of its end, because in her natural humility and self-distrust she could not believe that Tony would long prefer her above his boy friends.

One sunny Saturday Peggy and Tony set off on bicycles for Richmond Bridge, whence they purposed a row and a sail to Kingston. Peggy was dressed in her tennis array : a white piqué frock, white stockings, white canvas shoes, a panama hat with her school ribbon of blue and yellow, and her brown hair in a long plait tied with a yellow ribbon. Tony, pedalling along, looked at her. "I'm glad you're in your whites," he said. He himself was also in white, from his rubber-soled shoes to the open collar of his shirt. Hat he had none, and his hair was already ablow.

On reaching Richmond Bridge, they carried their cycles down amongst the boats, and Tony, looking learnedly along the unruffled stream and up at the cloudless and burnished sky, demanded of a man in a jersey and a peaked cap : "Any chance of a sail ? Looks deuced calm at present."

"She'll freshen later, I fancy," said the man.

"Good ! Shove the sail aboard. . . . Peggy, you'd better sit in the stern and steer, while I get her over to the other bank."

"Yes, that's best," agreed Peggy, relieved at the arrangement, for, though she didn't mind rowing when they were round a bend, she hated doing it before the eyes of the owner of the boat. So, before Tony could change his mind, she stepped expertly into the stern of the boat (held so comfortingly by the man in the peaked cap) and took the rudder lines. Tony, stepping in, stood in his place, and, pleasantly conscious of a few people watching from the parapet of Richmond Bridge, pushed his boat from the landing-stage. Then, sitting down, he took the oars and gave as fine a display of sculling as he could.

"Keep her head for the other bank, Peggy," he muttered, now ostentatiously feathering his oars on the water's smooth surface. "We're having a great popular success."

When he had pulled the boat out of sight of the bridge and opposite Marble Hill, he invited Peggy to come and scull behind him, adding rudely : "It's just the place for your style of sculling. The river's so nice and wide."

"All right," said Peggy. "But, Tony : I think I'll only row one oar, till I get used to it again."

"Righto !" Tony consented.

He bent his head and his body that she might step across him

to her place in the bows behind; and when he had seen that
her oar was properly in its rowlock, and her wrist-action was
shaping aright, and her back was straight and her stomach down,
he leaned forward on his own stroke-oar, and cried to her behind
him: " Now then, Bow, are you ready? Forty strokes to the
minute! *Go !* "

And he pulled with such force that Peggy's contribution to
the motive power was negligible, and the boat's head swung
round for the bank.

" Tony: we seem to be going in a circle," said she. It
was a habit of Peggy's always to apostrophize a person by his
name, before saying what she had to say. " Tony: it isn't
going properly."

" Pull harder, then," he roared.

Peggy, feeling sure in her fright that the bank was imminent,
strove to pull with even greater vigour than Tony, and so to
turn the boat's head. But this only resulted in her oar's blade
rushing along the top of the water and wetting the stern-
cushions, while her fists struck her breast and nearly threw
her on her back. Quite demoralized, she hastened to recover
herself, and, in an effort to get in time again with Tony, hit him
in the small of the back.

" Gosh ! " he exclaimed; but not in ill humour, since he
knew he had purposely pulled hard to demonstrate his superior
strength. " Now then, we'll pull together. You pull your
hardest, and I'll pull gently; " which he did, using but one hand.

The boat now travelled steadily; and the stillness of the
stream, the soothing *suff* of the boat's movement, the clapping
of the water against its sides, and the distant gossip of the
birds, all threw their enchantment over brother and sister, who
yielded themselves to mechanical rowing and silent thought.
Not even Tony cared to clown, as they passed the flowered
lawns, gold and green in the sunlight, whose weeping willows
were so tranced and still that it seemed they had never moved.
The silence that lives under the branches of willows on tranquil
noons, and flies to the dark heart of the fir trees when the wind
is up, was basking, this hushed hour, in the open sunlight on
lawn and far-stretching meadow. A water-rat's splash sent a
trembling through it, that endured for a little while, like the
ring of ripples on the shivered water. It was mid-day now,
and sometimes they passed a punt moored under the trees,
while its lolling occupants lunched on green things, beneath

a coloured awning. From higher up the stream came the twanging of a banjo, and a pleasant voice singing : " I *do* feel sorry that I *was* set free ; Massa and the Missus were so good to me." And once a kingfisher flashed by, in a quick flame of blue and gold.

" Thank God for the river," said Tony at last ; and it was the lyrical cry of his emotion.

The mid-day warmth reminded them of their plan to bathe before lunch.

" We'll just go through Teddington Lock," said Tony. " And soon we'll sail. I felt a breath on my cheek. She's going to freshen."

They would have saved much time had they hauled their boat over the rollers at Teddington, but whoever took to the rollers when there was a chance of being shut in behind lock gates, lifted up and up on the rising water, and then ushered out through the stately-opening doors on to the higher levels ?

" Gosh ! There's more breeze up here," cried Tony, as he pulled past the weir. (A boy is ever the slave of one exclamation, and " Gosh ! " had been Tony's master for years now.) He was keeping his eyes on the western and private bank, scanning it for a likely, if illegitimate, bathing place ; and at last he saw an ideal spot, where the trees, rising from undergrowth, bent to the water and their branches essayed to brush its surface. " There we are ! " he cried. " Gosh ! there we bathe ! "

" Yes, let's," Peggy assented. The bathe, in which she could display some skilful swimming, was necessary, she felt, if she were to recover that place in her brother's favour which must have been lost by her maladroit handling of her oar.

" Right ! Hop out," Tony commanded, holding the boat to the bank by a tuft of rushes ; and after she was disembarked, he jumped out too, and, taking the painter, moored the boat to an overhanging bough.

He picked up his costume and walked a little distance, to leave Peggy's disrobing to a private place. But, once out of sight, he was inspired to show her that he could undress and be in the water in less than sixty seconds. He dived in rather clumsily, and swam towards the middle of the stream where she could see him, but he did not turn his head till he heard her.

Peggy was a good swimmer, and was swimming with great resolution now, for the notion had entered her head that if she could cross to the other side and back again, she would indeed recover her reputation.   She had not felt sure that the task was within her power, but as she hesitated, it had suddenly looked easy enough, and now she was off on the venture, calling : " *I'm* going over to the other side."

" Are you ?   So am I," cried Tony, who did not like the idea at all.   But as Peggy's high opinion meant as much to him as his did to her, he started with a doubting heart to follow her.

And she, wishing she had never spoken, pursued her way into deeper waters and a wilder panic.

In fact, they both proceeded to crucify themselves on their desire for each other's praise.

Peggy's heart, when she found herself in the middle of the stream and saw that each bank was as far from her as the other, beat like an engine ; but, observing that Tony was swimming at her side, with no outward sign of fear, though his strokes were becoming rather laboured, and being quite unaware that he, like her, was wondering if his last hour had come, she struggled on, praying silently but frantically to God.   After twenty more strokes she was quite persuaded that the bank was as far off as ever ; and she had a deathly moment when she suspected that they were travelling sideways in the current. The engine under her breast now throbbed wildly and erratically as if its controls had slipped ; and her stroke increased to a panic velocity, her arms racing at times like a propeller above the water.   She splashed Tony with arms and feet ; and once they got entangled in each other, and both believed for the space of a second that all was over.

Still, neither would allow that it was not very enjoyable and easy.   Tony decided to make one final bid for life ; forty more strokes would he do, and if he were not in shallow water then, he would know that it was the end.   But he had only counted twenty-nine when his lagging and aching feet struck a stone, telling him that he was in his depth.   Turning round, he saw Peggy struggling home, and shouted :

" Come along ! Don't give in.   Gosh ! it's as easy as winking."

Peggy, on arrival, tried to stand up, but staggered in the water with weariness.

" I wasn't going to give in," she expostulated, rather annoyed at Tony's patronage.   " It was I who suggested it."

" All right," said Tony.   " Well, now we've got to go back."

Peggy felt ready to cry, but quite determined to do anything her brother did. After her bragging, she couldn't ask him to swim over to the boat and bring it across.

"I'll just get my breath," she said.

And while she sat on the bank and kicked the water, to hide her thoughts, she came to a bargain with God. She asked forgiveness for her ostentation and for being quite unable to abandon it before Tony, and she vowed she would not be guilty of it again, if God would get her across to the boat. And when she got into that state of " feeling " that her prayer had been heard and answered, she said with a fortitude that caused her some admiration :

"Tony, are you ready now? I am."

And she started back across the river, conceiving that she was being upheld by the Everlasting Arms. With a kind of fatalistic faith she rested in them, and it was strange how quietly and confidently she progressed, as she nailed her thoughts to faith, blinding them to aught else. They must not glance aside from God and His omnipotence, lest she sank like Peter on the lake. As long as she held tight to faith—oh, how steadily she was going, and how surely. Yes—wasn't it wonderful ?— power was undoubtedly visiting her ; and with power, exulta- tion ; and with exultation, the certainty of conquest. She went on and on, delighting in the answer to prayer, and in God ; the boat's side showed itself very near to her now, and, glowing with excitement, she reached it, panted a thanksgiving, and thought how beautiful it was that one could go through a great spiritual experience as one swam from bank to bank in the sunlight.

Tony had come up too, and was gripping the gunwhale.

"Why, it was stupidly easy," he declared, when his breath returned. " Gosh, I wish it had been twice as wide."

"So do I," began Peggy—but stopped, remembering her engagements with God.

"Shall we do it again ? " said Tony.

Peggy climbed out of the water.

"We shall hardly have time, shall we ? " she suggested, think- ing it was clever of God to pull her up so sharply on the instant of her fall.

"No, we shan't. . . . And, Gosh ! Peggy," he added, as he climbed the bank, and felt the wind on his wet costume. " She freshens ! Hurry up, and we'll sail to Kingston."

The wind was certainly rising; and under an obscured sun, the stream had turned slate blue. Tony was quickly back in the boat, erecting its mast and hauling up its sail. Then Peggy stepped into the stern and took the rudder lines; and Tony pushed off into a following wind, which immediately filled the canvas.

"Tony: look out!" cried Peggy, holding the lines taut as the boat careened and bore forward. "Tony: it's going."

"Of course it is," laughed he.

"Yes, but, Tony: it's going so fast."

"Of course it is. We've got the wind."

"Yes, but how do you stop it?"

"You don't stop it; you steer."

"But supposing we meet something?"

"Well, you steer round it."

"Oh, but when the moment comes, I always forget which rope to pull," pleaded Peggy, looking at her brother with a look rather like a dog's.

"In that case, we shall probably hit something," said Tony.

"Tony; I think you'd better steer."

"All right," conceded Tony, who was longing to take the lines.

And for the next hour he sent the boat scissoring through the water, as the scissors of a draper tear through a breadth of calico. He turned her head into the wash of passing steamers, to challenge that "sea-sick feeling;" he raced other less well-manned craft; while Peggy ate an overdue lunch, or dragged her fingers in the water, or stared dreamily at the houses on the banks, the people in the boats, and the swans on the stream. And then they sighted the white bridge of Kingston.

There were real yachts on the water at Kingston, so Tony let down his sail, and they paddled about for an hour and went ashore and drank tea. And when they were back in the boat, Tony said, resting on his oars: "It's five o'clock. I don't think we'll stay at Kingston——" He began to pull gently. "I'm for going back. Didn't someone say: 'It's better to journey than to arrive?'"

"I believe so," said Peggy.

"And we ought to try to make Richmond before dark, don't you think?"

Peggy nodding, he put the boat in the flow of the stream and pulled towards home. They said little. There was something sad about rowing at the day's end past river stretches they had sailed up at noon. Tony, looking sometimes at Peggy, was thinking : " No. One can manage a decent sort of friendship with a sister, but one can't work up anything more. Not with a sister. It can't be done. The Laon and Cythna idea is all a barney." Silence seemed a due deference to the lowness of the sun. The houses on the eastern bank, staring into the sun's face, were luminous themselves, and threw long, scintillating reflections across the water ; while on the other bank the sun-rays took stealthy cover and peeped from the undergrowth and the willows. And before the brother and sister reached Teddington Lock, the light on the waterside villas turned to rose.

" Tired ? " inquired Peggy of Tony, who was doing all the sculling.

" Not half ! " he answered. " Absolutely done in."

Twilight surrounded Eel Pie Island, as later they passed it. And when, with a sigh of relief, Tony bumped the boat against the landing-stage at Richmond Bridge, and fell forward on his oars, in imitation of an exhausted racer, darkness covered the river. Peggy awoke from a trance.

" It's been lovely," she said. " But I'm quite glad to be home."

CHAPTER II

ORESTES AND PYLADES

IN this year and this summer term Tony read Montaigne, "Of Friendship," and, as it so fell, construed with Mr. Jamieson Euripides' "Iphigenia in Tauris," wherein was set forth the deathless friendship of Orestes and Pylades; and these two writings, taken in successive mouthfuls, worked a powerful movement in his soul towards the building of a like friendship for himself. He began to look round for an Orestes. Privily, he decided to be in agreement with Montaigne that love with its "pricking and stinging" was a rash and wavering fire compared with true friendship, whose flame was "a general and universal heat, and equally tempered, all pleasure and smoothness." And he felt satisfied, though entirely without experience, that Montaigne was right in maintaining that "the ordinary sufficiency of women cannot answer this conference and communication, nor seem their minds strong enough to endure the pulling of a knot so hard, so fast, and durable." Let him then straightway build for himself a friendship on the model of Montaigne's; a friendship in which all things should now and henceforth be held in common: "wills, thoughts, judgments, goods, wives, children, honour, and life."

The Orestes of his choice was Raking. Raking walked home from school along Kensington Road to his mother's flat behind Olympia; which meant that he and O'Grogan Minor, when at length they converged, could make the greater part of their homeward journey side by side; and to this end they would wait for each other at five o'clock each evening, on the gravel that sweeps from the main doors of St. Paul's. An ill-assorted pair they looked; for Tony was now tall, the gracefulness of his childhood lengthening into the gracelessness of adolescence, while Raking was broad in the body and thick in the leg. He seemed maturer than Tony; adolescence had ripened quicker in him, and, as sometimes happens, it had widened his shoulders and his hips rather than lengthened his limbs. Like his figure, his face was big and coarse, with wide nostrils that moved much as he spoke, and little eyes that rarely looked at his listener—though this latter habit was due to no evasiveness, for he was unblushingly sincere in his talks with Tony, but to his simple ambitions, which kept his eyes resting on the future. It was of their ambitions that they talked on their homeward walk, with their schoolbooks under their arms.

Raking, who was on the Modern Side, would confess frankly that he had no sympathy with Tony's enthusiasms for poetry and painting and music: for him the open air; the army, if by any luck he could reach it; and if not, a poultry farm in England, or a ranch in Canada, or a plantation in Malay. A man's life should be lived, according to Raking, in riding-breeches and gaiters, with a gun slung behind his shoulders, and his shirt open at the breast, to the tanning of the sun and the wind. And when Tony suggested that he was not by any means convinced that a gamekeeper's life was the highest imaginable for man, Raking heard him not, but continued with a long, excited, spitting description of the finances of his poultry farm or the lay-out of his ranch. On little else, till the confidences deepened, did he speak well.

It did not dawn on Tony that a boy whose ambitions were so different from his own could never play the Etienne de la Boétie to his Montaigne. Sometimes, certainly, he felt a quick pain of frustration, when his ardent utterance of a difficult thought met nothing in his friend except incomprehension and boredom. And sometimes he was offended by a tinge of vulgar unscrupulousness in Raking; as when he said: " I don't see how you can blink your eyes to the fact that one can only get on by pushing others out of the road. You say friends are better than money—Yes, but the point is, you'll have far more friends if you're successful than if you aren't." To which Tony scoffed one word in answer, " Friends ! " But they were soon drawn closer together by another subject, on which both could talk eagerly, in some of the most thrilling conversations they had known.

Ever called by the large horizons, Raking would lead Tony to the green spaces that lie against London—on to the high, empty levels of Wimbledon Common, or down among the rolling green hills of Richmond Park—to any of those littered commons where Londoners, in their starved poetry, go to find the prairie. Always he must escape the pavement and the bricks. And tired and glowing delightfully after their swinging walk, they would recline under trees, in Richmond's coppices, or Wimbledon's hollows, or the woods that meet the Thames. And there, at first, they fell again to the planning of their future lives, Raking filling his with his steers and his stockyards, and Tony with libraries and pictures and the applause of men; or they dropped from this to a debate as to whether Tom Hayward could catch up with C. B. Fry's batting average, which looked like surpassing Ranji's of three years before; and this would lead them into a quarrel as to the perfect figure of an athlete, Tony averring that the best of them were always colossal in the chest and the shoulders but thin in the loins and the legs, and Raking insisting that all really powerful people must have colossal thighs. At any rate the thighs of Jumbo Hopgood, the Captain of the First XV, were absolutely too colossal for words.

But in secluded places secluded thoughts well up for interchange. And if their talk about their coming lives had thrilled, this new kind of talk had such a grip that it held them to their places till nothing but the darkness and a chill in the air compelled them to make their move for home. They felt exalted to a higher life-power as they talked thus; life tingled in their throats and their breath and their bodies. In Tony the talk was always accompanied by a slight trembling of the heart and of the limbs, and followed by a faint nervous exhaustion.

It threw a new intimacy over their union, which blinded him to any crudeness or inadequacy in his friend. It made him believe that at last he had a friend after the pattern of the books.

"Why—why—why should people be troubled like this?" was the half amused note of Raking. Though, to be sure, one wouldn't be without it, and its strange pleasure, he said; but it might have been arranged better; it was all rather a shame. Tony, when time after time this subject asserted its masterful claim over their solitudes, did more listening than talking. Much of Raking's argument was as passionately interesting to him as to his friend; but to some of it he did not fully respond.

When Raking admitted, in his stuttering language, that every girl with any beauty could trouble him to an unrest which was both a pleasure and a distress, and asked Tony if it were not the same with him, Tony shook his head and answered, No. This seemed to worry Raking, in whose talk there was far less of self-indulgence than of a bewildered search for fellowship. And didn't Tony, he asked, feel stimulated, when he was dancing, by the touch of his partner's waist and the resting of her hand in his. " Gosh, no ! " Tony smiled. And Raking muttered : " Good Lord ! " and dropped silent, as if he were unhappy about it, and felt alone.

" Well. . . . I don't know," said he at last. . . . " However, there it is. . . . There it is. . . . I suppose it'll stop one day."

It was inevitable that Raking, having led Tony adventuring into the remote green places, should lead him, sooner or later, on an adventure into these unmapped mysteries of the mind. The summer holidays had come then, and Raking had been invited to the cottage at Freshwater. Except with Keatings, who pronounced him a fool—a worser fool, even, than Derek— he was popular with the O'Grogan children, being, indeed, an Honorary Foof ; which is to say that they had conferred on him the Honorary Freedom of the O'Grogan Family, a distinction very seldom granted. There were not above twelve Foofs in the world, and Mr. Flote, the little verger with the walrus moustache, was the senior brother of the order. Andrews, the genial fisherman at Freshwater, was another, but Munster, his uncouth partner (who had poisoned his wife) certainly was not. Raking owed his election to the superlatives of Tony, abetted by those of Peggy and Joyce, who were much pleased with a certain timid admiration and gallantry in Raking, which he expressed, not by any " sloppy talk," but by little gifts of chocolates and flowers, and by frequent invitations to the Coronet Theatre, in which his mother had an interest. So all assented to Tony's persistent demand that Raking should come to Freshwater, especially since there would be plenty of room in the cottage, Keatings having joined a reading party of his Oxford friends in the Rhineland, and Joyce having induced her father to take her to the Lakes.

And Raking came ; and Tony met him on Yarmouth pier and brought him in triumph on the coach. Followed great days for memory's store : days of exploration to Brook, where the fossilized forest lay under the sea ; to Alum Bay, where the cliffs were of many colours ; to Totland, where the nigger minstrels chorused :

> " They do bite
> In the Isle of Wight,
> But you should try them in the Isle of Man ; "

and, best of all, to Compton Farm.

To get to Compton Farm you toiled happily up the slope of Afton Down and mouched along the skyline to the top of Tapnell Down, where you stood for a while, and looked below, to where the farm buildings huddled in a hollow, with their teeming fields tilted on the hills all round. " Isn't it absolutely the quintessence of farm-ness ? " Tony asked Raking once, as they stood looking at it thus. Raking demanded what the deuce he meant ; and yet he of all people should have caught a meaning ; for there stood the farm-house, with its flint walls and moss-rusted roof, its hay-stacks and barns, its round pond with the ducks swimming, and the cattle drinking ; and up here you could listen to the ceaseless barking of its farm dog and the cackle of its poultry, and even, with a little imagination, smell the pigs and the cow-droppings. You smelt these very distinctly when you had dropped from the hill and entered upon its farm-road, strewn with feathers ; and you accounted it a lovely smell.

One afternoon, pleasantly tired after their long walk, they sat in the front garden of the farm-house, between the privet and the porch, and drank their tea at an iron table, and ate as much new bread, farm butter, blackberry jam and cream as they desired, all for the charge of ninepence a head. Other visitors from Freshwater had come out for the same famous walk and the same famous meal, so that each of the six tables in the little yard had its company to tea. The table next that of Tony and Raking was entertaining two young girls, one black-haired and bold-eyed and blowsy and noisy, and the other of quieter colouring and less ample shape and voice, but ready with her eyes, none the less. They earned many a glance from Raking, but few from Tony, who was devoting himself to a shattering of all his previous records with the blackberry jam and the cream. When he could do no more, he pushed the jam-pot and the cream-plate behind the vase of flowers and begged Raking never to mention such things again, if he would avert an unseemly exhibition on the part of his companion. He unloosened the knot of the sash that held up his white flannel trousers ; and he sighed a long " Ah. . . ."

But Raking gave but a poor heed to this facetiousness ; his brain was behind the eyes that were watching the two girls, rather than in touch with the palate that was savouring the jam and the cream.

" You said there were ducks on this farm, O'Grogan," he observed. " I begin to think you're right."

" What ? Those two ? " Tony made a depreciatory *moue* with his lips. " Those aren't ducks, my boy ; they're a couple of waddling geese, and one of them's been fattened up for Christmas. *And*, if they knew how vile their Cockney quack was, they wouldn't let us hear so much of it. The dark one's been trying to interest you for the last ten minutes."

" I know," said Raking.

" Yes, it's strange, isn't it ? Strange in what funny stuff a goose will go nosing around ! Fancy choosing *you* for a conquest."

" I think she's rather pretty—in her blowsy way."

" I should think she was the daughter of Isaac Abrams Moses Gluckstein, of Whitechapel. But there ! I may be wrong. I am willing to admit so much—I am willing to admit that, in expressing this opinion, I may be wrong."

" Well, what about the little one ? She's rather sweet, isn't she ? "

Tony rested his elbows on the table and his chin on his locked fingers.

" I'll tell you all about 'em," he said. " Some big pot has taken a house here for the whole of the summer months—he's a lazy swine !—and he's brought with him about half a dozen maids. Your Rachel Gluckstein is the junior chambermaid, and the little one is the tweeny, and to-day is their afternoon off, so they're out on a beano."

" No, they're better than that," Raking demurred.

" Are they ? Well, anyhow, they're not worth worrying about."

" I'm not so sure. I rather like 'em."

Just then the dark blowsy girl, having listened with open mouth to a whispered story from her friend, let loose a shrill shriek of laughter, which she quickly suppressed behind her hand and converted into a giggle. Her eyes sought the two boys, to learn if the noise of her laugh had captured any interest there.

" Yoicks! she gives tongue!—whatever that means," muttered Tony. " Tally ho!—and all the rest of it."

But while he was speaking, both girls broke into such an absurd giggling, and swung their eyes away so hotly from Raking, and exclaimed so distinctly : " Oh, I sye!" that Tony immediately charged his friend, " By Jove! I believe you *wunk* at them."

" Certainly I did," acknowledged Raking.

Tony was more shocked at this than he had the courage to show ; he was glad of the cover of his buffoonery. Though there was frivolity and irreverence enough at his vicarage home, yet much of its professional puritanism had filtered into his being ; he was quite ready to break parental rules or shirk ecclesiastical duties, but wholly unfamiliar with the idea of breaking an unalterable social law. It had simply never occurred to him, in the ingenuousness of fifteen's childish side, that a boy of his class would wink at unknown girls of the servant class. This was the first time in his life that he had seen such a signal shot : had seen his sex, in the person of a public school-boy, calling to the other sex, irrespective of class; and he could not understand it.

The girls now got up and went into the front parlour of the farm-house to pay their bill and write their names in the visitors' book ; and Tony, supposing that their performance was at an end, reverted to the subject of his digestion, and the grave difficulty he would have in walking three miles home. Raking also appeared to have abandoned interest in the girls, and vouchsafed it to the food instead, which he attacked anew, under the loud protests of Tony. Nor, when the girls reappeared and walked out of the garden gate, casting glances behind them at the boys, did he direct towards them more than a resigned, " what might have been " expression. And, as soon as they were gone, he gave himself to the task of leaving the jam-pot and the cream-jug stainlessly clean. This achieved, they pushed back their chairs, stood up, and staggered towards the porch. While Tony settled their reckoning with the comely farm-mistress, Raking seized the visitors' book for the pleasure of adding his third signature that month. He wrote it, and passed over the book to Tony with the words, " Olive Fowler, and Emily Holt. So neither of them were Jewesses after all." And Tony, taking the book, read :

" Olive Fowler, 320 Chapel Street, Bethnal Green.

Emily Holt, 141 Longman's Buildings, Clerkenwell."
After the columns for the names and the addresses there was a
column for "Remarks," and here in Emily Holt's hand was
written, "A very nice Tea."

"They can't have many brains between them," said Tony,
"or they'd have thought of something a bit wittier than that to
remark."

And, having signed his own name, he chewed the penholder
while he composed a remark more symptomatic of brains.

"Come on," Raking persisted. "Come on. It's getting
late."

But Tony was not coming till his poem was complete.

"It'd have been better if you hadn't hurried me," he excused,
when he submitted it to Raking. "Still, you couldn't have done
anything half as good if you had tried. . . . You needn't look
so sniffy about it. I told you it was not my best form."

"It's pretty bally awful," was all Raking said, as he tossed
the book back on to its table. For Tony had written:

> "We sign our names so very badly,
> And wander home a trifle sadly,
> For bread and butter, jam and cream
> Are not as simple as they seem;
> But none the less our hearts are warm
> At every thought of Compton Farm."

When they were out on the hill-side again, they saw the two
girls high above them, and Raking was for giving them a
"Coo-ey!" but Tony said: "Good Lord, no! What on earth
for?" The girls, however, looking down, had seen them, and
it was evident from the lifting of their shoulders that they were
giggling stupidly. Soon they linked arms and began to sing,
because they were at the top of their climb, and had begun a
journey that would be level and quick, over the springy turf.
The tune, on their high treble voices, floated down to the boys
below—a popular tune of that year, to which the words fitted
themselves immediately:

> "Keep off the grass, keep off the grass, keep off the grass in the garden;
> Play at your ease, but if you please,
> Keep off the grass in the garden."

Neither Tony nor Raking was in any condition to climb fast
up the hill, and presently the girls were over the brow and out
of sight. Exhausted by the climb, the boys collapsed on the

summit of Tapnell Down, choosing their couch in the lee of some gorse. Here they lolled for an hour, pulling thistles and chewing clover, and wearing down many a topic of talk ; till, at length, the evening light on the hills lifted them to their feet and sent them briskly down the slope towards the Golf Links and Fresh-water Bay. And because the hills were empty, and the example of the girls had inspired them, they shouted in shameless voice the songs that London's barrel-organs had rolled out that year, and in the years gone by : " Bonn, Bonn, beautiful Bonn, Beautiful valley of Bonn," they sang ; and " Chick, chick, chick, chick, Won't you marry me, chick, Be my little wife, said he ; " and " She was a miller's daughter " and " Jack's the boy for work, Jack's the boy for play, Jack's the boy when girls are sad to kiss their tears away." Parts of the slope were very steep, tempting them into the exquisite terrors of a run which nothing could stop. " Never mind ! Here goes ! " shouted Tony, and, outstretching his arms to preserve his balance, and yelling : " With his one little, two little, three little, four little, five little, six little wives," he began his breakneck career. Raking followed ; and soon both were speeding to the bottom of the visible world and wildly ejaculating, " Crikey ! I can't stop ! I can't stop ! I shall hit one of the houses, which would be a pity ! " Then Tony, with a thrill both lovely and horrid, caught his foot in a rabbit-hole, and pitched and tumbled and rolled. A sharp, sweetly pleasurable pain in his ankle told him that it was sprained. Raking, unable to stop, ran on but fetched a compass and slowed down, as he turned up the hill to his fallen friend.

" Dead ? " he inquired.

" No, only slightly sprained."

" Can you walk ? "

" I dunno. I think, if you'll let me lean on your shoulder, I can. It's getting better every minute."

" Of course. Hang on to me."

Raking came close, and lifted him, and placed one of Tony's arms on his shoulder, and his own arm round Tony's waist. Thus supported, Tony limped down the hill, laughing at his clumsiness and his grimaces, and surprising in his hidden heart one of those thoughts that he was sure no one else indulged—a satisfaction that he and his friend should have been forced so close together.

The first of the stars were up as they stumbled on to the weast of grass and tamarisk behind the broken sea-wall. And here the two girls appeared from amongst the chunks of concrete, and smiled at their stumbling, and followed them a little way. The elder and bolder of them, perceiving that Tony's accident was real, came up with an offer of help. Raking paused.

"It's awfully good of you," he said, looking straight into her eyes, "but what could you do? He's only sprained his ankle."

"I don't know," the girl confessed. "We could run and get 'im a fly, I ser-powse."

"Oh no," protested Tony. "I'm not bad."

"Well, look here, O'Grogan," Raking suggested. "I vote we sit down a bit, at any rate. You're no light weight after all that tea. And we're too late for supper now, anyhow."

"All right."

"Is there anywhere we can sit quietly—Olive?" Raking asked of the girl.

"'Ark at 'em Oliving me! 'Ow did yer know my nyme was Olive?"

"Guessed it. Haven't you an olive skin and black hair? Why, my friend here guessed your name was Rachel."

"Ow, stow it! *I got it!* It was that there visitors' book. Lor! Fancy you troublin' to see what our nymes was!"

"Never mind all that. Where are we going to sit the wounded man down?"

"There're some seats in the New Road, ain't there, Emmy?"

The younger and fairer girl said: "Yes, there was, if 'e could walk so far."

"Anywhere, anywhere," Tony agreed. "It's passing off."

"Well, you look real pale," said the younger girl. "Won't yer rest yer'uther arm on me, too?"

"Oh, thanks," Tony smiled—awkwardly. "That's ripping of you."

Raking watched him as he put his arm on her shoulder.

"Golly!" he laughed. "It was worth spraining one's ankle for that." And he at once sprained his own, and seized it with his hand, and hopped for several paces in his agony. "Yoo-hoo. I've fairly done it in, this time. I can't walk. Won't someone lend me a shoulder?"

In a second the bolder girl had put her arm around his waist.

"Come along, pore boy," she soothed. "Now, down't holler. Lean on yer auntie."

" Oh, thank you, Auntie Olive. . . . By George, O'Grogan, it's an ill wind that blows nobody any good," laughed Raking, squeezing affectionately his new crutch.

" Down' be silly ! " the girl giggled.

And all four, interlaced together, walked and stumbled towards the New Road. When they had reached a seat under the hedge, Raking looked up and down the empty road and said :

" O'Grogan, we must reward these angels of mercy. Where can we get them some chocolates ? "

" We down' want no chocklits," Olive assured him. " You can be nice to us, that's all."

" What's ' being nice ' mean ? "

" Down' be silly ! "

" If it means a kiss, my child, here goes." And to Tony's amazement and discomfort, he seized the girl and kissed her, softly at first, and then hungrily. She accepted it, and even put her hand behind his head caressingly.

" I say, O'Grogan," said Raking, cuddling Olive close into his side. " It seems to me that that seat supports you as well as I can, and a rest'll do you good, with someone to nurse you a bit. I think Olive and I'll breeze along to the next seat. Eh ? Come on, Olive. I've a sprained ankle, too, and want to be comforted a bit. So long, O'Grogan—only for a minute or two."

He walked slowly away with Olive to a seat in view, where they sat like lovers.

Tony felt his companion lean against him, and, as if bound in duty to respond to her, he arranged an arm along her shoulders. This seeming inadequate, he forced himself to put a kiss on her hair. That would be enough, surely, till Raking returned. But the girl, after resting against him for a little while, suddenly looked up mischievously into his eyes, and shocked him into an embarrassment that turned his heart into a blob of air, by saying sarcastically : " *Well !* You aren't a softy, are you ? You don't overdo things, do you ? No. *Oh* no ! "

So unexpected this, and so out of key with the character he had given her, for he had conceived of her as shyer and sweeter than Raking's forward creature, that he blushed to his hair-roots, half withdrew his arm, and felt as eager for escape as ever in his life.

" There ! Don't take 'ard what I said," the girl consoled. " I think I like 'em better when they're not too saucy and coming-on, like. I like you, I do—*relly*. I like you a sight better than *'im*, what's with Olive." And she nestled back into his arm. " What's your nyme ? "

" O'Grogan."

" O'Grogan ! *Niaow !* Down' be as stand-orfish as orl that. Wot's your Christian nyme ? "

" Antony."

" Crimes ! I'm moving in the Upper Ten, I think. Wot outlandish nymes you swells do 'ave ! Though there's an Antony in our buildings, come to think of it ; but *'e's* a Roman Catholic, and besides, 'e's always called Tony. Mine's Emmy."

" Is it ? " Tony smiled an acknowledgment of this courtesy. " And what do you do when you're at home."

" Ow-jer mean ? "

" What's your—er—employment ? Have you a place of business, or do you work at home ? "

" You're not being funny, are yer ? "

" No." Tony's heart dropped again, lest he had used some phrase which, in the currency of Clerkenwell, might support a secondary meaning. " What's your job ? "

" Quite respectable. Olive and me works at a milliner's. I bin there two years nah, ever since I lef' school, where I was in the top standard, my dear—I'd 'ave yer know. Two years, exceptin' a month or two in service, which was no cop—no cop at all. I'm sixteen, yer see, and Olive's ight-een. We're 'avin' our week's 'oliday nah. We've saved up for it all the year. We come three days ago, so it's already nearly over, as you might say ; but lor ! it isn't 'alf being a treat. I never bin to the sea before. I bythed yesterday and this mornin'. *Ugh-h-h-h !* Cowld, but ever so jolly. I shall bythe to-morrer and the dye after, you bet—we've only jest those two dyes lef' ; we shell efta gow 'ome after that, worse luck. . . . And that there farm to-dye, where we sor you—it was 'eavenly ! 'Avin' our tea in the gardin, with the smell of the cows comin' over the 'edge—I liked it, I did."

A wave of compassion rose in Tony ; her words were a revelation—a peep-hole giving him his first view of a whole order of existence, over which pity might well be spent; he remembered her " remark " written in the Visitors' Book at Compton Farm, " A very nice Tea ; " and his arm drew her closer in sympathy.

" That's right," she said. " Nah we're gettin' relly friendly."

The compassion stayed—indeed, this night sowed the seed of it for ever—but it had not ousted the repulsion, or the fear; and he looked anxiously towards Raking, in the hope that he would soon be coming back. With intense relief he saw that those two had left their seat and were sauntering towards them, arm in arm. But the relief faded into anxiety again, when Raking said :

" I suppose we'd better not stop any longer now, O'Grogan. However, Olive and I have decided that this is too nice a friend-ship to let drop. We're going to meet again to-morrow night. At seven o'clock, by the gate of Tennyson's Lane ; you and Emmy, and Olive and I."

In their bedroom under the thatched eaves they talked till midnight, for Raking, inflated with memories of Olive's form in his arms, had introduced the old, dubious, disturbing, but exalting questions. Why—why—why should it be so? Wasn't it all funny ? If Olive and Emmy had been strange and common boys, he and Tony would have thanked them for their kindness and escaped as quickly as possible from their offending talk and their vile Cockney accent. But as it was. . . .

And then Tony surprised Raking, by assuring him across the darkness between the two beds, that he had felt exactly this repulsion from Olive's and Emmy's vacuous minds and their awful accent, and devil a hint of any other emotion.

" Good Lord ! " came Raking's surprised voice.

" Sorry ! But it's the truth."

" What, you felt nothing at all ? "

" No ; except that I felt frightfully sorry for Emmy when she said she'd never seen the sea before, and went so potty over having her tea at Compton Farm."

" Well, I don't understand. . . ."

" I think," Tony explained, not without pride in the coming words, " that I shall have to establish a mental affinity with a girl, before I can begin to love her, and want to hold her, and all that."

" Oh, *love* . . . yes," agreed Raking. " But I don't think I'm speaking of love. There's no love about this. I couldn't spend ten minutes with Olive, if we had to walk apart, but I could walk ten hours with her if I might just have my arm round her waist, and a kiss now and then. That's what's so funny. Do you mean to say you don't feel like that?"

"No."

"Good Lord!"

"Honestly," continued Tony, "I don't believe I shall ever want to touch a girl till I've learned to love her. Then——" his mind came alight, and his body a-tingle at the beautiful vision—"I'm sure I shall want to hold her closer than ever I can get her."

Raking was impressed.

"That'll be the real thing, of course. *I* shall want that, too. . . . Jove, yes! . . . But before it comes, don't you feel you want to kiss every beautiful face you see, and would like to have its eyes looking up into yours, waiting for you to kiss it again?"

It was certainly, at first mention, a pleasing picture; and Tony, lying there in the darkness, promptly re-painted it; himself standing in the New Road, and every girl he knew, one after the other, taking up the designed position. And after fair consideration, he replied:

"No, I could get no pleasure out of her kisses or her eyes, if I knew all the time that it was only a temporary sham."

"Good Lord!" muttered Raking.

And the darkness was empty of any voice, till he muttered again:

"Good Lord! *I* could."

He gave further thought to the mystery, and then asked:

"Doesn't the prospect of meeting Olive and Emmy to-morrow night hold any attractions for you, then?"

"No. I can't say that it does. . . . Except, as I've told you, that I feel frightfully sorry for Emmy. . . . I say, do you know Hobman Major—Hobman, C. E.—in the Lower Seventh, a rather clever ass, who's a Socialist and says so outright, in his speeches in the Union. . . . I think *I* shall be a kind of a Socialist. . . . It seems such a shame that a girl like Emmy should be sixteen years old before she's ever seen the sea. . . . Or had tea at a farm. . . ."

"Oh, you can't be a Socialist," Raking protested. "No gentleman's a Socialist—only the greasy rotters like Hobman. But never mind Hobman—he's putrid, and always was. . . . I say, you'll come to-morrow night, I suppose? I can't entertain them both. You see . . . what I hoped was, that you would go off and be happy with Emmy, and Olive and I could breeze off in another direction."

"Oh, I'll play your game for you all right," Tony promised—and suddenly added, "so long, of course, as it *is* playing the game."

"What do you mean?" Raking's voice had most noticeably side-stepped towards indignation.

"Oh, don't be huffy. I mean, so long as we *both*—well, *you* know."

"We'll be playing the game, so long as we don't force unwanted attentions on a girl. I'm not going to do that."

"Shall we? I dunno. After all, they're such ignorant little fools. . . ."

"We're only going to give them some fun."

"Yes, but—oh, I don't know. . . ."

And not knowing, he lapsed into silence.

"The fact is," came Raking's voice at last, and it was sulky: "It's easy for you to take the high line. You only seem to be half alive."

"All right, old man, all right," soothed Tony. "Don't let's quarrel. I'll go with you. It's all experience."

It was their first near approach to a quarrel, and Tony, for a moment, saw the gulf between them. But he turned from its contemplation. There was an aridity, a disappointment, in such thinking that wasted the heart.

Soon he was asleep.

The two girls were waiting for them, just before dark, at the gate leading into Tennyson's Lane. Tennyson's Lane had been chosen by Raking because it was locally known as "Lover's Walk." It was a rutty road, dark and dappled under its overarching trees, and spanned, after a few hundred paces, by a rustic bridge, over which the poet was wont to cross from one part of his garden to another. Olive was sitting on the gate, and Emmy leaning against it; and they grinned at their approaching swains.

"Get off!" Raking commanded Olive; and he lifted her bodily off the gate and kissed her mouth; provoking her to exclaim, "*Well!* Look at that now! He isn't a proper saucebox, is he?" and to add, as she touched her dress into order again, "No, don't you believe it, girls." Tony stood near Emmy, and wondered in disquietude if he ought to do something equally friendly by her. He felt like an actor in a home-made charade, who, wanting to acquit himself creditably, becomes increasingly conscious of his awkwardness and artificiality. All he could bring himself to do was to offer his hand in greeting to Emmy, at which reverence he observed that Olive suppressed a giggle.

"Well, I guess we'll walk up the lane, and on to the downs," said Raking.

"Righto!" assented Tony, eager to appear at ease.

"Yes, and—and—when we get to the foot of the downs, Olive and I'll go one way——" he drew her against him—"and you and Emmy the other. Two's company, but four's a crowd."

"Righto!" repeated the actor in the charade.

Then Olive, who had been watching Tony, said boldly:

"I believe he's afraid of us."

"Don't be silly," protested Tony, dropping at once into her idiom.

"Yes, he is. He's not struck on us at all, Emmy. I shouldn't wonder but what he's feeling all goosey about us. You needn't, you know. We're not *bad* girls; we only want a little fun sometimes, and we shan't split to anyone about you, see? You mustn't think we're a couple of tarts."

Raking roared with laughter at the word, but Tony recoiled inwardly; and Emmy said, "Give over, Olive—do."

"Well, does he *look* happy? I arst you!"

"Don't be silly," replied the tongue-tied actor; and with a strong, histrionic effort, he playfully smacked her cheek.

"Oh, he's coming on!" laughed Olive. "He'll be kissing me next."

Raking laughed too, and Tony felt more and more uncomfortable.

"Well, this is a bit public for these endearments, isn't it?" said Raking. "Children, come along. Up the lane and on to the downs."

With his arm round Olive he led the way for Tony and Emmy. The gate of Tennyson's Lane swung to behind them; and the adventure was begun. Tony, anxious to build a character for ease and assurance, not only grasped Emmy's waist, but drew her head against his shoulder; and, thus holding her, followed his friend some twenty paces behind. Still building, he laid question upon question, as they occurred to him; but he heard, in every sentence, his own insincerity and discomfort, and, hating that poor Emmy should hear it too, began to rake around, almost frantically, for solider material. He was silently busied on this research when she suddenly laid waste the whole uneasy building with the remark:

"What's the matter with yer to-night?"

"Nothing, silly. What do you mean?"

"Why, you're thinkin' of summin else all the time."

"I'm not."

"Yes, you are. You're *slow*."

"Slow to what?"

"Oh, I dunno. But you're not relly enjoying yourself."

"I am! What do you expect me to say or do?"

"*Expect!* It wouldn't surprise me to see you 'op it, any old moment; no more it wouldn't!" She moved sulkily. "Not if I give you 'alf a chance."

"Don't be stupid!"

After this interchange all sentences seemed more disastrously unreal than before. In compassion for her he raked in his mind for some arrangements of words that might sound convincing; but now a dull block of a thought was buffering his rake at every turn: "There's nothing in it. It's all too silly. . . . But oh, if Emmy were the girl one really loved, how absolutely gorgeous this walk would be!" And this sudden sweet vision of the real beloved walking with him in the lane drew him after it into a silence.

Half way along the green corridor of Tennyson's Lane, its trees opened to the sky, and there was a road which, turning to the left, ran through fields of wheat and mangolds to the footways of the downs. The two couples turned along it. Twilight had lowered down upon the earth, so that the downs, seen through it, were a long featureless undulation, silhouetted against the sky; and at sight of them, Tony, alarmed by his protracted silence, broke it with the first words that came into his head, which were some lines of Tennyson, whose bridge they had just seen. He began to recite:

> "Where far from noise and smoke of town
> I watch the twilight falling brown,
> All round a careless-ordered garden,
> Close to the ridge of a noble down."

"That's nice," said Emmy. "Po-try."

" Tennyson," Tony endorsed. " He wrote it about this
very place ; " and, lest the conversation slid away, he continued
anxiously :

> " For groves of pine on either hand,
> To break the blast of winter stand,
>   And further on the hoary channel
> Tumbles a billow on chalk and sand. . . .

Tumbles a billow on chalk and sand," he repeated to himself,
forgetting Emmy as he savoured the line. . . . " Tumbles a
billow on chalk and sand. . . ."

" 'E's dead, isn't he—Tennyson ? We use'ter do 'im in the
top standard."

" Yes. My father went to his funeral. They sang his own
' Crossing the Bar '—You know :

> ' Sunset and evening star '—

I wonder if he wrote that line on a night like this :

> ' And one clear call for me,
> And may there be no moaning of the bar
>   When I put out to sea,

> ' But such a tide as, moving, seems asleep,
>   Too full for sound or foam,
> When that which drew from out the boundless deep
>   Turns again home. . . .' "

" Oh, I *like* that," Emmy declared.

" Yes, it's pretty fine, isn't it : ' When that which drew
from out the boundless deep, Turns again home . . .' ? I
wish I'd written that line. . . ."

They were now on the turf at the bottom of the downs,
and Raking had turned along the track that led towards Alum
Bay. Tony, pleased that those in front should hear his voice
in a continuous flow and so believe him completely at ease,
hastily sent on the night air :

" There's another poem which they say he wrote at Alum
Bay, just at the end of this track :

> ' Break, break, break,
>   On thy cold grey stones, O sea !
> And I would that my tongue could utter
>   The thoughts that rise in me. . . .

> ' And the stately ships go on
>   To their haven under the hill. . . .' "

" That's *fine*," said Emmy.

" Yes :

> ' Break, break, break,
> At the foot of thy crags, O sea !
> But the tender grace of a day that is dead
> Will never come back to me.'"

But now Raking swung round.

" I say, O'Grogan ; this isn't a game of ' Follow my leader.' We love you and Emmy dearly, but this is our road, please."

" Oh . . . I see . . ." said Tony, momently nonplussed ; but he quickly called back with a well-made laugh, " All right, Emmy and I'll shin a little way up the downs."

They climbed twenty steps, and sat down. As in duty bound, Tony drew Emmy against him, and immediately the paralysis of speech sickened him again. And when the silence had amassed into an alarming size, he attempted a diversion by uttering his current thought.

" I wonder how they keep these endless miles of turf so close-cut."

Emmy sniggered in his arm.

" Reckon they come with a pair of nail-scissors twice a week," she suggested.

This was a lump of lead tossed into his heart, and sinking it horridly. The silence amassed itself again, while Emmy just lay against him, and he suffered. Over the skyline came the moon, laying its light down the slope of the hill and flooding the track at its foot, where the figures of Olive and Raking could be seen walking up and down in a lovers' hold. At last they too sat down together.

Emmy spoke next. And the sensitive Tony perceived that she had guessed he was foundering in this unfamiliar sea of flirtation and had thrown him a life-line.

" Tell me some more po-try," she said. " I like it."

He seized the line willingly. He spoke, and spoke well, of his enthusiasms. He quoted for her the greater part of Long-fellow's, " The day is done and the darkness Falls from the wings of night ; " and asked her if it wasn't " absolutely really rather superb." He spouted Milton's sonnet " On His Blindness ; " and swore that it was " absolutely conking." And, seeing that she was much impressed by his learning, he passed on to the " Iphigenia in Tauris," and enjoyed the ostentation of telling Emmy that he read it in the original Greek. " Lor !"

she ejaculated. "Yes," he said; and gave her some of the
Greek lines, both as a proof of his honesty and that she might
hear how absolutely wonderful they sounded; and she agreed
that they were very select—such was her word, and he marvelled
at it. He explained to her the Greek Genius, mainly in Mr.
Jamieson's words, but concluding with his own verdict in his
own tongue: "Oh, yes, Euripides is—is it—absolutely.
There's really no other word."

They could go no further, in this route: Emmy's intellect
had ceased to function. So she suddenly headed him into a
new field.

"Tell me all about your 'ome. 'Ave you a family of brothers
and sisters?"

"Good Lord, yes!" (Tony had lost the old "Gosh!" and
caught "Good Lord!" from Raking.) "There are five of
us."

"Tell me about 'em, one by one."

"My eldest brother's called Keatings. . . . Yes, he's called
after that, I suppose. . . . He's nearly twenty-one now, and
a dry sort of cove. Just gone to Germany for a holiday.

"Oh, how *lovely!* Crikey! Don't I wish I had money like
you."

"Yes . . . and then there's my eldest sister, Joyce."

"Ah, tell me all about her. How old is she, and is she
pretty?"

"She—she must be nineteen. I suppose she's pretty;
people say so. She's gone to the Lakes, to a place called
Grandelmere, with my pater, and she seems to be having what
she calls a ' scorgeous ' time."

Emmy did not interrupt: only listened, as a child listens to
a fairy tale, finding the simplest words enough for her imagination to paint with. And Tony, rattling on, wondered why he
should draw a pleasure from " showing off " before this girl;
why, since the painting of Joyce's good fortune must hurt a
little, he should be so willing to mix a brutality with his very
real sympathy.

"I suppose she's got a lotta lovely clothes?" asked Emmy.

"Oh, I don't know. Not so many," Tony answered, somewhat ashamed of his brag. "We're not so frightfully well
off."

"Oh, *no!* It don't sound like it, *do* it? Germany for your
brother, and the Lykes for your sister, and you dahn 'ere for

six old weeks.   No : you're starvin', of course. . . . And 'as she a boy ? "

" A what ? "

" A friend. A lover, if you like. I suppose she has. Shore to."

" Yes . . . well . . . we rather think there's a fellow who's a bit gone on her.   But it's only beginning."

" Ah, well, I 'ope she pulls it orf. . . . And 'oo comes after Joyce ?   Another gurl ? "

" No ; my brother Derek.   He's all right, I suppose, but we generally think he's rather a sidey swine.   Like all people with the brains of a wood-louse, he's dreadfully solemn and self-opinionated.   He's here with us, but my friend and I don't see much of him—he thinks we're altogether too juvenile."

" Lord-a-mighty !   He must be a nob.   I know the sort. We got 'em our way.   Does 'e go to College too ? "

" He'll be going to Oxford in a term or two. . . . And then there's my other sister, Peggy."

" Ah !   What's she like ? "

" She's seventeen now, and a curious kid.   Funny that I should always call her a kid, because I'm eighteen months younger.   But I feel older, somehow.   I think I like her best of all—she's not bossy like the others.   She's a bit too religious, perhaps, always wanting to go to church and to take you too ; and she can properly lose her wool sometimes, if anyone's rude to her.   But she's amazingly kind and generous and—and all that——"

" Is she pretty ? "

" 'S'pose so.   At least, *I* think so.   She's not generally considered to be as pretty as Joyce, but *I* think she's a dam-sight prettier.   *I* don't see what they rave about in Joyce. . . . At any rate, Peggy's *nicer*.   I like her best of all."

" I like Peggy best, too," said Emmy, after a pause.   " *I sye*, I must evva peep at her—to-morrow—oh, you needn't be afryde.   I shan't let on that I know you, or get you into any trouble.   I'll keep meself outa sight.   And the next dye I shell be gorne. . . . But I'd like to 'ev seen her.   You dow' mind, do yer ? "

" No, no," Tony laughed.   " Though I don't suppose she amounts to very much, really."

Emmy picked a wisp of grass and chewed it.

" And do you live in a big 'ouse in town ? "

" Not so big."

" How many rooms ? "

He told her ; and once again he found himself pleased to be stirring her envy by his talk of four different sitting-rooms, and to be aware that, in endeavouring to give her a true portrait of St. Austin's Vicarage, he had ended by presenting her with an enlargement of it. Their talk was interrupted by a quick exclamation of Emmy's, her grasp on his arm, and her fingers pointing to the turf road, twenty feet below them.

" *I sye !* 'Oo's that old codger walkin' down there ? Oh, my ! He's got long 'air, ain't he ? Crimes—— ! " she giggled loudly—" if that isn't a fair knock out ! Olive oughta see *'im*. What is he ? "

It was Captain Alum, strolling an easy serpentine course along the level grass, and humming gently to himself. His peaked cap was under one arm, and his black waved hair lifted in the wind from his brow and his shoulders. To-night his bundle dangled at his leather belt, and his boots flapped on his feet, leaving the stout stick, which so often had carried this baggage, free to pass behind his waist and under his jacket, while his elbows crooked around it. This forced the blue jacket behind him and allowed his thick, wide chest, clad no longer in the red jersey but in a grey shirt open to its last button, to come forward and meet the good breezes of Heaven. Tony did not catch what air he was humming, for the old man, on hearing the quickly suppressed giggle of Emmy, stayed his walk and his tune, and gazed up at them.

" The Lord be with you, my pretties," he said ; and straight-about pushed the stick into the turf and climbed the twenty feet towards them. Tony looked up at the black-bearded face, when it halted ; and Emmy looked down at the grass, in the agony of her giggle.

" It's very, very good to be young," said Captain Alum, shaking his head, as a man does who feels the full poetry of his words. " It is good to be as young as you are, and to love one another. . . . Be happy ; Be happy. . . . I shall praise God for the sight of you this night."

Tony being empty of a reply, and Emmy being yet in the gripe of her giggle, Captain Alum could only stare down at them across a silence ; till he offered for their information :

" I am an old man waiting on the mercy of God."

" How do you mean ? " asked Tony, finding his tongue.

" Well, sonny, it's like this : I've lived my life, and loved

like you, and lost sight of those that I loved; I've had my
troubles and my despairs, as *you* will, poor children, and sometimes I've even thought of putting a knife to myself.   I've
had my joys—and sinful, too, many of them were ; I've married
and had sons and daughters and seen them go from me, and
their very faces are not clear to me to-day ; I had a brother
and two sisters, and we played together, and *their* faces are
going from me too.   Everything departs and the Lord alone
abides, and His face grows clearer every day, and it is very,
very kind.   Yes, seventy years have I left behind me, and I
can hardly remember what filled them, so faded they are, my
dears ; and now I've nothing to do but wait for the end, and the
last mercy of God. . . . It is very beautiful, my children, to
wait."

" You don't look so very old," laughed Tony.   " You look
strong enough to tackle any two ordinary young men."

" Seventy-five," Captain Alum promptly informed him.
" Sixty-three years of sin, and twelve in grace.   I turned to the
Lord at sixty-three, and He forgave me all.   Since that great
and blessed hour, I have lived only for Him, and perfect happiness has been mine.   I pray you also may one day see His light
—and your little maid too.   But you're very young yet, and it
is generally to be found on the farther side of suffering and
punishment.   May your share be light ! . . . Dear, dear—— ! "
he beamed humorously upon them—" how the Lord must
love you both ! . . . Ah yes ! Yes ! God keep your share of
suffering light ! "

Emmy had now recovered command of herself, and was eager
to bury her offending giggle under her present goodwill.

" Do yer live here ? " she asked.

" I live wherever God is, my maid ; and that is wheresoever
I sit down to rest.   On a moonlight night like this, I find I
lie closer to Him on His hills ; but when I feel the rain coming
I go to where there are workhouses or lodging-houses, and
there I strive to meet Him in the souls of His less fortunate
children."

" Yes, but—— " Emmy persisted, now truly interested,
" How-jer *live*—I mean, how-jer buy your food ? "

Captain Alum smiled patiently.

" When I turned to the Lord and gave meself to Him, I took
Him at His word.   Doesn't He say in His Word, ' Take no
thought for your life, what ye shall eat, or what ye shall drink

nor yet for your body, what ye shall put on. The life is more than meat, and the body than raiment. Behold the fowls of the air, how your Heavenly Father feedeth them.' And again, in another place, ' Seek ye first the Kingdom of God, and all these things shall be added unto you.' Does anyone believe Him ? No. But *I* did, and I went out in perfect trust."

" And 'as He never let yer down ? " asked Emmy, not flippantly, but with earnest incredulity.

" Never. As the Scripture saith, ' Is He a man that He should lie ? ' I have tried to do His work for Him, preaching the gospel in season and out of season, as is commanded ; and the people, moved by Him, have offered willingly."

" Seems a pity they don't offer enough for you to 'ave a proper 'ome," Emmy suggested.

Again he smiled patiently.

" My child, I want none. When in obedience to His word, ' The labourer is worthy of his hire,' I have taken what little I need for my simple wants, I give the rest away, as He also tells me to do : ' Sell all thou hast and give to the poor, and come and follow me.' Why, this very day, missy, the pence came to me like His manna from Heaven ; twenty-three pence and one halfpenny ; and I looked at the sky and saw that I should need only enough for a sup, because I should sleep under the stars to-night ; so when I had bought my bread and cheese, I sat under a hedge and spread the pence that were left over, in a row along the grass, and said, ' There, Lord, that abundance is Thine. Thou wilt show me where I may give it.' And I got up and walked along, and soon I passed an old beggar, who had neither my happiness nor my strength, and I gave him enough for a bite and a bed ; and then I passed another, and gave to him too ; and then just as it was getting dark, I came across a man selling birds in cages, who told me he had done no trade for two whole days, so I bought one of his birds, and when I was out of his sight, I opened the cage door and bade the bird go to its freedom, and praise God. And it flew out, missy, wheeling and soaring into the sky ; so that now———" he smiled happily—" whenever I hear a bird singing, I shall be able to wonder if it is mine, and to remember that I have sent a perpetual prayer and praise into the heavens above me."

" Lor, fancy doing that now ! " said Emmy. " I should never'a thoughta that."

" I think it was rather a spiffing idea," Tony said, who was putting his hand into his pocket to find a sixpence, both because he wanted to show off before Emmy, and because he really liked the old man.

But Captain Alum refused the proffered coin.

"No, sonny. You keep your pence for your holiday, or for your maid. I have all I want for the day, and the morrow can care for itself. Buy something for the lass, and whatever you may do, be good to her. Be good to all maids." He was preparing to go, putting the peaked cap on his locks and the ferrule of his stick into the turf.

Tony stopped him for a minute. "I say," he ventured. "Would you let her hear you sing, as you go along? She's never heard you, but *I* have, and I thought it rather topping."

"No, no, no," laughed the old man, most unexpectedly turning bashful, like a child who has been asked to perform. "No, you don't want to hear me sing. Besides, it's a cracked old voice now, with no beauty for anyone except the Lord; though I used to be able to sing once, and in the days before I was converted, would sell God's gift for applause and money. . . . Well, God be with you, dears. And remember an old man's words: 'Keep innocency—keep innocency, for that alone shall bring a man peace at the last.'"

He lifted his peaked cap high, and trudged off.

"Well!" exclaimed Emmy, when she had brought round her face from staring after him. "Well, did you ever? Is he barmy?"

"Don't know," Tony replied. "We don't know whether he's a madman or a saint or a scoundrel. My pater says he's a bit of all three. But sometimes I can't help thinking that it must be rather wonderful to be just what he is. I mean, if one had the courage to care nothing about anything——"

He said no more; for Captain Alum, who had climbed upwards, had reached the skyline and decided, in that unabashing solitude, to humour Tony's request for a song. His voice bore down to them, diminishing as he passed beyond sight:

> "I heard the voice of Jesus say,
>   'Come unto Me and rest;
> Lay down, thou weary one, lay down
>   Thy head upon My breast:'
> I came to Jesus as I was,
> Weary and worn and sad;
> I found in Him a resting place,
>   And He has made me glad."

" Lor ! " Emmy breathed. " It fair gets you, don't it."

When the boys parted from the girls at the gate of Tennyson's Lane, they walked briskly home to the thatched cottage. Raking was evidently inflated by his adventure.

" By gad ! " said he, unconsciously quickening his step. " Olive is a rattling kid. She's perfectly frank : not pettish or condescending, but just admits honestly she enjoys a moonlight flirtation every bit as much as a boy does. She understands. . . . She—she was all I wanted her to be to me ; she was sweet. . . ."

" How do you mean ? "

" Oh, don't be alarmed. We didn't go the whole way. Though, I believe if we saw more of each other, she'd be perfectly honest and frank about that."

" But, good heavens ! you wouldn't—you wouldn't do it, would you ? "

" I don't know. I don't really see why not. I don't really see what's so hopelessly wrong about it. If nature makes us this way, she must take the consequences ; that's all. That's how I look at it."

Tony thought.

" In other words, we're to do whatever we feel tempted to do."

" N-no." Raking had no answer pat on his tongue. " No. If one took what one wanted by force, that would be a cad's business. But if the girl's happy about it too—why, no one's hurt—and two people are happier than they were. And there's not too much happiness in the world. So isn't there more good than harm in it—unless, of course, you're religious——"

" Which I don't think I am," interrupted Tony.

" No—well—I can't see that there's anything but religion to stop one. I can't see it really, O'Grogan. I *want* to see it. Honest, I do. What *is* it, O'Grogan ? "

But Tony, at fifteen, had no words in which to tell his thoughts, even if his thoughts were clear. Perhaps the words he wanted were : " It's all meaningless and repellent apart from love ; an expense of spirit in a waste of shame ; " or perhaps they were, " Be good to all maids." But he did not find them, and it may be that, had he done so, they would have been less sincere than his bewildered silence now. Raking accepted his silence as proof of defeat.

"You see," he claimed. "There's nothing to stop you apart from religion. So why hesitate?"

Tony snatched at an idea.

"But you might use the same argument in favour of suicide. One might want to do it, and there would be nothing to stop you except religion—and yet—and yet one doesn't do it."

"Oh, it isn't the same," protested Raking. "Your nature doesn't push you towards suicide, as it does towards this. Of course, I don't think you really understand yet, O'Grogan. I don't think you've properly come alive."

The little garden gate of the thatched cottage was now under view, and they spoke no further.

That evening Tony always regarded as the end of his friendship with Raking. The temperature-chart of their union had shown for twenty-four hours a steadily falling curve, and now the curve plunged to sub-normal. It was hardly a moral withdrawal on Tony's part, because morality in a young boy can seldom be strong enough for that; it was more of an æsthetic and intellectual withdrawal. In his blind way he began to feel the grating edge of Raking's insensibility, and to be chafed by it.

The next day, for example, Raking, having no use for Olive apart from the uses of flirtation, did not go down to the Bay to see them off by the Yarmouth coach, but Tony slipped guiltily there. And the first thing Emmy cried out, as she recognized him, was, "I sor' her! I sor' her! And yer brother too. Yes, I like Peggy. . . . Well, it was real nice of you to come and see the lambkins orf. And fancy you 'aving weeks more! Some people have all the luck! I shall think of you bything to-morrer morning, and 'aving your tea sometimes at that there farm. Oh, don't talk about it, girls, it makes me wanta weep." He helped them up the ladder of the coach, and lifted to them their cheap imitation-leather handbags. "So long!" sang Olive; and "Too-to-loo!" sang Emmy; to which Tony gave the correct reply, "Pip-pip!" And he gave wave for wave till the coach had rolled out of sight. Then he wandered home, feeling pleasantly unhappy about Emmy Holt, and the life of drudgery to which she must return, and her first "bythe" in the sea when she was sixteen years old.

With Raking he kept up a fine pretence of unabated friendship; and when the day of Raking's departure came, cycled cheerily by the side of the Yarmouth coach, talked cheerily as they walked up the pier, stayed with his guest on the Lymington boat till the very last second before the gangway was hauled ashore, and then, with a humorous handkerchief or hat, waved the boat into the far distance of the Solent. But when it was a mere toy in the haze, he walked thoughtfully down the long pier. He mounted his cycle and rode alone through the familiar lanes, whistling so as to send a peeping sadness to its lair again. His dam-silly picture of an ideal friendship with Raking had been an illusion—well, what of it? Life was long. And he began to feel a little conceited, as he examined what he had done : in his longing for a perfect intimacy he had given himself to the first dull youth who would encourage him, and chanced to walk the same road home.

Queer how absolutely alone every one was, if you came to work it out! Himself; whom did he really *love*? His father and mother? No; not as he ought to. His brothers and sisters; well, no; Peggy a little perhaps; but his affection for her was not the sort to give him satisfaction. His school-fellows? Lord, no! they were mere fellow-passengers in the same boat. No, one was absolutely alone, unless one loved somebody perfectly and was as perfectly loved.

He was cycling along a lane where the golden afternoon light fell through the trees on to the floor of the road; and he was surprised that the beauty of it sharply hurt him.

CHAPTER III

BY GRANDELMERE

THERE was published in the spring of 1905, when Tony was sixteen and a half years old, a novel that shall be nameless here, because, though lovely in texture, it was too frail to battle in the world's market and was met by only a few. But these few spoke of it among themselves, less as a novel to be weighed and valued, than as a strange and vivid experience to be accepted without questioning and remembered with a welcome pain. And one of those to whom it came as such an experience was Antony O'Grogan.

The book had been introduced into the Vicarage by Joyce and her father, who had heard that its scenes were set in the very lakeland district where they had spent a summer holiday the previous year. Dr. O'Grogan, after reading it, spoke of it slightingly, possibly because Archdeacon Gabriel had spoken of it highly ; Joyce enjoyed it, but chiefly, she admitted, because it was such fun identifying the hills and creeks where the heroine made love ; and Mrs. O'Grogan entered upon it but retired before the close of the fourth chapter, getting up and declaring that her patience with the heroine was exhausted. The book was left lying for some three days on the hat-stand in the hall, in the company of other novels that were awaiting their return to the Circulating Library ; and one night Tony, having finished his home-work and come out of the breakfast-room to stretch his limbs, glanced at it there and opened it. He read its first few pages, standing by the hat-stand, because he intended to return it to its place as soon as his faint curiosity was satisfied. But the book held him so firmly that he stood there for an hour, unaware of time ; and then, when his legs wearied, walked, still reading, to the sofa in the empty drawing-room, where he flung himself down to continue in his pain.

To describe in a few words the meaning of that book were impossible; it would need to be written again in its fulness, for the meaning was less in the story than in the luminous haze which lifted around it, tremulous with insubstantial sadnesses. Through its pages moved a wistful, round-eyed shepherd girl, with black hair, who wanted to take from life more than it could give and to offer it more than it could receive; and who, in the end, abandoned her search and withdrew her offering, and sat on the hillside alone, holding her knee between her hands.

Tony was still reading at ten o'clock; and he took the book up to his bedroom, and hurried into bed with none of his duties performed. He left the gas-light burning over the dressing-table—it could be controlled from the pillow by his own patent system of cords and pulleys; he drew the clothes luxuriously over his ears; and read on. When the last word was finished he put the book on the side-table, pulled the cord that douted the gas, and settled himself further under the clothes. In that warmth he had thoughts for no one but the Gerda of the story —Gerda, with her black hair and her defeated eyes, as she sat on her hillside above the lake, holding her knee between her hands.

That same spring had seen the publication of "The Hill," and the reading of this famous book had given Tony an experience similar to that which he was knowing now. He had carried his enthusiasm, and his inevitable verdict, "It's absolutely too wonderful for words," to his favourite master, Mr. Jamieson, under whose tuition he had come a second time, as he moved higher up the school; but he had met there a disappointment, for Mr. Jamieson had shaken his head, and expressed surprise that a boy who could respond with real understanding to Sophocles and Euripides could also respond so uncritically to a work which, pleasant though it was, pretended to no more than popular values. And Tony's faith in his own discrimination had taken an awkward blow. And now, when the morning woke him from his dreams of Gerda, his sensations of mixed glamour, sadness and happiness were so like those that had followed his immersion in "The Hill" that he wondered if once again Mr. Jamieson would condemn him. Oh, no, no! Surely he was not wrong this time. If this book was not beautiful, he would retire from discrimination. It was beauty for him.

Resolving that his doubt must be laid, he approached Mr. Jamieson's desk after class that morning, and began :

" Please, sir ? "

" Yes, O'Grogan," acknowledged Mr. Jamieson.

" Sir. Have you read——" and he named the book.

" No, but I've heard of it. It's good, isn't it ? "

" I don't know, sir. That's what I want you to tell me."

" Who is it by ? "

" No one knows. It's anonymous."

" But what do you think yourself ? "

" I think it's absolutely the most beautiful book I've ever read—so I suppose it's pretty awful."

Mr. Jamieson smiled.

" I will certainly read it. I had intended to do so."

" When ?—when ? " asked Tony eagerly. " I—I can't get the book out of my head. I could bring it to you this afternoon ; it's hidden in my bedroom."

" Why—what was it appealed to you so ? "

" I don't know, sir. I'm not even clear what it was about. I only know it seemed to say something I'd never heard said before—something that—oh ! I don't know—made me want to say ' Yes ! Yes ! ' all the time. . . . And yet it didn't say it ; it was—it was just behind all that it said."

" I know ! " nodded Mr. Jamieson.

" Oh, I hope you'll like it ! I couldn't bear—I should hate to lose faith in it now. And it wasn't like reading ' The Hill.' In that case I sort of fell in love with the characters, and wanted to imitate them, but here I—it wasn't exactly that I *loved* the heroine, it was that I—that I just *was* her—and one doesn't love oneself. . . . When do you think you'll have read it, sir ? "

" I think I shall have read it before to-morrow morning."

" Oh, good ! And oh, for pity's sake, try and like it."

Next morning Mr. Jamieson summoned Tony to his desk, as the other boys were leaving, and when the room was empty, said :

" Well, I've read it."

" Yes, sir," answered Tony ; and that moment there gripped him, with an actual physical effect in the shaking of his limbs, a nervous patience, a dulled resigned anxiety, such as might have filled the minute before hearing the result of a scholarship examination.

"It's an extraordinary book," continued the master, frowning as if his thoughts were fluttering in a high air, far away from words. "I—I see all that you meant. . . . Of this I am certain, that whoever wrote that book—and I think it was someone very young—wrote much better and much more than he knew. I don't suppose he had any idea of how big a thing he had done. . . . And yet 'big' isn't the word. . . ."

"My father said he thought it was *thin*."

"So it is. So it is," mused Mr. Jamieson. . . . "But then, gossamer is thin . . . and so is the wing of a dragon-fly. . . ."

"Mother said she thought it was silly."

"How 'silly'?"

"She said the heroine wanted a little common sense."

A smile spread on Mr. Jamieson's face.

"Your mother's fairly old, isn't she, O'Grogan? Well, I'm not young either, as you see . . . but I believe—I believe I haven't forgotten what it's like to be young. . . ." He seemed to search among his pens and pencils for further words. "Whenever I read a book of this peculiar quality I always think that the person who wrote it—in this case he, or she, was probably very young—was less of a conscious creator than a passive, suffering instrument. Like a—like a harp . . . on which the winds of the world have suddenly breathed—almost without its knowledge—and its strings give out a true chord . . . to which we all listen in a dumb, answering pain. . . ."

A dumb, answering pain; Tony, with his sense for words, stroked these over, to himself.

"There, O'Grogan. Are you satisfied? That's what I felt when I read your book."

The boy smiled his gratitude; and one of the absurdest things of this interview, so he reflected, was his keen joy when Mr. Jamieson used the words, "*your* book."

In many ways the O'Grogan family was at its bravest blossoming now. Keatings had finished his career at Oxford, and though he had only by desperate efforts and the pushing of a crammer won his pass degree, he had intelligence and humour in his eyes and was considered by all—even by his sisters now—to be a very presentable youth; Joyce had come of age in April and was beautiful, with her lively eyes, her lips ever parted for laughter, and her delightful curves at hip and thigh —which, to be sure, she often praised, calling them her " Ogee curves," as a tribute to the O'Grogan family. Derek was still an undergraduate, but doing large things in the athletic world; Peggy was eighteen, less pretty than Joyce, but with some ogee curves of her own, and a grave-eyed sweetness too— the fruit of a division in her nature between her leanings towards the celibate life of a nun and her tendency to fall in love with any young man who would give her encouragement; and Tony had recently taken his senior scholarship at St. Paul's.

And Dr. O'Grogan himself was in the highest fettle; he had this year been given his prebendal stall, and had immediately printed on his visiting cards " Canon O'Grogan," though, strictly, he had a right only to the title " Prebendary ; " he had received a record Easter offering and had consequently bowed to Joyce's loud demand that this summer he took " the whole O'Grogan outfit " to Grandelmere ; and he had hinted more than once that the imminent collapse of the Conservative Government (which came to pass in the following year) would brighten his chances of preferment. On Keatings' seeking illumination, Canon O'Grogan expounded to the dinner table that a Conservative Government only advanced those clergy whose sympathies were well known to be Conservative, and a Liberal Government those who, like himself, had unwaveringly professed a Liberal creed. Peggy was much shocked at this, and her father acknowledged : " Yes, my dear, it oughtn't to be so ; but there it is ! Your uncle, the Archdeacon, for example, owed more than one of his important livings to his well-known Conservative sympathies."

" And will his eye be dished now ? " demanded Keatings at once.

" Eye dished ? " repeated Canon O'Grogan, seeking illumination in his turn.

" I mean, when the Liberals come in, will his chance of a bishopric be stellenboshed for another ten years or so ? "

" I'm afraid so."

" Well, the Lord be praised ! That's the best news I've

heard for many a day.   And he may die before the ten years
are over."

"Hush, Keatings," begged his mother.   "There's many a
true word spoken in jest."

"Is there?   Good!   And, Father: are your chances of
getting a bishopric better now than Uncle's?"

The canon shrugged his shoulders, as much as to say: "It's
not for me to express an opinion."

"Well, do get one before Uncle," Keatings pleaded.   "That
would fairly steam-roll the Gabriels flat."

In this condition of present success and happy hopes the
O'Grogan family took train for Grandelmere.   Seven of them,
they filled a compartment.   Or, rather, since the only two
corner seats that looked over the passing landscape had been
given to their parents, five of them, for most of the day, occupied
the corridor.   A tall young man, Keatings leaned his hinder
parts against the walls of the compartment that his eyes might
fall below the tops of the corridor windows; and when, every
few minutes, he was obliged to lift these parts from their
support and allow those people coming and going to pass behind
him, he did it politely and with smiles, only making his unseemly
jests when they were out of hearing.   "Evidently travelling
doesn't agree with them," he would murmur, as they turned
the far corner of the corridor, and a door clicked; and Joyce,
who was next to him, would say: "Keatings, you've got a
sink of a mind!"   Beyond Joyce was Derek, and beyond
Derek, Peggy and Tony; because this family would arrange
itself naturally in its order of age, or, as Keatings preferred it,
in its order of merit.

During such times as they spent in the compartment, they
would play two popular parlour games that Keatings had long
ago invented.   The first of them was "Flatulent Conversations;" and consisted in keeping up just such an interchange of vapid remarks as occurred over the teacups on their
mother's "At Home" days; one "lost a life" if there were
a glimmer of wit or intelligence in one's contribution.   "I
like these summer days," began Keatings, "but it's a pity they
draw in so now."   "Yes," admitted Joyce, "each is shorter
now than the one before."   "Well, it can't be helped," said
Derek, "one must expect winter after summer."   "Yes,"
said Peggy, "and the nearer we are to next winter, the nearer
we are to next summer—really."   "Oh, *isn't* she an optimist?"

Tony gushed; "but you're right, my dear; it's so much better to look on the bright side." "It's characteristic of her unspoiled youth," said Keatings (for so often these games sideslipped into a bantering of Peggy). "Winter has no terrors for the young like her," Joyce offered; "it'll be time enough for her to be cynical when she's old like me." "Ah, it's good to be young!" sighed Derek. "I hope," said Peggy, "that I shall keep young in heart, right up to the end." "I wish it for you earnestly, my dear," said Tony, "but I pray God I may not meet you when you're like that." And there was a unanimous shout that he had lost a life, for he had said something quite intelligent.

Keatings began again. "How are all the children? They always look the picture of health?" "I think it must be so nice to have children always about one," said Joyce; "because they keep you so young." "Aye, but they be an expensive looxoory, that they be!" tried Derek. "Yes," Peggy gushed, "but you wouldn't be without them, you know you wouldn't! The dear things!" "Ah, but they grow up and leave one, and go their several ways," sighed Tony. "Ah, yes!" sighed all.

The second game was the game of "No Conceit;" and its intent was to counterbalance any vanity in the Family's members, by a steady pressure on their palpable, and probably sensitive, weaknesses. "Derek's nose is no longer this morning than it was yesterday—unfortunately—most unfortunately! It gives him such a pug-dog appearance." "Pug dog! His face is more like an apple in a bad fruit year." "Yes, and it deprives him of that *distingué* appearance which he secretly craves more than anything else." "Well, one would have thought that Keatings could have got at least a *pass* degree without all that fuss." "Pity Joyce's hair is not *naturally* curly. The horrid truth is revealed every time she bathes, when it's more like sea-weed than hair." "And Peggy's mouth!" suggested Canon O'Grogan, joining in. "Yes," Keatings groaned, "Oh, my God! Peggy's mouth!" All groaned, and nodded despairing heads. "It's so unpleasantly moist," Keatings pointed out, with offended nostrils. "God! it's awful."

And while they played the train was bearing them on to the vividest of all their summer holidays—the August at Grandelmere, when the O'Grogan family flourished in the world's face a brilliant and happy unity, before turning towards its failure and the first cracks of its dissolution. The train passed at one time through a storm of rain, and then on into sunlight ; so that in the brightness of Grandelmere station it stood like a long street of cabins which had brought on its roofs the rain of an unkinder world. On the platform in that fresher air, Dr. O'Grogan stood with his family about him. He could have had no knowledge then of the crack of disintegration that was coming, but Tony often wondered, in the later days when he loved to twist his mind round the uncompassable speculations of philosophy, whether a major event in a man's life, no matter how unforeseen it might be, could somehow be responsible for what happened before it in time. Reading the history, one might have assumed that Dr. O'Grogan, in his sadness before farewell, in his desire to give his children joy while such joy was possible, and in a plea to be remembered with kindness, had gathered them together in a lovely place and invested them with all the happiness he could buy. But perhaps it could not have been so ; and certainly there was no shadow on his laughing face when he assembled his family on the station at Grandelmere.

At the hotel Tony rushed up a hundred stairs to the room which he would share with Derek, and found that it commanded a view of the lake. He leaned from the window, swept the view with his eyes, and expressed his emotion in a wordless outburst, " Derek ! . . ."

The broad water lapped the gardens of the hotel ; on its farther side were wooded hills, the pines, where they were hidden from the homeward sun, enclosing a pitchy darkness, and, where they caught its rays, glinting a rosy splash from every trunk ; behind were loftier, bleaker hills, rolling into light and shadow ; and the sky behind all was a silken back-cloth lit with a primrose light. Tony stared at the treeless hills ; these were the pastures where Gerda had kept her sheep.

The promise of pleasure hung over all that he could see. Floating against the garden's brink was the private bathing-stage of the hotel ; farther along, where the main road ran, were moored the punts and skiffs and canoes ; and farther still lay the pier from which the pleasure steamers started for Fowl-horn. Even now a couple of skiffs, each holding a youth in flannels and a girl in a white dress, were pulling to their moorings, their rowers hungry for dinner. Tony's throat went dry with anticipated delights. He turned from the window to dress for dinner ; and this was the first of the delights.

On warm evenings dinner was served on the eastern end of the long veranda ; and as the O'Grogan family was rather late in approaching a table, since every member had been unwilling this first night to leave the ante-room till the whole clan was assembled, it created a most pleasant stir among the diners ; and well it might—this portly and striking clergyman, his distinguished if tired-looking wife, and his five handsome children. There was a flutter of turning faces, a marked stop in the conversation, and then a murmur of universal comment. Peggy blushed painfully ; Tony felt to see if his tie was straight ; Keatings whispered : " A success, children ; a success ! We've brought it off ; " and Joyce admitted : " Yes, we're certainly getting over."

On their fourth night there was a dance after dinner ; and Tony sat by the wall, because he was ashamed, and rightly, of his dancing. Keatings and Derek, proud rather than ashamed, were doing large things ; Derek, in his oppressive conscientiousness, shaming the more selfish young men by deliberately selecting all the stout, unpartnered ladies to waltz or polka or barn-dance with him. Joyce and Peggy had partners for every number. And Mrs. O'Grogan said at last to Tony : " Why don't you dance ! There's one little girl who'd make a lovely partner for you."

" Where ? " inquired Tony, with no more interest than a slight offence at being offered a " little " girl.

" Look. She's coming this way."

It was a barn-dance ; and a girl of about fifteen came by, her hand in her father's. Dr. O'Grogan watched her smilingly and vowed, as became an Irishman, that she " handled her feet well ; " but Tony gave her no second look. He had seen that her hair was dark, almost black, and tied at the nape of her neck by a green bow ; that her green dress was short-skirted and simple as a schoolgirl's party frock ; that her face was hot with the blushes of timidity ; and that, altogether, she was horribly young. He preferred them fair, he said.

Not till the Lancers were announced was Tony impressed into the dancing. Then a perspiring and noisy Master of the Ceremonies seized him and led him towards the schoolgirl. " Here's your partner ! Just the right size and age," shouted the fool, loud enough for half the room to hear. " Here you are. Joo know her ? It's Sibyl. Sibyl Chandry. Doe-know your name. Consider yourselves introjooced." And he shot away to other doubting and inquiring couples.

Tony bowed and smiled to his partner, who looked shyly into his eyes and coloured. Her diffidence was revealed by her manner of turning her head and looking at her left shoulder and down her arm, as for words. The glance that she had given him stirred in Tony, to his surprise, a quick, almost painful response ; for her face had all those soft lines and curves that could play along his heart-strings so familiar a refrain.

"That was a rather inadequate introduction," he opened. " My name's O'Grogan."

" Yes, I knew that," said the girl.

Tony sought desperately for words.

" ' Sibyl ' suits you," he found at last.

" Why ? "

" Oh, I imagine a sibyl as someone rather dark, and all that. . . I say, how old are you ? "

" I was sixteen two months ago."

" Great Scott ! You don't look it. You don't look much more than fourteen."

" No, I'm afraid I don't," she apologized.

" I suppose I ought to have said that my other name was Antony."

" Yes, I knew that, but I don't think Antony suits you a bit."

" Why ? " asked Tony eagerly. The conversation had become quite interesting.

" Oh, because. . . . Well, I imagine——"

" *Now then, First Figure !* " shouted the Master of the Cere-monies. " Come on, the music ! Now then, all of you. . . . No, that's not right. *You* and *you* advance and retire—and then both hands. . . . No, that's all wrong "—he had charged away to the rescue of another group—" No, turn her with both hands and retire. . . . Yes, that's it. . . . Now, Second Lady and First Gentleman. . . . Oh, wait "—he was off to disentangle the hopeless, shrieking, laughing confusion of a neighbouring set. " *That's* right. *You* and you—and *you* and you. . . . Repeat. . . . Yes, now you two." He pushed them round, and the first figure, it seemed, was complete. The music stopped, and all clapped heartily their own failure.

" You were going to tell me," Tony resumed, " what was wrong with my Christian name."

" It's just not my idea of you, that's all."

" Well, what's your idea of me ? "

" You ought to have something that's really Irish : Patrick or Michael——"

" Blazes ! *Why ?* "

" Well, I—I——"

" *Second Figure*," shouted the M. C. " Come on ! First couples advance. . . . Yes, *and* again. That's right. Perfectly simple. No, no, no, no, *NO !* You've got it all wrong. Lem-*me !* "

" Confound the man ! " muttered Tony. " Dreadfully silly dance, this, isn't it ? "

" No, I like it."

" Oh, sorry ! But you were going to tell me why I ought to——"

" *Now then :* all turn your partners round," shouted the M. C. " Don't stand talking there. No time for a conversazione. Swingeround ! " and Tony flung Sibyl round.

" You haven't told me where you live," he said, when they paused again.

" In India. At least, that's where I'm going to live from now onwards. Isn't it lovely ? "

" I should imagine so. Tell me all about it."

" I can't remember anything about it. I was born there. . . . Daddy's in the Indian Army, you see."

" And you were sent home ? "

" Yes, I was sent home when I was three. But Daddy always promised me he would take me back with him when I was sixteen. So this is our last bit of England before we go. That's why we came to this gorgeous place. Isn't it too perfectly thrilling ? "

" Not bad. . . . Well, go on about India." He had to encourage her talk which else would droop away from him.

" I've been learning riding at school and in the holidays, because I'm to have my own ponies. I can ride almost anything now."

" How long will you stop out there ? "

" Most of my life, I suppose."

" Won't you miss a lot of things ? "

" What things ? "

" Friendships and—and people—and——"

" But there are plenty of English out there."

" Yes, but they are always the same."

Now Sibyl looked away again, seeking down her arm for words. And when she did reply it was to lift her face and say a strange thing :

" I think one is bound to be lonely wherever one is, don't you ? "

The next figure of the Lancers took her from him ; and Tony, whose interest in her had been mightily heightened by the strange sentence, had no opportunity of returning to it till the dance's close. But then he invited crudely : " Here. Come and sit on the veranda a bit. I want to know what on earth you meant by what you said just now about being lonely. It rather interests me."

He led her to two wicker chairs on the veranda, and felt a certain pleasure in helping to arrange her comfortably in one of them. After which he pulled up the knees of his trousers, sat down, and laid one leg across the other that he might massage its black silk ankle and fiddle with the heel of its patent-leather shoe.

" What did you mean ? " he asked.

" Well, you see . . . one never . . ." Sibyl faltered, her eyes straying to the left, " one never gets out of anybody quite what one wants—does one ? "

" Extraordinary that you should say that," mused Tony aloud. " I was reading a book the other day, but I don't suppose you're likely to have read it——"

" You don't mean——" She had come quickly to life, and sat forward eagerly as she mentioned its name.

" Yes, I do, by Jove ! "

" Oh, don't talk of it—don't talk of it ! " said Sibyl. " It's the loveliest book I've read, but it's too—it's too unbearable. I can't get it out of my head. I've been walking with its atmosphere all round me ever since I read it. I read it just before we came here, because it was all about the lake."

" What made it appeal to you so ? "

" A story must appeal to you when you see yourself in it, mustn't it ? "

Her answer had come along her confiding, upward glance, and Tony met for a second her dark eyes that instantly flew away. The familiar blend of delight and pain was now active at his heart—and more insistently than it had ever been, at a first meeting.

"Yes, by Jove, you are like Gerda," he said.

"Oh, tell me you liked the book, too," Sibyl besought. "You did, didn't you?"

"I thought," Tony expounded, picking at the heel of his patent-leather shoe, "I thought that in its small way it was a very lovely piece of work. It's thin, of course, but then . . . so is gossamer . . . and so is the wing of a dragon-fly."

"Yes," Sibyl nodded, as soon as she understood.

"And I think I got the feeling," pursued Tony, "that the author, whoever he was, had done a bigger thing than he knew. What I mean is, he was not really a conscious creator so much as a passive instrument on which something outside him— larger than him—had played. Like a harp, whose strings have caught the wind outside it and have given forth a true chord . . . to which we all listen in a dumb, answering pain. D'you see what I mean?"

"I think so. I think I understand."

"But mind you," Tony added, "mind you, I reckon it was written by someone very young."

The best hour for the growth of a love is just after the lady who has stirred us is lost to sight, and we are recreating her picture in memory. Tony walked away from the door at which he had said good night, and sought the veranda where he might lean on the balustrade and gaze down at the lake or up at the dark mass of the opposite hills. He suspected that he had crossed the threshold of an exciting happiness. He was thinking especially of that moment, when, leading Sibyl to the last waltz after their talk on the veranda, he had suddenly remembered his words to Raking that the touch of no girl would stir him unless he loved her mind; and he had wondered, as he pushed open the ball-room door for her, if his holding of her waist and her hand would now delight him. And he had found it extraordinarily sweet to be enclasping her thus—so much so that its memory could send a thrill through his body. Oh, was he falling in love with Sibyl; was brilliance coming back into his life? Why, just to imagine this so desirable thing was to know that he must go forward and make it a reality.

And with Sibyl it would be different from—from the others. He would be able to possess her adoring mind as he had never possessed theirs ; he would get back from her what he was giving ; surely her eager silences as he talked had shown that ! O Sibyl, you lovely creature ! To have your adoration ! . . . Of course they would never speak of it to each other, because it was not in either of them to flirt ; their talk would be of their schools, their homes, their hobbies, and their ambitions for the future ; they would never clasp each other, except in the dances ; and certainly they would never kiss ; but each would know the other's thoughts, and be happy in the knowledge. Of course, too, it would stop at the end of a few weeks, and stop for ever ; and for him that closure, so completely would his imagination be in control by then (Tony knew much about himself) would be a sick ache. But he was prepared to make that payment as the price of his joy, and would think no more of it ; the beauty of the next few weeks would eclipse it from view. If Sibyl also suffered a little, why, that was lovely to think. O Sibyl, Sibyl, unhappy to be taken from me ! . . . How *wonderful !* His parents and his brothers and sisters and Major and Mrs. Chandry, and the people in the hotel would suspect no more than a holiday friendship ; they would never see it as love, for that would seem too utterly ridiculous. From beginning to end it would be the unspoken secret of himself and Sibyl.

Tony did not know that, before the end, a visitor was coming to the Grandelmere Hotel, who could penetrate to his secrets.

CHAPTER IV

MRS. EDEN WATCHING

THE hotel guests, sitting at the dinner tables on the veranda, saw in Mrs. Eden—as she walked to her place, followed by her husband—a tall, enlarging, well-dressed woman with soft, humorous eyes and hair silvering too soon. They judged her to be forty-eight or fifty.

Mrs. Eden, as she sat down and, lifting the inviolate table-napkin, glanced along the veranda with its chain of dining tables, was thinking thus : The first evening of a holiday is perhaps the best of all your thirty evenings. You see and measure the people whom you will meet for the next few weeks, and they see you in the dress to which—as always for a first appearance among strangers—you have given especial care. You trifle with the menu card, order your wine, eat and drink leisurely, and, when the last course has been served, watch the gradual departure of the other guests, studying their manner and deciding which are interesting, till at last you yourself arise and, pretending to be unconscious of anyone's glances, pass by the sitters in the wicker chairs to find seats at the farther end of the long veranda, while the string quartette tunes up for its evening programme. Before you stretches a month of such lazy hours and leisured careful dressing, with meals and service, like the glacial halls and marble staircases, at several points above your normal. It is a sensation that flatters and cozens you, but one to which every holiday-maker should rightly succumb. It's just a period of life more gaily dyed.

Evidently Mr. Eden, her husband, was thinking the same, for he expressed it with a merry rawness : " This is a bit of all right, Agnes," and clapped and rubbed his hands. She could

almost have predicted the words and the action, her husband
being a fairly prosperous, and therefore inarticulate, stock-
broker, whose honest round body was more happily tailored
than his mind; and such a manner of expressing his exalted
moment would have been the artless poetry of ninety and nine
of his breed.

"Fancy it being August," said he, spreading his table napkin.
"It's nearly as warm as Hell. But I suppose that's all this
glass. *Ah!*" This was the Wine List.

"Yes," answered Mrs. Eden, gazing through a glass screen
at the lake. "There's a lot to be said for an August that lets
you sit on a terrace and eat your dinner by the last light of the
sun—its best light—and by its last warmth, too."

"Yes," Mr. Eden agreed. "What shall we have?"

His wife lightly shrugged her shoulders. "I wish I were a
real connoisseur in wines. There ought to be a wine that
matches this scene—the hills, and the dense pines and the
afterglow on the water. I'm sure there ought."

"Yes," Mr. Eden answered doubtfully. "Well, what's it
to be?"

"Choose yourself, dear. It's something more tranquil
than champagne, I think."

"H'm, but champagne's a good word—an encouraging word
—oh, my Lord, yes! Agnes, an inspiring word. . . ." His
refrain dwindled into the column of champagnes.

Over her soup, Mrs. Eden gazed unobtrusively at as many
of the visitors as were within reach of her eyes. She had
looked forward to this. At the next table was a middle-aged
lady, without a companion and plainly expecting none, for there
was an open novel by her plate. Mrs. Eden leaned back to
get a glimpse of the book's title, in the hope that it might be
one particular book, but alas! it was not. The table beyond
was possessed by a family of seven—a good-looking, white-
haired clergyman, his handsome but sad-faced wife, two young
men, two young girls, and a schoolboy. She judged the
father to be a Canon at least, and placed the schoolboy at
Cheltenham or Harrow—a nice youth with fair hair laboriously
brushed with brilliantine, and a dinner jacket as neat as his
father's. From where she sat she could see his feet curled
round the legs of his chair, and remarked the black silk socks
and the brand-new pumps.

"I've found one nice family, at any rate," she murmured to

her husband. " No, don't look just yet. If you turn round,
they might guess I'd mentioned them. Now you can look.
They're talking to the people beyond them."

The people at the table beyond, to whom the whole family
was now talking, were a family of three—a father and mother
out of the same mould, and a schoolgirl daughter. The schoolgirl seemed no more than fourteen. Her dress was a simple
affair of green silk, and she wore neither necklace nor bracelet.
Her black hair was tied at the nape of the neck, and her eyes
gazed about with simplicity, as if this were her first visit to
a spot of quite such beauty, and she had not long been accus-
tomed to eating dinners and drinking red wine on a veranda.

" I shall certainly get to know them," Mrs. Eden announced.
It was pleasant to watch the chaff and the teasing that was being
tossed between the tables of the two families. " They are the
only two children here."

" Who ? " inquired her husband.

" The nice boy two tables away, and a fourteen-year-old
beauty three tables away. I'm sorry there are no others. You
want children about at an hotel to make you feel it's a holiday
place."

" I don't know." Mr. Eden was doubtful. " I don't
know so much about that. They're generally noisy and rush
about."

With pauses between the courses, and silences between the
conversations, the dinner floated by ; and after the fruit the
tables, one by one, emptied themselves of their sitters, the men
taking their smokes to the other end of the veranda. As Mrs.
Eden expected, the chairs of the two tables that particularly
interested her, were simultaneously pushed back and both
families rose. The boy stood aside to let his parents and his
brothers and sisters pass, and the girl stood aside to let—no,
Mrs. Eden was more than ever interested—the girl, conceal
it how she might, stood back to wait for the boy. She had done
it diffidently, covering her delay by playing with something on
the table. Just that—she had lingered. And by the manner
in which the two walked away together, behind their chattering
relatives, the girl looking at the windows of the billiard rooms
rather than at her companion, and the boy staring ahead and
keeping his hands in his pockets to affect a spurious self-possession, Mrs. Eden knew everything.

" They're in love."

"Who are?" queried her husband, selecting a cigar.

"That boy and girl."

"Don't be romantic." His head swung round to examine them. "Two whipper-snappers aren't in love because they walk away together."

"Oh, but these two are—I am sure of it. Not by their walking away together, but by their manner of walking, and by the exorbitant care the boy has given to his dress. There's not a speck of dust on his trousers, his pumps are like black glass, and his hair is plastered down—which is stupid enough, because I should say it was pretty hair. And *she*—she didn't do her hair in fifteen minutes. And then he finds it difficult to look at her, lest she catches him at it; and she looks anywhere but at him—but quite often at their reflection in the windows."

Mr. Eden's cigar was now alight, and his body turned comfortably round that he might face towards the moving people.

"Anything more you know about them?"

"Yes, both families have been here some time."

"How do you get that?"

"Why, the people in the wicker chairs are not in the least interested in them. When you and I pass those chairs, every head will turn and follow us along the veranda."

"Anything else?"

"Yes; I'm afraid—I'm very much afraid that the exceedingly good-looking parson ill-treats his wife."

"Damn, no! Parsons don't do that. Not allowed to."

"Oh, I don't mean that he knocks her down, but that he treats her with the utmost courtesy and indifference; which is the well-bred form of cruelty and desertion—isn't it? And now I've said something that sounds like a good thing, let's go before we drop to lower levels."

She pushed back her chair, and her husband did likewise. "Yes, we're almost the last at the tables," he said. "Looks bad." He tossed down the napkin with which he had dusted his front, and he and his wife strolled along the veranda, seeking a couple of chairs. Being late-comers, they had to walk far. They passed the piano and the chairs of the musicians. They passed the boy's parents and the girl's parents sitting together. They passed the clergyman's two elder sons, and his two daughters, all apparently rejoicing in a heated and humorous quarrel. They passed other people less recognizable, and still

they found no chairs.   They passed round the corner of the
hotel and on to the deserted side-veranda, hoping that there
might be chairs here which they could carry to the front.   But
suddenly Mrs. Eden whispered :

" If you're a sport, Peter, look straight ahead and mutter your
usual, ' There are no damn chairs,' and then let's turn gracefully
to the right-about.   We're being a nuisance."

A glance at one of the recesses formed by the side bay-
windows had shown her the boy and the girl seated—not very
close to each other—in wicker chairs.   The boy was lolling
back, and the one leg that was thrown over the other was gently
swinging its foot and showing the most of his silk sock.   The
girl was on his left, sitting almost sideways as she talked to him,
her elbows on the chair-arm, her chin in the cup of her hand,
and her legs bent under the seat.

" No," said Mrs. Eden, on second thoughts, " come away
and don't mumble anything about damn chairs, or that boy'll
certainly get up and offer us his."

" Well, why shouldn't he ? "

Just then the quartette opened its programme with a vigorous
march.

" Why ?   Why, a man who would disturb an idyll like that
would—would——" they were now round the corner again
and could see the musicians throwing their first energies into
the march—" I can't think of a sufficiently crushing simile—
would prick a bubble all opalescence and mystery one tenth of
a second before it must necessarily burst."

As they returned, they saw that the chairs beside the boy's
parents were now free, the girl's parents having gone within ;
and Mrs. Eden was quick to inquire : " Are you keeping these
seats ? "

The clergyman smiled politely.   " No, no ; take them, take
them."   He might have been smiling them into a private pew
at his church.

And so an intimacy began.   Mrs. Eden learned that her new
friends were Canon and Mrs. O'Grogan, that they had been at
the hotel three weeks and were staying another two, and that
all wise people should go on the excursion to Stagwater across
the lake, and to Red Dale in the opposite hills.   The conversation continued during intervals between the music and sometimes, it is to be feared, during the music too, after which they
offered perfunctory applause as an apology for this forgetfulness

And soon Mrs. Eden turned the conversation to the subject of Canon O'Grogan's youngest boy.

"Oh, Tony, you mean," said the father. "Yes, Tony's a good old fellow."

The words, though affectionate, seemed inadequate.

"I suppose he's still at school."

"Yes, he's only sixteen or so. He's at St. Paul's. And not doing too badly there."

"And who's the little beauty he goes about with?"

"Little Sibyl Chandry. You haven't met Major and Mrs. Chandry, have you? Indian Army people. Yes, I like Sibyl, and I'm glad she's here to amuse old Tony. In fact, there's no one else of quite his age in the place. They don't bring many children to a place like this, do they? I was afraid old Tony might be bored, but he and Sibyl seem to have amused each other."

Again Mrs. Eden wondered why the words were too prosaic to harmonize with her thoughts; she was reminded of a faint disappointment she took last summer when her husband described as "this old waterfall" one of those cascades above Stagwater on which the sun was casting pale, concentric rainbows. But then: an "old waterfall" was exactly what, in simple fact, it was. Anything more was given to it by the observer's eyes . . .

Canon and Mrs. O'Grogan were moving. It was dark now; and the warm air was interfused with cold, and the lights had gone up in the billiard rooms, and the balls were clicking and the glasses clinking, and the veranda, though the quartette was still playing, had begun to lose its people.

Next morning, when the sun was hot upon the lake, Mrs. Eden contended herself with sitting upon the veranda in one of the wicker chairs. On her lap were the scribbled sheets of a story she was struggling to build—but in discouragement and with fading purpose. For long months past she had been beating up against frustration; and this morning she seemed to know that she would write no more. Not even these lakes and hills which she so much loved would quicken an inspiration that was spent. Why the story of Gerda had visited her, and how she could have written it, who knew so little of the author's craft, and why, when she wrote it, she had trembled with an agitating conviction that it was true and good, must ever be something of a mystery to her. It had just been a pleasing and mastering day-dream that she had put upon paper, easily and without fret. And now her publishers were asking for a successor to Gerda, and she knew she had no more to give. Her return to Grandelmere in search of a second inspiration was a fond, vain step. Best know it, and rest, and turn from the writing of that which was bad to the reading of that which was good. She put the scribbled sheets on the table at her side, and took up her Wordsworth.

But she did not read for long, because the sound of voices down by the water's edge drew her eyes that way. It was Tony O'Grogan and Sibyl Chandry. They were standing in buff mackintoshes and bare legs, on the little bathing platform. From their laughter Mrs. Eden guessed that they were quarrelling who should enter the water first; and, fittingly, Tony threw off his mackintosh, poised on his toes, and took a header into the lake. Sibyl also discarded her mackintosh, but, lacking this strength of will, stood with her arms, for warmth's sake, folded across her breast, the hands grasping the bare shoulders. Her costume was a dark blue skin-tight costume like a man's, and Mrs. Eden had time to notice how her figure and limbs were just beginning to fill with maturity, before Sibyl, with a shriek of mixed amusement and apprehension, leapt into the water after Tony. Both could swim, the boy the better of the two, and anyone could see that, like a young cock-bird, he was displaying his over-arm stroke, his somersaulting, and his kick-churning for the admiration of his companion. Time and again he clambered on to the platform and dived over or under Sibyl, while she shrieked and laughed. Their voices seemed the only sound on the water or between the hills. When they both swarmed out on to the hard planks of the jetty, bringing costumes that were dark and shining with wet like the skins of seals, they lay supine in the sun, their hands behind their heads. On the weathered wood their limbs lay white.

But probably the sky dazzled their eyes, for they rose on their elbows and then sat with crossed calves, tailor-wise. Once Sibyl threw her legs straight before her and, placing her palms on the boards behind her, leaned back that the sun might beat on her breast. That Tony suggested diving in again was made clear by a quick, enthusiastic turn of his head, and that Sibyl repelled the unpleasant idea by a shiver of her shoulders. And then they stood up, put on their buff waterproofs, and leaving the jetty for the hotel, were lost to the watcher's view.

Mrs. Eden had read many pages of her book and passed away an hour before she wearied. It fell then to her lap; and she abandoned herself to idle staring across the water at the dense trees climbing the opposite hill. It was noon: the sun, high above the veranda, was exactly in front of the hotel, its light spread brilliantly over the face of the lake. This reflection on a water filmed with calm was so wide and dazzling that a little pleasure-skiff which had come from the hirer's stance near the pier and was about to cross it, seemed lost in an enchanted sea of stillness and light. The boat moved soundlessly. It was rowed by a man or a youth in tennis flannels and hatless; and in the stern a girl in a white dress held the rudder-lines. Tony O'Grogan and Sibyl Chandry. No voice could be heard at this distance, and, so far as could be seen, Sibyl was not moving at all, while Tony's rhythmic motion was a thing so regular as to be near to stillness. The boat passed on towards the east, diminishing and growing indistinct, till at last it rounded a little cape of trees.

Mrs. Eden remained thinking, wishing the boat would appear again. But it did not, and she relapsed into her book. Her interest revived, and it was not till lunch time that she was disturbed by voices and hurrying steps. Tony and Sibyl had returned from their row. Not knowing her, they would have passed, but she acted on an impulse and asked the boy with a friendly smile:

" Well, did you have a nice row ? "

" Yes . . thank you . . . topping ! We're going out again after lunch. Over to that village, Broadhaven. We shall have tea there and bathe."

" But you've bathed once already."

" Exactly ! "

" Won't you introduce your friend ? "

The boy blushed. " Yes. Sibyl, *here !* This is Sibyl Chandry. I—I don't know your name."

" Mrs. Eden. I only arrived last night. But you've been here quite a while."

It was Sibyl who answered.

" Yes, worse luck ! To-morrow's my last day. We go the day after—to India ! It's horrible ! "

" Horrible, going to India ? "

" Oh, no. Horrible leaving here quite so soon."

" You've enjoyed yourself, then ? "

" Oh, *rather !* I've never had such a perfect time in my life. I don't want to go a bit."

And the boy interrupted : " Oh, don't let's talk about it. You'll have all day to-day and all to-morrow."

Mrs. Eden, while he was speaking, had noticed his dress. His flannel trousers were pressed to a fine crease, his shirt was opened with a premeditated negligence at the throat, and his hair was as faultless as when he was in evening dress.

" I think I must go and get ready for lunch," said Sibyl.

" Righto ! " permitted Tony ; and she went.

" You can't say that *you* need to go, Mr. Tony," laughed Mrs. Eden. " I've never seen anyone so tidy in my life. Sit down, won't you ? "

He took the chair next to her, perhaps a trifle embarrassed. The obvious thing for Mrs. Eden to do, if he were to be made at ease, was to set him talking about Sibyl, so she began :

" That's a beautiful girl." (She had been going to say " little girl," but her wisdom saved her.)

" Who ? Oh, Sibyl. Yes, she's rather jolly. We—we've got an awful lot of interests in common. . . . Do you know, I think this ' Ships that pass in the night ' business is rotten, don't you ? I mean, I like all the people here ; I think they're a topping set. Well, you meet a lot of nice people on a holiday, and get to know them and like them, and in a week or two it's all over, and you never see them again. You may think you will, but you never do, do you ? "

" Oh, yes, sometimes."

The boy smiled and shook his head. " No, I don't think so. People just go out of your life. One never sees them again. One never does—really. . . . Especially when . . ."

" Especially when what ? "

" Oh, I was just thinking of the Chandrys as an example. We've all got to like them hugely. Major Chandry's one of the best, and so is Mrs. Chandry. And they're going to *India.*"

" Perhaps you'll go to India one day, and meet them there."

" No. One may imagine oneself doing these things, but one doesn't do them—really."

Knowing that he would be happiest if he spoke of Sibyl, Mrs. Eden repeated :

" Well, I think she's perfectly lovely."

" Who ? "

" Your friend, Sibyl."

" Is she ? Yes, I suppose she *is* pretty." If a person is spoken of admiringly, one's natural instinct is to exhibit any proprietary rights one may have in her, and the boy continued : " Yes, we always sit out and talk after dinner. She's the sort you can talk to. We've done it every evening, so that it's become quite an institution."

That minute Sibyl appeared out of a distant doorway, ready for lunch. Observing that Tony was sitting with Mrs. Eden, she pretended not to have seen him, and, walking to the rail of the veranda, leaned her hands upon its top and looked down upon the gardens below. That Tony saw her was plain to Mrs. Eden ; but his manners were too good to allow him to jump up at once, and he sat on abstractedly.

" Well, I must be getting ready for lunch," said she. " Good-bye for the present."

He stood up and opened a door for her, and she walked across the lounge to the lift, which raised her to her bedroom floor. In the bedroom was her husband, brushing his hair.

" That's a perfectly delightful little romance, Peter," she reported.

" What romance ? "

" The boy and the girl."

" Oh, that young fool ! There are always buckets-full of these budding romances at holiday hotels. I suppose he's making himself ridiculous."

But his wife shook her head.

" I don't find him ridiculous, somehow."

She was careful to be in her place on the veranda that afternoon, so as to see Tony's skiff pass along the lake, as he took Sibyl to her tea at Broadhaven. And since she was impatient for its coming, the time seemed strangely long before she saw it soundlessly moving over the glassed water, as it had done in the morning. It was at a greater distance from her, and the two white figures, one in the stern and the other rhythmically rowing, were two white specks.

" You have all this afternoon, and all to-morrow," she thought, " and then comes the day after."

For a long while she sat there ; the tea-hour came and passed ; the disk of the sun sank low on her right, and its far-flung rays laid a golden light on the water and touched the ruddy bark of the pines with fire. The opposite hills turned to indigo, as it went down behind them and drew home its light. Part of the time she was reading her Wordsworth, but mostly she was thinking of the calf-loves in her own youth, and of one especially—those six weeks in Thanet when she had loved Norman. Norman ! The name moved her lips to smile. He was Norman to her still, a self-conscious little dandy of sixteen. Thirty-five years ago ! They had walked together of summer nights, eating chocolates round the band-stand. There had been much less beauty there than here to trouble them with the need of love ; a meretricious beauty it had been —illuminations and carpet gardens and a red-coated band playing light, machine-made melodies. No broad and shadowed lake, reflecting the sun in its centre and pine hills under either bank ; none of this waiting stillness of Grandelmere. And yet that day ! That day before he had to go, when she had told herself, " I shall never see him again. I know I shan't. One never does." And she had not—in thirty-five years. Nor had they written, for both had been too shy to use a word like " love " and to exact promises in its name. Perhaps that had been as well, saving them from humiliation when letters flagged and failed. And Time had mended all, sure enough ; and it had only required a few weeks of time. That, she supposed, was what made it funny. And yet . . . Wordsworth was inter-fusing with her memories, and as she looked at the bare hills rolling behind the more trivial garnishings of valley and lake, her thoughts played less with humour than with those strange, eternal things that sometimes break through upon our earthly business.

Too quickly passed to-morrow, and in the evening, Mrs. Eden treated herself to but one glimpse of Tony and Sibyl, where, perfectly dressed, they sat on the wicker chairs, isolated round the corner of the veranda. They were still not close to each other, and she knew that Tony would be too diffident and awkward to offer Sibyl anything but the words of an ephemeral friend.

The Chandrys would be leaving, so Major and Mrs. Chandry told her that night, by to-morrow's three o'clock boat for Fowlhorn. She could have wished they were going earlier, so saving Tony a morning of dull sadness between breakfast and lunch.

And at three o'clock the next afternoon, Mrs. Eden, resolved to watch the end, was sitting in her place on the veranda, from which she could see the pier and the boat. She had heard Tony's light and laughing shout to Mrs. Chandry, " I'll come and see you people off all right ; " she had listened while Canon O'Grogan said : " Old Tony's actually refused to come on the excursion to-morrow, just so that he can see you off. Isn't that devotion ? " and now, from her chair set along the veranda rail, she saw the boy, in his white flannels and grey jacket, standing near the luggage on the pier and watching the crowd of passengers as it funnelled up the gangway. On the first-class deck stood Sibyl, in a wide Leghorn hat and a long fawn coat, pretending to talk and laugh suitably.

The siren sounded, and Mrs. Eden exclaimed at its brutality. Now the luggage was being carried aboard, and Tony was standing with his hands in his pockets, watching the porters. He stood alone, but on the other side of the gangway was a crowd of blithe souls, paying their last tribute to the intimacies of a holiday, with cheers and choruses and aped lamentations. Again the siren boomed. Tony brought one hand from his pocket in readiness to wave.

But the ropes were not yet cast back to the boat, and his hand returned to his pocket. He was no longer looking up at the Chandrys on their deck, but, as if impatient for the ship to be gone, studying a time-table placed on a pier notice-board. Once he pulled out his watch and looked at it. At last the boat began to move away, while the crowd on the pier, amid laughter and cheers, sang " Auld Lang Syne." Tony, standing aloof, waved a hand. Sibyl was waving hers—and so was Mrs. Chandry, for all the world as if her waves had a value equal to her daughter's. About Tony's hand-wave there was nothing fervent ; it was awkward and sufficiently full of effort to show his embarrassment with a courtesy so long drawn out. Doubtless he wished the boat could go quickly round the bend, like a train. Still, it was well under way, and fast diminishing. Tony walked towards the entrance of the little pier, then turned and waved again, in case he could still be seen. But the boat was beyond the throw of any signal, so he turned about, put his hands in his pockets, and climbed the hill to the hotel.

Immediately it broke upon Mrs. Eden that he would come on to the empty veranda to stare over the lake. "He'll want to stare at the bathing platform, and the pleasure skiffs—one particularly—and at Broadhaven yonder;" and quickly she shut her book, rose from her chair, and disappeared into the hotel.

During dinner that evening she watched again. Tony was talking merrily to his parents and his brothers and sisters at their table, though at times he sank into remoteness. Once he joined in the conversation with some new guests who had taken over the table of the Chandrys. And when the meal was finished and the chairs pushed back, he strolled jokingly along with the others, and sat with them when they took wicker chairs and entered into vivacious chatter with their neighbours. But after a while he got up and went forward to the veranda rail, on which he rested his hand, while he curled his foot behind his left heel. Mrs. Eden, by this time, was sitting with her husband in a chair not very far away; she could hear the muted but merry tune which he was whistling to himself. Studying him again—his hair as laboriously brushed, his tie as neat as yesterday, and his pumps like black glass—she found herself thinking: "I wonder if he got any pleasure in dressing to-night."

Now he was leaning forward to pick a stalk from an up-reaching clematis, which he might put in his mouth and leave to droop there, like a cigarette. And suddenly it trembled as if his teeth had set; to which quick grimace Mrs. Eden fitted her own words: "One never sees them again . . . one never does. . . ."

Well, there it was. A little of love, not much, but a sip of the dreadful cup, a prick of the sword that should one day pierce deep, a wounding touch of beauty as it passed, fugitive.

And her words to her husband seemed weak and unworthy: "Poor child! He's lost her now."

Mr. Eden surveyed him. "Awful little coxcomb, isn't he? . . . Oh, yes, I know you're smitten with him, but I like a boy to be a boy, and not a young cuckoo, simpering after a skirt."

"Oh, don't," begged his wife, "please, *please!*"

"*He'll* be all right in a week or two. A few good games of Rugger'll knock all that nonsense out of him."

" Of course they will," Mrs. Eden allowed, lifting her rope of pearls and examining it contemplatively.   " Of course they will—but why laugh at him now ? "

" Because it's the healthiest thing to do.   One should always laugh at folly as it flies."

" That's only a glib chain of words, Peter.   I could make as good a phrase.   ' Why should one laugh at pain as it passes ? ' Or, better still, ' Why should we not keep silence while beauty is passing by ? ' "

This was enough to bring Mr. Eden's head abruptly towards her.   " You have it badly to-night, my dear," he said.

" Yes, perhaps I have.   It's another wonderful night, isn't it, and such a wonderful spot, this."

Lights flared up behind them in billiard-room and lounge, for there was no quartette to-night.   They heard the fall and click of the billiard balls as they were decanted on the tables, and a clink of glasses at the bar, and men's voices.   Mrs. Eden's head moved resentfully, as at the return of something from which she had escaped.

" Well," said her husband,   " I'm going to have a game. Will you come and watch ? "

" Not just yet, my dear."

" Well, see you later."

" Yes.   Very soon."

CHAPTER V

THE DETONATION

IT was a Saturday afternoon in November. Tony was returning home from St. Paul's after playing in the Second XV against Merchant Taylors. He was exhilarated in mind and body. This was the first time he had been given a trial in the School Second, and he had borne himself not without distinction and applause in the conspicuous and dramatic rôle of scrum-half. Granted he had not scored a " try," which had been his secret ambition throughout a nervous morning, a nervous lunch, and a nervous ten minutes in the Changing Room, but he had more than once opened up the game for his three-quarters with a trembling quickness, and been the prime mover in the tries scored by other men. Congratulations had been tossed to him, when in the Baths the two teams were washing their feet or crowding under the showers. And he had overheard with averted face other comments on his success.

Now, excited and fatigued, he walked up the Hammersmith Road, with a stiffness registering along his limbs but only heightening the glow of fitness that tingled in his veins. The aching bruise on his thigh where he had been heavily thrown, the stinging cut in his left knee, the faint, pleasing sprin-paint in his right wrist, the dry thirstiness in his throat, and the resultant tendency to cough—these were not centres of radiating depression but focuses that captured the consciousness of health. Fatigue after work done with straining and extension ; fatigue and relaxation and thirst—few higher ecstasies are possible to men. Now for hot tea from a cruse that failed not, and a loaf of new bread, and a dish of butter. Not cake : cake was too sickly-sweet for such an appetite as his. Tea, tea ; and the whole top of a cottage loaf ; and the yellow butter ;

and a knife to spread it, and jab in the dish, and spread, and come again.

He pushed open the Vicarage door and threw down his kit-bag beside the hat-stand, as was the custom of the house. For a dozen years now the entrance hall of the Vicarage, with its tennis rackets, golf-clubs, string bags of tennis balls, cricket bats, last season's hockey sticks, a blazer or two, and, maybe, Joyce's white canvas shoes, had looked more like the Sports Department at Gamages than the vestibule to the audience chamber of the Parish Priest ; and over all the implements of play beamed the unheeded text : " GOD IS THE MASTER OF THIS HOUSE." Tony gave a glance at his face in the hat-stand mirror, and saw that his hair was moist and untidy, his eyes alight, his colour high, and his cheeks hollowed by the fatigue.

Then Joyce put her face out of the breakfast-room door—a frightened face—and took it back again, to say to the people in the room : " Yes, it's him." A chair was pushed back and Keatings came into the hall.

" I say, Tony," he began, quietly. " You'd better come in here. We're—there's a Family pow-wow in progress."

Like a barometer Tony responded instantly to the lowered pressure of the atmosphere. He did not know whether an uncomfortable alarm or a pleasant thrill was his uppermost sensation. And ashamed of either, he affected its opposite : a complete unconcern.

" Hang, no ! I'm hungry. It's not important, is it ? "

" About as important as anything can be."

" My eye ! What the devil's up ? "

But Keatings had returned into the breakfast-room. Tony, straightening his hair with his palm as if in respect for this sudden solemnity, followed. Besides Keatings and Joyce, Derek and Peggy were in the room. Keatings, with hands in pockets, was walking slowly up and down ; Joyce was seated disconsolately on the edge of the big mahogany table ; Derek was standing importantly on the fender, as might a Chairman of the Board ; and Peggy, with wide, absent eyes, stood by the plush curtain, gazing at the tarnished November garden.

" You look glum enough ! " laughed Tony. " Is there a death in the family ? Or have the Gabriels done something big again ? "

" *Cor*——! " muttered Keatings. " Don't mention the Gabriels. I had forgotten them."

" The Gabriels ! " repeated Joyce. " Why didn't they all
die first ? "

And she lifted her eyes from the ground to stare at the ceiling,
and Tony saw that they were wet ; saw also how beautiful they
were. Her lips were trembling.

" Joyce ! " he asked. " What's the matter ? "

" It's horrid," she answered. " . . . horrid. . . . ."

Keatings spoke ; perhaps deriving a small, compensatory
pleasure from the masculine directness with which he stated
the facts. " Father went abroad this morning with a woman
—a married woman—leaving a letter for mother and a letter
for me, and writing to the Bishop. He's—er—gone for
good . . . you understand."

Tony stared at his brother without speech ; all words stayed,
heavy and immobile, on the dark river-bed of his thoughts.

" It seems there has been some sort of connexion between
them for some time," pursued Keatings, " but the husband has
only just discovered ; he's a vulgarian, and he's made public
his vow to institute divorce proceedings. And Father's not
going to—Father's not going to defend the case ; and what's
more, he's sworn to acknowledge and protect the child that's
on the way."

" Good God ! " muttered Tony.

" Pretty awful, isn't it ? " said Derek, from the fender.

" Who is it ? Who is the woman ? "

" Mrs. Blayre, the wife of the vet. in Thomas Street."

" He didn't even choose a lady to disgrace himself with,"
said Derek.

" Oh, you shut up, Derek," snapped Keatings. " Your
contributions are neither pleasant nor helpful. . . . So Father's
just flown before the storm, and left us all. I don't suppose
we shall ever see him again."

" I sincerely hope we never shall," added Derek.

" Shut up, Derek, I tell you ! You're too infernally righteous.
Other men have done this sort of thing before ; and probably
the only thing that'll keep you from doing it yourself will be
your confounded interest in your own career and your own
reputation. I daresay you'd do it fast enough, if you thought
it a help instead of a hindrance."

" That may be," Derek allowed, with precisely the note that
had accompanied the " Had on ! " of his childhood ; " but I
shan't be preaching purity every Sunday morning, and pro-

nouncing absolution, and knowing all the time that I've got a
baby coming by someone else's wife."

"Oh, don't . . ." pleaded Joyce " . . . it's horrid . . .
horrid."

"And I shan't leave a wife and five children in the lurch.
If I'm fool enough to marry, I shall stand by my obligations."

"Father had to choose which obligations he would accept,
as he says in his letter to me. And he chose to stand by a woman
who would otherwise be completely left, and by a—a child.
He says we're old enough to stand on our own feet and care for
one another, and for mother. Under the circumstances I
don't feel at all sure that he chose wrong."

"Oh, Father *would* cover his choice with fine words and
phrases. He's a dab at that," suggested Derek. "They don't
deceive me. A common elopement with another man's wife
is a common piece of self-indulgence and no more."

"It isn't as simple as that," Keatings denied. "Just think a
bit, if you can. . . . Father must have had a pretty awful time
when he knew that he was found out and that the fat would have
to go into the fire."

And now Peggy spoke for the first time. From her place
by the window she whispered : "Of course."

"And, honestly," Keatings continued, "I believe in much
of his letter. He finds the best words to justify himself, no
doubt, but—I don't believe he's been wholly bad in his choice.
I don't . . . somehow."

And Peggy whispered again : "Of course not."

All this while Tony had been sitting on the arm of a chair
and staring round the room. To him, everything in the
room had put on, like an unwelcome garment, a heavy significance it had never expected to wear : the time-piece presented
by the congregation, the family photographs on the mantel-
shelf in their plush and silver frames, a college group hanging
on the wall, the pious Doré pictures, the arm-chair that had so
often held his father, his ash-tray, and, saddest of all, perhaps,
the vase of flowers that stood in the centre of the table to give
the room good cheer.

"It must have been a hell of a choice for him," he said.

Derek pshawed. "He should never have put himself into a
position where he had to make such a choice."

"Of course he shouldn't !" Keatings admitted. "And *I*
shouldn't have poured glue into my tutor's keyhole at Univ. ;

and Joyce shouldn't—shouldn't spend hours titivating her face in front of the glass, and you shouldn't be the pompous prig you are ! We all do what we shouldn't sometimes—even you. After all, Father's rather a fine old bull, with life pretty active in him, and . . . well, Mum must have been pretty dull for him sometimes. It was fairly obvious they didn't get on, and I expect it's pretty difficult for a strong, healthy man——"

"I should stop there," interrupted Derek, with a laugh. "You're getting too realistic. There are sisters in the room."

"Oh, rot ! It's not a moment for squeamishness. We all know each other's thoughts and they're pretty realistic this evening. I reckon——" Keatings's face went hot at what he was going to say—"I reckon that if Joyce and Peggy are to find reasons for judging Father more gently, it's their brothers who must tell them that men are—are sometimes driven harder than most girls can understand."

Joyce fixed her eyes on the floor, and Peggy turned a little nearer the window, and Keatings, catching their discomfort, grew redder.

"I want them to understand, that's all. All nature shows that——"

"All right. You needn't go on," said Joyce, lifting her wet and beautiful eyes. "I understand what you're trying to say."

"Father's a fine strong creature in his way. I used to notice it and feel rather glad that I was his son. I—I don't think I feel any the less glad now."

It was at this moment that Peggy dropped on to a chair, laid her arm along its back and, burying her face in the crook of her elbow, cried, "Daddy. Oh, poor Daddy. . . ." Responsive tears leapt to Keatings's eyes, and Tony struggled with the lump in his throat.

"It's going to be damned awkward for his son in the future," Derek persisted, but more gently. "I should think we'll all have to change our name."

"My name's good enough for me," said Keatings, hardly mastering a sob.

"After the divorce there'll be a case in the Church courts, and he'll certainly be inhibited if not unfrocked. Then I suppose they'll proceed against him in the civil courts."

"Don't be more of an idiot than you can help," Keatings scoffed, who seemed to get relief by directing his conflicting emotions into a common effort against his brother. " A Church court'll find him guilty, certainly, and the Bishop'll deprive and inhibit him, but what the devil have the civil courts got to do with it ? Don't you realize that it's only because Father's a parson, and because parsons set themselves a highei standard than laymen, that he's done anything technically wrong at all."

" Wife-desertion's an offence, isn't it ? "

" Certainly not. They can compel you to provide foi your wife, and Father's done that. He had about six hundred a year of his own, and he's promised that Mum shall have half of it. He says he'd have give it all to her, only he had nothing else, and there was this kid, and it'll be difficult enough for him to find work."

" What a mess ! What a mess ! " sighed Derek.

Joyce spoke in an even voice. " So three hundred a year is all that we've got between us and penury ? "

" That, and our brains," agreed Keatings.

" Finish, Oxford, for me," said Derek.

" *You're* not so badly off. It's ' finish school ' for Tony."

" And it's ' finish, Joyce's little affair,' " reminded Derek.

All looked towards Joyce, for they knew to what hope he was alluding. They left their own troubles for a moment, and passed through the doorway into hers, and, standing there, were silent. Joyce, too proud to break down like Peggy, stared ahead with her eyes no longer wet and her lips moving to a smile of acceptance.

Keatings spoke first, and it was clear that he felt awkward in this attempt to comfort a sister.

" It'll test the fellow," he suggested. " And if he doesn't stand the test, I reckon Joyce is worthy of someone rather better."

But Joyce made no comment, and Peggy suddenly left her chair, and came and sat by her sister's side, taking her hand. The young men turned their eyes uncomfortably away.

" He shouldn't have run," said Derek abruptly. " He should have stood his ground."

" Oh, my God, what a fool you are ! " sighed Keatings, glad to escape from sympathy into contempt. " Talk about fine words and phrases ! You're a slave to them. What could he do but run ? Could he stand up and face the congregation to-morrow ? Could he walk about the——"

" Of course not," Tony burst in. " Derek's got about as much imagination as a horse."

" Could he walk about the streets, knowing that everyone who passed him would turn round, and that people would rush to their windows to see him pass ? Could he face the servants ? Could he face *us* ? "

" Oh, don't . . . ! " pleaded Joyce. " It's all so terrible."

And Peggy, tearless now, pressed her sister's hand.

" Where's Mother ? " asked Tony.

" Upstairs in her room," Derek answered.

And a silence fell : none of them seemed to know what to do about their mother.

The three boys began to talk plans for the future. Joyce took no part, gazing in front of her. And Peggy, who had been restless since the mention of her mother, got up and went quietly out of the room. For a few minutes she stood in the empty hall, undecided. None of these children found it easy to be endearing or intimate with their mother, and Peggy, longing to go to her with comfort, hesitated. There was a real heart-bursting sympathy in her to-night, and not a little of her habitual self-dramatization, too. She was hurt and ashamed to think that, in such an hour as this, she should have been filled with a most pleasing picture of herself entering like a messenger of solace into her mother's room, and should have rushed from the others so as to win the credit of being first at her mother's side. But when someone moved in the breakfast-room, perhaps to come out and anticipate her in this kindly work, she hesitated no longer ; the impetus sent her hurrying up the stairs. At her mother's door, she knocked, and, feeling a kiss of love and pity mounting to her lips, she turned the handle and entered.

It was Tony who had moved in the breakfast-room. Let Keatings and Derek continue their planning, in which manifestly they were not unhappy. He himself was feeling that stiffness in his limbs and a new tiredness in his eyes. The bruise on his thigh, the cut on his knee, and the faint sprain in his wrist were no longer centres aching with well-being. Rather did some of the lassitude and sickness of the world seem to have found an expression there. The thirst had left this throat, and he had little desire for tea. He rose, left the breakfast-room, picked up his kit-bag of football-togs and carried them up to his room, where, loving a dramatic action, he tossed them into a corner like superannuated things. Then he rested his weary body on the bed and tried to think out the future. But his thoughts, too tired to cut into new country, roamed languidly about the past.

" Could he face the congregation to-morrow ? Could he face the servants . . . and us ? " He was thinking of a far-off day when as a small boy he had decided that he could not face the street or the congregation or the servants and had walked away from his home, in a dull pain. And this same father had found him and brought him back, with an arm round his shoulder. And now this father himself was suffering all that stunned bewilderment, that fear of being seen, that sick decision that he must wander off. Hardly the right pains for a portly man of fifty and more; they were a schoolboy's pains. " O God, help him." Tony, who had long ago abandoned prayers, except in sudden emergencies, found himself muttering this, as his imagination hurt him with vivider and vivider pictures of his father's suffering. Sharp, for his own relief, came the petitions, " O God, help him. . . . O God . . . help him."

It was soon seen that when Canon O'Grogan evacuated a position impossible to hold, he had acted wisely. By resigning his benefice he saved himself and his family from the disgrace of deprivation ; by his retirement to a cheap resort in Belgium and an undertaking that he would not, at least while living with Mrs. Blayre, come seeking a priestly cure in England, he enabled the Bishop to hold his hand from disciplinary action. Canon O'Grogan just disappeared from St. Austin's, Kensington, and a Canon Eadie administered the parish till the benefice should be filled. The curates remained ; and Mr. Flote the verger still superintended the cleaning of the church, and kept its registers, and doled out its hospital letters, and polished the sacred vessels, and saw that the flowers were on the altar, and guarded the vestments for whosoever should be called to wear them.

The O'Grogan family, for so long the noisy centre of parochial life, disappeared quickly too. Archdeacon Gabriel bore down upon them like a successful dreadnought steaming to the boats of a foundered liner, and took them into his own house, till such time as they found a home for themselves. And St. Austin's Vicarage, with its furniture gathering dust in the untenanted rooms, stared blind and silent at the long road. Keatings accepted the Archdeacon's salving operations with a good grace and a quiet courtesy, explaining to his brothers and sisters, " He means well.   He can't help his manner or his face.   Of course he's enjoying his benevolence, but it's a good job someone's happy."

" *I* think he's bossy and bumptious ! " Derek pronounced. " It's humiliating to have to accept their benevolence."

" Certainly, certainly," agreed Keatings.   " But we've managed to get into a position where humiliations abound. Can't be helped. Did I tell you, by the bye, that I was engaged on my autobiography which is to be entitled ' Disgrace Abounding ' ? "

" But I always hoped," Peggy bewailed, " to come to *his* assistance when he should be in disgrace."

" Well, there's still hope," said Keatings.

They were obliged to find a home for their furniture quickly. The new Incumbent, the Rev. John Cambridge, and his wife, had already entered upon their duties, dangling their diplomacy wherever they went, and lubricating their movement about the parish with a tact that was almost excessive, and being no more than discreetly (if ubiquitously) vocal about " their difficult position."   These good people were waiting to fill the Vicarage with righteousness again.   So Mrs. O'Grogan, on the Archdeacon's advice, rented a small, forty-pound-a-year house in Cullingham Avenue, Chiswick, where the speculative builders had lately been cutting up the old gardens of the Royal Horticultural Society into streets of red-brick villas. The family moved into No. 17 Cullingham Avenue on a day before the Christmas of 1905.

There had been debate among them as to who should go back to the Vicarage and see the furniture into the vans.

" It's going to be pretty awful, standing on the steps with every eye in the road peeping round the curtains," said Tony, " and the passers-by not knowing whether to smile pleasantly at us or pretend they've noticed nothing."

" Yes," Peggy agreed most cheerfully.   " And the postman'll probably explain to the removal men what it's all about."

" Bless him ! " said Joyce.   " Let him be happy."

" Mother mustn't go," said Derek, always ready for the grand manner.   " One of us must take it all off her shoulders."

" Well, I don't know what you people are quarrelling about," Keatings languidly commented.   " *I'm* going.   Derek'll look

after the old lady and take her to Chatsworth Towers—"
this was his sub-humorous name for the little jerry-built
affair at Chiswick—"and see the first van-load home, while
Peggy makes her a cup of tea. And I'll cycle to the Vicarage
and watch that everything goes aboard, and then go the rounds
and see that nothing's been left behind—not even a—" he
mentioned a humble fixture on a secluded wall—"and then
I'll come out and lock the door quietly behind me, and all will
be over."

"And I'm going with Keatings," declared Joyce. "This
sort of job needs an intelligent woman. And what's more, I'm
not going to hide in shame behind the hall-door. I shall dance
up and down the steps and ripple with laughter every now and
then, and let everyone see that I'm enjoying the fun immensely."

"Certainly, certainly," Keatings endorsed.

"Besides," added Joyce, "I like removal men. They're
always the sweetest souls."

So Keatings and Joyce arrived and opened the deserted
Vicarage about half an hour before the two pantechnicons backed
against the pavement. Keatings, pipe in mouth, strolled back
and forth from the house to the tail-boards of the vans; gave
a helping hand with the piano; instructed the men which
articles of furniture they might smash so that he could have the
insurance money; and chaffed the errand boys who stood about,
baskets on shoulders, picking their teeth with the straw that
dropped from the crates. Joyce, if an acquaintance passed,
smiled merrily; she fondled the four great horses whose lips
were busy in their nose-bags while their eyes were busy with
her; she made tea in the kitchen for the last time, and sent
it out to the men; and she demanded of Keatings if they
weren't too perfectly adorable when they sat down on the tail-
boards of their vans and drank it, and cut up their bread and
cheese with their jack-knives.

By three o'clock the last article was shipped and the van
doors closed. Keatings and Joyce pulled down the blinds of
the Vicarage, beginning at the upper room which had been
their nursery. They took a farewell look at the empty breakfast-room and hall, and came out and locked the door, and
carried the keys to Mr. Flote, in his office in the church. The
little old man pressed their hands significantly as they said
good-bye, but, with his natural tact, he offered no word of
compassion.

Then Joyce walked along the pavement to take a Chiswick bus in the Kensington Road. Ahead of her, down the long vista of the street, whose tall uniform houses and intermittent lamp-posts seemed the very framework of her childhood, ambled the second pantechnicon, with its crew lolling on the tail-board. It was the only vehicle in the street, and she doubted not that people were half rising from their chairs by front windows to watch the retreat of the O'Grogans. If they watched her they should see only a brisk and happy girl. Before she reached the Kensington Road, Keatings, pursuing the pantechnicon, passed her on his bicycle and waved. " See you at Chatsworth Towers," he called ; and she laughed and waved back.

PART III

CHAPTER I

THE O'Grogan Family, quickly recovering from its stroke, sat up to enjoy its convalescence. As with other convalescents, its members were soon asserting their strong appetite for life, and examining the larder. Keatings decided with some satisfaction that he was now the Regent and declared that he must live at home so that he could "look after the old lady." Through the Archdeacon's influence he obtained employment in a Clerical Assurance Society, and disliked his work richly; but it enabled him to return each night to the little villa in Cullingham Avenue, where, when the sixteen-year-old maid was having her "evening out," he would help his mother lay the supper against the arrival of his sisters, and help them all to clear it away afterwards, and take his turn at "wiping up," only allowing himself the murmured protest, "I'll do it; I'll do it, mind you; but I'd have you know it's Woman's Work." Joyce, after a term in a Chiswick High School as a junior mistress, which she pronounced "a perfectly poisonous occupation," found something much more to her fancy when she commercialized her good looks and her social gifts by becoming a Society Reporter for the *Chiswick and Gunnersbury Times*. "It's lovely," she said, on returning from a wedding or a ball or a political tea-party. "They all see that I've a note-book in my hand, and they seek me out. They dance in front of me that I may see their frocks. They leave themselves about, in my immediate vicinity, hoping for the favour of my eye; and I always make them happy by writing down something, whether I publish it or not. Besides, it sells the paper. Even the local celebrities are not above flitting around me and angling for my favours.   I am one of the most sought-after persons at every assembly." Derek, with St. Paul's and Oxford behind him, had no difficulty in earning his " sixty pounds a year resident " at an Eastbourne preparatory school.   Peggy became a Lady Almoner for a Benevolent Society, and went to see if the applicants for aid were scamps or not.   She much enjoyed this " going about doing good " at other people's expense, but she was probably the worst servant the Society ever employed, for she could not bear that the enormous, fat, slatternly women whom she visited and questioned should do anything, next time she called on them, but rise up and call her blessed, so she sent in enthusiastic reports about them all.   Her dislike of being disliked must have cost the Society immense sums ; and her conscience did not fail to submit to her, twice or three times a day, that it was wrong, very wrong, thus to buy a wide popularity with public funds.

The Archdeacon had been emphatic that Tony should continue his promising career at St. Paul's, at least till the end of the next summer term.   That would bring him to the threshold of his eighteenth birthday, and if he could attain, as seemed likely, to one of the Eighth forms, his chance of getting a junior mastership would be handsomely increased.   Keatings, the self-appointed guardian of his youngest brother, agreed ; but when the Archdeacon offered to pay Tony's fees, he declined with grave thanks, assuring his uncle that he could find the money himself.   And he did so ; and Tony and his schoolbooks took a District Railway train daily to Hammersmith throughout the spring and summer terms of 1906.   He did well in those terms, less from conscientious effort, than because he could not help it, and he took the Halley Prize in the Apposition which crowned his school life.

" Pity he couldn't go on with it," said Keatings to his sisters. " A damned shame.   He'd have got a better scholarship to Oxford than either of the Gabriels, and a fellowship before he'd done ; and that would have deflated the Archdeacon properly.   I was counting on him more than any of us to do the trick.   Now he'll only be a wretched usher at a preparatory school, while John and Warner Gabriel are throwing their weight about Oxford."

" There's plenty of time," said Joyce.   " I've a sort of feeling that I'm going to do something rather bright.   And there's Derek, too. He's got bounce and push enough for anything."

"Oh, he's a fool," said Keatings.

There were in those days three outstanding firms of scholastic agents in London: Landseer, Thyme and Co., Leman and Finchley, Ltd., and Mr. Peidestros. The first two stood out as the agents with the best schools on their lists; and Mr. Peidestros stood out as the man to come to if your qualifications were dubious. The first two, as their names suggested, were business-like firms; Mr. Peidestros was less a firm than a person. Landseer, Thyme and Co., and Leman and Finchley, Ltd., had good premises with several neat rooms; Mr. Peidestros had what Tony called " a room and a bit," and both untidy. He was a tall, clean-shaven old man with huge features and a mop of waving blue-grey hair. To echo and emphasize this striking embellishment of hair he always wore a grey morning coat, and grey trousers, and a grey stock round his high collar, and a single dark pearl in its centre. The grey morning coat was always buttoned at the waist, so that its lapels bulged out above and gave his figure the appearance of possessing, not a chest, but a breast. When he stepped out from his offices into the winter air, he wore grey spats and a grey sombrero hat; and when into the summer sun, white spats, a white panama with a brim like an awning caught in the wind. And yet he was hardly a dandy, for the whole grey symphony was a little disordered; and incisive eyes could detect behind the pearl pin and the grey stock a very cheap flannel shirt.

His skin had an olive tint that set his clients guessing at his nationality. Some thought him Spanish; some, influenced by his name, averred that he must be Greek; Derek, who had met him before securing the Eastbourne post through Leman and Finchley, voted him Sicilian; and Tony suspected that he was a Turk. But all his clients were sure that he was a Dago; and this not bitterly, except when his promises had failed to materialize. His office was a long, rectangular room, the first-floor-front of a Wimbury Street house; and it held his desk at the end near the door, and on the rest of its floor the littered tables of three girl-typists—"his daughters" as Mr. Peidestros smilingly called them. At the far end a door led to a second room which was little more than a converted cupboard, and this was the place of interviews between headmasters and their prospective assistants. So it was that Tony defined his premises as " a room and a bit."

Landseer, Thyme and Co., and Leman and Finchley, Ltd., shook doubtful heads over Tony, and explained that as a rule they dealt only with graduates, and preferably with Oxford and Cambridge men, but they would certainly inform him if they heard of any likely situation; Mr. Peidestros met him, literally, with open arms; that is to say, he rose from his desk and extended at the level of his breast two fin-like hands, palms upward, as if he were Sir Henry Irving welcoming before an audience a son long lost; then swung the hands, without bringing them into contact with his visitor towards a vacant chair in front of his desk, while he said in even tones, " Come in, sir; come in, come in. Be seated." Still with the grace of an actor, he dipped one of the fin-like hands into a drawer and took out a box of Russian cigarettes in coffee-brown paper and offered one to his new juvenile lead; he struck a match and held it to Tony's cigarette, as if this were a sacramental ceremony before business could be inaugurated; then pulled up the knees of his trousers and sat down in his arm-chair and leaned back to survey his guest.

He opened a cross-examination; and his gay and noisy questions to Tony about his past life and his future hopes much embarrassed the youth, in the presence of the girl typists; who, however, were marvellously indifferent and clicked away at their instruments as if unconscious of their principal's hearty laughter and ingratiating cross-examination. It was the tender, encouraging, put-you-at-your-ease cross-examination that a counsel reserves for his own witnesses.

" *Yurse*—yes, yes." Mr. Peidestros breathed encouragement and confidence in a manner half a clergyman's and half a doctor's. " Yurse; we'll get something for you—certainly. You'll do all right. We want your sort. But you're young, you know. You look very young. I can't promise you a good stipend. Get you plenty of jobs ' on mutual terms,' but you can't do with that, can you ? "

Tony inquired what " on mutual terms " might mean.

" Hospitality in exchange for services rendered, but no salary," explained Mr. Peidestros.

Tony shook his head, saying he couldn't do with that; and Mr. Peidestros nodded his, saying, " *No*, no ; *no*, no, of course not. Must have pocket money, I suppose ? "

Tony said that he didn't see how he could do with less than about fifty pounds a year.

" *Wurl*—well, well," considered Mr. Peidestros. " Yes, we ought to be able to get you something like that. Let's see what subjects we can put you down for." He took a sheet of foolscap and, plunging a long hand into the cavity behind his bulging lapels, drew a gold pencil from somewhere. This he laid down on the paper, that he might rub his hands and wrists together before writing, which he did for a long time, and slowly, like a fly rubbing his forelegs on the side of a plate. " Well. You can teach Classics, can't you ? "

" I think so," answered Tony, diffidently. " At least, I ought to be able to teach prep-school boys. I've done nothing else at St. Paul's for the last three years."

" Quite so, quite so," encouraged Mr. Peidestros. " I'll put you down as Classics. Were you really high in the school ? . . . Probably pretty high," he quickly suggested, before Tony could reply.

" I was in the Middle Eighth."

" That's not the top form, is it ? "

" No. Just below it. The Upper Eighth is the top form."

" Well, we'll say you were in the Eighth at St. Paul's. If you were as high as that, you ought to be able to teach Classics to Scholarship standard."

" Oh, I don't know. . . ."

" Well, we'll put you down ' Scholarship Standard.' They may not ask you to do it. Almost sure not to, with a junior master. Can you teach French ? "

" No. I've forgotten all my French."

" Oh, but didn't you do French at St. Paul's ? "

" Not for my last two years."

" But you did it at your preparatory school ? "

" Oh, yes."

" Well, we'll put you down for French. They don't want much at preparatory schools." He wrote it in a large hand, very free with the paper-space and magnificently independent of the ruled lines. " And Mathematics ? What about Mathematics ? "

" No, I shouldn't like to teach Maths."

" But you must have done your Euclid and Algebra once ? "

" Yes, but——"

" We'll put you down Elementary Mathematics. Now about English."

" I ought to be all right with Literature, I think."

" Good. Fond of Literature, are you ? Good. English Literature is coming on, as a subject, these days. Well, the other English subjects are simple enough. We'll put you down All English Subjects. Divinity, now ? You ought to be rather special with Divinity."

" Why ? " Tony laughed.

Mr. Peidestros spread a palm towards the ceiling. " Are you not a parson's son, and a parson's nephew ? "

" I suppose I could teach Scripture," admitted Tony.

And Mr. Peidestros nodded most encouragingly and breathed, " *Yurse*—yes, yes. We'll put you down Divinity. Don't know any Book-keeping or Shorthand, do you ? "

" Good Lord, no ! "

" Oh, well. They're not much in your line. But sometimes we get a school that makes a feature of a commercial education. But they're not your sort of schools. Not the best sort. No, you want something of a better class than that. Now there's Games. How are you off for Games ? You look as though you could play most Games. Get yer colours or anything at St. Paul's ? "

" I was not bad at Rugger. I was tried for the Second XV."

" That's good enough. ' All Games.' " He picked up the list of attainments and scanned it contemplatively. Now Mr. Peidestros differed from other men in contemplation, who often pull their chins, in that he would finger his fine nose long and strokingly, as if pleased to be reminded of its line and mass ; and would take his cigarette from his lips and wave its scented smoke under that nose, as if offering a tribute of incense to a magnificent organ. It was an action more suited to a cigar than a cigarette, even as his high manners and his dignified morning coat were suited to something better than a soiled flannel shirt. " *Wurl*," he said, having performed these cere-monies, " your subjects look promising enough. Classics to Scholarship Standard, French, All English Subjects, Divinity, Elementary Mathematics, All Games. Now—wait a minute—we've got to get certain details about yourself. What's your height ? "

" I'm five foot eleven in my boots."

" Say ' Six foot in your socks '—you haven't stopped growing yet. When an applicant is as young as you are, its best to compensate for it in height. They've more faith in your discipline then. Your age is what?"

"I shall be eighteen in September."

Mr. Peidestros shook his head.

"Is that all?" He blew some smoke through his lips. "Better say nineteen." And after surveying Tony for a second or two, he showed, by a nodding of his head, that he was satisfied with the wisdom of his decision. "Yes; you can carry off nineteen all right; and you'll be it soon enough. What's your religion?"

"Oh, Church of England."

"Good. That's good. You're not High or Low, or anything like that, are you? It's just as well not to be. Or, at any rate, don't make a noise about it, if you are."

"No. I think I'm just plain Church of England."

Mr. Peidestros was more than ever satisfied and encouraging. "*Yurse*—yes, yes. It's best. It's best in the long run. Then you can accommodate yourself to whatever turns up."

"Of course I don't think I'm anything, *really*," Tony explained.

"Oh, nonsense, nonsense. You must have some religion. We can't get you any posts without religion. Naturally not." Mr. Peidestros left that point as too obvious for discussion. "Now about your references. There's your Headmaster at St. Paul's——"

"The *High* master," Tony corrected. "Mr. Walker was High master all my time, but he'd certainly be rude to anyone that wrote to him. He's rather given than way."

"*Yurse;* some people are like that. It's a pity, I always think. It's so easy to be pleasant. . . . Pity we can't use him—a great pity . . . !"

"There was another master who would speak rather well for me, I think; a Mr. Jamieson."

"H'm." Mr. Peidestros was doubtful, and stroked his nose three or four times. "Better someone high-sounding, you know."

"There's my uncle, Archdeacon Gabriel——"

"Of course! Of course. We'll put him first. Clergymen always go down—especially the—er—the higher ranks. Any army men?"

"My mother's uncle's a big pot at the War Office—General Warham."

"*Is* he? Is he, now? Why, excellent, excellent! Nothing

better. General Warren, is he? Fancy that! *Warham*—yes, I meant Warham. I shall certainly put him down, and I think we might safely put his address as the War Office, London——"

" But I don't at all know that he'll consent to——"

" Oh, yes, he will, my boy. He won't let you down. Besides, very likely they won't write to him at all. Oh, yes, I've not the least doubt I shall be able to find you something. You should score well in an interview, you know ; you've a good presence—quite a good presence. Well, I'll let you know as things turn up." They had now risen and were approaching the door. " And there's a little registration fee we charge—to cover postage and so on——" Mr. Peidestros waved such a prosaic subject away with his palm, to somewhere beyond his left shoulder. " Yurse. Just a half-crown. But send it along any time, my boy. Don't exercise yourself about it. Send it any time." It was the tone of a large creditor doing the big and generous thing by his debtor ; and on this happy arrangement they parted. " *Good*-bye ; *good*-bye," said Mr. Peidestros, in a smiling benediction, and closed the door, still nodding automatically.

And certainly for every typed sheet that Landseer, Thyme and Co. or Leman and Finchley, Ltd., sent to Tony, Mr. Peidestros sent seven. Each sheet contained details of a vacancy in what Mr. Peidestros called " a good class preparatory school for gentlemen's sons," or " a well established school for the sons of business and professional men ; " and after the details came the words, " Write promptly but carefully to Mr. ——," or perhaps, " Write promptly and carefully to Miss ——," for not a few of Mr. Peidestros's schools seemed to be conducted by women. Often, at the bottom, there was a piece of advice pencilled in the agent's large and generous hand.

Tony, however, was not served ill by Mr. Peidestros. There were one or two of the better headmasters who realized that you could often draw a promising fish out of the Peidestros backwater, and accordingly left a tentative line there, as well as in the main stream of Landseer, Thyme and Co., and Leman and Finchley, Ltd. Such a one was Mr. Sugden, of Stratton Lye, Hurst, Sussex, and he had the additional wisdom to perceive that you got a man cheaper from Mr. Peidestros. A correspondence, passing between Tony and Mr. Sugden, increased in interest and good will, till at length an interview in

Mr. Peidestros's little cell crowned it with the offer of a junior mastership, and its acceptance.

Mr. Sugden was a huge pylon of a man, widening downward from his small head and his narrow sloping shoulders to his big chest and bigger loins.   On the same plan his hands and wrists seemed too large for the narrower upper arm.   But the voice that came from the top of this pylon was loud and friendly, and the eyes could twinkle up there, like the light on the Tower of Pharos ; and if he bragged somewhat about his school, well, that was an amiable fault.   " I think you'll be happy in your work," he kept repeating.   " They're delightful boys, delightful ; " and when he and his new master emerged from the cell, he called over the heads of the girl typists to Mr. Peidestros : " The trick is done, Peidestros.   O'Grogan is coming to us. I think he'll be very happy in the work ; it's a delightful lot of boys we've got just now, truly delightful."   And Mr. Peidestros rose and extended both his hands towards Tony with a gesture that might have been borrowed from an Egyptian wall-painting, and said : " Well, well, well.   Didn't I say so ? Yes, I think I found the right man for you. . . . Now isn't that excellent ? " and then he placed a paternal hand on Tony's shoulder and shepherded them both to the door, as a kindly and talkative registrar might shepherd a newly-married couple into their future happiness.   So huge was Mr. Sugden in his black clothes (making even the agent look small) and so helpless and light felt Tony, under the guiding pressure of this hand on his shoulder, that he had little hesitation in deciding which of the couple was the bridegroom and which the captured bride.

CHAPTER II

THE SECRET CORRIDOR AGAIN

IN the train on that Tuesday afternoon, when he was journeying to Hassocks Station to take up his work at Stratton Lye, Tony was apprehensive and restless; his body and breathing were troubled by a conflict between his nervousness of what he was going to and his impatience with the train for its halting approach. But he had no notion that in days to come he would look back upon this journey, as do all men upon one or two journeys in their lives, and think: " Strange that I never knew when I stepped into the train or gazed out at the passing landscape that I was travelling to *that !* " And yet he was fast moving into a stretch of the old, unquiet brilliance, so desired.

The train slowed into a station, and his breathing went to pieces : it was Hassocks. The train stopped, but not this panicky fluttering of his heart. The fussiness on the platform and a blend of voices disarrayed his thinking, and he hardly knew what he did, as he bundled out with his gladstone bag. There were quick high voices belonging to young boys who were probably his future pupils, and the steadier but very disturbing voices of their parents. There were isolated men and women waiting on the platform, or walking with a smile to a marooned passenger; and any one of them might be a colleague of his, or any of the ladies might be Mrs. Sugden herself. That hard-bitten old coachman; perhaps he was a retainer of Stratton Lye.

There were at least six little groups of boys and elders, and he wondered whether carriages had been provided for them in the station yard. Would he be able to elude them all and drive up to the school alone ? But even as he resolved to conquer for himself this last lane of privacy, a powerful hand gripped his shoulder. It was Mr. Sugden hurrying by.

"Hallo, O'Grogan. Good! I'll be back to you in a minute. You can come up in my fly."

"Oh, thanks," murmured Tony, but Mr. Sugden was some distance away, a high black lighthouse, surged about by a sea of boys in red and yellow caps.

To go up in Mr. Sugden's fly, with, perhaps, a strange parent and a brace of strange boys, was the last thing he had wanted to do. The bright and intelligent remarks he had prepared for his first meeting with his principal or his pupils were quite unsuited to their juxtaposition together, within the embrace of a station fly; those adapted to Mr. Sugden had been for his ear alone, and the jests composed for the boys might even displease their headmaster; and his intellect felt too battered now for the invention of more appropriate felicities. Instead of appearing impressive and vigorous—a positive character, as he had rehearsed—he would appear dull and negative.

But Mr. Sugden gave him little time to worry. Possessing a hustle that one could scarcely have foreseen in a human column so massive and tapering, he was far more engaged in appearing hearty and effective before the parents than in observing whether his new master was positive or negative. "Come along, O'Grogan. Come and see how you like us. We'll take Mrs. Galloway and young John up with us. Young John's a new boy. Mrs. Galloway, this is Mr. O'Grogan, my latest addition to the staff. A brilliant youngster who's going to do great things for the boys, yours included. Come along, all."

The dusty fly, with its ambling irregular horse, rolled out of the station yard, jolting up and down on its springs and dandling Mr. Sugden into a few minutes' silence, as a cradle might. He and Mrs. Galloway vibrated quietly in the back seat, and Tony and the new boy in the seat facing them. Their road took them over a crossways and along a ridge of high ground, from whose height the whole of North Sussex fell away. On their left was a narrow stretch of weald, and then the long swell of the South Downs, lifting and falling like a high sea till, with the rearing of a tidal wave, it struck the earth in the great curve of Wolstonbury. Wolstonbury Hill, round as the top of a world, magnificently placid under the evening sun, dominating the more volatile hills by the splendour of its individuality, reigning over all the country at its base by the simple right of its own lofty, serene, self-sufficient integrity—Wolstonbury, at this first presentation of itself, imposed upon Tony a fealty that he never forswore. He loved Wolstonbury in that hour, and loved it all his days.

"Yes, that's Wolstonbury," said Mr. Sugden. "Not the highest of the Downs, but the grandest to my thinking. There are plenty higher—Chanctonbury and Ditchling Beacon and Firle—but they haven't the majestic isolation or the perfect roundness of Wolstonbury. All the South Downs are noblemen, I always tell the boys, but Wolstonbury's the one perfect gentleman of the lot. I like to think that Stratton Lye is at its foot."

Mr. Sugden, Tony had observed, had a habit of turning everything in the world, from a mountain to a measles epidemic, into credit for his school, and he seemed now, in the presence of the parent, to be cashing Wolstonbury into the same good money.

They were passing some modern red-brick houses, dotted at intervals along the road, and Mr. Sugden deplored them. "Dreadful! Dreadful! Like splashes of Croydon tossed out here. No style. No taste. It's just because there's a railway station at Hassocks. This part of Hurst is the gift of the railway, just as Egypt is the gift of the Nile. . . . But it's healthy," he added, remembering the parent at his side. "Everybody says it's one of the healthiest spots in Sussex. All this rapid growth is a tribute to its healthiness. And it gets better as we get out of it. You'll think the neighbourhood round Stratton Lye very picturesque, I think."

"The air seems good," Tony obliged, most anxious to say something. "Wonderfully fresh after London."

"Yes, everyone notices that," agreed Mr. Sugden, hastily cashing the winds. "We're quite high here : a hundred and fifty feet above sea-level. And, whenever possible, we get the boys on to the top of Wolstonbury."

Seemingly he was impressed by Tony's obliging remark ; and, rather than waste time while he had a parent in the carriage, he proceeded to cash Tony himself ; he alluded to his junior and senior scholarships at St. Paul's, and to his supposed prowess in cricket and football ; and, bethinking himself of St. Paul's and its great and terrible High Master, Mr. Walker, he promptly cashed that gentleman, explaining to Mrs. Galloway that " Walker had turned out more classical scholars than any man of his time ; " and, determining like a good business-man that before he had finished with Tony he must have exhausted the last halfpenny of his value, he gave a little time to thought, after which he remembered Archdeacon Gabriel, and cashed him. So profitable a ten minutes had this been that the next thing to do was obviously to use the parent for Tony's benefit; and he spoke to Mrs. Galloway of Captain Galloway, her husband, and of his prospects of an early majority in the Blues, and of their house in town which he so much admired ; and he told Tony that young John's father had twice been mentioned in despatches during the Boer War.

The road, widening through the village of Hurst had left the ugly and recent villas, and was narrowing into quaintness, if not into beauty. A few large houses stood behind their stone or brick walls ; a few shops of irregular pattern fronted the pavement, and a church with a tall steeple loomed ahead. Tony stared at the shops and the houses and the church ; and, often, in after months, when it became his habit to take an evening walk from Stratton Lye into Hurst, he would wonder that the pavements and garden-walls and shop-faces could be so different from the strange, agitating pictures of his first evening. The leisurely horse bobbed on and on, beyond the pavements into the country, till, about three-quarters of a mile from the village, it turned through an iron gate. Tony had just time, before they went into a darkness beneath large untidy yews and blown Scotch firs, to notice that the garden of Stratton Lye was bounded along the road by a wall of stone and flint, behind which rose a lofty screen of trees. Nothing of the house could be seen from the road, and, truly, the garden's grey wall and the gloomy rampart of trees promised little but some dark, old, damp-green mausoleum. The carriage drive, dark beneath the yews and firs, was rough and stony, and its borders were widths of sparse grass carpeted with ivy. The trees, though not dense, yet bullied one another for room, and at one place the outer growth of a yew had surrounded the trunk of a poplar tall as a steeple.

But, suddenly, as the drive bent, the house and its lawns broke upon the view ; and both were beautiful. The lawns were trimmed and sun-shot, with clumps of rhododendron and two magnificent clipped yews that might have been lifted from the picture of some marbled pool in Greece ; and the house dreamed above its garden, a rambling place of deep red brick,

with windows of brown wood, and roof of Horsham stone, and
irregular chimney stacks, now noosed in the sun's long rays.

" A goodly sight, isn't it ? " Mr. Sugden inquired of Tony.
" I always think it's so desirable that young boys should be
brought up in beautiful surroundings, instead of in your banal
modern residences, as they do in the Eastbourne preparatory
schools." He had commercialized its loveliness straightaway.

Next minute Tony had lost Mr. Sugden and was being led by
a butler towards the Common Room.

He entered a large, oblong room, with a big table in its
centre and some torn leather chairs round the fireplace. A
large engraving of the Coronation of King Edward VII.
hanging over the marble mantelpiece, was the only picture in
the room. A baize notice-board, a tall, half-empty bookshelf,
and the Parish Almanack broke the bareness of the distempered
walls. Three lofty windows, cheaply curtained, looked out
upon the kitchen gardens. Two men sat in the fireside chairs,
and one lounged on the support of fender and mantelpiece.
Those in the chairs were alarming to Tony, for one had a
moustache and the other a grey beard. But the one on the
fender was comforting ; he was clean-cheeked, clear-eyed,
and certainly no more than two years older than Tony.

" Oh, are you O'Grogan ? " asked the moustached man.

" Yes, I believe so," answered Tony, in a terrible effort at
humour, which made him blush.

They forgave him this, and introduced themselves : the
moustached man as Browning, the grey-haired man as La Motte,
and the tall, merry-faced youngster as Winter.

" Though we generally call him Cyril," added Browning,
" because he's a child."

" Well, I'm no longer the Baby of the Staff—now," laughed
Winter.

Tony covered his misliking of the jest with a merry :

" Why, how old are you ? "

" Twenty. And don't say you're twenty-one, because anybody can see you're not more than eighteen."

" I'm nearly twenty," Tony assured them.

A gong sounded in the entrance hall, its reverberations
diminishing beneath the crescendo of young voices and hurrying feet.

" The feet of the sweet things who'll devastate the next few
months of your life," sighed Browning. " It's Tea."

That first tea was a confused memory to the new master; he carried away from it to his little bed-chamber in the roof an impression of a large hall, with long trestle tables feeding sixty talkative boys, none of whom individualized himself. The masters sat at the heads or feet of the tables, and one young governess presided over a table of very small boys. Maids bustled about, and a sailing, overdressed woman who was, it appeared, the Lady Matron, made a royal visitation of the tables and the kitchens. Up in his slope-roofed bedchamber Tony unpacked his trunk, moving shirts from trunk to drawer in that dull, automatic drift that signifies an acceptance of loneliness. He was surprised that a picture of Peggy which he placed at an angle on his dressing-table could raise such a melancholy.

Next came an interview with Mr. Sugden, in which his duties were explained. And when it was over he felt tired with his long-sustained effort to be impressive. " Why can't one be natural ? " he thought, and wandered back to the Common Room.

In the Common Room he gravitated naturally to the master of his own age, finding him the one solid piece of comfort in Stratton Lye. They filled the evening with talk. The talk pricked Tony with alarm at first when the duties of the masters were mentioned, but presently it changed its character and became very pleasing, very engrossing—a series of confidences surprising for a first night, but rich with the promise of sympathy and kinship. It was just before supper. Browning was on duty in a class-room ; La Motte had taken a stick and gone for a walk ; and Winter, left in the armchair with Tony opposite him, had begun, most plainly, to turn his thoughts from the subject in hand to the closed door of the room and the sounds outside. He seemed to be anxiously looking for somebody, and at the same time to be anxious to hide his anxiety. And Tony, for a moment, grew uncomfortable again, wondering if he were in the way.

" Are you expecting somebody ? " he asked, feigning a laugh.

" Oh no . . . no," answered Winter, hurriedly. " Some of the boys come in to say good night sometimes. They're decent kids, you know. Really affectionate."

" I suppose so," said Tony, dutifully.

" Yes. . . ." Winter hesitated, opened his lips to speak again, but abandoned the words. He filled a pipe instead.

But it was clear that his thoughts were playing around the truncated end of the conversation, and after a silence he stuttered to give them shape.

"Yes. We've extraordinarily wrong ideas about boys—about some of them, at any rate—especially when they're about twelve or thirteen, haven't we?"

"Wrong? How do you mean?"

"Well, even the brightest and cheekiest have a rather feminine quality—some of them. But we don't like to allow it."

"Feminine?"

"Yes. . . ." Winter's clear and open face reddened, but his eyes looked directly into his new friend's, as if defying him to think him other than the straightest, sanest and least senti-mental of masters. "For instance, there's a boy here—he's—he's extraordinary! He's quite a useful athlete, he's probably the most impudent boy in the school, and he's reasonably good at his work. Not a scholarship case, but you've only got to hear him talk and—" Winter's lower jaw straightened, as he waited for words—" and study his irrepressible personality to know that he's worth ten of most of the boys who take the scholarships."

Winter paused, but Tony made no comment. Watching and listening, he had guessed from memories of his own that Winter was dilating on a person he loved to speak about.

"He's the last kid you'd call 'soft' or 'soppy,' O'Grogan. You'd be much more likely to call him 'forceful.' And yet he's got an absolutely feminine power of devotion. Hangs about you, and all that."

"Hangs about whom?"

"Well. . . ." Again Winter reddened, and conscious of this betrayal in his cheeks, flung a merry laugh in front of it. "About *me*. Strange, isn't it? That's what I mean, O'Grogan."

"Do you like it?"

Winter knocked the top ashes out of his pipe.

"Yes . . ." he said. "Why shouldn't I be frank about it? Yes. I don't think I've ever experienced anything I've liked better. . . . I don't see why one should be ashamed to confess that, do you?"

"No. . . ." supplied Tony.

"I mean—everything that I feel for young Frank is good. I feel I want to do everything I can to help him. I feel I'd sacrifice myself an awful lot if it would advance him in the least, and I'm jolly careful all the time that it doesn't degenerate into favouritism. . . ."

Tony mused. " I've often . . ." he began.

Observing his abrupt stop, Winter encouraged him.

" You've often what ? "

" I've often felt an affection for somebody that seemed so stupid that I was ashamed to speak of it—and yet I didn't quite see why it should be stupid——"

" Exactly ! Exactly ! " interrupted Winter enthusiastically.

" ——Except," continued Tony, "in so far as I knew it would have to be transitory . . . and so one was stupid, perhaps, to let it mean so much to one. But it's generally been all on my side. . . . Except once. . . ." and he slid from the subject to a memory of Sibyl Chandry and the veranda at Grandelmere.

" It's certainly not all on my side with young Doyly," said Winter, not without triumph. " That's his name : Doyly—though I usually call him Frank. I bet you anything you like that he won't go to bed to-night without slipping away from the others and coming here to say good night to me. Well, that's rather pleasant, you must admit."

" I do, certainly," Tony smiled.

" You'll see ! I'm expecting him any minute. The younger boys have gone to bed, but he's one of the elders—nearly thirteen and stays up longer. They'll be making a move for bed any moment now. Of course he may *not* come."

There being no possible reply to this, Tony attended to his pipe, whose control, since he had no previous familiarity with the instrument, was proving an art that needed about as much mental concentration as an infant gives to its first walk. With his right hand he held the bowl firmly, with his teeth he secured the mouthpiece, and with his lungs he drew and drew and drew, just holding his own against a powerful resistance in the pipe. There was very little smoke anywhere to wave a triumph over his efforts.

The door of a distant class-room opened ; a noise of feet and voices was disgorged into the hall and distributed up the stairs and along the lobbies ; the voice of Browning called to someone ; Winter quickly turned his ear towards the sounds ; and at the same time the resistance in Tony's pipe settled down to its victory.

One voice was louder than the others, as it approached the

Common Room door; a merry voice: "Don't piffle more than you can help, old Protheroe. . . . Of course I know you were born mad, but that's no reason why you should be proud of it. . . What? . . . Oh, *did* you. . . . Well, who cares? . . . No, I shan't be long. . . . Shan't tell you, so sucks! It's no business of yours. It's private business of mine. Good night. Sleep well. . . . I shall see some more of you during my stay, I expect—but, *I say!*—not a bit more than I can help—you bet! . . . Good night."

The voice was now outside the door. The steps belonging to it paused and there came a hesitant knock.

"Come in," called Winter, in a tone deliberately commonplace. He was now leaning back in his armchair with a newspaper extended before him; and Tony suspected that he had quickly assumed this careless posture, to conceal from his visitor that he had expected his coming. Tony knew the grammar of these disguises; none better.

Winter did not turn his eyes from his paper as Frank Doyly entered, but sent them down a column of print: that was part of the stage business. Tony looked straight at the visitor. He saw a slim but well-shaped boy, whose hair would have been fair, had he not, after the fashion of dawning adolescence, pomaded it tight to the scalp. The cheeks were still smooth and clean as a child's; the nose firm and small; the eyes lit with anticipated impudence. It was such a face as would, at any time, have stirred an unrest in Tony, and a faint pain; and its power had been doubled now by the talk that had introduced it. A swell of good-will to the boy lifted in him.

Winter looked up from his paper.

"Hallo, Frank. Settling down, eh?"

"No, sir."

The boy was standing with his fingers linked behind his back, while he jerked up and down from his toes to his heels.

"What do you mean? Of course you are settling down! Here you are, delighted to be back in school, burning to get to work——"

"Not half!"

"What do you mean—'Not half!'? Don't bring your vile Cockney jargon back here."

"I never get settled down from the hols. till about half-term, and then it's time to get unsettled with the next hols. So I never settle down at school at all—really."

" Can't have anything of that sort this term.   Your Common Entrance is less than a year off."

" Oh, a year's a long time."

" Not an hour too long for all that you've got to learn. Mr. La Motte says your Latin Prose is a disgrace to the school, and your Greek worse."

" Oh, but old La Motte—*Mr.* La Motte, I mean—says that of everybody.   It's his idea of being funny."

" Have you met Mr. O'Grogan yet ? "

Frank Doyly became suddenly shy.

" No, sir."

" Well, you'd better present yourself.   This is Frank Doyly, O'Grogan—probably the laziest good-for-nothing in the school." (How quickly Tony sensed the affection in the abuse !)

The boy offered a hand ; and Tony, hardly less shy, took it. He was uncomfortably abashed by the boy's gaze which, because of his very diffidence, looked nervously straight into his.

" I don't know exactly why Frank should be honouring us with a visit to-night," continued Winter facetiously.

" I've come to say good night.   You know that perfectly well," explained Doyly, released again into impudence.

" We should probably have enjoyed a fair rest without your good wishes."

" Oh, dash ! don't be too funny.   It's no good trying to do that sort of thing unless you do it well."

" Confound the child ! " cried Winter, and, throwing out a hand, seized him by the wrist.   " We won't put up with that brand of sauce, will we, O'Grogan ? "

" Let me go," laughed Doyly, struggling to free himself. " You asked for it."

Winter brought his other hand into play, and soon captured Doyly's other wrist.   The boy pulled and pushed and twisted, and even pretended to bite the imprisoning fingers, but at the end he was still in Winter's grip, breathless, and staring with defiant impotence at his master's grin.   Tony, watching with a smile, could feel what affection was being conveyed to the boy by Winter's tight-holding hands.

" You're beginning the term very badly, Frank Doyly," warned Winter.   " This is mutiny, you know."

" I don't care," assured the breathless boy.

" I think I shall report it to Mr. Sugden."

" And I think I shall report you for ill-treatment."

" Not ill-treatment, my boy.   Legitimate discipline."

" Oh, *is* it ? "

" Yes.   I have a witness here.   Mr. O'Grogan is a stern believer in discipline."

Immediately at this reference to the new master Doyly turned shy again.   He had no answer.   Then, in one of Winter's unguarded moments, he jerked himself free, and put both hands into safe custody behind his back.   Winter stared him up and down, as if deploring every aspect of his appearance.

" You look as though you'd come to spend the evening."

" No, I haven't.   I've something better to do."

" Well, nothing's detaining you.   Good night, child."

" Child !   *Child !*   You're not so frightfully old yourself, sir."

Winter turned to Tony.

" What's to be done with him, O'Grogan ? "

" You're only about twenty-one," continued Doyly, " if that.   And if you're not as much as that, you're still an ' infant ' in law, and not responsible for your actions."

" Doyly, go straight to bed."

" All right, sir.   It's dull enough here."

But he still stood, with his hands behind his back, and rising up and down on his toes, and seeming in no hurry to go.

" Say good night to Mr. O'Grogan first."

Again Doyly proffered his hand to the new master, saying with perfect respect : " Good night, sir," and nervously sending his eyes into Tony's ; eyes at once shy and impudent, hesitant and advancing.   There pricked at once in Tony the pang of a desire to possess for himself the hero-worship now given to Winter, and to meet it with one of those inward and hidden devotions, compact of doubts and hopes, glamours and jealousies.   Life was not life till such an experience filled it ; it lay fallow and empty, waiting for the visitation. . . . But no, it would be a poor game, robbing Winter of an affection in which he delighted.   Winter was a good, simple fellow, and his frank confidences had won a quick and keen liking from Tony.   Tony dropped Doyly's hand, and dropped the picture with it.

Doyly turned from him to Winter.

" Well, good night, sir."

" Good night, Frank, old man."

There was such simple affection in Winter's tone as made Tony glad of his decision.

But a seed of thought, once sown, may germinate of itself, despite all efforts to cancel it ; and Tony was always powerless against this particular seed.   Next morning, as he sat down at the foot of one of the long trestle tables for breakfast, he found himself looking around for the one figure in Stratton Lye which had attracted him.   There was Frank Doyly, quarrelling with other boys for the privilege of eating his breakfast on the left hand of Winter.   He easily won the coveted place, seated himself there triumphantly, and opened a happy and probably impudent conversation ; and Tony, to his surprise, heard himself thinking : " Not for long ! " just as if competition had begun between him and Winter.   And the idea of the competition was wonderfully pleasing.   It made him both ashamed and happy.

After breakfast, when the boys and masters went out for half an hour's play in the field, Doyly walked hanging on Winter's arm.   And while the other boys played Touch and Hot Rice, or strolled about in couples with an arm on each other's shoulders, Doyly kept his favoured place by his master's side.   A bell rang high up on the bricks of the back wall, and all flowed into the class-rooms.   Tony spent the morning teaching Elementary Latin and Elementary Mathematics to the younger boys, and discovered that the occupation could be full of interest.   He saw nothing of Doyly, and wondered if the boy went to any of Winter's classes.   Lunch ; and there was Doyly standing in proud possession of his place by Winter's chair, before anyone could oust him.   Winter was late, entering after Grace, and Tony saw Doyly bantering him.   A ludicrous sentence shaped itself, unasked, in his head : " Well, I haven't had a chance to fire any of my guns yet."

The afternoon was hot with a mid-September sun, inviting to cricket rather than to football.   But the Michaelmas term yielded no jot of its claim to football, and by two o'clock the boys were all gathered in the West Room, where they were being sorted by Mr. Sugden into three " Games," a " Senior Game," a " Middle," and a " Junior."   Mr. Sugden expounded it all to Tony.

"The unfortunate Master on Duty takes the Junior Game, as it's the most harassing task ; that's La Motte.   I like, whenever possible, for the Junior Masters to ' change ' and play with the Senior boys.   So you and Winter'll look after the Seniors, will you ?   Perhaps you and Winter'll pick up from them."

"Good !" thought Tony, for his thoughts were independent of his will.   " I shall have my chances during football."

Winter tossed a coin and won : he deliberately picked a tall boy named Crosbie, though Doyly had palpably put himself forward to be chosen, and was now looking anxious lest Mr. O'Grogan should pick him.   But Tony, after asking advice, picked a powerful young creature called Rogers.   Doyly, much relieved, laid himself in front of Winter's eyes again, but with no success ;   Winter selected another.   Doyly muttered his disappointment, and turned his anxious eyes towards Tony.

"Doyly," called Tony.

With a grimace of philosophic acceptance, Doyly marched to the new master's side.   " Not long," went Tony's autonomous thinking.   " It'll be a different story soon."

The sides selected, they ran out excitedly to the playing-field. Over it lay a brilliant sunlight in which the birds were rejoicing with competitive songs.   In a few seconds that which had been an empty meadow was dotted with running boys, whose red-and-yellow shirts and flashing white knees heightened its greenness and their own brilliance.   The singing of the birds withdrew behind the noisier shouting of the boys, and the pounding on the ground of the ball, which flew low sometimes, and high sometimes, and once so high that none could see it, for the sun was looking at it too.   It thumped and pounded again, drawing after it a riot of red-and-yellow shirts, and the racing white shirts of Winter and Tony, and even the black monument of Mr. Sugden, who had come to bless the opening of the game—a ball—a ball dancing and bouncing on the grass—the one Pied Piper that draws all Englishmen at a run to its music.

Everywhere light, and liveliness, and sparkling air !   Tony, feeling the breeze break on his knees and his naked throat, and pass through his hair, was lifted to a keenness, a restlessness, a breath-taking impatience to be away and about with the game.   Come on !   Come on !   Let's get started.   He felt charged with energy, bursting with goals ;   confident that he could play this game against its kings.

The two young masters placed the men.

"Where do you generally play, Doyly?" asked Tony.

"Inside Right, sir."

"Well, you'll have to put up with a pretty awful Outside Right, because if I can play anywhere in this infantile game, which I doubt, it's there. Keep me properly fed, and I'll feed you."

"Right you are, sir!"

They had started. Tony ran up and down his wing, shouting instructions to his side. Now his full-back had sent the ball with a powerful kick far ahead of him, and he was racing for it, with a speed no other pair of legs on the field could equal. Tony had been known for speed and deftness on the Rugger fields of St. Paul's, and, though he was strictly no Soccer player, these qualities clothed him now (to the easy worship of boys) with the glitter of an International. His foot met the ball just before Winter, the opposing full-back could take it; and with a neat feint, he had outwitted Winter and was racing for the goal. He heard the voice of Doyly, his Inside Right, shouting: "Oh, good, sir, *good!* Well played, I say! . . . Oh, played, sir! *Played!*" Easily he might have run towards the centre and scored, but instead he looked behind, passed the ball to Doyly, and cried, "Shoot, kid! Shoot!" Doyly immediately shot the ball fifteen feet wide of the goal. A groan from his own side met a shout from the other, and all walked back for the goal-keeper's kick, the younger boys debating whether or not the new master "could be an International if he liked."

Ten and a dozen times this happened: a rush by the new master down his wing; some skilful footwork that left his opponents standing; and merry cheers from the boys behind. Every time did he hold back from scoring, and transfer the ball to his Centre Forward or his Inside Right; and twice did Doyly, now much excited, score from the pass. There was little room in Tony's mind for any remembrance of his contest with Winter, but once when a cannon-ball shot from his own foot sent the ball through the goal-posts, and past the goal-keeper who had no hesitation about dodging it instead of meeting it, and a great part of the way towards Wolstonbury, and when Doyly screamed with joy and laughter, and the smaller boys behind did Indian war dances, the thought peeped, "I'm outgunning him this afternoon."

" By gad, sir," said Doyly, when they were walking back to the centre line, after this murderous goal. " I thought you said you couldn't play Soccer."

" Nor I can.   I'm a Rugger player."

" Well, you're better than any master we've ever had."

" Stuff ! " demurred Tony.

When the game was over, the enthusiastic Doyly, with three goals out of six to his account, walked back at the new master's side ; he wanted to talk about the game.   But Tony, giving a quick glance behind, saw Winter strolling home alone, and Pity halted him.   He waited for his colleague to come up and join them.   And Doyly, seeing Winter and remembering his existence, went immediately towards him, in sorrow for his neglect, and with that attractive affectionateness, so like a girl's. But the automatic register in Tony, working despite his inter-dict, recorded that the capture of Doyly's allegiance would be none too difficult an operation, did he choose to advance. The very first assay appeared to have carried the outer works.

That night he chanced to be in the passage outside the class-rooms just before the elder boys would be dismissed to bed. He waited a minute that he might say good night to Doyly, but there was no sound as of the boys preparing to come out, so he told himself to pursue his road to the Common Room.   But he was powerless to move from the passage.   He looked at the pictures on the wall, studied the newel of the staircase, and trifled with some exercise books lying on a hall table.   Twice and thrice he bade himself begone, but still stayed.   What was he waiting for ?   He hardly knew. . . . To say good night to Doyly, away from the eyes of Winter ? . . . He supposed so— and unspeakably silly it sounded. . . . Yet why ?   Why ? . . . How could one control the longings of one's heart ?   They went one's way, laughing at one's efforts at prohibition or direction.

And then Doyly emerged with a troop of other boys, and, seeing him, ran up to say good night.

" Oh . . . good night, Doyly," answered Tony, feigning surprise.   And, taking the boy's hand, he gave it a pressure that would hint at his dawning affection.   He knew his subject : for Doyly flushed a little, looked eagerly into his eyes, and returned the pressure with a significance unmistakable.   He even hung on to Tony's hand when it was for drawing itself away.   Tony's heart leapt.

CHAPTER III

TONY was interested and happy at Stratton Lye. He liked to wander, when his work was done, in the roads and lanes, and watch the game of racing shadows which the clouds played on the long green bareness of the downs; or to cycle at an angle towards these hills and to see how they changed their shapes as he drew nearer and nearer along the winding road; to see a smooth and gentle face becoming a high shoulder, and a steep escarpment swinging into an easy gradient, and Wolstonbury lifting its breast, like a proud chief at the head of his column. Strangely moved, he would exclaim aloud: "There's nothing quite like them—nothing!" Or he would clamber alone to the top of Wolstonbury, and look down upon the whole weald, and see the last sunlight on the slants of tillage and pasture and on the roundness of the trees.

He liked the boys; he liked the work of teaching them and the duty of playing with them; he liked Winter and Browning and La Motte; and he was amused by, and consequently not without a fondness for, Mr. Sugden. And no one was to know that this general happiness had been given the one needful light, when the class-rooms, playing-fields, passages and stairways of Stratton Lye became the theatre of a secret game. No one was to know that his thoughts were lit, in the daytime and the night time, by the drama of forging a link between Doyly and himself.

Winter had had no chance against the varied artillery that Tony, almost unwillingly, had arrayed against him. The new master, having won the enthusiastic suffrages of the boys by his performances on the football field, by his entertaining lessons in the class-rooms, and by the stories he would tell them on Sunday walks, so that they quarrelled to walk at his side, had but to disclose his favouritism to Doyly, occasionally to withdraw it, and then to vouchsafe it again, for the boy to accept it with delight, be jealous of its possession, and come seeking it when he thought it had slipped away. Winter accepted his loss, and as he was of coarser make than Tony, probably felt it less than his supplanter would have done. "Frank has a craze for you now," he said, one Sunday afternoon when they returned from a walk with the boys, throughout which Doyly had hung on Tony's arm; and Tony, reddening, replied: "What rot! He likes us all."

Though ashamed of his submersion in the game, he would sometimes wonder why. How could there be anything wrong in it? As Winter had once said, the thoughts that gave him the greatest pleasure were those of doing the boy service, of influencing him along the highest ways, of stirring up his intellect and maturing his taste, of being a power for good whom he would remember in later years. Surely love, wheresoever and howsoever it lifted its face, must be a good thing.

And yet to no one—not even the most sympathetic and least conventional judgment in the world—could he have told some of the hidden pastimes in which his game involved him. Could he have told that at evening time when, not being on duty, he was free to take a walk in the country roads, he would escape before Winter or Browning could suggest himself as a companion, so that he might indulge long thoughts of his pupil; and that in the hours when he dressed himself for football or church, he had the admiring eyes of Doyly in mind; or that at night when the elder boys were just getting into bed, he would pass along the passage humming, so that Doyly might hear him and rush out, as he often did, with his "Good night, sir," and then in the silence and half-dark of the passage he would give and receive from the boy that significant pressure of the hand? He knew too that the tacit understanding, now established between himself and Frank, was not only a delight to both of them but had passed, to the boy's knowledge as well as his own, into the regions of secrecy.

To stage in imagination dramatic scenes in which he plunged to Doyly's rescue, or stood loyally by the boy when all the world ostracized him—was it, or was it not, contemptible? Ninety-nine out of a hundred people would certainly laugh such imaginings to scorn, but which of them had not done precisely the same thing when a single person reigned in their minds?

Of only one of his moods was he confident that a wrongness flushed it. He was worried to learn again that, as in the old days when his desire to possess another person had first visited him in the shape of little Wavers, the thought of punishing Doyly was a pleasant thought, not lightly to be driven away. Stories he had read of kindly and popular masters punishing boys, and then with a swift change to gentleness converting their resentment into gratitude—some similar experiences of his own at Colet Court and St. Paul's—came into his mind and stayed there assertively. He thrust the thought into duress; but as so often happens, the pent dream, when an opportunity presented itself, sprang out and shaped into action, before he knew what was happening.

It was one evening during Preparation. Tony, as Master on Duty, was sitting in a leisurely attitude at his table. The boys were working before him, the younger at smaller desks in front, the elder at larger desks behind. The silence was disturbed only by the scratching of nibs, the rustle of book-pages, and the occasional shuffling of feet. Tony's glance falling on the bent head of Doyly, he judged from the movement of the boy's pen that he was not writing but drawing. He kept him under observation, and saw him pass his completed drawing to his neighbour, Rogers, with a suppressed giggle. Rogers grinned and passed the paper to the next boy, Chapman, who, grinning in his turn, was about to do the same friendly office for his neighbour, when Tony addressed him:

"Chapman, don't pass it on. Bring it up to me instead."

Chapman, glancing up, pretended an ignorance of the master's meaning; and Tony spoke sharply.

"Don't gape like a fool. Bring that paper to me."

Reddening, the boy stepped out of his desk, walked to the master's table, and laid down the paper. Tony picked it up. It held a crude representation of all four masters sitting in the Common Room; their mortar-boards and gowns hung on hooks by the door, the clock showed the hour to be eight o'clock, the moon through the window suggested that it was night, and below was written:

> The Saints of God, their wanderings done,
> No more their weary course they run,
> O happy saints, for ever blest,
> In that dear home how sweet your rest.

Tony compressed his smile, and said : " This is your work, Doyly, isn't it ? "

" Yes, sir."

There was too much promptness about his answer to please Tony, too much confidence in his master's easiness, too little apology.

" All right," he said unsmilingly. " Then you had better come up here instead of Chapman."

Doyly, perceiving at once the unexpected hardness in the voice, exchanged places with Chapman ; and, at the same time, his confident air retired in favour of a grinning foolishness.

" This is a very fine picture," said Tony, after examining it thoughtfully, " and it must have taken you a considerable time to draw. I suppose you have given up the last half-hour to it."

Doyly had no answer beyond his awkward grin.

" Well, you'll admit," continued Tony, " that you owe me a half-hour of work, in addition to which you deserve half an hour's punishment for disturbing your neighbours. I imagine it'll take you about an hour to learn by heart the first fifty lines of your Æneid, Book VI. I will hear you say them to-morrow. Thank you. Go to your seat."

It was a severe punishment, as Tony saw, immediately he had announced it ; the conning of fifty difficult Latin lines would certainly pack a good hour ; but he resolved that he would not retreat from what he had said ; and to establish himself in such a punishment, chose to think very seriously of Doyly's offence, and to endorse his own justice in showing no favouritism.

Doyly's face heated with surprise and rising anger.

" Fifty lines, sir ? "

" Yes. Fifty lines. That was what I said."

" I can't do that in an hour, sir."

" Then do it in two."

" But you said——" began the boy.

" Go to your seat, and don't argue."

Flourishing sullenness like a flag—muttering a declaration of war—Doyly turned about and walked towards his place while Tony, rather weakly, began to justify his anger further. "I don't like boys who when they've had their fun and are found out, begin to bleat."

Round came Doyly's face and the flash of his eyes. " I'm *not* bleating." There was no " sir " now.

Tony took no notice, but ostentatiously opened a book and read. He felt hot and unreasonably eager to utter stinging words; and withal, happy, alive, exulting. Why was it always an exultant hour when you were quarrelling with the person you liked? Why was it certain that Doyly, in his surging vindictiveness, felt happy, alive and exultant too? Why did both know that they meant more to each other than ever when they squared up for battle?

Mr. Sugden had instructed Tony to hear the " Latin Repetition " of the elder boys at the close of Preparation, so, at eight o'clock, he summoned them to stand in a row before him and recite " *O fons Bandusiæ, splendidior vitro.*" Doyly took his place sulkily in the row, and when his turn came to recite the ode, muttered three lines and petered out into silence.

" Go on," said Tony quietly.

" I can't."

" Why ? "

" Because I don't know it, I suppose."

Tony was cool now, and remembered that there were times when cold water was more painful than hot.

" I'm sorry. I'll secure you a few quiet moments to learn it, when Preparation is over. I will stay here and help you."

There was a strange allurement in the prospect of holding the boy imprisoned, and playing in an empty class-room this game of quiet master and rebellious pupil.

When, five minutes later, he announced to the other boys that they could go, Doyly rose to go too, as if he had failed to understand, or declined to take seriously, his master's suggestion that he stayed behind and learned the ode.

Sharp as a sergeant's command shot Tony's words: " *Sit down*, Doyly ! " It overawed Doyly, who sat down. The boys filed out, and they were alone.

Doyly's head was bowed over his book; not once did he look up, and Tony was free to stare at that favourite head and savour with pleasure the resentments and rebellions that were seething there. The clock on the wall, from being unheeded, now became a major presence, ticking away the minutes, with a noisy indifference to the conflict beneath its gaze. When fifteen of these minutes had been ticked and dismissed, and the long hand lay horizontally on the quarter, Tony, acting an ignorance of his victim's rebellion, called pleasantly :

" Let me see if you can repeat that ode now, Doyly."

With an obedience insolently mechanical, Doyly rose heavily from his seat, approached the table, and stood there, wordless.

" Fire away," commanded Tony, maintaining his offensive high spirits.

" *O fons Bandusiæ, splendidior vitro. . . .*" Doyly recited the same three lines, his parrotry boldly underlined. At the end of the third line he stopped, defeated, and stared at the wall ahead.

" You don't seem to know it yet."

" No."

" How is that ?   Has your brain ceased to function ? "

" I don't know."

Looking at the sullen, averted face, Tony told himself that he had never liked it so well. " You wouldn't trouble to fight anyone else but me," he thought. " Stupid kid ! You're proving everything that you want to disprove." And he decided that a swift change from sarcasm to kindness might be ventured now.

" Aren't you being rather foolish, Frank ? "

No answer, but perhaps a swelling beneath Doyly's averted eyes.

" Why not learn it, my boy, and get it over ? "

For an instant Doyly turned his eyes towards his master's face, as if he were about to surrender ; and a lesser insight than Tony's might have guessed that the boy was longing to rush back into the mutual favouritism which he loved, and to find it deepened by this quarrel. But sullenness had rooted quick and tightly, and was not to be dislodged at the first prod of the weeding hook ; so he turned his eyes adrift again, to stare unresponsively at the maps on the wall.

" You persist in being a mule, then ? "

A silence ; reminding Tony of his own dumbness before the masters at Colet Court ; flattering him with the thought that his rôle was now changed from pupil to master.

" Come along, old man ; let's do it together, and forget all about it."

" I'd do it if it were fair," said Doyly suddenly.

" *Fair !* What do you mean ? "

The boy conceded no explanation.

" Now, Doyly, I should be perfectly justified in doubling your imposition for that piece of impudence, but I won't put more on the mule's back that he can bear. Sit down and learn that ode. I shall return at Prayer-time, and hear it. If you don't know it then, we can easily pursue our efforts in our spare time to-morrow."

With the same mechanical action which so successfully robbed obedience of its essential quality and converted it into mutiny, Doyly returned to his seat; and Tony, parading his ease and good spirits, walked out of the door, closing it on a prisoner. At Prayer-time, as he expected, the rebel proffered no more of the ode than before. Deciding to swing back to anger, Tony looked with a set jaw into the boy's face. He met a gaze that was now addressed defiantly to his own, as a sword-point stares at a sword-point. And there was a pink flush on Doyly's forehead.

"This knot gets tighter, doesn't it?" said Tony. "It looks as though it will need a cane to cut it. . . . Good night."

Doyly's eyes threw to him, for a good night, the sharpest stiletto that savagery could whet. It pierced Tony with delight.

Between Tony and any other of the boys, that threat of a flogging could have meant no more than a report to Mr. Sugden and a request for the intervention of his cane, since it was no custom of the assistant masters to administer corporal punishment. But to Tony and Doyly, who knew that their relationship had passed beyond the commonplace traffic of schoolmaster and schoolboy into a region where both could trust that their movements would be for ever secret to themselves, the words had suggested a liquidation of the debt in a private caning administered by Tony. And as that evening wore on, Tony, blinding his own insight which might have whispered uncomfortable truths, persuaded himself that in such a proceeding there could be found an adjustment that would satisfy the honour of both; he would offer to the boy, when his rebellion should be melting, the choice of three cuts with the cane as an alternative to his heavy impositions; and Doyly, who was as histrionic as most boys, would see at once which was the picturesque road and take it unhesitatingly, preening himself on his fortitude. Tony read Doyly perfectly, because Doyly was so like what he himself had been as a boy.

In the morning at breakfast Doyly, who had recently fought
for and conquered a seat at the new master's side, most ostentatiously went to his old place on the left of Winter, and there
talked and laughed noisily.   And when the meal was over he
made it his task to be seen of Tony, hanging on Winter's arm.
" Little ass ! " laughed Tony to himself, much gratified at
these patent snubs.   In the half-hour before Classes, in the
Break, in the half-hour before Lunch, Doyly persisted in
his sullenness, marching obediently into the class-room, but
learning nothing ; and all the while Tony, acting no less,
flaunted before Doyly his occupation with a hundred matters
much more important than a pupil's sulks.

It was after lunch, when all the other boys had gone out to
football, that he made his move.

" Come here, Doyly," he called to the only boy left in the
room.   And Doyly, a machine without a will, came and stood
before him.

" You want to go out and play football with the others too,
don't you, Frank ? "

" Not particularly."

" Oh yes, you do.   Well, hadn't we better see how we can
solve our little trouble ?   I understand, old man, exactly what
you're feeling ; you don't want to give in, and nor do I.   It's
all very natural.   Shall we put our heads together and see
what's to be done about it ? "

Doyly had turned his face away, and was looking out of the
window.

" You said I wasn't fair.   Well, let's think it out.   You will
admit that you deserved some punishment for drawing sketches
during Prep, and disturbing your neighbours with them.   Of
course you will.   But because you chose to think my punishment rather severe, you have been unpardonably rebellious
ever since, refusing to learn your Horace, and refusing to do my
impositions ; and what's happened ?   I have added nothing
to your punishment for all this, because I understood your
feelings, so you haven't come off too badly, have you ? "

Tears were embarrassing Doyly's eyes, and he had no way
to deny them, except by bringing his face round to his master's,
and letting a smile break at the lips.

" Well, Doyly, we must put an end to this frowsty staying indoors over a book.   I'll make a fair offer to you : would you
prefer to take from me three strokes of the cane, instead of

your impositions ? If you like to do that, I'll consider all our accounts squared. . . . I can't doubt which alternative a boy of your calibre'll choose. What do you say, Doyly ? "

Yes, Tony had read his man well : Doyly, pleased with the compliment, and eager to play the heroic rôle, replied brightly : " Of course, sir, I'll take the caning."

" I thought you would," said Tony approvingly. " Go then and wait in the Third Form class-room."

" Yes, sir." And with the smartness of a soldier who goes fearlessly to the firing squad, he walked out of the room.

Like many young men in those days Tony possessed a " swagger cane," whose purpose was less to advance his walking by a pressure on the ground than to encourage his thinking by a twirling in the air. After allowing a few minutes to pass he strolled into the lobby and took this cane from the masters' hatstand. The deeper parts of him, which were in protest against his actions, had no chance just now of rising above the strange pleasure that occupied his mind. What was there wrong in this proceeding ? Nothing. Rather was there generosity and understanding in it, as Doyly had immediately seen. Only a foolishly introspective person like himself would notice this strange enjoyment and worry about it ; a normal person would be satisfied with his skilful management of a difficult, if affectionate, pupil. What rider was ashamed of using rein and whip on a high-mettled pony ? With his cane in his hand, he entered the Third Form class-room.

The afternoon sun was slanting on to the walls through the tall windows ; and the voices of the footballers and the whistling of the referees came floating over their lowered sashes. A breeze lifted a blind and slacked it again, so that its acorn beat sleepily on the glass ; and a trail of clematis, tumbled from the trellis work above, peeped against a pane, like an eavesdropper. Why the sunlight, and the happiness of the voices and the peace of the swaying clematis should deject Tony he could not say ; nor must he betray any malaise now. Doyly, with his hands in his pockets, was looking out of a window at a bird on the lawn ; and he turned round, on his master's entrance, and formed with his lips a suppressed grimace, in humour's cause. And Tony, in a manner supremely natural and friendly, said :

" We'll get through this quickly, Frank. Bend over that desk."

A shade paler, the boy obeyed. He obeyed with promptness

lest he should appear afraid. But in his right knee, as Tony
noticed, there was an involuntary vibration.

Sharply came the cane's first cut—so sharply that Doyly
quivered. And Tony, seeing that quiver, caught his breath
in an instant sympathy. Shame sent the blood to his brow,
where a moisture broke. The next two cuts were formal—
no more.

Maintaining his affectation of merriness and ease, he said :
" There ; that's over, Frank, and thank goodness. Our
accounts are all square now."

Doyly straightened himself and smiled his gratitude. It was
certain that *he* was feeling nothing except a gratification with
himself and a deeper affection for his master ; Doyly, at all
events, would never see in this incident aught of what Tony
was seeing ; he would have forgotten it in an hour's time, or
would recall it only with satisfaction.

But not so Tony. By sustained effort he flew all that afternoon his flag of naturalness and good spirits. He talked gaily
with Doyly and the other boys, when they walked back from
the football field ; and none of them knew that it was a strain
for him to hold his thoughts on the surface, and not to sink
them into profound questionings.

But when Tea was over and he was free, he hurriedly took
his stick—the same stick that he had employed in the Third Form
room that afternoon—and escaped from Stratton Lye for a
walk alone. And soon he found that he had left the houses
and cottages behind him and was following a meadow track
towards the Downs. The sun, dropping beside the western-
most reach of the downs, was washing their cheeks with colour
and filling their folds with shadow. Wolstonbury, round as
the top of a world, loomed ahead of him, with all its surface,
save for one wedge of light, mantled in a dark serenity ;
Wolstonbury, quiet, self-sufficient, contemplative, and remote
from the bewilderments of the men at its foot. Angry tears
could have spurted to his eyes ; his distaste for the afternoon's
memory, now free to enlarge, had lifted and swelled till it became
a sick disgust with himself—a disgust that so rejoiced in its
complete triumph that it would allow no validity to countering
arguments, but bore them down with oaths, giving quarter to
none. " Oh *damn ! damn !* Why did I do it ? Why, when
I care for the boy . . .? Damn ! " The oath, bursting aloud
from him every time he faced the memory, became at last

rhythmic and melancholy, and he would accompany it with angry swishes at the tall yellow grasses. For a moment, as his cane lopped off a head, he had a fancy to snap the weapon savagely in pieces, as a violent ratification of his " Never again ! " But he refrained, for a part of his disgust was with all fine scenes that his imagination staged. The thought came to him : " Well, there it is ! Why worry ? What's done can't be undone, and I suppose we've all got things in our past that we should be ashamed to tell to a living soul. . . . Why are we made like this ? " But he refused the comfort of excuses and extenuations, and, running over the old words : " Why did I do it ? *Why ?* " walked on and on, his worry unhealed.

CHAPTER IV

HOME AGAIN

THE memory of this day, washing like an acid over Tony's affection for Frank Doyly, graved it deep. Dwelling again and again on his surrender to the disquieting things that muddy our human love, he would exclaim : " No, dammit, no ! When I love, I love too well for *that*. I don't want to hurt Frank. I want to help him, and to give much to him."

And in this idea of helping Doyly he discovered both a balm for his conscience and a pleasant pastime. On the football field he gave pains—rather noisy pains—to training the boy ; in the Preparation Room he helped him with his Latin Elegiacs and Greek Conditional Sentences (not averse to showing that, though he took only a junior form, he was more than master of these senior subjects), and he knew that he disentangled the boy's difficulties with a lucidity and sympathy above that of Browning and La Motte, since his imagination and youthful keenness were brighter than theirs ; and on Sunday walks, when the loyal Frank was hooked on to his arm, he would talk for hours of the passages in literature that delighted him, while Frank, ever ready to take fire at enthusiasm, would sparkle with pleasure when he understood, and rumple his brow with frustrated desire when he was failing to understand.

Doyly had no talent for speaking aloud of the affection he obviously felt. But, so odd and English was his make-up, he was as ready to show it by actions as he was shy of mentioning it in words. He had never any hesitation in fighting to walk by Mr. O'Grogan's side, or in emerging from his dormitory to say a second good night, if he heard Tony's voice in the passage ; but he drew back from the language of affection, preferring the language of impudence and mock-rebellion. That he wanted his affection told, but by other lips than his, was proved one day when Tony lifted from the tray in the hall a letter in an unrecognized hand. He opened it curiously, and turning first to the signature, read the name of Doyly's father.

" *Dear Sir* (the father had written),

" *My boy, Frank Doyly, is very enthusiastic about ' the new master,' and writes in almost every letter to tell us of the great pains you have taken with his work and games. My wife and I feel we should like to thank you for this, and to assure you that Frank himself is more than grateful. Perhaps the simplest way to assure you of this is to quote the following sentence from the latest letter of this odd youth : ' I often wish,' he writes, ' that I could tell him that I am frightfully pleased, and all that sort of thing, but it would sound so silly, wouldn't it ? ' Why it should sound silly is not as clear as the sunlight to us, but perhaps that is because we are getting old and have forgotten what it was like to be thirteen . . ."*

Tony always counted the arrival of this letter as one of the richer moments of his life.

So the term waned, and the five weeks of the Christmas holidays crept closer till they stood at a distance of days only. They brought a dim disappointment to Tony, for they showed that in Doyly's mind Christmas and Holidays weighed heavier in the scales than any adoration staged at school. Sometimes, remembering that even the boy's father had failed to see anything silly in the frank admission of good-will, he would play with the idea of speaking out to Doyly, in simple, direct words, something of his affection and his eagerness to help him. The phrasing of the sentences and the picturing of the scene would engross him during his lonely walks in the country roads. He placed the scene a class-room, where he and Frank would be standing alone just before they parted for the holidays, and there he would extend his hand and begin : " Look here, Frank, I've long believed that we all of us make our lives the poorer, because of our sickly fear of saying things that savour of prettiness. There's no sense in holding them back really. Life isn't so full of good things that we can afford to deny our friends anything that will please them. So I am jolly well going to say to you what I want to say : it's just this ; I've learnt this term—somehow or other—God knows why—to feel a very profound affection for you. Well, I just want you to know that

that affection's there, and that its one desire is to serve and help you——" here he would smile kindly—" in every possible way. I always think, don't you, that for all of us there is a wonderful support in feeling behind us someone's very real and quite unshakeable affection." And Frank, in wordless gratitude, would smile and give his answer through the pressure of his hand. Then Tony would say : " Good-bye, old man ; have a good holiday." And Frank would reply : " Good-bye, sir ; thanks most awfully for all you've done——" which Tony would interrupt, putting a hand on his shoulder and pushing him to the door. " There, there. That's nothing, that's nothing, old chap. Good-bye."

Whether he would say these things he could not determine ; he longed to do so, and would tell himself that, as a good Irishman, there was no need for him to be a slave to the accursed shyness that ruled among the inhabitants of this quaint and foggy England, and that even laid its ban on so bright and full a nature as Doyly's. Poor old England ! Amusing and rather lovable old England ! But the O'Grogans were Irish, and properly demonstrative ; all except Derek, who had solemnly donned the whole panoply of English conventions— Derek, the family's one compleat Englishman ! Poor old Derek ! Amusing and rather lovable old Derek ! But why shouldn't he, Tony, do his diligence to be himself ? And yes, he would ; be damned to it, he would.

The last day came, and he wondered if he would produce his little act, not in the bustle of next morning's departures, but in the quiet of some class-room that evening, as he was saying good night to Doyly. The opportunity came. Bed time had announced itself noisily, and Doyly, last out from Prayers, was standing opposite him in the empty hall, all the others, including the Master on Duty, having bounded up the stairs, like a herd of chamois at the promise of food.

" Good night, sir."

" Good night, Frank. . . . Good night."

And there ! . . . the opportunity had gone.

It was as well. To-morrow morning would be the right time ; to-morrow just after breakfast, when the long procession of station flies appeared on the drive.

And the next morning he strolled about the class-rooms and passages, and when he imagined he was hearing the flies in the distance, walked into an empty room, in the certainty that

Doyly would find him there, to bid him farewell.   And Doyly burst in, almost immediately behind him.

"Hallo, Frank," he greeted.

"Hallo, sir."   The boy dropped into diffidence.   "I—I thought I'd come and say good-bye before the cabs come."

"Oh, yes. . . . Well, good-bye.   Have a good holiday," said Tony ; and no more.

He returned home to learn from the busy lips of Keatings, Joyce and Peggy, whose indolent pens had told him nothing, a full tale of some remarkable changes in the lives of two of the family—Joyce and Derek.   In enlarging on these changes Joyce's lips were the most active, while Derek's were not active at all ; nor even present, for the most part, because Derek seldom took his seat in the Family parliament.   Joyce had "started on her own," she said, "as a free-lance Lady Journalist." She had her own typing paper, headed :   "Joyce Duveen, The Authority on Women's Affairs," and on this she typed "bright and attractive pars" for half a dozen of the most popular London dailies.   These were paid for and even commissioned, but the similar leaves which she scattered on the penny weeklies, such as *Home Talk* and *The Gossip* and *Queries* were less success- ful ; some of them dropped into safe resting places, but many of them floated out of her sight and were heard of no more.   Still, she was making better money than the pound a week, at which the *Chiswick and Gunnersbury Times* had valued her pen.

The Women's Affairs, on which, with no justice whatever, she had announced herself to be the Authority, consisted, it seemed, in information about the private lives of the great. She attended what she called "functions ;" four, five, or six of them a day ; and seeking out the celebrities in the room, made them sit by her side and deliver up to her notebook their habits, their hobbies, their past and future movements, and any of their domestic secrets that might be marketable.   "Please— please—you must give me a story," she would protest, and she would put an expectant pencil to her lips in a way that was quite irresistible—or so she said.   "It's a blood-sucking business, certainly, but hugely jolly, and I'm hugely good at it."

The celebrities whose blood was most saleable, said Joyce, were Society Ladies and Literary Men. Bishops and Archdeacons went well, but not Deans, and no clergy of lesser title. " Can't sell the ungaitered at all ! " Criminal lawyers were brisk, but not such a good line as Criminals. Indeed, she'd put murderers at the top of the list, only there were so few of them, unfortunately. No, Society and its fauna were the kind of malarial country which bred such pestilent mosquitoes as herself. And there was a remarkable parallel, my Tony, between the career of a Society " par " and the career of the Society lady about whom it was written ; if it contained ever so little a title it started life with the brightest of chances, but if it held a thumping big title, it was sure not only of immediate acceptance, but of high prominence and high pay. Only draw the blood of a Duchess or a Marchioness, and you could spend its proceeds before you had even posted it to the newspaper. Which was partly right (maintained Joyce, with a sideways nod) because these ladies were distinctly press-shy and difficult to conquer. Whereas the literary men—ah, the literary men were a very different story.

" Oh, I've taken some jars ! It's been the biggest shock of my journalistic career. There's no difficulty with most authors, my children ; if you don't go and hover about them, bless their sweet little hearts, they come and hover about you. People whose names in my childhood stood only one degree below God's I now draw to my side with no greater effort than a parade of my notebook and my pencil. Up they come, bursting with information about their forthcoming books. They waddle up in files, like geese coming to drink. Sometimes I'm half afraid they'll queue up. But they're rather sweet with their pretence that they don't care for publicity, so I do what I can for them. I hope I've helped one or two. And they sell well—that's the funny thing. Nobody'd want to read about them if they could see them, and yet they sell next best to the murderers and the duchesses. And here's another funny thing : with Women's Suffrage all the noise, you'd think that the Authority on Women's Affairs ought to do a big trade in the private lives of the Suffragettes, wouldn't you ? but they don't sell at all. It's only their public lives that are marketable, and of course the reporters have netted all that. For every Suffragette I sell to a Woman's paper, I could get rid of half a dozen male novelists, and oh, three dozen duchesses. And, of course, Royalty, if only you could get them . . ." she added wistfully.

But if Joyce wanted to discourse on her own activities,

Keatings and Peggy were more eager to tell the mystery of Derek. And Joyce, once she saw that this secondary, but quite interesting, topic had displaced her own, accepted the disappointment and launched her chatter into the new waters with an eagerness no less than her brother's and sister's. Derek, they explained, had quarrelled with his Headmaster, resigned his post, and steamed for home, with all the flags of his *amour propre* flying high on the mast. "So he says, but he most probably got the sack," suggested Keatings, over his pipe.

"No, he didn't," Peggy denied. "He told the Headmaster what he thought of him, and gave notice straight away."

"That's the way he puts it."

"Well, why not believe him ?" Peggy pouted.

"Because," Keatings submitted, "he's a born liar."

"He isn't ! He's much too proud to tell lies. He's got more character than any of you."

"That's true, thank God. Character in such quantities becomes uncomfortable for everybody."

"It means he isn't a liar, at any rate."

"Oh, he doesn't *know* that he lies, poor lad. That's his weakness ; he persuades himself that he's done something very fine, and misrepresents facts accordingly."

Peggy rustled with annoyance. "I can't see why you shouldn't believe that what he says is true. After all, he's ours, and the Headmaster isn't." Always Peggy's resolve to believe in her family was a little like her struggle to accept the dogmas of her Church ; she believed, and prayed the Family to help her unbelief. "And anyhow," she added, "he had decided to leave at the end of the term. He says there's no money in schoolmastering, and no future."

Keatings turned to Tony.

"You must understand that Peggy's going through a period of adoration for Derek. But it can't last."

"And she's only doing it," Joyce explained, "because she's having a highly religious season just now, and thinks she ought to love everybody she detests."

"Idiots !" said Peggy, flushing.

"Yes, but what's Derek doing now ?" asked Tony, anxious to recover the main point.

Joyce looked at Keatings, and Peggy looked at Joyce and Keatings, and both girls broke into laughter.

"No one knows," said Joyce. "He goes out after breakfast

every morning, and he seems to have more money in his pocket that can have been honestly come by, but if you try to get out of him what his job is, he only grins."

" He's a fool," Keatings pronounced.

" Fool or not, he's making money," said Peggy.

" Oh, yes," agreed Keatings. " That type does."

" But what do you *think* he's doing ? " persisted Tony.

" I've my suspicions," Keatings began ; but before he could uncurtain them, Joyce intruded *her* suggestion ; she whispered it, as if it were a suggestion of murder.

" I think he's money-lending."

" No." Keatings shook his head. " No. It's not that, though doubtless he'll take to that soon."

" Well, he dresses up to the eyebrows. Is he a shopwalker, do you think ? "

" God, no ! Nothing so *déclassé* and honest as that."

" Well, what is it ? What's *your* suspicion ? "

Keatings knocked out his pipe and began to fill it, teasing her with delay.

" Oh, *what*, confound you ! " she demanded impatiently.

" I think it's Daylight Burglary." Having offered this, Keatings put a match to his pipe, and added between his puffs : " At least that's all I can think of. He's probably been reading too much ' Raffles.' He's a gentleman cracksman. Yes, I'm sure of it."

" Oh, how ripping ! " cried Joyce. " But no, that's not my idea."

" Well, what's yours ? "

Joyce's mouth took the first steps towards a mischievous smile, but fell back to solemnity again. Her eyes stared with admirable gravity into the trouble ahead.

" I'm afraid—I'm dreadfully afraid," she said, " that it's the White Slave Traffic."

That Joyce, in her new adventuring with her notebook, was happy, and that Keatings, in his quiet, undistinguished work at the Insurance Office, was not unhappy, Tony saw ; but he was less satisfied about Peggy's happiness. All her smiles were decorative and obliging rather than sincere, and her high spirits had none of the naturalness of Joyce's, and perished much quicker. She would sink easily into her own depths, and, when charged with it by the others, would come to the surface with a flush, a smile, and a radiant denial.

"Peggy has all the symptoms of a Secret Sorrow," said Tony to Keatings and Joyce.

"It's probably Derek," suggested Keatings.

But it was not Derek. It was simply that she was let and hindered in the current lap of her spiritual race. Peggy had discovered soon after their arrival in Chiswick, a church, distant not three-quarters of an hour in the bus, where the ceremonial was so richly suggestive, the music so luxuriously soothing, and the pious gestures and posturing of the congregation so satisfying if you quietly copied them, and the vestments of the clergy so flattering to them, and the idea of calling these kindly ascetics "Father" such a last irresistible attraction that she longed to surrender herself to these things with a perfect understanding and the serenest faith. And her sin was that she had promptly surrendered to them, but with the most imperfect understanding and without a speck of serenity in her faith. It had been a pure dive into self-gratification, and she had the spiritual vision to see this.

Last Easter Sunday Keatings had wandered into its High Mass, curious to see this church of Peggy's. And there had been "Hail, Festal Day!" carried round the church with trumpets and incense, and with cantors and choristers and copes and dalmatics and tunicles; and an orchestra up in a gallery had accompanied some extraordinary performances in front of the altar with Gounod's "Messe Solennelle;" and the whole congregation had more than once succumbed to the floor, leaving Keatings upright and conspicuous, and when he had copied them rather than feel a fool, they had all risen again and left him kneeling; and at the end of the service Peggy, delighted to see her brother there (he had not been difficult to see), had rushed up to inquire how he had liked it. Keatings who had a marked talent for summing up a complex impression in a sentence, replied: "I'm going home to get a plain dry biscuit." And Peggy, to her discomfort, was conscious of her immediate intellectual agreement. Then Joyce insisted that she must come too, and on Low Sunday, when, according to Peggy, the whole performance would be encored because it was within the octave, Joyce watched it all from a seat by the West Door. The impressions she brought away dealt mainly with the clergy; the tall, middle-aged Senior Assistant Priest, Father Saffery, who had entered from the rainy street with an Inverness cape over his cassock, so that he appeared to be hung about with three skirts, she styled " The All-Weather Model," or " The Three-Decker ; " and the young chubby-faced Junior Priest, Father Williams, she described as the " Good-with-Men-and-Lads-one." Peggy sank into further thought.

What a curse was her clear spiritual vision ! Others could have settled themselves into the lap of such a church if it soothed them, and could have been happy there, and because happy, good. But not she : she was conscious of a hundred falsities ; she knew that her enthusiastic aligning of herself beside the most polemical of the church's workers, and her fervid, well-documented, sometimes insulting advocacy of the church's usages, were acted things ; she knew, too, that just as a man, who is aware of his financial insolvency but conceals it, might involve himself in deeper and deeper waters, so she, who was horribly conscious of her spiritual insolvency but had covered it with this fine costume of logical conviction and proselytizing zeal, was swimming on sadly into desperate seas ; for it was now Christmas time, and all the Church's best members were going to their confession, and she would certainly have to go too. Yes, she must go, for how could she, who had contended against all comers in defence of the Sacrament of Penance, and had even, when hard put to it and rather heated, declared her certainty that it was divinely ordained—how could she diverge from its terrors and slip round it unvisited ? So she swam hopelessly on ; she who could hardly keep afloat swam on in the costume of a champion, towards this disaster.

And to think of all that she would have to confess in the dreadful hour ! Under such spiritual limelights as hers the smallest sin threw a well-marked shadow, and all—all would have to be confessed, else would the confession itself be a sin with a shadow like a mountain's. She would have to speak out all her hypocrisy, and her persistence in it ; she would have to say : " I have only come to Confession to-day because I knew it was expected of me and I was afraid not to. I don't know that I really believe in it at all. I have no real faith that after you, Father, have pronounced absolution, I shall be any more forgiven than I was before I came. In fact, I am not at all sure that I am not committing another sin in coming to you like this. When in the *confiteor* just now I said that I confessed ' to Blessed Mary Ever Virgin, Blessed Michael the Archangel, Blessed John the Baptist, the Holy Apostles Peter and Paul, and all saints, and to you, Father,' I fancy I added another sin to be confessed, because I am not at all sure, really, what I think about the saints. By my hypocrisy, by all my play-acting, by my wilful forcing of my own mind, by the violence I have done to my intellect when arguing with others (it would sound like a litany) I've got myself into such a state that I no longer know which are the things I really believe and which are those I am pretending to believe. And this confession—I've no idea in which category it comes. Honestly, Father, I think if I cleared my mind of all the fog, I should have to say that I believed—yes, it would be the truth—that a simple confession to God in the privacy of my bedchamber, and a promise to Him that, by way of reparation and amendment, I would never come near this High Church again, would leave me with a much greater feeling of pardon and release and confidence than this amazing thing I am doing now."

And difficult, worrying, brow-crumpling as all this was, it was as nothing to a further sin which would surely have to be confessed—though very guardedly and very indirectly. How—in pity, how was she to admit that not only had she forced herself into her present Advanced Beliefs, but also she had been forced there by the action of her heart? The matter was thus: after only a few weeks of attendance at the church she had found her thoughts more and more occupied and her heart more and more monopolized by Father Michael Saffery, the middle-aged but handsome Senior Assistant Priest. And the complication that this unfortunate element introduced into her confession was an extraordinary one; because—explain it who might—or, rather, let no one do so, since the explanation were doubtless horrid—the idea of enumerating her sins and analysing the state of her soul before him, and of asking his counsel and absolution, was so strangely pleasant that it mingled with her fears a delight which transcended them. Here was a problem that threw a huge cross-shadow, and made confusion indeed!

Of course she might have escaped from this additional worry by arranging to make her confession to one of the other priests whose presence did not quicken her heart-beats at all, nor throw a delight over the whole procedure; and she had finally resolved to do this; only Father Michael had come up to her one day and instructed her, as a neophyte, that she should seek the Sacrament of Penance before Christmas morning, and she, bewildered by his proximity, had said, Yes, certainly, she would be delighted to do so; and when he had asked her what arrangements he could make for her and what priest she would desire as her Director, her whole heart had, by a sudden *coup*, overthrown reason and conscience and will, so that she had instantly lifted her eyes to him and said, " Oh, *you*, please." And he, saying " Certainly, my child," had made, while her heart raced in disorder, an appointment for noon on the morning of Christmas Eve. It was all done, and written down in a diary, and committed to his waistcoat pocket before she could say, " No, I didn't mean that. Please—please, I don't want *you*," or think of some less uncivil equivalent.

What was she to do now ? Most certainly she had sinned in thus collapsing before a sweet temptation ; and most certainly such a sin ought to be confessed and its nature explained if absolution were to be valid—but how ? If she were to do real justice to her offending, she ought to say : " When I asked to come and confess my sins to you, I really emptied the confession of all worth by converting it from a misery into a delight. I can only get it back into a misery again by telling you this frankly, but even so, I am not at all sure that it cancels out properly." (Had Peggy been able to submit her troubles to Tony, and he to submit his to her, and had they both had a larger wisdom than was theirs at eighteen and nineteen, they might have seen at last the odd parallel and contrast in their experiences of love—how he in its blindness wanted to wield the whip, and she, in the same blindness, to put herself under one.)

But this was not all. Her conscience was fretted by the wholly sinful desire, in which she trapped herself often, that Father Saffery should be impressed by the exhaustive character of her confession and the profound spiritual insight it revealed. Certainly her manuals and the instruction she had received had taught her that the priest, on these occasions, was no more than an impersonal instrument of the Church, a mere automatic channel of God's grace, but her mind, which could be as acute as her conscience, told her that Father Michael Saffery in the confessional would still be Father Michael Saffery and would know that it was Peggy O'Grogan speaking, and so there must inevitably be a difference in Father Saffery's estimate of Peggy O'Grogan at 12.30 on Christmas Eve from that which he held at noonday. And she was minded that if he must know all the wickedness in her he should have an eye also for the good ; and, meditating on this, she would catch herself preparing the congratulatory words he would address to her : "Before proceeding, my daughter, to counsel and absolution, let me, as the voice of your Mother Church, compliment you on your full and courageous confession. . . ." To have thoughts like this, was it another sin that must in honour be announced ? Must she say, "In this confession which I am now concluding, Father, I have been guilty of a strong desire to impress you."

And if this, the sum of difficulties enveloped in her confession, were not enough to withdraw her from the liveliness of Keatings and Joyce into the fastness of her own thoughts, there was ever with her the sad certainty that she had fallen in love with a priest dedicated to celibacy, who must never—never so much as suspect the inclination of her heart. She had made a ship-wreck of her life.

After protracted meditation in the quiet of her room, she decided, with a sudden shake of the head, that the path of Auricular Confession was entangled enough without the complications introduced by the feet of Father Saffery, and that the only course before her was to escape somehow from her appointment with *him*. It would not be easy, for there was no possibility of explaining her change of front, but there it was : the difficult step ahead of her was her punishment for having yielded so easily to temptation. With no clear idea of what she was going to say, she waylaid the Father next Wednesday night, as he stood at the West Door of the church in his cassock, cape and biretta, after the Service of Preparation for Communicants.

"Excuse me, Father," said she. "May I ask you something ? "

He turned to her, while still shaking hands with the ladies and the children who had queued up to bid him good night. "Yes, my child. Will you wait just a minute ? "

Peggy stood aside, and gazed at the darkness of the distant chancel where the sacristan had already extinguished the lights. Only one light was glimmering at the end of the arches, the little red lamp that hung before the tabernacle on the Lady altar. And while she waited more lights went down in the nave, so that now there was only one burning from each column, and one over the tower door. The nave was a trough of twilight in which two rows of haloed lamps converged towards the blackness of the chancel. Now the last of the congregation had gone, the sacristan was far up the church, walking between the chair-rows to pick up the scattered papers and straighten the disordered hassocks, and Father Saffery was free to turn to her again. " Well, my child, what is it ? " he asked, giving Peggy that smile of especial tenderness which, she sometimes believed, he rested on her alone. As he asked it, he pushed each hand and wrist up the opposite sleeve, and laid the sleeves, thus joined, along the front of his cincture.

Peggy's eyes swung away ; and, feeling that his gaze had fixed on her, her wayward blood rushed to her brow and down her neck and throat. Speak she must, but what ?

" Please, Father, would you mind if I made my confession to someone else ? "

Oh, he was staring at her, not answering her at once : had she offended him, or had she—worse still, making her colour deeper—had she revealed anything to him ? "

" Certainly, my child, but why ? "

" Oh, I don't know, but . . ."

No more—she could think of no more to say—what a fool she had made of herself !—why hadn't she prepared properly a whole chain of lies, even if she had to confess them afterwards to whoever should take his place ?—he must be suspecting all— his way of looking at her proved that he was doing so—oh, she must escape from this church and never visit it again—couldn't she go as a missionary somewhere—to some islands in the Pacific. . . . ?

" That's all right, my child. I'll ask Father Williams to hear it at the same place and hour."

" Oh, thank you. . . . You don't mind, do you . . . ? "

" Oh, no, no. Penance should be a strictly impersonal matter, of course, but there's no reason why you shouldn't seek direction from the person who you think will help you most."

" Oh, it's not that, but . . ."

" What is it, then . . . ? "

" Oh, I don't know. . . . Yes, I'd like Father Williams."

" Well, that will be all right. I'll see him about it."

Peggy put out her hand.

" Good night."

" Good night, my dear."

There was a fondness very marked in his holding of her hand, and Peggy carried out into the dark streets, and for many miles on the blowy top of a bus, not only her confusion and heat, but the germ of a terrifying happiness.

CHAPTER V

SUMMER TERM

SUMMER again; summer lying golden under the downs, its sun so high, and beating such a light on the naked hills that they had shadow and substance no longer, but only shape, and waved along the glowing sky like a stream of cloud. The Summer term in possession of Stratton Lye, and burning a tract in Tony's memory that was pleasant for ever. To be nineteen and a pupil no longer but a master, and, moreover, a master of nearly a year's standing; to be no longer the lips that said " Sir," but the ears that heard that flattering address; to be nineteen and to smoke one's pipe as openly and unceasingly as forty smokes it, and to lift one's tankard at the inn with the ripest men; to live in the present and have no more care for the future than nineteen feels; to have money in one's pocket, not overmuch, but enough to buy cigarettes and pffective socks and ties—here were franchises that spread a erivate joy over Tony's days.

In the Summer term the sun fell slantwise into the Preparation room at eight o'clock at night, and drew one from one's desk to listen to the singing of birds. In the Summer term there were the long evenings of Fielding Practice on the trimmed grass of the cricket field, when he and twenty boys would go out under the falling sun, and the boys would fan out in a wide circle, and Tony would stand in the centre and with his cricket bat smack the ball—than which no more glorious privilege has been allowed to men—to this far-distant fieldsman and that one; while the boys' voices came back, shouting that it was their turn now, sir, or shrilling the explanation of their failures, or flinging a laughter at other people's, and Tony's voice would follow the racing ball with loud instruction, " Judge it ! Judge it, boy ! Feet together now. Back him up, you other. . . . Oh, mercy,

mercy, what a fool ! " And behind it all would be a smell of mown grass from the corner of the field, where the groundsman had piled it, or the smoke of its slow fire drifting towards the orchard ; and then, as the light failed, the ball would reach his hand wet with dew, and holding on its surface all the smell and touch of evening.

In the Summer term there were those talkative approaches to the great Saturdays when a First XI match was to be played ; those last dwindling hours of noisy speculation, at meals, on walks, or in dormitories ; that last Net Practice on Friday night when Tony bowled and shouted untiringly to the batsmen who must uphold our honour to-morrow (Mr. Sugden and half the school looking on) and was as happy as any rowing coach screaming his imprecations to the Oxford crew. There were the Cross Country runs, which himself had introduced, with boys as umpires at all the main points in the eight-mile course ; when the younger boys would be given their long start, and then the middle group would take off, and then the starred cluster of favourites, and lastly, many minutes later, himself, at a steady, confident, unstraining stride. Nothing quite like this : to run into the soft warm air, naked save for a thin white vest and scanty running shorts ; to become conscious of one's rippling muscles as the breeze played on them ; to feel the peer of any Olympian Greek ; to break across a meadow and turn the eyes of some lonely ploughman and see (as we called it) the " gorblimey ! " look therein ; to go on through the dancing midges and to indulge for a second a poet's thought : to-night was one not being as simple and wise as they ? The umpires at the first base would give him a cheer, and if that base were a low stile he would entertain them and earn a second cheer by taking it at a leap ; by the second base he would be near the favourites ; by the third he would be among them, chaffing and encouraging the broken-winded, and drawing the survivors on with him to the conquest of those ahead.

And then that walk back into the school buildings, when to a mind such as Tony's, fatigue after exercise presented itself as one of the loveliest things in the world, and therefore as one of the most significant. How exquisite it was—this heaving of one's breast, this intaking of short quick breaths through a mouth that would not close, this cooling of the sweat on fore-head and neck as the air touched it coldly, this ache and stiffness settling in the muscles of calf and thigh, this treacherous " give " of the weary knees, this drying and powdering of the earth on his palms, this delicious thought of a long drink, a cold bath, a cigarette, and a succumbing of one's body on to a bed! Tony, lying on his counterpane, girdled only with a towel, the cigarette at his lips and his hands behind his head, would wonder whether the body in these moments shot into men's consciousness a quicker revelation than ever their minds, dulled by too much thought, could place there, of the goodness which was the essence of life. Was Fatigue a mystical ecstasy?

The final brilliance was given to this summer term by the presence in it of the two things which best illuminate men's days. One of these was artistic creation. Tony was busy on a mighty poem. He had begun to believe, though he faced no ridicule by uttering the belief aloud, that he could be a poet, and a poet in no small way either. Sometimes, when creation was strong in him, he suspected that in Tony O'Grogan, a great poet had at last appeared in England. So many things could halt him in his path, and send him probing deep for their furthest import. And not only the things that delighted everybody, such as a rose-garden or a sunset—for every man was a poet in the presence of a Gloire de Dijon or on the summit of Wolstonbury at the droop of a fine midsummer night—but everything, everything. As he lay on his bed now, look! A candle on the table, the ordered pattern of the rug on the floor, the light falling on his carafe of tooth water, the Roman lettering of the title on a book's spine, the damp and decay in a corner of the room wall, all these, did he care to think about them, could point the thought-road to ideas as ultimate as the mind of man could stand in without vertigo. Was this to be a poet, and different from other men? Did Mr. Sugden ever walk to the brink of Eternity through his tooth glass, or Cyril Winter tread the road to God by staring at a circle in the pattern of the linoleum? They did not. Then let him secretly believe in himself; let him develop the intellectual energy and the physical stamina, and he would write his poetry with the best.

The aspiration had rooted quickly and was now mastering and draining the soil of his mind. He had started on the great poem. Having only one subject that he knew anything about, school life, he was writing, such was his austere devotion to truth, about that. What matter if novelists by the hundred had tooled in this quarry before him? No one had thought of carving an epic out of it. It was his own idea—absolutely!

A thrilling secret, this. Nonsense to say that the subject had not the magnitude that an epic claimed : old Aristotle was wrong ; the magnitude of a subject depended, not on the exalted rank of its persons or the vastness of its conflicts, but on the poet's vision of their significance. And to get an Iliad out of little subjects was greater than to get it out of the Siege of Troy ; it needed a nobler vision and a more miraculous art. With all the ocean-deep ambition of nineteen Tony was hardly content with a seat at Homer's side ; his thoughts fell covetously on one step higher.

And so creation had commenced. And now it was making his lonely walks down the shaded roads, when he was off duty, or when Sunday had shut the cricket bats behind their cupboard doors, into hours warm with the strain and excitement of mental sport. How he looked forward to these creative walks ! There were no times like them ; they were the hours best worth living.

And the other thing that lit up his days was the knowledge of his complete capture and occupation of Doyly's mind ; and this light was heightened by the suppressed, censored memory that in a few weeks time, with the close of the term, it must be put out for ever. Doyly went to Marlborough next term. But Tony lived in the current happiness, as he had done with Sibyl Chandry, and did not allow himself to think of its end. And Frank Doyly, with his own sidelong thought for the guillotine that must fall at the term's end, was most deliberately proffering the evidences of his worship ; never from his lips ; but, as a dog or a pony might, with his shoulder and the inclination of his body. On a Sunday walk, only let Tony and Frank drop behind the long straggling flock of boys, so that a corner of beech trunks or a curve of high hedge covered them from their fellows in front, and Frank, hanging on Tony's arm, would lean against him for the six short paces of privacy. Or in church, when all sat themselves for the sermon, Frank, at Tony's side, would accord three minutes to the orator, and then move two inches closer to Tony, who, glancing his way, would see him looking up impudently.

Once on a cross-country run, Frank caught his foot in the mouth of a rabbit burrow, and pitched magnificently into the tussocky grass, and lifting himself with elaborate stage-business, limped to the hedgerow. Was it deliberate ? He had certainly staged it when he was twenty yards in front of Tony. Tony fell out of the run to examine the injury.

" Are you hurt, Frank ? "

Doyly, in his pain, answered nothing, but with many a grimace and with suitable pauses, limped to a gate some fifty paces distant. There he placed his hands on the top bar and leaned forward, his injured foot pawing on its toe like the hoof of a lamed horse. At last, as he got used to the pain, he bravely threw up his face and tossed back his hair.

" Hurt ? " repeated Tony, who had followed.

" Oh, no ; it's nothing much, sir. I've sprained my ankle a little, I think. I always think a sprain's rather a topping feeling, don't you ? "

" I don't know about that."

" I'm enjoying it awfully, really."

He made a move to sit on the gate, but this involved placing the injured foot squarely on the ground, and such a movement —apparently—was not possible without the vilest suffering.

" Oh, damn ! " he said.

" Shut up, Doyly ! " commanded Tony.

" Yes, but it hurts," protested Doyly, in justification, and he looked up brightly. " Do you think it's broken ? "

" Get on, you boys," ordered Tony, to some of the lazier stragglers who, having seen the accident from their unenthusiastic rear, had begun to run seriously for the first time, and were now gathered round, glad to exchange the doubtful pleasures of a foot-slog over ploughed fields for the delight of gaping at a hospital-case. " Run on. I'll stay with Doyly. Go on. I mean it."

Reluctantly they turned away, and produced a jog-trot to the order of their master ; and as they ambled on, they looked back frequently at the entertainment they had forgone. Doubtless, when they were safely round the hedge's curve, they introduced variety into the monotony of a cross-country run by a period of walking.

" Will you be able to limp home all right ? " asked Tony of his patient.

" Oh, yes," Doyly opined. " It's getting better already."

" It'll swell up, I expect," Tony sympathized.

" Will it ? " Doyly looked a little alarmed. " Do sprains always swell ? "

" Of course."

" H'm. . . . Well, I suppose it will then." Doyly, apparently, had decided to hold his fort, with or without ammunition

" I'll help you back."

The boy got off the gate ; and as the foot touched the ground, he bent at the knee and screwed up his face with the anguish of it all.

" *Hell!* I'm sorry, sir.   But it hurts like blazes."

" Come on," said Tony encouragingly, putting an arm round his back and under an arm-pit.   " We'll manage it all right."

" How far are we from home ? " asked Doyly, his brows lifted and his eyes resigned, as he accepted the labour before him.

" About two and a half miles."

" I'll do it."   It was a hero's word.

" Come on, then.   It'll be getting dark."

" You won't mind going slow, will you, sir ? "

" No, no.   You set the pace."

They began the homeward journey, Tony's arm supporting Doyly, and Doyly limping rhythmically, grimacing often, and following the grimace with whistles, since he must not swear.

" It'll be better when we get off this rough ground on to the smooth road," Tony promised.

" Will it ?   I'm glad of that. . . . Is it far to the road ? "

" Only about a hundred yards."

" I'll do it."

They passed through a swing gate on to the hard macadam of the Wolstonbury Road.

" Ah, that's better," agreed Doyly.   " That's ever so much better."

And after they had gone a few dozen paces in silence, he leaned his body against Tony's, and put an arm ostensibly for support about his waist.   Tony understood ; and the hand under the boy's arm-pit gave its acknowledgment of pressure. This being the consummation that the boy desired, he said no more ; he was quite happy, and Tony was quite happy ; there was nothing more to do or to say ; once or twice Frank looked up at Tony's profile, and Tony affected not to see this ; and thus linked, they walked home together under the darkening trees to Stratton Lye.

It was as the term's last day shortened its distance from them that Tony discerned the change in Doyly's attitude.   He read the boy's thoughts as the boy himself could not have done : Doyly, he saw, had realized that his pleasant game of mutual adoration must stop on the term's last day, and, accepting its closure with the ease that was natural to him, had begun already to sink back from adoration to mere friendliness.   The summer holidays with their interests were hard at hand, and in the light thrown by their approach, Stratton Lye and Mr. O'Grogan were already fading into figures of the past.   And this fading had no wound for him ; he just accepted it and acted as common sense demanded, withdrawing from the game and turning his thoughts towards the stretch of holiday and the rise of Marlborough beyond.   That there was not a hint of unhappiness about him—this was the sharp point for Tony.

He took it away with him on his solitary walks, and in its company slashed his cane cheerily at the heads of the cow-parsley and the plumes of the tall grasses.   " Of course ! Whether Frank knew it or not at the time, he was only playing a game.   *I* know—who better ?—that it's the pleasantest pastime in the world.   He was only playing at it. . . ."   As he said it, Tony struck with merry savagery at a frond of bracken, for it was no painless thrust that he was baring his breast to. " Only playing at it. . . . I suppose I was too, but—I don't know—I'm such a poisonous ass that I let it get hold of me too much, till it passes beyond a game. . . ."   Did all men deliberately work themselves up into love, and then suffer ?   Was love never anything but a self-suggested thing ? . . . Was it nothing at all, really ?   Was there no such thing ? . . . He would get over this, of course.   Next term might hurt a bit, when he saw the class-rooms where they had acted their game together, and the football field, and the gate in the hedgerow where Frank had rested his ankle.   But in a month or two he would be cured.   Yes, that was what would happen, and therefore he could not really believe in his love—or in his hurt. Self-suggested things.   And yet it *did* hurt and ache. . . . Oh, it was all absurd. . . . Men were idiots. . . . idiots ; they pretended that love was everything, and it was nothing but auto-suggestion. . . .

But if there was no love, if it was all imagination, then was life worth living ? . . .

" Oh, I don't know," said he, finally.   And, beaten in thought, he turned about on his tracks.

Too proud to show that he had noticed Doyly's diminuendo,

he maintained with him a cheery friendliness.   And under his laughing talk he was thinking : " We have sunk to friendliness. Ha ! ha ! "—this in mockery at himself—" and it is the whole drop from the zenith to the level of the ground. . . . Well, there it is. . . ."   And he and Doyly continued their jokes together ; and upstairs in his bedroom, he turned to his poem that he might escape into that melancholy pleasure of creating on paper the things one longed for in real life and failed to win.

The division between them widened, as Doyly's excitement about the holidays increased with the approach of the last week. Why worry ?   He wouldn't worry.   He would be as happy and indifferent as Doyly was.   But when on the eve of the day of departure he walked out on his usual stroll and found himself rehearsing a dramatic farewell-scene for the morning, could he believe then that he was not worrying ?   Did his warm head and the irregular action of his heart suggest that he was quite happy and indifferent ?   And his conviction that, though his reason saw the childishness of this rehearsed scene, he would certainly go through with it, lacking the will to turn from it, did that look like anything but a wilful dive into pain ?

This was the scene that he was composing for the morrow. At ten o'clock the station flies would come up the drive and all the boys whose destination was London—Doyly among them —would rush out of the school to clamber aboard ; but as Tony would not be accompanying them, because he had charge of a later shift which was going to Brighton, he would keep himself hidden from Doyly's sight so as to force the boy to give one last proof of his affection by his coming to seek him out.   And the room where he would keep out of sight would be the empty New Room, from which he could watch the cabs and the crowd on the drive ; here, to anyone who took the least trouble, he could easily be found ; and, on the other hand, if Doyly showed no signs whatever of remembering him, he could watch the cabs disappear and suffer the completest torture.   Lunacy, all of it ; as his mind could easily see. But he was wretched, and in its power.

And, sure enough, next morning he was standing in the New Room, well back, so that he could see the people on the drive and not be seen by them.   The cabs were there, and many of the boys had taken their places, and Doyly was standing on the threshold of Stratton Lye, jesting with a friend who had mounted a box-seat.   Ah—sharp sickening of the heart !—he had left the threshold and was walking along the gravel of the drive : was he going to jump into one of them without a thought for Tony ? Now he was talking to Winter—talking with a glee that was without flaw—good God ! had the boy no feeling at all ? Winter was saying good-bye to him ; Doyly was looking up with real gratitude into Winter's face and pressing his hand— pressing it hard, as Tony could see, and that pressure was a constriction at his heart. But *now* . . . yes ! Doyly was running back into the school ! He was coming, then ; of course he was coming ! One might have known he would. This was all Tony wanted now—that Frank should seek him out and perhaps say something that it would be happiness to remember. Even if Doyly had only been reminded of another master's existence by his good-bye to Winter, still Tony would be satisfied. . . . Doyly's feet were outside the New Room door —but they passed—they passed into the South Room where was his locker. Tony walked furtively to a corner from which he could command a view across the passage into the sunny South Room. Doyly was at his locker—*gosh !* had he only come back for something he had left ? The locker lid slammed down—Tony stepped back out of sight—his heart pounded, as Doyly emerged from the South Room—would he come looking anywhere else for him ?—if so, Tony must pretend to be doing something—but Doyly's steps went quickly, unhesitatingly down the hall to the cabs outside.

Hurriedly Tony returned to his window, still standing far back like a spy. Was it believable ? Doyly was climbing into a cab, and he was not coming ; he had forgotten every thing in that merry moment. . . . Tony stared . . . and continued to stare. . . .

The first cab was moving, and the boys roared their cheers, as they always did. The second cab moved too, and the third, and the fourth, in which sat Doyly. Ah, he would at least look round, before the cab turned the bend in the drive and was hidden in the tunnel under the trees—he would look round and remember at the last second. If he would only do that much now, Tony would be satisfied. . . .

The string of cabs went on, and the fourth cab took the curve and passed out of sight. Tony stared a few minutes longer at the empty drive, and then swung round and began to whistle merrily.

CHAPTER VI

PEGGY RECEDES

THERE is no wheel that swings round the circle of the year so quickly as the three-spoke wheel of a school's three terms. Tony soon discovered this. If the gay Summer term went quickly, the summer holiday went quicker still : and here they were, before the bathing dresses were wholly dry, in a term they called the Christmas term, with the thought of holly already in the air. And round came the spoke of Christmas, bringing the Lent term after it, and the groundsman was at work on the cricket pitch, because the Summer term was lifting again. Was it really true that he was speeding towards the end of his second year at Stratton Lye ? Yes, it was true enough. Well ! he who would fly over time with the smooth, swift flight of a bird, let him seat himself in the scholastic chair.

And to see the year swing round like this, a man must sit in the country. Tony, who had lived all his previous life in London, now learned a new interest, to which he gave the whole of his enthusiasm, and a naïve applause. Wasn't it simply wonderful to be able to watch the changing beauties which the months hung on the countryside ? September, and already the frost was busy, and the cobweb lace was strung with pearls, and the lawns every morning were washed over with a watery milk. October, and the leaves took the sky like birds, crossing the warp of the rain in transverse lines ; or if the day were sunny as summer, the wind shook the tracery of yellow leaves on the branches, till they dazzled the eyes like sequins. Full winter, and the naked trees were dark in the hollows, and pools of sky-light lay in the water-logged meadows. Spring, and the young larches filled these woodlands with the youngest green in the world, and the wild cherry put out its blossom of fawny white. This being his mood, what was his excitement and his proselytizing zeal when he, twenty himself, discovered A. E. Housman, and " A Shropshire Lad ? " Not a master nor a senior boy but must attend, as he quoted with heating cheeks and brightening eyes :

> " Now of my threescore years and ten,
> Twenty will not come again,
> And take from seventy springs a score,
> It only leaves me fifty more.

> " And since to look at things in bloom
> Fifty springs are little room,
> About the woodlands I will go
> To see the cherry hung with snow."

And so it came to Eastertide, and he was home again. And one evening, when the air outside, even in that new-built Chiswick avenue, was aglow with the young Easter sun, and festooned and spangled with the song of birds, and he and Joyce were face to face over a game of chess, the girl upright and bored, for she was being beaten, and himself bent and engrossed, for, as far as he could see, he was only six moves from the mate, Keatings entered and delivered himself of a most valuable opening sentence. He said : " Gather round, children, gather round. Here be news." His voice was lifted no higher than usual ; if anything it was quieter ; but Joyce, who stared at him, and Tony, who looked up, saw that he was acting the quiet, phlegmatic, well-bred man whom no news, however astonishing, could explode into excitement.

" Oh, what is it, what is it, Kay ? " Joyce exclaimed, who had never any objection to exploding.

" Is one of the Gabriels dead ? " asked Tony.

" No. I don't know that it is as good news as that." Keatings drew a chair and sat down, grimly smiling.

" Oh, what is it then—you fool ? " persisted Joyce. " Derek's in gaol. He's been caught in some nefarious traffic at last."

" Derek does nothing more nefarious than sell motor cars on commission. I should have thought that was proved to all our satisfactions. He may like to pretend that he has other more picturesque irons on the fire, but then—he always was a fool."

" Oh, but I believe he has. I believe the motor car business is only a blind. They're a gang, I'm sure. You can't make as much money as he does by selling cars."

" Oh, yes, you can—if you've got enough bounce and a gift for plausible language, and a natural tendency to lie."

" But I've got all those gifts," Joyce demurred. " And I don't make so much money."

" Check ! " called Tony.

" Oh, damn *check !* " grumbled Joyce. " He's always checking me. I resign. You've won. I want to hear Keatings's news. What is it, Kay ? "

" It's rather magnificent. Thinking it over, I've decided that it's rather magnificent. I was coming home in the train this afternoon—its coaches by the way were the old-fashioned District Railway type—and at Earl's Court, where they hold you up an infernal time, I looked out of the window, and I saw two people get into a first-class carriage—a tall man and a girl——"

" How thrilling ! " interrupted Joyce. " ' A tall man and a girl ! ' Now if it had been a little man and a tall girl, it'd have been dull."

" Or if it had only been a third-class carriage," suggested Tony.

" And when I add that the man was a parson," continued Keatings.

" Ah ! " breathed Joyce, appreciatively.

" . . . and that the girl was extraordinarily like Peggy, it becomes really succulent. Not in any spirit of curiosity, but simply because my limbs were stiff, I got out and walked up the platform. As I passed the first-class compartment I looked in. There was no one in it except the parson and the girl, and the girl's head lay on the man's shoulder, and I fancy (I'm not sure, mind you, because I was so abashed that I walked on quickly), but I *fancy* his arm was round her waist. The girl was Peggy."

" Kay ! The little slut ! It wasn't—it couldn't have been Father Michael ? "

" It certainly was : as you shall see."

" And is he *in love* with her ? Why, he's not been in the house more than twice, and he's met none of us. Coo ! what fools we've been. I thought he was just her spiritual director."

" He was very much in love with her in the train. I stretched my legs again at Hammersmith, and well, it might have been a soldier and a nursemaid, on a seat in Kensington Gardens."

" But, Kay ! isn't he supposed to be a celibate ? She was at great pains to tell us that. They all are, at that church."

" He may be a celibate, or he may not, but he's engaged to Peggy."

" Engaged ! Oh, and I had serious thoughts of being the one myself, who should lure him from his vows."

" Is Peggy *engaged* ? " demanded Tony, feeling a mild blow in the thought.

" Yes ; hear me out. We all dismounted at Chiswick Station, and I tried to hide myself behind the fat porter, but Peggy was looking up and down the platform, obviously in the hope of seeing me, and she ran up with the news. She was all red and trembling—you know what she can do in that line—and we all shook hands and felt fools, and then walked back together, the Father talking genially all the way, and Peggy speechless, and myself (I confess) somewhat hung up for conversation. But the Father rambled on in a fine, hearty, bedside manner ; and now—and now he and she are upstairs telling Mother."

Joyce and Tony just stared, while Keatings took his case of cigarettes, tossed one to his brother, lit another for himself, threw the match into the grate, and tossed the box to Tony.

" But he must be over forty," Joyce objected suddenly.

" What does that matter ? Wouldn't that suit Peggy's ideas down to the ground ? . . . And, Joyce, my dear, do you realize that he's a baronet's son ? "

" Is he ? *Coo !* . . ."

" And what's better still, he's the eldest son—Peggy spluttered it all at me when she was leading me to him—and I don't suppose his old father'll live long—at least we can hope not—the silly old gaffer ! "

" I devoutly hope not," Joyce endorsed.

" And child ! the Gabriels ! " Phlegm deserted the well-bred Keatings, and delight surged into his eyes. " Gor-lummy ! it's a fair knock-out ! "

" I suppose it is."

" Course it is ! Elsa and Theresa are both older than you and Peggy, and has a single follower come dangling round them ? Devil a one. Nor will one. In three years' time they'll have turned to Good Works or Suffragetting. But Peggy by then ought to be Lady Saffery—with any luck."

" Coo ! I *am* glad," said Joyce. " But I wonder how she does it. It's her dog's eyes, I think."

The door opened ; and Derek entered : perfectly dressed ; his hair groomed down, his morning coat well-cut, the opening of his waistcoat outlined by a white slip, his trousers grey-striped and neatly creased, and his boots strapped in their grey spats, like a couple of valuable whippets in their jackets, when the east wind blows.

"Lord!" exclaimed Keatings. "Here's the Manager of the Lingerie Department."

"I suppose you've heard the news, Derek," said Joyce.

"What news?"

"Peggy's engaged to a wealthy baronet."

Derek, lacking the humorous imagination of Keatings, saw no necessity to act the well-bred man whose calm nothing could ruffle. His eyebrows lifted, and he stared at Joyce, and turned to Keatings for confirmation. But inasmuch as he *was* phlegmatic, he released no louder outburst than, "Goodness! is that so? Or are you being funny?"

He sat down and crossed one leg over the other, first dusting its knee and calf. Always Derek arranged his well-clad legs as if he were handling two perfect art-pieces.

"She's going to marry that Father Michael of hers."

"*Him?* But he isn't a baronet." One felt that Derek was relieved. Secretly delighted at being the most successful one of the family, he had no desire to be suddenly dethroned by his younger sister.

"He's a baronet's son," Keatings exclaimed readily.

"I didn't know that," said Derek.

"No, there are a lot of things you don't know—strange as it may seem."

Derek ignored this, as he always ignored Keatings's snubs; could he not afford to, while he was the inventive and successful man of business and Keatings remained in the dull rut of an Insurance Office?

"But he can't marry her. He's a celibate."

"That's what's so magnificent," Tony submitted. "To marry a baronet's one thing; but to marry a celibate baronet's very much finer."

"But *he*—he, a High Church parson, who probably believes that yielding to feminine charms is yielding to sin! Why, he won't know what to do with her when he gets her."

"He seemed to know what to do all right in the train," Keatings suggested. "I couldn't have done it better myself."

"Why? What happened in the train?"

Keatings repeated his story with gross exaggerations. And Derek, after hearing with parted lips of the hungry kisses, the long caresses and the strokings of the cheek that Father Michael had given to Peggy, paused before commenting : " Fancy anyone wanting to do that with Peggy ! "

" I suppose she's attractive enough to *others !* " Joyce proffered.

" I can never see much in her, myself," said Derek. " And why did she want to be so secretive about it ? How long do you suppose they've been cuddling without our knowledge ? She's been attending that church for two years. Has it been going on all the time ? "

" No," Joyce suddenly pronounced. " I see it all. He proposed to-day and cuddled her for the first time in the train. He waited till after Easter : he would naturally wait till Lent is over. Lent is a time of abstinence."

" I think Joyce is about right," Keatings approved.

" When will they marry ? "

" They'll marry——" Joyce, now considering herself a kind of metereological expert, cast her eyes up to the ceiling, as if it were a sheet on which she could work out her arithmetic. " They'll marry in about a year. It's now Easter ; they'll hardly marry in the winter ; so it'll be just before Lent. Before Lent, for the above-mentioned reasons. That means I ought to be a godmother by Christmas. Oh, do you think it'll be born on Christmas Day ? I hope it is, the darling ! We'll call it Noel—Noel Saffery."

" What's its father's Christian name ? " asked Derek.

" Michael, you ass ! Doesn't everyone call him Father Michael ? "

" You think you're clever," sneered Derek, " but it doesn't follow that it's his Christian name at all. These High Church priests often call themselves after angels."

" True," Tony interpolated. " There's Father Ignatius. He was really an Old Pauline, of the name of Joseph Leycester Lyne."

" Well, anyhow, it *is* his name," Keatings clinched. " So we've a Michael to match their Gabriel now."

" Ass ! " laughed Joyce.

" And as he's to be our brother, we shall have to call him Mike. Or Micky. It won't come easy to me——"

He stopped for the door handle was turning. Peggy and Father Michael entered ; and all the family pushed back their chairs and stood up, as if a headmaster had come into the room.

Tony noticed that the blood-red flags of shame flying in Peggy's cheeks and down her throat had almost disfigured it.

" Here are some of them," she began. " No, they're all here. That's lucky."

" I have to be presented," explained Father Michael, behind an embracing smile. " There's Keith. Well, I know *you* already. Won't you introduce me to the others ? "

Keatings pulled Joyce forward by the arm.

" This is Joyce."

Father Michael took her hand, held it a little while, and then drew her to him, and kissed her cheek. " What a beautiful sister ! " he said. Joyce blushed richly, and her eyes sparkled. The three brothers felt foolish : Derek looked at his finger-nails which were in excellent condition, Tony made a comic grimace to Peggy, and Keatings hastened to lift the general embarrassment by proceeding :

" And this one's Tony. He's supposed to be the brainy one. But I don't think there's much in it."

Tony extended his hand awkwardly. " How do you do, sir ? "

" For mercy's sake don't call me ' sir,' " protested Father Michael, shaking his hand.

" And this is Derek. He's the only one of us who makes large money."

" How do you do ? " said Derek, with perfect ease.

Then Keatings, feeling very uncomfortable, essayed facetiousness. " That's the lot—with Peggy. Not much of a lot, all told," which sounded to him so absurd that he in his turn ran up the flag that was in Peggy's cheeks.

Since all were standing, and none, least of all Joyce, who was feeling about thirteen years old, liked to be the first to sit down, it fell to Father Michael to cut the tension by suggesting : " Let's all sit down."

At once they all sat down, exactly as if they had been his congregation and he had said : " Let us now read God's Word for a space." Father Michael, putting his hand in Peggy's arm, guided her to the sofa, where he sat at her side and took her hand on to his lap that he might stroke it. Keatings looked anywhere but at this process ; Derek dropped his eyes to his boots and adjusted his spats and gave his subsequent interest to the window ; Tony thrust his hands deep into his trouser pockets, and with compressed lips and vibrating mouth, kept a giggle safely out of sight; and Joyce saw his predicament, and immediately turned red and rigid with the same effort.

A perfunctory talk ensued, in which, after the first five minutes Derek played by far the most distinguished part, taking up the Father's points and endorsing or disallowing them with the assurance of a contemporary. Keatings was conscientious, laborious, but unhelpful; Joyce ventured one or two insertions, of which, to judge by her blushes, she was completely ashamed, and some of them she failed to finish properly, because of her impeding giggle; and Peggy and Tony remained throughout in their safe but unhonourable tents of silence. The ordeal of this necessary convergence and conversazione was closed by Father Michael: he rose and offered his most smiling farewells; and Peggy at once rose after him. All stood as he opened the door for her and followed her out, laying his hand upon her shoulder.

No one spoke. Keatings wiped his forehead. Derek grimaced. And Tony flung himself back on his chair, and released the turbulent giggle, which came out in the shape of an uproarious laugh.

"You did look a row of imbeciles," he said at last.

Keatings sighed. "It was bright and brotherly—what?"

And Joyce declared: "Oh, I *think* he's rather sweet; I *think* he's rather a lamb. . . . Yes, I'm delighted with my new brother. He's better than any I've had so far."

And Derek was beginning: "I think Peggy might have done worse. He seems a gentleman——" when Peggy reappeared at the door.

"Keatings," said she, keeping hold of its handle.

"Yes, child?"

"Keatings, you've been communicating with Daddy recently, haven't you?"

"Yes."

"Well, don't write to him about this, till I've had a chance to. I'm going to write this evening. I want him to hear of my engagement from me myself, and within an hour or two of its happening. Don't you think he ought to? Poor, darling Father—he'll be out of all the fun. And he would have enjoyed it so. Promise you won't?"

"Of course I won't."

"Oh, thanks. Well, good-bye. Michael's waiting."

And she was gone again. But her visit had moved Derek

to the decision that he also must be going, and to a very heavy comment. Lighting a cigarette and strolling towards the door, he said : " Peggy's having no father available means that one of us'll have to discuss the marriage settlements. We'll have to look into the position much more thoroughly than ever Mother'll do. I think this man takes it for granted, rather coolly, that we're going to give our sister to him, don't you ? Still, all that'll wait."

He disappeared, and Keatings stared after him.

" God ! what a fool ! " he exclaimed.

Peggy was a winter bride, married in December, when the appointment of Father Michael to an incumbency in Southend had opened a vicarage to their feet. At the word " Southend " Joyce had wrinkled her nose, but Peggy had exclaimed : " It's lovely ; it's all cockles and costers and East End trippers. Next to Whitechapel or Bethnal Green, there's no place I'd like better. Michael and I'll convert them all." A leaden sky overhung the wedding, and the promise of snow ; and Tony had a fancy that, against the still, opaque, charged background of the embracing sky, the tall bridegroom in his black clothes, and Peggy herself, had a preternatural clearness. His own thoughts also, when Peggy had been driven away, and he was returning alone to his station, seemed to have become preternaturally clear.

And as he sat in his train, shut from the view of the country by the darkness of the December evening, and discouraged from reading by the swooning gaslight in his compartment, he saw only the clear figure of Peggy (now Peggy Saffery) in her going-away dress, and the clear figure of the tall man who had taken her away. And he thought. He thought how unreal, in spite of his solidity, was this Michael Saffery, who had come and gone—a name, a visible face and figure, a chain of pleasant greeting and banter ; no more. The real Michael Saffery he had never seen. . . . Peggy had seen him, perhaps. . . . Or did anyone ever see a real man ? . . . All Michael's kindliness and banter were really only a standardized garment that revealed nothing more specific, nothing more proper to the man himself, than did his standardized, priestly attire. To Tony this man, though Peggy, his sister, weighted and helpless with love, had dived into the depths of him to find her life, was no more than a tall, spare parson, with an ascetic but genial face, and a visiting manner. Surely out of the many sentences that he had spoken and the " business " that had gone with them, a simple, straight, sincere man would have created, as an actor creates, a character for his audience to read. . . . Or no : a clearly created character might have meant no more than a brilliant piece of acting ; probably most of the marked characters of the world amounted to no more than this.   Michael's inability to create himself for others might suggest that he was an unbrilliant and unhypocritical soul, lonely and hidden, behind his standardized garments.

Could one ever know the real truth of anybody ?   Of his most intimate friends did Tony know only just a little more than he knew of these two passengers who chanced to have jostled into this train with him ?   One was a lined, pondering, weary old virgin of fifty, with her reticule containing no doubt a sovereign or two, and a florin or two, to support her in her meaningless course ; and the other was a palpable " commercial gent," with a bag of dull business on the rack above him, and a desire, always strong in commercial gents, to break the tedium of a journey by opening a conversation.   The window provided him with a card to lead.

" A damned dark night," he said.

" Yes, it is," Tony agreed.

" And cold.   This cold before snow always penetrates into my bones.   It's always better when the snow's come."

" Yes, I suppose it is."

" You gotta go far ? "

" I get out at Hassocks."

" Yes ; a slow train, this ; stops everywhere, doesn't it ?   I get out at East Croydon, thank goodness—trains are too parky on a night like this.   I been up to Stockport to do a bit of business and brought it off, too ! "

" Big, was it ? "

" Not too bad ; not too bad."   The man sucked his teeth. " I ought to clear my twenty out of it."

" I'm so glad."

" Yes. . . . You come from far ? "

Tony explained that he had come from marrying his sister ; and the man said : " Really ?   Go on ! " and talked about married life, and how it was the thing, really, with all its ups and downs, and how—this in a knowing whisper, for the old virgin's sake—a man didn't make himself a man till he'd filled a man's part, and how he expected Tony'd be finding the right girl for himself soon, and sincerely wished him joy of her—and the train slowed into East Croydon. He fetched down his bag of dull business. " Well, good night to you."

" Good night."

" Yes. Pleased to have met you. Hope you have a good journey and the snow keeps up, till you're safely home. Good night, again."

" Good night."

He faded into the darkness.

Could one ever know anything real of anybody ? Peggy. His relation to her and his knowledge of her differed only in degree from his knowledge of these strangers huddled in the same box with him for an hour. He had met her a few more times than once ; he had seen into her just a little further than her outer garments ; but not very far. Nor she into him. And now she had gone out of his life almost as completely as this good fellow who had left the train. There would be a letter now and then, a flying visit to her house, and some interchange of talk at a family reunion ; and both would always know that they had not shown more than the fringes of themselves to each other.

There had been no essential change ; all that had happened was that Peggy had gone a little further outside his life than she had always been. Every living soul, even the one nearest to us, was outside our lives. The vast wilderness of our inner lives was untrodden by any foot save our own ; its fringes alone were visited. And we were all silent ; only our fringes speaking. He thought of Wavers, that little figure of long ago, who had first stirred in him the yearning for another person ; of old Raking, with whom he had imagined a perfect friendship ; of Sibyl Chandry with her dark hair, her oval face, and the unspoken love in her eyes ; of Frank Doyly, so recently gone, and yet nearly forgotten now ; of his father, his mother, and Keatings and Joyce and Derek and Peggy. And he thought of the girl he would marry. They would only be dear strangers, he and she. He shivered in his seat. He was fronting the truth of the utter solitariness of every man ; and it is a truth whose face is so intolerable to look into that we may praise God that the stress and laughter of life but seldom part their curtains to disclose it to us.

What was the meaning of it all ? Sixty or seventy years of complete loneliness, with never a hope of that perfect mutual absorption with another soul, which was the only satisfying thing in the world. One's body was forever prompting one to it, and yet, to a moment's clear thought, it was seen to be as unattainable in this world as the shimmering water of a mirage in the wilderness. Would it be attained hereafter in some less limited order ? The fact of sex hinted that it was the goal of man—to pour himself into some other person, to press his whole body thitherward, as if he would melt into her, to yield her all that he could of his very life. (Almost for the first time Tony's body stirred at the thought of the girl who would take from him all of himself that he was able to give. When was she coming ?) And yet this blending only left one frustrated again, and issued —how strange !—in another being who was destined to the same loneliness and frustration.

And supposing that in some spiritual world this perfect unity were attained, would it be with only one person ? Why, he could imagine a love—he could even feel the seeds of it in himself—which could never be content unless it had achieved its perfect unity with every living soul—which could not bear that one soul should be outside its embrace. Would this, the only perfect fulfilment, ever be granted one ; or would death close the mockery with annihilation ?

No, no ; not annihilation. This love, this dim craving, was itself a strong hint that annihilation could not be. A thing like this must have meaning ; and what meaning had it, if it just lifted its head in the world, met its frustration, and perished for ever ? No, nothing could be so meaningless as that. " I believe then—but in what ? "

His thoughts swung to a testing and distillation of his religion. What did he honestly believe ? Like most sons of an English vicarage and an English public school, he had accepted and discharged the performances of religion with a shrugging resignation that shirked thought. Once, during the month that followed his confirmation he had secretly lived the religious life, and very happy—nay, more than happy, blessed—those few weeks seemed to him now. But the light had dulled and died, and thereafter the services in church had become again a mere concession to propriety, as void of interest and emotion as the *Preces* gabbled by six hundred boys at five o'clock in the Great Hall at St. Paul's. " No, I cannot honestly say that I believe in any of those dogmas and practices. Not at present. But I have faith in something—I have just said so. I don't—I can't believe any of the details of Christianity, but I have faith in a Purpose. There must be purpose in everything ; if I were to deny that, I should do violence to the laws of my thought."

But how vague ! " Faith in a Purpose : " there was nothing there to give him again that inner serenity and blessedness which, for a few weeks, he had experienced. And he would like it again ; oh, how he would like it again ! All men would. Let them ridicule religion as they liked, let them fly the title " saint " as it were a title of shame, yet all who had once known what " peace in believing " meant, all who had glimpsed the beauty of holiness, all who had ventured the experiment of hiding their life with Christ in God, all would rather discover that quiet garden again than the richest pleasure-grounds of the world.

Redhill Station.

The lined and weary lady fumbled with the door, and he leapt up and opened it for her, and handed out her heavy suit-case, and smiled deprecatingly, when she said : " Oh, thank you. Thank you so much. Good evening."

" Good evening," then he slammed the door on himself to keep out the cold.

If only he could believe it all ! If only he had the simple belief which it was to be presumed was Peggy's, why then—suddenly he saw it—his course would be clear. Highly sensitized this evening to the loneliness of all living people, he saw that nothing mattered except to love as many of them as possible, to serve them, to bring them peace, to draw them closer and closer to him, and to one another, with bands of love, and to do this work while it was yet day, for the night came apace, in which perchance no man might do this work any more ; and all this painted one picture—the portrait of a priest. All those who in Christ's name had loved the whole world and laboured for it were making a winning appeal to Tony to-night, as he sat in his railway carriage—St. Francis of Assisi, St. Aidan of Iona, the blessed Curé d'Ars, Father Damien, Tolstoy, Father Ignatius, even old Captain Alum—and a few, a tiny few, of the clergy he had known in his father's days—not your Dr. O'Grogans and your Archdeacon Gabriels—but men like Mr. Crabb whom the children had loved, or like Mr. Russell, the saintly evangelical, who had so often been seen in his slums with a fish-basket of comforts swinging against his shabby frock-coat, or like Father Murray, the High Church missioner of the Mirfield community, of whom it was said that you could not come into his presence without being converted.

And as the representative of those to whom the men of consecration go, another figure appeared out of his past : little Emily Holt, the Cockney child, whom he had picked up one night at Freshwater Gate, and, on another night, held for an hour against his side. He could hear her voice again : " I bythed yesterday and this mornin'. *Ugh-h-h-h !* Cowld, but ever so jolly. I never bin to the sea before. And that there Comptin Farm to-dye, where we sor you—it was 'eavenly ! "

Three Bridges Station ; and an old gentleman whose kind eyes, grey moustache, and Shakespeare collar gave him the appearance of a chapel elder, padded into the carriage softly and patiently—as softly and patiently as he spoke, rubbing together his hands cased in white woollen gloves :

" A cold night."

" It is rather."

" Ah well, it is not far to Brighton now."

" I get out at Hassocks."

" Some lovely country that way ; but I'm going on to the sea."

" Yes ? "

And the train, moving, lulled them both into their thoughts.

Ah, if only he could believe ! That was all he wanted. Then, have done with this hunger for a single love ! He would join some community like the Mirfield Fathers and seek, not to get the adoration of a single person, but to give himself and all that he was worth to the whole world. He pictured himself in a cassock, visiting the sick and the sinful, a basket on his arm.

Or the picture changed : and he was very like Tolstoy—a tough old man with a long beard, who, after proclaiming his creed of communism, universal love, and non-resistance to evil, had sold all his possessions and given them to the poor, and was now labouring in a smock-frock by the side of the peasants he loved.

But such a life could not be lived—he saw this—without an intense inner life of prayer—and one could not pray without belief. " And I don't believe. I can't. . . . And I have a fancy that I never shall—not in that way—not with the conviction that would give me the spiritual and intellectual ease for such work. . . ."

What to do then ? His present schoolmastering would lead to nothing ; it was a temporary drift that he must soon arrest, if he were to make a position and reputation and money. (Making money ! Like a broken-winged bird he had dropped instantly from the skies to the earth.) Would it not be best to make a move soon ? In a few months he would be twenty-one. But what move ? Pretty obscure, not to say gloomy, his prospects. Then, of a sudden, he remembered his poetry. Could he not consecrate himself to his art, as a monk consecrated himself to religion ? (He began to wing aloft again.) His poetry could even be conceived of as a priestly task, since it was both interpretation and ministration. It was interpretation, because he would probe hard into the depths of thought, using, perhaps, this craving to merge oneself into other persons as a key to all understanding ; and it was ministration, because he would pour the world's loneliness into his songs, and thereby give it a voice and the healing of speech. Yes, yes ; if he were to consecrate himself thus, there would be no better bread-winning occupation than his present mastership, with its quiet healthy days, its freedom from strain and care, and its long holidays. The Gabriels might say : " Fancy ! despite the promise of his schooldays he hasn't risen beyond a prep-school mastership ; " and Derek would certainly despise him ; and no girl would be able to marry him on his low stipend—but what of all this ? After all these things did the Gentiles seek. He would, if necessary, despise money and position and—most difficult of all—family praise. The future ! Let the future care for itself. He would not make the timid creature's bid for security. Worldly security was a dull business, like the dull business in the bag of the commercial gentleman ; it was valued only by your commonplace souls—by your Dereks. Rather he would make a kind of monastic vow of poverty and celibacy and go forward as a servant and friend, whether recognized or unrecognized, of this world of solitaries. It was a pleasing idea, and he felt happier now—happy with a resolve rooted and already stirring—as the train bore into Hassocks station and delivered him for his humble tasks at Stratton Lye.

" Good night, sir," he said to the old gentleman in white woollen gloves.

" Oh . . . good night, good night."

CHAPTER VII

WHEN TOLSTOY RETREATED

AND so Tony, happy with his poverty and his celibacy, made a long halt at Stratton Lye. He could hardly believe, when the time came for a violent change, that he had delayed there five quiet years. Years wholly pleasant they were; years of successful teaching, praised by Mr. Sugden, for with the departure of Browning and Cyril Winter, he had assumed their seniority and, on taking over the higher forms, had helped to bring a whole procession of scholarships to the doors of Stratton Lye; years of engrossing creation, for he would give his spare evenings to his verse-craft, and there was no happiness quite like this, and of the lyrics which he had cut and polished, two or three—though he had sent twenty or thirty to the editors—had been accepted for tail-pieces in the magazines, and paid for with half guineas.

His acceptance of poverty and celibacy was stable enough, probably because at present he did not want anything more; but his indifference to reputation and family praise was very insecure. The days of his lyrics' publication, as they drew near, had been days under a searchlight's beam; the nights that introduced them had been restless with excitement; and with the morning the shutters were scarcely down from the newsagent's shop before he was inside purchasing copies of the magazine for his mother, for Peggy, for Derek, who was abroad, and for friends. Many letters to else forgotten friends did he write on these days, beginning: " How are you, old man ? " and ending: " There's a little effusion of mine in this month's *Windsor*." And once he almost fell into the coils of a Vanity Publisher. Compiling a type-script of twenty of these lyrics, he had sent it to a Mr. James Eustace Ltd., a firm with a most convincing address near St. Paul's Cathedral; and Mr. Eustace had replied in person, expressing his enthusiasm for the work and his readiness to publish the book if Mr. O'Grogan would contribute thirty-five pounds towards the cost of production, in consideration of which outlay he would receive fifty copies of the book for himself for circulation among his friends. Thirty-five shillings being nearer Tony's spending power, the negotiations fell through; but ever afterwards he was able to say " I received *one* offer for their publication."

That year should succeed year in this noiseless tread, without crowning his brows with fame, did not seriously disturb him as yet: between eighteen and twenty-three all life seemed to stretch before him.

In the summer of 1910 two things of moment happened; and they were brought about by a letter from Frank Doyly, the first for two years. All Frank's old high spirits were in the letter, and not a small dose of his old affection; he was writing most clearly under the bright light and the impulse of a plan that rejoiced him. There was a confounded conspiracy, said he, among his masters and parents to make him read Euripides, Horace, Catullus, and other old bounders, during the summer holidays. He had put up a fine defence, inflicting no small losses on the enemy—mainly losses of patience and good manners and (he hoped) self-respect—but he was now surrendering on his own terms, which were that he was to choose his own tutor. That tutor was a certain Mr. O'Grogan who was the world's best classical master. And now it seemed that his father, breathless and weary from the fights, was going to communicate with this master and beg him to accompany the family on an August holiday in Belgium and give to the distinguished prisoner of war some two hours' sweat a day. " Please do," concluded Doyly, shedding suddenly the grand metaphorical manner and standing in his naked boyishness, " oh please, *please* do. It'll be hell if you don't."

Mr. Doyly's letter came two days later, inviting him to the task with much courtesy and suggesting " as a possible inducement " the discharge of all his expenses and an honorarium of four guineas a week. And Tony who felt more ashamed to take four guineas a week than anxious to haggle for more, replied that he was perfectly satisfied with Mr. Doyly's most generous offer and would do all he could to be worthy of their confidence.

Anticipation of this holiday was now the dominant pleasure in his mind. Something of his old love for Frank returned, but very different in character from the aching obsession of three years before; it had quieted into a gratified attachment, which, moreover, showed an odd tendency to spread over the whole of this unseen family. What was Doyly at seventeen going to be like? What were his parents and his two elder sisters like? Odd that a family could be a lovable unit like an individual! Perhaps one of the sisters. . . .

It was with a restless keenness that one August afternoon he stood on the platform of Ashford Junction, waiting for the London-Dover train to roll in, and bring the Doyly family to its meeting with him. More and more impatient he became as the minutes passed; nervousness began to trouble his breathing. Absurd, but when the breast of the engine roared towards him and its breath smote his cheek, the nervousness tugged at his heart like a man's hand. The curving of the train brought into view a youth's head and shoulders far extended from a carriage window, and his hand outrageously waving; and before the train was still, or Tony had recovered from its strepitous onrush, the youth, perhaps one inch under six feet and with an athlete's waist and a blacksmith's shoulders, was walking with a grin towards him.

" Hallo, sir."

Tony put forth a hand and an answering smile. But heavens! was this young Hermes the fawning Doyly of three years back? A flush accompanied the smile on Tony's face; he shook Frank's hand and curtained his thoughts with laughter, for he was feeling uncomfortable at the memory of certain passages between them, and a little repelled to think he had experienced a lover's hunger for the touch of this boy's hand and shoulder. But there was nothing of this embarrassment in Doyly; never had Doyly known a moment's criticism of his master's affection.

" You haven't changed a bit," said he.

" And you aren't recognizable," laughed Tony, for he had nothing to say. And again he studied Doyly's face and figure. One had no original thought as one looked at him, on Ashford platform; one just remembered Praxiteles and Greece.

For a mile along the Dover railroad, the Doylys' reserved compartment was a drawing-room in which Tony, standing with the help of the luggage rack, was being presented to a grey mother in one corner seat, a grey father in another, and two sisters, one surprisingly old and matronly, and the other very pleasant but far from beautiful. " She isn't here," thought Tony.

Ostend was the family's base during their holiday, and here, if the sun shone, they consigned Frank's lessons to the nights, and spent the days either on the sands and in the sea, or visiting Ghent, or Malines, or Dixmude, or Ypres. At the last place they heard so much talk in the *pâtisserie* about the interest and beauty of Furnes that Frank was vehement for proceeding there the very next day. But this was their third week, and the family shook its head. By now they had tired of this cathedral visiting and picture staring, and this joggling in a carriage over cobbled roads ; and Mr. Doyly drew a " Hear, hear " from his wife and daughters, when he boldly pronounced that if you had seen one of these old Flemish communes you had seen them all.

" You're a lazy lot," complained Frank. " Dull and heavy —that's what you are. No spirit of exploration. I want to see something new every day. I'm going to Furnes ; it's part of my education. And so is Mr. O'Grogan. In fact we are going to-morrow. If necessary we'll walk there."

" I'm ready," Tony assured him.

" Of course," agreed Frank. And his voice hinted that the family ought to feel the contrast between Mr. O'Grogan's vigour and their lassitude.

He opened the Baedeker and spread its map on the *pâtisserie* table. But after measuring the mileage to Furnes with the back of a knife, he was obliged to shake a sorrowful head and say : " No ; can't be walked. Not in a day."

" But look here," said Tony, placing a finger nail on the town of Nieuport. " There's one of these roadside railways running from Nieuport to Furnes. What's wrong with walking along the coast from Ostend to Nieuport, taking a return ticket to Furnes, and walking back from Nieuport to Ostend in the starlight of evening."

" There's nothing wrong with it," Frank allowed crossly. " And what's more, it's what we're going to do. We'll do it to-morrow, if the weather's obliging."

The weather was more than obliging the next morning ; it beamed a brilliant benediction over them ; and, indeed, its warm enthusiasm became almost embarrassing, so that Frank and Tony had pushed their jackets into their ruck-sacks, when they issued out of Ostend on to the long straight road to Nieuport. Under the sun it lay like a taut tape between the sand-dunes and the sea.

Given a flat road through country monotonously the same—sand-dunes and coarse grass nearby, and Dutch elms and church spires along one horizon, and the sea sparkling on the other—let its course be so straight that it is empty of surprises and doubts, for its few pleasure towns, its Mariakerke, and Middelkerke and Westende, are alike in their spruce vulgarity—let these be the conditions of the road, and two people, walking it, will swing into their rapidest stride, and, over the unhesitating rhythm of their motion, will release a talk so high and absorbing as to be counted among the memorable things of life.

The talk of Tony O'Grogan and Frank Doyly this morning was all about the certainty of an early war with Germany. It was the year 1910, when the war-scare fashion was at the crest of one of its waves. And though Tony, as a young intellectual, was more than half a Tolstoyan with a loud hatred of militarism, yet there was a stirring in his young blood at this distant call of war, and this growing appetite had dictated a conqueror's terms to his theories, instructing him to expound the view " that they would have to fight *this* war—they would have to teach Germany, as the arch enemy of pacifism, that pacifists were prepared to take up arms in one great final battle for their faith." Mr. Robert Blatchford, the Socialist editor who had proclaimed exactly this message, had been of great help to Tony in this satisfactory compromise.

Was there no chance of the war's being avoided, inquired Frank.

" Absolutely imposs.," declared Tony. " No, it's absolutely imposs., I'm afraid. The Germans are perfectly frank about it. Last summer holidays Mr. Sugden had the bright idea of making a little more money by having some foreign students as parlour boarders, and he asked me to stay with him during August to talk English to them. There were six Germans, one Frenchman, and myself ; and we talked of little else except the war. One day I had taken them for a walk along the downs from Ditchling Beacon to the top of Wolstonbury, and two of them, two shaven-headed coves called Strauss and Wedekind, as we stood and looked over the weald, laughed and said, ' Next time we come over this brow it will be from the sea, and with half a million men deployed along the skyline. We shall march down this slope and make your school our Corps Head-quarters.' And I said, ' *Will* you? You won't get over the top of the brow, because we shall be waiting for you, and all along the line of the downs, ten million strong.' And he said, ' *Nein, nein,* you've got no army,' to which I replied, ' No, but most of us can fire a gun, and I shall have much pleasure in shooting Strauss first and then hitting Wedekind over the head with the butt end.' We had a most jolly talk about it. Did you read Robert Blatchford's articles in the *Daily Mail?* "

" No," Frank admitted. " But I heard about them. Didn't he say——"

" Well," Tony broke in, unheedingly, " there was a Socialist writing. No red-hot Conservative like your father—no bullet-headed Tariff Reformer like my brother Derek; and *he* said that it was inevitable, and the sooner we trained every able-bodied man in the kingdom, the better. That from a Socialist, mind you. He sees what the triumph of Germany would mean——"

" That's what Lord Roberts is always saying, isn't it——? "

" Yes. Yes, of course," Tony admitted, but as if doubtful of this new ally. " But he says it from a different point of view. He's frankly a militarist. For my part, I shan't be fighting for a nation or a flag, so much as for a principle. It'll just be an accident, of which I shall be jolly glad, that my nation will have ranged up on the side of the principle. But whether you look at it as a pacifist and an internationalist —which is what I think I am—or as a howling patriot—as *you* probably are—I should have thought it perfectly obvious what was afoot. Teddy saw it all along—Teddy being our late lamented sovereign, Edward VII. What do you suppose his *entente cordiale* with France was about, and this alliance with Russia, and our overtures to Japan? The foreign offices are getting shoulder to shoulder, but the people won't see it. I've no particular use for the *Daily Mail*, but in this particular instance it happens to be right—absolutely right; but I doubt if it's really making much impression—the English people being, bar none, the most mentally indolent and unimaginative on the face of the globe——"

" Damn, no! " Frank burst in.

" Yes, but—interrupting you for a moment—they simply won't see it; they don't want to believe anything so disturbing, so they shut down their imaginations and walk straight on, whistling and refusing to see a cloud that's black with the thunder-storm. Oh, how I should like the job of stumping the country and waking them up to their peril! Only I shouldn't speak to them of the threat to their country, so much as of the threat to humanity. I should appeal to their altruism rather than to their selfishness."

" You'd do it thundering well! Will it come soon, do you think? How ripping! "

" Those German students seemed to think so. Wedekind said that next year was the appointed hour. Nineteen-eleven, he said——"

" Oh, I hope it's not quite so soon as that," Frank interrupted, a little skip of excitement intruding itself into his stride. " I shall be only eighteen then, and I suppose that's too young to get a commission in the army."

" You needn't worry about that. I've no doubt we shall want every man from eighteen years old and upwards. Robert Blatchford says so."

So went the thrilling talk, and the miles were swung beneath their stride : the sand dunes went past their right shoulders, unconsidered, and the glistening Channel accompanied them on their left. Scarcely did they see the sparse houses of Westende and Lombartzyde as they strode through them, their speed quickened with talk and their inward eyes engaged on a picture of war. From the sand dunes came no word of prophecy ; they did not whisper that among them would run the long en-tanglements of barbed wire, and the chain of concrete *mebuses* with their machine guns pointed seaward in expectation of the invading English, and their searchlights commanding the Channel ; they could not murmur, " You are marching into No-Man's-Land."

Nieuport was in front of Frank and Tony now, its red roofs, its crow-step gables, its flèches and bell-turrets rising behind the masts and the ruddy sails on the Yser river, which were veiled in turn by a fringe of trees. Frank and Tony had just spoken their pleasure in the red sails, when a loud, palpitating hum, low in the sky behind them, turned both their heads as one. A huge clumsy biplane was flying towards Nieuport, not three hundred feet above the ground.

" Great Snakes! " shouted Frank. " It's an aeroplane. Would you believe it, it's the first I've seen."

" Yes, it's from Ostend," Tony explained. " I heard there

was one coming to give a demonstration on the sands. I expect the whole population's on the beach to see it."

They stood still and stared with parted lips at the machine roaring overhead. They could see the doll-like head and shoulders of the aviator. Above their watching faces the aeroplane traced a semicircle as it turned its nose again for Ostend. It flew straight away from them, almost as if their two faces had been the points it had selected for its hairpin bend. So rapt were they by this unfamiliar sight that they said nothing till the machine had diminished to a speck, motionless against the blue, and its roar had faded into a hum that was sounding less in their ears than in their memories. They never thought of it as a visitor out of the future, bringing a murmur of a great noise that the future held in its keeping, and turning about and receding into the future again. Instead they recommenced their walk, and quickly found the happy, easy stride.

And walking on, they disputed whether in the coming war, aeroplanes could be employed to any good purpose; whether in their comparative clumsiness they wouldn't be shot down like grouse on the wing; whether they would ever be capable of sufficiently sustained flights to bomb the reinforcements marching up to the battle. And talking thus, they crossed the bridge that spanned the Yser; but it held its secret. Left and right of its entrance was a belt of trees and pasture, with here and there a farm building: No-Man's-Land; No-Man's-Land where, four years later, the two battle lines would meet, clash, and finally, since neither would yield it up, entrench themselves for a fifty months' quarrel; where the Véry lights would shoot up at night and outline these trees, now shivered and blasted and thrown; where the searchlights would sweep round and illumine the old piers of the bridge; where thousands of men would take their bullet or their shell-splinter and shut their eyes on this, their last picture of the world they had known.

Frank and Tony passed on into Nieuport, and chose a café on the Yser's bank, for the refreshing of themselves with some *syrop de groseilles*. Frank sat himself down by an iron table on the pavement to guard the long glasses and reserve the chairs, while Tony went in search of a *pâtisserie* and cakes. Five minutes later the cakes were spread upon the table, seated on their paper bags: *swedois, meringues, bateaux marrons, tartlettes au fruits, babas* and *éclairs ;* sixteen in all; eight each; and they devoured them every one without distress, for their stomachs were like their minds and at an age of enthusiasm and receptivity. And while they digested the cakes and called for more *syrop* and fingered the long glasses, they continued the talk; and so did its stirring images occupy Tony's mind that he took little count of the real back-curtain against which they were raised—the Yser with its red-sailed barges and the flat country stretching behind to the outlines of Westende, now bathed in a haze from the Channel. On the film of his memory came only a vague impression that the café was a corner building, and that if he turned his head, he could look up a long, lifting street and see at its top the tower and roof of *Les Halles*, where they sold the butter and eggs. And that at the end of the embankment was the little station of the *Chemins de Fer Vicinaux*.

"I don't want to mount the train yet," Frank maintained. "We talk better walking. Can't we walk further?"

Tony produced the map and spread it on the table.

"We might walk to Coxyde or Oost-Dunkerque—Oost-Dunkerque sounds promising. It seems we can pick up that road-side train anywhere."

"Well, let's," said Frank; and suiting the action to the word, he stood up and shook his flannel trousers into place. "I love these Belgian villages."

Tony drained his glass and rose too; and together they began the long tramp to Oost-Dunkerque. With so brilliant a subject of conversation it would seem but an easy stretch. And sometimes behind the conversation, Tony, delighting in this new intimacy with Doyly and perceiving that the boy would soon be of an age with him as he was already of a height, wondered if a friendship was beginning between them that would last through the whole of two long lives—such a friendship as was to be hymned, a few years later, in the song, "Friend of Mine," which Tony always cond mned as sentimental, while his whole nature answered thrillingly to its sentiment:

> "And when the night falls tremulous,
> And the last lamp burns low,
> And one of us, or both of us,
> The long, lone road must go . . .
> Whatever fate our souls await,
> Let me be there, let me be there with you."

On then with his friend to Oost-Dunkerque, creating his pictures of what they would do in the coming war; but never seeing the strangest picture of all, which, even after it had established itself as the truth, forever seemed too strange for believing; never the picture of himself marching at the head of his company, after its withdrawal from the battle of Paschendaele into a "quiet" sector for a few weeks' rest—marching on and on, till he recognized the cobbled road from Coxyde to Nieuport—reaching Nieuport at night and seeing under the autumn stars that it was nothing now but some acres of undulating brick-rubble, a few gutted walls, and the shell of a church standing in a picturesque ruin against the sky—clambering down into his Company Headquarters which were some cellars beneath the rubble—and with the daylight next morning setting out to find the spot where he and his friend had sipped their *syrop*, eaten their cakes, and prophesied this war—finding it easily, because he had only to go down the remains of the street which dipped from *Les Halles* to the quays—and standing there and thinking, "Yes, under this mound of rubble that café lies, and there are actually weeds growing over its grave; that's the old Yser, right enough, though there are no red sails on it now, and its concrete walls have been shelled into the water; there's all that's left of the little station of the *Chemins de Fer Vicinaux*; and look! there's even the rusty ruins of one of its tram-like railway carriages! Just to think of it! To think that we should have sat here, discussing this war, on a *trottoir* that would be buried beneath its desolations, and within a stone's throw of the cellar that would be my Company Headquarters, and—O Frank, Frank!—hardly more than a cannon's shot from the place where the better of us should die. . . . And you said, I remember, 'I love these Belgian villages.' . . . Well. . . . I wonder where the *pâtisserie* was. . . ."

CHAPTER VIII

THÉRÈSE OF OSTEND

AT the end of August the Doylys left for Paris to spend the last fortnight of Frank's holidays merrymaking. Paris had been the noisy demand of Frank; his sisters had immediately endorsed it, and Mr. Doyly, after protesting that September was no season for the boulevards, had decided abruptly : " Well, it'll be hot, it'll also be cheap ; " whereupon the whole family packed up their baggage. Tony made his farewells on the platform of Ostend station, agreed to a hundred plans for reunions in England and other travels together, gave the train a humorous push to help its slow starting, and waved to Frank and the sisters, who leant in turn from the windows and waved back, till borne out of sight. A sudden sense of loneliness gripped him.

The bank-notes of Mr. Doyly, fattening his pocket, persuaded him to delay during his remaining two weeks in Ostend. He gave the mornings to the sands, first bathing, when he would wilfully swim out far enough to set the *sauveteurs* shouting and blowing their trumpets, and then reclining with his pipe in a hammock chair and watching the gaiety of others. Often his note-book came out of his blazer pocket, that inspirations might be feverishly jotted down, for few things moved him quicker to that questioning compassion which is the tilth of creation than the sight of a multitude of people happy, boisterous, and buffooning, under the tonic of the sun.

One thing, perhaps, touched yet more vitally the germinating seeds ; one thing never failed to fill his head with a fine drugging rhythm of ambition, idle dreaming, and active, warm creation ; and this was the massed music of the Kursaal orchestra, as it filled every night the high, wide roof of the Grande Rotonde. In that garish and pillared mosque of pleasure, with the portraits of the great composers looking down from their painted medallions on the ceiling, and the flags of all nations drooping from the encircling gallery, and a thousand well-dressed people seated at their tables, and the tall mirrors on the left reflecting a distorted canvas of the whole scene—here, in an air heavy with the smoke of men's cigars and the scent of women's *Peau d'Espagne*, he would sit alone at his private table, lipping his own cigar, and not unconscious of his dinner jacket and patent leather shoes, and fix his eyes on everyone's focal point, to wit, the black back and passionate arms of M. Hellesens, the conductor, who, in his little brass pulpit that jutted from the orchestra's balcony, was poising and plunging and swinging and swaying and crouching and rising and brandishing fists before the tempest of music, like King Lear evoking the storm and acclaiming it with a dithyramb.

But Tony's brain only half apprehended M. Hellesens, for in the infinite spaces behind his staring eyes the music had set a whole school of young poets and phrase-makers to their tasks ; and M. Hellesens only came back into full possession and scattered the school when his ravening gymnastics and passionate forward-reaching seemed like to rend him in twain or to lift the whole excited audience through the air on to his back—or when a throbbing metronomic excitement suddenly began to beat in his shoulders, as the brass and wood-wind blared out a warrant for a universal madness among the instruments, and the forty fiddlers entered upon a wild acceleration, all going mad together, and a brain-storm swelled and swelled in the drummer till he was a terrifying lunatic abandoned to the percussion of everything within reach, and the music was a thunder and an earthquake and a doomsday, in which it seemed the whole orchestra must perish together, like the wild spirits they were, with M. Hellesens diving after his performers, baton uplifted, into the fellowship of their damnation. And just when Tony felt that his brain must burst, and knew that every other of the thousand listeners was in the like condition, their brains crying an answer that was both, " Oh, let it go on ! let it go on ! " and " It will stop in a second ; it will stop ! it will stop ! " lo ! it finished in a last frenzy of the drummer and a crash—and M. Hellesens was still alive, and facing round upon all and smiling and bowing, and the fiddlers were quiet and wiping their bows or their foreheads, and the horn-players were spitting down their instruments, and the drummer was a perfectly sane young man—even a bored young man—as he laid his weapons down.

Then, in his excitement, Tony felt as if much of that power which had been released from the balcony had entered into his own being, and he was himself a full-charged store of power, a genius in endowment and a giant in will. And when the music began again, his confidence mounted to a knowledge that he would create larger and larger poems—larger poems than man had yet produced—superhuman poems; he could hear their periods rising and falling and answering one another and soaring to majestic climaxes, like the waves of sound; and then his emotion would change, and he would perceive the inability of literature to attain to the balance, the pattern, the dense texture of orchestrated music, or to express so perfectly the wistfulness of life and its wordless longings, and he would deplore that, in his chosen art, he must ever express so much less than he could feel and see. Oh, there was only one thing worth being and that was a giant among composers; the Beethovens and Wagners of the world were its greatest voices, and he could not be content to rank below the greatest to-night.

Here came a plump soprano to sing to them, and the orchestra were preparing to weave a tapestry of sound behind her; she began; her voice came effortlessly from her lifted face and wound above them, sounding the world's sorrow and making it beautiful; the people listened and stared; and Tony, moved to a new delight, told himself again and again that here, surely, was the divinest thing that had been given to men, a woman's voice to sing to them; here was one of those many things that went so far towards balancing the ills of life. Oh, with what a myriad of such enjoyments the gods had endowed the world! When would grumbling men see it, and stop bleating for their few hours of pain? Just hark to this outburst of enthusiastic applause: wasn't it another wonderful thing? This generosity and gratitude surging up from a thousand people, wasn't it absolutely glorious? Why, they loved the plump soprano in this moment, the good souls! A universal "Bravo!" a storming, stamping "Bravo!" it simply put a lump in your throat, if you thought about it—its generosity, its goodwill, its happiness. And didn't they see that every "Bravo!" they gave to a singer, or a symphony, or a goal at a footer match, or the close of a book, or the march of a good dinner, was a "Bravo!" to life, that would take a lot of cancelling. By gad, there was a poem lurking here, surely! Now for his pencil and notebook.

And many such thoughts did he think, sitting at his worship of M. Hellesens's orchestra.

But his loneliness in these weeks—to his surprise and discomfort—bred other imaginings than philosophies of life and dreams of fame. He was alone in a crowded city of pleasure, and feeling more completely alone as the days built up the fortnight. And when on the sands in the mornings he watched the caresses of the courting couples, or in the streets at night the spurious caresses sold by the courtesans, a hunger moved his body and a temptation visited the threshold of his mind. Though he made more and more room for it, as each summer night removed another day from his holiday, he chose to believe that it would remain a debate in his mind and nothing more. He wouldn't really succumb, he supposed. So he listened—listened long and pleasantly to his own arguments. "I am over twenty-one now, and I have a right to know. . . . There cannot be many who haven't found out before this. . . . If ever I am to write I need experience. . . . It's not that there's any danger of *me* becoming a libertine. If I could once learn what this thing is, I don't suppose I should ever want to explore it again. It might be wise to explore it once, and so put one's imagination to rest."

On his last night, as he sat in the Grande Rotonde of the Kursaal, a silent figure among hundreds of laughing groups or happy couples, and the music from the balcony sang and thundered over his head, this ingratiating temptation worked into fuller and fuller occupation of his mind, till at last the crowded people around him were no more clearly seen than figures in a dream and the loudest of the music might have been miles away. "It'll have to be to-night, or not at all. . . . I have a right to know. . . . If ever I am to take this step, it had best be now, while I am in a foreign town. . . . Furtive? . . . Yes, I suppose it is. . . . But how can it ever be done, except furtively? . . ."

The vocalist tripped down the tiers of the balcony and stood at M. Hellesens's side for her song. She was very young, and her diffidence and anxiety were clear to Tony, as she glanced with a trembling smile at the vast audience. All about her was modest : her dress a simple robe of salmon pink, her brown hair parted in the middle and drawn from her brow to a coil at the nape of her neck, her brown skin flushed with nervousness, and her eyes straying to the paintings on the roof. She stood, a splash of pink and brown against the black and white of the orchestra. Her voice shook as it swam into Donizetti's *Air de Lucie de Lammermoor*, but it found its confidence, and then she rested her hands on the cushion of her bosom and sang happily. As her feeling swelled, she pressed them together or opened them a little way apart in invitation ; and her voice, so fresh and clear and exquisitely feminine, sang its way into Tony's hidden and shadowed debate, as if it were the call of the voice of all her sex. He bent his head from her, ashamed that his body should feel empty of all except a weakness and a trembling. Oh, the mystery of it all, for love and pity and infinite tenderness were so large a part of this trembling desire ! In it all that was best in him and all that was worst in him seemed to have met and mingled at a single point. How close was the best to the worst ! He was poised between the depths and the heights, and he could touch the depths or touch the heights, with a movement scarcely measurable.

The debate was still a warm sea in his head, its waves swelling and falling and buffeting one another and settling to no calm, when the orchestra clashed to its last climax. M. Hellesens bowed to the applause, and disappeared. Tony rose with the rest, and fell into the slow stream of people pouring to the doors. He was hardly aware if he went onward or stood still. In the same abstraction he went down the wide staircase and gathered his hat and light overcoat from a steward, and passed under the marble portico into the darkness of the pavement that fronted the courtyard and the carriages. " I have not known. . . . One must arrive. . . . It has to be furtive. . . . Why need I think of it as despicable if I go into it, not as a poor piece of self-indulgence, but as a step in pursuit of knowledge ? . . . Is that rather specious ? . . . Perhaps it is . . . I don't know. . . ." He crossed the courtyard towards the gates and the *Place* beyond, where so many lamp-lit streets converged. " And then, on the other hand, isn't all this timidity rather contemptible ? . . . If I do it at all, why not do it boldly, instead of in this conscience-shaking way, like a nervous girl. . . . I don't know. . . . I don't think I'm ashamed of faltering on the brink. . . ."

So he goes, lost and seeking, as every soul in the world.

He emerged from the Kursaal gates on to a pavement of the *Place*. It was only ten o'clock, and through a night bright and warm under a star-sprinkled sky the people were coming and going, in their carriages or on the pavements, in numbers as large and wraps as light as those of the sunny morning hours. Ten o'clock. Inevitably Tony's eyes, directed by his recent thoughts, swung along the pavements to see if any of the ladies of the night were yet abroad. Almost at once he met the merry, inviting eyes of a young girl, whose face had swung back to him over her shoulder, as she walked steadily onward, round the railings of the Kursaal. Her gait continued the invitation, her steps becoming jaunty, as if the heels of her shoes were exceptionally high; her hips swinging. And she turned her face and looked again. A blush burned at Tony's cheek-bones, and his glance shot away into the road. Then he walked off in the opposite direction. But the pavement, describing a circle round the Kursaal, carried him to the Digue, where he stood to look at the dark shapes of the bathing machines, and the ripples of the sea, as they sighed in luxurious laziness up the sands. All nature was tinctured with his thoughts to-night: the air was velvety and warm like a caress, the languor of the sea was a lover's languor, and even a sail that had filled with the breeze was round and smooth and disquieting. He turned about and saw a young girl's spare figure, walking towards him from the other side of the Kursaal; walking with a jaunty step that flashed its explicit invitation. Its dark coat and white fox fur he recognized at once as belonging to the girl who had already sent him the invitation of her eyes. Her face swung to him again; she passed and tossed over her shoulder the same merry smile. As far as he had seen by the light of an arc-lamp, it was an oval face, soft and childish above its froth of white fur; such a face as always went straight to his heart. His throat dried, his inner trembling quickened and he followed.

" Good evening, dar-leeng," she greeted him, in her foreign accent, when he was passing her.

Discomfort was again hot on his cheek-bones, but he answered her with as much ease as possible.

" Good evening, Mademoiselle."

" You come for a walk—no ? It is a lovely night."

He smiled down at her, and she archly up at him.

" Yes," he decided. " If you care to."

" Oh, I love to come. Thank you vary much."

" You are Belgian ? " inquired Tony, as they walked on.

" Noh. French, dar-leeng."

" But you speak English very well."

" Ah, yes. I have been in England during two years."

" You seem very young ? "

" I am twenty-two, dar-leeng."

" You look sixteen."

" Ah, I like you. I like you vary much." And she quickly put her arm round his waist, and looking up at him, whispered, " I think I like you vary much, dar-leeng."

How that " dar-leeng " hurt him ! It surprised him that a word could hurt so. And chasing after his thoughts, even as he walked and talked with her, he supposed it was because he had longed all his life for this word to be given him in a real surrender, and now he had bought it for money.

" What's your name, little one ? "

" Thérèse."

" It's a beautiful name, and it suits you—Thérèse."

" I like you to call me ' little one.' "

" Do you ? I am glad—my little one."

The word was a tool that cut him as he used it. Turning his eyes down to this little girl's face, which looked up so often from its white fur, he felt no dislike of her—nay, almost an affection, and certainly a quick-beating desire, but his endearing word repelled him like the feel of a false half-crown when it is light as aluminium.

" Oh, but put your arm round my shoulders, will you not ? " she pouted. " Hold me close. No one will mind."

Tony blushed that she should have to tell him the rules of procedure like this ; and he tried to commute his awkwardness into ease by a gay laugh and the words, " Why certainly, *ma petite ;* " and he gathered her small shoulder in his hand, and drew her tight against him. The touch of her body gave him a tremor of pleasure (how different he was from the boy who had been so embarrassed when Emmy Holt, of the Freshwater night, cushioned herself under his arm !) ; it seemed extraordinarily tender and sweet to hold a childish figure close and protectingly ; but the pleasure was marred by a sudden hunger for the real, complete, ecstatic self-giving that he had wanted, and by a disappointment that this spurious performance was not it.

Suddenly she asked him a strange question, and his pride hinted that he lied to her; but he quickly recoiled from a pride so poor, and answered frankly: "No, you're the first, my little one."

And her response was a tight hug.

"I will be good to you," she said.

Their walking along the digue for the next few hundred yards was enclosed in a lovers' silence; and under that silence Tony's mind, darkening with sadness, was shutting its eyes and trying to imagine that the slight body, pressed against his and abandoned to his will, was the much-loved body of the girl who would one day worship him and desire him. She who would be Juliet to him . . . or Heloise. Let his imagination be strong enough to conceive of Thérèse as her, and then the actual holding of Thérèse should give the same joy, for the touch of one young feminine body must be like the touch of another. But his heart fell as it told him that this was *not* the same—that it was as different as a foggy twilight from a full noon—and he was surprised to find himself seeking a comfort in his disappointment by drawing closer to him this little trivial Juliet —this little paid deputy for Heloise.

"Shall we go now?" she asked.

"Yes, if you like. Is it far?"

"Noh. Only just behind the Kursaal. We have been walking away from it."

"It is not half-past ten yet, little one."

"*Ah, n'importe.*"

They turned about, and, interlacing again, walked back along the digue.

"I return to Bruxelles to-morrow, or the next day," said Thérèse.

"Why? Don't you live here?"

"Oh, noh. I come here for the season. And Ostend is finished now. Ostend is always finished after the first week in September."

"Are your—your friends, then, always the visitors?"

"Yes, oh, yes. Nearly always the English boys."

She had said it wistfully, and Tony took a slight shock.

"You like the English?" he asked, feeling for an answer that would balm the bruise.

"Yes, vary much. They are always the kindest and the most generous."

" And you think you will do better in Brussels than here ? "

" But yes ! *Naturellement.* It is difficult here. There are not many houses where we can get a room in Ostend. It was not so once ; but it is now. They are afraid of the police. In Brussels—no."

The police ! Fear joined the many thoughts in Tony's mind and was for a time the loudest visitor in that room. He sickened with shame : shame that he should be engaged in a traffic that offended the police of Ostend, and a greater shame that he should play the coward about it. Truly there was little but shames to be found down the road he was treading now.

Behind the Kursaal they walked into a street of arc lamps, she unafraid of the people's eyes, and he, though feigning a self-possession and a gaiety, anxious to escape under cover. She drew him across a road that was still a-rattle with horse-hoofs, and stepped into a quieter street that ran at an angle from this main thoroughfare. It was a street of shops, but their plate-glass windows were now dark and blinded, and the pavements under them were almost deserted. One or two of the windows on the upper floors were alight ; and one or two people walked rapidly along the echoing flags to their homes. Each of these lighted windows and each of these people was a spring of fear to Tony. At a tall narrow door between two of the glass shop-fronts, Thérèse stopped and rang ; and together they stood on the pavement, the girl's feet jigging merrily, and Tony's lips rounded for the shaping of a light, unheard tune.

Now a semicircle of light had created the fanlight over the door ; the handle was being turned, and the door pulled with difficulty from its jamming. It disclosed the figure of a tall, full-bosomed girl, who met them with some casual phrase that sounded like, " *Entrez, mademoiselle.*"

Leaving the door agape, she walked back to the first room on the right to open it for them and switch on its electric lamps.

" Come in, dar-leeng," said Thérèse.

They both followed the tall, capable girl into the ground-floor front room that she had illumined for them. In its bright light Tony saw that it was a typical Ostend *chambre à louer :* a large mahogany bed pushed against the further wall, with a mahogany dressing-table shouldering its side against the back of the bed ; a mahogany and horsehair sofa against the nearer wall ; heavy curtains over the windows, and a huge gilt mirror leaning above the mantelpiece and reflecting a tilted segment of the room. The tall, capable girl, her back to them, was busying herself for their comfort, drawing closer the folds of the curtains, lifting off the counterpane of the bed, pummelling the cushions on chairs and sofa. Tony was shocked at the indifference and efficiency of this young, comely creature. Thérèse, meanwhile, had gone opposite the gold mirror and was removing her hat and touching her curls. He saw now that she was pretty above most, her forehead broad and crowned with fair, curled hair, her features small, her cheeks full and smooth under their powder, her lips shapely and apart and lovable, even under their borrowed vermilion.

Now the tall, capable girl, her tasks completed, came to Tony with an open palm. Nonplussed and frightened, he did not catch her meaning; but Thérèse explained.

"Oh, I see," Tony acknowledged. "Thank you;" and with a blush of shame for his ignorance, he fumbled for his pocket case, drew it out, and with insecure fingers disengaged a ten-franc note.

"That will do," he said, in what was meant to be a lordly fashion, as he handed it to the girl. "Never mind the change."

And immediately the girl, as if eager to escape with her luck, departed without a word of thanks or demurring.

"Oh, you fool!" Thérèse rebuked, but gently, and with a charming glance from under her eyebrows. "You give her too much. She laugh at you."

"Can't be helped," answered Tony jocularly, though saddened at this chaffering.

Thérèse doffed her coat; and Tony's heart began to race with fright . . . with shame . . . and with quickening desire. This was the first time that a girl had unveiled herself before him. But almost before his shaking hands had laid away his overcoat Thérèse had jumped upon his knee and was caressing his cheek with her hand and saying, "Dar-leeng!" His hand felt her waist and breast, and suddenly all his distaste and heartache were forgotten, and he drew her into his hunger, pressing—so strange it was!—both the worst of him and the best of him upon her lips: pressing thither not only his lust but his whelming humanity too.

A quarter of an hour later, and he was conscious that there was nothing left in him but pity and tenderness. The worst being satisfied the best could play. He asked her gently how she entered upon her present life, and she told him a story which, though it conformed to a standardized shape, came from her lips with the simplicity of truth. She had had a fiancé who had left her with a baby—" *Ah, mais il est brave, mon bébé* " —and she had fled from her parents and put the child with some cottagers, and come to Brussels to find money enough for herself and him. " If I work in a shop, I do not make enough, but now—in a few years I shall have enough to start a little business of my own, and he will live with me. *Voilà !* " Tony preferred to believe it true.

There was a silence, and then she said, " You go now—no ? "

" Well, yes, I suppose so," he laughed.

Quickly she slid from his arms and switched up the light. The clock on the mantelpiece showed them that it wanted half an hour to midnight. To his surprise Thérèse began to dress hurriedly.

" You too, darleeng," she hinted, with a smile.

Then he understood : she was going out into the street again. The former distaste came back and constricted his heart, but he cloaked it under merry sentences and gave her her wish. To his merry talk she returned but formal answers, so busy was she with her fingers and her comb and her mirror, so eager to complete this attiring and to take her place on the pavements again, before her sisters should have forestalled her. Once, sitting down to draw on her stocking, she made a grimace and said, " Oh, my foot, my foot ! " and held it out for him to see. It was a pretty little foot, but inflamed. " Too much walking; too much walking," said she. " Ah, well ; " and she hurried on the stocking.

He too dressed quickly, not wishing to be a hindrance to her. Coming to his pocket case, he gave her, in a sudden uprush of generosity, and remembering what she had said about the English boys, one of Mr. Doyly's five-pound notes.

" *Voilà*," said he, smiling as he tried his French. " *C'est pour vous et pour votre bébé*."

She recognized the value of the note and cried, " *Ah, vous êtes gentil, vous êtes gentil !* " and folded it happily into her handbag ; after which she turned to the mirror that she might powder her face and finger her mouth with her lip-salve.

Standing behind her and tracing the childish lines of her

figure, he wondered what he thought of this girl who for a space had taken him into so intimate a union and was now hurrying out of his life for ever. None of the sentimental admiration which some of his favoured authors had pronounced, nor any of the contempt which the righteous must affect; but a deep compassion, certainly, and a swelling gratitude that was emotional rather than reasoned. As he drew on his overcoat and picked up his hat, he recalled the scene in Dostoievsky's *Crime and Punishment*, where Raskolnikov knelt before a harlot-girl and kissed her and said, " It is not before you that I am kneeling, but before all the suffering of mankind." Only a Russian could say a thing like that, but he felt that when, in a moment now, he must say good-bye he would like to kiss her in this wise, not amorously, but reverently. To her little shallow mind, his kiss would mean no more than that she must believe in his gratitude rather than his contempt, but to his own thinking, it would be a ceremonial kiss, offered as a recompense and a plea for forgiveness from all his kind.

He walked up to her and put his arm about her shoulder, while she was giving the last touches to her hair and her hat in the mirror. With his other hand he turned up her chin that he might print his ceremonial kiss on her mouth.

" Good-bye, my little one."

But before he could reach her mouth, she had turned her face to one side and presented to him her full cheek.

" Not there," she smiled, pointing to the newly painted lips. " Not there. You spoil them. Kiss me on the cheek—do you mind ? "

Dulled by this unexpected rebuff to his fine thinking, he kissed the cheek perfunctorily ; and together they walked to the front door, where she shook his hand and smilingly repeated her " *Vous êtes gentil*," and ran up the street in the direction opposite to his own.

PART IV

CHAPTER I

HALF-TERM had gone by, and the Christmas holidays were drawing towards Stratton Lye fast as a cantering horse; and ahead of them came a flying missive from Peggy: Tony must, *must*, MUST give his four weeks to them in their Southend vicarage. In her lively words there was a new affectionateness which lit an instant response in him, but, after a second and third reading, made him wonder if it sprang from a disappointment and a loneliness. Surely this warm letter had burst from a pain suppressed. And when on the 19th of December he alighted from the train on to the Southend platform, he caught from her eyes the same expression of a new-born interest. She was a little shy, and so was he, and they shook hands with roaming glances; but each felt that, hidden behind their shynesses, two new affections were indulging in a mutual peep.

" O Tony, it's jolly," she exclaimed. " It's ripping of you to come. It's years since I've seen you. Hundreds and hundreds of years."

" It's three months, to be accurate."

" Yes, but I mean *properly*. I haven't seen you properly since I was married. We're going to have enormous talks. I want to talk about old times and our holidays at Freshwater and funny old Captain Alum and our life at the old Vicarage, and that summer at Grandelmere and—oh, heaps of things. Do you mind ? "

" I shall survive it, I expect."

" Yes, do if you can." The ice broken, her talk flowed over him like rapids. " Tony: I so seldom see any of the Family now. And they're the world's worst correspondents; I *do* think they ought to write sometimes to the one member of the Family who's left them for this outpost of civilization. You see, *you're* all together in the holidays and have all each other's news ; you ought to send some of it along to poor *me*, who wants some of the crumbs that fall from the rich man's table, and the dogs licked his sores. This is my taxi. Hop in. . . . Tony: Joyce has only written about three times, Keatings once, and Derek not at all. Do you know, I've felt it so much that I suddenly realized how beastly we'd all been in not writing regularly to Father, and I send him a long letter every week, and he writes lovingly back—my only relative who writes to me. He knows all about your coming, and says he's going to think of us together on Christmas Day, and lift his glass to us, his two youngest—bless his dear old heart ! He's still in Belgium, living on the cheap. I hoped you might run into him, when you were over there in the summer."

" Belgium's rather a large place. One can quite easily miss people."

" Yes, I suppose you can. But, Tony: even if he is living in sin, he's a darling. I love him much better now than ever I did when I lived in the same house. So I do you. I suppose that's often the way. It's a dreadful indictment on the human race, isn't it ?—that it's almost impossible to live with each other and to love each other. What pigs we must be ! "

Tony put his hand on the taxi door. " Here, I'm going back. I don't want to be hated."

" No, don't be a donkey : it takes more than four weeks. I can endure you and love you for that period. I wouldn't vouch for five weeks, though ; and, Tony: you must promise you'll let me know directly I get on your nerves, and you begin to loathe the way I cut up my meat, and the way I move my mouth when I eat, and the way I fall into the same sentence again and again, and always with the same horrid expression of the eyebrows, and the insincere notes in my laugh which always runs up the same scale, and the endless rattle of my voice, and its habitual high pitch, and the way I sit down and the way I stand up—you know the way you can——" She stopped and continued : " You know, in theory I love everybody in the world, and I think I really do. *Really*. I find the smelliest tramps quite adorable, and O Tony ! as for the East End costers who crowd down Southend High Street on a Bank Holiday with their toy balloons and ' tittlers ' and their ladies in ostrich feathers and their choruses and their hoarse-throated jests, and their patience—oh, I defy anyone to see them without wanting to kiss them all."

" I know what you mean," said Tony.   " They have an effect on me, but they don't make me want to kiss them.   They make me want to write greater poetry than the world has ever seen."

" Yes, I suppose that's the way it takes you—exactly the same thing and entirely different.   Don't you sometimes think you and I are very much alike ?   *Do* say you do."

" I don't know."

" Oh yes, we are.   I was quite sure of it during the Communion Service last Sunday.   And I gave more thought to it in the evening when I had to go to some old meeting in the town—for the Society for the Prevention of Missions to Seamen—or one of those things.   And I decided that yes, it was so.   But to return to me.   I really love everybody in the world, but I want to live with nobody.   It's fear : fear of not loving *one*. By the by, did you know that I was a Christian Socialist ?   I didn't know myself till I discovered that Michael was one and expected me to be.   I was delighted.   Good gracious !   I haven't talked so much for years ; it's topping, and here we are ! "

St. Blaise's Vicarage, a gabled house of red brick and red tiles, stood within the square asphalted yard of St. Blaise's Church, and proclaimed its legitimate cohabitation with the church by a Gothic front door.   To this door Peggy ran ahead, and flung it open with her latch key.

" Enter, Tony.   Come right in to tea."

Tony had not completed his glance at her drawing-room before he knew that the whole place, with its cushions, its flowers, and its tea set out on an occasional table, was on parade for him : the silver was new-polished and standing at rather conscious attention ; the sugared cakes had been lovingly chosen and were arrayed in a pleasing pattern ; the flowers had come from the florist's that morning and were posed like coryphées when the curtain lifts on the ballet.   And he was sure that Peggy, before she set out to meet him at the station, had given one last look to her room, and had stepped back and rearranged a flower or a cushion.

" Is Michael coming ? " he asked, as he sat in a corner of the long Chesterfield.

" No, he's out somewhere."

" Busy, I suppose, just before Christmas ? "

" Oh, yes, I expect so."   (Was she speaking with less ease ?)

" You've never told me how you like being a Vicar's wife."

" Oh, it's awful fun. Especially the more vulgar parishioners, and Tony: they *can* be adorably vulgar in these parts. And some of those who aren't quite as vulgar as the others, are dreadfully snobbish about it—but that's rather sweet too, isn't it ? One or two of them are saints of God, as you always find."

" And you're a success ? "

" Rather ! Yes, I've no doubts on that score. They say I'm a ' nice little person.' They like me—but not as they do Michael, of course. He starts with the enormous advantage of his cassock and his cape and his carburettor—his biretta, that is. I can't catch *those* up. They worship him. There's an awful lot of priest-worship in these here ' Catholic ' churches, Tony."

" And are you as madly in love with him as ever ? "

At once he knew that he had been tactless : Peggy's eyes, glancing at him, had been frightened before they smiled.

" Yes, of course."

A silence dropped, fortunately disturbed by the sound of the hall-door shutting. Peggy's voice called : " Michael. Come and see Tony."

" Right-ho ! " The reply was as genial as ever, and Father Michael came after it into the room : a tall figure in an untidy cassock and cape ; thin-featured and friendly-eyed, but—how was it ?—he had advanced much further into middle age than was warranted by the two years since Tony had last seen him. In two short years he had collected its greyness over the ears, its thinness on the crown of the head, and its chickeny skin at the adam's apple in the throat. From several symptoms— from the yellowness on the rim of his clerical collar, the absence of a cuff at his wrist, a razor cut on his cheek and another under his chin, the latter having spotted his collar—Tony suspected that this man who had appeared when presented to the O'Grogans as so brisk and dapper was in truth relaxed and lazy. His geniality was the same, however. He offered his right hand to Tony, and placed his left hand on the boy's shoulder, and said : " Well now ; this is excellent."

" Michael : don't you think my Tony's growing rather fine ? " asked Peggy, when their polite exchanges were releasing them to sit down.

" *Please*, Peggy," her brother demurred.

" Well, you *are* ; and I am ever so proud of you. I'm long-ing to show you off in church." As she said it, she took her handkerchief and removed a grease stain from her husband's cassock, an attention which he received with a smile.   Now the talk played again behind the teacups, but it had lost its spontaneity : brother and sister both perceived that it had become a traffic in formal inquiries and feigned interests, and Peggy soon withdrew from it into silence.   Tony, though aware that he was not interesting Father Michael very much, pushed in front of him his ambling information, and knew that it was moving with as little ease as a hobbled donkey in a field.   His old embarrassment in this stranger's presence grew upon him till it was a darkness ; and when Peggy suggested that he and she went up to his room to unpack, he experienced a quick relief, like shutters opening to the daylight.

Up in the bedroom pleasure burst into noisy life again, Peggy sitting on the bed and starting a hundred hares of conversation, and Tony hanging up his suits and observing with a new tenderness, now that Thérèse of Ostend had healed a myopy in his eyes, the line of her shoulders, the long straightness of her arms, the swell of her breast and the round grace of her hip as she crossed one leg over the other.   Strange that this new sight of his should add a tenderness to his affection !

Michael left them to themselves again after dinner, proffering his sermons as an excuse, and they talked the evening away. It was after ten o'clock when Peggy said : " Go and see what Michael's doing ; " and Tony walked out and across the hall to the study.

" Oh, come in, come in, old man," Michael's voice called to his knock, and Tony pushed open the door.

Father Saffery's study was a small square room, too heavily assertive of its master's calling.   It always made Tony think of a short, fat man, recently converted to Anglo-Catholicity and displaying with more zeal than intelligence, in button-hole, on watch-chain, in his tie and on his fingers, the insignia and trinkets of a dozen Catholic guilds.   In the corner that faced you as you entered was a statuette of the Madonna, bright with blue and gold paint, and you felt that she was meant to be the presiding genius of the room ; a big crucifix, reaching to the picture rail, bent forward over the Vicar's littered desk, as if blessing all that might be transacted there ; in their gold frames a gallery of Raphaels and Leonardos hung round the walls and watched the blessed work of the room ; a *prie-Dieu* with another crucifix and candlesticks and several black manuals, stood in a corner like a mercy-seat where God Himself might be approached for his assistance in the work; a "Churchman's Almanack" hung from the bell-push to give the work direction; in the tall shelves innumerable theological books, including all Father Faber's books and many volumes of Liguori's "Moral Theology," ranged themselves untidily for the work's advising; and, extended in the single arm-chair, with his knees higher than his chin, reclined the Vicar himself, engaged on a sixpenny paper-backed novel.

"Hallo, Tony," he greeted, half rising. "Here; have this chair, won't you?" and on Tony's declining, he sank back relieved. "Well, sit down somewhere. Yes, I'll come and see Peggy soon, but let's have a talk first."

He laid the novel face upwards on his lap, put his elbows on the arms of the chair, locked his fingers together, and disposed himself for conversation. Tony pulled up the chair from the writing-table, and sat down, resting his elbows on his knees. But despite Michael's amity, naturalness would not sit itself between them; and the talk only slipped its hobbles when it discovered itself as an argument on Anglo-Catholicism and Socialism. Then the Vicar expressed himself with an amazing fluency and a bursting utterance that was, however, always held in courteous check and always patient of his visitor's views. But, even so, Tony had that curious sense that nine-tenths of Father Michael's arguments were designed for the decoration of himself rather than for the conversion of his visitor, and that, however courteously he might wait till Tony's interpolation had concluded, he was not really listening to any other words than his own, but was inwardly threading a necklace of new sentences with which to add to his own decoration when his turn should come. For nearly an hour this argument must have continued; and it was still bouncing to and fro as they walked back to the drawing-room. Tony entered first, and took a knock of sorrow to see Peggy sitting in a gilt chair with sad and distant eyes, her elbow resting on its arm, and her cheek sleeping in her tired hand. Arousing herself with a start, she sloughed off the sadness like a bad dream, and met them with smiles.

The days convinced Tony: Peggy and Michael, behind a window-dressing of good humour, content, and even affection, had sundered. And the knowledge set him brooding. Peggy had loved this Father Michael with all that perfection which Tony himself longed to take from someone and to pour back in return, and in two years it had sunk down into an empty tolerance. And in so sinking had it not disproved itself? Was there then no such thing as a love which endured? He had believed, and still believed, that a perfect union with another fellow-creature was the one thing which could give completion to life, and that without it all else in the world must dim its beauty and don shadows of pain; and was it nowhere to be found? Were we all cheated by a transient gleam ahead? No, no! Peggy had been unfortunate; that was all. If it had not endured for her, then Michael was not her true love. Twenty years older than she! She had blundered. One must not give up faith in the perfect thing, because a sister had guessed wrong. One must not blunder; that was all.

Tony was seeing Michael's character now. In the old days before the marriage, the Father's manner, like his dress, had been tidy and well-ordered, and none of his character had come past it; but now he was wearing his own clothes. And it was no very unamiable character; just an ordinary one; but by its ordinariness it had failed Peggy. Like many priests who had no taskmaster over them, he was indolent—but then so were most men. On week mornings, ten minutes before eight, when the bell of St. Blaise's had for some time been ringing the people to Mass, Tony would hear the Vicar leaping out of bed, bustling about his room, opening his door and running downstairs like a late schoolboy; and at breakfast Tony would keep his eyes from the too evident fact that St. Blaise's priest that morning had ministered at the altar unshaved. Indolent —but then so were most men. He was irritable sometimes with his wife—but then how many husbands were not? His High Churchmanship and his Socialism were decorative rather than sincere—but then, wasn't it possible that this was clearer to Tony's keen insight than to his own lazy thinking? In his sermons he acted a part—but then, what else was it possible for him to do. His profession had cast him for the part, and he must play it out.

None the less, these sermons, delivered so quietly and with such an effect of packed emotion, of restless spiritual yearning, and of insatiable love for souls, affronted Tony, who knew how much of the preacher's time was spent on his bed or in his arm-chair. Did many commonplace priests, after their long course of half-unconscious hypocrisy, attain to this very real histrionic power, their one remarkable gift? Just remember his own father, or look at this brother-in-law of his ! Once inside the walls of his church and vested in alb and amice and stole, he could create his part as perfectly as the most accomplished character actor. And always the Peggys of the world—not only the foolish women but the Peggys—would come to the feet of such men, and believe, and perhaps break themselves there. Why, Father Michael's rôle in church would have deceived Tony himself, had he not seen the actor in his dressing-room.

And if all its tinsel and buckram could be revealed to him by a few days' intercourse, how quickly it must have hurt a clear spiritual vision like young Peggy's. Poor Peggy! He didn't like to think of Peggy being disappointed.

Many times he found himself catching her thoughts and feeling a hurt in them. Her conscience sent her to every service her husband conducted, and into her modest seat at the back of the church ; and Tony's new fraternal affection sent him along with her, and on to the hassock next hers ; and if it were ten minutes before Low Mass, he felt Peggy's knowledge that the celebrating priest, in his Vicarage across the yard, had not yet hurled off his blankets and hurried into his bedroom slippers ; and if it were sermon time at High Mass and Father Michael were preaching very earnestly, or if it were a Communicants' Guild service and he were giving an exceedingly devotional address, he saw her eyes avoid the pulpit, and knew that the addresses wounded her. Sometimes he went with her on her round of the parish streets, and when the simple women, to whom she had brought some comforts, came to the doors and greeted her with : " O ma'am, what a *lovely* sermon yer 'usband give us last night ! " he watched her answer with a grateful smile, and knew that, behind the smile, her sense of truth had been chafed. Sometimes he sat in the drawing-room and listened while silly ladies, over her teacups, enlarged on her husband's saintliness, or on her good fortune in being his wife, or on her wonderful privilege of assisting in the noble work of a priest " who was always going about doing good," and he almost felt the laugh that trembled in Peggy as she bethought herself that Michael, at the moment, was shut up in his study with a sixpenny novel.

So Peggy had flowered into nothing more uncommon than

a *hausfrau*—Michael's *hausfrau*, doing the better part of her husband's work in the streets of his parish. Was it good enough ? Had not Peggy been a seed of brighter promise than that ? But then : was it not true of nearly all people that they were made for more than they achieved ? The forest was packed with seeds of which only one or two had the luck or the room to grow into tall trees. And to the larger minds were not the many unfulfilled seeds as lovely and as interesting as the few fulfilled ? If there was going to be nothing epic about Peggy, well, perhaps one could see her as the more beautiful for that, because she was going to be typical of the great majority.

Peggy uncovered herself to him before he departed. He had encouraged her to it. A polite silence extending over the last days between her and Michael had told him that, behind their window-dressing, there had been a sharper breach than usual ; and he was so touched by her gaiety in front of him and her remoteness when she supposed he wasn't looking that his romantic desire to act the strong supporting brother swelled up in him, and he resolved to lure her into speech ; it would relieve her, he thought ; it would lift for a while the burden of her hypocrisy.

He began by discussing her religion. Could she really swallow all the paraphernalia of Catholicity—the penances and the priestcraft, the masses and the Mariolatry (he was rather proud of these words). " Frankly, Peggy, can you ? "

And she seemed delighted to pour out her spiritual history ; she settled down to it on the sofa, throwing her arms along its back and looking at him with laughing eyes. She told him how, in her childhood when she was terribly shallow, she had firmly believed all the dogmas of the Christian faith, but had doubted most gravely her own goodness ; and then, when she was eighteen and a little less shallow, she had suddenly doubted all the dogmas as well, so that she was left with nothing but a despairing desire to be good ; and then, one day, a sentence in one of Michael's sermons—" Michael's, of all people ! Wasn't that strange, Tony. I always like to think it was *his* sermon "—had given her a complete release from mental worry. He had been speaking of dogmas and ceremonies, and he suddenly said : " You must always remember that the best in this kind are but parables ; parables shadowing forth truths that could not otherwise be hinted to our finite minds ; "

and the minute he said that everything had leapt into clearness.

"Tony: it was wonderful. I suddenly saw the Mass in a new light, as the most lovely parable ever devised to teach us about our unity with God and our dependence on Him and our need of renewal, and all that sort of thing. . . . I saw that whatever we believe and practise down here, we shall find, when we die and enter upon a larger vision, that it was all terribly childish. And Tony: I saw that in this respect the most intellectual conceptions of the modernists were probably no nearer the real, untellable truth, and not half so expressive, and not half so simple, and not half so free from pride, and not half so emotionally satisfying, as the comparatively crude sacramentalism of the Catholics of all ages. I saw they would never satisfy me. Perhaps they ought to—but I can't help it —I'm not made that way. I've a sort of a feeling that the rejection of sacramentalism as childish is really less profound than its acceptance. Tony: it's like this : to the very shallow, to peasants and children and so on, Catholicism is a most marvellous system of discipline and faith, dovetailing extra-ordinarily with all one's emotional needs ; to the rather less shallow—those are the rationalists and modernists and you, I expect—it's a stumbling block and an offence ; and then as you get to something like profundity—that's me—you see the parable idea, and rest quietly in it. I'm sure you don't understand what I mean, but *I* do. You see, I'm incurably Christian at heart ; I am—*really !* By that I mean that everything Christ said and did, and everything the best of his followers said and did, has always, all my life, simply *screamed* its truth at me ; so the only question was, what sort of religious practice and discipline was I to go in for ? And I have chosen that which was good enough for the Catholics of all the ages. And honestly, Tony, it dovetails most marvellously with my nature, such as it is."

Tony thought long on all this, and at last commented :

"So you're perfectly happy, are you ? "

"Happy ! " She glanced up, and immediately sent to him that artificial smile which was always at her service now. "Oh, yes."

"Really happy ? "

"Yes. . . . Why should you ask ? Don't I look it ? "

"Not always."

" Oh, I'm sorry to hear that ! "   She settled herself into the corner of the sofa, to look at him better.   " I thought I was one of the world's bright and cheery souls.   But I'm glad you told me.   I'll start at once the Brighter Peggy Movement."

" Don't be facetious, when I want to be serious.   Are you as happy as you expected to be ? "

If she were to abandon facetiousness she must withdraw her stare from him ; she directed it into the fire and did not answer.

" Are you, dear ? " he repeated.

" No, Tony. Of course not. We never are. Not as happy as we expected to be."

Silence succeeded this ; and Tony's gaze had gone the same way as hers—into the fire.

" But, Tony, I'm quite fairly happy, all the same."

" Tell me what's missing."

Her unanswering silence proved her desire to speak.

" Tell me, Peggy. Tell me what's missing."

" Oh, nothing," she murmured. " Nothing much. Only perfection, and we're fools to expect that."

" Perfection of what ? "

" Love," Peggy murmured.

He broke the silence again. " I understand, dear. Go on."

" Tony : when I was in love with Michael, I—I am very fond of him still, of course, but so differently !—when I was in love with him before we were married, I'm sure I loved him as utterly as it was possible for one human being to love another. My mind was never at peace, unless my thoughts swung back to him . . . and I was quietly happy if I could rest my eyes on him. And now—so soon—it's all different. I—sometimes my mind's only at peace when I swing my thoughts away from him ; and—and, apart from duty, he means so little to me—that's what's so awful—that the change can be so quick. . . . Oh, it won't bear thinking on, Tony."

She was near to breaking down, and he gave her a pause in which to recover.

" Things'll get better and better, I'm sure," she continued, " as we get more used to each other, and dependent on each other. And if we have children. . . . I say, Tony ! have you ever remembered that we've got a little brother in Belgium ? I've made up my mind that if I never have any children, and if anything should happen to father, and if the mamma is compromised a bit by the boy, I shall go over there and beg to be allowed to adopt him. Don't you think that that would be rather nice?"

Inwardly Tony was conscious of his loving and pitying smile. This was the real Peggy; Peggy, leading her commonplace life, and arranging the picturesque and beautiful deeds that she would one day do.

He restored the talk to Michael.

"But you say you're still fond of Michael, only in a different way?"

"Oh yes, yes. I think I am. Of course I am. I want to love everybody, and to put him first. . . ."

"Won't things come perfectly right again?"

She shook her head.

"Not back to where they were when we first discovered one another. I can imagine many things, but I can't imagine that. They'll get better and better, as I've said, but they won't get back to their beginning again. They're really almost as right as they'll ever be now, Tony; and it's not so bad. We've both of us learned a lot of wisdom. He accepts the position and sees my good points, and I've heaps of them; and I accept all his good points, and he's got heaps of them, too . . . and I'm grateful to him for much . . . and fond of him, so that . . . but, Tony"—her lip trembled—"I wanted to *love*, not to *accept*. That's what breaks my heart, if I dare to think: I wanted to *love*, not to accept."

And she turned her face away that he might not see her tears. He stayed in his chair, till a conflict within him had settled; the lifting of her shoulders, and her hand feeling for her handkerchief, made him long to comfort her—one ought, he thought, to take her in his arms—but his whole nature, to his bewilderment, was shrinking from doing such a thing with a sister; even to take her hand and stroke it would be difficult; however, let him conquer this English revulsion. He got up and went and sat on the sofa by her side, and put an arm round her shoulder. Instantly Peggy showed that no such revulsion troubled her; she threw her arms about him and kissed his cheek.

CHAPTER II

AND STILL THEY PUT FORTH IN HOPE

A ND then Joyce married at Easter; not a novelist, as she had once vowed she would do, but Len Daubeny, of the Indian Army, and the son of a retired Indian Army general, who lived in an old house on Chiswick Mall. Len Daubeny had been observed drifting in front of their windows, back and forth again, with an innocence too pronounced to be innocent; and Joyce, after examining him in detail from behind her lace curtains, and deciding that his height was six feet and that his eyes were the kind, blue eyes that India gave, and that his skin was the interesting sallow brown with which that country also decorated its servants, told Keatings to go out and collect him. Keatings had little difficulty in effecting the acquaintance, for poor Len Daubeny was desperately offering himself for capture—his leave from India would not last for ever. This was in early spring, and thereafter he was a daily companion of Joyce and a nightly visitor at their house. And on Palm Sunday, after church, which Joyce, impressed by the Major-General's sidesmanship, had begun to attend again, he asked her if she would return with him to India and share a poor man's bungalow at Rawal Pindi or Peshawar. And Joyce looked frightened for a moment, and then said she would love to.

So in Easter week they were to be married by special licence in Chiswick Parish Church, by the river. And Derek, as dispassionate as ever, but fortunately no less pompous, announced that his present to the bride would be to pay all the expenses of a large Reception at Chiswick Town Hall; which caused Joyce to fling her arms around him and kiss him as " an old darling, too good to live," and him to protest that it was nothing, that she was his sister, after all, and that twenty pounds would go a long way ; and when he was released from the embrace, he rearranged his suit and smoothed down his hair. And to Tony, who was home again for the Easter holidays, Keatings commented : " With Peggy and Joyce both gone, I've made up my mind to remain a bachelor and stay at home and look after the old lady. Derek'll go off as soon as it suits him ; that's certain enough ; he'll retire to bachelor chambers of his own, or he'll marry a fat woman with a large enough fortune. But I'm glad young Joyce is marrying. The Daubenys haven't much money, but they're Sahibs, and it's another jar for the Gabriels."

The little riverside church was crowded for the wedding, so popular had Joyce made herself in Chiswick and Fleet Street ; and an Easter sunlight streamed upon the heads of the people. The dust motes were alight and jubilant in its rays. Why dust motes, dancing in their beam of light, should express melancholy rather than jubilation Tony was not prepared to consider, but as he stood, elaborately dressed, in his front pew on the bride's side of the church, and gazed at Joyce's slim white back and the folds of her falling veil, and the trembling of the spring flowers in her hand, and then at the square, sober shoulders, well braced, and the neat head of Len Daubeny, he filled with pity. Joyce, from the nape of her neck to her high-poised heel, with her shoulders steady but her arms faintly vibrating, was beautiful as a gazelle tense for alarm ; and so was Len Daubeny ; beautiful as a still, curbed horse. Tony sank into brooding. What might be the prank of the gods in making for themselves these shapely playthings, so exquisitely nervous and tuned for pain, and then driving them together, and leaving them to break ? If you thought of it, there was a splendid foolhardiness about all young men and young women who married, for, though in their heart of hearts they suspected that all their predecessors who had put to sea on this venture had foundered out of sight, yet always they volunteered to undertake it again, and put forth in the plucky hope that with them at least it would be different. And a crowd of brave, uncomplaining people, all of whom believed in secret that these new adventurers were doomed like the rest, assembled to support them in their start and to flourish gallantly a soiled old creed of success. " It is all rather splendid," thought Tony.

But Joyce would be happier than Peggy; not as happy as
she expected to be, for sure; but happier than Peggy, just
because she was less intense and had never been vexed by these
same playful gods with too much spiritual sight. Always her
vitality would burst up into high spirits, as surely as Peggy's
flowed into brow-crumpling thoughts. And therefore she
would be an easier wife than Peggy—laughing and self-sufficing
and unexacting. But for *him*, give him a wife like Peggy,
hungry for perfections, and with grave eyes that looked beyond
the world to immortal goals.

But no. In his present rebellion against the gods, he was
almost persuading himself that he, for one, would not play
their game for them; *he* would not allow them to breathe this
lying mist of love on to the clear sight which was with him now.
And he was just blowing up an anger with himself for having
been, so far, one of the keenest, aptest, forwardest exponents
of their game, when his eyes fell on the back of the youngest
bridesmaid.

It was a back as beautiful as Joyce's—nay, more beautiful,
he thought. Those wide little shoulders, square with the
little nape, and emphasizing the neat waist, and then answered
by the widening hips—it was rather " ravishing "—the word
jumped into sight. Len Daubeny's two sisters were to be the
bridesmaids, so he had been told; and ravishing indeed they
looked, with their dresses of pink silk and old lace, their large
picture hats over gold-shot hair, and their bouquets of pink
tulips in their white-gloved hands. The elder one was tall
and slender as Joyce; the younger a little shorter and broader,
but with a schoolgirl's figure, nevertheless; and it so happened
that, tired of looking at Archdeacon Gabriel, the Vicar of Chiswick, and the Rev. Warner Gabriel who were praying over
Len and Joyce, she turned round to see the congregation, and
met Tony's eyes staring at her. As if on a spring, her face
went back to its duties; but from that minute Tony's eyes were
tethered to her rose-clad figure; he forgot Joyce and Len in
front and the congregation behind, and watched her only,
as she stood beside her taller sister, or walked up to the altar,
or played abstractedly with the bouquet of pink tulips in her
hand.

The Town Hall, decorated under the inspiration of Derek,
drew approving gasps from the people, as they crowded in
to their tables. Everywhere among the green palms and ferns

was the bridesmaids' pink : it appeared in tulips and hydrangeas and carnations, and the platform was as a florist's shop or a flower show on Hydrangea Day. And thus the two pink bridesmaids, sitting at the central table, seemed the heart of the room, rather than the white bride, and the jokes flying towards them from the other tables, either demanded whether they had been dressed under the personal supervision of Derek, or prophesied that that when the feast was over and the guests dispersed, they would be carried away with the other flowers in the florist's van. And after the toasts had been pledged, after Archdeacon Gabriel had made a graceful, if a rather sanctimonious speech, and Derek had made a pompous one, and Keatings had looked down on his plate in a general shame for his relatives, and the tables had broken up, and the guests had threaded themselves into new groupings, and Len and Joyce had quietly disappeared, and that faint air of sadness was mixing with the afternoon sunlight in the room, Tony, who had been watching the younger bridesmaid all the time, walked up to her where she stood alone by a tall window, staring down into Sutton Court Road. She brought her face round to his approach.

" I suppose you are my sister now," he said.

After looking him up and down, she allowed her eyes to fold with amusement.

" Oh, I hope so ! "

The words shot into him a thrust of delight.

" And I too," he said.

" You're Joyce's brother, aren't you ? She's talked a lot about you. Of course : you're Tony."

" And I don't even know your name ! "

" Don't you ? " She feigned a hurt. " Well, you ought to. Len ought to have talked a tremendous lot about me to all of you people, but that's just the sort of thing he wouldn't do : the chump ! And hasn't Joyce mentioned me at all ? "

" No, I'm afraid not. Not to me."

" Oh ! " She made with her lips a pout of displeasure. " That *is* disappointing. Well . . . can't be helped. . . . I suppose I made no impression on her. I suppose I'm not really a vivid personality."

" I think you're the vividest person here."

This retort, instant and automatic, surprised himself and lifted a colour to his cheek as well as to hers.

" Oh ! " When she had recovered and could play at humour again, she laughed. " Thank you. You've saved my day from disaster."

" What *is* your name ? "

" Honor. And if you want me to respect you, for pity's sake, don't say ' I could not love thee, dear, so much, Loved I not Honour more,' because—do you know, I've lived twenty years in the world, and I've never met a single person who didn't make an idiot of themselves sooner or later, and say that."

" Any other names ? "

" No other that I'm not ashamed of."

" What is it ? "

" Mary. But I don't answer to it."

" ' Honor Mary Daubeny.' What a lovely succession of syllables ! ' Honor Mary.' "

" Oh, but it sounds so like *Hail, Mary,* doesn't it ? And I'm sure ' Honor ' doesn't suit me at all. I'm not frightfully honourable really. I always cheat the railways and the buses, if they let me. I know I oughtn't to all the time, and I don't want to, but I simply can't help it. It's in my blood. Let's see : ' Tony.' I can't make fun of your name. ' Antony.' Oh, yes, I can, though. There was a saint called Antony, wasn't there ? "

" Yes. He sold all he had and gave it to the poor, and went and lived a hermit's life in the Egyptian desert."

" But how dull ! "

" And there he was visited in person by the devil who sorely tempted him."

" Oh, that was better. And do you think you are like him ? "

" No. . . . At least, only in being sorely tempted just now."

" How ? Do tell me. I love hearing about other people's temptations. I've told you mine."

Mischievously he looked into her eyes and on to her cheek and mouth. " Lots of ways. But most of them I can't tell you. Here's a minor one. I've been tempted for some time to break off one of those tulips from your bouquet and steal it for myself."

" One of my tulips ? Why should you want one of them ? "

" Because—well, since you ask it, because you are looking

rather beautiful, and one of your tulips would remind me of what you looked like to-day. . . . Oh, don't be huffy; it's quite impersonal. Any beautiful picture would make me feel the same about it. I should buy a little photogravure copy of it before I left the gallery. There's no sense in being angry, if you dress yourselves up to make fools of us, and we promptly oblige." And, having explained the nature of the temptation, he yielded to it. "Thank you," he said, holding the tulip in his hand.

"Well!" exclaimed Honor, rather inadequately, but pretending to amazement at his impudence.

"And now let's talk about something else," said Tony.

Honor rearranged the flowers of the bouquet so as to conceal its wound. "Tell me something about yourself, brother, what you do, and all that."

"Officially I teach small boys in a prep-school; actually I try to write."

"To write what?"

"I hardly like to say. It sounds so dreadful. But I try hard to write poetry."

Honor seemed much interested.

"Oh, you must show me some of it. I've a sort of feeling that it's quite good. Yes, I should have thought you were a poet."

"God help us, no! I hope I don't look like one, do I?"

"No, but you talk like one."

"Do I? Not usually, I think. When I have a subject before my eyes that would inspire a clod, perhaps I do."

"Oh, be quiet. . . ."

"And what do you do for a living? Anything?"

"No. What can one do in this backwater of civilization called Chiswick? But I've got to do something soon, because we've no money, which is always so awfully tedious, isn't it? In Chiswick, and with no money, nothing desperate or dangerous can possibly happen, and I feel I want something like that. As it is, I'm going to be made into a secretary."

"I should have thought that you were more likely to be made into a wife."

"Lordy, no! That would be almost as dull. I'm never going to marry."

"Why not?"

"Because I hate domesticity. I help Mummy with the

housekeeping, and though I don't show it to her, I loathe it, and loathe it and loathe it and loathe it."

A shrill voice called her, "Honor! Honor!" and they swung round their heads to see her sister bearing through the people like a graceful yacht. "Honor. They're off. Len and Joyce are off; their car is at the door. And we're going immediately after them——" She paused, recognizing that Tony had been in conversation with her sister, and looked apologetically at him. And Tony observed how like she was, this taller and slenderer sister, to Honor; she was Honor in oval shape.

"Jill, let me present your brother to you," said Honor. "This is Tony O'Grogan. He's most anxious to be a good brother, and he's begun by stealing one of my angel flowers."

Jill and Tony made their bows to each other, but little was said, for Jill drew them to the steps of the Town Hall to throw confetti and rice and banter at the departing couple. Tony joined in the riot, but beneath the surface of clowning and shouting, his thoughts were running in an underground stream on the little wide-shouldered bridesmaid whose voice was still in his ears. He hastened back to her side that he might help her into her car; and he waved his tulip at her triumphantly when she was borne away, waving too.

All that evening he was apart from the others and restless: reason was shut down: will and direction had gone from his thoughts: he just floated and drifted on his memories of Honor: pacing up and down his room, with a heart deliciously irregular and a throat deliciously alight. As soon as darkness fell, he could hold himself no longer but went out that he might pass by, and loiter near, the windows of her house on the Mall. He saw nothing of her, not even a shadow behind a blind, but he was hardly disappointed; it was enough to be alone in the cold air with his thoughts of her—of her shoulders and back, of the movements of her mouth, and of her eyes folding with amusement; it was pleasant to walk home with them, and to escape to his bedroom, where he could put out the light and get into bed behind a closed door and sink into the warmth of these thoughts, in the hope that they would take shape as dreams, or fly from his window on telepathic waves and visit her sleep.

In the morning after breakfast, the sun still blessing the spring day with a summer heat, he was loitering in the road that gave on to the Mall, that he might see her if she left her house. And in mid-morning she appeared, with a string bag for her shopping in her hand: he knew immediately that those wide little shoulders were hers and not Jill's. He retired under cover, allowed her to pass, and followed at a distance, awaiting his chance to contrive a natural meeting. She had turned down Chiswick Lane to make for the shops on the Chiswick High Road, and he fetched a compass round a parallel road and encountered her on the crowded shopping pavement with a surprised and delighted, " Hallo ! my sister ! "

She laughed to see him.

" Is that our Tony ? Are you housekeeping like me ? "

" I'm shopping. . . . No, I'm not. I'll be honest in Honor's presence : I'm acting."

" Acting ? "

" Yes, I'm pretending I met you by accident, whereas I've been waiting all the morning for you to appear, and cursing you for your delay."

" But what on earth for ? "

" What on earth for ? I wonder. Is it peace, Jehu ? What hath Zimri to do with peace who slew his master ? I suppose I came because I thought I'd like to be a brother to you, and help you with your loathèd housekeeping. Give me that bag to carry."

She gave it to him, protesting, " But brothers don't do that. They're not nice enough."

" Is it to the milliner's we go first, or to the modiste's ? "

" It's neither ; it's the greengrocer's. Lordy, how I hate it all ! A greengrocer's is a disgusting place. No one should have to go out and collect the roots that they're humiliated into eating—and the branches, and the seeds. It's work that should be hidden from sight and done by slaves."

" One of your slaves shall carry for you to-day."

" That's why I'm never going to marry. Not unless some hugely wealthy nabob buys me at a figure——"

" Oh, yes, you will. Joyce said much the same sort of thing, and she succumbed to Len at once."

" Yes. Fancy anyone feeling like that about old Len ! "

" Will Len say, I wonder, when someone succumbs to you,
' Fancy anyone feeling like that about Honor ! ' "

" Yes, I expect so.   Yes, that's just the sort of thing he
would say."

" The blind, blind idiot ! "

" Thank you, brother.   You've an astonishing gift of making
pretty compliments, haven't you ? "

" None.   I hate compliments.   I speak only the dazzling
truth."

" Oh, shut up !   Here's the beloved greengrocer's, and there
are the roots for Daddy and all of us to graze on to-night.   Will
you wait outside ?   Please do.   I might get a giggling fit if
I felt you were watching me."

" Yours to command," said Tony.

In such a fashion they spent the whole forenoon, Tony
waiting outside shop doors and imagining with inner inflations
that he was attending on his wife, and Honor (as he knew full
well) extending the shopping, which ostensibly she so disliked,
far beyond the plans which she had brought down the steps of
her house.   She would issue from the shops and push her
parcels into the bag, or suspend them by the string loops over
his fingers, and say, " This is magnificent.   I never expected
to have a brother like this."   And when the Mall and the
river, glimpsed at the top of Chiswick Lane, threatened them
with severance, Tony demanded quickly :

" I say, couldn't we do something together this afternoon ?
The sun has entered my blood.   Couldn't we go on the
river ? "

" I'm supposed to go calling with Mummy this afternoon."

" Can't you dodge it ? "

" I suppose I could.   As I told you yesterday, I've no sense
of honour."

" Well do.   We'll bus to Kew Bridge and get a skiff from
the boat-house at Strand-on-the-Green.   Could you be ready
by two ?   Meet me at two in Chiswick churchyard, by Hogarth's
tomb."

" Yes.   Yes, I think I could, with a little management.   Jill's
is a sweet nature."

" Praise God for Jill ! "

" Then for an hour or two, good-bye.   And thank you a
thousand times for holding all my parcels.   I'm most terribly
pleased with my new brother.   I am—truly."

To this he answered with no clownish repartee, but with a flush and silence.

Ever since, the afternoon before, he had parted with Honor, there had been a pause in Tony's reasoning. He who in the church had been a vessel filling with pity and thought, was now a vessel charged with exultation only. And he would not suffer a footstep of thought to come near and disturb his exultation. God, no! Who, of his own will, would be healed of an opiate's ecstasy? The sun this day, with its July face, played on his skin a tingling warmth which was the exact physical accompaniment to the queer, white, shadowless excitement within. His reasoning stilled, he felt insubstantial as air. He was feelings, not thoughts. And Honor : he knew—simply knew—that her thinking, too, had been dispersed into a mist of feeling. What might not happen on the river?

Here he was in the skiff with her, casting off from the boat-house at Strand-on-the-Green. What had happened between his good-bye two hours before and this reunion now he had little knowledge. He had changed into tennis flannels, cold though the April evening might turn ; would he not willingly pay a price of pneumonia for the happiness of dazzling Honor with his white flannels ? And Honor had changed her morning dress for a summery green frock and a large Leghorn hat— changed, undoubtedly, to feed his eyes. And now she lay at ease and at full length, on the sun-heated stern-seat, and he quickly sculled the boat into slacker water under the bank, for the tide was running down at a good four miles an hour. He did not speak. He looked at the old tiled houses, with their green shutters and their dormer windows and their forward tilt which gave them the appearance of poising on their toes to pitch into the water, upper stories first. He looked at a pair of swans sailing near the mud. He passed the Isle of the Two Chestnuts, and saw that it was fully green now, and that its chestnut trees were already in blossom. He passed under Kew Bridge ; and beyond its spans the river broke beautiful : the tall trees of Brentford Eyot on one side and the tall trees of Kew Gardens on the other ; and the water green with their reflections beneath the banks, and widely silver in the centre, where the strong tide ran. " I shall kiss her here," he thought.

It was Easter, and the young low trees on Brentford Eyot were yellow-green, but the tall old trees behind them, spreading their bare branches against the sky, looked like seaweed pressed against the blue page of an album.   The whole stretch of the river was empty, as it always is in the youth of the year, this side Richmond Lock.   And the towing path, running like a ribbon between the old grey wall of Kew Gardens and the willows bowing to the water, was empty too.   And the stillness of the budding trees, the half-heard sibilance of the birds, blending with the unreal sound of far-away voices, and the rhythmic flutter of his feathering oars, confirmed his silence, and laid on her a silence of sympathy.

Once she turned and saw him gazing at her, and to deny her confusion she laughed and said :

" You haven't spoken a word since Strand-on-the-Green."

He spread his lips into a smile and lifted his brows.

" Why speak ? " he asked.

And she turned again to her watching of the Kew bank where, between lofty chestnuts, came glimpses of rhododendron in every shade of red.   Under the spread of one tree sat a painter on his stool with his easel before him.

" The artists are out ! " she ventured humorously.

But Tony did not answer.

The silence held them till they were round the bend of Syon Park, and here the river seemed wider, because the trees were everywhere lower, and the green reflections had withdrawn to the banks.   The breadth of the river was silver now, and visited the narrow green reflections with patches of silky sheen.

" You aren't always so dull," said Honor at last ; and Tony's eyes twinkled, as he offered something which he had searched out the night before.

" ' Can Honor's voice provoke the silent dust ? . . . ' "

" If you begin the Honor quotations, I shall get out," she declared.

" Get out, my dear," Tony consented, turning the boat's head quietly towards mid-stream.   " I'd love to see you."

" All right, *Saint* Antony.   By the by, did you know that Saint Antony was the patron saint of pigs ? "

" I didn't.   How did you know ? "

" I looked him up last night."

" Oh, did you ?   And haven't you discovered that there was another Antony, who was no saint ? "

" What was he ? "

" He was a lover."

" Mark Antony, you mean ? "

" Yes.   Wait. . . ."   He ran over something in his memory, and then, fixing his gaze on Honor as she reclined on her cushion, spoke in a low voice, level and smooth as the water, and as lit with a peculiar light of its own :

> " The barge she sat in, like a burnished throne,
>   Burned on the water : the poop was beaten gold ;
>   Purple the sails, and so perfumèd that
>   The winds were love-sick with them.   The oars were silver
>   Which to the tune of flutes kept stroke, and made
>   The water which they beat to follow faster,
>   As amorous of their strokes.   For her own person,
>   It beggared all description : she did lie
>   In her pavilion, cloth-of-gold of tissue,
>   O'erpicturing that Venus where we see
>   The fancy outwork nature. . . .
>   O, rare for Antony ! . . ."

He sighed with satisfaction.   " Yes, rare indeed for Antony ! "

" Is that something you've written ? " asked Honor.

" No, sister.   It's an earlier master's : Shakespeare's."

" Oh, I'm sorry.   I ought to have known, I suppose."

" It's his description of the woman Antony loved—his Cleopatra."

This turned Honor's face away ; but since Tony did not proffer an explanation, she was driven, by a strengthening impulse, to inquire why he had quoted it.

" Why ?   I should have thought that was obvious.   Because you recalled it to me."

" But I'm not like Cleopatra, I hope.   She was a brown hook-nosed creature, I'm sure."

" She was beautiful in her own kind, and whatever is beautiful must be like you."

" Don't be absurd."

" I will not be, and I have not been.   As a matter of fact, that was a bit of rather obvious philosophy.   You *know* you are beautiful of your kind—and so is the movement of this boat through the water, and the shudder of my oars, feathering the surface, and—and what else—— ? "   he looked round for beauties comparable with Honor's—" and the darkness under those trees, and the sun on that lawn.   When anything decides to be beautiful, it enters on its kinship with you."

" Ah, well," Honor sighed. " I suppose it's nice to have a poet for a brother."

" It's nice to have an inspiration for a sister."

" I don't know what you mean now. . . . But do let's stop. It's getting tedious."

" I'm dull when I don't speak, and tedious when I do," he grumbled. " There's Richmond Lock. I'll row you up there where there are plenty of pleasure boats and people to amuse you. *I* shall hate it."

" Why ? "

" I hate the river where it's got flashy embankments and tea-gardens and crowds of noisy people who don't really love the river, but only flirt with her. I hate all flirters."

" Don't let's go," murmured Honor. " Let's go back to where the river's empty."

Touched by her quick assent to his outburst, and by the glimmer of a hint that she would rather be alone with him, he turned his bows without a word, and, hardly paddling, let the boat drift down the running stream. He would let the stream carry it down to that lovelier reach where he had first promised himself he would kiss Honor. And there he would keep his promise to himself. So agitating was the thought that he could speak no word, and a half hour passed in silence before they were in the empty stretch that flanks Kew Gardens wall. He cast his eyes around for a place where he could moor, and selected a patch of still water under the droop of a willow. They ducked as the nose of the boat poked into this cool shade, and Tony, unshipping his oars, kneeled on the seat and looped the painter round a splintered bole. Then he returned to his seat, and with a sigh bent his head and rounded his back to provide a dumb-show of exhaustion.

" Tired ? " inquired Honor gently, from where she lay low in the stern.

For answer he went and sat in the stern-seat by her side, resting his arm along its back. She straightened her legs and crossed one foot over the other. Soon his arm had fallen to her shoulder, and since she did not resist him, he drew her a little closer. " I'm tired too," she said, as if justifying her consent ; and she removed her hat into her lap, and let her head rest in his neck. And in gratitude for such a use of him, he tightened his grasp. They spoke nothing, but Honor stared at her crossed feet, and Tony stared at her gold-shot hair.

Many minutes passed, and he wondered if she could feel the knocking of his heart. He hoped she could, and tried to place her so that it could tell its own story. And on a sudden, hardly aware of what he was doing, he had dropped his lips in a moth-soft visit to her hair.

She moved her head and looked up.

"Honor," he whispered into her eyes. "I love you."

The eyes folded for amusement.

"Tony, you *are* the most ridiculous person I've ever met. You know nothing about me."

"I know that I love you."

"Do you realize that it's only twenty-four hours since we first met?"

"Twenty-four seconds or twenty-four centuries are the same thing where Eternity is. To be in love is to be high above time. Time ended and Eternity began the minute I saw you in the church, before I had even seen your face. I have known you twenty-four centuries."

"You are talking a lot of nonsense."

"I wonder."

Her face was still upturned to hear and to rebuke his unintelligible words; and he dropped his lips in the moth-soft visit, not to her hair, but to her mouth. "That is to be in Eternity," he muttered, his speech quickened. "What has time to do with that?"

But she had averted her face.

"Don't, Tony. . . . Not like that."

And he, offended, armed himself in silence; whereon she looked up again and added:

"I want to like you, you see."

"Like! *Like!* I don't want you to *like* me. I don't like you. I don't know enough about you to like you, but I love you—O Honor, I love you—I've never known anything like this before—I've not been sane since the first sight of you —I've felt unreal, as if I had died and crossed into some other life—it's either love or madness. Don't begin by liking me, Honor. Begin by loving me. Tell me one thing, dear—I say! forget about being modest, and don't mind hurting me, if you have to—but tell me the honest truth, did you feel anything when you first saw me?"

Her face, rather frightened, was still staring at him, and she did not answer.

" Tell me, dear," he repeated.   " Wouldn't it be rather wonderful to be the first girl in history who left all the silly coyness out and spoke the truth ? "

Her lids closed over her eyes, and her smile broke into the words, " I admired you, I think."

" Oh, won't you have the courage to say more than that ? "

" I admired you very much."

He hugged her tight now, and her body was willing.

" Did you think about me after you had gone ?   I know it's not generous to ask, but I don't care.   I don't feel generous. *Did* you ? "

" I thought about you a bit."

" All night ? "

Again her eyes closed that they might play no part in the nodding of her head.

" Yes."

" O Honor. . . . Honor. . . ."

" I have told you the truth, Tony, but I don't know what it means."

Tony hardly spoke again that afternoon ; but rowed her quietly home through the sunset and the dusk.

CHAPTER III

THAT evening after his kiss on the river, he paced up and down his room ; and in the riot of his thoughts, a faith in his love was the cause that carried all before it. An orator stood on a platform in his mind and fanned and fed the cause with rhetoric. " I believe in this. I believe in this. I love her. I love that child. And it is the real thing. It was too quick and unsought and overwhelming to be a delusion. And because it is the real thing it will last. I am going to enter upon this love and see that it lasts—always—always. There is going to be one love in my life and one only ; and it is going to be this. I am going to love her passionately all through our wedded life, and right up to the last. Oh, I know that others have hoped to do this and failed, but I'm going to be one of the few that do it. Most men have no wisdom or skill to tend their love and keep it aflame. If there's an art in these matters I'll discover it. It would be cowardly not to go forward just because so many have failed. Thousands are being killed daily, trying to fly in the air, but still the others come on. I'm going on."

But in the morning an axe fell upon the neck of his elation, and nearly severed it. He met Honor and walked with her ; and he went home from the walk, darkened by the knowledge that, though her talk had been studiously merry, she had rebuffed him. It was so, was it not ? Examine again every word she had spoken and every detail of her manner. Could they be otherwise read ? No, she had firmly rebuffed him. *Hell !* what did it mean ?

He took the worrying question up to his room. Of course : she was angry with herself for having been too willing the previous afternoon; she was going to play the conventional game of " not making herself too cheap; " she was going to put him back in his place. Conventional little fool! After all, everything around her had always been conventional: her Anglo-Indian, churchwarden father; her churchmanship; her High School; her Chiswick home. Despite all her fine talk about the unadventurousness of her Chiswick life, she was going to be no heroine of love, who could scout conventions as for an hour he had hoped she was going to be, after her heroic confession on the river.

He met her once or twice more, and was received with the same cheery discouragement, and sent home to the privacy of his room, declaiming angrily. Damn! he wasn't going to stand for this. Did she love him, or did she not? In eight or nine days he must return to Hurst, and she could play with him in this fashion! If she did love him, she must stop this fooling; if she did not, he would snap the rope that bound him to her—snap it then and there. Up and down the room, up and down the same track; or now seated for a space, and now standing by the window and looking out and seeing nothing; with his brain heated under his hair, and the skin of his temples and cheeks tingling with warmth.

He mumbled the sentences of a passionate and offensive letter he would write to her. And the literary artist in him, rejoicing in the full-charged phrases as they leapt ready-made into thought, bade urgently that he released them from their mere dream existence and gave them the active life of words that have taken shape on notepaper and gone beneath the eyes of their victim. And the lover in him—the lover that had hurt Wavers and struck at Doyly—was restless till they had administered their wound. He seized pen and wrote.

" *Honor* " (no *dear* or *dearest*),
      " *In a week from now I go back to Hurst. Whenever in the last few days I have met you, you have suppressed me if I spoke of anything except commonplace gossip or childish pleasantries. And in the presence of this rebuttal, my courtesy with you, which is the expression of a reverence deeper than any emotion that has come into my life before, has not suffered me to tell you of a love that is burning and searing my heart. I write it. And if you do not wish to read it, you can turn from the letter and put it away from you as you have so often turned from me and dried up the words on my lips. I don't*

know if you will read it, but I feel that I must write it if I am to know any mental rest.

"*I have told you that I love you—the word 'passionately' I will not use, for it has been cheapened below any use for me. I will simply say that I love you with the only love I shall ever give to anyone; that I am satisfied that there is no delusion or self-deception in my love; that I believe that it will last through life, only deepening and strengthening and refining itself, as it quiets from its early fervour; that, if you will meet my love with your own, you will be for me the solution of all the riddles of life—you will be my fulfilment—the answer to the question, 'Why was I born?' I write such words after weighing them and deciding that they add no single touch of meretricious ornament to the beauty of the simple truth.*

"*In these words you will see that I have had no truck with 'expediency,' or the fear of 'making myself cheap'; nor have I ever, as so many lovers do, tried to heighten your interest by letting you doubt my love and awaking your jealousy. I have just told you the truth of my complete abandonment to you. And I want a similar frankness from you, and a similar superiority to the ordinary trickery. I love you much too painfully to be in any mood for the shallying treatment you may think it right or pretty to adopt. I am not going to be led at the end of any threads of caprice, nor whistled to at six o'clock and sent about my business at seven. Nor shall I accept the position of a useful and amusing second or third string to your bow. I must be all or nothing. And I feel I must know now which I am to be. I ask you to reply to this letter with a simple answer to my question, 'Do you love me?' And if you say 'No,' as you have every right to do, I shall trouble you no more. I would rather cut adrift at once. And if you say 'Not yet,' I think I shall be wisest to do the same, because I feel sure that if you are destined to love me as I you, you must have responded by this time to my approach. You must have known your partner as I knew mine. I shall never be content with a built-up love.*"

Doubting the wisdom of delivering this letter, but powerless to resist the drive in his imagination, he went out after dark, lips set and reasoning silenced, and pushed the envelope through the letter-box of the house on the Mall. The lid of the letter-box clapped down on a deed irretrievable.

That was on Monday night, and he must return to Sussex on the Tuesday of the following week. Next day he waited at windows for a glimpse of herself or her messenger, bringing her answer. His thoughts and his hands were impotent for other work. And the day passed with never the one letter that mattered tumbling to the doormat. Not the time to despair yet : she might have posted it ; the letter would be among those of the first post to-morrow. And there were two letters for Tony on his breakfast plate—ah ! one would be hers ! The top one came from Cyril Winter—curse him ! Then the under one might be hers. Dared he look ? No, it was from a Stratton Lye boy—oh, drat the child ! How little interest had any Stratton Lye boy for him now !

Still, there was another post at twelve ; perhaps a local letter was more likely to come at that hour. For three hours after breakfast he fretted restlessly to and fro, often visiting the window in the hope that Honor might be in the road, and always seeing the same dull avenue of houses. Eleven-thirty. Only half an hour now. If it did not come by the noon post he would know his fate : she would have snubbed him and let him go. Did thirty minutes ever creep so slowly ? Had twenty of them gone yet ? No, only six. . . . What said the watch now ? Only a quarter to twelve ? . . . And now, after this wait deliberately prolonged ? Ah, it was five to twelve. Forthwith that sinking and heightening of the heart, as one longed for and dreaded the postman's coming ! His knock, higher up the street, quickening one's pulse-rate : his approach with nearer knocks ; his knock next door ; *now !*

Could he be passing across the front of their house instead of coming up their threshold ? " Oh, he can't be, he can't be." But he was ; he was turning into the gate of the house beyond.

" *My God !* All right ! . . . Then it's over. . . . I know now. It was best to know. . . . It's all over. All right, Honor : you'll see no more of me. I shall not again offer myself. You don't know with whom you are dealing. And, O Honor, I loved you. That much I shall always know. I loved you, little one, with all the love that is possible to men. And I'd have been good to you if you'd have taken me. Well, one can turn to one's books now. The suspense is over."

Read he could not ; but he could write. Never had he felt so eager to write. He found relief in turning to the poem he had begun last term, *Regnauld and Mélisse*—a poem very like Shelley's *Revolt of Islam*, because it was to tell the story of a passionate and enduring love—and in altering the features and the voice of Mélisse into the features and the voice of Honor. No use had he for the poem which had occupied the years before, wherein the two heroes were very like Frank Doyly and himself—how nonsensical now seemed that piled-up tale! The days passed over his new work. Each morning, the first post having failed to bring him the letter, he went up to his room, where his table was, and out of a settled sadness tapped the springs of creation. Only the quarter of an hour before twelve o'clock cut across his work, for then the mid-day postman must be looked for down the road. Most he enjoyed writing the scene where Regnauld first espied Mélisse and knew her for his love immediately, and the scene where the ardent Mélisse, without coyness or shame, avowed to the hero that " the tide of her love for him ran as high as his for her." In the afternoons he broke off from this writing at three o'clock when the postman came again ; but he went to the foot of the stairs without hope ; and the wound was not too severe as he returned with empty hands.

Saturday morning showed on his plate a letter that might be hers. No expression passed over his face as he sat down before it ; no lift of the brow or dart of the eye that Keatings and Derek and his mother might observe, though suspense was making his heart knock hammer-strokes and shaking the fingers that cut this envelope addressed in a girlish hand. The same fingers dropped sugar into his coffee as he began to read.

" *My dear Tony*

" *Will you do something for me. You must ! ! ! There's a too truly wonderful Fancy Dress Ball to-night at the Apollo Rooms Kensington, the Easter Ball, Jill and my cousin Gerard Harvey are going and I could have two more tickets for the asking but I have no brother to take me now that Len's gone. Will you take me. I have been wanting to ask you all the week but I haven't had the courage and you see, Len and Jill brought back from Italy some years ago a perfectly priceless set of Commedia dell' Arte dresses, an Isabella an Arlecchino a Columbina and a Spavento Somebody who was the Braggart Captain, and Jill is going as the Isabella and I as the Columbina and Gerard wanted to go as the Arlecchino but I insisted that he was to be the Braggart Captain so that you could be the Arlecchino ! ! ! It would fit you perfectly and you would look topping in it, it's a marvellous particoloured affair with a wide brimmed hat not the least like the pantomime harlequins ! You won't mind being a zany, will you.*

One reason why I insisted on you being Arlecchino is because I wanted to see a lot of you before you go back to your beastly old school, and Arlecchino always plays opposite Columbina as of course you know being so learned ! ! I got Columbina's dress out of our property basket this afternoon, and oh Tony it was so thrilling that it simply gave me courage to ask you.   And now I am going to melt your heart by being terribly pathetic ! !   Tony I have hung up both garments that the smell of camphor may evaporate.   Dont make me have to put them back in the basket tonight unworn and wet with my tears.   Dont you go back on Tuesday.   How bestial.   Do let us have this spasm of gaiety before you go.

" *My love,*

" *Honor.*"

Tony read it again ; not knowing whether it was weighing him down with disappointment and resentment or inflating him with tenderness and joy.   Not a word of answer to his late appeal, nor allusion to it, even !   To treat it as a piece of foolishness best forgotten !   By heaven, he wouldn't stand that ! It was another of her cheery rebuffs, and he was finished with them.   To write in this merry, care-free style when he was living daily with anguish !   To treat as nonsensical his assurance that, unless he could be all-in-all to her, he must go out of her life for ever !   What a lesson for her if he, in his turn, left her letter unanswered !   Or, better still, if, too lofty to stoop to a tit-for-tat, he sent her a courteous answer, declining her invitation.

But " Will you take me ? "   These little words went straight as a shaft to his protectiveness.   " Will you take me ? "   What a meaning might be hidden behind them !   And : " I insisted on you being Arlecchino."   This deliberate choice of him as her partner !   And at the end of it all : " My love."   What did those two words mean, left in the air like that ?   He had ashed her : " Do you love me ? " and she had replied : " My love.   Honor."

He took the letter upstairs to pore over it in solitude.   " Will you take me ? "   " O Honor darling, how can I turn my back on that ?   But am I then to eat the snub you gave me when you refused to answer my letter ?   And after all I said, am I to let you think that you have but to whistle and I shall come to your heel ? "—the orator had mounted the platform in his mind again—" No, you had best take the wound and understand me. No, my dear, I don't take rebuffs so easily. I do not lay the whole of my love at a girl's feet, for her to pass by with her head in the air. And then perhaps to come back and take that little portion which, for the nonce, is of use to her. I do not come a second time."

This last sentence drove him straight to his table and his notepaper.

" *My dear Honor,*
        " *I am sorry I cannot accompany you to the dance you mention, but I shall be busy to-night making preparations for my return to Sussex——*"

But Honor reading that ! The hot tears welling to her eyes ! Oh, no, no. One must forgive, that was all, rather than administer such a disappointment as that. He would cheapen himself once more. And perhaps, perhaps, she might answer his question to-night. Honor, in her Columbina's dress, might give him his " Yes," and languish in his arms. " I will come again once more," the orator declaimed for him, and stepped down from the platform.

And he took his pen and wrote : " Why, Honor dear, of course I will take you to the dance. Look for me this afternoon. . . ."

And there he stopped. Yes, no more than that. That much was good. And it should be delivered quickly that she might have time to reflect on its reticence. She would see in it both dignity and mystery, and be left wondering.

The Ball was in full swirl when Jill and Honor Daubeny, and Gerard Harvey and Tony added an Isabella and a Columbina, a Braggart Captain and an Arlecchino to the fringe of the scene. Honor's dress was anything but the Columbine of the harlequinade : it was a voluminous creation of red and gold brocade, with a tight waist that lifted up her breasts and showed above the low bodice a little of the fold between them—to the final rout of Tony ; Jill's was of the same pattern, but in white and gold ; Tony's was a striped jerkin, and hose and pointed hat ; and Gerard Harvey's Braggart Captain was more like a swashbucklering Toby Belch than anything else. Gerard

Harvey had proved a man much older than Tony had foreseen, and all agreed that he was the chaperon of the party. The four stood by the door, and spent a few minutes in recognizing the costumes of the crowded dancers eddying beneath the great chandeliers.

All those guests who revisit the earth when a Costume Ball calls them to a night of life again were there : Queen Elizabeth and Mary Tudor, Nero and Marie Antoinette, Robin Hood and Friar Tuck, Prince Charlie and Dick Turpin and Lady Jane Grey—so many of those, as Tony pointed out, who had died violently and sought new life in a Costume Ball ! And the figments were as alive to-night as the dead men : The Queen of Hearts, Don Quixote, the Vicar of Wakefield, Ophelia and Hamlet and Carmen. And all the nations, such is their courtesy on these occasions, had sent their usual delegates : a Dutch Girl, a Mandarin, a Geisha or two, a Matador, two Cossacks, and Uncle Sam himself. And those of the Immortals too, who love the dancing time of men, were mixing in the revel : a scarlet Mephistopheles and a black devil, a Puck and an Ariel and a Pan. And our brothers, the animals—yea, and the flowers as well—jostled with the rest to prove how kin they are to men and immortals, when all are dancing. Little wonder that the Braggart Captain, infected by such festivity, seized Isabella round the waist and disappeared ; and Tony, with never so much as a by-your-leave, spirited off with Columbina.

Having bumped into Satan and apologized to Puck and descried a perspiring Dionysus, he thought it worth while to remark to Honor that none but the wicked or mischievous Immortals ever fraternized with men on their gala nights. Where were the Watchers and the Holy Ones ? And this led him into metaphysical profundities, whereby he struggled to explain to Honor that all opposites were equally true, that man was at once a solitary and a herder, and that St. Antony was the truth of his solitariness and Puck and Dionysus the truth of his good company. And for this lapse he apologized.

Honor looked up into his face. " What a strange mind you've got, Tony ! " she said. " It doesn't seem to work like anyone else's."

" How so ? "

" Oh, I've noticed it again and again. You so often seem less excited by the things themselves than by the strange ideas you can find behind them. I'm afraid *my* brain can only move among the things themselves."

It was a pleasant rebuke and he acknowledged it with a pleased smile.

"Probably the ideas behind are much more real, and therefore much more exciting, than the things in front."

"There you go again! It'll take me all the evening to find out what you meant by that. And I shall take it to bed and keep awake with it. It's a strain sometimes, Tony."

He danced on, probing for a special meaning in these last words.

"Have I often been a strain on you, dear?"

"Oh, no. Once or twice."

"When was the last time?"

She looked up, both pardon and a plea for pardon in her eyes.

"You know when, don't you?"

And his hand behind her waist drew her nearer for a second's fraction. She had alluded to his letter; almost she had asked pardon for not answering it. "She will speak to-night," he thought. "She will make an opportunity to say, Yes, she loves me with a completeness no less than mine. But I shall give her no prompting. She must come of her own."

"Don't let's talk any more now," he said. "Let's dance and dance."

"Oh, yes. I like just to float on the music—" and she began to hum:

> "Waltz me around again, Tony,
> Around, around, around;
> Waltz me around again, Tony,
> Don't let my feet touch the ground;
> It's lovely and dreamy,
> It's peaches and creamy,
> And I forget what comes next, don't you?"

"Hush!" he murmured. And they danced in silence till the music ceased.

He partnered Jill in the next dance, while Gerard Harvey guided Honor in and out of sight, through the jostling crowd. Often, as he talked to Jill, his eyes were seeking Honor, and once—twice they found her face and earned her lively smile. It was some time before he discovered that he was dancing more

fluently than ever in his life, and that this was both because the
taller and slender Jill fitted his height, and because she was the
lightest dancer who ever flattered a partner into believing himself
better than he was.

"Confound it!" he said. "Is it I who am dancing so perfectly or is it you?"

"You are dancing very nicely."

He looked down into her face—the oval version of Honor's
face. Well, if he could not now talk *to* Honor, he could talk
about her to this sister of hers—what did he care if Jill espied
his infatuation? Besides, was there not a peculiar kindness
and understanding in Jill's eyes, when sometimes he trapped
them watching him?

"Jill, don't you think Honor looks lovely to-night?"

"Yes, I think she looks adorable."

"What a generous sister you are! But there! You can
afford to be generous."

Jill laughed the compliment away. "Generous or jealous:
I wonder which."

"Ah now!" Tony rebuked her. "That won't do.
You're well aware that you've no reason to be jealous. Besides,
you're exactly like Honor, only in a different shape. I always
think you're like two dishes out of the same dinner service—
one round and one oval."

"Enough! Enough!" laughed Jill. "But the fact remains
I've always wanted to be small and round-headed like Honor."

"Well, that's very silly of you," said Tony.

"Look at Honor's shoulders," Jill advised.

"I have. I always am," Tony admitted.

"Well, then," said Jill, as if the case were proved.

"Do you two sisters really admire and like each other so?"
asked Tony. "That's rather wonderful, isn't it?"

"It's always been the fashion in our family to admire Honor.
She's the family babe, and all that."

"I'm in the family now, dammy," Tony reminded. "I
say, don't you think that families often go in pairs? I mean,
there's a family like ours, and sooner or later another family
comes along that exactly fits it, and then the two families become
almost one. I think we shall sort of sail side by side now."

"Yes, it often happens like that. But Tony, if that's so,
you must try and understand—us."

"What do you mean?"

" Well, Honor, for example.   You must understand that she's
awfully young and simple, really—not dazzlingly clever.   But
absolutely truthfully, she's the sweetest and merriest and lovingest
child imaginable."

How much did this adorable sister know ?

" And you ?   What about you ? " he asked.

" Oh, I expect I'm much about the same."

At the close of that dance they went to the chairs under the
stage where Honor and Gerard were sitting.   Honor, flushed
and excited, greeted them with : " Oh, isn't it too unbearably
lovely ? "   Jill collapsed merrily into a chair.

" Jill's expiring, and so am I," Honor declared.   " I'm off
to get lemon squashes."

" You're not ! "   Tony forbade.   " I will go."

" No, you shan't, you harlequin ! "

And Honor jumped up, but before she could escape, Tony
had caught her hand as one might catch a bird in one's fist, and
closed his fingers on it painfully.

" We'll both go."

" Let me go, you zany ! "

" Certainly.   Come on."

He drew her, running and sliding with him, across the empty
floor ; and a hundred pairs of eyes from the costumed figures
and the chaperons along the walls turned in pursuit of their
linked flight.   A fan or two, and some monocles and lorgnons,
followed them.   Honor gave a skip.

" We make a nice little pair," she said.   " Everybody's
saying it, I can see."

" Mine is a reflected light."

" No, it isn't.   You look quite nice in trunks and hose.
And so do I in these voluminous folds.   Oh, nobody's lived
till they've dressed up in an outrageous costume and run amok
with hundreds of other lunatics.   Only I wish I had tights
like you."

" Honor, Honor ! "

There was a crowd at the counter in the buffet, and Honor
was crushed close to Tony as they struggled to the front, and
he protected her with an arm about her waist.   But once at the
front the four drinks jumped on to the counter as quickly
as if he had slapped it with Harlequin's wand.   And Tony
and Honor, each holding two, ran a non-spilling race back to
Gerard and Jill.   They watched the next dance through.

And then, to shrieks of alarm and laughter, the lights began
to dim, and from the lime-lights high up in four corners of the
room coloured beams played on the centre of the floor.   The
violins sang a waltz very softly, and the atmosphere of
the Easter Ball changed from that of a scherzo into a
nocturne. Into the darkness outside the dancing splashes
of lights, and often across their white shafts, Tony waltzed
with Honor ; and neither spoke. From the darkness and the
pale-hued lights and the soft caressing music, sentiment
saturated into them, as the electricians and the musicians
designed it should. The worst of their bumps into laughing
neighbours could not destroy this sentiment nor disturb their
silence. They danced on and on, so restfully that time meant
nothing. Tony felt Honor lean towards him, and he thought,
" O Honor, you love me to-night as much as I love you. You
will tell me so before the night is over. Perhaps you are wondering now how you can say it." And when the music ceased
after the second encore, and all the couples withdrew to the
walls, he kept her waltzing in the darkness for a few seconds
more.

But as he was dwindling to a pause it happened that two of
the lime-lights went out in the expectation that the chandeliers
would immediately go up. Two were left playing. One had
a dazzle-pattern glass before it, so that it laid a splash of many-
coloured fragments on the floor ; and the other had an open
light, so that it threw a white ellipse by the side of the fragments. Tony saw his opportunity for a very fine parable, and
was not the man to miss it.

" Behold the ruins of poor Arlecchino ! He lies in a thousand
lovely fragments on the floor. The white light is Columbine,
perfectly intact ! Ah ! "—the dazzle glass had been removed—
" all that was Arlecchino is gone now and forgotten like something that has never been." And the chandeliers flashed up,
eliciting a humorous cheer from the crowd along the walls,
and every person in the room turned blinking eyes towards the
source of light. " Both are extinguished now," said Tony.
" They are lost as though they had never been. All their story
is over. So it was, and so it ever shall be."

" Zany ! " Honor scoffed.

Never are the hours so quickly kidnapped as behind the backs
of dancers, and the large hand of the clock on the gallery had
already crossed the hour of midnight when Tony, who had

been dancing with Honor half the night and telling himself
that he could feel her love pouring over him, saw the lateness
of the hour with a chill of fear. " Oh, surely she will speak
to-night," he thought, and unwittingly drew her closer in invitation. " At one o'clock we break up the Ball and it will
be too late. And on Tuesday I go. O little Honor, you cannot
be going to send me away unanswered. Is it an opportunity
you want ? "

His feet slowed and ceased.

" Oh, don't stop," she begged. " I don't want to stop."
And the words hurt him. Had she no such thought as was
filling him, of escaping together to a quiet place ?

" Honor, let's find somewhere to sit this out ? "

" Oh, must we ? "

" No."

Sharply disappointed, he seized her and resumed the broken
dance. Though she said nothing, he knew that she had observed his manner ; and a few minutes later, she, in her turn,
disengaged herself and stopped.

" Yes, let's sit this out somewhere. I'm really quite tired."

So they strolled out of the doors under the gallery, she slipping
an arm into his, and he in acknowledgment pressing it against
his side with his elbow. The corridor was as public as the ball-
room, so numerous were the couples seated on the plush settees,
and so inquisitive the gaze they directed to these passers-by.
Through one glass door after another Tony peeped, but all
the rooms had their occupants, and he sighed.

" Is there never a quiet place anywhere ? "

The doors at the end of the passage opened on to the landing
above the wide staircase.

" Let's go down," he proposed. " I don't care what I
arrive at so long as I escape from these beastly crowds."

Honor was ready ; indeed she put her further hand over the
one she had linked on to his arm, and, thus bound to him, she
footed it down the thick carpet. His hopes had soared into
certainties now : he was walking to the incredible moment
when she would say : " Tony, yes . . ." and they would seal
it with a passionate kiss.

The wide staircase debouched on to the large first landing.
Facing the staircase-floor were large doors evidently leading
to an empty room, for no light showed through their stained-
glass panes. He pushed open one, and by the invading light

of the arc lamps in the street saw the outline of graceful French settees and sofas in gilded wood and brocade.

" This is a retreat, if you like. We have a whole drawing-room to ourselves."

She entered without demur, letting the door swing behind her.

" We won't put on the lights," added he, " lest anyone discovers this place of our privilege. Come, sit down by me."

Leading her to the nearest of the settees and seating her beside him, he put his arm round her shoulder and with his other hand gently caressed her cheek, her chin, and her throat. She dropped her head on his shoulder. Not for a long time did he do more than touch her face or turn it up to his and look down into her eyes, whose brilliance was just visible in the blue-grey darkness of the room. Then he began to imprint quiet kisses on her forehead, and she suffered it. Quick little sentences shaped themselves unsought in his mind : " It is done. . . . We are there. . . ." And in one of these times when he was holding up her chin that he might see her eyes—at last, as if he could hold no longer his gathering ecstasy of anticipation, he passed his arm right round her shoulder, drew her up to him, and placed his lips down on hers. His hold became an inescapable lock, and the touch of his lips a hardening pressure.

She twisted her face from him, and her body pulled to be free.

" Don't, Tony ! "

At once he unclosed his hold a little that she might droop away from him, and asked : " ' Don't.' Why ' Don't ' ? "

" You've no right to kiss me like that."

" No right ! " On a sudden one hand fell limply to his side, and the other drew away from behind her. " What do you mean by ' no right ' ? I love you more than words can show, and that is the only way I can express it."

" Oh, I don't know, Tony." She put her hands together and dropped them between her knees. " It may be right for you to offer kisses like that if you love me as you say you do, but is it right for me to take them if I don't love you in quite the same way ? "

Ten seconds of silence, and he stood up ; stood dubious ; and then walked towards the door.

" Come. We must go back."

" O Tony, what's the matter ? What have I said ? "

He only opened the door and let the light from the landing

spread its fan into the room. "You'd better come away quickly. There's only half an hour more. I'm sorry I made a mistake just now."

"Tony, you wouldn't have me tell you untruths, would you? I'm awfully fond of you, but——"

"Please . . . please . . ." begged Tony, with suffering in his voice.

By the fan of light he saw that she had dropped her face into the palms of her hands. But he only walked on to the landing, waiting for her to come. Many fine denunciations and sarcasms came near his lips, but the fullness of his despair saved him from uttering them. And they danced a disorderly ballet in his head. "You hang about me as if you loved me, you rest your head on my shoulder, you let me touch your face and kiss your brow, you raise my hopes to the highest pitch, only to dash them to the ground again. If you mean nothing with me, for God's sake let me alone. Let me go my way. I want no pretty letters from you. . . . I've told you I will not be half-and-half. Hell! I love you with all my being, but I'll not flirt with you, or be flirted with. . . . You don't love me, that is obvious. I misread all those phrases in your letter, and have cheapened myself on their strength. 'My love. Honor' —it was no more than you would send to a corpulent uncle in the city. . . . I've humiliated myself by coming a second time to your whistle. Not again, little one. Not again. . . . Gosh, she's nothing! She's too light to be capable of love —and I love her!"

With a tired toss of her head Honor joined him, and the two wordless children passed into the light of the stairs. And the light recreated their pantomime dresses, which the darkness had extinguished that they might be Honor and Tony alone. Tony, inwardly laughing a bitter laugh at his merry-andrew dress, led the way up the stairs; and Honor, who had come down them on his arm, now followed one step behind.

As they approached along the corridor to the ballroom, they heard laughter and screams and wilder music than ever; and the picture framed by the arched entrance showed that the dancers were in paper hats and caps and toy masks and false moustaches and Ally Sloper noses, to celebrate the last dances; that each had a "face duster" made of a hundred coloured strips of paper, or a "tittler" made of a peacock's feather, or a toy balloon; and that some were blowing toy trumpets and hooters, and that others were tossing long streamers of paper which entangled themselves round necks and feet and the high chandeliers, and broke and dangled ; and that Gerard and Jill were as uproarious as any, and buffooning with the best. Honor hesitated diffidently on the brink of this wild circle, and Tony stared into it. But he could not bear that she should loiter unpartnered outside the rioters. Nor must people look at her and wonder at her wistfulness, nor Jill and Gerard suspect a quarrel.

" Come ; we had best dance," he said.

And without an answer she came into his arms, and they danced into the midst of the rioters. With acted liveliness he seized the first face-duster he could reach, and played a laughing and violent part with it. He snatched a peacock's feather and put it into Honor's hand, but she could not play up as he could, and it hung unemployed at her side. The splendid unfitness of what he was doing exactly suited his mood ; or was it a splendid fitness ? that he should be dancing, dressed up like an idiot, with a girl whom he had been tricked into loving and would assuredly quit on the morrow—amid a crowd of other coupled fools. His heart was sicklier in its beats than he had ever known it, for he fully believed now that in the matter of Honor he had guessed wrong, and the certainty jumped up intermittently and stabbed him with an intolerable thrust, beneath his clowning and laughter.

CHAPTER IV

TONY'S body returned to Hassocks in the train, and took a car to Hurst, and laughed a greeting to boys and colleagues in the hall of Stratton Lye, and climbed the stairs to the bedroom under the roof; and all the while his mind was away in an empty nowhere and engaged with his thoughts of Honor. It had been a long debate between his thoughts—almost a business meeting; and he had presided over it with a gloomy impartiality. And now his body sat on the bed, and his mind, before leaving the distant meeting, summed up its verdict: " She does not love me ; that is plain. She has none of that overwhelming assurance of love which is mine. She likes me, and I might be able to make her do a little more, but that is not what I want. A love that has to be planted and reared is not the plant I dreamed of. Most men can rear it in a girl, but I doubt if it is ever more than the blossom of a few sunny days. I must accept the truth: she was no Juliet waiting for me. Good then ; I pursue her no more."

And this resolution being a point at which he could well dismiss the meeting, he got wearily off the bed, took out his keys, and began to unpack. But, as often happens with a meeting when its chairman has dismissed it, its members did not adjourn ; and soon he was sitting on the bed with rounded shoulders and presiding over them again.

" Failure ! I have failed with Honor. I begin to suspect that only Joyce and Derek have Daddy's talent for success, because they're content with success as the world counts it. Aren't they saner in this than Peggy and I ? Joyce saner than Peggy ! No. No, I'd rather be Peggy. . . . Besides, just because I've failed with Honor, it doesn't mean that I'm going to fail with everything else.   I'm going to make a success of my writing.   I *feel* it."   The irrepressible confidence of youth surged up.   " I feel abso*lutely* confident about that.   Much of it is great stuff, I know.   And it'll be greater for all I've gone through in the last week.   So good-bye, Honor.   I'll get to work at once."   And he dismissed the meeting again.

And in the following weeks nothing but his writing could lift him out of the blackest despairs.   He tried to tell himself that these despairs were largely a black miasma arising from auto-suggestion, but the information helped little.   After all, to the reason alone, love *was* auto-suggestion ; auto-suggestion was a technical diagnosis of it ; and to give the cause of a disease another name didn't do much towards altering the disease.   And with a powerful imagination like his, the anguish could drive onward into extreme places ; he would sit on his bed, elbows resting on his knees, and picture Honor in the possession of another man and giving him all her love, and then he would understand why some lovers had become murderers, or had let their whole lives tumble to waste.   The weeks passed, and she did not write to him, nor he to her ; and sometimes when the pain had got a deadening clutch on him, he would throw all fine resolutions to the wind, and think : " I can't go on with this.   I can't.   If she were to write one word of encouragement to me, I should have to skulk back to her.   Pride or no pride, if she were to ask me to come back to her, I should have to go. I've only enough strength left not to take the first step myself. And even that may not hold out."

The writing was a temporary anodyne.   He wrote in his bedroom after school hours, walking up and down, and chewing a pencil and rushing with sudden inspirations to his scribbling paper.   Or he wrote on his walks down the country roads, a notebook waiting in his pocket to receive the lines when they were chiselled and polished to their last perfection.   Many must have seen him pausing in the road and scribbling furiously, or revising his notebook and perhaps colliding with a hedge or a lamp-post.   Or he wrote sitting half-way up the slope of Wolstonbury Hill.

Mock-modesty is a partner of ours only when we have company ; when we are alone we cut him dead.   There were times when Tony, after pouring his inspirations over twenty pages, would lay down his pencil from a cramped hand, and shoot up into a standing position and exclaim : " Oh, it's great ! It's magnificent ! " There were times of soaring faith when Tony the critic told Tony the author that his *Regnauld and Mélisse* was really superior to Shakespeare's *Romeo and Juliet*, because Shakespeare, by killing off both his children, had shirked the problem of a passionate love's endurance, whereas he, in *Regnauld and Mélisse*, had faced up to it, and had shown, with no facile evasion of the difficulties, how his hero and heroine triumphed. But at other times he would abruptly arrest his bedroom walking, stand still, and ask himself : " Do I honestly believe that my story, with its triumph, is possible ? I must be sure that I do, because whenever the suspicion enters that I am writing lies, the fountains of creation droop and dry up. Yes, yes. I do believe in it. I do believe that all I am writing is possible. It must be, since all the world dreams of it."

And then he would sink back into thoughts of Honor, and of what they might have built together, had her passion equalled his own. The thinking lowered him into the pits of despair again. For, after attempting to believe that he had been too hasty with her and reminding himself that most men had to woo a girl's love and wait for it, he would be compelled to shake his head and mutter aloud : " *No !* To woo it into view, perhaps, but not into existence. I'll serenade for a love that's hiding coyly behind the window curtains, but not for one that isn't at home. And it isn't. It isn't. I did try to woo it out, and she told me it wasn't there. Nor is it. . . ." Then the anguish gripped him again, and for all the summer evening he lay on his counterpane, with his hands linked behind his head, knowing that he was beaten by it, and that if Honor by the frailest hint gave him his chance of escape, he must take it. " If only she would write to me. If only she would send me the smallest word of hope. . . ."

She wrote to him when July broke in a blaze of dog-days.

" *Tony dear——* "

The arrangement of the words was his first sharp prick of hope.

" *—We've such an absolutely gorgeous plan Jill and I and we'll never forgive you if you don't fall in with it ! ! ! You know Joyce was always raving to us about the happy times you used to have at Freshwater when you were children well we've been able to rent the very cottage that used to be yours, we have got it from now till the middle of September and we are off next*

Wednesday and the question is are you coming to stay with us directly your holiday begins and to stop just as long as you like. And the answer is Yes you are ! ! Both Jill and I are so frightfully keen on it and Daddy and Mummy solemnly invite you dedicating the pleasant duty to me as I insisted they should, and Oh Tony dear, you must ! ! you will be able to show us all round and introduce us to the natives and besides, now that the desire has got firmly fixed in our heads, Jill and I, we shall suffer horribly if we dont get it. So you simply must because we suffer when we are thwarted, its all Daddy's fault, he was so soft with us when we were young. Jill you know is awfully fond of you, she wont hear a word against you, not that anyone ever hears anything against you but she has announced that she wouldnt if she did. But let me have a little credit too, this enormously brainy idea originated with me. I just whispered it beneath my breath one day, and she replied quite calmly, Oh thats settled, and Daddy said, Is it to be sure, and she said, Yes to be sure it was, and didnt pursue a subject that was closed. So you see this is not so much an invitation as information. Its Jills orders. And mine qui t'aime."

In the tumult of pleasure that was Tony's thinking just then a score of different delights was jostling in humorous horseplay : one wanted to kiss the letter and murmur : " You exquisite darling ! I love every word that you write as I love every movement of your lips," or a like extravagance ; another wanted to flourish the letter overhead and cry : " If I'm beaten, so are you, little one ! Joke as you like, you had to summon me, and in your letter you had to hint more than once at the love which you denied. ' The idea originated with me.' Why did you tell me that ? ' It's Jill's orders. And mine, *qui t'aime.'* Your latest version of ' My love. Honor.' Then the words *did* mean something ! That separation of yourself from Jill—almost the only full-stop in your letter—tells nothing to those who suspect nothing, and tells everything to me." He rushed to his paper and wrote an enthusiastic reply, sending to Jill " his unlimited love ; " for, in truth, he was feeling a love for that very dear girl—that strong, full, expansive love which a man can only feel for the woman he is not in love with.

So a happy noon in late July saw his face at the window of a train that was screaming through the New Forest to Lymington ;

but his eyes hardly saw the noon, for he was thinking of those old days when he and Peggy and Derek and Joyce, their heads full of " The Children of the New Forest " or " Tales of the Norman Kings," would crowd to the window to look out on these old trees in the hope that, down one of the long vistas, they might see the House of Arnwood, or the Intendant's cottage, or the tree from which the arrow glanced that slew the Red King, or some of the deer that the King loved as if he had been their father.

Soon his eyes saw nothing at all, for the memories of that crowded family had turned all his thoughts inward. Odd how the Family, in those very early days, would move as a unit ; if one went to the train window, all went to the train window ; if one ate chocolate and rolls from the luncheon basket, all ate chocolate and rolls ; if one blew paper bags into balloons and burst them, all seized paper bags and did the same ; if one threw the paper into the wind that tore past the train, all jumped up to do likewise ; if one was sentenced by Father to silence and immobility, all withdrew into their seats and into themselves. " Silence in the pig-market ! Let the old sow speak first ! " And not a word was uttered till Brockenhurst ; though perchance one giggled, and then all giggled.

And now Peggy was a Vicar's wife in Southend, and Derek lived alone and reticently in his flat in Artillery Mansions, Westminster, and Joyce was half-way to India, and Tony himself, in his mind at least, ranged far from the thoughts of the others, and their father had disappeared years back, and the servants who were with them then, were they even alive now ? Only Keatings remained at his mother's side—Keatings, the unbrilliant, but the humorous and the stable.

The sun had lit the Solent to a sherry gold when his little ship chunked out to it from the mud-flats of the mainland ; and he stood in the head-wind to stare at the island, of which almost the whole outline was visible. On that little strip of land floating in the haze, was Honor now ; waiting in one of the hollows under the hills, impatient and nervous, surely. A word kept framing itself on his lips : " Powerless. . . . Powerless when *this* calls. . . . Powerless to be proud and turn away from the chance of love. I always have been. . . . Powerless to resist you, Honor ; " and he rejoiced in his powerlessness. Would those hills which must have looked down on a million roaming lovers in their time watch yet another embrace ?

Rich, elating, breath-taking thought ! . . . The church and houses of Yarmouth Town took larger and squarer shapes, and its long, white pier, if you half closed your eyes, seemed to breast up towards the ship and grow larger as it came.   There were people waving on its edge, and surely one of them was Honor !   Was it ?   Yes, it was.   Honor alone—what a sister was Jill !—Honor in a white dress and a large straw hat.

As he stepped with grins and other comic grimaces on to the pier, they shook hands, and both were about to speak, when speech most treacherously deserted them.   It pretended to be there for half a second, and then deserted them both at the same moment, and left them in their discomposure.   They looked round for it, but it was not in sight. Tony summoned it to return, and it returned unwillingly, bringing a very commonplace face indeed.   They walked down the pier, and it lingered and halted between them, and once they thought it had slipped away again. Honor couldn't discipline it at all and would have let it escape if it liked, but Tony forced it to walk sensibly between them. In the hired car which waited at the pier's foot, it sat itself between them, as dull and perfunctory as if it disliked the rôle of separating chaperon.   And both of them at last, after being polite with it, began to look away from so dull a companion. Tony took his pleasure in awaiting the landmarks on the familar road.   At intervals the chaperon, bound in duty to break a too long silence, explained what he was doing ; but it failed to break one interminable silence, and Tony, looking round towards Honor, perceived that it had finally escaped from the car.   He put out his hand in search of hers, and she allowed hers to be found straying about, and to sit in his for all the rest of the journey ; so there was no longer a seat for speech between them.

In the cottage, General Daubeny rose from his chair and welcomed them, as he was compelled to do, for the front door opened straight into the living-room where he was smoking. He was a spare man of moderate height, with that skin which India first browns and then etches with the record of her suns. His spruceness was a soldier's : even on holiday, his grey shepherd's plaid trousers were sharply creased, his black jacket was as speckless as a uniform's tunic, his collar was of regulation pattern, white and starched, and his bow-tie was rigid.   The neat, grey moustache was in review order, each bristle of it facing the right way and ready, as it were, for a king's inspection-

The eyebrows were less orderly; they might have been likened to two groups of civilians craning their necks to watch the review on the Indian plain. The eyes themselves could stare piercingly ahead and around, but anyone knew that they were seeing no more than a soldier sees; and when they were not engaged on this sharp scrutiny, they were simple and humorous and kind. The inevitable monocle went easily to his eyes; and, in fine, he was as perfectly typical a product of his calling as any you could find in the Yacht Club on the Bund at Bombay or in the United Services Club on Pall Mall.

Tony, prepared by his daughters, was always diverted by the way the General's manner would stay smooth and humorous and loquacious, till some unordinary remark, or a knock at the door, or an unexpected apparition surprised him, when his head would swing with a bird-like quickness to the interruption, and some such exclamations as: " What-what? Be damned! Good God!" would spring from his lips, and his hand would lift his monocle to its " stand to!" in his eye, and his eyes would stare like machine guns at whatever was toward. Watching this little series of reflex actions, Tony always built around him his Indian Orderly Room, and saw his Adjutant entering to inform him of a misdemeanour in the Lines, or, worse still, of the imminent approach of the Divisional General. Jill called it " Daddy's Stand to;" Honor, loving the whole series, nicknamed her father, " Whatwhat-damn-damn;" and Len, using the residue of his expressions, called his governor " Good God."

General Daubeny had liked from the first " that Irish boy," as he described Tony; and now he showed a real pleasure in his arrival.

" Here you are at last! She's brought you safely, has she? Did you have a pleasant journey? I meant to come and meet you myself, but Jill issued different routine orders. You'd better understand at once that Jill's the C.O. here, and I'm her Orderly Sergeant, or her sweeper, or something. It was she who detailed Honor to meet you. I do hope these two girls won't be too much of a nuisance to you. They seem to want to monopolize you, but don't hesitate to give them the slip when they bore you, and we might have a round of golf or a long walk together. The Links on the Downs are quite good. . . . Honor, go and find your mother. . . . The Memsahib's about somewhere, O'Grogan, and she'll be in in a

minute. Sit down, sit down. Honor, go and find your
mother——"

But at that moment Jill entered the room with such a burst
that her father exclaimed : " What-what ? " and Honor added,
" Damn-damn ! " while his hand fumbled for the monocle.

" Tony ! " cried Jill. " This is ripping. So here you are,
and did you have a pleasant journey ?—oh, what a pair of stupid,
uninspired remarks ! "

" Be damned, they're not ! " the General interrupted.
" They're not stupid at all. I made them myself just now."

" How did you leave England ? " Jill tried instead. " *That's*
more original."

" Very empty," said Tony gallantly.

The General laughed. " England indeed ! The Isle of
Wight isn't a foreign part. ' How did you leave England ? '
Good God, what will the girl say next ? "

Then came Mrs. Daubeny, with a welcome no less generous,
and an invitation that he came and saw his room. " Though
you must know your way about better than we do," she smiled.

" Why, why ? " the General inquired, his monocle on sentry
duty and challenging this passing remark.

Honor explained.

" Because he used to live here himself, ducky. Hasn't that
soaked in yet ? "

The monocle challenged this new statement, and accepted
it for a friend.

" Oh, of course, of course. . . . Well, let the boy have a
rest. Get him some tea. I don't suppose he's had any tiffin
yet."

" Don't be absurd, father," Jill broke in. " He'll be much
more interested in seeing his old home than in chatting to you."

The monocle swung round to this third voice, and was
satisfied with its good faith.

" Oh, yes, I suppose so. . . . Well, I'd better show him the
rounds. . . . Oh, no, he knows his way round, as you say.
Carry him off, then."

And he sank back into his chair, letting the monocle fall.

Over the tea-cups Tony perceived an interesting battle,
though it was veiled by the good manners of all. There were
two topics of conversation skirmishing for the capture of the
meal, the General's heavy battalions and the daughters' light
cavalry. The General was evidently fearful lest the light

chatter of his children should bore his guest, and the children held similar views about their father's long arguments and anecdotes. The General talked of India, and described the voyage of Len and Joyce thither, lecturing reminiscently on Gib., Malta, Port Said, Port Tewfik and Aden; and his daughters, at every opportunity, attacked on his flank with their plans for the morrow, the colour of their bathing dresses, the blackberry jam at Compton Farm, and the prawns at low tide. Tony divided his attention as evenly as possible between the combatants, strangely moved to perceive the loving shame with which each generation regarded the conversational talents of the other. But the huge reserves of the General were too many for his daughters, and his battalions began to march forward unendingly, while Jill and Honor were reduced to a guerilla warfare on his rear. Finally they were left behind in a great silent desert, and the Indian Army marched off with Tony.

The girls waited in their chairs, sighed once or twice, and at length quitted the room with their mother.

The General seemed highly pleased. One feels an especial affection for a boy one has rescued, and he offered Tony a cheroot and arranged both of themselves into chairs, for the enjoyment of a masculine conversation. He discussed the position of the British in India, and pointed out that India was not a single nation, capable of political self-consciousness, but a continent of hostile races and religions. He explained the quarrel between Lord Kitchener and Lord Curzon, and the damnableness of the *Bombay Chronicle* and Mrs. Annie Besant, and the necessity for the Strong Hand. He enumerated all those politicals whom he wouldn't trust an inch further than he could see them. He spoke of the machinations of the Germans, and the meaning of their friendship with the Turks and their Bagdad Railway, and the chances of a Jehad among the Moslems. He described punitive expeditions against the frontier tribes, and his experiences in China during the Boxer Rebellion. He described life in Lahore, Delhi, Jhansi and Jhelum. He told amusing stories of Babu clerks, laughed heartily at them, and yielded to the temptation which attacks us all, to recite the really laughable climax a second time. And all of this Tony answered and parried and endorsed with admirably feigned interest, longing all the while to be off into the summer evening with Honor and Jill, and listening with his other ear for the sound of their voices or their footsteps.

At last, thinking that if he could not be with them, he would at least savour the pleasure of talking about them, he sent the General's conversation divagating towards his daughters, and heard how Jill (the *burra wallah*) was one of the world's beautiful natures, but it was Honor (the *chota wallah*) who had fascinated her father ever since her sparkling and impudent childhood. This flowed naturally into a chapter on life in Rawal Pindi and an appreciation of the loyalty of Indian ayahs to their charges, and the fondness for children shown by his Indian bearer, and a character study of a certain Subadar Major of the regiment, towards the close of which Tony's other ear began to suspect the slither of furtive movements in the garden outside. He said, " Really ? " and " Good Gracious ! " and " Ha, ha ! " when they fitted into the discourse, and decided that the movements were accompanied by suppressed giggles and were situated to the left of the lattice window. Or were they even closer ? Were they not under the sill and disturbing the sunflowers and marguerites and the faded foxgloves that peeped in through the panes ? As he wondered, the two faces of Jill and Honor, the oval face a little higher than the round one, framed themselves in the flowers and the creepers all round the casement, and Honor called out : " Good God ! Damn, damn ! " and Jill pleaded, " I say, Daddy : let him go now. He's come to see *us*, not you. We've let you have him for an hour."

" What, what ! " exclaimed the General. " Be damned, what ? " and up went his monocle to examine the visitation.

" Good God ! " he said.

Tony looked at the monocle and then at the visitation, and wondered if that little gold-rimmed window, which in its day had been directed towards the lake of Kandy and the valley of Kashmir, had ever faced a pleasanter picture than this.

In the morning Honor and Jill bore him off before the General could suggest a round of golf, and together (as Jill said) they went down the corridor of the past and revisited his childhood : they went up to the roadside tree from which the O'Grogan children had once held up the Royal Mail, and Honor touched its smooth bark ; they went into the grocer's to ask where was that old postman now with his spade-shaped beard and his ambling governess-cart, and learned that he lived in a toddling retirement near the churchyard ; they went down to the beach and inquired amongst the boats and the bathing machines after Andrews, the blond and genial fishman, and old Munster, the dark and surly one, who, according to legend, had poisoned his wife. Andrews was still active, this very hour, and was out paddling with his boat among the lobster-pots, but Munster had long ago gone gloomily to his account and the reproaches of his murdered wife.

They lay on the beach till the sea went down, and then clambered over the rocks to the Western caves, and lo ! Tony was almost too tall now to crouch his way through the Emergency Exit. The Frenchman's Hole was still there, a dark and forbidding shaft in the Western Wall. And walking back to lunch, Honor broke a pause with : " I iike living in your childhood ; " for which most gratifying word, Tony took her hand and pressed it.

And in the afternoon they dodged the General's invitation to Tony " to come and stretch his legs with him in a long walk, having done his duty by those two girls ; " and instead Tony stretched the girl's legs and his own along Tennyson's Lane, and up the downs to the Monument, and there dared them to roll down the slopes as Joyce and Peggy were always ready to do. But neither accepted the challenge, so all three linked arms and ran down till the strain on their coupling was too great, and they broke up in laughter, and Honor went shrieking on towards the grass road at the bottom, and Jill, as was fitting in one of her name, fell down, and Tony, leaving her to her wounds in blackguardly fashion, raced after Honor and beat her by a dozen lengths. Then along the turf road to Alum Bay, where an alfresco tea, if memory were no liar, could be drunk beneath its rainbow cliffs.

On the downs between Compton Farm and Freshwater there is a rolling summit from which the country falls away in billow upon billow of pasture and tillage ; and here, as you halt in your homeward walk, with the falling sun in your faces, you can view the sea on both sides of you, and know that you are on an island. Yonder, to the north, the River Yar meanders under the yoke of Yar Toll Bridge to the Solent, which glistens in a placid ribbon, with the hills of the mainland rising blue behind it ; here, under Freshwater cliffs, the Channel plays in the same light, and Highdown cliff thrusts into it a towering corner, like a ship's bows, with a little rock at its foot. Sometimes if you are so late that the sun drops before your eyes under Tennyson's Down, you may turn towards the Solent and see that it is still a silver ribbon and that the buildings on the mainland have come into bold relief, while to your south the light on the Channel is narrowing out.

And not once nor twice, in the next few days, but evening after evening—so it were fine—did these three top that summit at its best hour; for you can cross it returning from Compton Farm, after a visit to learn if teas, with blackberry jam and cream, are still sold there at ninepence a head; or from Brook where you have gone to examine the stone forest under the sea and to ascertain how much may be left of that old wreck among whose bones you once played hide-and-seek; or from that little village which is the setting of " The Silence of Dean Maitland "—a book about which you have every right to be rebellious, does one of you, on its mention, wrinkle his nose, and every right to be triumphant when, staring up at the Maitland's Vicarage and Church, he appears as interested as any of you. Or you can reach it if you have stolen from among the General's golf clubs each of you one, and have taken them up on to the high, free turf above the links, where there are none to laugh at you, and where Jill, who can really play this difficult and dangerous game, has given you a lesson and many beaming rebukes for your screams and your tomfoolery and your military oaths.

That day they reached this summit on their return from Brook, they were very weary in loin and limb, so they stood there awhile that their disordered breathing might slacken to the standard rate again. To aid this recovery Tony put an arm round each of their waists, and Jill looked away over the two seas, and Honor pillowed her head in his neck, announcing that her purpose was sleep. Tony was just thinking that this was hardly the best way for her to steady his disordered breathing; he was telling himself that he loved Jill and Honor both, and ought to be allowed to marry two sisters, if he wanted to ; and, more seriously, he was promising himself that this quiet pause up here would be listed among the fine things in his memory, when Honor abandoned her plan of sleep, because the pillow, she said, was bony; which indictment drew " 'Sdeath ! " and " 'Sblood ! " from Tony, and started a long controversy as to its truth.

That second time they reached it, on their return from Compton Farm, Honor and he were alone, for Jill had declared that she must give her adorable father one good game of golf, or he would not be as happy as he deserved to be; so here in the evening light came only two people, pushing their spiked walking-sticks into the turf; and the evening light was empty, because they had dawdled in the yard of the farmhouse and among the gorse bushes, and along the brinks of the cliff, so that it was later than usual when they reached the highest place and looked at the two seas.

" *Sapristi !* " Tony exclaimed. " What a light ! "

Their lifted eyes had noticed, as they climbed to a view of the sun's face, that one vast pattern of tiny clouds was spread across the sky, from horizon to horizon, in the shape of an angel's wing; and now, with a gasp, they saw that it was more like a wing than scoffers would ever credit, for it tapered in long streamers to a point behind the Solent. The sun was down below the opposite hills, leaving all the wing's plumage tipped with rose. Gold lay the Solent's strip; and square as a doll's toys stood the coastwise buildings of the mainland. Some of their windows which could still see the sun were flashing this message in gleams of light. There was a moving in the quiet air, and note of trouble in the beating of the sea, though a schooner, many miles out, seemed as still as a model in an old mariner's room. The movement in the air was stealthy, and one had the strange idea that the mist which had already erased the horizon could be felt on the cheek which was turned towards it. From some red-jacketed golfers down on the links came their voices in a mountain clearness; they had long ago abandoned their game in this impossible light and were calling : " Who goes home ? "

Tony examined the sky with his mouth open.

> " Mackerel skies and mare's tails
> Make lofty ships carry low sails,"

he quoted. " The weather'll be all wrong to-morrow."

Honor placed her hands on the crook of her stick behind her, and sat on them.

" Never mind. We can stay indoors and play."

" But I don't want any bad days. I shan't have too many of them."

" Your vac. goes on till the middle of September, doesn't it ? "

" Yes, but I can't stay here all that time."

" Why ever not ? "

" I don't think I ought to stay more than a month."

" Tony ! Why ever not ? "

He shrugged his shoulders and did not answer.

" Oh, if you don't want to. . . ."

" Honor, you know I want to. . . ."

" Then why are you being silly ? You'll stay here till the last possible moment."

" No."

She dismembered her stick-and-hand chair, and came up to him.

" Yes, you will—*please*."

Putting both hands on her shoulders he held her before him as a father might.

" God ! Honor," he mumbled. " I . . ."

" What ? "

" Oh . . . nothing . . ."

" What were you going to say ? "

" Nothing, dear . . . nothing . . ."

She asked no more, but looked up at him, as at a stranger. Fool that he was, his eyes had filled in a way that must be visible and must be explained—with a part of the truth. " You should have seen yourself as you looked up just then, Honor. For a moment you seemed like an incarnation of all the beauty of the evening. You—you seemed like an ideal become momentarily real, and it only left one with a sense that nothing is attainable and nothing lasts. . . . Everything's so fugitive and insecure. . . . It must be wonderful to carry, as a rose does, hints of eternal things in one's face. . . . Oh, I don't know what I am talking about. . . . These things can only be felt, not told. . . . This light is unreal, isn't it ? Or the world is unreal, and we know it in a moment like this. . . . Honor, I . . ."

" What, Tony ? "

" No. . . . Not again. . . ."

" Tony, do say what you were going to say—*please*."

" No."

To that she could add nothing. She turned away, but let his arm feel lightly for her waist. And thus, side by side, they gazed at the beauty before them. The light was changing under their eyes, and they watched that lustrous gold on the Solent's strip go out like a lamp; it was as quick to leave as the rose-tints on the clouds were slow, for these tip-toed away. The brilliance had died in the Channel, and an indigo darkness was spreading over it from the east; but the schooner had not moved. Down in the bay they could see old Andrews in his boat coming home from the lobster-pots. The air chilled; and, still holding each other, they began to walk down the hill-side very slowly, speaking no word, but exchanging a smile now and then. Darkness fell about them before they were near the cottage, but never once had they completely broken their mutual hold or their mutual silence.

CHAPTER V

AND SO TO KRUGER'S GRAVE

WHEN they entered the living-room of the cottage, the General glanced up.

"Eh, you're late, Honor. Have you kept the poor young man out all this time? He wants his supper, if *you* don't. I'm sure he's got something better to do than dance attendance on Jill and you all day. O'Grogan, you mustn't let these selfish girls take advantage of your good nature."

"I won't," Tony agreed.

"I think of stretching my legs in a long walk to Newport to-morrow. Would you care to come?"

"Well, yes. . . . Yes, thank you very much."

"We might get there in time for tiffin, and then get the train back, in time for supper."

"Yes . . . yes, that would be splendid."

"How's that, Honor? I shall at least have got him a whole holiday from his bear-leading of you two cubs."

"It's all right; you won't get him," said Honor. "It's going to rain like billy-oh! to-morrow."

"Eh, *what*?" The General put up his monocle to bear on this point.

"There's a mackerel sky and a most unnatural light."

"Rain be damned!" He took his monocled eye to the window. "I see nothing. The weather looks to me to be 'Set Fair' if ever weather did. What says the glass?"

His monocle was now staring into the barometer, which his knuckle was tapping. Nothing happened in the barometer, and he tapped it again, his head, but not his eyes, turning a little to one side, as if he would bring a ear to the aid of the eyes.   The action was bird-like and reminded Tony of a thrush listening for worms.

"The glass is high and stationary," he announced, dropping the monocle.   "You needn't worry, O'Grogan, we shall get our walk all right."

"But, Daddy darling," Jill submitted.   "You know that that barometer is exactly like your eye-glass: it never sees a storm till it's actually arrived.   Then it jumps about in the most extraordinary fashion."

"Ha, these girls!" the General smiled to Tony.   "It amuses them to think they're much wiser than us.   Well, we like 'em to be happy, don't we?"   Always he seemed to forget that one of his daughters, Jill, was a year older than his guest; or perhaps he regarded Tony's sex as amounting to ten years' seniority.   "But I'm not going to have them sacrificing you too far.   Directly they begin to bore you, you mustn't hesitate to say so.   They seem to think you've got nothing to do but amuse them.   Well, now, for pity's sake, call the Memsahib and let's have supper."

There was no walk on the morrow, for the weather broke in the night, and a procession of rainy days went gloomily by, like the shrouded figures of Banquo's kings.   They stayed indoors, with their faces watching the rain patterning the panes of the lattice windows and beating down the flowers; till, under Tony's command, they procured oil-skins and sou'-westers from old Andrews and rowed out in his boat a mile from shore, where they paid out their line till it touched the bottom, and drew up the rock-whiting with monotonous regularity.   Or they accompanied the old fisherman when he went out to his lobster pots, and Honor characterized the staring lobsters and the worried, escaping crabs as "too perfectly sweet" and detected likenesses in them to the sidesmen of Chiswick Parish Church.   Or beneath the unremitting rain they bathed in unmannerly seas—the only people in all Freshwater with the courage to do so.   Or when August passed, they went out in their waterproofs and picked wet blackberries.

One day was fair, just before August closed, and they were mightily relieved to find that its clouds were broken, because there had been an excited hope among them that on this day a famous old friend from Tony's past would appear again in Freshwater.   Tony had not been a day in the island before making inquiries whether Captain Alum was still alive and could

be exhibited to newcomers singing his hymns along the skyline
of the downs. And the people told him that though the old
man's visits were rarer than they used to be, he was almost sure
to be on Afton Down on the 28th of August. And why that
day of all others, Tony inquired. The people told him why,
and he hid their counsel from the girls.

The afternoon of the 28th, if clear of rain, was windier than
it need have been, and they set forth in overcoats, with hands
pushed deep into pockets and collars turned up. Tony guiding
them, they passed through the gate that closes the Military
Road, where it drops into Freshwater Bay after its downland
journey from Chale and Brixton and Brook. They climbed
it a little way and then, breaking across the turf, paddled through
the prickly gorse to the verge of the cliff. Here, looking down
the precipice, they saw the sea bullying the rocks below, and
stepped hastily back lest vertigo overthrew them. They walked
along the turf to a little, low, dark obelisk which stood in its
square of railings only a few paces from the precipice's brink.
No other persons were near it, and Honor scoffed, " I don't
believe he's coming. I don't believe there's anything in it."

" If he's alive, he'll come," said Tony. " He has too great
a sense of drama not to appear at exactly his given moment."

" But you'd think that other people would have heard of it,"
Jill objected. " And there's not a soul in sight."

" I don't know anything about that," said Tony, shrugging.
" The local savages don't take him seriously, and a new generation of visitors has arrived which knows not Joseph."

" Probably it's the weather," said Honor.

They were now standing by the little obelisk, and inevitably
they read again the words cut upon its face that looked towards
the sea. Or rather the girls read it, and Tony watched their
expressions.

" Erected
In Remembrance
Of a Most Dear
And Only Child
Who Was Suddenly
Removed into Eternity
By a Fall From
The Adjacent Cliff
On the Rocks Beneath
28th August, 1846."

" Poor mite ! " Jill whispered ; but Honor exclaimed :

" Twenty-eighth of August !   Why, that's to-day ! "

" Yes," said Tony.   " That's why he comes."

" Oh, then I think he must be rather a dear," said Jill, and Honor murmured, " Eighteen forty-six !   Sixty-five years ago ! " and they observed the discoloration on the stone of the obelisk and the rust on its unpainted railings.

" Here are some people coming."

It was Jill who had spoken ; and the others, looking down the slope, saw a figure climbing towards them, with a little chain of children hopping and skipping behind him, as a kite-tail flutters behind a kite.   Further back a few staider adults followed the track of the children.

" It's the Captain himself," Tony announced.   " Of course ! One might have guessed !   He's hardly the man not to collect his audience from the beach."

Jill and Honor's gaze had now run to meet the approaching captain, and was accompanying him up the hill, while their lips parted in admiration and amusement.   The old man's long, waving hair and beard, both grey now, were rioting in the wind. His blue reefer jacket, perhaps given him by some coastguard, did not meet across his soiled white sweater and was kept in place by a huge leather belt, for he was much fatter than when Tony had last seen him, and so seemed shorter and stockier than ever.   The peaked cap was in the same hand as his stick, which pierced the turf at every forward step of his left foot. The other hand grasped a book.   And behind came the laughing and wondering children, as if they were playing in a charade of the Pied Piper.

" Oh, isn't he perfectly *sweet*," cried Honor.   " I'm sure St. Paul looked just like that."

With such resolute steps did Captain Alum approach the obelisk that Tony, Jill and Honor were soon, of their shyness, retreating to a score of paces away, where they stood to see what should happen.   First Captain Alum scanned the inscription, nodding several times in his profound appreciation of its sadness.   Then he leaned his stick against the low railings, and hung his cap upon them, and clasped his hands in front of his breast, as far as the book between them would allow, and silently prayed.   Which done, he invited the children, with a very sweet smile, to come a little closer, for they needn't be afraid of an old man who loved all God's pretty ones.   And they obeyed.

"Children," he began—and Tony and the girls came a few steps nearer to hear, "sixty-five years ago, which is before your dear fathers and dear mothers were born, a little child in the midst of a happy August holiday fell from this cliff here and met the dear Lord on the rocks below. 'Fear not,' I think He said, 'it is I.' And this stone marks that God was very close to this place one day, when he came to lift up a little bairn by the hand. It is like the stone which Jacob erected in the wilderness, saying, 'Surely God is in this place and I knew it not. And this stone which I have set up for a pillar shall be God's House.' Sixty-five years ago to-day! and I cannot think that the dear heartbroken parents who followed the blessed patriarch's example and lifted a stone to their God instead of a curse—as if with the blessed Job they would say, 'The Lord gave; the Lord hath taken away; blessed be the name of the Lord'— I cannot think that they are yet alive; they have rejoined their 'dear and only child' in the beautiful heaven above. But in their love they placed this tiny monument here, no higher than a child, that when they should be gone from hence, there might still be people who would remember their little one. And shall we disappoint them? Shall it be nothing to us who pass by? No, no, my pretties; we will let our hearts be softened, even in the midst of our happy playtime, by the memory of a great and terrible pain that was suffered on the very ground where you are standing now; and we will think about God; and we will learn from these dear parents the lesson that in our afflictions we must not rebel, but bow our heads and say, "Surely God is in this place.' 'Out of our stony griefs, Bethel we'll raise.'"

So the sermon went on; and there were large tears in the old preacher's eyes; and Tony preferred to believe that they sprang as much from a good heart as from the overwrought imagination of an actor. Captain Alum had not the vigour of body or mind that he had shown in the years before; his talent for phrase and his humour had weakened; he repeated himself in the distressing way of senility; but Tony still found that familiar words spoken by him, perhaps because of the picturesqueness of his figure and of his setting, filled themselves with a peculiar potency. Never before, though he had heard his father, in the grandest voice, close a dozen church-years with the same lesson, did noble words mean so much to him as when Captain Alum, at the close of his address, opened his book with the shaking hands of an old man, and read—he who once would have trusted his memory and declaimed the words with an ingratiating smile : " Remember now thy Creator in the days of thy youth, while the evil days come not, nor the years draw nigh, when thou shalt say, I have no pleasure in them ; while the sun, or the light, or the moon, or the stars be not darkened, nor the clouds return after the rain."

The lesson read, Captain Alum asked his congregation to think of the lost child, and to pray silently. And when he had given them time enough to pray, he suddenly—for at least in his dramatic sense there was no weakening—burst without warning into a hymn. In a voice far less powerful than of old and troubled by breathlessness, he sang :

> " There's a Friend for little children
> Above the bright blue sky,
> A Friend Who never faileth,
> Whose love will never die ; "

and to Tony listening, a hundred Sunday afternoons, most of them wintry in atmosphere, came visiting memory.

Captain Alum had hoped that the children, knowing the hymn by heart, would join in, but they only stared silently, and some giggled. So he began to conduct them with his shaking hand, and, meeting with no response, dropped the hand and continued alone :

> " Our earthly friends may fail us,
> And change with changing years ;
> This Friend is always worthy
> Of that dear name He bears. . . ."

Tony was staring now with chin dropped and fixed eyes. " Our earthly friends may fail us, And change with changing years. . . ." Wavers. . . . Raking. . . . Sibyl Chandry. . . . Doyly. . . . Cyril Winter. . . . Peggy. . . . Jill and Honor. Jill and Honor ; they had failed him in his first twenty years, in so far as they had not come into his life, and one day they would fail him again, departing from him—or he would go from them—even though . . . The thought swelled his love for Honor, and he looked down sideways at her. How he wanted her, for the little while allowed them. Honor, let's make the most of the time. And Jill. Strange that the thought of losing Jill could be so sharp a pain.

Captain Alum, sustaining his hymn alone, carried it to its

end with a steadily diminishing interest and energy. His
"Amen" was hardly heard, and suggested disappointment.
He picked up his stick from the railings round the obelisk and
put on the peaked cap, and turning his breast towards the
upward slope of the hill, trudged away, singing quietly to himself the words of his unsuccessful hymn :

> "There's a home for little children
>   Above the bright blue sky,
> Where Jesus reigns in glory
>   A home of peace and joy ;
> No home on earth is like it ;
>   Nor can with it compare,
> For every one is happy,
>   Nor could be happier, there."

A few days later the weather recovered its high spirits, and
a wheel of suns swung round the heavens ; but each chased the
other far too quickly, for it was September now. There was an
evening when Jill and her parents had gone to a foursome on
the links, and Tony and Honor were alone with their novels
in the living-room, and the two facts of September and a sunset,
both blazing through the window, were oppressing Tony so
heavily that his eyes would stray from the pages of his book to
the crown of his companion's head ; and he was thinking,
"Surely she will not let me go without speaking." The one
remnant of his old irrationality was this fixed idea that Honor,
having repulsed him twice, must now take the first step if they
were to declare their love.

"Tedious ! Dull stuff !" he grumbled, tossing his book on
the table ; and Honor said promptly, "Let's go out," just as
if this conception had been occupying her mind for the last
half-hour.

They took their sticks from the corner of the room and went
out into the horizontal light. It lay on the green boles of the
beeches, and down the ruddy barks of the pines ; it rested
along the curved top of the quick-set hedges and splashed the
western fronts of the houses, so that they saw the shapes of
nature in their roundness and the buildings of men very square.

With few words, and they banal, he led her through the gate
of Tennyson's Lane into a dappled darkness under that vault
of trees. "This evening, this evening," he kept saying to

himself as they strolled along in uncommunicative dreaming.
He remembered how when he was fifteen he had walked unhappily up this lane with Emily Holt, and had dreamed then of
the time when he would be walking in a solitude with the girl
he loved. And here they were together in the same lane.

There is a chalk-pit at the foot of the downs if they are
reached by the road that branches from Tennyson's Lane ;
and across the semicircle of its floor a long turfed ridge, like a
giant's grave. To the O'Grogan family this long heave of
turf was known as Kruger's Grave, because Derek had once,
in a boyhood much impressed by the South African War, employed the flints and stones and chalk-chips lying around to print
along its top, " Here lies Kruger, R. I. P." That was a dozen
years ago, and the first high wind had swept his inscription
away, but otherwise Tony and Honor found the long heave as
undisturbed and unchanged as the grave of a great man has a
right to be. Only the bramble bushes which had then been
but a knee's height had grown into tall entanglements and made
a covering for the giant's feet. They sat together near the
grave's head, which was a hummock higher than the rest of it,
as if the giant beneath had lifted his head and pillowed it above
his shoulders. Honor reclined with an elbow on this hummock ;
and Tony, leaning both elbows on his knees, drew patterns on
the ground with his stick.

" I wish you weren't going," said Honor.

" I must. And I can't think how you have endured me so
long."

" The lad fishes for his compliment."

" He does nothing of the sort. I——"

" You know you've just *made* our holiday. Having ten times
our brains—or at least ten times mine—you've made our holiday
out of your extraordinary imagination, just as you make one of
your old poems. And you know we're properly grateful."

" Grateful ! " In a low voice he scoffed at the bloodless
word.

" Oh, I *hate* you sometimes."

" That's better."

" I'm trying to be nice. What do you want me to say ? "

For answer he looked into her face, and she met his glance
with unflinching eyes, her brows uplifted as if at a loss for his
meaning. But the colour at her cheeks was in poorer control.
He turned away with a sigh ; and she sat upright.

"Tony . . . oh, *isn't* this dreadfully awkward . . . ? I want to say what you want me to say, if only you'll tell me what it is."

Tony's silence proclaimed his pride.

"If you don't tell me, Tony, I can't, can I ? "

He drew a sweeping circle with his stick, and, beating points along its circumference, submitted:

"I've told you twice—once in a letter which you ignored, and once at a ball when you stopped me like a child who was going too far. . . . I cannot tell you a third time and take a third reprimand. You may like administering them, but it hurts me."

"Tony, how *can* you ? . . . I couldn't say I loved you till I was sure——"

"Till ! " He had not raised his eyes from his geometry on the ground, but the word "till " had dropped into him like yeast, raising a fermentation. " *Till* you were sure ? Honor, what does ' till ' mean ? "

"Did I say ' till ' ? Lordy, I wonder what I could have meant by that ? "

"Did it mean all that I wanted ? "

"I don't know," she parried. "It might have done."

"Honor, did it, dear ? "

". . . Yes. . . . Oh, yes, Tony. . . ."

Enough : she was in his arms and taking his kisses ; and her hand was passing over his head, and holding the column of his neck, and stroking his cheek and feeling for his back and his shoulders ; and beneath this touch which was that of a girl who, lost from thought, was sending him thus the whole of her love, his passion stretched beyond the reach of words, and he poured back his answer through a tremble in his arms ; and his ecstasy, very near to pain, communicated itself more and more to her, till, between her kisses which were now vying with his in their hard assault, she began to gasp, " Tony . . . ! O Tony . . . ! "

In that suppressed, impassioned cry, he imagined he was hearing an answer from the world outside to that need of his which had been crying to it all his life ; and strange triumphant thoughts leapt like lightnings about his mind : " I have found it. . . . This is to be satisfied at last. . . . One can rest, having known this. . . ."

The last of the light was gone, and in the dusk, as he relaxed his hold, he knew a second of sadness that this supreme moment should be already over ; he glimpsed again the fugitiveness and insecurity of all things ; but the sadness could not last in his unbelievable joy, and now holding her lightly, he asked :

" We are engaged, Honor ? "

" Yes, yes."

" When shall we marry ? "

" Oh, when *can* we, darling ? "

" At once. . . . Or very, very soon."

" But, Tony, how—how ? "

" We shall be poor."

" Oh, I don't mind.   I've never been used to much."

" I think we can do it.   I shall get a non-resident post at another school.   Perhaps a hundred and fifty pounds a year.   I know others who have done it.   And we shall have a tiny house——"

" O Tony, it'll be too unbearably lovely."

" Let's go home and tell them all."

" Had we better tell them just yet—'cept Jill ?   Daddy'll never understand."

Tony stood up, saying, " He must understand ; " and taking her hand, he raised her to her feet.   " Come, let's hear what he says."

But before they started on the homeward walk, he drew her for another embrace.   And they kissed but gently now, like old lovers.

CHAPTER VI

THE CAMPAIGN

HIS parley with the General was not a success.
When the two men were seated together after supper, he said " Yes, yes," and " Quite so," to a dissertation by his host whose subject matter had eluded him ; and when the dissertation halted, he proffered a diffident, " Sir. . . ." This unusual mode of address, together with its unusual tone, lifted the General's head.

" Eh, yes, yes ? What ? " said the General, unconsciously frowning at him.

" Have you any objection, sir, to my being engaged to your daughter ? "

" What, what ? "

The General could hardly have faced a thing more remote from his speculations, had his Adjutant entered his Orderly Room with information that a junior subaltern of B Company was seeking permission to marry the Quartermaster. He fumbled with a trembling hand for the support of his eyeglass. The words he intended to use were " Good God, no ! " but in his confusion he fixed the eyeglass and said, " Engaged to my daughter ? Which one ? "

" Honor, sir."

" Honor." He repeated the name, and then perceived that its introduction had done nothing to relieve his bewilderment. " But you're not in love with each other, are you ? " he inquired, floundering backwards to a first cause.

" Yes, sir."

" Since when ? I've known nothing about this. My wife's known nothing about it."

"No, sir. We only . . . we only told each other this evening."

"Told each other this evening! Did Honor say so, too, then?"

"Yes, sir."

"Good God!"

Tony was conscious that though the monocle was staring at him from beneath eyebrows drawn together, the eyes behind were hardly seeing him, for the brain was occupied with righting itself.

"Engaged? I thought you were just friends. 'Their brother,' the girls always called you."

"I loved Honor from the first moment I saw her, sir."

"And when was that?"

"At Joyce's wedding."

"But that's not five months ago. No, my boy, this is too quick work altogether." His brain was clearing. He got out of his chair and went to the hearth-rug and turned to stare again at the seated Tony. Being quite unoriginal, he had no dislike of triteness, and no ear for it, if he heard it. "You can't know your own minds yet."

"By heaven, I do, sir."

"Of course you think you do, but you don't. And be damned, Honor doesn't! She's only a baby. She doesn't come of age for three months."

"She says she's ready to marry me."

"God . . . ! To-morrow, I suppose? . . . Oh, I see now why you've been so willing to put up with her all this holiday. Ha, ha! So you've been imagining yourselves in love with one another. Well, I never!"

"*No*, sir," snapped Tony, rather angrily. "We've imagined nothing."

This new note slightly startled the General.

"*What?*"

But he recovered. "Oh, come, my boy, don't be silly. How can she marry you? I understand you've only a small stipend."

"I believe I can get a hundred and fifty pounds a year, if I take a non-resident post."

"The whole thing's ridiculous, my boy," the General pronounced, lifting his eyebrow and scattering the monocle on his vest, as if he would drop the subject with it. "I'm sorry to sound harsh, but you can't marry on a hundred and fifty pounds a year. Besides, it's too quick altogether. You'll have forgotten it in a year's time."

Protestations rushed to Tony's lips, but he held them back, and only asked in a voice not free from hauteur :

" So I'm to understand, sir, that you refuse your consent even to a long engagement ? "

" Certainly. I can't have her tied up as early as this."

" Then, I think, sir, you'd better forbid me to see her, too. Because I don't feel that I can give any undertaking that I shan't try to hold her to me."

" What ? " The General's mouth went rather angrily to one side to snap this out : " Whad'd'you mean ? " It was the tone he had used in his Orderly Room to remind a subaltern that Battalion Orders were Battalion Orders, and not an opening for argument. And probably in those days, the subaltern's answer had been a smart salute and a departure from the room. But not now. Tony rose from his chair and began to explain his meaning with an outer ease and an inner pride in his language.

" I mean I can't promise that I won't try to persuade Honor that, even if we mayn't be engaged *de jure*, we are *de facto*."

" De *what ?* " demanded the General. " Good God, what language you boys do use ! De *hell !* put in plain English,. that means that your asking for my consent is all a farce because you intend to be engaged to her in any case—ur ? That's your drift, is it ? "

Tony began to feel uncomfortable : he was a guest in this man's house and must withdraw his majestic horns rather than prod the old gentleman with them. He dropped from grandeur into boyishness.

" No, sir ; not quite. It—it means that I want your consent most frightfully, but I can't—I simply can't pretend that if you allow me to see Honor, I shan't treat her as the girl who has promised that she will marry me. I only want to be honest."

" Look here, O'Grogan—or Tony, as I suppose I must call you. I'm not going to quarrel." The General replaced the monocle that his last words might receive the emphasis and dignity of ceremonial utterance, and inwardly applauded the manner in which he, as a man of the world who had been a diplomat more than once during his Indian career, was going to handle the situation. " I like you far too well. I like your openness and your eagerness—and your simplicity, if you'll forgive me for saying so. And to show you that I am not in the least afraid of your very honest threats, I shall *not* forbid you to see Honor. Honor takes her orders from me, and not from you. See her as much as you like. You couldn't marry her for years so there's nothing in all that nonsense. It'll probably be best for you to see each other and not work yourselves up into some idiotic love-sickness. And in a little while you'll know that I've been completely reasonable. And now let's all be good friends together. Ha, ha, I can't have your family taking *all* my chickens, can I ? "

Tony went out to find Honor. His mind was not clear as to his future course ; but this much he saw : that, let the General treat the recent interview as lightly as he cared, for himself it had meant the opening of a war, and that, in the coming campaign, though the enemy had all the material advantages, he at least possessed two immaterial ones—an excellent British General's grave over-confidence, and Honor's certain loyalty. Her deliberate and wordless kiss when she heard his tale confirmed his assurance. He found himself thinking in the grand manner. " I shall touch her love to heroism," he thought, recalling an old phrase. " She said, ' Nothing desperate or dangerous ever happens in Chiswick.' Well, something damned desperate is going to happen in Chiswick soon, if you ask me." What the phrases portended he had yet to determine ; but they excited him, who was more encouraged by phrases than he would have liked to admit. " I have warned the General," he decided. " I've fairly and honestly warned the old bird, and now I can go ahead."

Home again in Chiswick, he had still no clear vision of the campaign in front of him, except that he must open it at once and prosecute it with set teeth. In theory this is but a poor state of mind from which to launch your attack, but it has been known, not seldom in the history of these islands, to be successful.

The very morning after his arrival home he was in the train, with his teeth set, as he rumbled towards the offices of the scholastic agents : Landseer, Thyme and Co., Leman and Finchley, Ltd., and Mr. Peidestros. Landseer, Thyme and Co. and Leman and Finchley, Ltd. took his name and requirements with less head-shaking than they had shown five years earlier, for he was now twenty-three, and looked it, with his tall, stable figure, his wide shoulders, and his skin printed with the lines of thought and humour. Also his five years' experience at Stratton Lye and his tale of scholarships went no little way towards balancing his lack of a degree. These firms were hopeful. But he felt an easier heart when he was mounting the iron-bound stairs to the office of Mr. Peidestros; Mr. Peidestros being a warm and living, if roguish person—not a firm.

Mr. Peidestros's own voice answered his knock; and when he entered, Mr. Peidestros himself stood up to welcome him, rising from behind a desk so untidy that it looked as if the waste-paper baskets and ash-trays had been emptied over it. Mr. Peidestros had not changed in five years, which was well for Tony, who thereby took no shock, for he had entered the room, expecting the same tall, straight figure, the same grey suit, the same mop of curly iron-grey hair, the same smooth olive skin, and the same smiling good nature.

" Good morning, Mr. Peidestros," he greeted him.

" Good morning, good morning, Mr.—yes—of course, I remember you well—Mr. Chambers, isn't it, for whom we found that post at Loughborough. How are you doing there, my boy ? I heard excellent accounts of you from the Reverend Soule. Do be seated." He addressed both his fin-like hands, palms upward, towards the chair by the desk.

Tony sat down and explained that he was not Mr. Chambers who went to Loughborough, but Mr. O'Grogan who went to Stratton Lye.

" Oh, yes, certainly ! I remember you well. But you were much younger then. About seventeen. I was a bit apprehensive of you, you looked so young, but you've filled out "—he flapped Tony on the breast with the back of his right hand—" and you've done well, haven't you ? I heard excellent accounts of you from Mr. Sugden, when he was last here. I sent him some French and German students, didn't I, one holidays. You're not leaving him, are you ? Good ! Must make changes sometimes, and we'll find you something— *we'll* find you something. Have a cigarette."

He offered his client one of the Russian cigarettes in their coffee-coloured paper, and took one himself; and across the smoke of these cigarettes—Mr. Peidestros's cigarette often waving about—Tony outlined his present needs. As before, he was not a little sensitive to the presence of the girl typists ; who, however, clicked on indifferently as clocks.

" A non-resident post." Mr. Peidestros rounded and threw forward his lips, shaking his head. He drew at the cigarette and waved it to one side. " Not so easily got, my boy. It's a different class of work. Older boys, you see, at grammar or cathedral schools."

" I shouldn't mind that."

" Yes, but you offer Classics chiefly, don't you ?—Have you got Mr. O'Grogan's file, Miss Cape ? Thank you. . . . Yes, you offer, I see, Scholarship Classics, French, All English Subjects, Divinity, Mathematics, All Games. . . . Come, that's not so bad."

" Yes, but you offered all that," Tony smiled. " *I* didn't."

" With perfect faith, my boy ; perfect confidence. And you've justified it. Pity you can't offer Modern Languages. That's one of the best horses to ride now, if you haven't a degree. The schools are clearing out the French and German masters, and quite right too. Foreigners are no good with English boys. You couldn't, I suppose, nip over to France for a month at Christmas, and polish up your Modern Languages. A little hard work, and you ought to be able to offer Modern Languages to Sixth Form Standard."

Tony didn't think this was possible.

" Wurl. . . ." Mr. Peidestros lifted resigned eyebrows. " Pity ! Of course we may be able to do something on your Classics and French and English. And you score in an interview, my boy. But why do you want to leave prep-school work ? *That's* your line."

" I want to marry."

" *Oh-hh-h-h-h-h !* " It was a very long, very knowing " Oh ! " It mooned up into Mr. Peidestros's treble and down again ; and Tony felt the girl typists becoming horribly real. Mr. Peidestros nodded several times. " *Yurse*, now we see daylight. . . . Marry ? . . . H'm. . . . If you want to make a home for the lady, I should try to get a partnership, or a school of your own, not a non-resident post. If you could raise the capital, I could do something good for you in that line. Has the lady any money ? "

" No," answered Tony, refusing to mind the girl typists.

" They so seldom have," sighed Mr. Peidestros. " Pity ! So seldom. I could have set up a young couple like you very nicely. I should have liked to. . . . You know some men borrow money, start a school and go bankrupt. . . . But I don't want you to do that; no, I don't want you to do that. It's not strictly honest, I suppose. . . . Still, you don't propose to live on one hundred and fifty pounds a year, do you ? "

" I thought I could get a house, and do some private coaching as well."

" That's not strictly allowed under agreements . . . but you can do it ; bless my soul, you can do it."

" I have known several who have done it," Tony explained.

" *Yurse*—yes, yes." Mr. Peidestros nodded. In a rich voice, as of a father blessing all their enterprises, he repeated : " *Yurse*, yes, yes. Certainly. . . . But if you're going to do that, I should recommend you to read for a London degree. It impresses the parents. It's the letters, B.A., that go down. You needn't put ' Lond.' after them. Couldn't you read for a London degree ? "

Tony looked at the point of his cigarette and thought of his poetry ; must he desert that like a tree that could yield him no fruit, or should he hold to his labour with a fine trust that one day it must blossom. No, he would not desert it yet : it was his real work, and Honor would stand by him in it ; the hour in the campaign had not yet come that would call for its sacrifice. So he shook his head, and said he wouldn't have time to read for a degree as he had another fish to fry in his spare hours.

" Really ? " asked Mr. Peidestros, quite interested. " Any money in it ? "

" Can't say," Tony laughed. " Shouldn't think so. But it's got to be done."

" What is it, if I may ask ?   I might be able to help you."

Tony was far more ashamed of proclaiming to the girl clerks his spare-time occupation than of announcing his marriage— of which, to say the truth, he was rather proud.

" I try to write," he confessed.

Mr. Peidestros threw forward his lips in distrust of such a pastime.

" Oh, *writing*. Not much in that. The *Daily Mail* pays well, I believe, but there's a terrible crowd at the gate. . . . Some people bring it off sometimes, of course," he mused.

" But mine is Poetry," Tony corrected, offended at this mention of the *Daily Mail*.

" Poetry ? H'm . . . well . . ." Mr. Peidestros left the subject as no longer susceptible of treatment. " You'll be wanting this post next term, I suppose ? "

" If you can get it for me. I want to marry as soon as possible."

" *Yurse*, yes, yes. Of course you do," assented Mr. Peidestros in a richly sympathetic voice. " Naturally, naturally. I'll look round at once. I'm most interested in all you tell me. You must bring your little lady to see me, before you go back to Mr. Sugden. Yes, bring the little lady. Is she handy ? "

" She'll be back from her holidays in a few days."

" Bring her round, my boy. She's beautiful, I suppose ? "

" She's not bad."

" Ha, ha ! ' Not bad.' You've seen worse, eh ? Is she in the scholastic way, too ? "

" Lord, no ! She's only twenty, and she's so far stayed at home with her father who's a retired Major-General."

" *Is* he. *Is* he now ? " Up went Mr. Peidestros's eyebrows. " Couldn't we use him as a reference ? "

" No, I shouldn't do that. No, don't do that, please."

" No ? Well, praps not, praps not. And, to be frank, we don't find military men of great use as references. They seem to think it bad form to write enthusiastically about young men, and they always think themselves compelled in honour to mention any little shortcomings one of our clients may have—which is no good to anybody. Only the other day a Colonel-man knocked a magnificent post out of my hands "—Mr. Peidestros stretched forward the offended hands, palms upward and empty—" just as they had closed on it, by admitting that the boy was rather young for such work. Wurl ! . . . we don't want references like that, do we ? No, clergy are the people : they like to do a good turn by their young parishioners, and they're used to writing things up, with their sermons and all. And they go down, too. Better than anybody else, almost. It's funny. I can't see why, but there it is ! But now, my boy, wouldn't this father-in-law of yours put up a little something towards starting you in a partnership ? "

" I don't think so. He's not very well off. Retired Indian Army, you see."

" Oh, Indian Army, is he ? Yes, there's not much in that. Well, we must do what we can for you." They had risen, and his hand was on his young client's shoulder. " I feel an interest in you quite apart from business. I no longer think of it as business. Good-bye, my boy."

A few days later, Tony led Honor, who was inclined to giggle and hang back, up the iron-bound stairs to see Mr. Peidestros, not so much to please Mr. Peidestros as to divert Honor, who, he felt, would pronounce the handsome old agent " perfectly adorable."

On their entry Mr. Peidestros rose ; recognized them ; put both his long hands together like the folded wings of a butterfly ; opened them like the same wings taking to the air again ; and, smiling such a smile as a god might give to two of his children, said : " *Wurl*, well, well."

Hastily Tony began to talk business.

" No, no," Mr. Peidestros demurred. " Oh, no. Don't let's talk business. I'll do what I can for you, be sure, but not in business ; in friendship. Sit down, dear lady. . . . So you two are engaged, are you ? " and, sinking into his chair, he stared at them as if they were the loveliest sight he had seen for many a day. It is possible that, in that office, they were so.

Honor did not answer him, but Tony was prompt with his " Yes."

" And you want to get married soon ? "

" Yes."

" Well, we must find a place for him next term, dear lady, mustn't we ? And you must give him a term to get settled in, and to look round for a little house, and then we'll marry you in the Easter holidays. How will that do ? "

Tony said it would do excellently.

" Parents all agreeable, eh ? "

" Not frightfully," said Tony.

" Aren't they ? " Mr. Peidestros raised his eyebrows. " Not as agreeable as they might be ? They so often aren't. Still . . . you're going ahead, no doubt ? "

" Perhaps," nodded Tony ; and the agent nodded back to him.

" *Yurse*, yes, yes. Quite right. If you wait till you've got five hundred a year in this profession, you'll wait a devil of a time, and all the bloom'll be off the flower. Yurse, you go ahead and take your chances. Life opens all sorts of gangways to a little bluff—that's what I always say. The *fait accompli* is what you've got to aim at, dear lady. I've nearly always found it successful with my headmasters ; if they've been diffident about some young client of mine, I've seen that they've engaged him before they quite realized what was happening, and once they've got him, they find that he's as good as another.   Yurse, every bit as good.   Most people are.   That's what you'll find your parents'll do, my dear, if you present our young friend to them as a *fait accompli*.   Of course they will !   And it's what you'll find out about yourselves, if ever the first bloom departs, which I hope it won't.   I'm sure you look made for each other."

He beamed on them ; and Tony saw that after a lifetime spent in affecting engagements, he was compelled to play his part in bringing off a similar piece of business in a different market.

" Let's see : you've come of age, my dear, haven't you ? "

The fingers of one hand were smoothing his long nose to a point as he asked this ; and when Honor said she was still three months away from her majority, the hand waved six inches to the right, to dispose of so small a technicality.

" *Wurl*, that's as good as makes no difference.   And when you're a little older, I dare say I shall be able to get him somewhere where he can be a housemaster. . . .   Make a lot of money out of boarders, if you know how. . . .   You'd like to be a housemaster's wife, wouldn't you, my dear.   But "—he gave the *grand seigneur's* wink to Tony—" you read for that degree, my boy.   Then I shall be able to do much more for you.   It'll be heavy going, I dare say, but she's worth it, isn't she, ha, ha ! . . .   Well, well, this is magnificent."

Out on the pavements again, Honor exclaimed with a skip : " O Tony, he's too good to be true.   Where *did* you find him ? I'm sure he's the Devil ; the Devil would be just as handsome and have those wicked and benevolent eyes.   O Tony, do you think we've sold ourselves to the Devil ? "

" No," said Tony, affecting seriousness.   " No, I don't think he's the Principle of Evil.   He's the Principle of Mischief, I think.   We've sold ourselves to that."

" So thrilling ! " exclaimed Honor with another skip.   " But, Tony, what are we really going to do ? "

" I'm not clear yet.   First of all I'm going to establish myself in a better strategic position for arguing with your father."

Honor was satisfied.   As long as plans were as indefinite as this she could enjoy them without fear.   " Oh, I hope the Principle of Mischief does something quickly," she said.

But Mr. Peidestros was not destined to dance more mischievously into this affair than with his encouragement, his sanguine plans, and his blessing. Tony went back to Stratton Lye and told the full truth to Mr. Sugden, in the course of tendering his resignation. And that excellent pylon of a man, that monumental automatic cashing machine, was disorganized and perturbed by the news, to a degree most flattering to a young master. Mr. Sugden accepted his resignation, but begged him to consider his steps carefully, and characterized them as " surely rather wild," and shook his head sadly over each one of Tony's plans as it was submitted to him ; and he would have been quite unable to analyse, had he ever thought to do so, by how many parts, in this mixture, his self-interest exceeded his paternal solicitude. From all the unselfish standpoints he could think of, he put the case for Tony's staying where he was : he put it from the point of view of Tony's future ; he put it from the point of view of the girl ; he put it from the point of view of the girl's parents ; he put it from the point of view of the peculiar nobility of prep-school work ; he put it from the point of view of the Housing Problem, and of coal and rates and confinements and Life Insurance ; and, in short, it was perfectly obvious that Mr. Sugden thought that the loss of Tony would be a serious wound to Stratton Lye.

He certainly did think so. He knew that the school's rich raiding in the scholarship fields was largely due to the exceptional flair for classical literature in this young man, and to the infectiousness of his enthusiasm ; he knew that when Mr. O'Grogan was teaching Eclogues or Elegiacs, he was not task-mastering among slaves but proselytizing among aspirants ; so he begged him to beware of early matrimony.

But Tony's teeth were set—he was taking his classes and conducting his football games with teeth set—and the head-master was at length obliged to swallow and digest the un-palatable draught ; after which, somewhat impressed by his own stoicism, he promised every help to his departing colleague. And Tony had several flying afternoons in town, for the inter-viewing of headmasters, on whom he was sensible that he had made a favourable impression ; and about half-term he was offered a post at St. Bede's Prebendal School, Colborough. Mr. Sugden was much worried by this news and came into the Common Room to inquire the stipend which had been offered him. When he heard it was one hundred and fifty pounds non-resident, he seemed to debate within himself a minute and then go out with an inward groan at so huge a sum. "Take it if you think it wise, *I* don't," were his last words.

It was then about eight o'clock, and the post did not leave Hurst again till the next morning; and at half-past ten Mr. Sugden entered the room again, glanced round, and seemed pleased to discover that Mr. O'Grogan was still here, and alone —writing at the table. But he didn't like to see him writing. He fell into a chair: he was tired, for he had spent the last two and a half hours walking up and down his study, like a financier whose stocks were falling or a general whose battle went ill.

"About that post, O'Grogan. I've been thinking it over, and I've a proposition to make. I've never had a non-resident master before, but I really don't see why I shouldn't. I give you a hundred resident now. What do you say to stopping here if I offer you a hundred and fifty non-resident? That really amounts to a large rise in salary, because naturally your board doesn't cost me fifty pounds a year."

Tony stood up, his face alight.

"There's nothing I should like better, sir."

This eagerness was a tactical error; only a little hesitation or even a silence of thirty seconds, and Mr. Sugden would have mentioned the possibility of earning a little more by capitation fees. He did, in point of fact, mention it now, but it was to make clear that the possiblity must be regarded as out of the question. "Of course, that's a large salary, and it'd have to cover everything; capitation fees, for instance."

"Oh, quite," agreed Tony. "Of course."

Again an error; for had he demurred, Mr. Sugden would have mentioned the hope of a "rise" later on. He did mention it, but to destroy it. "And you'd have to treat it as a rise, covering the next few years. It's a large salary for a prep-school to pay a man of your age."

"Quite," agreed Tony. "I think it's awfully nice of you."

"No, no: I want to help you in any way I can. Your duties would be just the same; you would just feed and sleep at your own home."

"Yes, yes." Tony was ready to excel Mr. Sugden in generosity; to meet him, not half way, but at his very door-step. The words "at your own home" sent an exhilarating shiver about his body. They returned when the headmaster had gone; and they painted a cottage somewhere down one of these lanes; a lonely cottage, with windows that looked towards the great crown of Wolstonbury Hill; with Honor behind its dimity curtains or sleeping in its dimity bed. The lines of a song that had rolled from every barrel-organ that year, to stir all hearts, whether in broad squares or in narrow slums—so they were young hearts on the sunny side of disillusion—rolled over and over in his mind, as if that were a barrel-organ too; and he felt no shame in the delight thay gave him, for they were true, exquisitely true, to the emotions within him

> " There are arms that will welcome me in,
> There are lips I am burning to kiss,
> There are two eyes that shine, just because they are mine,
> And a thousand things other men miss."

And next time he wrote to Honor, he called her " his thousand things," inviting her to discover the allusion.

He wrote also to Mr. Peidestros, but Mr. Peidestros, like a man deeply hurt, returned no answer for a long time. When at last his answer came, it proved to be no congratulatory letter, but a formal bill " for clerical and other expenses."

Now in his evening walks he sauntered down the lanes to direct his eyes to the outside of cottages which, were their occupants but to die or to depart, could take the centre of his picture very pleasingly. He composed no verses as he sauntered; he was too satisfied and too serene; instead he composed sitting-rooms and bedrooms; his imagination burned no longer with metaphors and literary ornaments, but with books and china and pictures; no longer with inversions of sentences, but with rearrangements of furniture, and with wall-papers and curtains and chintz.

One evening he struck westward across the Brighton Road and found himself in a little lost hamlet of half-timbered cottages, most of which, turning their backs on the great highway which had been of little importance in the centuries ago when they were built, looked placidly westward; while the others, which were obliged to face eastward, shyly hid themselves behind the houses opposite. It was Albourne Green. But all these cottages had curtains in their windows, and he walked on up a road whose name, so an old labourer told him, was Benfelly

Lane. The name charmed him, who had once made researches in Domesday Book for the purposes of his poetry, because he instantly suspected that in the " Benfelly " of this labourer the old Domesday " Benefelle " survived after nine hundred years. And then to see " Beanfield Farm " painted on a gate was a further thrill, and he walked on towards Twineham. He had almost forgotten the object of his journeying, when he suddenly realized that he was passing a cottage, and that it was empty. " Gosh ! " said he.

It had no beauty except the beauty of age : it was but a rectangular building with a roof to it—a Noah's ark with a chimney stack at either end. The porch was in the middle and its pillars were two tree trunks painted brown ; on each side of the porch was the sashed window, painted white, of a sitting-room ; and above, at equal distances, were the three sashed windows of the bedrooms. They were not even dormer windows, nor did they hide far back under the eaves, and they were absurdly small. But age, using this barn-shaped dwelling as a palate, had daubed and dusted it with all the colours of the surrounding landscape. On the roof which was unusually steep—steep with the steepness of a voice that has soared to its top-note, and with the same vibrato—it had turned the tiles to a meadow-brown, and either powdered them with the grey-green of the beech boles or patched them with clumps of rusty moss from the roadside. The bricks which had once been red it had darkened to a neutral tint, and slavered some with the yellow-green of wheatfields, and hidden others with the golden, velvety pile of its moss. At one corner it had bound the house to the earth with an old ivy's limbs, nigh dead, but knotty and strong as a wagoner's arms, and with ankles as hairy as a stallion's fetlocks.

Tony pushed at the little gate in the hedgerow, and discovered that age had played with this a livelier part : it had made it an ancient and disreputable drunkard which clung to the support of its post, and, if encouraged forward, moved with a week-kneed slither along the quarter of a circle and then stopped defeated. While he was pausing there, the old labourer who had given him the name of Benfelly Lane, slouched past.

" Ev'nun, zur."

" Good evening. This cottage is empty, isn't it ? "

The labourer halted, that the whole of his brain might be

devoted to a correct treatment of this question. Though he must have passed the cottage every evening of his life on his homeward journey, he looked now at its closed windows, its smokeless chimneys, its weedy brick-path, and the high grasses in its garden, and his eyes recorded the slow working of a Sussex brain.

"Aye, her be empty all right."

"What's it called?"

But the labourer had not yet disentangled himself from the previous question, and he announced, after a further examination of the house, that he was ratified in his first opinion.

"Aye, her be middlin' empty, bayn't she?"

"Yes, but what's it called?"

The labourer now looked at Tony, to get this new question properly into focus.

"Called? Sheep's Eye, her be." He was completely sure of it. "Aye, Sheep's Eye, that's her name."

"Sheep's Eye?" Tony ransacked his memory. "Is that a corruption of Shipley, or Sepelei, as it used to be?" he asked learnedly.

"Shipley? Noah, Shipley's eight or nine mile or mower from here, on t'other side of the Adur. Sheep's Eye, her be."

"But perhaps she wasn't always called that."

"It's bin that as long as I known it, which is nigh on seventy years."

"One could rent it, I suppose?"

The labourer's answer was unconsciously devastating.

"Aye, she's bin rented afore now."

Tony smiled.

"It's the sort of place I should like to have myself."

When the full implications of this remark had passed through the labourer's staring eyes into his brain, he rather surprised Tony by expressing no surprise.

"Aye, a gen'l'man had it once afore—though I don't know that he was by good rights a gen'l'man. However, he lived there without working; he wrote for the papers, they said, though I never see owt of his meself, and he gave talks on platforms. After him Dummelow had it, who was Farmer Orde's man, him of Thatcher's Spinney Farm. Then Cardy had it who works on the roads for the Council. 'Tain't properly a gen'l'man's cottage, I don't call it."

" I must make further inquiries."

" Aye, you could do that. Well, I must be getting along hoam, I must now, if you'll excuse me."

" Certainly. Good night."

" Night, zur."

Tony passed through the gate, and walked in the garden. It was much overgrown and weedy, and evidently the late occupant had used all of it for vegetables. But there were well-grown shrubs up either side of the brick path : veronica and laurestinus and berberis and mock-orange ; and beside the porch was a box-tree cut into the shape of a cone.

" One could turn all this front into grass," he thought.

He walked along the untidy hedge on the left that separated the garden from a meadow, and he counted the hedge-plants which had quarrelled for its making : hazel and thorn and elder and blackberry and sloe, with columbine and deadly nightshade and honeysuckle involved among them, and ivy and bracken at their feet. This brought him behind the house, and he learned that the back garden was separated from another meadow only by a fence of oak posts and wire, so that one could look down the grassland as it fell gently away to a dark spinney. There was a large plum-tree here, and several apples and pears. Turning towards the back wall of the house he saw that it was a wall of creepers, whose overgrowth fell to the ground, some long and wispy, some fluffed and entangled, like a woman's new-washed hair.

Now let him look through the front windows : very small but very possible were these ground-floor rooms with their big fireplaces. What of the bedrooms ? Could one mount to their windows ? He looked at the tough branches of the old ivy, and decided that something could be done. It was done very easily, and soon he was suspended like a fruit below the sill of a bedroom window and peeping in. Yes, much could be made of little rooms like these ; and what of the view from up here ? Turning his head to the left so that he was facing south, he saw over a flat stretch of weald the whole pack of the downs coming towards him, with Wolstonbury king of the pack. An endorsement jumped at his heart. Turning quickly to the right for what might greet him there, he saw a broad and undulating stretch of the weald which led to rising ground well-wooded, whose masses of rounded trees, this early autumn, resembled woods embroidered on a tapestry. And at that point his muscles protested against holding him longer, and he hastily and clumsily descended.

Then he went out through the gate, latching it behind him carefully, like one who had a proprietary interest in this enclosure.

The Christmas vacation was a holiday, not only from Stratton Lye and work, but from time itself—a four weeks' delay in the supra-temporal nowhere of love. No doubt the bodies of the youngest O'Grogan and the youngest Daubeny were to be seen in the Chiswick streets, or on Wimbledon Common when the frost came, or in Richmond Park when the snow was down—in which time their bodies might even have been seen face downward on a toboggan—or in the Daubeny's house on the Mall for the Christmas party, when these same bodies were decorated so carefully that one might have supposed them the loyalest residents of this, our temporal world; but, none the less, the truth remains that all this outward gaiety was largely a concession to the tenants of an order other than that in which Tony and Honor were living, and that, at every possible moment, they escaped into this silent region of their own, and dwelt there with linked hands.

Welcoming her lover at Victoria Station, Honor dispersed that considerable structure at a breath—the breath of a kiss. Every trace of it faded out, with all its population and its porters and its locomotives, like the insubstantial pageant it probably is—as, her arms about his neck, she whispered her ecstatic : " Tony ! Tony ! " Through such a gateway she led him to his four weeks' sojourn in a district too still, too soundless, too empty of all but its own golden light for any thinking man to account it a part of our present changing world.

And the translation of Antony O'Grogan and Honor Daubeny to these unreal planes (or more real planes, according as different philosophies may esteem them) explains why, for the present, the difficulty of the Major-General, her father, did not assert itself. There is no disrespect in saying that, to this state of existence, he was quite irrelevant. He would have been the first to avouch that such a tom-fool country, where neither the British tables of measurement nor even the metrical system were valid, was a place which he had never visited and had no desire to visit. If philosophers deposed that such a place existed; that, indeed, it was God's Own Country; that, moreover, such human beings as the bhikshu, the neo-platonist, the saint, the poet, the child, and the lover—and possibly the epileptic and the drunkard and the idiot—were able sometimes to linger on its frontiers, well, all he could say was that, when they returned to the realms of sense again, he would be prepared to renew pourparlers with them, and to negotiate on the principles of British Justice. "For if ever there was a three-dimensional person, it's dear old General Daubeny," thought Tony, and would have said as much to Honor, could she have understood him; since, in his fondness for decorating himself with these blinding metaphysical terms, he was no better than his fathers.

Together on an early January day these two dwellers in eternity put their bodies in a train that would stop at Hassocks Station, and took them out when it got there, and walked them along the brisk and frosty roads, four miles or five, till they stood outside Sheep's Eye cottage, in Benfelly Lane; at which point it may be said that the dwellers left heaven and dwelt very much in their bodies and very much in terms of time. And Wolstonbury Hill watched them from over the weald, as three hundred years before it had watched the homespun labourers, leal subjects of Elizabeth, building this cottage, and for three hundred years had watched its home-makers coming, in Stuart and Puritan, Augustan and Georgian times—all of them as foolish as their forerunners, with their dreams of the perfection it would hold. Well might Wolstonbury, had it not been too near an eternal thing to know the weakness of emotion, have lifted an eyebrow, as it watched to-day the gentles impropriating Sheep's Eye and bringing to it no more wisdom than the churls who had gone before. But Wolstonbury rose against the sky, its surface as smooth as a sphere and its line a perfect arc; and with these symbols of eternity in its shape it remained austere, impassive, indifferent.

The General became relevant again when, at the end of the holiday, Tony drifted down to the hard earth and the General's study, like Browning's angel into the cell of the boy Theocrite, and begged once more that he might be openly engaged to Honor.

"*What?* . . . Damn, you're not still harping on that, are you?" the General ejaculated, with that angry thrust of his mouth to one side. "Engaged to Honor? Good God, no.

Haven't you got shut of that fancy yet? I thought you were learning to be happy children together." He seemed angry that they had not doffed the idea, like the fancy dress of a single night. "No, I won't hear of it. That's enough." It wasn't worth leaving his chair for, or running up his eyeglass to, in salute.

"I am quite sure, sir"—Tony always found himself adopting this formal mode when he stepped into the rather enjoyable pomps of a suitor's audience—"that I love Honor and always shall, and that therefore I want to marry her; and that she loves me, and always will, and that therefore she wants to marry me. That's all I know."

"And how often have you been sure of that before, when you've spent a few weeks with a pretty girl?"

"Never, sir. Never once before. When I was sixteen, I was attracted by a little girl, but I half knew all the time that it was a transient thing. I do not feel that with Honor. No, I can honestly say that no one's been to me what Honor is."

"Then," the General laughed, "that's all the more reason why you shouldn't tie yourself up to the first pretty girl who throws you off your balance. *I* had many such attacks before I settled down. Bless my soul, I began at school: I had some idea of marrying the doctor's daughter, and, as far as I remember, she was quite ready. Honor isn't going to marry the first good-looking youth who stirs her fancy. . . . That's the whole trouble, nothing more and nothing less, that you're both good-looking children."

"Well, I don't know about that in my case," Tony demurred, "but of course it's true of Honor. But isn't it always the beginning of the trouble, sir? After all, the highest love is only sublimated sex."

"Is only *what?*" The General's mouth shot to one side. "What the hell does that rigmarole mean?"

To explain its meaning briefly to a completely virgin mind was not easy, and Tony looked towards the window for help. But inasmuch as on the subject of these Viennese doctrines, now first percolating into England, he had lately been enjoying supper-to-midnight discussions with a long-haired master at Stratton Lye, he was able to find some words.

"I don't think that it makes love any the less glorious, sir, but rather more so, to think that men have raised out of their natural procreative instincts the loveliest thing in the world, and the solution of nearly all their frustrations. I mean to say, the rose isn't any the less beautiful, or any the less a striking evidence for theism, because it has its roots in the earth."

The General had stared at him during these propositions, as if he were staring at them rather than at him; and he did not remove his gaze for some time. Then he said:

"Well, I don't know what all that flummery's about, and I'm sure I'm content not to. But to come down to brass tacks"— the General's language always ran, sooner or later, on to familiar tram-lines—"my own opinion is that you and Honor, in spite of all your fine talk, are more than usually innocent and simple. You're young for your years. Honor, in any case, is extra-ordinarily young. Now, if it were Jill, there might be more in it."

"More in it!" Tony reiterated, in potent bitterness. "More in it, my God! . . . Forgive me, sir; but how can you know?"

"The whole thing's too quick, by a long chalk. Too quick."

"Quick! What have quickness or slowness to do with real love? They are irrelevant terms."

"Irrelevant? Damn! Why?"

Now at last the General had put up his monocle.

"Because love, if it's the real thing, lifts itself above our spatio-temporal order. . . . Or that's what I believe. . . . But anyhow, sir, I've loved Honor for nearly a year now. And, sir, I didn't decide lightly that it was she, and only she, for me. Nor did she come easily to the same decision about me."

"Stuff and nonsense! She's come to no such decision."

"Ask her, sir."

"I shall not ask her. Of course she'd say she'd either marry you or go into a nunnery; and after being given an opportunity to say it, she'd begin to believe it. I don't want any stagy scenes with her. I shan't forbid her to see you, or shut her up, or take her round the world, or any tommy-nonsense like that; which would only convince her that she was dying with love for you. I'll have no stagy scenes with her or with you." He opened his eye-cavity, and scattered the monocle and all such scenes with it. "That's the end of it."

Tony's cheeks heated.

"But supposing, sir, that's not the end of it?"

"Eh what? Whad'd'you mean?"

Tony, who was sitting near the table, fiddled with some papers on it, and tossed them down again.

"Honor and I don't want to do anything without your

consent, sir. We've both agreed that our happiness 'll be horribly spoiled if we don't have your consent when we get married."

The general began to fumble for his monocle with a trembling hand : evidently one of the unpleasant scenes which he had scattered with it would have to be recovered.

"*When* we get married ! God ! . . . *When* we get married ! Which you won't do, O'Grogan. What are you thinking of ? Are you going to Gretna Green in a post-chaise ? Are you going to live on air ? Pfoo ! "—the monocle was now " standing to "—" Don't oblige me to get angry with you, my boy ; I've tried to deal with you gently and diplomatically over this affair. I've welcomed you to my home the same as ever, and I expect you to justify my trust in you——"

" I warned you not to trust me, sir."

" What ? Whad'd'you mean ? "

" I told you, sir, four months ago, that if you allowed me to see Honor, I couldn't pretend that I wouldn't treat her as the girl who had given a definite promise to marry me. I don't want to come into your home on false pretences. As soon as I can make a home for her, I shall feel justified in taking advantage of her promise."

" Oh ! " It was a good sarcastic " Oh ! " as round and damaging as the staring monocle. And after delivering it, the General rose, shook down his trousers, and dusted them. " That's a declaration of war, is it ? "

" If you like to put it so dramatically——"

" Dramatically ! Ha ! the pup accuses me of drama. Which of all things I am most anxious to avoid. . . . My dear boy, I don't want to quarrel with you——"

" I'm afraid I'd rather you did, sir. If we are to remain friendly I can't with honour steal Honor from you "—confound the clashing of the words !—" but if we are openly at war, and I can improve my position sufficiently to justify my setting up a home of my own, I shall then be able to ask anything of her without loss of honour "—oh, damn the word ! Surely it were wise of all fathers to call their daughters Honor, and so catch the feet of their threatening suitors in these hampering gins ! Tony stumbled hastily to an end. " And that's the position I shall labour for now, sir."

" I see. And when you've got into this position, you'll snatch her, will you ? "

"I suppose I shall have to, sir."

"Very good.   Very good."   The General was now standing against the fireplace.   His chest lifted a little, and his shoulders adjusted themselves.   Magnificently calm, he dispensed with the monocle, being above such adventitious aids.   "Well, the opening of hostilities gives *me* advantages as well as you.   It frees you to talk very big like this, and it frees me to say what friendliness forbade me to say before; and that is, that if you wait till you are in a position to make a home for Honor, you'll wait quite long enough to suit my book.   It may interest you to know that I have spoken with your mother and your uncle, Archdeacon Gabriel, and I understand your circumstances pretty well.   Now it is fortunate that you go back so soon to your schoolboys, because it relieves me from the unpleasantness of forbidding you my house.   When you return, I daresay you will come and see me as usual; in three months, this little scene will seem very absurd, if, indeed, we haven't forgotten it."

Tony moved towards the door, halted as if to say something, and moved on again.   All he could find to say as he opened the door was: "I am more serious than you think, sir."

"You are," the General laughed.   "Painfully serious. But it gets better."

General Daubeny was pleased with his strategy, and doubtless it would have been the wisest, if based on a right estimate of his opponent's character; but on this matter his Intelligence was bringing him the most mistaken information.   It was mistaken too in the weight it allowed to the loyalty, the timidity, and the decorum of Honor, his daughter.   Loyalty, timidity, and decorum were all in Honor, and, despite her romantic utterance about "nothing desperate or dangerous ever happening in Chiswick," were more natural to her than their opposites; she had been frightened when Tony once mooted the question of a secret marriage; but she was more frightened—this was what the General did not know—by the suffering which appeared in Tony's face if, by word or action, she seemed less than the heroic lover he wanted.   He could always win her to his will by the way his eyes roamed unhappily abroad when he was disappointed in her.

And Tony was more offended by the General's humorous

toleration than he would have been by his violent obstruction. For a second time he went back to Stratton Lye with teeth set, and with teeth set took his classes, and with teeth set acquired a five years' lease of Sheep's Eye, as from the twenty-fifth of March. With a grim smile he acknowledged the concession that it should be completely redecorated, and that he might begin work in its garden at once. With an untrembling voice he announced to Mr. Sugden that he would move into his new home before the Summer term. With the same purposeful air he set a jobbing gardener to dig in the vegetable patches of Sheep's Eye and prepare them for grass.

Very pleasant was it, perhaps more serenely pleasant than anything he had ever known, to mount his cycle on fine evenings when the spring was stirring and see how the new grass seeds were germinating or the old shrubs breaking. Easter fell in April's first week that year of 1912, and Mr. Sugden had asked him to give a fortnight of the holiday to Stratton Lye that he might coach some scholarship boys who were remaining at the school for that period. This suited him well : it put new money into his pocket and gave him the long April afternoons for work in his garden—warm, wet spring afternoons when grass really grows and creepers and flowers and shrubs really break and bloom. To-day the clematis montana would be just so much greener than yesterday, and the leaves of the jessamine quite noticeably larger ; and the Japanese honeysuckle had grown an inch at least, and see ! the yellow wall-flowers were open as well as the red. The flowering currant was as pink as a child beribboned for a party, and the dome of the veronica was all sprinkled with new green. That quickset hedge ! Only a day or two ago it showed its bare branches, and now it was all green. This hedge, one might say, had changed its sex and age : only last fortnight it had looked brown and bristly and hostile as a tetchy old hedgehog, and now, at ten paces away, it looked round and smooth and soft as a young female thing. In the back garden the big plum tree, with all its white finery on, stood against the dark bareness of Thatcher's Spinney like a splash and a stippling of Chinese white. And under the dull old ivy leaves new shoots were peeping and pressing themselves against the wall.

One afternoon, seeking a pleasant titillation, he trailed his hand down the leaves of the box-tree which the last tenant had cut into the shape of a cone ; and he started back as he heard a flutter inside.   With a lovely swoop and rise a frightened thrush flew out and sped away into Thatcher's Spinney.

" Hallo ! " said Tony ; and he parted the leaves and peeped in.   Yes, here was her nest with the blue eggs resting in the smooth lining of clay and its little festoon of berberis round the brim for decoration and good cheer.   " Well now, isn't that nice of her ! " he thought, surprised how flattered and grateful he could feel that she had chosen his box-tree for her nest.

With the falling of dusk he would cycle back to his supper at Stratton Lye, delighting in the young, innocent greenery of the roadside hedges, and in the light emerald of the larches down in the woodlands, and the fawny white of the wild cherry's blossom ; for his eyes had been touched to a keener and more affectionate sight by the fingers of his own garden.   And in his bedroom under the tiles, if he heard the rain pattering down at night, or saw the sun bright in the morning, he rejoiced in both, for both swung his thoughts to his distant garden and showed the rich earth drinking the water or the grass straining upwards under the sun.

CHAPTER VII

A LATE April day, and Sheep's Eye Cottage waited. In its every room a fire waited, tossing its flames about and playing a game of leaping lights and dancing shadows on the whitewashed walls. The flames, when stronger than the daylight, threw on floor and wall the shadows of the simple furniture that Tony, in his steadfast, untrembling deliberateness, had bought in Hurst or had caused to be made by an old carpenter in Albourne Green. To left and right swung the flames, in the draught from the wide-open windows and doors ; to and fro swung the shadow of each piece of furniture, like a compass needle. The light of the fires touched with an erubescence the folds of the dimity curtains that Honor had sewn with nervous fingers. And above the roof, the smoke of the fires went up from the two chimney stacks, to tell Albourne and Twineham that the new tenants were coming into Sheep's Eye to-night.

The garden outside waited, for the young gentleman, who was renting Sheep's Eye, had come early that morning and put it in final trim, raking the earth round the shrubs, training with hammer and nail any tumbled wisp of creeper, clipping the quickset hedge, and standing well back in the roadway to see the completed picture. Beyond Sheep's Eye—but perhaps forgetful that this was the day—Hurst and Albourne, Twineham and Ansty waited, for Tony, with his calm deliberateness, had seen to it that not only a cottage and a garden should be waiting for Honor, but a circle of friends and the assurance of many interests and many diversions. After five years at Stratton Lye he had built his popularity in the houses where there were young people and tennis lawns and hockey fields and bridge-tables and ping-pong boards and picnic baskets. And he had canvassed the mistresses of them all that they should leave Honor no time for loneliness in Sheep's Eye Cottage. So good had his staff work been, while the General at Chiswick was waiting for an infatuation to perish !

There had been more than the slanting blue smoke to tell the nearer neighbours of Sheep's Eye that this was the day of its occupation, for Mrs. Fyfold, the old carpenter's wife, who was now in the cottage, ministering to the fires and preparing the tea, had told them all about her young gentleman that just now she was " doing for," and the dear young lady he would be bringing there as his wife, come tea-time on Thursday. With an anxious watching she tended those fires, determined that at the right moment they should be flaming high ; and with a lively affection she prepared the " country tea " which her young gentleman had commanded with his happy laughter that " was so taking : " poached eggs and toast, and new bread and butter, and some of her own plum jam, and sixpen'north of fresh cream from Mr. Orde of Thatcher's Spinney Farm. Ever and anon she left the kitchen and, talking to herself, peeped through the living-room door, to make sure that all was right ; or, lifting her skirts, she climbed the stairs to the little bedroom, to see that the draught was not upsetting the flower-vases or littering the place with petals and leaves. For her young gentleman himself had come early that morning and decorated both living-room and bedroom with blooms from his garden : wallflowers and daffodils and anemones from the beds ; ladysmock and primroses from the hedge and ditch ; and branches of flowering currant and plum-blossom from the shrubs and trees. And Mrs. Fyfold, after he had gone, had brought a handful of blooms along too.

It was sundown now, and at every sound of footsteps or wheels in Benfelly Lane, she went to the cottage door. Once it was to see the passing of the old labourer who had introduced Tony to Sheep's Eye ; and he greeted her as he trudged by.

" Ev'nun, Mrs. Fyfold."

" Evening, Jo."

The labourer decided that he might halt his trudging.

" Seeing 'em in, eh ? "

" Aye."

" They bayn't come yet, then ? "

" No.   Not yet."

" They won't be so long now, dessay."

" No.   When I heard your steps I wondered was you they ? "

" Noah, I'm not they."   He seemed immoderately tickled by the idea.   " But Sheep's Eye do be looking proper alive again, don't she ? "

" Aye."

" And to think that I was by when first he set eyes on it. ' That there cottage do be empty, bayn't it ? ' he says to me ; and I says, ' Aye, it were empty right enough.'   And 'e says, ' What's her called ? ' and I says, ' She do be called Sheep's Eye, by rights.'   ' Reckon that's the same as Shipley,' 'e says, and I says, ' Noah, Shipley do be a mile or mower from here.'   ' Mebbe I could rent it,' 'e says ; and I says, ' Aye, it could be rented all right, but it's no house for a gen'l'man, to my thinking.'   However, he took it, and here he be coming right away, he be ; this very night.   Mr. Fyfold better ? "

" Yes, he's none too bad this weather."

" Well, I must be getting alone hoam, I must now.   Night, Mrs. Fyfold."

" Good night, Jo."

In the train Antony O'Grogan and Mrs. O'Grogan (was it possible that Honor was Mrs. O'Grogan ?) sat side by side, sometimes touching each other's hands or limbs, but not speaking much, for there was a tall man in the compartment all the way from London to Haywards Heath, who studied them rather carefully, and when they spoke it was of commonplace matters, such as the shell-pink blossom of the orchards they were passing, and the bright, stainless green of the hawthorn and the larches that broke the bare old woods with a shock of youth.   But from Haywards Heath to Hassocks they were alone, and Tony took her hand in both of his and asked her : " Happy, dearest ? " and she who had been rather pale throughout the journey lit up a most deliberate sparkle in her eyes and flew a smile to convince him.

Only one suit-case was on the rack, and in it were enough of Honor's garments for a night or two, no more ; the rest waited at the mercy of her parents.   Before the day was much darker her parents would know of the wedding : a letter signed " Antony and Honor O'Grogan " was awaiting their return from an afternoon's visiting.   Antony and Honor had signed it thus an hour or two before they went to the Registrar's Office ;

and Honor had said : " Oh, isn't it unlucky to write my married
name before it's properly mine ? Let's write Tony and Honor."
But Tony had laughed at superstition and insisted on the
" O'Grogan." Like a single bell this name would sound the
fait accompli finally but kindly, and proclaim to all readers
without another hurtful word that the guardianship of Honor
was legally changed. Not Jill nor Peggy knew of the wedding,
because Tony, though he had longed that both should be in the
secret, had determined to incriminate nobody.

Hassocks. They were there ; and Honor's hand was shaking
a little, as her husband aided her to the platform. A car, with
all the speed of indifference, drove them through the bright
evening to Sheep's Eye ; and only once in the cab did Tony,
holding her hand, speak to her. " It was wonderful of you to
do this," he said. She smiled back at him. " For *me*, by gosh ! "
he muttered, half to himself. " Gosh, I'll not forget it ! "

In the cottage porch Mrs. Fyfold stood to welcome them.
Of the garden, the living room, and the bedroom, all lively
with flowers, Honor could find but one thing to say : " O
Tony, it's perfect ! " Then when they were about to sit down
to tea, Mrs. Fyfold looked from one to the other, and much to
her own surprise, was moved to utterance.

" Well, there now ! . . ." she began, and glanced again from
Tony to Honor, while she fumbled in her apron-pocket for a
handkerchief with which to dab at her eyes and her nostrils.
" Well, there now ! Forgive an old woman, but—you've fair
upset me—you do be two pretty young things, and no mistake
. . . and may I say as my heart is with you, my dears—and I
wish you well from the bottom of me heart, I do now. . . ."
She patted her eyes. " Well, it's a great day for you, a'nt it ?—
you must excuse me because you've properly upset me : I
never thought I should take on like this. . . . There, sit down
and have your tea, and don't take no notice of me—but perhaps,
miss, you'd let me give you a kiss first, just to show you what
I can't say very well—will you ? . . . Oh thank you, my dear ! "
—this was as Honor came laughingly into her embrace, and
returned it—" well there, well there. . . . God bless you. I
can't say more than that, can I ? God be good to you. . . ."

It was dark when Mrs. Fyfold came to bid them good night,
and the same fond interest was in her eyes.

" I just come along to say good night, sir. Good night,
miss. I'll be round early in the morning, and don't you worry

about nothing. It's a real pleasure for me to be doing for you at a time like this. Just you think of nothing but your two selves, and if there's any little odd job Mr. Fyfold can do for you in the morning, just you let him know. He's proper interested in your home, and he's handy in his way. Good night, sir. . . . Thanks, I know my way out right enough. You stay with the young lady. Good night, miss, and God bless you."

The darkness fell deeper, and Tony, taking the lamp, led Honor up to the little bedroom. There he watched her as she undid her leather belt and took off her blouse of lawn and lace and her skirt, and stood before the dressing-table in her moirée petticoat and a petticoat-bodice of white nainsook and lace, from whose short sleeves her long bare arms reached up to unpin her hair. The long amber hair fell down her back ; and drawing up a chair, she sat before the mirror to comb and brush it. Then Tony who had been sitting on the bed, got up and came towards her and took the brush without a word from her hand, and brushed the hair, and felt its surface with his hand— as a man might tend and polish a possession long coveted and lately won. And suddenly the swelling of his love overpowered him, and he flung himself on his knees at her side, and buried his head in her lap. She stroked his hair and kissed the nape of his neck ; and he, lifting up his face to hers in a worship so still as to be almost unseeing, took her kisses on his mouth and forehead. Desire was less urgent than worship when he fumbled with his fingers at the button of her white bodice and exposed her breasts, whereover he passed his lips, then resting his cheek against them. And with both hands she pressed his head against them.

PART V

CHAPTER I

TWO YEARS AFTER

IT was a Saturday in the early July of 1914, and the household of General Daubeny was arraying itself for happiness. From base to roof the red house on the Mall had completed the dressing of its less important rooms, and the flush of anticipation could be imagined in their faces : there were flowers in their available button-holes ; their linen was stiff and glistening from the hot-air cupboard, and perhaps a trifle self-conscious about its freshness ; their doors were ajar like ears that listened for sounds below ; and their windows were open and gaping into the Mall, like foolish and happy mouths. The most important member, the dining-room, was not yet fully attired ; its door was resolutely, even rudely, shut, and one could understand an apprehension in the other rooms lest it were late for the festivities. The kitchen was fussed and fashed ; everywhere its populace was in excess of its legal accommodation ; there were more saucepans on its range than had any right to be there, and more crockery, canisters, castors and cutlery on its table ; there were too many finger bowls, dessert dishes, wine glasses and fruiterers' bags on its dresser ; and certainly too many feet on its linoleum.

And all this because Miss Joyce (or young Mrs. Len, as the cook called her) was home from India after three years' absence, with her baby and its fat brown smiling ayah. A gathering of the clans was afoot : Mrs. O'Grogan was already in the drawing-room with the General and Mrs. Daubeny and Joyce herself ; Derek and Keatings would arrive as soon as their London offices released them ; Peggy and Michael Saffery would appear next, in the Vicar's car, from Southend ; the six Gabriels were coming—the Archdeacon and his lady, the Rev. Warner Gabriel and Mr. John Gabriel, and the Misses Elsa and Theresa; and lastly, Honor and Antony O'Grogan, hot-foot from Sussex. Seventeen would sit down to dinner.

In the drawing-room over emptied tea-cups, Joyce, radiant with her excitement, was talking so disastrously fast that her sentences, like children crowding out of school, shouldered one another aside, and the little ones were knocked over and forgotten, and the bigger had to recover their balance and come up late, and only the strongest ran straight and true to their full-stop; and meanwhile the three parents listened and loved, and Jill Daubeny leaned forward admiringly.

"Oh, but we mustn't let the talk beat everlastingly around that wretched child," said Joyce, alluding to Antony Leonard whom the ayah had removed upstairs for his bath, "because it gets—but I *am* glad that I got in with him first—before Peggy got in with hers—because it means that my boy's the first of the new generation—Peggy was so beastly slow about getting busy. —*I* didn't take nearly three years to produce a baby, and hers was pure plagiarism, wasn't it? because she'd no sooner heard of Antony Leonard than she produced one herself, just as if the idea'd never struck her before. I couldn't have done it more promptly, could I?"

"No," the General agreed, who was sitting forward on a stiff chair, his fingers spread on the knees of his smart shepherd's-plaid trousers, and his monocle aloft and addressed towards his daughter-in-law. "Dammit, no! The blighter got himself gazetted at the earliest possible moment. He wasn't going to miss a day's seniority, if he could help it."

"Yes, he couldn't have got through Sandhurst quicker," acknowledged Joyce, delightedly; and the General looked a thought uncomfortable that she should have developed his little parable thus. But he only gave the sharp, nervous nod that was growing on him as he got older.

And now Jill entered the conversation.

"But why did you call him *Antony* Leonard? You never told us."

"Leonard for your family, Antony for mine."

"Yes, but why Antony, when Keatings was his godfather?"

"Oh, I don't know. I think we were all rather fond of Tony. I could never understand why Peggy didn't call hers after Tony, instead of 'Michael Derek,' because Tony was always her favourite. And fancy calling anyone after Derek!"

Mrs. O'Grogan, sad and withdrawn as ever, here broke her silence. " I think she called him Michael Derek because she felt Derek was getting left out in the cold."

" Oh ! " Joyce shrieked. " Isn't that Peggy all over ? And I suppose Derek's being an appallingly pompous and high-principled godfather—he's rather enchanting in his way—but what about Honor and Tony ? They ought to give us something soon now—how dreadfully slow all these people are !— oh, but wasn't it wonderful about Tony and Honor ? I was thrilled when I heard it. Tony would be the only one of us to elope and do something original."

The General, with another nervous motion that was growing on him, lifted his chin and shot his lips forward for a second.

" Is a run-away marriage original ? "

" Now don't pretend you're still angry with them, because we all know you're not," Joyce teased. " We know you forgave them long ago."

" It's a principle of the army that one always forgives success. When we saw that he was going to make a success of the marriage, we decided that we must overlook a technical breach of orders——"

" Who's ' we ' ? " This was from his daughter Jill.

" Eh, what ? " He swung round to Jill and away again. " And I must say that at the Court Martial young Jill here proved a most eloquent Prisoner's Friend. And, as it's turned out, the marriage has been the making of Tony. He's——"

" Stuff ! " This from Jill again. " Tony didn't need any making."

" Of course he did ! He was rather a feckless, dreaming, happy Irish boy, wanting to write poetry, before—and with no sense of affairs at all——"

" Pooh ! " Jill scoffed.

" —But when he found himself saddled with a wife and a house, he buckled to, working at his school all day and reading for a London degree at night, and he took his Intermediate with a couple of lengths to spare. He's quite safe to pass his Finals, and then it seems he may hope for a Headmastership."

" *Which* he's too good for," said Jill. " He should have gone on with his writing."

" And starved, I suppose ? " The General turned on her sharply.

" They had enough to live quietly," Jill retorted, almost

passionately. "They should have done the heroic thing, instead of tamely bidding for security——"

"That's some of Tony's thunder," the General explained with a laugh to Joyce. "Jill has always stolen it."

"Well"—Mrs. Daubeny was breaking in—"*I* think he showed up awfully well. He came to us, before we were really reconciled, and promised us that he was going to justify the step he had taken and give us no cause to regret it. And he's lived up to his promise. He's made her wonderfully happy, with lots of friends, and as Daddy says, he's slaved like a nigger. And now you really must excuse me, because I'm getting jumpy about the dinner and the dining-room table."

And she disappeared.

Joyce returned to the subject of Honor and Tony.

"And do they still love each other as romantically as at first?"

To which the General, who, like so many of his kind, had given the long, hot hours of his Indian days to a camp-bed and the lightest of novels, and was therefore as romantic, when it came to other people's love, as any housemaid, replied very deliberately:

"He has eyes for no one else."

"How nice!" said Joyce inadequately—and at that moment Keatings and Derek were shown into the room.

Both were in evening dress, and feminine eyes saw at once that Keatings's jacket was shiny and wrinkled, while Derek's was a tailor's masterpiece. Joyce jumped up from her chair, ran to her eldest brother, seized both his hands, cried: "My one and only Keatings!" and kissed both his cheeks.

"Save us!" Keatings grinned. "You usedn't to be so demonstrative. . . ."

"O Keatings, it's—it's—well, it *is*, really! I had to go to the other end of the world to learn that I was quite fond of you all. I'd never supposed that I really liked you like that. I used to find you rather tedious, but I simply loved your cable when the kid was born. It was the best of all my cables. Do you know, I nearly wept when I got it! Sloppy of me, wasn't it?"

The General, who had risen for the irruption and was examining it through his monocle, demanded what the cable had said.

"Oh, you wouldn't understand. Nobody'd understand. Only the Family—isn't that so, Keatings?"

" But what was it ?   Damn, what was it ? "

" Oh, it just said : ' One more jar for the Gabriels ; ' and I cried over it—away out there in my outpost of empire.   There ! I've told the truth : I *did* cry.   I cried all over the kid.   Now why should a stupid remark like that make me cry ? "

" You can search me," said Keatings, in despair of an answer.

Joyce had now gone to her second brother and kissed him, but more diffidently.

" And Derek !   Funny old Derek.   I got quite fond of you, too, when the monsoons were about and the mosquitoes.   I realized you were all I'd got.   Are you a millionaire yet ? "

" Not doing too badly," Derek grinned.

" Badly ! " grunted Keatings.   " He's a blooming partner now.   A motor magnate."

" Oh, are you really, Derek ?   Then won't you give me a car to take back to India.   *Do*."

" You won't go back to India," said Derek significantly.

His words and manner were strange ; and Joyce dropped her hands from his elbows.

" Won't go back ?   What do you mean ? "

" You won't be able to *get* back for many years."

" Derek !   I'm going back to my lord and master in six months.   Nothing less than the end of the world'll stop me."

" Something very like the end of the world is going to stop you, if the rumours in the city to-night are correct."

" Keatings, what's he talking about ?   Oh, isn't he maddeningly mysterious ?   Derek, you haven't changed a bit.   What *do* you mean ? "

" He's got some donkey's notion that all Europe's going to war in a month's time," Keatings explained, with fraternal shame.   " He heard it to-night, and he's very proud of it."

" Father, do you hear that ? "   Joyce had turned to the General.   " Derek says Europe's going to war next month."

" War ?   Good God ! " exclaimed the General, fumbling for the monocle which he had abandoned.

" Oh, let's sit down and hear all about it," suggested Joyce. " It sounds rather jolly.   Sit down, all.   Now, Derek darling, what is it ? "

Derek, sitting straight in a high-backed chair, told to an attentive audience—attentive all except Keatings, who had heard the whole in the road and now stared with impatience and shame at the pictures in the room or at his shoes—of a rumour current in the city that Germany was hatching a plot on the Austrian frontier to establish a *casus belli* with Servia, Russia and France, and that Great Britain was secretly re-affirming her engagements to France. " So, if the trail fires," he concluded, " we've booked a nice place for the explosion. In other words, if none of the powder proves to be damp, all Europe will be at war in a month."

The silence that met his silence was like a wide mirror staring at him.

Jill Daubeny knocked it to pieces.

" I don't believe a word of it."

" No sensible person would," Keatings endorsed.

" My dear boy." The General, removing the monocle from the subject as if it were no longer worthy of his scrutiny, supported them. " I've heard that story at regular intervals for forty years—ever since 'seventy."

" Of course," breathed Keatings.

And Joyce added : " Well, anyhow, Len's the only soldier among you, and he's in India, so it won't affect him. All the rest of our men are men of peace, thank goodness. And now I wish Peggy and her parson'd come. I want to show them Antony Leonard."

But the six Gabriels came next ; all together, so that Keatings, standing back, murmured to Joyce : " Lord ! what a crowd ! We must hold together." One by one the Gabriels presented themselves to the Daubeny family, who were now in their dinner dress ; first, Mrs. Gabriel, large and full, and quite un-aware that she was a rather stupid woman married to a clever husband ; then the Archdeacon, tall and well-fleshed, silk-vested and silk-voiced, with all that feminine graciousness with which the Church often overlays a natural masculine aggressive-ness, thereby producing a faint aroma of insincerity—which was so offensive to Keatings that he started Joyce's giggles by muttering something about a hermaphrodite ; then Elsa and Theresa, less dowdy than one might have expected and desired, but faintly wrong to a sensitive observer, none the less, since their dresses were neither wholly of the world nor wholly of God ; then the Rev. Warner Gabriel, who had, in truth, much of his father's good looks but possessed also a retreating chin —which was lucky for Keatings, who muttered to his sister : " God ! He looks like a chicken trying to cough up a seed ; "

and then John Gabriel, but he, unfortunately, was every inch a man.

The Archdeacon being fluent, and Mrs. Gabriel not less so, and the two girls and the two young men being adepts at social gatherings, the three O'Grogans—Keatings, Joyce and Derek —were driven from the field of conversation and into one another's companionship; and Keatings whispered to Joyce: "Never mind; we shall have reinforcements when Peggy and Tony come. We'll flatten them out then. Meantime they're an entertaining study."

Peggy and Michael Saffery arrived at half-past six; Tony and Honor half an hour later; and the O'Grogan tide, now at the full, lapped for a polite minute at the Gabriels, and then turned to beat round Joyce, the heroine of the evening; and in the midst of its lively play, Keatings was able, with whisperings, to outline the Family's campaign: "This is the scheme, my children: whenever the Gabriels get on top of the conversation at dinner, I shall cough twice, and that'll be a signal for the O'Grogans to talk at the tops of their voices about something —doesn't matter what—about snowdrops if you like—but to talk like the deuce and drown 'em. This is Joyce's show, and Joyce is Us, not Them. Honor, you're an O'Grogan; you're on our side."

"Rather!" whispered Honor, with a skip.

"And Jill too!" Jill herself claimed. "Jill's your ally."

"Of course you are," said Tony, putting his arm round this allied waist and squeezing it, in formal confirmation of the claim.

Dinner was announced; and as the seventeen people entered the dining-room, there rose a clamour of congratulations to Mrs. Daubeny for her decorating of the table. "Tables," she corrected; and they saw that two tables, end to end, were hidden under the lake of white linen. In the centre was a pyramid of fruit; silver vases of roses ran in single file down the length of the cloth; among the dishes of sweets and almonds, and the crossed crackers, chains of artificial ivy leaves meandered; everywhere fairy lamps sparkled like jewels; and from the electric chandelier that hung over the centre, streamers of Christmas tree tinsel dropped to the four corners, giving to the whole table-top the likeness of a basket of good things, gaily festooned for presentation to a leading lady.

"It's like Peter's cloth let down from Heaven," the

Archdeacon commented. "But are Christmas decorations wholly seasonable in the Trinity season?"

"Not so unseasonable as they may appear," Mrs. Daubeny laughed. "Joyce will recognize them: they are those that have decorated her Christmas table ever since she could remember. Mrs. O'Grogan has kept them all these years, and we borrowed them from her."

"Darling old mother!" said Joyce.

"And Mrs. O'Grogan is going to take the foot of the table, while I take the head," the General ordered. "This dinner symbolizes the union of the two clans. It symbolizes it damn well, as a matter of fact, because there's not a little of the O'Grogan crockery and cutlery united to ours."

"There's a fellow upstairs who symbolizes it better," suggested the Archdeacon, as all with noisy chatter found their places and sat in them. "Your Antony Leonard, Joyce dear. You ought to have put him, sleeping in his crib, in the centre of the table, as the *pièce de résistance* of the decorations— ("Jever hear such damned rot?" muttered Keatings, on the right of Joyce)—or perhaps he ought to have presided. Yes, that's better; he ought to have presided where you are, General. He's much more important than we are, because he's got all his life in front of him. But there he is, asleep upstairs, and quite unconscious that he's a symbol of anything. Sucking his thumb, I doubt not, and conscious only of a pleasant repletion under his nightgown——"

Most clearly Keatings coughed twice.

Joyce leapt to the call. She had nothing to say, but she said the first thing that came into her head. "I've a great scheme," she cried. "Keatings shall marry Jill. Why he hasn't done it before I can't imagine. Then the dove-tailing'll be a perfect artistic whole. Three O'Grogans married to three Daubenys. Of course I don't suppose Jill wants him for a minute, but she ought to sacrifice herself in the cause of art. Pass those almonds. Derek'll be left without a Daubeny, like a lion without a martyr, but then he always did travel on his own, didn't you, old dear? Oh, and we must make Antony Leonard an Honorary Foof."

"Honorary! He's a Foof by right of birth," shouted Peggy. "He's a Roman born."

"What on earth's an Honorary Foof?" begged the Archdeacon.

" An Honorary Freeman of the O'Grogan Family," Keatings explained.

This introduced ten minutes of bantering, full of quips and allusions which were unintelligible to the Gabriels; and Tony, who was sitting next to Jill Daubeny, decided that he could leave the victorious field and plunge, as he always loved to do, into an engrossing talk with her.   Before the soup was cleared away they were deep in the things that interested them ; they spoke of books they had lately read, and of books that Tony ought to write ; of homes they would like to build and how they would furnish them ; of travel routes they had mapped, and of ideal holidays ; and in such thrilling talk both lost consciousness of the food on their forks and the wine in their glasses and the loud chatter around them.   A sudden nudge at his elbow awoke Tony to the knowledge that the Archdeacon's voice had lately been booming, with effective flank support from Mrs. Gabriel, and that Keatings had coughed a second time. He jumped with the first thing handy to the Family's rescue.

" What's all this talk of yours about war in a month, Derek ? Jill's just been telling me about it."

" Yes, tell us the latest news from the city, Derek," Peggy called.

" War ? " queried Keatings.   " Civil war in Ireland do you mean ? "

" No, he doesn't mean anything so paltry," Joyce explained to her brother.   " Tell them, Derek."

" Not Ireland," Derek laughed.   " The troubles in Ireland'll be forgotten in a day when we find ourselves facing half Europe.   They'll have played their part, though.   It's because Germany thinks our hands are full in Ireland that she's secretly moving now.   At least, that's what the city thinks——"

The table was Derek's ; handed to him by Tony.   He gave the Great Rumour at considerable length, adducing in its support the latest secrets of diplomacy and recent incidents on the frontiers.   He substantiated it from personal experience.   He declared that the Motor Industry was feeling the first breath of a storm that would blow them great good, for Russia and France were inviting tenders and placing contracts for tractors and lorries and staff cars and motor pontoons and lighters and aeroplanes and Heaven knew what.   His own firm, he said, had undercut an American firm, to capture a large French contract, and though they would be selling at cost price, it was worth it, for they would then have their footing with their clients and when war started, there would be no quibbling about prices. He denied Tony's assertion that Fortune appeared to have adopted him as her own child, and expounded that good fortune was only another word for good foresight ; as an instance of which he told them how his firm had already begun the designing of new aeroplane engines and of low-geared lorries for heavy ground, in case the war went on for years.

It was a useful effort in the Family's behalf ; and before the Archdeacon could be delivered of some sentiments on the morality of making money which was the price of blood, Keatings got hold of the ball and proved by a series of syllogisms that his brother had been talking rubbish. Joyce followed with the assertion that she would make her way back to Len, were Keatings or Derek right, and emphasized her resolve by picking some of the table decoration as a souvenir for the absent one.

This skirmish successfully achieved, Tony fell to talking with Jill again, and heard little of anyone else's voice till one sentence detached itself from the uproar. Mrs. Gabriel was speaking to Honor diagonally across the table.

" So you're very happy, I hear, Honor," she was saying.

" Rather ! " Honor answered ; and no one could doubt that she meant it.

Tony, breaking from the talk with Jill, looked quickly at his wife ; and Jill, surprised at so sudden a movement and at his momentary departure into remoteness, looked up at his profile. He appeared to feel her glance on his cheek, and at once returned to their laughing talk.

And now the General was on his feet, a fact they were welcoming, since he seemed about to make a speech, with cheers and clapping and a hammering of spoons on the table. Joyce hammered with a wine-glass and broke its stem. Honor cried : " What-what. Damn-damn." The Archdeacon leaned back in his chair, fingered his glass and beamed at his host. Father Michael, anticipating a toast, refilled his glass. Keatings also filled his glass, but less for the toast at the speech's end than for his diversion during its progress. Peggy chose a banana, as her accompaniment to the speech. And Jill and Honor gazed down in embarrassment at their plates and refused to face the world, as most female relatives do when one of their men embarks upon an after-dinner speech.

"I think," said the General, "that before we break up, someone ought to give a sort of—shall we say—official welcome to our daughter Joyce—for she *is* the daughter of both our families—which, as the padre said, she has been the first to unite for ever in her young scamp upstairs—and *he's* a Sahib, I can assure you !—and it's her coming home that has been the—the *casus belli* of this muster ; so we shall want to drink her health and the health of the young Turk upstairs " (Humorous *Hear, hears* and '*Ear*, '*ears* from various parts of the table), " and since we are talking of *casus bellies*——"

" But are we ? " interrupted Joyce, obliging the speaker to turn towards her and ask :

" What-what ? " before he could continue :

" Since we are talking of *casus bellies*, it's occurred to me that if young Derek should ever be right and England should need all her sons to defend her—well, now——" He put up his monocle and surveyed the table—" I see before me Keith, Derek and Antony O'Grogan——"

" Who are Irish," reminded Tony, to keep humour, which was threatening to slip from the room, at the board.

" Eh ? " snapped the General. " Irish ? Yes, yes, but *loyal* Irish. Good God, yes—dammit—*loyal* Irish—not the poisonous traitors who never lose an opportunity of stabbing us in the back——"

" Hear, *hear !* " shouted the Tory Derek. " Hear, *hear !* "

" They've done it before," continued the General, thus encouraged, " and they'd do it again, if ever we went to war —you can be sure of that."

" Yes, yes," Tony soothed, and wondered if his interpolation had been helpful.

" But the loyal Irish—there've been no nobler servants of the Empire than the loyal Irish. There was Wellington. And there's Roberts now." The mention of these great names mollified him into equanimity again, and he proceeded with a smile : " And I see before me three such loyal sons of the Empire in Keith, Derek and Antony O'Grogan. I see John Gabriel, and I am reminded by Joyce's presence of my own dear boy, already a soldier ; I see two excellent padres in Warner Gabriel and Mr. Saffery, and dammit ! I remember *myself* who am not too old to teach the drill-book, if need be—and so I say, that if ever England should have to defend her frontiers we could put a very honourable little company into the field."

All gave loud cheers to this, partly for the sake of being up-roarious, and partly to express an affection for the good old man. Someone even tried to break into " Rule, Britannia," but it perished in the jollier business of hammering the cutlery.

" But "—began the General, when he could begin again —" but there'll be no war, you can take my word for it." The monocle, that magnificent aid to oratory, dropped. " The Germans'll wait till they've a navy equal to ours, and if they wait till then, they'll wait quite long enough to suit my book——"

Instantly Tony's thoughts shot indoors to puzzle out : " Oh, where have I heard that before ? Where ? Where ? Was it he who said it to me, or someone else ? " And soon the pictures came before him : one of the General facing him and saying : " If you wait to marry Honor, you'll wait quite long enough to suit my book ; " and another of Jill facing the General and saying : " That barometer's just like your eyeglass, Daddy ; it never sees a storm coming till it's actually arrived."

" However "—the General was continuing—" however, all that hasn't much to do with Joyce. Joyce, my dear, we raise our glasses to you, and to Len in his absence, and to your rap-scallion upstairs."

" Joyce." They were giving the toast boisterously.

" Joyce."

" Joyce, God bless her ! "

" Len."

" Len, God bless him."

" Antony Leonard."

" Antony Leonard, God forgive him."

And then they called on Joyce for a reply ; and Joyce, turn-ing quite red, enjoined them : " Don't be idiots ! How on earth could I make a speech ? " but they persisted in their clamour, and at last, to a terrific hammering on the table, she half rose and said : " Thanks frightfully for what Father said. And now my idea is that when dinner's over, we all dance." " Yes, yes ! " " Hear, hear," came the cries ; and Joyce, forgetting that she was formally acknowledging a toast, explained the plan with volubility, gradually degenerating from a stand-ing to a seated position. " Yes, do let's ! We'll dance in the drawing-room and out in the hall. Have you noticed we're exactly right in numbers : eight men to nine women, and one of the women'll have to strum on the piano. So come along as soon as possible. I want to dance. We can only be young once, and I'm beginning to feel frightfully old—I've passed thirty, do you realize it, people ?—it's a shocking thought—and as the end draws nearer, I begin to see more and more that nothing matters in the world but palliness and kindnesses " —this irrelevant and unexpected moral drew loud laughter and the statement that the wine had got into her head, which she readily allowed. " Yes, I'm sure it has. I began to suspect it some time ago. But come along, do ; cut your smokes and your gunpowder talk as short as possible, won't you ? "—the ladies were rising—" I give you ten minutes. You've got to come, all you boys, when you hear the music start."

In a quarter of an hour the loud, imperious playing of Mrs. Daubeny summoned the men to their attendance ; and the dancing began. The General partnered Mrs. O'Grogan ; the Archdeacon twinkled his gaitered feet in and out of Joyce's flying shoes ; Tony seized his wife with a preference so marked that it enchanted that houseful of romantics ; Warner Gabriel bowed before Peggy and led her into a restrained, clerical waltz ; Father Saffery, quite untroubled by clerical dubiety, captured Jill Daubeny with a promptitude that annoyed both Keatings and Tony ; Derek, obeying his lofty conceptions of duty, took Theresa Gabriel and danced with her an unadventurous measure ; John Gabriel took his sister Elsa ; and Keatings, left with Mrs. Gabriel, embraced her firm and weighty mass with great gallantry, and directed it with great skill. From the drawing-room into the hall and back again the couples waltzed, with a communal singing of the waltz's air, not all of it in tune ; with collisions in the doorway, some of which were less accidental than deliberate ; and with insistent, uncompromising, rhythmic yells for the tune's continuance, when Mrs. Daubeny's hands fell exhausted to her lap and her head bowed collapsingly over the keys.

Mrs. Gabriel took the piano. And Father Saffery shouted to Tony : " It's not fair that you should monopolize your wife all the time. Let us old men have a treat sometimes," and abducted her straight away ; Tony then had no hesitation in snatching Jill, the Father's late partner ; the other couples reshuffled themselves in the mêlée ; and once more a driving, swirling and bruising (so Joyce complained) but impenitent scrimmage filled the house with its screams and laughter. The servants came to the top of the basement stairs to watch.

In the third dance Peggy, defying the proprieties, came to Tony, took his hand, and announced that he was her partner ; and as they swam together into the vortex, she bewailed : " I hardly ever see anything of you. It's a year since we met."

" Too busy," he grinned. " Hard work."

" Don't you ever write now ? "

" No. No, there's oceans of time."

Peggy danced several steps without speaking.

" Tony : may I say something ? It's quite nice."

" Why not ? "

" Tony : I've long wanted to say "—it was apparently diffi-cult to say, for she sent her eyes adrift—" that—just that I'm so terribly glad that you're happy. Yours was what every marriage ought to be, wasn't it ? If you've got what you've got, you've got everything."

She gave her eyes to him again, and he smiled into them gratefully.

" Yes."

" Of course Joyce is happy, I think," Peggy went on. " But then she *would* be. She'd make it her business to be, which is amazingly sensible. . . . But I was a little afraid for you, Tony. I was afraid you'd either be unutterably happy—or the other thing. . . . And you're happy ! I'm thrilled about it."

" Thank you."

" And Honor's a darling," she added.

" She is," said Tony simply.

" Tony : why have you never asked me to stay with you in your cottage ? I'm cut to the quick about it. You've had Mother and Keatings, but never me once."

This protest she had sent along a direct, steady, but merry glance ; and that merry glance melted into a second's bewilder-ment, as it trapped a frightened look on Tony's face—a look which had passed quickly into brightness again. It was like a ripple which shudders, half seen and half imagined, over a sheet of water, when a whisper of visiting wind has disturbed the still and sunny day.

" *I* didn't entertain them," he laughed. " I was far too busy. Honor looked after them. And she hardly knows you, does she ? "

" All the more reason——"

" Exactly ! You shall come at the end of July, when the school breaks up. I'll take the first week of August as a holiday."

And then that dance ended.

It was not likely that such strenuous dancing would long be maintained among brothers and sisters and husbands and wives ; and Charades supplanted it. The older generation retired to a row of chairs, and the younger to the wardrobes and the trunks upstairs. A superior fecundity in Tony's mind now lifted him to the mastership of the ceremonies ; and not ten minutes of wrangling were needed before his yelled inspirations had carried their sheer merit to triumph. The Charade was to be a series of five scenes, of which the first three should enshrine a word of three syllables, and the last two a word of two. The first three scenes were to be Potted Opera, and the last two Potted Shakespeare.

The first potted opera was the opening scene of *Carmen*, in which Tony, after the custom of actor-managers, played the principal rôle himself : he was Carmen, dressed in some stockings of Jill's, an old red petticoat of Mrs. Daubeny's, an old-fashioned zouave jacket, a false fringe, and a red rose between his lips ; and he brought down the house on his first entry. Derek was a noble Don José, in the General's sword ; and all the others were soldiers or cigarette girls. The dialogue consisted almost entirely of Carmen crying : " O Don José, how I love you ! " and Don José replying : " O Carmen, how I do the same ! " and both, while embracing, breathing " Oh, oh, oh ! " in their mutual ecstasy. It had been an audience of defectives which had not suspected " Oh " for the hidden syllable here.

Faust followed *Carmen*. Here Jill was the young Dr. Faust, wearing long stockings, bloomers for trunks, an old black coat of her mother's, and the General's sword. John Gabriel was Mephistopheles, but a black Mephisto, since the available feminine hose and bloomers were all black ; and Keatings was Marguerite, in a skirt and blouse with a pillow in his chest to make a bosom, and a pillow slung behind to complete his figure. Keatings's was the triumph this time ; the room rocked when Faust punched Keatings in the bosom and on the pillow behind, and exclaimed : " Marguerite, how you do grow ! " The syllable was submerged beneath the laughter and none so quick as to salve it.

No scene of opera could be recalled to enshrine the third syllable, so Tony invented a fictitious opera called *The Gods and Ganymede*; and explained to a doubting audience that it was one of the lesser known works of Verdi. " Opus 358," he said. Its first act was magnificent: all the Gods and Goddesses were seen on Olympus, with Jove on the throne, in a dressing-gown, a paper crown from the crackers, and the General's sword; and Honor, in male attire and bearing a tray, was Ganymede, the lovely Phrygian boy whom Jove had recently translated to Heaven to be his cup-bearer.

Her identification was easy, for Tony kept summoning her with the genial apostrophe: " Gan, dear, bring the nectar," and Honor ran to his feet with the Bass or the Guinness, which he drank as a God should drink.

Now the two Shakespearean scenes; and here in the first the secret must inevitably out, even to those who had not as yet disentangled it—such as Mrs. Gabriel and the staring General. When Viola discussing with Olivia whether her face was all God's handiwork, expostulated: " I call it a daub, anyhow," the General shouted his guess with great delight, confirmed it with a " Good God, yes! Of course!" and lowered his monocle as if his acumen had put an end to the business. But he was adjured by his daughters to shut up, or he would ruin the last scene, so he put up his monocle again to study it. It proved to be a gorgeous Eastern affair, with Honor as Cleopatra, and Antony as Antony, and Jill as Charmian, and Warner Gabriel as Enobarbus. But when Antony began to address Enobarbus as " Enny, old bird——" the scene was broken up beneath a tidal wave of laughter and applause. " O'Grogan-Daubeny, very fine, very fine!" clapped the General; " Very apposite, very apposite!" congratulated the Archdeacon; " Most amusing," said Mrs. Daubeny; while Father Saffery explained the riddle's answer to Mrs. Gabriel, and the steps by which it had been built up.

Then the Archdeacon, having heard the clock strike eleven, rose to withdraw himself and his family. To-morrow was Sunday, he said. So the Gabriels departed, and Father Saffery went with them. But the rest of the young people refused to break up. They lit a fire, not so much because the night was cold as because a fire was good fun; and they turned out the lights, and sat all around it, on sofas and chairs, and carpet and cushions, and talked of their childhood.

CHAPTER II

THE RETURN

NEXT morning, after church, Tony, Honor and Peggy set off on a voyage whose inspiration and captain were Peggy. They mounted a bus in the Chiswick High Road, rushed for its front seats, captured them, and sat there, while the vehicle rattled them into King Street and over Hammersmith Broadway into the Hammersmith Road. But not till the red-brick Gothic of St. Paul's school, creepered and mellow behind its railings and its lawns, dominated one side of the road, and the red-brick pastiche of Colet Court tried to dominate the other, did they feel that the bus was passing through a gate into the country of their exploration.

From now onward the streaming pavements and the branching side-roads were the tracks of their schooldays, and every house and shop was a friend—except these places which were offensively new. There was the old North End Road which had been one of the paths to Earl's Court Exhibition; there was Avonmore Road—did Peggy remember young Peter Brand, that ass, who lived down there. Yes, and Phyllis Maple had lived three doors further. Remember that riotous party at her house, when the Ming vase was smashed? Hallo, there was Olympia. Remember Barnum and Bailey's? Remember the Freaks—the Fat Lady, the Bearded Lady, and the Skeleton Dude? Remember Derek being quite unable to tear himself away from gaping at the Man with Two Bodies, and Alice, the maid, saying it fair turned her stomach round?

But how empty seemed all these roads on a Sunday. Nowhere was there a big boy in a St. Paul's cap or a small one in a Colet Court cap, who on weekdays were the very natives of the road.

Stay, though: that was a Pauline, wasn't it, returning with a model yacht from Kensington Gardens. Yes, and the pity of it! his cap was changed now from the gay affair of Tony's days, with its red and white ribbon and its heraldry in gold and silver wire. This black cap with its white circle was a dull, uninspired concoction, Tony thought. Now the bus had only to go over the hump of the bridge and it would drop them at St. Austin's Road. But it sailed past their corner, and they rushed for the steps, and hurried or slipped down them, and jumped off dangerously on to the stationary road.

How quiet it was on a Sunday. Tony took Honor's arm and Peggy's arm, and directed them—rather like a policeman directing a couple of disorderly women—towards the corner. "There! There, Honor, my dear; in a house right at the top of that long road was born the famous Tony O'Grogan and the hardly less famous Peggy O'Grogan."

They stood at the bottom, looking up the road. How small the houses looked, and surely the vista used to seem much longer. Why, to-day one could see Uxbridge Road at the top of it quite easily, and yet one's memory had suggested that Uxbridge Road, from this end, was generally lost in the mist of another world.

"Tony," Peggy pleaded: "Tony: say I'm not right in thinking that it's a little squalid."

"I wasn't thinking that," Tony answered. "I was thinking how was it that I lived here sixteen years and more, and never once knew what a gorgeous sight the sky could be at the end of a long London road."

Peggy and Honor looked. The road tapered and diminished to the scene in the sky, like a straight highway running to a pageant. The lowest part of the sky was a leaden hill-range capped with light; above was a splash of golden brilliance mixing rather angrily with the grey cloud masses; above that the cloud-masses shaped themselves into grey cumuli which became smaller and smaller towards the zenith till they were as tiny and individual as the curls of a ram.

"Peggy, say you never noticed that sort of thing when you lived here."

"Never," Peggy admitted.

There was no one in the road, church time being past; so Peggy was able, as they walked towards the vicarage, to rhapsodize over the coal-holes which stretched in the same old dotted line along the pavement; over the faded pink geraniums in the window-boxes ; over the accumulations of blown dust which had collected in the sagging of the pavement flags and in the interstices between them ; over the pillar box. And Tony was able to point out the sad privets, some golden, and the few rusty trees—all of a most unhealthy complexion to eyes now trained by the country ; and to bewail that the front doors had now split themselves into *two* doors, so as to admit to flats and maisonettes ; that the area-doors opened into basement flats, no longer into roomy kitchens that held cooks in powder-blue cotton and parlour maids in black dresses and aprons and caps with streamers ; that the " Apartments " cards were up in many a window ; that a London which had been, was gone. Only ten years, and it had faded into this, as one lantern scene fades into another.

Standing in front of the vicarage, they ran their eyes from its hearth-stoned steps to its sham Corinthian portico, and the stucco balcony above, and the window above that, and the dormer window in the roof. " Wasn't it any bigger than that, and was it really so ugly ? " asked Peggy ; and Tony replied, " Well, it's by the mercy of God that children are not fastidious ! " The door was plainly unlatched, and Peggy dared him to push it open a little further and see into the hall. He did so. All was changed : the chocolate dado and the tiled paper were gone, and the gas fixtures ; only the applied leaf ornament still ran round the cornice of the ceiling.

Then the three entered the church. In the porch were the cards of the clergy with their hours for hearing confessions, and there was not one name that belonged to ten years ago. And this smell of incense was new too. They passed from the porch to the west end, and again exclaimed in surprise that the church should be no bigger, that the clustered columns were no further apart, and the vaulted roof no higher. But if the material structure of the church had shrunk, its spiritual professions had soared. This was not the " Moderate High " Church of Dr. O'Grogan's days ; it was " Cartholic " of the " cartholics." Six candles guarded the golden tabernacle on the altar, mosaic Stations of the Cross ran round the walls, a crucifix hung on the column opposite the pulpit, and curtained confessionals stood in the corners. " It seems almost a law that as a neighbourhood goes down the church should go up," Tony whispered to Honor—not to Peggy, for she had dropped to her knees in the nearest pew.

Steps were heard crossing the chancel, and a little cassocked man, with a white walrus moustache, passed through the sanctuary rails to the altar, where he lifted the missal and placed it on the retable.

Peggy had risen, and she exclaimed, " Tony : it's Mr. Flote. Oh, it's Mr. Flote."

They all went up to the chancel, where Peggy called, " Mr. Flote, Mr. Flote, *won't* you recognize me ? "

He turned, and screwed his eyes at the intruders. Recognition opened them wide, and he came down from the altar with outstretched hands, as a diminutive and playful king might come down the steps of his throne.

" It's Miss Peggy ! Miss Peggy ! And Mr. Antony ! Well, this is—no, go easy with that arm, dear boy—that's where my arthritis troubles me. And how are the other dear children ? How's the dear boy Mr. Keith ? And Miss Joyce ? "

They began to answer him, but he turned to Honor.

" And is this—am I guessing right ?—is this your little lady, sir ? *Well !* Well, Mrs. O'Grogan—or Mrs. Antony, may I call you ?—well, you've got one of the best boys, if you'll pardon my expressing an opinion. Miss Peggy here, and Mr. Antony were always the best of the dear Vicar's family, to my thinking. Not but what they were all scamps, madam. I could tell you a story or two ! Well I mind Master Keith at a children's service pretending to be blind, and being led in by Master Derek, and bumping into all the other dear children, and falling over chairs and hassocks and the like. Oh, ho, ho ! He sat with his eyes tight shut the whole service through, and was led out by Master Derek, bumping into everything again. I said to him, when they come near the door and tried to bump me, I said, ' Go along with you. I wonder what your father'd say, if he saw you playing up like that. It'd be the strap, and you know it.' But I couldn't help but laugh. But come downstairs and I'll make you a cuppa tea. . . . O yes, you must. . . . Often enough I've made our present curates laugh with tales of those old times. Very pleasant boys they are—nice natural boys. . . . Come along. . . . This way, Mrs. Antony."

Mr. Flote went ahead of them down the narrow stairs to the vestries. He walked rather stiffly, the shoulder of his arthritis arm lifted higher than the other. " I heard all about you from Miss Joyce, who wrote to me from India. I hadn't heard nothing of any of you for years when all of a sudden a letter come from India, and I said to my daughter, I said, ' That's funny ! Who wants to write to me from India ? ' and it was Miss Joyce's, with all the news about the dear boy she'd married, and her little one, and your and Mr. Antony's elopement, and all the like of that. I *did* take it kindly of her to remember me out there, and I sent her all the latest, though I find it hard writing nowadays, with my arm so sadly. . . ."

" Phew ! " Tony broke in from the rear. " The same old smell down here. It's the only thing that hasn't changed. Honor, this smell has removed twenty years off my shoulders. It makes me feel about five."

" Yes, it's always a shade damp down here," Mr. Flote acknowledged. I daresay that's what brings the arthritis. But I can't complain. I'm pretty perky for eighty. Come in."

His peculiar burrow, between the Clergy Vestry and the Muniment Room, was another thing that had not changed : there was the same raffish desk, the same decrepit arm-chair, the same gallery of faded and curling photographs pinned all over the wall, the same oak table littered with a cash box, a wafer box, a **pi**le of collection plates, purificators, a chalice veil and a corporal, and the same gas stove with its drunken asbestos and its rusty iron. He lit the trivet and set the kettle on the flame. Some new photographs pinned among the others— that was the only change. Tony, running his eyes along them, chaffed him. " Flote, you haven't dusted this place in the ten years since I left you. And as you hadn't done it in the twenty years before that—hallo ! what's this . . . ? " He was looking at a photograph of the interior of Antwerp Cathedral. . . . " Peggy, look at this."

Peggy came up and looked over his shoulder, and Mr. Flote came too, bringing in his hand the bread-knife with which he was cutting them some thin slices of bread and butter. He explained the card to them. " Yes, your dear father sent me that two years ago, come Christmas. You see what he wrote below, don't you ? " Screwing up his eyes, he traced under the words with the point of the knife. " ' To a faithful old friend. Psalm 84, and especially verse 11.' A nice, natural man, your father was."

" What's Psalm eighty-four ? " asked Peggy.

" It's that there one about ' How amiable are thy dwellings thou Lord of Hosts. My soul hath a longing to enter into the courts of the Lord '—and all the like of that. . . ."

" And verse eleven ? " It was Tony who asked this in a soft voice, for Peggy could not speak.

" Oh, he was always very apt-like with his quotings, wasn't he ? your dear papa. We haven't had many preachers the like of him. It's that there one about ' a doorkeeper in the house of the Lord.' It proper moved me, I *will* say, when I looked it up, coming from a big man like he was. And see what he says on the back : oh, he was always a good speaker, he was ; and he had a big heart, if I may say so—your father. He says—look here : ' I often think of you in your burrow underground, dear old friend ; and sometimes I tell myself that they placed you well, those who put you down there, among the foundations of the church.' "

They stayed a little longer with Mr. Flote, drinking his tea and munching his bread and butter, while he discoursed on the changes in the church.

" The congregation isn't like what it was. Not that it's smaller but it's not the same class. The collections aren't a half of what they was in your time. We don't see a sovereign in the plate from one year's end to another, except perhaps 'Ospital Sunday. And the Vicar's Warden is the baker in High Street—I wonder what your dear father'd have thought of that ! And we never have no bishops preaching here now like we used to ; except the dear Bishop of London—*he* comes sometimes. You'd hardly think it was the same church, but it *is*. I've seen some clergy come and go in my time, and they've all had their different little ideas, the new ones never reckoning much to the ones before 'em or their ways, and wanting it all different, and I've had to play up to them all, which I do, because they're all the same sort of gentlemen at the bottom—nice, natural gentlemen, for the most part."

When they rose to go, he took Honor's hand and said, " Well, dear Mrs. Antony, I take it kindly of you to have come and looked me up, like you have. And if you'll believe me, you've picked one of the best in young Mr. Antony."

" I know I have," laughed Honor.

" And I see *he* don't regret his bachelor times. I see *he's* never been so happy before, in all his born days."

" That's about the truth, Flote," laughed Tony.

CHAPTER III

TONY took Honor back to Sheep's Eye the same night, because he had to go on duty at the school early the next morning. They took the latest train and when they walked up the brick path to the porch of the cottage, it was eleven o'clock of a perfect night—such a night as is often foreshown by the sky they had seen over the London roads. They entered and lit a lamp. Clean and comfortable and very pleasing seemed the little room, with its polished wood, its chintz chairs, its shining ornaments, and its whitewashed walls.

"Looks nice when you come back to it," Tony remarked.

"Sweet," agreed Honor.

She did not remove her coat, as Tony was doing, but put up her face for a good-night kiss.

"I'm tired after last night. I'm going straight to bed."

"Good night, dear." He kissed her, rather absently, and felt for his pipe.

"I shall sleep like a log, Tony. You won't wake me if you're late, will you?"

"No, my child. I'm only going to have one pipe, or two at the most. Good night."

She was gone, and soon he heard her footsteps on the floor overhead. When his pipe was lit, he opened the front door quietly and stepped on to the threshold. What a night! The whole sky from the northern woods with their tapestry trees to the long southward wave of the Downs was emptied of cloud or haze, garnished with the summer stars, and blanched with a brilliant moon. Not a leaf rustled; no owl hooted; no bird fluttered wakefully in the foliage, nor bat made a shudder in the empty air. Every wall and tree and shrub laid its shadow out of sight of the moon.

Pipe in mouth, he walked to his gate and leaned on it; and the sound of his feet and the creak of the gate seemed a trespass on such stillness. He turned round and looked at his house. In Honor's bedroom window was a square of light, and he watched it till it blacked out. Then, hands in pockets, he began to wander round the little garden. The antirrhinums and the stocks; the few roses in their beds or on a rustic rose-screen; the shrubs so handsomely grown since first he saw them three years ago; the grass patch, a trim thing of his own creating; the country stretching away to the rise of Wolstonbury, clear against the lustred sky; and, above, the star-pageant—why had each of these things, as he looked at it, a dull blow for him? Each the same dull blow.

"God, what a fool I am!" he muttered. "Why can't I accept it? Just accept it. I'm a thousand times more fortunate than most, and know it."

He walked on till he came to the little orchard at the back. Here an apple tree which Honor and he had planted a month before their wedding, now grown well and hung with young fruit, gave him, not á dull blow, but a stab. He ridiculed himself with a dead laugh. Ha! such an old story, such a universal story, and he was making a tragedy of it! Why, people always made a comedy of it. Hadn't he any humour at all? It was no more than the matter of an old jest, everywhere accepted: that honeymoon rapture didn't last; that passion must sooner or later sink into friendship; that the lure of his wife's body must often lose its potency for him, though not, it seemed, for other men; that her little intellectual failures and feminine cowardices, which had once possessed a charm for him, could sometimes now be irritants; that she whose nearness a year or two ago was necessary for his ease and content could sometimes now give him the best quiet by her absence—"O God!" he gasped, having forgotten that it was a comedy. That he who had once loved Honor so, should be able to desire her only seldom now, and when a physical need was upon him—if this were so, and it *was*, then he could believe no longer in the love he had hunted for. For if the love he had felt for Honor were not this thing, then he must trust no other passion that might visit him, because it could never surpass what he had felt for Honor. And this being granted, it followed that a man must ever be alone in the world—alone among good friends.

" A love that is an everlasting mutual absorption is the only perfect thing in the world—and there is no such thing."

Well, could he say that he accepted it ? To a nature such as his what followed from acceptance ? Strolling up and down and pulling at his pipe, he surveyed the whole face of the world to see the results of his acceptance ; and he saw that every beautiful thing in it partook of the injury. Every beautiful landscape and evening sky would hurt, for they always stirred this sharp hunger for a perfect human love. The exquisite lines of women's faces would hit him the same blow, for they pointed to something that wasn't there. The curves of children's cheeks would rejoice him for a moment, and then— remind him that they must grow up and want this thing that existed in dreams alone, and take their disappointment. All the love-lyrics, and the whole literature of love, would come with the same pain, for his heart would resist them and say, " There is no such thing." And lastly, if there were no such thing, there was nothing to write about, for it had touched everything with its light, and the light was out.

Well, could he say, " I accept it," and laugh ? He walked to the gate and leaned his back against it, and looked up at Honor's window. He pictured her lying asleep on the double bed, and he knew that he was very fond of her. He imagined himself standing by the side of the bed and looking down on her untidy auburn head and her closed lids : " I'll be good to you, Honor ! You shall never know these thoughts of mine ; you couldn't understand them if you did—you're too simple and sensible and lively. And there'll never be anyone else, Honor —you can be sure of that—because I shall believe no more in any love that may try to enter."

He knocked out the pipe on the gate, saying briskly, " I shall get used to it," and walked back into the house. Closing the door quietly he climbed with the hall-lamp up to the room. He held the lamp above her, his palm shading the light from her face. Yes, he loved her, but a little differently—that was all. He'd be an idiot to make a tragedy of a little change like that ! " It's trite, God bless my soul ! " he thought, trying a laugh. But an irregularity in his heart rebuked the laugh and whispered, " Even a trite event can lose its triteness to him who is suffering it. The laughter is always the onlooker's." " No, no," his will answered. "It's a comedy with a little passing pain in it. I shall get used to it. It only hurts till I've got my readjustments right. There's nothing big in it. There's no unfaithfulness on her part or mine—nothing that might be a tale worthy of all this fuss; no love turned to hate; no illness born of despair; no life of misunderstanding and mutual degradation stretching before us; nothing big; in fact, there are no incidents at all—it's simply not a tale worth the telling!" And yet—he drove his elbow against his heart to control a pain there—and yet the meaning was gone from beauty everywhere, and all the shrines were empty.

CHAPTER IV

ON WOLSTONBURY

WHEN Tony first discovered that such a love as he had felt for Honor could wane, and that adoration could yield ground to irritability, he did a powerful deal of thinking. He thought first that he would go back to his writing, but when he read through the piled manuscripts of *Regnauld and Mélisse*, with all its " more-than-Romeo nonsense " as he now called it, he sickened at the wrongness he could find in it. *Regnauld and Mélisse !* the very lushness of the title was lyrical with wrongness. Well, the thing to do was to throw away all this unreal stuff and start again : let him acquiesce in life as it was—an affair that amused itself by disappointing one's inborn craving for perfection—and toss *Regnauld and Mélisse* on to the flames as a kind of sacrament which should confirm his acquiescence and stiffen his shoulders to carry it. Tony was always tempted to picturesque ceremonies. And then he would write about other things. But he could find nothing else to write about : it was no good writing unless one could see a perfect beauty somewhere and struggle to capture it in words, and he could no longer—at least for a time—see it anywhere ; it was all wounded for him, and drooping. And his pencil hung idly above his notebook, with nothing to say. So both his passions had gone. Honor, innocent and lively little Honor, had laid both of them low. Then it was that he decided to cast over his previous plans and to set to work on reading for a degree and on building a better home for Honor, whom, though he didn't love her as he had wanted to, he could still resolve to love better than anybody else.

And he did not burn the old manuscripts, because a new idea was glimmering in the distance. Perhaps the perfection of human love might be found one day in some such form as the saints had found it—in a love not for a person but for the world, a love that sought nothing but gave all. If one day all his disintegrated ideas should resettle into some such discovery as this, then beauty would certainly come back again to the earth. And then perhaps all these descriptions of a youth's more limited and earth-bound passions might be the early cantos of a work much bigger and much further-reaching than the one he had first planned. . . . At twenty-five the lure of the grandiose can still be felt, even through repulse and disillusion.

So he had begun to work for his degree; and his brain, long extended by traffic with brow-furrowing thoughts and with worthy phrase-making, had made a small matter of his set books and his examination papers. And the summer of 1914 found him with his Intermediate well behind him and his Finals looming in front.

The school term ended on July 29th; and on the Friday, the last day of the month, not Peggy alone, but Jill Daubeny as well, came driving down to Sheep's Eye, for a long week-end. Monday was August Bank Holiday. Father Michael, more attracted to Jill than Tony cared to watch, drove them down in his little black coupé, but was resolute to return to Southend the same night, where he must make his preparations against the Sunday. They alighted into Tony and Honor's joyous welcome, and Peggy, looking up at the creepered cottage and round at the flowered garden, and away at the sweeping landscape and the high crown of Wolstonbury, shot her soaring beatitudes over all, like jets from a fireman's hose.

Their talk was chiefly of their plans for the next few days. Only Father Michael was disposed to be political, and he expatiated somewhat on the Irish quarrel and the failure of the conference which the King had summoned to Buckingham Palace, and his hopes that if it came to Civil War between the Catholics of the South and the detestable Orangemen of the North, the Catholics would have the best of it. Of Russia's bickering in the Near East with Austria he spoke hardly at all; as between the Greek Orthodox Church and the Roman Church he was impartial, he said; both were Catholic. Besides it would come to nothing.

Tony was not interested in either topic. He was hardly acquainted with them, because when term ended and holidays began, he was apt to get newspapers but irregularly in his remote cottage. Instead, he told his plans to the three girls. "My staff has drawn up its schemes for every minute of your stay," he said. "And I promise you, you've got to get up at an early hour to-morrow. To-morrow we walk for miles and miles, and picnic on Wolstonbury."

They went out early the next morning into weather set for heat, and the four of them marched with a will, the girls in stout shoes and swinging their sticks, and Tony in shorts and an open shirt, with a rucksack slung at his shoulder blades ; not clear, as he grumbled, whether he was the colonel of the regiment or its baggage train. They walked from Albourne Green to Muddleswood, and from Muddleswood to Fulking, and so on to the shoulder of the downs where the chain is cleft by the Adur Valley. It was on Fulking Hill that the great view of the Weald first laid itself before them.

"Look," commanded Tony.

Peggy rewarded him with a gasp, and Jill with a silence. From the escarpment's foot all the Sussex Weald billowed away in tillage and meadow and woodland, the hedgerows crossing it in a net-work of squares and diamonds, and the tree-masses lying athwart them in patches of dense embroidery. All the distant North Downs, from Ide Hill in Kent to Clandon in Surrey, passed beneath the sweep of their eyes ; and two great headlands came marching forward on to the weald, Black Down and Leith Hill. And round the rim of this vast basin, six other counties laid their contribution to the prospect, before they closed it in.

But Tony would not suffer the girls as yet to fix the names on the picture map before them, but led them away from it to the folds behind the Devil's Dyke ; and they walked and walked, the spring in the turf putting a spring into their stride and a lightness into their hearts. The riders were out on the downs this Saturday before the August Holiday, and it was plain that their horses rejoiced also in the turf and the upland air : their hoofs pawed and their mouths strained for licence to canter or gallop ; which given, they went like the wind, till they were specks on a distant crown.

The downland crowns behind the Devil's Dyke make a sea of infolding hills ; and it was among these ways that Tony and his party walked—not to the Dyke itself, for the bank holiday crowds were assembling there—but by the inland route and quickly, towards the solitude of the brow above Seddlescombe, where they could look down on that toy village, nestling among its screening trees on the face of the bluff. Not a soul moved in that shelved hamlet, and no voices rose to the watchers above ; it lay like a morsel blown from three hundred years before ; and only the smoke of its chimneys told them that it was still inhabited. Then he led them by Newtimber to his best loved Wolstonbury, and from its summit they saw the view again, under an afternoon sun, and this time they drew their pleasure, not from the great expanse as a whole, but from the little individual things ; they picked out Stratton Lye, and Albourne Green, and Sheep's Eye, and the twisting lanes and the straight roads, the clustered villages and the far-off spires, the barns and the stacks, and the men and horses moving upon the fields. The enthusiasm of the girls swelled into fine frenzies, and Tony indorsed them ; they did not know that the beauty of all these things was drooping for him.

Hotter than ever broke the Sunday, and Jill, standing with Tony in the garden and looking towards Wolstonbury, said, " she was mad for the downs again." " I must go back, I must go back," she cried ; and Tony, in an instant agreement, rushed into the house to announce that lunch would be served on Wolstonbury. But the faces of both Peggy and Honor were doubtful and demurring ; and Peggy explained at last that " she had thought of going to church ; " and Honor said, " Yes, Peggy shall pray for you Sabbath breakers, and I'll stay and see that she's fed. You and Jill go, and I'll make up your lunch." So Tony, driving down a peeping sense of delight and relief, marched off with Jill, heading for the slopes of Wolstonbury.

The morning had not worn very far when the sun, now in their faces, went behind the only cloud afloat in the heavens, and by so doing, left all its downward rays clearly outlined against a primrose sky, those directly above Wolstonbury falling to its top like the lines of a visible shower. Above the cloud the abating radiance perished in a vast serenity of Cambridge blue. Then the sun emerged and quenched all that momentary apotheosis with its brilliance ; and it climbed and topped its curve before the toiling couple had topped the summit of Wolstonbury.

" Ah ! " Jill sighed, as Tony flung down his rucksack, and both sank happily on to the turf. " Here I spend the afternoon. We will eat our lunch in the presence of nine counties. And then we'll just talk."

And they talked—one of those talks that drink up the hours like minutes, that raise an exhilarating glow in the head and light a tingling warmth on the cheeks and spread a strange peace in the heart. Did Tony do most of the talking ? Neither knew, for the listener who perfectly understands and enthusiastically responds, especially if she is a feminine listener, enjoys as big and happy a part as the one with the words ; and moreover, such talks as these do not lend themselves to measurement in terms of time. At what point Tony began with spluttering words to expound his creeds, and by what tracks they had come to these ultimate topics, neither ever remembered ; but at some time or another Tony was saying :

" I've been struggling for months past with an idea which I can't put into words. I can only kind of see and feel it. But these downs always help me to see it in a picture. There are two kinds of beauty before us now, aren't there ? "

" Are there ? " Jill inquired, with eyebrows humorously arched.

" Yes. There's the rather luxuriant and rather too obvious beauty down in the valley there—a matter of orchards and flowers and creepers and rambling roses—like all that I've tried to put into my garden—a matter of small individual things, and, seen as a whole, rather lush. And then there's the graver and cooler and lonelier beauty of these bare downs—' bleaker ' I suppose is the word—a matter of line and mass and shadow, and so on. We climb from one to the other. Well, I'm beginning to find the one rather finicking and personal, and the other more satisfying, just because it's spacious and impersonal and lonely. D'you understand me ? "

Jill, staring ahead, nodded an affirmation. " I think I understand."

" Well, I sometimes wonder if in life we have to climb from one to the other—do you see ? And perhaps this wide, simplified, un-individual—if there *is* such a word—this wide un-individual beauty of the downs is only a first step towards an austerer beauty still—I mean, the beauty of snowfields and glaciers, and so up and up to the completest beauty of all—which is—I dunno—something bleaker and colder than poor human minds dare imagine. That's the idea. I don't know if there's anything in it. And I'm sure you don't understand me."

" Yes, I do. I do—I think."

Tony, looking up at her profile, loved her outward-gazing eyes, so grave now, and her lips set for thought.

" I dunno," he complained. " Pushed to its furthest, the idea seems to lead to the end of our individuality—our personality. . . . But sometimes I think that whenever we approach perfection, whether in our thinking or in our behaving or in our loving, we approach that end. I mean, if I think aright, I am not thinking in any way personal to myself, but according to some universal law ; and if I were to love aright, I should love selflessly, like God. It seems to me that if we are one day to reach this absolute perfection we shall have to shake off the last shred of personality. . . . I dunno. . . . It's bleak, but if it's true, we mustn't funk it ; and as I say, sometimes it appeals to me as the greatest beauty. . . . Nirvana. . . . Oh, how wonderful Buddha was, and Christ ! . . ."

Always the talk of youth, in its stammering earnestness, fetches up at last to Buddha and Christ.

" They've all said the same thing really, Jill : that the only road to serenity is over that exceedingly unpleasant mountain, the complete annihilation of self. . . ."

" I think I see what you mean," Jill nodded. " A little, anyway. And I shall think about it an awful lot."

It was late afternoon now, and he clambered to his feet.

" We must be going. They'll wonder what has become of us. Come on."

Picking up Jill's hand from her lap he raised her too, sending through the significant pressure of his fingers a man's affection for the girl who will talk of the things he loves.

When they pushed open the door of the cottage they stepped into a buzz of voices. A car waiting outside had inflated their curiosity and steadied their minds for alarm ; but they expected no such excitement as was here. Honor ran out to them, saying : " Mr. and Mrs. Sugden have come with extraordinary news. We were hoping you would arrive soon," and returned with them following quickly. Mr. Sugden lifted his great obelisk of a body, and even as he heard his introduction to Jill, told his young colleague that Germany had declared war on Russia and was concentrating her armies on the French and

Belgian frontiers and aiming at the English Channel, in the certainty that France must come to the aid of her ally, Russia. Yes, yes, she was only waiting for France to signify her intention of supporting Russia, so that she would have the right to invade France. Good God alive, there was nothing so far as he could see, except the unprepared French armies, to stand between the magnificent German hosts and the Channel ports, from which they would present a pistol at the heart of England. " I'd got some German students coming over for the holidays," Mr. Sugden spluttered, " and they've all cancelled by wire. The one young fellow who's arrived leaves to-morrow, if he can get back. Called up, you see, to fight us."

" Good heavens ! " Tony exclaimed. " Is all this certain ? "

" Absolutely ! Absolutely ! You'll see it all in to-morrow morning's papers."

" And if Germany moves against France, what then ? "

" We shall have to join in with France. Of course we shall ! We have promised to, and we can't have the Germans at Calais and Boulogne. Allowing for diplomatic exchanges, I calculate that by Wednesday next Germany and Austria will be at war with France and Russia, and that England will be at war with Germany and Austria, and Italy too, possibly, and that Turkey may have joined Germany against us, which'll mean that Stratton Lye'll have no boys next term. Why, it's as likely as not that they'll evacuate the civilian population from these coastal districts. Parents won't send their children here."

Jill gasped.

Peggy said : " Yes, there were prayers about it in church this morning. They prayed that the nations of the world might be guided aright, and they sang ' O God, stretch forth thy mighty hand, And guard and bless our Fatherland,' and they finished up with the National Anthem."

" Really ? " Mr. Sugden exclaimed. " I wish I'd been."

" And the Vicar preached about the terrible choice that might be offered to England in the course of this week, and how she must put honour before expediency, and that if she were called to suffering and sacrifice, she must steadfastly set her face to go to Jerusalem. His text was ' He set His face to go to Jerusalem.' "

" Yes. It's a—it's a——" Mr. Sugden's lips were trembling to reassert his captaincy of the conversation. " It's a question of Stratton Lye and next term, O'Grogan, and what we're all going to do, supposing the Germans are held off from the Channel ports and ordinary civilian life can still go on in these parts.   People are saying that every man under thirty-five will have to volunteer, so it seems to me that in any case my life's work at Stratton Lye is going to tumble like a house of cards.   I was hoping to get some undertaking from you that you would stay at least for a term or two."

" Me ? " Tony echoed.   He had not so quickly related himself to the war.

" Yes, in case the worst comes to the worst, we must talk it over.   Could you come and see me to-morrow ? "

" We're supposed to be playing tennis to-morrow, aren't we, Honor ? "

" Yes, at the Armstrongs. And on Tuesday at the Trevelyans."

" It's hardly a time for tennis," Mr. Sugden objected.   " Why, I've—I've half my investments in German securities.   And Indian Railways.   God knows if we shall be able to keep India."

" How'll this do ? " Tony proposed.   " I promise that *if* we declare war, I'll cancel all tennis and come and see you. Meantime I must consider my guests."

" Guests ! "   Mr. Sugden was not impressed with the word. " We'll have Germans for guests in a month or two.   Enemy officers billeted in our best bedrooms. "

Tony laughed.   " Well, that'll at least save us from worrying about Stratton Lye.   All'll be in the melting-pot then."

" Yes, yes, but we shan't let them in."   Mr. Sugden could not conceive that the Allied Countries would allow Stratton Lye to be ruined.   " We shall hold 'em.   We shall hold 'em all along the French frontier.   That's where the worst of the fighting'll be.   And quite the best thing that the older men like myself can do for our country will be to keep our establishments afloat within the lines.   Dammit, education, of all things, mustn't stop."   And from every unselfish point of view—from the point of view of England who would need that her boys of to-day should be educated into the men of to-morrow—from the point of view of the boys themselves whose fathers would be taken from them to fight—he expounded to Tony why it was his duty, for the time at least, to give his services to Stratton Lye.   He begged him to come and talk it over.

" I will," said Tony.   " On Wednesday, if not before."

" Yes, do. Yes, do. If all the others weren't away on holidays, I'd have 'em down for a Council of War. ' Council of War,' that's the word. We must save Stratton Lye."

" We'll all do our best, I expect."

" Yes, I know you'll help me. Well, we must be going soon. We thought we'd motor into Brighton and see the crowds."

The Sugdens went into the hall, carrying the electric conversation with them; they delayed there ten minutes while it sparked again; they took it down the brick path and continued it by the footboard of the car, to the accompaniment of the engine which Mr. Sugden had started unconsciously, during a lecture on the strategic advantages of a march through Belgium and Luxembourg; and then the car rolled away, leaving a cloud of blue smoke, like a symbol of the last counsels of Mr. Sugden.

And, indeed, the smoke of Mr. Sugden's conversational exhaust hung about the cottage all that night, its smoke-blacks lying like dooms on the furniture, the flowers in the garden, and the stretching countryside. At the first possible moment after breakfast Tony rushed out to buy a paper and learn news. It was a hot Bank Holiday, and every man and woman was standing in some idle and talkative group at gateways or on thresholds. Any passer-by who chose to join in their debates was not only tolerated but welcomed. Tony marvelled that the shy, reticent English, who could so seldom bring themselves to speak to a stranger, should all have become brothers, and demonstrative, talkative brothers, as the great threat lifted in the sky. From these people Tony learned a score of unsubstantial rumours and two substantial facts : that the German declaration of war with Russia was confirmed, and that the Foreign Secretary would make a speech in the House that afternoon to define England's place in the swinging and nervous balance of Europe. With this he had to be content.

After lunch the four young people from Sheep's Eye went to their tennis at the Armstrongs as if nothing menaced; and in the excitement of their games forgot that Germany existed and that the Foreign Secretary was at that moment asking of the people's representatives in Parliament whether Britain's promises to France and Belgium should be honoured. The countries beyond the wire-netting of the tennis court were extinguished, but they came into existence again at tea-time, filling the conversation; and again at the close of play, when Mr. Armstrong returned from London with grave shakings of his head. On their return home they found a hand-delivered letter from the Trevelyans cancelling to-morrow's tennis, because young Trevelyan, who was a subaltern in the gunners, had been ordered by wire to report at once.

And the next morning, it being useless to fret and inflame their aching need of news, Jill suggested of a sudden what they must certainly do. "We must climb Wolstonbury again, and see as much as possible of England. I feel I want to look again at those farmlands and church spires and the smokiness over London. I feel I shall look at her with new eyes this morning. I shall understand her for the first time. Don't you feel rather like that?"

Tony, after staring at her whimsically, announced : "I speak as a fool, but I submit that Jill is a poet."

"Not a poet," she protested. "Or if I am, I've caught it from you. But I think I'm one who can understand what the poets try to get at."

"And how they must love you for existing," Tony suggested.

Peggy and Honor being equally enthusiastic, they all set out once more for the climbing of Wolstonbury. They approached it from behind, toiling up past the chalk-pit of Newtimber lime works. From its foothills to its crown no human figure was seen on it, for the day's excitement had held the people to the pavements of their towns or the thresholds of their cottages. Only the ragwort marched in a golden procession up its shoulders, and the field-scabious and the devil's-bit scabious ran beside it in a mauve array. On the first ridge where they rested they watched the chalk-blue butterfly scintillating along a purple streamer of thistle and knapweed and viper's bugloss. Their road up to the mysterious earthworks of Wolstonbury lay along a sunken footpath, where the wayfaring tree, at every few paces, held out to them its coral berries, like a gypsy peddling beads. On their right a flank which had once been worked for wheat, but since given over to grass, shimmered in the wind and the sun, and the white butterfly danced over it.

By the first great earthwork which portends a platform to dominate the Newtimber valley and the beechwoods and lemon-green slopes of Fulking Hill beyond, Tony paused and said : "What a gun-position this would be!" and he remembered how the German students at Stratton Lye had said that they would appear as invaders over the whole line of the downs.

Ten minutes more of climbing, and they were on the top where was nothing seen except the clumps of wind-brushed thorn; and the tall grasses obscuring the holes of England's earliest inhabitants, the cave-dwellers; and the field-scabious and the harebells and the toad-flax and the thyme. A meadow-brown butterfly flitted ahead of them, and all around was the music of the cicala.

Now they judged themselves to be on the highest point, and stood to see the spread of England beneath them. Not yet was the great view in its fullness unveiled, for the mist of a hot August day had curtained the distant North Downs and was even hiding the foot of Chanctonbury Hill, which rose from the diaphanous haze like a promontory out of the sea. But the effect of this mist was to increase the sense of distance, so that Chanctonbury, though a headland from their own chain of hills, seemed as if it were on the other side of England.

They sat down, rather silent, and waited; and it was not long before all the mists had gone. Now all that ever could be seen from Wolstonbury was before their eyes, in detail clearly drawn : the tessellated floor of meadows and hedgerows, splashed with the thick embroidery of tapestry trees; the far-off villages and towns; the line of the North Downs with Hindhead and Box Hill and Leith Hill in front; and the smoke over London.

"In the old days," said Tony, "they would have lit the warning beacon here, and Leith Hill would have answered it, and a ring of fires would have sprung up, from Ide Hill to Black Down, and shot away to the West."

The girls did not answer.

Tony looked at the hundreds of fields on the vast floor beneath him. Some were red with standard wheat, some were the dead cream of oats or barley, and some were spiked with the shadows of wheat in shocks. Others were close-cropped sunburnt meadows, and others were hayfields faded into grey. One was particoloured in five stripes, like a harlequin's leg; first the cream of corn, then the bright green of mangolds, then the brown of fallow earth, then the dull green of aftermath clover, and lastly a spotted strip where the corn stood in shocks. The ricks stood newly thatched by the sides of barns and in the meadow-lots near the gates. From any part of the scene came, now and then, a prick of light, which was the sun flashed from a window twenty or thirty miles away or from the wind-screen of a car on an unseen road. And that blueness beneath those elms—was it the blue smoke of a bonfire, or a pond among the trees ? "

" How quiet it all looks ! " said Honor.

They began to talk together. So quiet it all looked down there, and yet it was all astir, everywhere, with anticipation and excitement and fear ; astir to-day as it had never been in its history before, because its population was so much bigger than on the eve of previous wars, and the threat was so much darker. To think that every soul under those trees and those roofs, as far as they could see, was waiting—waiting for the same news ! And those three horses drawing the reaping-machine in the oat-field—perhaps they would be taken to draw the guns, and even to die for the fields they had served.

Peggy was the only one with the courage to speak the emotion quivering in her.

" Dear England ! " she murmured.

And Tony nodded. " Yes, we may be Irish, but I feel extra-ordinarily English to-day." And he thought of adding : " I suppose one's nationality is really determined, less by the place where one's parent was born than by the country which has been the playground of one's childhood ; " but he did not.

The birds down there—look ! The birds were not easily seen from these heights at first, but with an effort they could be distinguished, dipping and banking and hovering, like the notes, despite all, of Nature's unconquerable joy. Some of them knew, one might guess, that they were winning admiration from four people on Wolstonbury Hill, and disported them-selves for further praise. How was this for a dipping arc, and this for a cleaving uprush ? And there were two, higher up and farther away, which showed a twinkling delight in making themselves visible and invisible, by catching the sun for one moment and then shaking it adrift again. They went in and out, two intermittent and evasive lights, in the peaceful air. The birds, dipping and switchbacking and hovering over their parcel of England, as if in love with such a place for play.

CHAPTER V

DOWN AMONG THE PEOPLE

WEDNESDAY, war being declared, Father Michael came to fetch Peggy home, there being many things he was anxious to arrange and discuss, because he had that morning written to the Chaplain-General to offer his services as a chaplain. He seemed to think he might be called up before lunch time to-morrow.

Tony, Honor, and Jill were restless all day, and suddenly, as the darkness gathered, Tony said to the two girls: "Look here, *you*. Go and get your hats and coats on. We're going to Brighton. We are going on the pier, which is sure to be absolutely crowded, and we'll hear the bands playing the National Anthems of the Allies. These be historic scenes, not to be missed."

" O Tony ! " They both jumped with delight. " O, do let's. How gorgeous ! "

" Let's ! There's no ' Let's ' about it. The order has gone forth. Hurry up, hurry up."

And two hours later they were jammed in the crowds on Brighton pier.

Who will forget those first nights of the war in places where the bands played—such a night as this into which came Tony, Jill and Honor ? The band drumming out the airs that held the Englishman's patriotism and sentiment ; the crowds, as far as a turning head could see, rolling up the choruses : " Hearts of oak are our ships, Hearts of oak are our men ! Steady, boys, steady ! We'll fight and we'll conquer again and again ; " " Land of Hope and Glory, Mother of the free, How shall we extol thee, Who are born of thee ? " and the indifferent stars looking on. The women as inflamed as the men, but with moist and swelling eyes ; the children on their parents' shoulders, cheering they knew not what. " Drake is going West, lads, His ships are in the bay ; " " If the Dons sight Devon, He'll quit the port of Heaven, And drum them up the channel, As we drummed them long ago." The cheers when a man came amongst them who was already in his khaki ; and when two grinning Jack Tars pushed their way down the pier. The pier illuminations, in the still night, a necklace of fairy lamps, so soon to be put out for four years ; across the water, the crowds seen moving under the arc lamps of the esplanade and the lighted windows of the sea-front houses—a sea-front which was soon to face the sea, dark as a lonely cliff-face. The noise of the crowds on the esplanades rolling over the water to the crowds on the pier. The crowds on the pier shouting a chorus that the whole town might hear. " Should auld acquaintance be forgot, And never brought to mind, We'll tak' a cup of kindness yet, For the sake of Auld Lang Syne." And the music of the National Anthems : the " Marseillaise "—" *Aux armes, citoyens ! Formez vos bataillons ! Marchons, marchons* "—the " Brabançonne," the Russian hymn, and " God save the King." And, over all, the indifferent stars looking on.

Tony, Honor and Jill were as flushed as the rest, Tony even intoxicated with a new thought that was surging in his head. It had come bearing into him on the waves of music and emotion. All martial music speaks of sacrifice ; and to some natures the sight of a great multitude speaks the same message. By Jove ! —for the first time he was hearing it, as the band played " The March of the Men of Harlech," and the crowd, not knowing any words, roared the melody—by Jove ! this war meant that the time was over for personal matters. With what splendid timeliness, after his strange talk with Jill, had the hour struck for serving other than personal ends ! He must think this out ! Yes, there was something calling here.

And when the music was over he held his wife's arm and Jill's all the way up the thronged pavements from the pier to the station, and poured into the ears of both of them, though aware that Honor did not understand him as well as Jill, his conception of this war as an escape from poor little local and personal " beauties " into something bleaker and grander and lonelier. Compelling them almost to run beside him, so fast went his feet in the accompaniment to his words, he expounded that life didn't square with logic at all ; that though your Tolstoys and your pacifists could put up a colossal case in the realms of reason and religion for refusing to support a government in a war, yet something in him was crying: " You must go !

You must go, not because you want to inflict suffering on your enemies, but because you want to share it with your friends." This led him to expound that the English, with all their faults, would probably fight this war a little more nobly than anyone else, just because they didn't go into wars to give blows so much as to take them, which was the very reason why they were so much better in stubborn defence than in dashing attack ; that while the Germans would fight it coldly and scientifically, and the French hotly and emotionally, the English would fight it complacently and jokingly and sufferingly, and that therefore they would probably win, because their attitude would square with life, whereas the German attitude would only square with reason and the French attitude with emotion ; that, moreover, he had little doubt that though the German cause was by no means perfectly black and the English perfectly white, yet the English cause was the whiter of the two, because the German leaders, if not their people, had committed a crime against the world, and must take their lesson ; and lastly— what he was talking about now was quite unintelligible to Honor—that when a man found he had left behind him his potty little personal and unsatisfying loves and was marching towards a love for the whole world—a love which sought nothing but gave all—Beauty would come back again to the things of earth.

It was an inflamed, distorted talk, but flashed sparks of truth, as all emotional utterance does : it was like the outburst of one who stands on a hill and sees for the first time a wider and stranger country than any he has conceived. Tony was eager to rush towards what he saw. For twenty years he had hunted his happiness in egocentric loves, his clear intellect critical of the enterprise but his emotions driving him on ; and now he gave his allegiance to something, hazily glimpsed but intuitively recognized, whose centre was outside himself. He was but one of thousands such, and they found their spokesman, as the world knows :

" Oh, we who have known shame, we have found release there . . .

" Now God be thanked Who has matched us with His hour,
    And caught our youth, and wakened us from sleeping . . .

" Dear ! of all happy in this hour, most blest
    He who has found our hid security. . . ."

Jill was soon summoned home by her father ; doubtless the old gentleman, catching the fever in the air, had yielded to the crazy rumours about the War Office commandeering all the South Coast railways for the movement of troops. Tony took her to Hassocks station, whose usually quiet booking office and platforms were a-bustle and a-fluster with holiday-makers hastening home. And while they waited there, a mysterious train, its wagons chalked " W ↑ D " and their loads hidden under tarpaulins on which sat an occasional soldier, rumbled slowly but unstopping through the station, stared at by hundreds of eyes, above gaping mouths. As Jill's train was sighted, Tony, who had long been examining her with a sideways look, put out his hand.

" Good-bye, Jill."

" Good-bye, Tony," said she, taking his hand and looking up into his face. " I've had a wonderful time. I shall remember our talks always. I was thinking about them all night."

" I wish you weren't going. . . ."

" So do I. . . ."

" Give me a kiss, Jill. You've never given me a kiss."

At once she put up her face, and when his arms embraced her with a tightening affection, her body, in a moment's uncontrol, pressed hungrily against his. Those watching must have thought them lovers, had he not quickly lifted his lips from hers.

" Good-bye, my dear . . . and, Jill, remember I . . ."

" What ? . . ."

" Remember I value your friendship more than any other I possess."

" And I yours, I think, Tony."

The carriages of a crowded train were alongside, and he put her into the least uncomfortable he could find. From the window she broke an embarrassed silence with talk of common things, and his answers drifted along the same daily surface. The train started with a jerk ; he pressed her fingers in a parting and humorous benediction, and, the separation widening, both gave their hands to waving. The train out of sight, Tony swung quickly about and walked out of the station into the glow of the late afternoon.

He walked the whole way back to Sheep's Eye with a stride deliberately merry. It was the kind of merriness that is designed to brow-beat and laugh out a fear. All that road he was answering some question in his mind with a " No, no ; " and again, " No, no. No, no, *no !* " Sometimes his lips framed the word, and his head shook. Sometimes he uttered it aloud with an expletive : " My God, no ! " No, he would not succumb to the old craving—he believed in it no more. One thing he would always know : he could never love anyone more than he had once loved Honor. *That* was love, so he had had his experience of it. He wouldn't try it out again.

But the old craving was strong ; it tugged at his heart with its promise of the familiar pains, joys, anxieties and anguishes which heightened life so gloriously. Who could turn from such a promise ? It almost had him down, and he laughed rather bitterly to think that, within twenty-four hours of all his fine words to Jill and Honor about the necessity of transcending mere personal craving, he should be in its grip again. He realized that if he could throw this assailant now, it might prove in the end to have been a decisive conflict. " Once make this step, and I shall have crossed over into easier country. And I can do it, I can do it. . . ."

He looked round about him for help, on the road that he was walking. It was the road that he had first taken in a station fly with Mr. Sugden, when he came as a nervous seventeen-year-old master to Stratton Lye. The Sussex weald falling away on his right, and the Downs, with Wolstonbury as their captain, marching towards the sunset on his left. It was the road down which he had eloped with Honor in a motor car, holding her hand and saying : " It was wonderful of you to do this. For *me !* gosh ! I'll not forget it."

That settled it. That last memory settled it. He made his decision and believed that he had taken the vital step out of the lush valleys on to the colder foothills ; and, as often happens in such moments of belief, the joy of conquest exceeded the pain of renunciation. He heard himself exclaiming—for he fell easily into phrases : " I am free. I am free. . . ."

In the cottage he broke a fine plan that had been germinating during the last mile. " Honor. Honor, hurry up with some food. We're off for a jaunt together to Brighton again. We must, we simply must see those crowds and hear the bands again. I can't say why, but the sight of it all just *gets* me. I want to go back and feel once more all that I felt last night."

And Honor repeated her enthusiastic approval : " O yes, do let's, do let's."

"Come on, then. But I say, Honor, you can give me a kiss, if you like. You look pretty to-night."

She, as Jill one hour before, came to his arms, and he hugged her as if she were the best thing to hang on to. "Do you know, you're quite a pretty thing! You look as pretty as I've ever seen you to-night. Come on, let's go and hear the music again, and feel ready for anything."

CHAPTER VI

" TIME " IS CALLED

ONE by one the men of those two families went to the war's fronts. An autumn filled with the rumblings and movements of war hinted to the discerning that the early falls and trickles must soon become a landslide of English things eastward to Europe and the Levant. The recruiting posters appeared on every hoarding. " Surely you will fight for your King and Country," said one, marvellously ignorant of the way to appeal to Englishmen. Another turned the face of Lord Kitchener, the Secretary of State for War, and his pointing finger towards every man in the street, and gave the words below : " Lord Kitchener wants *You !* " It was enough to make any Englishman stay where he was. But later, after Lord Kitchener had died, when the same face and the same pointing finger stood above the words, " Carry on ! " it was enough to make any man ready to go. They had learnt better by then. They had taken down from the front of a big shop in London the long streamer which said : " Who lives if England die, Who dies if England live ? " They had removed the poster which insolently cried : " Why are You not in Khaki ? " and they were trying instead, " Sign on for the Great International between England and Germany," and " 'Arf a mo', Kaiser ! " For the Englishman's patriotism is of such a kind that it must not be shown ; it must come abroad veiled as humour. The face of Lord Kitchener, and his finger pointing at each shy creature in this island, probably achieved far less than the staring face of the dispatch-rider, and his finger pointing behind him to the battle and the fired houses and the stretcher-bearers. " They want more men " was his simple statement.

The air was full of songs ; but it was the same story with them. Keatings, completely Englished by this time, could sit

445

in a theatre and listen with a despairing grin to the *ingénue* lady
who came before the curtain and sang, of her impertinence,
" We don't want to lose you, But we think you ought to go ; "
and he even declared that he, for his part, was going to stay
long enough to make a really decent collection of the white
feathers which the feather-brained young ladies were presenting
to the young gentlemen still in their " civies." He wanted
enough to frame. Self-appointed laureates wrote songs for
marching recruits ; but was one of them sung ? Not one.
Nor the old songs either, once the first mad nights of the war
had passed. The recruits marched in every street of every
village and town of England ; they marched on the Brighton
Road, past Albourne Green where Tony and Honor could
watch them ; in the Southend roads past the gate of Peggy's
vicarage ; in the Chiswick roads past the houses of Mrs.
O'Grogan and General Daubeny ; in the Westminster streets
past the windows of Keatings's offices ; and they were never
singing " Land of Hope and Glory " or " Rule Britannia,"
but :

> " Who were you with last night ?
> Oh, who were you with last night ?
> Who was the dreamy
> Peaches and creamy
> Vision of pure delight ?
> Was it your little sister, mister ?
> Answer me, honour bright.
> *Will you tell your wife in the morning*
> Who were you with last night ? "

or, with a great roar as they rounded the corners :

> " Hello, hello, hel*lo !* it's a different girl again
> Different eyes, different nose,
> Different hair, different clothes ;
> Hello, hello, hel*LO !* it's a different girl again."

Tony could remember the old days of the South African War
when the barrel organs rolled out, " Cook's son, Duke's son,
son of a hundred kings," and " Good-bye, Dolly, I must
leave you." That was a war when the mass of civilians sang
about the soldiers ; this was a war when the mass of civilians
were soldiers themselves and, being Englishmen in uniform,
knew that they must sing irrelevancies :

> " If you were the only girl in the world,
> And I were the only boy,
> Nothing else would matter in the world to-day,
> We would go on loving in the same old way."

For the Englishman out of uniform can sometimes talk patriotism; in it, never; he had rather by far talk sedition. It is his strange inverted poetry.

The air was full of sounds. Peggy, in her Essex home, could hear the guns at practice in Shoeburyness near by, and at Sheerness across the Thames. Tony heard them at points along the Sussex coast. All England heard the hum of aeroplanes overhead. The noise of artillery on the roads and in the lanes was an unmistakable sound, mixing the clapper of horses, the jingle of spurs and harness, and the rumble of steel-girt wheels. The long convoys of motor lorries were easily distinguished, too—so many heavy vehicles all travelling at the same pace; and people came to their gates to watch the procession go by; to stare at their uniform elephant-grey paint, their " W ↑ D " on their hoods, and the khaki soldiers at their steering-wheels, on their roofs, and on their tail-boards.

At night one imagined that one could distinguish the slow rolling of troop trains from the sound of all other trains.

Much faster than the lorries went the purring ambulances and the dispatch-riders on their motor bicycles; and the streets were a day-long drama. Especially those that led down to the ports : down them in riotous song went the sailors returning after shore-leave to their ships; the German prisoners, marching between guards with fixed bayonets, to their prison hulks in the river; the ambulances and private cars in their hundreds to meet the hospital ships as they came in; the men in heavy equipment and service caps marching to the French steamers; the men in light equipment and pith helmets marching to the big eastbound transports; the ammunition columns; the R. E. columns with pontoons; the R. N. A. F. columns with aeroplanes; the R. F. A. columns with mysterious guns hidden under tarpaulins; the detachments of nurses in grey and red; the A. S. C. convoys, and the Red Cross stores

And with this eastward landslide of English things the men of the two families went one by one. General Daubeny battered daily at the War Office for work, however modest, and was sent at last to a large city in France as its Town Major, an appointment over which he huzza'd like an undergraduate. Father Michael, after spending months in anticipation of his chaplaincy and in censure of the Chaplain-General as a Protestant who denied to Catholics their proper representation in the army, suddenly abandoned his oft-repeated dogma that " he who held the chalice should not hold the rifle," and enlisted in the Essex Regiment as a combatant, with an unequivocal lie about his age. He seemed so happy in his new life that Tony always suspected that he had been glad to escape from priestly duties and a hidden spiritual malaise. Warner Gabriel obtained his chaplaincy almost at once—much to the indignation of Father Michael, who declared that it was because the child was a broad churchman and had an Archdeacon for father. John Gabriel was a subaltern in the London Scottish and took part in their charge which rang through the land, much to the annoyance of Keatings. Len Daubeny wrote that he was going with an Indian Brigade to France, and that Joyce must stay with her child in England till the troubles settled. Before September was on the wane Derek received his commission in the Army Service Corps (Motor Transport Section), and in the same month Keatings enlisted as a private in the London Irish; and the difference between the competent and intense young officer and the humble, cynical private was the difference between Derek and Keatings. "Derek'll be a Colonel before the war's over; he's got all the bounce," said Keatings. And there was no doubt that Derek, wearing gravity and despairs more often than humour, enjoyed his part in the saving of the Empire; whereas Keatings frankly detested *his* part, and when asked how he liked the World War, disposed of it in a sentence: "I never did like gardening."

Derek was splendidly magisterial in these early months. He convened a meeting of the whole family, whereat his common-place romanticism, if somewhat ponderous in its phrasing, did him honour as a son of the O'Grogan house (so the Family agreed at last) and as a son of Britain. That his firm should be profiting by the war, said he, and would profit still more, was an undeniable fact that kept his conscience uneasy, and he honestly felt that some of his income ought to be devoted to the prosecution of the war. Let Keatings therefore have no anxiety about his mother, nor Tony about his wife. Honor, when Tony went, could live with their mother and Joyce and Peggy; and he, Derek, would instruct his bankers to pay the women all that they could need. "And in the event," added poor Derek, blushing for the first time, "of my—er—death, my executors will hold my estate, such as it is, in trust for the Family. You see—er—I've nobody else. . . . And if Keatings should be the one to fall, or Tony, I should like—I should like, if you will allow me, to regard the care of their dependants as a first charge on myself." When the meeting was over, Joyce said to Keatings, not without tears, " Really, old Derek's rather magnificent. I don't think we've ever appreciated him properly ; " and Keatings, also a little moved, replied, " Yes, he's a fool, of course—a pompous, unimaginative ass, but I expect it's his type that's going to save England now—and all of us."

Tony, though the first to be eager, was the last to go. Mr. Sugden, restlessly worrying and rooting round Stratton Lye, like a mother brontosaurus round her nest of little reptiles as the hurricane blows up, begged Tony to consider only his duty to his wife, which was manifestly, said he, to remain quietly at his present job of teaching for Mr. Sugden. At any rate till such time as all the single men had been conscripted for the army, and the married men were being summoned ; because conscription was coming, mark his words—and well it might ! " Single men first ! " Mr. Sugden proclaimed. Finding that this did not carry full conviction to his young colleague, he begged him to consider only his duty to his country, which was clearly to stay where he was and teach the children in the absence of their fathers. He pointed out that the East Coast schools would certainly be ruined by the German air-raiders, and it was up to the South Coast schools to hold the educational fort for England. " Business as usual," he said ; and Tony had an immediate sense that Mr. Sugden, who cashed everything, was glad that he could do his duty to his country now and cash the misery of the East Coast dwellers. Then he begged Tony to consider his duty to himself, which was clearly to stay in England, and at Stratton Lye, till such time as he had passed his Finals, when he would get a good commission and be of much greater use to the nation as an officer than as a private.

This last reason was the only one that carried much weight with Tony, and it kept him in England till early 1915 when, having passed his Finals, he joined the Artists Rifles O.T.C. Derek, Keatings, and Len Daubeny were already in France, Father Michael was leaving for " the Mediterranean," Warner Gabriel was in Egypt, and John Gabriel was dead. " In which matter they've gone ahead of us once again," said Keatings grimly. " The Gods have ordained that they shall always be first."

The friends of Tony's past were all at their places. Little

Wavers was a guardee subaltern in France; old Raking, as might have been expected of him, was just as far afield as he could get, having left a Malay plantation to accompany Townshend to Kut; there was a Colonel Chandry, so Len Daubeny wrote, in his Indian Brigade; Cyril Winter had fought with the Royal Naval Division at Antwerp and was now under orders for " the Mediterranean; " Frank Doyly had fought at Neuve Chapelle and was still " somewhere in France." And all those boys of Stratton Lye whom Tony had first seen gathered together round the dining-tables of the school—all of them being now any age from eighteen to twenty-four—were scattered abroad like chaff tossed into the drive and the caprice of the eastward gale. They were on foreign soil and on unnamed seas, and many of them were in the air. He was jealous of their precedence.

He went at Midsummer. In July he had been drafted as a Second Lieutenant to a battalion of Lancashire territorials, wherein he had hardly learned his ropes, or the names of the men in his platoon, before the cry of Gallipoli summoned the whole brigade to " the Mediterranean." It was on two early August days that he went on his last leave to those of his family who were still to be found in England. And they were Jill Daubeny, nursing at a hospital in Leicestershire, Peggy and Joyce living at his mother's house with their two little boys, and Honor who was to make her home with Mrs. Daubeny. Not unconscious of his subaltern's uniform, whose buttons were polished to a precious brilliance and whose Sam Browne belt reflected portions of the first-class compartments and the taxis, he travelled first to Jill's hospital, where he had but an hour; and Jill, touched to melting by his quick swoop to her side, gave him the sweet memory of her kiss, her hand-pressure, her quivering mouth and her last strange bursting word: " You still count me the first of your friends after Honor, don't you? . . . I want to be that. . . . O Tony, I suppose everyone has always loved you."

Then he went home to the little house at Chiswick, where his mother and Peggy and Joyce and Honor awaited him. Joyce tried all night to be her lively self, whose loyalties and affections used to be hidden under a bright glaze, but the glaze showed a split when suddenly she said: " We shan't have a man left, now Tony's going. Just Mother and Peggy and I —just the O'Grogan women left uselessly at home. Ah, well,

I suppose we should have been still more apart, if there had been no horrid old war ; it's dispersed the men, but it's assembled the women of the Family again. Like old times. I vote we all live close together if—if all of us—when this business is over. We'll all live on top of each other in some English village. Peggy must have the Vicarage, and Tony a prep-school of his own, and Derek (bless him !) the Great House and Park, and old Keatings'll be there with Mother in a cottage somewhere, like the funny old family anchor he is, and Len and I'll retire young and breed pigs and poultry. Then all our infants can play together. Between us we'd make the village sit up. Don't you think it's a good idea, Tony ? I do, because as I keep on telling you, only you *won't* listen, I realize more and more as I get so horribly old that nothing matters in life except palliness and human relationships and—well, you know what I mean. . . ."

Peggy concealed her feelings all the evening, but had no intention of concealing them a minute too long. She was silent while they were all together, leaving the talk to Joyce and Honor, but in mortal fear lest her youngest brother should leave without hearing from her all that she longed to say. She begged him in an aside, when at a late hour they were separating for bed, to come and say good night to her in her room. So Tony, going into the little narrow chamber that used to be Keatings's burrow and still held round the walls his school and college groups, sat on Keatings's iron bed at Peggy's side. Michael Derek in his cot slept by them as they talked. The talk deepened in intimacy and widened in range till they were speaking of large general things : of religion and art and love and marriage. At first they had spoken impersonally as if their words related not at all to any experiences of their own but Tony, before he could make up his mind to go, had confessed in a sentence to this, his best loved sister, that he had learned a lesson like hers.

" Peggy, there's no such thing as the perfect union one dreams of."

" Oh, surely ! " Peggy protested.

" No. Only for the may-fly's hour. It's a drooping thing at best. Everyone has always said so, but one must go through with it before one will believe it, and so the world wags on."

Peggy kept silence. This was a confession from her brother, and an answer would not come easily to her lips.

" That's why," continued Tony, " I'm grateful to this war for one thing at least : it has suddenly drawn life in a larger manner for us. And by bringing death so near——"

" Oh, don't ! Tony——"

" It has shown some of us that there are much more important things than little disappointments like that—primary, fundamental things—husbandhood, I mean, and paternity. It has given us a big lift towards getting out of our excessive ' personalness.' "

Peggy frowned over this without understanding, she being one who must be personal or perish.

" But, Tony : there *is* a personal love that is completely and eternally satisfying, and that only becomes more and more wonderful as one lives longer with it."

" Have *you* found it ? "

" Yes."

He looked sharply at her. " How do you mean ? "

" I mean—I mean, if one can't have a perfect union with a fellow creature, one can always have it with God."

" Oh. . . ." He understood. " But, Peggy dear—I hate to shake your faith—but supposing that's only another and bigger illusion ? "

" Tony : it can't be ! " she proclaimed, her fingers clenching on her conviction. " No, that would be too awful to think. I *must* keep my faith in that : if there's not that, there's nothing. . . . As you say, there's nothing. . . ."

" I don't want to rest my life on an illusion," Tony persisted. " I'd rather stand quite alone."

" I couldn't stand quite alone," Peggy admitted, shaking her head. " No, I don't think I should ever be strong enough to do that."

And Tony thought a long time before breaking in again. " I see that if people can believe in God as you do, they can be perfectly happy. They can pour all the love that is in them over their fellow-creatures, loving all the world instead of one, and they can receive back all they need from God."

" Yes, that's it," Peggy nodded.

" It must be magnificent, that. But I haven't the faith. God ! don't I wish I had ? I'd know what to do then."

" Tony : perhaps that's what you're destined to do."

" No, no. But I sometimes think that—if I come back from this—I shall do social work of some sort I've been half a Socialist ever since at fifteen years of age I met little Emily Holt, who'd never seen the sea or had tea at a farm."

And his thoughts passed to another child, Thérèse of Ostend, who had shown him her foot, inflamed with too much walking.

" Tony : have you quite given up your writing ? "

" Yes, rather ! " he exclaimed, succumbing to the weakness of being dramatic ; then he drew himself into a worthier attitude. " At least, in the old way. You see, the old light that was on everything went out. But I think I'm beginning to catch another sadder kind of radiance on the edges of things, that would be worth writing about, if I could see it more clearly and if I could catch it in words."

Just then little Michael Derek stirred in his cot, as if he heard voices in the room.

" Hush ! " laughed Tony, rising. " I must go. Youth is restive against such nonsense."

But Peggy, rising too, held on to the lapels of his khaki jacket, to keep him a few minutes more.

" You didn't destroy all that you wrote, did you ? "

" No, I nearly did, but——"

" Then, Tony, will you let me have it to keep ? That's what I wanted to ask."

" It's worthless."

" It isn't. And I want it for a very special reason."

" What is that ? "

" I've always believed you're going to be enormously famous one day, and then I'm going to write your life. I've set my heart on it. So I shall want your early thoughts, please."

" If it's never published till someone wants to read my life, there's not much danger of its ever being given to the world."

" We shall see," said the faithful Peggy significantly.

" Certainly you can have it, my dear : but if ever it did see the light, you would make it clear, wouldn't you, that the fool forswore it all when he grew up—that it was only a young man's romanticism."

The child stirred.

" Good night, Peggy." He laughed again, and pointed the moral. " Youth stirs in its sleep at the mention of romance. Let us not wake it too soon. Good night. Honor'll think I'm never coming."

" Good night, Tony," whispered Peggy.

Honor alone accompanied him to the station and the platform

and the train door ; and holding her the last time for many a year, perhaps, he could hardly speak ; nor she ; but his thought was : " She is the elemental fact." He realized this better, somehow, as he recovered a sense of his surroundings and saw that they were only one pair out of a hundred such, on that streaming platform. All that Honor could tell him she told in her last long, unreleasing kiss ; and then the train broke the hand-hold which was their last contact ; and he was one face out of hundreds laughing, and one hand out of hundreds waving.

Four days later he moved down the water from Southampton Docks into the Solent, misty and pale-tinted with morning, and, though one of five thousand officers and men on the third largest liner in the world, knew the meaning of loneliness for the first time in his life. A crowd of Tommies, lolling on the deck, were singing in lazy chorus :

> " If you were the only girl in the world
> And I were the only boy,
> Nothing else would matter in the world to-day . . ."

and when they passed another ship on the water, they burst into a greeting :

> " Hello, hello, hel-*lo !* it's a different girl again . . ."

The lifting summits of the Isle of Wight rose out of a bank·of mist, just as Chanctonbury and the downs had risen that morning when he and Honor and Peggy and Jill had stood on Wolstonbury to look at England's last day of peace. He hoped that the mists would open and vanish that he might see the church tower and white pier of little Yarmouth, and the red villas of vulgar little Totland, and the coloured cliffs of Alum Bay. Such little spots they seemed now. And the great ship, escorted by destroyers, went with a slow majesty down the Solent, so that his wish was granted and he saw the places of his boyish holidays and his youthful love. They hurt him, but not unbearably ; almost there was a pleasure in their pain, as with the pain of a healing bruise. There were the Needles, flat as jagged shards in the direct light of the sun ; and beyond, the open sea glistening. He remembered all the people he had known here : Emily Holt, old Raking, his father, Captain Alum ; all those who had appeared for a space in his life and gone out of sight. How Captain Alum, were he alive

now, would have loved to stand on a spur above Alum Bay
with his black curls blowing in the wind, and to sing the great
transports out to sea !

> " God be with you till we meet again ;
> By his counsels guide, uphold you,
> With his sheep securely fold you :
> God be with you till we meet again.

> " God be with you till we meet again ;
> Keep love's banner floating o'er you,
> Smite death's threatening wave before you :
> God be with you till we meet again."

" I had a brother and two sisters," Captain Alum had said,
" and we played together ; and now even their faces are going
from me." Keatings, Joyce, Derek, Peggy ; it was possible
that he had looked his last upon them. Jill ; and Honor, too,
his wife. Nothing was stable, nothing permanent—unless Peggy
were right. And yet how could one endure without something
stable, still, perpetual, in time but not of it, nor knowing its
touch? Southward turned the ship, and now the underside of
the island swung towards them, a long wave of white cliffs
folding inward to the shadows of Freshwater Bay. The bay
opened and he could descry the houses that he had known.
The wrench at his heart easing with the minutes, he fell to
wondering that the exigencies of war should have sent his
great ship down the Solent and round the Needles instead of
down the eastern channel and out by Spithead, and so allowed
that Freshwater's little cove, of all the places along England's
sea-line, should be the last to stand forth as a picture, with
details clear and intimate. For now the cliffs were diminishing
to a ribbon under an immense sky, and the world was becoming
a world of sea. And a " funny man " among the officers began
to salute the fading hills with a song:

> " We don't want to lose you,
> But we think you ought to go . . ."

Like a thousand others on that ship Tony stayed watching the
cliffs till they were gone into the past, and then turned to
face the empty and heaving path ahead, so pitilessly pointed
out by the bows of the ship as they forged onward, but
mercifully revealing naught.

Portway Reprints

The following titles have been reprinted at the request of the London & Home Counties Branch of the Library Association and can be obtained from Cedric Chivers Ltd., Portway, Bath.

Non-fiction

Braddock, Joseph	HAUNTED HOUSES
Cardus, Neville	DAYS IN THE SUN
Cobbett, William	COTTAGE ECONOMY
Edmonds, Charles	A SUBALTERN'S WAR
Gibbs, P.	FROM BAPAUME TO PASSCHENDAELE
Grant, I.F.	ECONOMIC HISTORY OF SCOTLAND
Harris, John	RECOLLECTIONS OF RIFLEMAN HARRIS
Hitchcock, F.C.	STAND TO: A DIARY OF THE TRENCHES
Jones, Jack	GIVE ME BACK MY HEART
Jones, Jack	UNFINISHED JOURNEY
Jones, Jack	ME AND MINE
Lowe, George	BECAUSE IT IS THERE
Price, Harry	THE MOST HAUNTED HOUSE IN ENGLAND
Spain, Nancy	THANK YOU, NELSON
Stamper, Joseph	LESS THAN THE DUST
Tangye, Derek	TIME WAS MINE
Tangye, Derek	WENT THE DAY WELL
Thompson, P.A.	LIONS LED BY DONKEYS
Villiers, Alan	SONS OF SINDBAD

Fiction

Ainsworth, W. Harrison	GUY FAWKES
Barke, James	THE END OF THE HIGH BRIDGE
Barke, James	THE SONG IN THE GREEN THORN TREE
Barke, James	THE WELL OF THE SILENT HARP
Blaker, Richard	MEDAL WITHOUT BAR
Broster, D.K.	SHIPS IN THE BAY
Broster, D.K. & Taylor, G.W.	CHANTEMERLE
Broster, D.K. & Taylor, G.W.	WORLD UNDER SNOW

Buck, Pearl	THE MOTHER
Buck, Pearl	THE PROUD HEART
Burney, Fanny	CAMILLA - in 5 vols
Caldwell, Taylor	THE EAGLES GATHER
Caldwell, Taylor	TENDER VICTORY
Caldwell, Taylor	THE BEAUTIFUL IS VANISHED
Collins, Wilkie	ARMADALE
Cookson, Catherine	COLOUR BLIND
Cookson, Catherine	FIFTEEN STREETS
Cookson, Catherine	KATE HANNIGAN
Cookson, Catherine	FANNY McBRIDE
Cookson, Catherine	MAGGIE ROWAN
Cookson, Catherine	ROONEY
Cordell, A.	RAPE OF THE FAIR COUNTRY
Corke, Helen	NEUTRAL GROUND
Crockett, S.R.	THE GREY MAN
Croker, B.M.	THE YOUNGEST MISS MOWBRAY
Cusack, Dymphna & James, Florence	COME IN, SPINNER
Darlington, W.A.	ALF'S BUTTON
Davies, Rhys	THE TRIP TO LONDON
Davies, Rhys	THE BLACK VENUS
Dehan, Richard	THE DOP DOCTOR
Dumas, Alexandre	THE LADY OF THE CAMELLIAS
Dumas, Alexandre	THE CORSICAN BROTHERS
Eca de Queiroz, José	COUSIN BASILIO
Ewart, Wilfrid	THE WAY OF REVELATION
Ferrier, Susan	THE INHERITANCE
Firbank, T.	BRIDE TO THE MOUNTAIN
Godden, R.	BLACK NARCISSUS
Golding, Louis	MAGNOLIA STREET
Golding, Louis	CAMBERWELL BEAUTY
Golding, Louis	THE LOVING BROTHERS
Gunn, Neil	BUTCHER'S BROOM
Gunn, Neil	THE GREY COAST
Gunn, Neil	THE KEY OF THE CHEST
Household, Geoffrey	THE THIRD HOUR
James, Henry	WHAT MAISIE KNEW
Jenkins, Robin	HAPPY FOR THE CHILD
Jones, Jack	RIVER OUT OF EDEN

Portway Reprints

The following titles have been reprinted at the request of the
London & Home Counties Branch of the Library Association and
can be obtained from Cedric Chivers Ltd., Portway, Bath.

Non-fiction

Braddock, Joseph	HAUNTED HOUSES
Cardus, Neville	DAYS IN THE SUN
Cobbett, William	COTTAGE ECONOMY
Edmonds, Charles	A SUBALTERN'S WAR
Gibbs, P.	FROM BAPAUME TO PASSCHENDAELE
Grant, I.F.	ECONOMIC HISTORY OF SCOTLAND
Harris, John	RECOLLECTIONS OF RIFLEMAN HARRIS
Hitchcock, F.C.	STAND TO: A DIARY OF THE TRENCHES
Jones, Jack	GIVE ME BACK MY HEART
Jones, Jack	UNFINISHED JOURNEY
Jones, Jack	ME AND MINE
Lowe, George	BECAUSE IT IS THERE
Price, Harry	THE MOST HAUNTED HOUSE IN ENGLAND
Spain, Nancy	THANK YOU, NELSON
Stamper, Joseph	LESS THAN THE DUST
Tangye, Derek	TIME WAS MINE
Tangye, Derek	WENT THE DAY WELL
Thompson, P.A.	LIONS LED BY DONKEYS
Villiers, Alan	SONS OF SINDBAD

Fiction

Ainsworth, W.Harrison	GUY FAWKES
Barke, James	THE END OF THE HIGH BRIDGE
Barke, James	THE SONG IN THE GREEN THORN TREE
Barke, James	THE WELL OF THE SILENT HARP
Blaker, Richard	MEDAL WITHOUT BAR
Broster, D.K.	SHIPS IN THE BAY
Broster, D.K. & Taylor, G.W.	CHANTEMERLE
Broster, D.K. & Taylor, G.W.	WORLD UNDER SNOW

Buck, Pearl	THE MOTHER
Buck, Pearl	THE PROUD HEART
Burney, Fanny	CAMILLA – in 5 vols
Caldwell, Taylor	THE EAGLES GATHER
Caldwell, Taylor	TENDER VICTORY
Caldwell, Taylor	THE BEAUTIFUL IS VANISHED
Collins, Wilkie	ARMADALE
Cookson, Catherine	COLOUR BLIND
Cookson, Catherine	FIFTEEN STREETS
Cookson, Catherine	KATE HANNIGAN
Cookson, Catherine	FANNY McBRIDE
Cookson, Catherine	MAGGIE ROWAN
Cookson, Catherine	ROONEY
Cordell, A.	RAPE OF THE FAIR COUNTRY
Corke, Helen	NEUTRAL GROUND
Crockett, S.R.	THE GREY MAN
Croker, B.M.	THE YOUNGEST MISS MOWBRAY
Cusack, Dymphna	
&James, Florence	COME IN, SPINNER
Darlington, W.A.	ALF'S BUTTON
Davies, Rhys	THE TRIP TO LONDON
Davies, Rhys	THE BLACK VENUS
Dehan, Richard	THE DOP DOCTOR
Dumas, Alexandre	THE LADY OF THE CAMELLIAS
Dumas, Alexandre	THE CORSICAN BROTHERS
Eca de Queiroz, José	COUSIN BASILIO
Ewart, Wilfrid	THE WAY OF REVELATION
Ferrier, Susan	THE INHERITANCE
Firbank, T.	BRIDE TO THE MOUNTAIN
Godden, R.	BLACK NARCISSUS
Golding, Louis	MAGNOLIA STREET
Golding, Louis	CAMBERWELL BEAUTY
Golding, Louis	THE LOVING BROTHERS
Gunn, Neil	BUTCHER'S BROOM
Gunn, Neil	THE GREY COAST
Gunn, Neil	THE KEY OF THE CHEST
Household, Geoffrey	THE THIRD HOUR
James, Henry	WHAT MAISIE KNEW
Jenkins, Robin	HAPPY FOR THE CHILD
Jones, Jack	RIVER OUT OF EDEN

Jones, Jack	BLACK PARADE
Jones, Jack	BIDDEN TO THE FEAST
Jones, Jack	RHONDDA ROUNDABOUT
Jones, Jack	LUCKY LEAR
Jones, Jack	SOME TRUST IN CHARIOTS
Jones, Jack	OFF TO PHILADELPHIA IN THE MORNING
Jones, Jack	LILY OF THE VALLEY
Jones, Jack	THE MAN DAVID
Jones, Jack	COME NIGHT : END DAY
Kersh, Gerald	NINE LIVES OF BILL NELSON
Kersh, Gerald	THEY DIE WITH THEIR BOOTS CLEAN
Keyes, F.P.	VAIL D'ALVERY
Kirkham, Nellie	UNREST OF THEIR TIME
Kyle, Elizabeth	THE PLEASURE DOME
Lawrence, Margery	MADONNA OF SEVEN MOONS
Lewis, Hilda	PENNY LACE
Lewis, Hilda	THE DAY IS OURS
Lindsay, Philip	PUDDING LANE
Lofts, Norah	REQUIEM FÔR IDOLS
Lofts, Norah	WHITE HELL OF PITY
MacDonell, A.G.	HOW LIKE AN ANGEL
Mackenzie, Compton	POOR RELATIONS
Macpherson, I.	SHEPHERD'S CALENDAR
Macpherson, I.	LAND OF OUR FATHERS
Macpherson, I.	PRIDE IN THE VALLEY
Macpherson, I.	HAPPY HAWKERS
Macpherson, I.	WILD HARBOUR
Masefield, Muriel	SEVEN AGAINST EDINBURGH
Maturin, Henri	MELMOTH THE WANDERER - in 3 vols
Myers, Elizabeth	A WELL FULL OF LEAVES
Neill, Robert	MIST OVER PENDLE
D'Oyley, Elizabeth	LORD ROBERT'S WIFE
D'Oyley, Elizabeth	YOUNG JEMMY
D'Oyley, Elizabeth	EVEN AS THE SUN
Oliver & Stafford	BUSINESS AS USUAL
Oliver, Jane	THE LION AND THE ROSE
Oliver, Jane	NOT PEACE BUT A SWORD
Oliver, Jane	IN NO STRANGE LAND
Oliver, Jane	THE LION IS COME
Oliver, Jane	CROWN FOR A PRISONER

Ouida	UNDER TWO FLAGS
Ouida	MOTHS
Pargeter, Edith	MOST LOVING MERE FOLLY
Pargeter, Edith	ORDINARY PEOPLE
Pargeter, Edith	THE HEAVEN TREE
Pargeter, Edith	THE GREEN BRANCH
Pargeter, Edith	THE SCARLET SEED
Phillpotts, Eden	THE RIVER
Phillpotts, Eden	CHILDREN OF THE MIST
Phillpotts, Eden	THE MOTHER
Phillpotts, Eden	THE HUMAN BOY
Phillpotts, Eden	THE HUMAN BOY AGAIN
Procter, Maurice	NO PROUD CHIVALRY
Shellabarger, Samuel	CAPTAIN FROM CASTILE
Shiel, M.P.	THE LAST MIRACLE
Sienkiewicz, Henryk	THE DELUGE - in 2 vols
Sienkiewicz, Henryk	PAN MICHAEL
Smith, Betty	A TREE GROWS IN BROOKLYN
Soubiran, André	THE DOCTORS
Sutton, Graham	NORTH STAR
Sutton, Graham	THE ROWAN TREE
Tunstall, Beatrice	SHINY NIGHT
Vaughan, Hilda	HARVEST HOME
Walpole, H.	FORTITUDE
Walpole, H.	KATHERINE CHRISTIAN
Warren, R.P.	AT HEAVEN'S GATE
Wells, H.G.	MR. BLETTSWORTHY ON RAMPOLE ISLAND
Wilkins, Vaughan	SEVEN TEMPEST
Wilkins, Vaughan	A KING RELUCTANT
Wilkins, Vaughan	CITY OF FROZEN FIRE
Young, Francis Brett	DR. BRADLEY REMEMBERS